Three by Marquis De Sade

Justine
The 120 Days of Sodom
Florville and Courval

Three by Marquis de Sade

Justine
The 120 Days of Sodom
Florville and Courval

by Marquis de Sade

Wilder Publications, LLC.
PO Box 3005
Radford VA 24143-3005

ISBN 10: 1-60459-420-9
ISBN 13: 978-1-60459-420-1

Justine
or 'Good Conduct Well Chastised'

To My Dear Friend

O thou my friend! The prosperity of Crime is like unto the lightning, whose traitorous brilliancies embellish the atmosphere but for an instant, in order to hurl into death's very depths the luckless one they have dazzled.

Yes, Constance, it is to thee I address this work; at once the example and honor of thy sex, with a spirit of profoundest sensibility combining the most judicious and the most enlightened of minds, thou art she to whom I confide my book, which will acquaint thee with the sweetness of the tears Virtue sore beset doth shed and doth cause to flow. Detesting the sophistries of libertinage and of irreligion, in word and deed combating them unwearyingly, I fear not that those necessitated by the order of personages appearing in these Memoirs will put thee in any peril; the cynicism remarkable in certain portraits (they were softened as much as ever they could be) is no more apt to frighten thee; for it is only Vice that trembles when Vice is found out, and cries scandal immediately it is attacked. To bigots Tartuffe was indebted for his ordeal; Justine's will be the achievement of libertines, and little do I dread them: they'll not betray my intentions, these thou shalt perceive; thy opinion is sufficient to make my whole glory and after having pleased thee I must either please universally or find consolation in a general censure.

The scheme of this novel (yet, 'tis less a novel than one might suppose) is doubtless new; the victory gained by Virtue over Vice, the rewarding of good, the punishment of evil, such is the usual scheme in every other work of this species: ah! the lesson cannot be too often dinned in our ears!

But throughout to present Vice triumphant and Virtue a victim of its sacrifices, to exhibit a wretched creature wandering from one misery to the next; the toy of villainy; the target of every debauch; exposed to the most barbarous, the most monstrous caprices; driven witless by the most brazen, the most specious sophistries; prey to the most cunning seductions, the most irresistible subornations for defense against so many disappointments, so much bane and pestilence, to repulse such a quantity of corruption having nothing but a sensitive soul, a mind naturally formed, and considerable courage: briefly, to employ the boldest scenes, the most extraordinary situations, the most dreadful maxims, the most energetic brush strokes, with the sole object of obtaining from all this one of the sublimest parables ever penned for human edification; now, such were, 'twill be allowed, to seek to reach one's destination by a road not much traveled heretofore.

Have I succeeded, Constance? Will a tear in thy eye determine my triumph? After having read Justine, wilt say: "Oh, how these renderings of crime make me proud of my love for Virtue! How sublime does it appear through tears! How 'tis embellished by misfortunes !"

Oh, Constance! may these words but escape thy lips, and my labors shall be crowned.

The very masterpiece of philosophy would be to develop the means Providence employs to arrive at the ends she designs for man, and from this construction to deduce some rules of conduct acquainting this wretched two-footed individual with the manner wherein he must proceed along life's thorny way, forewarned of the strange caprices of that fatality they denominate by twenty different titles, and all unavailingly, for it has not yet been scanned nor defined.

If, though full of respect for social conventions and never overstepping the bounds they draw round us, if, nonetheless, it should come to pass that we meet with nothing but brambles and briars, while the wicked tread upon flowers, will it not be reckoned - save by those in whom a fund of incoercible virtues renders deaf to these remarks-, will it not be decided that it is preferable to abandon oneself to the tide rather than to resist it? Will it not be felt that Virtue, however beautiful, becomes the worst of all attitudes when it is found too feeble to contend with Vice, and that, in an entirely corrupted age, the safest course is to follow along after the others? Somewhat better informed, if one wishes, and abusing the knowledge they have acquired, will they not say, as did the angel Jesrad in 'Zadig', that there is no evil whereof some good is not born? and will they not declare, that this being the case, they can give themselves over to evil since, indeed, it is but one of the fashions of producing good? Will they not add, that it makes no difference to the general plan whether such-and-such a one is by preference good or bad, that if misery persecutes virtue and prosperity accompanies crime, those things being as one in Nature's view, far better to join company with the wicked who flourish, than to be counted amongst the virtuous who founder? Hence, it is important to anticipate those dangerous sophistries of a false philosophy; it is essential to show that through examples of afflicted virtue presented to a depraved spirit in which, however, there remain a few good principles, it is essential, I say,- to show that spirit quite as surely restored to righteousness by these means as by portraying this virtuous career ornate with the most glittering honors and the most flattering rewards. Doubtless it is cruel to have to describe, on the one hand, a host of ills overwhelming a sweet-tempered and sensitive woman who, as best she is able, respects virtue, and, on the other, the affluence of prosperity of those who crush and mortify this same woman. But were there nevertheless some good engendered of the demonstration, would one have to repent of making it? Ought one be sorry for having established a fact whence there resulted, for the wise man who reads to some purpose, so useful a lesson of submission to providential decrees and the fateful warning that it is often to recall us to our duties that Heaven strikes down beside us the person who seems to us best to have fulfilled his own?

Such are the sentiments which are going to direct our labors, and it is in consideration of these intentions that we ask the reader's indulgence for the erroneous doctrines which are to be placed in the mouths of our characters, and for the sometimes rather painful situations which, out of love for truth, we have been obliged to dress before his eyes.

2

Madame la Comtesse de Lorsange was one of those priestesses of Venus whose fortune is the product of a pretty face and much misconduct, and whose titles, pompous though they are, are not to be found but in the archives of Cythera, forged by the impertinence that seeks, and sustained by the fool's credulity that bestows, them; brunette, a fine figure, eyes of a singular expression, that modish unbelief which, contributing one further spice to the passions, causes those women in whom it is suspected to be sought after that much more diligently; a trifle wicked, unfurnished with any principle, allowing evil to exist in nothing, lacking however that amount of depravation in the heart to have extinguished its sensibility; haughty, libertine; such was Madame de Lorsange.

Nevertheless, this woman had received the best education; daughter of a very rich Parisian banker, she had been brought up, together with a sister named Justine, by three years younger than she, in one of the capital's most celebrated abbeys where, until the ages of twelve and fifteen years, the one and the other of the two sisters had been denied no counsels, no masters, no books, and no polite talents.

At this period crucial to the virtue of the two maidens, they were in one day made bereft of everything: a frightful bankruptcy precipitated their father into circumstances so cruel that he perished of grief. One month later, his wife followed him into the grave. Two distant and heartless relatives deliberated what should be done with the young orphans; a hundred crowns apiece was their share of a legacy mostly swallowed up by creditors. No one caring to be burdened with them, the convent's door was opened, their dowry was put into their hands, and they were left at liberty to become what they wished.

Madame de Lorsange, at the time called Juliette, whose mind and character were to all intents and purposes as completely formed then as at thirty, the age she had attained at the opening of the tale we are about to relate, seemed nothing but overjoyed to be put at large; she gave not a moment's thought to the cruel events which had broken her chains. As for Justine, aged as we have remarked, twelve, hers was of a pensive and melancholy character, which made her far more keenly appreciate all the horrors of her situation. Full of tenderness, endowed with a surprising sensibility instead of with her sister's art and finesse, she was ruled by an ingenuousness, a candor that were to cause her to tumble into not a few pitfalls. To so many qualities this girl joined a sweet countenance, absolutely unlike that with which Nature had embellished Juliette; for all the artifice, wiles, coquetry one noticed in the features of the one, there were proportionate amounts of modesty, decency, and timidity to be admired in the other; a virginal air, large blue eyes very soulful and appealing, a dazzling fair skin, a supple and resilient body, a touching voice, teeth of ivory and the loveliest blond hair, there you have a sketch of this charming creature whose naive graces and delicate traits are beyond our power to describe.

They were given twenty-four hours to leave the convent; into their hands, together with their five score crowns, was thrown the responsibility to provide for themselves as they saw fit. Delighted to be her own mistress, Juliette spent a minute, perhaps two, wiping away Justine's tears, then, observing it was in vain, she fell to scolding instead of comforting her; she rebuked Justine for her sensitiveness; she told her, with a philosophic acuity far beyond her years, that in this world one must not be afflicted save by what affects one personally; that it was possible to find in oneself physical sensations of a sufficiently voluptuous piquancy to extinguish all the moral affections whose shock could be painful; that it was all the more essential so to proceed, since true wisdom consists infinitely more in doubling the sum of one's pleasures than in increasing the sum of one's pains; that, in a word, there was nothing one ought not do in order to deaden in oneself that perfidious sensibility from which none but others profit while to us it brings naught but troubles. But it is difficult to harden a gentle good heart, it resists the arguments of a toughened bad mind, and its solemn satisfactions console it for the loss of the bel-esprit's false splendors.

Juliette, employing other resources, then said to her sister, that with the age and the figure they both of them had, they could not die of hunger Ä she cited the example of one of their neighbors' daughters who, having escaped from her father's house, was presently very royally maintained and far happier, doubtless, than if she had remained at home with her family; one must, said Juliette, take good care to avoid believing it is marriage that renders a girl happy; that, a captive under the hymeneal laws, she has, with much ill-humor to suffer, a very slight measure of joys to expect; instead of which, were she to surrender herself to libertinage, she might always be able to protect herself against her lovers' moods, or be comforted by their number.

These speeches horrified Justine; she declared she preferred death to ignominy; whatever were her sister's reiterated urgings, she adamantly refused to take up lodging with her immediately she saw Juliette bent upon conduct that caused her to shudder.

After each had announced her very different intentions, the two girls separated without exchanging any promises to see each another again. Would Juliette, who, so she affirmed, intended to become a lady of consequence, would Juliette consent to receive a little girl whose virtuous but base inclinations might be able to bring her into dishonor? and, on her side, would Justine wish to jeopardize her morals in the society of a perverse creature who was bound to become public debauchery's toy and the lewd mob's victim? And so each bid an eternal adieu to the other, and they left the convent on the morrow.

During early childhood caressed by her mother's dressmaker, Justine believes this woman will treat her kindly now in this hour of her distress; she goes in search of the woman, she tells the tale of her woes, she asks employment . . . she is scarcely recognized; and is harshly driven out the door.

"Oh Heaven I" cries the poor little creature, "must my initial steps in this world be so quickly stamped with ill-fortune? That woman once loved me; why does she cast me away today? Alas! 'tis because I am poor and an orphan, because I have no more means and people are not esteemed save in reason of the aid and benefits one imagines may be had of them." Wringing her hands, Justine goes to find her cure; she describes her circumstances with the vigorous candor proper to her years . . . . She was wearing a little white garment, her lovely hair was negligently tucked up under her bonnet, her breast, whose development had scarcely begun, was hidden beneath two or three folds of gauze, her pretty face had somewhat of pallor owing to the unhappiness consuming her, a few tears rolled from her eyes and lent to them an additional expressiveness...

"You observe me, Monsieur," said she to the saintly ecclesiastic... "Yes, you observe me in what for a girl is a most dreadful position; I have lost my father and mother... Heaven has taken them from me at an age when I stand in greatest need of their assistance... They died ruined, Monsieur; we no longer have anything. There," she continued, "is all they left me," and she displayed her dozen louis, "and nowhere to rest my poor head . . . . You will have pity upon me, Monsieur, will you not? You are Religion's minister and Religion was always my heart's virtue; in the name of that God I adore and whose organ you are, tell me, as if you were a second father unto me, what must I do? what must become of me?"

3

The charitable priest clapped an inquisitive eye upon Justine, and made her answer, saying that the parish was heavily loaded; that it could not easily take new charges unto its bosom, but that if Justine wished to serve him, if she were prepared for hard toil, there would always be a crust of bread in his kitchen for her. And as he uttered those words, the gods' interpreter chuck'ed her under the chin; the kiss he gave her bespoke rather too much worldliness for a man of the church, and Justine, who had understood only too well, thrust him away. "Monsieur," said she, "I ask neither alms of you nor a position as your scullion; it was all too recently I took leave of an estate loftier than that which might make those two favors desirable; I am not yet reduced to imploring them; I am soliciting advice whereof my youth and my misfortunes put me in need, and you would have me purchase it at an excessively inflated price." Ashamed thus to have been unmasked, the pastor promptly drove the little creature away, and the unhappy Justine, twice rejected on the first day of her condemnation to isolation, now enters a house above whose door she spies a shingle; she rents a small chamber on the fourth floor, pays in advance for it, and, once established, gives herself over to lamentations all the more bitter because she is sensitive and because her little pride has just been compromised cruelly.

We will allow ourselves to leave her in this state for a short while in order to return to Juliette and to relate how, from the very ordinary condition in which she sets forth, no better furnished with resources than her sister, she nevertheless attains, over a period of fifteen years, the position of a titled woman, with an income of thirty thousand pounds, very handsome jewels, two or three houses in the city, as many in the country and, at the present moment, the heart, the fortune and the confidence of Monsieur de Corville, Councillor to the State, an important man much esteemed and about to have a minister's post. Her rise was not, there can be no question of it, unattended by difficulties: 'tis by way of the most shameful, most onerous apprenticeship that these ladies attain their objectives; and 'tis in all likelihood a veteran of unnumbered campaigns one may find today abed with a Prince: perhaps she yet carries the humiliating marks of the brutality of the libertines into whose hands her youth and inexperience flung her long ago.

Upon leaving the convent, Juliette went to find a woman whose name she had once heard mentioned by a youthful friend; perverted was what she desired to be and this woman was to pervert her; she arrived at her house with a small parcel under her arm, clad in a blue dressing gown nicely disarrayed, her hair straggling carelessly about, and showing the prettiest face in the world, if it is true that for certain eyes indecency may have its charms; she told her story to this woman and begged her to afford her the sanctuary she had provided her former friend.

"How old are you?" Madame Duvergier demanded.

"I will be fifteen in a few days, Madame," Juliette replied.

"And never hath mortal . . ." the matron continued.

"No, Madame, I swear it," answered Juliette.

"But, you know, in those convents," said the old dame, "sometimes a confessor, a nun, a companion... I must have conclusive evidence."

"You have but to look for it," Juliette replied with a blush.

And, having put on her spectacles, and having scrupulously examined things here and there, the duenna declared to the girl:

"Why, you've only to remain here, pay strict attention to what I say, give proof of unending complaisance and submissiveness to my practices, you need but be clean, economical, and frank with me, be prudent with your comrades and fraudulent when dealing with men, and before ten years' time I shall have you fit to occupy the best second-story apartment: you'll have a commode, pier-glass mirrors before you and a maid behind, and the art you will have acquired from me will give you what you need to procure yourself the rest."

These suggestions having left her lips, Duvergier lays hands on Juliette's little parcel; she asks her whether she does not have some money, and Juliette having too candidly admitted she had a hundred crowns, the dear mother confiscates them, giving her new boarding guest the assurance her little fortune will be chanced at the lottery for her, but that a girl must not have money. "It is," says she, "a means to doing evil, and in a period as corrupt as ours, a wise and well-born girl should carefully avoid all which might lure her into any snares. It is for your own good I speak, my little one," adds the duenna, "and you ought to be grateful for what I am doing." The sermon delivered, the newcomer is introduced to her colleagues; she is assigned a room in the house, and on the next day her maidenhead is put on sale.

Within four months the merchandise is sold successively to about one hundred buyers; some are content with the rose, others more fastidious or more depraved (for the question has not yet been decided) wish to bring to full flower the bud that grows adjacently. After each bout, Duvergier makes a few tailor's readjustments and for four months it is always the pristine fruits the rascal puts on the block. Finally, at the end of this harassing novitiate, Juliette obtains a lay sister's patents; from this moment onward, she is a recognized girl of the house; thereafter she is to share in its profits and losses. Another apprenticeship; if in the first school, aside from a few extravagances, Juliette served Nature, she altogether ignores Nature's laws in the second, where a complete shambles is made of what she once had of moral behavior; the triumph she obtains in vice totally degrades her soul; she feels that, having been born for crime, she must at least commit it grandly and give over languishing in a subaltern's role, which, although entailing the same misconduct, although abasing her equally, brings her a slighter, a much slighter profit. She is found agreeable by an elderly gentleman, much debauched, who at first has her come merely to attend to the affairs of the moment; she has the skill to cause herself magnificently to be kept; it is not long before she is appearing at the theater, at promenades, amongst the elite, the very cordon bleu of the Cytherean order; she is beheld, mentioned, desired, and the clever creature knows so well how to manage her affairs that in less than four years she ruins six men, the poorest of whom had an annuity of one hundred thousand crowns. Nothing more is needed to make her reputation; the blindness of fashionable people is such that the more one of these creatures has demonstrated her dishonesty, the more eager they are to get upon her list; it seems that the degree of her degradation and her corruption becomes the measure of the sentiments they dare display for her.

Juliette had just attained her twentieth year when a certain Comte de Lorsange, a gentleman out of Anjou, about forty years of age, became so captivated by her he resolved to bestow his name upon her; he awarded her an income of twelve thousand pounds and assured her of the rest of his fortune were he to be the first to die; he gave her, as well, a house, servants, lackeys, and the sort of mundane consideration which, in the space of two or three years, succeeded in causing her beginnings to be forgot.

It was at this point the fell Juliette, oblivious of all the fine feelings that had been hers by birthright and good education, warped by bad counsel and dangerous books, spurred by the desire to enjoy herself, but alone, and to have a name but not a single chain, bent her attentions to the culpable idea of abridging her husband's days. The odious project once conceived, she consolidated her scheme during those dangerous moments when the physical aspect is fired by ethical error, instants when one refuses oneself much less, for then nothing is opposed to the irregularity of vows or to the impetuosity of desires, and the voluptuousness one experiences is sharp and lively only by reason of the number of the restraints whence one bursts free, or their sanctity. The dream dissipated, were one to recover one's common-sense mood the thing would be of but mediocre import, 'tis the story of mental wrong-doing; everyone knows very well it offends no one; but, alas! one sometimes carries the thing a little farther. What, one ventures to wonder, what would not be the idea's realization, if its mere abstract shape has just exalted, has just so profoundly moved one? The accursed reverie is vivified, and its existence is a crime.

Fortunately for herself, Madame de Lorsange executed it in such secrecy that she was sheltered from all pursuit and with her husband she buried all traces of the frightful deed which precipitated him into the tomb.

Once again become free, and a countess, Madame de Lorsange returned to her former habits; but, believing herself to have some figure in the world, she put somewhat less of the indecent in her deportment. 'Twas no longer a kept girl, 'twas a rich widow who gave pretty suppers at which the Court and the City were only too happy to be included; in a word, we have here a correct woman who, all the same, would to bed for two hundred louis, and who gave herself for five hundred a month.

4

Until she reached the age of twenty-six, Madame de Lorsange made further brilliant conquests: she wrought the financial downfall of three foreign ambassadors, four Farmers-general, two bishops, a cardinal, and three knights of the King's Order; but as it is rarely one stops after the first offense, especially when it has turned out very happily, the unhappy Juliette blackened herself with two additional crimes similar to the first: one in order to plunder a lover who had entrusted a considerable sum to her, of which the man's family had no intelligence; the other in order to capture a legacy of one hundred thousand crowns another one of her lovers granted her in the name of a third, who was charged to pay her that amount after his death. To these horrors Madame de Lorsange added three or four infanticides. The fear of spoiling her pretty figure, the desire to conceal a double intrigue, all combined to make her resolve to stifle the proof of her debauches in her womb; and these mis-deeds, like the others, unknown, did not prevent our adroit and ambitious woman from finding new dupes every day.

It is hence true that prosperity may attend conduct of the very worst, and that in the very thick of disorder and corruption, all of what mankind calls happiness may shed itself bountifully upon life; but let this cruel and fatal truth cause no alarm; let honest folk be no more seriously tormented by the example we are going to present of disaster everywhere dogging the heels of Virtue; this criminal felicity is deceiving, it is seeming only; independently of the punishment most certainly reserved by Providence for those whom success in crime has seduced, do they not nourish in the depths of their soul a worm which unceasingly gnaws, prevents them from finding joy in these fictive gleams of meretricious well-being, and, instead of delights, leaves naught in their soul but the rending memory of the crimes which have led them to where they are? With what regards the luckless one fate persecutes, he has his heart for his comfort, and the interior ecstasies virtues procure bring him speedy restitution for the injustice of men.

Such was the state of affairs with Madame de Lorsange when Monsieur de Corville, fifty, a notable wielding the influence and possessing the privileges described further above, resolved entirely to sacrifice himself for this woman and to attach her to himself forever. Whether thanks to diligent attention, whether to maneuver, whether to policy on the part of Madame de Lorsange, he succeeded, and there had passed four years during which he dwelt with her, entirely as if with a legitimate wife, when the acquisition of a very handsome property not far from Montargis obliged both of them to go and spend some time in the Bourbonnais.

One evening, when the excellence of the weather had induced them to prolong their stroll beyond the bounds of their estate and toward Montargis, too fatigued, both, to attempt to return home as they had left, they halted at the inn where the coach from Lyon stops, with the intention of sending a man by horse to fetch them a carriage. In a cool, low-ceilinged room in this house, looking out upon a courtyard, they took their ease and were resting when the coach we just mentioned drew up at the hostelry.

It is a commonplace amusement to watch the arrival of a coach and the passengers' descent: one wagers on the sort of persons who are in it, and if one has gambled upon a whore, an officer, a few abbots and a monk, one is almost certain to win. Madame de Lorsange rises, Monsieur de Corville follows her; from the window they see the well-jolted company reel into the inn. There seemed to be no one left in the carriage when an officer of the mounted constabulary, stepping to the ground, received in his arms, from one of his comrades poised high on top of the coach, a girl of twenty-six or twenty-seven, dressed in a worn calico jacket and swathed to the eyes in a great black taffeta mantle. She was bound hand and foot like a criminal, and in such a weakened state, she would surely have fallen had her guards not given her support. A cry of surprise and horror escaped from Madame de Lorsange: the girl turned and revealed, together with the loveliest figure imaginable, the most noble, the most agreeable, the most interesting visage, in brief, there were there all the charms of a sort to please, and they were rendered yet a thousand times more piquant by that tender and touching air innocence contributes to the traits of beauty.

Monsieur de Corville and his mistress could not suppress their interest in the miserable girl. They approached, they demanded of one of the troopers what the unhappy creature had done.

"She is accused of three crimes," replied the constable, "'tis a question of murder, theft and arson; but I wish to tell your lordship that my comrade and I have never been so reluctant to take a criminal into custody; she's the most gentle thing, d'ye know, and seems to be the most honest too."

"Oh, la," said Monsieur de Corville, "it might easily be one of those blunders so frequent in the lower courts... and where were these crimes committed?"

"At an inn several leagues from Lyon, it's at Lyon she was tried; in accordance with custom she's going to Paris for confirmation of the sentence and then will be returned to Lyon to be executed."

Madame de Lorsange, having heard these words, said in lowered voice to Monsieur de Corville, that she fain would have from the girl's own lips the story of her troubles, and Monsieur de Corville, who was possessed of the same desire, expressed it to the pair of guards and identified himself. The officers saw no reason not to oblige, everyone decided to stay the night at Montargis; comfortable accomodations were called for; Monsieur de Corville declared he would be responsible for the prisoner, she was unbound, and when she had been given something to eat, Madame de Lorsange, unable to control her very great curiosity, and doubtless saying to herself, "This creature, perhaps innocent, is, however, treated like a criminal, whilst about me all is prosperity... I who am soiled with crimes and horrors"; Madame de Lorsange I say, as soon as she observed the poor girl to be somewhat restored, to some measure reassured by the caresses they hastened to bestow upon her, besought her to tell how it had fallen out that she, with so very sweet a face, found herself in such a dreadful plight.

"To recount you the story of my life, Madame," this lovely one in distress said to the Countess, "is to offer you the most striking example of innocence oppressed, is to accuse the hand of Heaven, is to bear complaint against the Supreme Being's will, is, in a sense, to rebel against His sacred designs... I dare not..." Tears gathered in this interesting girl's eyes and, after having given vent to them for a moment, she began her recitation in these terms.

Permit me to conceal my name and birth, Madame; without being illustrious, they are distinguished, and my origins did not destine me to the humiliation to which you see me reduced. When very young I lost my parents; provided with the slender inheritance they had left me, I thought I could expect a suitable position and, refusing to accept all those which were not, I gradually spent, at Paris where I was born, the little I possessed; the poorer I became, the more I was despised; the greater became my need of support, the less I was able to hope for it; but from amongst all the severities to which I was exposed at the beginning of my woeful career, from amongst all the terrible proposals that were made me, I will cite to you what befell me at the home of Monsieur Dubourg, one of the capital's richest tradesmen. The woman with whom I had lodgings had recommended him to me as someone whose influence and wealth might be able to meliorate the harshness of my situation; after having waited a very long time in this man's antechamber, I was admitted; Monsieur Dubourg, aged forty-eight, had just risen out of bed, and was wrapped in a dressing gown which barely hid his disorder; they were about to prepare his coiffure; he dismissed his servants and asked me what I wanted with him.

"Alas, Monsieur," I said, greatly confused, "I am a poor orphan not yet fourteen years old and I have already become familiar with every nuance of misfortune; I implore your commiseration, have pity upon me, I beseech you," and then I told in detail of all my ills, the difficulty I was having to find a place, perhaps I even mentioned how painful it was for me to have to take one, not having been born for a menial's condition. My suffering throughout it all, how I exhausted the little substance I had... failure to obtain work, my hope he would facilitate matters and help me find the wherewithal to live; in sum, I said everything that is dictated by the eloquence of wretchedness, always swift to rise in a sensitive soul . . . . After having listened to me with many distractions and much yawning, Monsieur Dubourg asked whether I had always been well-behaved. "I should be neither so poor nor so embarrassed, Monsieur," I answered him, "had I wished to cease to be."

"But," said Dubourg upon hearing that, "but what right have you to expect the wealthy to relieve you if you are in no way useful to them?"

"And of what service are you speaking, Monsieur? I asked nothing more than to render those decency and my years will permit me fulfill."

"The services of a child like yourself are of no great use in a household," Dubourg replied to me. "You have neither the age nor the appearance to find the place you are seeking. You would be better advised to occupy yourself with giving men pleasure and to labor to discover someone who will consent to take care of you; the virtue whereof you make such a conspicuous display is worthless in this world; in vain will you genuflect before its altars, its ridiculous incense will nourish you not at all. The thing which least flatters men, that which makes the least favorable impression upon them, for which they have the most supreme contempt, is good behavior in your sex; here on earth, my child, nothing but what brings in gain or insures power is accounted; and what does the virtue of women profit us I It is their wantonness which serves and amuses us; but their chastity could not interest us less. When, to be brief, persons of our sort give, it is never except to receive; well, how may a little girl like yourself show gratitude for what one does for her if it is not by the most complete surrender of all that is desired of her body!"

"Oh, Monsieur," I replied, grown heavy of heart and uttering a sigh, "then uprightness and benevolence are to be found in man no longer!"

"Precious little," Dubourg rejoined. "How can you expect them still to exist after all the wise things that have been said and written about them? We have rid ourselves of this mania of obliging others gratuitously; it was recognized that charity's pleasures are nothing but sops thrown to pride, and we turned our thoughts to stronger sensations; it has been noticed, for example, that with a child like you, it is infinitely preferable to extract, by way of dividends upon one's

investment, all the pleasures lechery is able to offer Ä much better these delights
than the very insipid and futile ones said to come of the disinterested giving of
help; his reputation for being a liberal man, an alms-giving and generous man, is
not, even at the instant when he most enjoys it, comparable to the slightest
sensual pleasure."

5

"Oh, Monsieur, in the light of such principles the miserable must therefore
perish!"

"Does it matter? We have more subjects in France than are needed; given the
mechanism's elastic capacities for production, the State can easily afford to be
burdened by fewer people."

"But do you suppose children respect their fathers when they are thus despised
by them?"

"And what to a father is the love of the children who are a nuisance to him?"

"Would it then have been better had they been strangled in the cradle?"

"Certainly, such is the practice in numerous countries; it was the custom of the
Greeks, it is the custom in China: there, the offspring of the poor are exposed, or
are put to death. What is the good of letting those creatures live who, no longer
able to count upon their parents' aid either because they are without parents or
because they are not wanted or recognized by them, henceforth are useful for
nothing and simply weigh upon the State: that much surplus commodity, you see,
and the market is glutted already; bastards, orphans, malformed infants should be
condemned to death immediately they are pupped: the first and the second
because, no longer having anyone who wishes or who is able to take care of them,
they are mere dregs which one day can have nothing but an undesirable effect
upon the society they contaminate; the others because they cannot be of any
usefulness to it; the one and the other of these categories are to society what are
excrescences to the flesh, battening upon the healthy members' sap, degrading
them, enfeebling them; or, if you prefer, they are like those vegetable parasites
which, attaching themselves to sound plants, cause them to deteriorate by sucking
up their nutritive juices. It's a shocking outrage, these alms destined to feed scum,
these most luxuriously appointed houses they have the madness to construct
quite as if the human species were so rare, so precious one had to preserve it down
to its last vile portion! But enough of politics whereof, my child, you are not likely
to understand anything; why lament your fate? for it is in your power, and yours
only, to remedy it."

"Great Heavens! at the price of what!"

"At the price of an illusion, of something that has none but the value
wherewith your pride invests it. Well," continued this barbarian, getting to his feet
and opening the door, "that is all I can do for you; consent to it, or deliver me
from your presence; I have no fondness for beggars . . . ."

My tears flowed fast, I was unable to check them; would you believe it, Madame? they irritated rather than melted this man. He shut the door and, seizing my dress at the shoulder, he said most brutally he was going to force from me what I would not accord him voluntarily. At this cruel moment my misery endowed me with courage; I freed myself from his grasp and rushed toward the door:

"Odious man," said I as I fled from him, "may the Heaven you have so grievously offended some day punish your execrable heartlessness as it merits to be. You are worthy neither of the riches you have put to such vile use, nor of the very air you breathe in a world you defile with your barbarities."

I lost no time telling my hostess of the reception given me by the person to whom she had sent me; but what was my astonishment to have this wretch belabor me with reproaches rather than share my sorrow.

"You idiotic chit!" said she in a great rage, "do you imagine men are such great dupes as to dole out alms to little girls such as you without requiring something for their money? Monsieur Dubourg's behavior was far too gentle; in his place I should not have allowed you to leave without having had satisfaction from you. But since you do not care to profit from the aid I offer you, make your own arrangements as you please; you owe me money: pay it tomorrow; otherwise, it's to jail."

"Madame, have pity!"

"Yes, yes, pity; one need only have pity and one starves to death."

"But what would you have me do?"

"You must go back to Dubourg; you must appease him; you must bring home money to me; I will visit him, I will give him notice; if I am able, I'll repair the damage your stupidity has caused; I will convey your apologies, but keep it in mind, you had better improve your conduct."

Ashamed, desperate, knowing not which way to turn, seeing myself savagely repulsed by everyone, I told Madame Desroches (that was my landlady's name) that I had decided to do whatever had to be done to satisfy her. She went to the financier's house and upon her return advised me that she had found him in a very irritable mood, that it had not been without an effort she had managed to incline him in my favor, that by dint of supplications she had at least persuaded him to see me again the following morning, but that I would have to keep a strict watch over my behavior, because, were I to take it into my head to disobey him again, he himself would see to it I was imprisoned forever.

All atremble, I arrived; Dubourg was alone and in a state yet more indecent than on the previous day. Brutality, libertinage, all the characteristics of the debauchee glittered in his cunning glances.

"Thank Desroches," he said harshly, "for it is as a favor to her I intend to show you an instant's kindness; you must surely be aware how little you deserve it after your performance yesterday. Undress yourself and if you once again manifest the least resistance to my desires, two men, waiting for you in the next room, will conduct you to a place whence you will never emerge alive."

"Oh Monsieur," say I, weeping, clutching the wicked man's knees, "unbend, I beseech you; be so generous as to relieve me without requiring what would be so costly I should rather offer you my life than submit to it . . . . Yes, I prefer to die a thousand times over than violate the principles I received in my childhood . . . . Monsieur, Monsieur, constrain me not, I entreat you; can you conceive of gleaning happiness in the depths of tears and disgust? Dare you suspect pleasure where you see naught but loathing? No sooner shall you have consummated your crime than my despair will overwhelm you with remorse . . . ."

But the infamies to which Dubourg abandoned himself prevented me from continuing; that I was able to have believed myself capable of touching a man who was already finding, in the very spectacle of my suffering, one further vehicle for his horrible passions! Would you believe it, Madame? becoming inflamed by the shrill accents of my pleadings, savoring them inhumanly, the wretch disposed himself for his criminal attempts! He gets up, and exhibiting himself to me in a state over which reason is seldom triumphant, and wherein the opposition of the object which causes reason's downfall is but an additional ailment to delirium, he seizes me brutally, impetuously snatches away the veils which still conceal what he burns to enjoy; he caresses me . . . . Oh! what a picture, Great God I What unheard-of mingling of harshness... and lewdness! It seemed that the Supreme Being wished, in that first of my encounters, to imprint forever in me all the horror I was to have for a kind of crime whence there was to be born the torrent of evils that have beset me since. But must I complain of them? No, needless to say; to his excesses I owe my salvation; had there been less debauchery in him, I were a ruined girl; Dubourg's flames were extinguished in the fury of his enterprises, Heaven intervened in my behalf against the monster before he could commit the offenses he was readying for, and the loss of his powers, before the sacrifice could occur, preserved me from being its victim.

The consequence was Dubourg became nothing if not more insolent; he laid upon me the blame for his weakness' mistakes, wanted to repair them with new outrages and yet more mortifying invectives; there was nothing he did not say to me, nothing he did not attempt, nothing his perfidious imagination, his adamantine character and the depravation of his manners did not lead him to undertake. My clumsiness made him impatient: I was far from wishing to participate in the thing, to lend myself to it was as much as I could do, my remorse remained lively. However, it was all for naught, submitting to him, I ceased to inflame him; in vain he passed successively from tenderness to rigor... from groveling to tyranny... from an air of decency to the profligate's excesses, in vain, I say, there was nothing for it, we were both exhausted, and happily he was unable to recover what he needed to deliver more dangerous assaults. He gave it up, made me promise to come the next day, and to be sure of me he refused absolutely to give me anything above the sum I owed Desroches. Greatly humiliated by the adventure and firmly resolved, whatever might happen to me, not to expose myself a third time, I returned to where I was lodging. I announced my intentions to Desroches, paid her, and heaped maledictions upon the criminal capable of so cruelly exploiting my misery. But my imprecations, far from drawing the wrath of God down upon him, only added to his good fortune; and a week later I learned this signal libertine had just obtained a general trusteeship from the Government, which would augment his revenues by more than five hundred thousand pounds per annum. I was absorbed in the reflections such unexpected inconsistencies of fate inevitably give rise to, when a momentary ray of hope seemed to shine in my eyes.

Desroches came to tell me one day that she had finally located a house into which I could be received with pleasure provided my comportment remained of the best. "Great Heaven, Madame," I cried, transported, throwing myself into her arms, "that condition is the one I would stipulate myself Ä you may imagine how happy I am to accept it." The man I was to serve was a famous Parisian usurer who had become rich, not only by lending money upon collateral, but even by stealing from the public every time he thought he could do so in safety. He lived in the rue Quincampoix, had a third-story flat, and shared it with a creature of fifty years he called his wife and who was at least as wicked as he.

"Therese," this miser said to me (such was the name I had taken in order to hide my own), "Therese, the primary virtue in this house is probity; if ever you make off with the tenth part of a penny, I'll have you hanged, my child, d'ye see. The modest ease my wife and I enjoy is the fruit of our immense labors, and of our perfect sobriety . . . . Do you eat much, little one?"

"A few ounces of bread each day, Monsieur," I replied, "water, and a little soup when I am lucky enough to get it."

"Soup! Bleeding Christ! Soup! Behold, deary," said the usurer to his dame, "behold and tremble at the progress of luxury: it's looking for circumstances, it's been dying of hunger for a year, and now it wants to eat soup; we scarcely have it once a week, on Sunday, we who work like galley slaves: you'll have three ounces of bread a day, my daughter, plus half a bottle of river water, plus one of my wife's old dresses every eighteen months, plus three crowns' wages at the end of each year, if we are content with your services, if your economy responds to our own and if, finally, you make the house prosper through orderliness and arrangement. Your duties are mediocre, they're done in jig time; 'tis but a question of washing and cleaning this six-room apartment thrice a week, of making our beds, answering the door, powdering my wig, dressing my wife's hair, looking after the dog and the parakeet, lending a hand in the kitchen, washing the utensils, helping my wife whenever she prepares us a bite to eat, and daily devoting four or five hours to the washing, to mending stockings, hats, and other little house-hold odds and ends; you observe, Therese, 'tis nothing at all, you will have ample free time to yourself, we will permit you to employ it to your own interest, provided, my child, you are good, discreet and, above all, thrifty, that's of the essence."

6

You may readily imagine, Madame, that one had to be in the frightful state I indeed was in to accept such a position; not only was there infinitely more work to be done than my strength permitted me to undertake, but should I be able to live upon what was offered me? However, I was careful to raise no difficulties and was installed that same evening.

Were my cruel situation to permit me to amuse you for an instant, Madame, when I must think of nothing but gaining your compassion, I should dare describe some of the symptoms or avarice I witnessed while in that house; but a catastrophe so terrible for me was awaiting me during my second year there that it is by no means easy to linger over entertaining details before making you acquainted with my miseries.

Nevertheless, you will know, Madame, that, for light in Monsieur du Harpin's apartment, there was never any but what he got from the street lamp which, happily, was placed opposite his room; never did Monsieur or Madame use linen; what I washed was hoarded away, it was never touched; on the sleeves of Monsieur's coat, as well as upon Madame's dress, were old gauntlet cuffs sewn over the material, and these I removed and washed every Saturday evening; no sheets; no towels, and that to avoid laundry expenses. Never was wine drunk in her house, clear water being, declared Madame du Harpin, the natural drink of man, the healthiest and least dangerous. Every time bread was sliced, a basket was put beneath the knife so that whatever fell would not be lost; into this container went, also, and with exactitude all the scraps and leavings that might survive the meal, and this compound, fried up on Sunday together with a little butter, made a banquet for the day of rest; never was one to beat clothing or too energetically dust the furniture for fear of wearing it out, instead, very cautiously, one tickled about with a feather. Monsieur's shoes, and Madame's as well, were double-soled with iron, they were the same shoes that had served them on their wedding day; but a much more unusual custom was the one they had me practice once a week: there was in the apartment a rather large room whose walls were not papered; I was expected to take a knife and scrape and shave away a certain quantity of plaster, and this I next passed through a fine sieve; what resulted from this operation became the powder wherewith every morning I sprinkled Monsieur's peruke and Madame's hair, done up in a bun. Ah! wouldst to God those had been the only turpitudes of which this evil pair had made habits! Nothing's more normal than the desire to conserve one's property; but what is not normal is the desire to augment it by the accession of the property of others. And it was not long before I perceived that it was only thus du Harpin acquired his wealth.

Above us there lodged a solitary individual of considerable means who was the owner of some handsome jewels, and whose belongings, whether because of their proximity or because they had passed through my master's hands, were very well known to him; I often heard him express regrets to his wife over the loss of a

certain gold box worth fifty or sixty louis, which article would infallibly have
remained his, said he, had he proceeded with greater cleverness. In order to
console himself for the sale of the said box, the good Monsieur du Harpin
projected its theft, and it was to me he entrusted the execution of his plan.

After having delivered a long speech upon the indifference of robbery, upon,
indeed, its usefulness in the world, since it maintains a sort of equilibrium which
totally confounds the inequality of property; upon the infrequence of punishment,
since out of every twenty thieves it could be proven that not above two dies on
the gallows; after having demonstrated to me, with an erudition of which I had
not dreamt Monsieur du Harpin capable, that theft was honored throughout
Greece, that several races yet acknowledge it, favor it, and reward it for a bold
deed simultaneously giving proof of courage and skill (two virtues indispensable
to a warlike nation), after having, in a word, exalted his personal influence which
would extricate me from all embarrassments in the event I should be detected,
Monsieur du Harpin tendered me two lock picks, one to open the neighbor's front
door, the other his secretary within which lay the box in question; incessantly he
enjoined me to get him this box and, in return for so important a service, I could
expect, for two years, to receive an additional crown.

"Oh Monsieur!" I exclaimed, shuddering at his proposal, "is it possible a master
dare thus corrupt his domestic ! What prevents me from turning against you the
weapons you put into my hands? Du Harpin, much confused, fell back on a lame
subterfuge; what he was doing, said he, was being done with the simple intention
of testing me; how fortunate that I had resisted this temptation, he added... how
I should have been doomed had I succumbed, etc. I scoffed at this lie; but I was
soon enough aware of what a mistake it had been to answer him with such
asperity: malefactors do not like to find resistance in those they seek to seduce;
unfortunately, there is no middle ground or median attitude when one is so
unlucky as to have been approached by them: one must necessarily thereupon
become either their accomplices, which is exceedingly dangerous, or their
enemies, which is even more so. Had I been a little experienced, I would have
quit the house forthwith, but it was already written in Heaven that every one of
the honest gestures that was to emanate from me would be answered by
misfortunes.

Monsieur Du Harpin let more than a month drift by, that is to say, he waited
until the end of my second year with him, and waited without showing the least
hint of resentment at the refusal I had given him, when one evening, having just
retired to my room to taste a few hours of repose, I suddenly heard my door burst
opens and there, not without terror, I saw Monsieur du Harpin and four soldiers
of the watch standing by my bed. "Perform your duty, Sirrah," said he to the men
of the law, "this wretch has stolen from me a diamond worth a thousand crowns,
you will find it in her chamber or upon her person, the fact is certain."

"I have robbed you, Monsieur!" said I, sore troubled and springing from my
bed, "I! Great Heaven! Who knows better than you the contrary to be true! Who

should be more deeply aware than you to what point I loathe robbery and to what degree it is unthinkable I could have committed it." But du Harpin made a great uproar to drown out my words; he continued to order perquisitions, and the miserable ring was discovered in my mattress. To evidence of this strength there was nothing to reply; I was seized instantly, pinioned, and led to prison without being able to prevail upon the authorities to listen to one word in my favor.

The trial of an unfortunate creature who has neither influence nor protection is conducted with dispatch in a land where virtue is thought incompatible with misery, where poverty is enough to convict the accused; there, an unjust prepossession causes it to be supposed that he who ought to have committed a crime did indeed commit it; sentiments are proportioned according to the guilty one's estate; and when once gold or titles are wanting to establish his innocence, the impossibility that he be innocent then appears self-evident.

(o ages yet to come ! You shall no longer be witness to these horrors and infamies abounding!)

I defended myself, it did no good, in vain I furnished the best material to the lawyer whom a protocol of form required be given me for an instant or two; my employer accused me, the diamond had been discovered in my room; it was plain I had stolen it. When I wished to describe Monsieur du Harpin's awful traffic and prove that the misfortune that had struck me was naught but the fruit of his vengeance and the consequence of his eagerness to be rid of a creature who, through possession of his secret, had become his master, these pleadings were interpreted as so many recriminations, and I was informed that for twenty years Monsieur du Harpin had been known as a man of integrity, incapable of such a horror. I was transferred to the Conciergerie, where I saw myself upon the brink of having to pay with my life for having refused to participate in a crime; I was shortly to perish; only a new misdeed could save me: Providence willed that Crime serve at least once as an aegis unto Virtue, that crime might preserve it from the abyss which is some-day going to engulf judges together with their imbecility.

I had about me a woman, probably forty years old, as celebrated for her beauty as for the variety and number of her villainies; she was called Dubois and, like the unlucky Therese, was on the eve of paying the capital penalty, but as to the exact form of it the judges were yet mightily perplexed: having rendered herself guilty of every imaginable crime, they found themselves virtually obliged to invent a new torture for her, or to expose her to one whence we ordinarily exempt our sex. This woman had become interested in me, criminally interested without doubt, since the basis of her feelings, as I learned afterward, was her extreme desire to make a proselyte of me.

Only two days from the time set for our execution, Dubois came to me; it was at night. She told me not to lie down to sleep, but to stay near her side. Without attracting attention, we moved as close as we could to the prison door. "Between seven and eight," she said, "the Conciergerie will catch fire, I have seen to it; no question about it, many people will be burned; it doesn't matter, Therese," the evil creature went on, "the fate of others must always be as nothing to us when our own lives are at stake; well, we are going to escape here, of that you can be sure; four men Ä my confederates Ä will join us and I guarantee you we will be free."

I have told you, Madame, that the hand of God which had just punished my innocence, employed crime to protect me; the fire began, it spread, the blaze was horrible, twenty-one persons were consumed, but we made a successful sally. The same day we reached the cottage of a poacher, an intimate friend of our band who dwelt in the forest of Bondy.

"There you are, Therese," Dubois says to me, "free. You may now choose the kind of life you wish, but were I to have any advice to give you, it would be to renounce the practice of virtue which, as you have noticed, is the courting of disaster; a misplaced delicacy led you to the foot of the scaffold, an appalling crime rescued you from it; have a look about and see how useful are good deeds in this world, and whether it is really worth the trouble immolating yourself for them. Therese, you are young and attractive, heed me, and in two years I'll have led you to a fortune; but don't suppose I am going to guide you there along the paths of virtue: when one wants to get on, my dear girl, one must stop at nothing; decide, then, we have no security in this cottage, we've got to leave in a few hours."

"Oh Madame," I said to my benefactress, "I am greatly indebted to you, and am far from wishing to disown my obligations; you saved my life; in my view, 'tis frightful the thing was achieved through a crime and, believe me, had I been the one charged to commit it, I should have preferred a thousand deaths to the anguish of participating in it; I am aware of all the dangers I risk in trusting myself to the honest sentiments which will always remain in my heart; but whatever be the thorns of virtue, Madame, I prefer them unhesitatingly and always to the perilous favors which are crime's accompaniment. There are religious principles within me which, may it please Heaven, will never desert me; if Providence renders difficult my career in life, 'tis in order to compensate me in a better world. That hope is my consolation, it sweetens my griefs, it soothes me in my sufferings, it fortifies me in distress, and causes me confidently to face all the ills it pleases God to visit upon me. That joy should straightway be extinguished in my soul were I perchance to besmirch it with crime, and together with the fear of chastisements in this world I should have the painful anticipation of torments in the next, which would not for one instant procure me the tranquillity I thirst after."

"Those are absurd doctrines which will have you on the dung heap in no time, my girl," said Dubois with a frown; "believe me: forget God's justice, His future punishments and rewards, the lot of those platitudes lead us nowhere but to death from starvation. O Therese, the callousness of the Rich legitimates the bad conduct of the Poor; let them open their purse to our needs, let humaneness reign in their hearts and virtues will take root in ours; but as long as our misfortune, our patient endurance of it, our good faith, our abjection only serves to double the weight of our chains, our crimes will be their doing, and we will be fools indeed to abstain from them when they can lessen the yoke wherewith their cruelty bears us down. Nature has caused us all to be equals born, Therese; if fate is pleased to upset the primary scheme of the general law, it is up to us to correct its caprices and through our skill to repair the usurpations of the strongest. I love to hear these rich ones, these titled ones, these magistrates and these priests, I love to see them preach virtue to us. It is not very difficult to forswear theft when one has three or four times what one needs to live; it is not very necessary to plot murder when one is surrounded by nothing but adulators and thralls unto whom one's will is law; nor is it very hard to be temperate and sober when one has the most succulent dainties constantly within one's reach; they can well contrive to be sincere when there is never any apparent advantage in falsehood... But we, Therese, we whom the barbaric Providence you are mad enough to idolize, has condemned to slink in the dust of humiliation as doth the serpent in grass, we who are beheld with disdain only because we are poor, who are tyrannized because we are weak; we, who must quench our thirst with gall and who, wherever we go, tread on the thistle always, you would have us shun crime when its hand alone opens up unto us the door to life, maintains us in it, and is our only protection when our life is threatened; you would have it that, degraded and in perpetual abjection, while this class dominating us has to itself all the blessings of fortune, we reserve for ourselves naught but pain, beatings, suffering, nothing but want and tears, brandings and the gibbet. No, no, Therese, no; either this Providence you reverence is made only for our scorn, or the world we see about us is not at all what Providence would have it. Become better acquainted with your Providence, my child, and be convinced that as soon as it places us in a situation where evil becomes necessary, and while at the same time it leaves us the possibility of doing it, this evil harmonizes quite as well with its decrees as does good, and Providence gains as much by the one as by the other; the state in which she has created us is equality: he who disturbs is no more guilty than he who seeks to re-establish the balance; both act in accordance with received impulses, both have to obey those impulses and enjoy them."

7

I must confess that if ever I was shaken it was by this clever woman's seductions; but a yet stronger voice, that of my heart to which I gave heed, combatted her sophistries; I declared to Dubois that I was determined never to allow myself to be corrupted. "Very well!" she replied, "become what you wish, I abandon you to your sorry fate; but if ever you get yourself hanged, which is an end you cannot avoid, thanks to the fatality which inevitably saves the criminal by sacrificing the virtuous, at least remember before dying never to mention us."

While we were arguing thus, Dubois' four companions were drinking with the poacher, and as wine disposes the malefactor's heart to new crimes and causes him to forget his old, our bandits no sooner learned of my resolution than, unable to make me their accomplice, they decided to make me their victim; their principles, their manners, the dark retreat we were in, the security they thought they enjoyed, their drunkenness, my age, my innocence Ä everything encouraged them. They get up from table, they confer in whispers, they consult Dubois, doings whose lugubrious mystery makes me shiver with horror, and at last there comes an order to me then and there to satisfy the desires of each of the four; if I go to it cheerfully, each will give me a crown to help me along my way; if they must employ violence, the thing will be done all the same; but the better to guard their secret, once finished with me they will stab me, and will bury me at the foot of yonder tree.

I need not paint the effect this cruel proposition had upon me, Madame, you will have no difficulty understanding that I sank to my knees before Dubois, I besought her a second time to be my protectress: the low creature did but laugh at my tears:

"Oh by God !" quoth she, "here's an unhappy little one. What! you shudder before the obligation to serve four fine big boys one after another? Listen to me," she added, after some reflection, "my sway over these dear lads is sufficiently great for me to obtain a reprieve for you upon condition you render yourself worthy of it."

"Alas ! Madame, what must I do?" I cried through my tears; "command me; I am ready."

"Join us, throw in your lot with us, and commit the same deeds, without show of the least repugnance; either that, or I cannot save you from the rest." I did not think myself in a position to hesitate; by accepting this cruel condition I exposed myself to further dangers, to be sure, but they were the less immediate; perhaps I might be able to avoid them, whereas nothing could save me from those with which I was actually menaced.

"I will go everywhere with you, Madame," was my prompt answer to Dubois, "everywhere, I promise you; shield me from the fury of these men and I shall never leave your side while I live."

"Children," Dubois said to the four bandits, "this girl is one of the company, I am taking her into it; I ask you to do her no ill, don't put her stomach off the m,tier during her first days in it; you see how useful her age and face can be to us; let's employ them to our advantage rather than sacrifice them to our pleasures."

But such is the degree of energy in man's passions nothing can subdue them. The persons I was dealing with were in no state to heed reason: all four surrounded me, devoured me with their fiery glances, menaced me in a still more terrible manner; they were about to lay hands on me, I was about to become their victim.

"She has got to go through with it," one of them declared, "it's too late for discussion: was she not told she must give proof of virtues in order to be admitted into a band of thieves? and once a little used, won't she be quite as serviceable as she is while a virgin?"

I am softening their expressions, you understand, Madame, I am sweetening the scene itself; alas! their obscenities were such that your modesty might suffer at least as much from beholding them unadorned as did my shyness.

A defenseless and trembling victim, I shuddered; I had barely strength to breathe; kneeling before the quartet, I raised my feeble arms as much to supplicate the men as to melt Dubois' heart . . . .

"An instant," said one who went by the name of Coeur-de-fer and appeared to be the band's chief, a man of thirty-six years, of a bull's strength and bearing the face of a satyr; "one moment, friends: it may be possible to satisfy everyone concerned; since this little girl's virtue is so precious to her and since, as Dubois states it very well, this quality otherwise put into action could become worth something to us, let's leave it to her; but we have got to be appeased; our mood is warm, Dubois, and in the state we are in, d'ye know, we might perhaps cut your own throat if you were to stand between us and our pleasures; let's have Therese instantly strip as naked as the day she came into the world, and next let's have her adopt one after the other all the positions we are pleased to call for, and meanwhile Dubois will sate our hungers, we'll burn our incense upon the altars' entrance to which this creature refuses us."

"Strip naked!" I exclaimed, "Oh Heaven, what is it thou doth require of me? When I shall have delivered myself thus to your eyes, who will be able to answer for me?..."

But Coeur-de-fer, who seemed in no humor either to grant me more or to suspend his desires, burst out with an oath and struck me in a manner so brutal that I saw full well compliance was my last resort. He put himself in Dubois' hands, she having been put by his in a disorder more or less the equivalent of mine and, as soon as I was as he desired me to be, having made me crouch down upon all fours so that I resembled a beast, Dubois took in hand a very monstrous object and led it to the peristyles of first one and then the other of Nature's altars, and under her guidance the blows it delivered to me here and there were like those of a battering ram thundering at the gates of a besieged town in olden days. The shock of the initial assault drove me back; enraged, Coeur-de-fer threatened me with harsher treatments were I to retreat from these; Dubois is instructed to redouble her efforts, one of the libertines grasps my shoulders and prevents me from staggering before the concussions: they become so fierce I am in blood and am able to avoid not a one.

"Indeed," stammers Coeur-de-fer, "in her place I'd prefer to open the doors rather than see them ruined this way, but she won't have it, and we're not far from the capitulation . . . . Vigorously ... vigorously, Dubois . . . ."

And the explosive eruption of this debauchee's flames, almost as violent as a stroke of lightning, flickers and dies upon ramparts ravaged without being breached.

The second had me kneel between his legs and while Dubois administered to him as she had to the other, two enterprises absorbed his entire attention: sometimes he slapped, powerfully but in a very nervous manner, either my cheeks or my breasts; sometimes his impure mouth fell to sucking mine. In an instant my face turned purple, my chest red . . . . I was in pain, I begged him to spare me, tears leapt from my eyes; they roused him, he accelerated his activities; he bit my tongue, and the two strawberries on my breasts were so bruised that I slipped backward, but was kept from falling. They thrust me toward him, I was everywhere more furiously harassed, and his ecstasy supervened . . . .

The third bade me mount upon and straddle two somewhat separated chairs and, seating himself betwixt them, excited by Dubois, lying in his arms, he had me bend until his mouth was directly below the temple of Nature; never will you imagine, Madame, what this obscene mortal took it into his head to do; willy-nilly, I was obliged to satisfy his every need . . . . Just Heaven! what man, no matter how depraved, can taste an instant of pleasure in such things . . . . I did what he wished, inundated him, and my complete submission procured this foul man an intoxication of which he was incapable without this infamy.

The fourth attached strings to all parts of me to which it was possible to tie them, he held the ends in his hands and sat down seven or eight feet from my body; Dubois' touches and kisses excited him prodigiously; I was standing erect: 'twas by sharp tugs now on this string, now on some other that the savage irritated his pleasures; I swayed, I lost balance again and again, he flew into an ecstasy each time tottered; finally, he pulled all the cords at once, I fell to the floor in front of him: such was his design: and my fore-head, my breast, my cheeks received the proofs of a delirium he owed to none but this mania. That is what I suffered, Madame, but at least my honor was respected even though my modesty assuredly was not. Their calm restored, the bandits spoke of regaining the road, and that same night we reached Tremblai with the intention of approaching the woods of Chantilly, where it was thought a few good prizes might be awaiting us. Nothing equaled my despair at being obliged to accompany such persons, and I was determined to part with them as soon as I could do so without risk. The following day we fell hard by Louvres, sleeping under haystacks; I felt in need of Dubois' support and wanted to pass the night by her side; but it seemed she had planned to employ it otherwise than protecting my virtue from the attacks I dreaded; three of the thieves surrounded her and before my very eyes the abominable creature gave herself to all three simultaneously. The fourth approached me; it was the captain. "Lovely Therese," said he, "I hope you shall not refuse me at least the pleasure of spending the night with you?" and as he perceive my extreme unwillingness, "fear not," went on; "we'll have a chat together, and I will attempt nothing without your consent. "O Therese," cried he, folding me in his arms, " 'tis all foolishness, don't you know, to be so pretentious with us. Why are you concerned to guard your purity in our midst? Even were we to agree to respect it, could it be compatible with the interests of the band? No need to hide it from you, my dear; for when we settle down in cities, we count on you to snare us some dupes."

"Why, Monsieur," I replied, "since it is certain I should prefer death to these horrors, of what use can I be to you, and why do you oppose my flight?"

"We certainly do oppose it, my girl," Coeur-de-fer rejoined, "you must serve either our pleasures or our interests; your poverty imposes the yoke upon you, and you have got to adapt to it. But, Therese, and well you know it, there is nothing in this world that cannot be somehow arranged: so listen to me, and accept the management of your own fate: agree to live with me, dear girl, consent to belong to me and be properly my own, and I will spare you the baneful role for which you are destined."

"I, Sir, I become the mistress of a -"

"Say the word, Therese, out with it: a scoundrel, eh? Oh, I admit it, but I have no other titles to offer you; that our sort does not marry you are doubtless well aware: marriage is one of the sacraments, Therese, and full of an undiscriminating contempt for them all, with none do we ever bother. However, be a little reasonable; that sooner or later you lose what is so dear to you is an indispensable necessity, hence would it not be better to sacrifice it to a single man who thereupon will become your support and protector, is that not better, I say, than to be prostituted to everyone?"

"But why must it be," I replied, "that I have no other alternative?"

"Because, Therese, we have got you, and because the stronger is always the better reason; La Fontaine made the remark ages ago. Truthfully," he continued rapidly, "is it not a ridiculous extravagance to assign, as you do, such a great value to the most futile of all things? How can a girl be so dull-witted as to believe that virtue may depend upon the somewhat greater or lesser diameter of one of her physical parts? What difference does it make to God or man whether this part be intact or tampered with? I will go further: it being the intention of Nature that each individual fulfill on this earth all of the purposes for which he has been formed, and women existing only to provide pleasure for men, it is plainly to outrage her thus to resist the intention she has in your regard. It is to wish to be a creature useless in this world and consequently one contemptible. This chimerical propriety, which they have had the absurdity to present to you as a virtue and which, since infancy, far from being useful to Nature and society, is an obvious defiance of the one and the other, this propriety, I say, is no more than a reprehensible stubbornness of which a person as mettlesome and full of intelligence as you should not wish to be guilty. No matter; continue to hear me out, dear girl, I am going to prove my desire to please you and to respect your weakness. I will not by any means touch that phantom, Therese, whose possession causes all your delight; a girl has more than one favor to give, and one can offer to Venus in many a temple; I will be content with the most mediocre; you know, my dear, near the Cyprean altar, there is situate an obscure grot into whose solitude Love retires, the more energetically to seduce us: such will be the altar where I will burn my incense; no disadvantages there, Therese; if pregnancies affright you, 'tis not in this manner they can come about, never will your pretty figure be deformed this way; the maidenhead so cherished by you will be preserved unimpaired, and whatever be the use to which you decide to put it, you can propose it unattainted. Nothing can betray a girl from this quarter, however rude or multiple the attacks may be; as soon as the bee has left off sucking the pollen, the rose's calix closes shut again; one would never imagine it had been opened. There exist girls who have known ten years of pleasure this way, even with several men, women who were just as much married as anyone else after it all, and on their wedding nights they proved quite as virgin as could be wished. How many fathers, what a multitude of brothers have thuswise abused their daughters and sisters without the latter having become on that account any the less worthy of a later hymeneal sacrifice! How many confessors have not employed the same route to satisfaction, without parents experiencing the mildest disquiet; in one word, 'tis the mystery's asylum, 'tis there where it connects itself with love by ties of prudence . . . . Need I tell you further, Therese, that although this is the most secret temple it is howbeit the most voluptuous; what is necessary to happiness is found nowhere else, and that easy vastness native to the adjacent aperture falls far short of having the piquant charms of a locale into which one does not enter without effort, where one takes up one's abode only at the price of some trouble; women themselves reap an advantage from it, and those whom reason compels to know this variety of pleasure, never pine after the others. Try it, Therese, try, and we shall both be contented."

8

"Oh Monsieur," I replied, "I have no experience of the thing; but I have heard it said that this perversion you recommend outrages women in a yet more sensitive manner . . . . It more grievously offends Nature. The hand of Heaven takes its vengeance upon it in this world, Sodom provides the example."

"What innocence, my dear, what childishness," the libertine retorted; "who ever told you such a thing? Yet a little more attention, Therese, let me proceed to rectify your ideas.

"The wasting of the seed destined to perpetuate the human species, dear girl, is the only crime which can exist Ä such is the hypothesis; according to it, this seed is put in us for the sole purpose of reproduction, and if that were true I would grant you that diverting it is an offense. But once it is demonstrated that her situating this semen in our loins is by no means enough to warrant supposing that Nature's purpose is to have all of it employed for reproduction, what then does it matter, Therese, whether it be spilled in one place or in another? Does the man who diverts it perform a greater evil than Nature who does not employ all of it? Now, do not those natural losses, which we can imitate if we please, occur in an abundance of instances? Our very ability to provoke them, firstly, is an initial proof that they do not offend Nature in the slightest. It would be contrary to all the equity and profound wisdom we everywhere recognize in her laws for them to permit what might affront her; secondly, those losses occur a hundred hundred million times every day, and she instigates them herself; nocturnal pollutions, the inutility of semen during the periods of woman's pregnancy, are they not authorized by her laws, enjoined by them, and do they not prove that, very little concerned for what may result from this liquid to which we so foolishly attach a disproportionate value, she permits us its waste with the same indifference she herself causes it every day to be wasted; she tolerates reproduction, yes, but much is wanting to prove reproduction is one of her intentions; she lets us go ahead with our reproducing to be sure, but it being no more to her advantage than our abstaining therefrom, the choice we happen to make is as one to her. Is it not clear that leaving us the power to create, not to create, or to destroy, we will not delight her at all or disappoint her any more by adopting toward the one or the other the attitude which suits us best; and what could be more self-evident than that the course we choose, being but the result of her power over us and the influence upon us of her actions, will far more surely please than it will risk offending her. Ah, Therese ! believe me, Nature frets very little over those mysteries we are great enough fools to turn into worship of her. Whatever be the temple at which one sacrifices, immediately she allows incense to be burned there, one can be sure the homage offends her in no wise; refusals to produce, waste of the semen employed in production, the obliteration of that seed when it has germinated, the annihilation of that germ even long after its formation, all those, Therese, are imaginary crimes which are of no interest to Nature and at which she scoffs as she does at all the rest of our institutions which offend more often than they serve her."

Coeur-de-fer waxed warm while expounding his perfidious maxims, and I soon beheld him again in the state which had so terrified me the night before; in order to give his lesson additional impact, he wished instantly to join practice to precept; and, my resistances notwithstanding, his hands strayed toward the altar into which the traitor wanted to penetrate . . . . Must I declare, Madame, that, blinded by the wicked man's seductions; content, by yielding a little, to save what seemed the more essential; reflecting neither upon his casuistries' illogicalities nor upon what I was myself about to risk since the dishonest fellow, possessing gigantic proportions, had not even the possibility to see a woman in the most permissible place and since, urged on by his native perversity, he most assuredly had no object but to maim me; my eyes as I say, perfectly blind to all that, I was going to abandon myself and become criminal through virtue; my opposition was weakening; already master of the throne, the insolent conqueror concentrated all his energies in order to establish himself upon it; and then there was heard the sound of a carriage moving along the highway. Upon the instant, Coeur-de-fer forsakes his pleasures for his duties; he assembles his followers and flies to new crimes. Not long afterward, we hear cries, and those bandits, all bloodied over, return triumphant and laden with spoils.

"Let's decamp smartly," says Coeur-de-fer, "we've killed three men, the corpses are on the road, we're safe no longer." The booty is divided, Coeur-de-fer wants me to have my share; it comes to twenty louis, which I am compelled to accept. I tremble at the obligation to take such money; however, we are in a hurry, everyone snatches up his belongings and off we go.

The next day we find ourselves out of danger and in the forest of Chantilly; during supper, the men reckon what their latest operation has been worth to them, and evaluate the total capture at no more than two hundred louis.

"Indeed," says one of them, "it wasn't worth the trouble to commit three murders for such a little sum."

"Softly, my friends," Dubois answers, "it was not for the sake of their purses I exhorted you not to spare those travelers, it was solely in the interests of our security; the law's to be blamed for these crimes, the fault's not ours; so long as thieves are hanged like murderers, thefts shall never be committed without assassinations. The two misdeeds are punished equally; why then abstain from the second when it may cover up the first? What makes you suppose, furthermore," the horrid creature continued, "that two hundred louis are not worth three killings? One must never appraise values save in terms of our own interests. The cessation of the victims' existences is as nothing compared to the continuation of ours, not a mite does it matter to us whether any individual is alive or in the grave; consequently, if one of the two cases involves what in the smallest way affects our welfare, we must, with perfect unremorse, determine the thing in our own favor; for in a completely indifferent matter we should, if we have any wits and are master of the situation, undoubtedly act so as to turn it to the profitable side, entirely neglecting whatever may befall our adversary; for there is no rational commensuration between what affects us and what affects others; the first we sense physically, the other only touches us morally, and moral feelings are made to deceive; none but physical sensations are authentic; thus, not only do two hundred louis suffice for three murders, but even thirty centimes would have sufficed, for those thirty centimes would have procured a satisfaction which, although light, must necessarily affect us to a much more lively degree than would three men murdered, who are nothing to us, and by the wrongs done whom we are not in the least touched, no, not even scratched; our organic feebleness, careless thinking, the accursed prejudices in which we were brought up, the vain terrors of religion and law, those are what hamper idiots and confound their criminal careers, those are what prevent them from arriving at greatness; but every strong and healthy individual, endowed with an energetically organized mind, who preferring himself to others, as he must, will know how to weigh their interests in the balance against his own, will laugh God and mankind to the devil, will brave death and mock at the law, fully aware that it is to himself he must be faithful, that by himself all must be measured, will sense that the vastest multitude of wrongs inflicted upon others cannot offset the least enjoyment lost to himself or be as important as his slightest pleasure purchased by an unheard-of host of villainies. Joy pleases him, it is in him, it is his own, crime's effect touches him not, is exterior to him; well, I ask, what thinking man will not prefer what causes his delectation to what is alien to him? who will not consent to commit this deed whereof~ he experiences nothing unpleasant, in order to procure what moves him most agreeably?"

"Oh Madame," I said to Dubois, asking her leave to reply to her execrable sophistries, "do you not at all feel that your damnation is writ in what you have just uttered? At the very most, such principles could only befit the person powerful enough to have nothing to dread from others; but we, Madame, perpetually in fear and humiliated; we, proscribed by all honest folk, condemned by every law, should we be the exponents of doctrines which can only whet the sword blade suspended above our heads? Would we find ourselves in this unhappy position were we in the center of society; were we to be where, that is to say, we ought to be, without our misconduct and delivered from our miseries, do you fancy such maxims could be any more fitting to us? How would you have him not perish who through blind egoism wishes all alone to strive against the combined interests of others? Is not society right never to suffer in its midst the man who declares himself hostile to it? And can the isolated individual fight against everyone? Can he flatter himself he is happy and tranquil if, refusing to submit to the social contract, he does not consent to give up a little of his happiness to insure the rest? Society is maintained only by the ceaseless interexchange of considerations and good works, those are the bonds which cement the edifices; such a one who instead of positive acts offers naught but crimes, having therefore to be dreaded, will necessarily be attacked if he is the strongest, laid low by the first he offends if he is the weakest; but destroyed at any rate, for there is in man a powerful instinct which compels him to safeguard his peace and quiet and to strike whosoever seeks to trouble them; that is why the long endurance of criminal associations is virtually impossible: their well-being suddenly confronted by cold steel, all the others must promptly unite to blunt the threatening point. Even amongst ourselves, Madame, I dare add; how can you lull yourself into believing you can maintain concord amongst ourselves when you counsel each to heed nothing but his own self-interest? Would you have any just complaints to make against the one of us who wanted to cut the throats of the others, who did so in order to monopolize for himself what has been shared by his colleagues? Why, 'tis a splendid panegyric to Virtue, to prove its necessity in even a criminal society... to prove for a certainty that this society would disintegrate in a trice were it not sustained by Virtue!"

"Your objections, Therese," said Coeur-de-fer, "not the theses Dubois has been expounding, are sophistries; our criminal fraternities are not by any means sustained by Virtue; rather by self-interest, egoism, selfishness; this eulogy of Virtue, which you have fabricated out of a false hypothesis, miscarries; it is not at all owing to virtuousness that, believing myself, let us suppose, the strongest of the band, I do not use a dagger on my comrades in order to appropriate their shares, it is because, thereupon finding myself all alone, I would deprive myself of the means which assure me the fortune I expect to have with their help; similarly, this is the single motive which restrains them from lifting their arms against me. Now this motive, as you, Therese, perfectly well observe, is purely selfish, and has not even the least appearance of virtue; he who wishes to struggle alone against society's interests must, you say, expect to perish; will he not much more certainly perish if, to enable him to exist therein, he has nothing but his misery and is abandoned by others? What one terms the interest of society is simply the mass of individual interests unified, but it is never otherwise than by ceding that this private interest can accommodate and blend with the general interest; well, what would you have him cede who has nothing he can relinquish? And he who had much? Agree that he should see his error grow apace with the discovery that he was giving infinitely more than he was getting in return; and, such being the case, agree that the unfairness of the bargain should prevent him from concluding it. Trapped in this dilemma, the best thing remaining for this man, don't you agree, is to quit this unjust society, to go elsewhere, and to accord prerogatives to a different society of men who, placed in a situation comparable to his, have their interest in combating, through the coordination of their lesser powers, the broader authority that wished to extract from the poor man what little he possessed in exchange for nothing at all. But you will say, thence will be born a state of perpetual warfare. Excellent! is that not the perpetual state of Nature? Is it not the only state to which we are really adapted? All men are born isolated, envious, cruel and despotic; wishing to have everything and surrender nothing, incessantly struggling to maintain either their rights or achieve their ambition, the legislator comes up and says to them: Cease thus to fight; if each were to retreat a little, calm would be restored. I find no fault with the position implicit in the agreement, but I maintain that two species of individuals cannot and ought not submit to it, ever; those who feel they are the stronger have no need to give up anything in order to be happy, and those who find themselves the weaker also find themselves giving up infinitely more than what is assured them. However, society is only composed of weak persons and strong; well, if the pact must perforce displease both weak and strong, there is great cause to suppose it will fail to suit society, and the previously existing state of warfare must appear infinitely preferable, since it permitted everyone the free exercise of his strength and his industry, whereof he would discover himself deprived by a society's unjust pact which takes too much from the one and never accords enough to the other; hence, the truly intelligent person is he who, indifferent to the risk of renewing the state of war that reigned prior to the contract, lashes out in irrevocable violation of that contract, violates it as much and often as he is able, full certain that what he will gain from these ruptures will always be more important than what he will lose if he happens to be a member of the weaker class; for such he was when he respected the treaty; by breaking it he may become one of the stronger; and if the laws return him to the class whence he wished to emerge, the worst that can befall him is the loss of his life, which is a misfortune infinitely less great than that of existing in opprobrium and wretchedness. There are then two positions available to us: either crime, which renders us happy, or the noose, which prevents us from being unhappy. I ask whether there can be any hesitation, lovely Therese, and where will your little mind find an argument able to combat that one?"

9

"Oh Monsieur," I replied with the vehemence a good cause inspires, "there are a thousand; but must this life be man's unique concern? Is this existence other than a passage each of whose stages ought only, if he is reasonable, to conduct him to that eternal felicity, the prize vouchsafed by Virtue? I suppose together with you (but this, however, is rare, it conflicts with all reason's informations, but never mind), I will for an instant grant you that the villain who abandons himself to crime may be rendered happy by it in this world, but do you imagine God's justice does not await that dishonest man, that he will not have to pay in another world for what he does in this? Ah! think not the contrary, Monsieur, believe it not," I added, tears in my eyes, " 'tis the misfortunate one's sole consolation, take it not away from us; forsaken by mankind, who will avenge us if not God?"

"Who? No one, Therese, absolutely no one; it is in no wise necessary that the misfortunate be avenged; they flatter themselves with the notion because they would like to be, the idea comforts them, but it is not on that account the less false: better still, it is essential that the misfortunate suffer; their humiliation, their anguishes are included in what Nature decrees, and their miserable existence is useful to the general scheme, as is that of the prosperity which crushes them; such is the truth which should stifle remorse in the tyrant's soul or in the malefactor's; let him not constrain himself; let him blindly, unthinkingly deliver himself up to causing every hurt the idea for which may be born in him, it is only Nature's voice which suggests this idea; such is the only fashion in which she makes us her laws' executors. When her secret inspirations dispose us to evil, it is evil she wishes, it is evil she requires, for the sum of crimes not being complete, not sufficient to the laws of equilibrium, the only laws whereby she is governed, she demands that there be crimes to dress the scales; therefore let him not be afraid, let him not pause, whose brain is driven to concerting ill; let him unheeding commit wrong immediately he discerns the impulsion, it is only by lagging and snuffling he outrages Nature. But let us ignore ethics for a moment, since it's theology you want. Be advised then, young innocent, that the religion you fall back upon, being nothing but the relationship between man and God, nothing but the reverence the creature thinks himself obliged to show his creator, is annihilated instantly this creator's existence is itself proven illusory. "Primitive man, terrified by the phenomena which harried him, had necessarily to believe that a sublime being unknown to him had the direction of their operation and influence; it is native to weakness to suppose strength and to fear it; the human mind, then too much in its infancy to explore, to discover in Nature's depths the laws of motion, the unique springs of the entire mechanism that struck him with awe, found it simpler to fancy a motor in this Nature than to view Nature as her own mover, and without considering that he would have to go to much more trouble to edify, to define this gigantic master, than through the study of Nature to find the cause of what amazed him, he acknowledged this sovereign being, he elaborated rituals to worship it: from this moment each nation composed itself an overlord in conformance with its peculiar characteristics, its knowledge, and its climate; soon there were as many religions on earth as races and peoples and not long after, as many Gods as families; nevertheless, behind all these idols it was easy to recognize the same absurd illusion, first fruit of human blindness. They appareled it differently, but it was always the same thing. Well, tell me, Therese, merely because these idiots talk drivel about the erection of a wretched chimera and about the mode of serving him, must it follow that an intelligent man has got to renounce the certain and present happiness of life; like Aesop's dog, must he abandon the bone for the shadow and renounce his real joys for hallucinations? No, Therese, no, there is no God, Nature sufficeth unto herself; in no wise hath she need of an author; once supposed, that author is naught but a decayed version of herself, is merely what we describe in school by the phrase, a begging of the question. A God predicates a creation, that is to say, an instant when there was nothing, or an instant when all was in chaos. If one or the other of these states was evil, why did your God allow it to subsist? Was it good? Then why did he change it? But if all is now good at last, your God has nothing left to do; well, if he is useless, how can he be powerful? And if he is not powerful, how can he be God? If, in a word, Nature moves herself, what do we want with a motor? and if the motor acts upon matter by causing it to move, how is it not itself material? Can you conceive the effect of the mind upon matter and matter receiving motion from the mind which itself has no movement? Examine for one cold-blooded instant all the ridiculous and contradictory qualities wherewith the fabricators of this execrable chimera have been obliged to clothe him; verify for your own self how they contradict one another, annul one another, and you will recognize that this deific phantom, engendered by the fear of some and the ignorance of all, is nothing but a loathsome platitude which merits from us neither an instant of faith nor a minute's examination; a pitiable extravagance, disgusting to the mind, revolting to the heart, which ought never to have issued from the darkness save to plunge back into it, forever to be drowned.

"May the hope or fear of a world to come, bred of those primordial lies, trouble you not, Therese, and above all give over endeavoring to forge restraints for us out of this stuff. Feeble portions of a vile crude matter, upon our death, that is to say, upon the conjointure of the elements whereof we are composed with the elements composing the universal mass, annihilated forever, regardless of what our behavior has been, we will pass for an instant into Nature's crucible thence to spring up again under other shapes, and that without there being any more prerogatives for him who madly smoked up Virtue's effigy, than for the other who wallowed in the most disgraceful excesses, because there is nothing by which Nature is offended and because all men, equally her womb's issue, during their term having acted not at all save in accordance with her impulsions, will all of them meet with after their existence, both the same end and the same fate."

I was once again about to reply to these appalling blasphemies when we heard the clatter of a horseman not far away.

"To arms !" shouted Coeur-de-fer, more eager to put his systems into action than to consolidate their bases.

The men leapt into life... and an instant later a luckless traveler was led into the copse where we had our camp. Questioned upon his motive for traveling alone and for being so early abroad, upon his age, his profession, the rider answered that his name was Saint-Florent, one of the most important merchants of Lyon, that he was thirty-six years old, that he was on his way back from Flanders where he had been concerned with affairs relative to his business, that he had not much hard money upon his person, but many securities. He added that his valet had left him the preceding day and that, to avoid the heat, he was journeying at night with the intention of reaching Paris the next day, where he would secure a new domestic, and would conclude some of his transactions; that, moreover, he was following an unfamiliar road, and, apparently, he must have lost his way while dozing on his horse. And having said that, he asked for his life, in return offering all he possessed. His purse was examined, his money was counted, the prize could not have been better. Saint-Florent had near unto a half a million, payable upon demand at the capital, had also a few gems and about a hundred gold louis . . . .

"Friend," said Coeur-de-fer, clapping his pistol to Saint-Florent's nose, "you understand, don't you, that after having robbed you, we cannot leave you alive."

"Oh Monsieur," I cried, casting myself at the villain's feet, "I beseech you not to present me the horrible spectacle, upon my reception into your band, of this poor man's death; allow him to live, do not refuse me this first request I ask of you."

And quickly resorting to a most unusual ruse, in order to justify the interest I appeared to take in the captive:

"The name Monsieur has just given himself," I added with warmth, "causes me to believe we are nearly related. Be not astonished, Monsieur," I went on, now addressing the voyager, "be not at all surprised to find a kinsman in these circumstances; I will explain it all to you. In the light of this," I continued, once again imploring our chief, "in the light of this, Monsieur, grant me the unlucky creature's life, I will show my gratitude for the favor by the completest devotion to ail that will be able to serve your interests."

"You know upon what conditions I can accord you what you ask, Therese," Coeur-de-fer answered; "you know what I demand from you..."

"Ah, very well, Monsieur, I will do everything," I cried, throwing myself between Saint-Florent and our leader, who was still about to kill him. "Yes, I will do anything; spare him."

"Let him live," said Coeur-de-fer, "but he has got to join us, that last clause is crucial, I can do nothing if he refuses to comply with it, my comrades would be against me."

Surprised, the merchant, understanding nothing of this. consanguinity I was establishing, but observing his life saved if he were to consent to the proposal, saw no cause for a moment's hesitation. He was provided with meat and drink, as the men did not wish to leave the place until daybreak.

"Therese," Coeur-de-fer said to me, "I remind you of your promise, but, since I am weary tonight, rest quietly beside Dubois, I will summon you toward dawn and if you are not prompt to come, taking this knave's life will be my revenge for your deceit."

"Sleep, Monsieur, sleep well," I replied, "and believe that she whom you have filled with gratitude has no desire but to repay it."

However, such was far from my design, for if ever I believed deception permitted, it was certainly upon this occasion. Our rascals, greatly overconfident, kept at their drinking and fell into slumber, leaving me entirely at liberty beside Dubois who, drunk like the others, soon closed her eyes too.

Then seizing my opportunity as soon as the bandits surrounding us were overcome with sleep:

"Monsieur," I said to the young Lyonnais, "the most atrocious catastrophe has thrown me against my will into the midst of these thieves, I detest both them and the fatal instant that brought me into their company. In truth, I have not the honor to be related to you; I employed the trick to save you and to escape, if you approve it, with you, from out of these scoundrels' clutches; the moment's propitious," I added, "let us be off; I notice your pocketbook, take it back, forget the money, it is in their pockets; we could not recover it without danger: come, Monsieur, let us quit this place. You see what I am doing for you, I put myself into your keeping; take pity on me; above all, be not more cruel than these men; deign to respect my honor, I entrust it to you, it is my unique treasure, they have not ravished it away from me."

10

It would be difficult to render the declarations of gratitude I had from Saint-Florent. He knew not in what terms to express his thanks; but we had no time to talk; it was a question of flight. With a dextrous movement, I retrieve the pocketbook, return it to him, and treading softly we walk through the copse, leaving the horse for fear the sound of his hoofs might rouse the men; with all possible dispatch we reach the path which is to lead us out of the forest. We had the good luck to be out of it by daybreak, without having been followed by anyone; before ten o'clock we were in Luzarches and there, free from all anxiety, we thought of nothing but resting ourselves .

There are moments in life when one finds that despite one's riches, which may be great, one nevertheless lacks what is needed to live; such was Saint-Florent's case: five hundred thousand francs might be awaiting him in Paris, but he now had not a coin on his person; mindful of this, he paused before entering the inn . . . .

"Be easy, Monsieur," I said upon perceiving his embarrassment, "the thieves have not left me without money, here are twenty louis, take them, please, use them, give what remains to the poor; nothing in the world could make me want to keep gold acquired by murder."

Saint-Florent, whose refinements of character I at the time did not exactly appreciate, was absolutely unwilling to accept what I tendered him; he asked me what my expectations were, said he would make himself bound to fulfill them, and that he desired nothing but the power to acquit himself of his indebtedness to me.

"It is to you I owe my life and fortune, Therese," he added, kissing my hands, "I can do no better than to lay them both at your feet; receive them, I beseech you, and permit the God of marriage to tighten the knots of friendship."

I know not whether it was from intuition or chilliness of temper, but I was so far from believing that what I had done for the young man could motivate such sentiments as these he expressed for me, that I allowed him to read in my countenance the refusal I dared not articulate; he understood, insisted no further, and limited himself to asking what he could do for me.

"Monsieur," said I, "if my behavior is really not without merit in your view, for my entire recompense I ask nothing more than to proceed to Lyon with you and to have you find me a place in some correct household, where my modesty will have no more to suffer."

"You could do nothing better," said Saint-Florent, "and no one is in a better position than I to render this service; I have twenty relatives in the city," and the young trader then besought me to divulge my reasons for having left Paris where I had mentioned to him I was born. I told my story with equal amounts of confidence and ingenuousness.

"Oh, if it is but that," said the young man, "I will be of use to you before we reach Lyon; fear not, Therese, your troubles are over; the affair will be hushed; you will not be sought after and, certainly, less in the asylum where I wish to leave you than in any other. A member of my family dwells near Bondy, a charming region not far from here; I am sure it will be a pleasure for her to have you with her; I will introduce you tomorrow."

In my turn filled with gratitude, I approve a project which seems so well suited to me; we repose at Luzarches for the rest of the day and on the morrow, it is our plan, we will gain Bondy, but six leagues distant.

"The weather is fine," Saint-Florent says to me, "trust me, Therese; it will be most enjoyable to go afoot; we will reach my relative's estate, will tell of our adventure, and this manner of arriving, I should think, will make you appear in a still more interesting light."

Having not the faintest suspicion of this monster's designs, and far from imagining that I was to be less safe with him than I had been when in the infamous company I had left, I agree to everything; we dine together; he not so much as murmurs when for the night I take a chamber separate from his, and after having waited until the warmest part of the day is past, certain of what he tells me, that four or five hours will suffice to bring us to his relative's, we leave Luzarches and strike out on foot for Bondy.

It was toward four o'clock in the afternoon when we entered the forest. Until then Saint-Florent had not once contradicted himself: always the same propriety, always the same eagerness to prove his sentiments for me; I should not have thought myself more secure had I been with my father. The shades of night began to descend upon the forest and to inspire that kind of religious horror which at once causes the birth of fear in timorous spirits and criminal projects in ferocious hearts. We followed mere paths; I was walking ahead, and I turned to ask Saint-Florent whether these obscure trails were really the ones we ought to be following, whether perchance he had not lost his bearings, whether he thought we were going to arrive soon.

"We have arrived, whore," the villain replied, toppling me with a blow of his cane brought down upon my head; I fell unconscious... Oh, Madame, I have no idea what that man afterward said or did; but the state I was in when I returned to my senses advised me only too well to what point I had been his victim. I was darkest night when I awoke; I was at the foot of a tree, away from any road, injured, bleeding... dishonored, Madame; such had been the reward of all I had just done for the unlucky man; and carrying infamy to its ultimate degree, the wretch, after having done to me all he had wished, after having abused me in every manner, even in that which most outrages Nature, had taken my purse... containing the same money I had so generously offered him. He had torn my clothing, most of it lay in shreds and ribbons about me, I was virtually naked, and several parts of my body were lacerated, clawed; you may appreciate my situation: there in the depths of the night, without resources, without honor, without hope, exposed to every peril: I wished to put an end to my days: had a weapon been presented to me, I would have laid hands on it and abridged this unhappy life full only of plagues for me... the monster! What did I do to him, I asked myself, to have deserved such cruel treatment at his hands? I save his life, restore his fortune to him, he snatches away what is most dear to me! A savage beast would have been less cruel! O man, thus are you when you heed nothing but your passions! Tigers that dwell in the wildest jungles would quail before such ignominies... these first pangs of suffering were succeeded by some few minutes of exhaustion; my eyes, brimming over with tears, turned mechanically towards the sky; my heart did spring to the feet of the Master who dwelleth there... that pure glittering vault... that imposing stillness of the night... that terror which numbed my senses... that image of Nature in peace, nigh unto my whelmed, distraught soul... all distilled a somber horror into me, whence there was soon born the need to pray. I cast myself down, kneeling before that potent God denied by the impious, hope of the poor and the downtrodden.

"Holy Majesty, Saintly One," I cried out in tears, "Thou Who in this dreadful moment deign to flood my soul with a celestial joy, Who doubtless hath prevented me from attempting my life; O my Protector and my Guide, I aspire to Thy bounties, I implore Thy clemency, behold my miseries and my torments, my resignation, and hear Thou my entreaties: Powerful God I Thou knowst it, I am innocent and weak, I am betrayed and mistreated; I have wished to do well in imitation of Thee, and Thy will hath punished it in me: may Thy will be done, O my God I all its sacred effects are cherished by me, I respect them and cease to complain of them; but if however I am to find naught but stings and nettles terrestrially, is it to offend Thee, O my Sovereign Master, to supplicate Thy puissance to take me into Thy bosom, in order untroubled to adore Thee, to worship Thee far away from these perverse men who, alas I have made me meet with evils only, and whose bloodied and perfidious hands at their pleasure drown my sorrowful days in a torrent of tears and in an abyss of agonies."

Prayer is the misfortunate's sweetest comfort; strength reenters him once he has fulfilled this duty. My courage renewed, I raised myself up, I gathered together the rags the villain had left me, and I hid myself in a thicket so as to pass the night in less danger. The security I believed I enjoyed, the satisfaction I had just tasted by communing with my God, all combined to help me rest a few hours, and the sun was already risen high when I opened my eyes. For the wretched, the instant of awakening is hideous: the imagination, refreshed by sleep's sweet ministrations, very rapidly and lugubriously fills with the evils these moments of deceiving repose have smoothed into oblivion.

Very well, I said as I examined myself, it is then true that there are human creatures Nature reduces to the level of wild beasts! Lurking in this forest, like them flying the sight of man, what difference now exists between them and me? Is it worth being born for a fate so pitiable?... And my tears flowed abundantly as I meditated in sorrow; I had scarcely finished with my reflections when I heard sounds somewhere about; little by little, two men hove into view. I pricked up my ears:

"Come, dear friend," said one of them, "this place will suit us admirably; the cruel and fatal presence of an aunt I abhor will not prevent me from tasting a moment with you the pleasures I cherish."

They draw near, they station themselves squarely in front of me and so proximately that not one of their words, not one of their gestures is able to escape me, and I observe... Just Heaven, Madame, said Therese, interrupting herself, is it possible that destiny has placed me in none but situations so critical that it becomes quite as difficult for Virtue to hear them recited as for modesty to describe them? That horrible crime which equally outrages both Nature and social conventions, that heinous deed, in a word, which the hand of God has so often smitten, rationalized, legitimized by Coeur-de-fer, proposed by him to the unhappy Therese, despite her wishes consummated against her by the butcher who has just immolated her, in brief, I did see that revolting execration carried out before my own eyes, together with all the impure gropings and fumblings, all the frightful episodes the most meditated depravity can devise. One of the men, he who gave himself, was twenty-four years old, of such a bearing and presence one might suppose him of an elevated degree, the other, of about the same age, appeared to be one of his domestics. The act was scandalous and prolonged. Bending over, supported by his hands, leaning upon the crest of a little hillock facing the thicket where I lay, the young master exposed naked to his companion in debauch the impious sacrificial altar, and the latter, whom the spectacle filled with ardor, caressed the idol, ready to immolate it with a spear far more awful and far more colossal than the one wherewith the captain of the brigands of Bondy had menaced me; but, in no wise intimidated, the young master seemed prepared unhesitatingly to brave the shaft that was presented to him; he teased it, he excited it, covered it with kisses; seized it, plunged it into himself, was in an ecstasy as he swallowed it up; aroused by criminal caresses, the infamous creature writhed and struggled under the iron and seemed to regret it was not yet more terrible; he withstood its blows, he rose to anticipate them, he repelled them . . . . A tender couple lawfully connected would not have caressed one another so passionately... their mouths were pressed together, their sighs intermingled, their tongues entwined, and I witnessed each of them, drunk with lust, bring his perfidious horrors to completion in the very vortex of delight. The homage is renewed, and in order to fire the incense nothing is neglected by him who cries aloud his demand for it; kisses, fingerings, pollutions, debauchery's most appalling refinements, everything is employed to revive sinking strength, and it all succeeds in reanimating them five times in swift succession; but that without either of them changing his role. The young lord was constantly the woman and although there was about him what suggested the possibility he could have acted the man in his turn, he had not for one instant even the appearance of wishing to. If he visited the altar corresponding to the one in him where sacrifices were performed, it was in the other idol's behalf, and there was never any indication the latter was threatened by assault.

11

Ah, how slowly the time seemed to pass! I dared not budge for fear of detection; at last, the criminal actors in this indecent drama, no doubt surfeited, got up and were prepared to start along the road that was to take them home, when the master drew near the bush which hid me; my bonnet betrayed me... he caught sight of it . . . .

"Jasmin," said he to his valet, "we are discovered... a girl has beheld our mysteries . . . . Come hither, flush the bitch into the open, let's find out why she is here."

I did not put them to the trouble of dragging me from my sanctuary; I stepped forward immediately and, falling at their feet,

"Oh, Messieurs!" I cried, stretching my arms toward them, "deign to have pity upon an unhappy creature whose fate more deserves your compassion than you may think; there are very few misfortunes which can equal mine; do not let the posture wherein you discover me cause any suspicion to be born in you; it is rather the consequence of my misery than of my faults; do not augment the ills which overwhelm me, be so kind as to diminish them by making available to me the means to escape the furies that hound me."

The Comte de Bressac (that was the name of the young man into whose hands I had fallen) possessed a mind containing a great fund of wickedness and libertinage; no very abundant amount of sympathy dwelled in his heart. Unfortunately, it is only too common to find men in whom pity has been obliterated by libertinage, whose ordinary effect is to harden: whether it be that the major part of his excesses necessitates apathy in the soul, or that the violent shock passion imparts to the nervous system decreases the vigor of its action, the fact always remains that a libertine is rarety a man of sensibility. But in addition to this harshness native to the species whose character I am sketching, there was also in Monsieur de Bressac a disgust for our sex so inveterate, a hatred so powerful for all that distinguishes it, that I encountered considerable difficulty introducing the affections into his soul wherewith I strove to move him.

"My little dove," said the Count, severity in his tone, "if you are looking for dupes, improve your style; neither my friend nor I ever sacrifice at your sex's impure temple; if it is money you are begging, look for people who are fond of good works, we never perform any of that description . . . . But, wretch, out with it: did you see what passed between Monsieur and me?"

"I saw you conversing together upon the sward," I replied, "nothing more, Monsieur, I assure you."

"I should like to believe it," said the Count, "for your own good; were I to imagine you had seen anything else, never would you emerge alive from where we are . . . . Jasmin, it is early, we have time to hear the girl's adventures, and afterward we will see what's to be done with her."

The young men sit down, they order me to sit near them, and thereupon very ingenuously I make them acquainted with all the woes that have afflicted me from the day of my birth.

"Well, Jasmin," said Monsieur de Bressac as soon as I had finished, "for once let us be just: the equitable Themis has doomed this creature, let us not suffer the Goddess' designs to be thwarted so cruelly: let us expose the delinquent to the death penalty she has incurred: this little murder, far from being a crime, will merely take its place as a reparation in the moral scheme; since sometimes we have the misfortune to disturb that order, let us at least courageously make amends when the occasion arises . . . ."

And the cruel men, having laid hands upon me, dragged me toward the wood, laughing at my tears and screams.

"We'll tie each of her members to a tree Ä we need four trees placed in a rectangle," said Bressac, tearing off my clothes.

Then by means of their cravats, their handkerchiefs, their braces, they make cords wherewith I am tied instantly, in keeping with their plan, that is to say in the cruelest and most painful position imaginable. I cannot express to you what I suffered; it seemed they were rending me limb from limb and that my belly, facing downward and strained to the utmost, was about to split at any moment; sweat drenched my forehead, I no longer existed save through the violence of pain; had it ceased to compress my nerves, a mortal anguish would surely have seized me: the villains were amused by my posture, they considered me and applauded.

"Well, that's enough," Bressac said at last, "for the time being she may get off with a fright.

"Therese," he continued as he untied my hands and commanded me to dress myself, "show a little judgment and come along with us; if you attach yourself to me you shall never have reason to regret it. My aunt requires a second maid; I am going to present you to her and, upon the basis of your story, undertake to interest her in you; I shall make myself answerable for your conduct; but should you abuse my kindness, were you to betray my confidence, or were you not to submit yourself to my intentions, behold these four trees, Therese, behold the plot of earth they encompass: it might serve you for a sepulcher: bear it in mind that this dreadful place is no more than a league's distance from the chateau to which I am going to lead you and that, upon the least provocation, I will bring you back here at once."

I forgot my sufferings instantly, I embraced the Count's knees, tears streaming down my cheeks, I swore to behave myself well; but quite as insensible to my joy as to my pain,

"Let us be off," said Bressac, "your actions will speak for you, they alone will govern your fate."

We advance; Jasmin and his master exchange whispered remarks; I follow them humbly, without saying a word. In less than an hour we arrive at Madame la Marquise de Bressac's chateau, whose magnificence and the multitude of servants it contains make me see that whatever the post I must hold in the house, it will surely be more advantageous to me than that of drudge to Monsieur du Harpin. I am made to wait in an office where Jasmin most obligingly offers me everything conducive to my comfort. The young Count seeks out his aunt, acquaints her with what he has done, and a half-hour later himself comes to introduce me to the Marquise.

Madame de Bressac was a woman of forty-six years, still very beautiful, and who seemed highly respectable and sensible, although into her principles and remarks somewhat of austerity had entrance; for two years she had been the widow of the young Count's uncle, who had married her without any fortune beyond the fine name he brought with him. All the riches Monsieur de Bressac was able to hope for depended upon this aunt; what had come down to him from his father barely gave him the wherewithal to buy his pleasures: to which income Madame de Bressac joined a considerable allowance, but that scarcely sufficed; nothing is so expensive as the delights to which the Count was addicted; perhaps they are purchased at a cheaper rate than others, but they far more rapidly multiply. Fifty thousand crowns was the Marquise's revenue, and young Monsieur de Bressac was its sole heir. All efforts to induce him to find a profession or an occupation had failed; he could not adapt himself to whatever diverted his attentions from libertinage. The Marquise passed three months of the year's twelve in the country; the rest of the time she lived in Paris; and these three months which she required her nephew to spend with her, were a kind of torture for a man who hated his aunt and considered as wasted every moment he passed outside the city which was the home of his pleasures.

The young Count bade me relate to the Marquise the matter with which I had just made him acquainted, and as soon as I was done:

"Your candor and naivete," Madame de Bressac said to me, "do not permit me to think you untruthful. I will inquire after no other information save what will authorise me to believe you are really the daughter of the man you indicate; if it is so, then I knew your father, and that will be one more reason to take an interest in you. As for the du Harpin affair, I will assume responsibility for settling it with two visits paid to the Chancellor; he has been my friend for ages. In all the world there is no man of greater integrity; we have but to prove your innocence to him: all the charges leveled against you will crumble and be withdrawn. But consider well, Therese: what I promise you now will not be yours save at the price of flawless conduct; thus, you see that the effects of the gratitude I require will always redound to your profit." I cast myself at the Marquise's feet, assured her she would be contented with me; with great kindness she raised me up and upon the spot gave me the post of second chambermaid in her service.

At the end of three days, the information Madame de Bressac had sought from Paris arrived; it corresponded with what I desired; the Marquise praised me for having in no wise imposed upon her, and every thought of unhappiness vanished from my mind, to be replaced by nothing but hope for the sweetest consolations it was permitted me to expect; but it did not consort with the designs of Heaven that the poor Therese should ever be happy, and if fortuitously there were born unto her some few moments of calm, it was only to render more bitter those of distress that were to succeed them.

We were no sooner arrived in Paris than Madame de Bressac hastened to work in my behalf: the first president judge wished to see me, he heard with interest the tale of my misfortunes; du Harpin's calumnies were recognized, but it was in vain they undertook to punish him; having made a great success of trafficking in counterfeit banknotes, whereby he ruined three or four families, and whence he amassed nearly two millions, he had just removed to England; as regarded the burning of the Palace prisons, they were convinced that although I had profited from the event, I was in no way to blame for causing it and the case against me was dropped, the officiating magistrates being agreed, so I was assured, that there was no need to employ further formalities; I asked no questions, I was content to learn what I was told, and you will see shortly whether I was mistaken.

You may readily imagine that as a consequence of what she did for me, I became very fond of Madame de Bressac; had she not shown me every kindness as well, had not such steps as those she had taken obligated me forever to this precious protectress? However, it was by no means the young Count's intention that I become so intimately attached to his aunt . . . . But this seems the moment for a portrait of the monster.

Monsieur de Bressac had the charms of youth and the most attractive countenance too; if there were some defects in his figure or his features, it was because they had a rather too pronounced tendency toward that nonchalance, that softness which properly belongs only to women; it seemed that, in lending him the attributes of the feminine sex, Nature had introduced its tastes into him as well . . . . Yet what a soul lurked behind those effeminate graces! All the vices which characterize the villain's genius were to be encountered in his: never had wickedness, vindictiveness, cruelty, atheism, debauchery, contempt for all duties and principally those out of which Nature is said to fashion our delights, never had all these qualities been carried to such an extreme. In the midst of all his faults predominated another: Monsieur de Bressac detested his aunt. The Marquise did everything conceivable to restore her nephew to the paths of virtue; perhaps she put too much rigorousness into her attempts; the result, however, was that the Count, further inflamed by that very rigor's effects, only the more impetuously gave himself up to his predilections and the poor Marquise gained nothing from her persecutions but his redoubled hate.

"Do not imagine," the Count would often tell me, "that it is of her own accord my aunt acts in all that concerns you, Therese; believe me, were it not for my constant badgering she would quickly forget what she has promised to do for you. She would have you feel indebted to her, but all she has done is owing exclusively to me; yes, Therese, exactly, it is to me alone you are beholden, and the thanks I expect from you should appear the more disinterested, for although you've a pretty face, it is not, and you know it very well, after your favors I aspire; no, Therese, the services I await from you are of a radically different sort, and when you are well convinced of what I have accomplished in behalf of your tranquillity, I hope I will find what I think I have the right to expect from your spirit."

So obscure were these speeches I knew not how to answer: however, reply to him I did, on a chance, as it were, and perhaps with too great a facility. Must I confess it? Alas! yes; to conceal my shortcomings would be to wrong your confidence and poorly to respond to the interest my misfortunes have quickened in you. Hear then, Madame, of the one deliberate fault with which I have to reproach myself . . . . What am I saying, a fault? It was a folly, an extravagance... there has never been one to equal it; but at least it is not a crime, it is merely a mistake, for which I alone have been punished, and of which it surely does not seem that the equitable hand of Heaven had to make use in order to plunge me into the abyss which yawned beneath me soon afterward. Whatever the foul treatment to which the Comte de Bressac had exposed me the first day I had met him, it had, all the same, been impossible to see him so frequently without feeling myself drawn toward him by an insuperable and instinctive tenderness. Despite all my recollections of his cruelty, all my thoughts upon his disinclinations toward women, upon the depravity of his tastes, upon the gulf which separated us morally, nothing in the world was able to extinguish this nascent passion, and had the Count called upon me to lay down my life, I would have sacrificed it for him a thousand times over. He was far from suspecting my sentiments... he was far, the ungrateful one, from divining the cause of the tears I shed every day; nevertheless, it was out of the question for him to be in doubt of my eagerness to fly to do his every bidding, to please him in every possible way, it could not have been he did not glimpse, did not have some inkling of my attentions; doubtless, because they were instinctive, they were also mindless, and went to the point of serving his errors, of serving them as far as decency permitted, and always of hiding them from his aunt. This behavior had in some sort won me his confidence, and all that came from him was so precious to me, I was so blinded by the little his heart offered me, that I sometimes had the weakness to believe he was not indifferent to me. But how promptly his excessive disorders disabused me: they were such that even his health was affected. I several times took the liberty to represent to him the dangers of his conduct, he would hear me out patiently, then end by telling me that one does not break oneself of the vice he cherished.

12

"Ah, Therese!" he exclaimed one day, full of enthusiasm, "if only you knew this fantasy's charms, if only you could understand what one experiences from the sweet illusion of being no more than a woman! incredible inconsistency I one abhors that sex, yet one wishes to imitate it! Ah! how sweet it is to succeed, Therese, how delicious it is to be a slut to everyone who would have to do with you and carrying delirium and prostitution to their ultimate period, successively, in the very same day, to be the mistress of a porter, a marquis, a valet, a friar, to be the beloved of each one after the other, caressed, envied, menaced, beaten, sometimes victorious in their arms, sometimes a victim and at their feet, melting them with caresses, reanimating them with excesses . . . . Oh no, Therese, you do not understand what is this pleasure for a mind constructed like mine . . . . But, morals aside, if you are able to imagine this divine whimsy's physical sensations, there is no withstanding it, it is a titillation so lively, it is of so piquant a voluptuousness... one becomes giddy, one ceases to reason, stammers; a thousand kisses one more tender than the next do not inflame us with an ardor in any way approaching the drunkenness into which the agent plunges us; enlaced in his arms, our mouth glued to his, we would that our entire being were incorporated into his; we would not make but a single being with him; if we dare complain, 'tis of being neglected; we would have him, more robust than Hercules, enlarge us, penetrate us; we would have that precious semen, shot blazing to the depths of our entrails, cause, by its heat and its strength, our own to leap forth into his hands . . . . Do not suppose, Therese, we are made like other men; 'tis an entirely different structure we have; and, in creating us, Heaven has ornamented the altars at which our Celadons sacrifice with that very same sensitive membrane which lines your temple of Venus; we are, in that sector, as certainly women as you are in your generative sanctuary; not one of your pleasures is unknown to us, there is not one we do not know how to enjoy, but we have in addition to them our own, and it is this delicious combination which makes us of all men on earth the most sensitive to pleasure, the best created to experience it; it is this enchanting combination which renders our tastes incorrigible, which would turn us into enthusiasts and frenetics were one to have the stupidity to punish us... which makes us worship, unto the grave itself, the charming God who enthralls us."

Thus the Count expressed himself, celebrating his eccentricities; when I strove to speak to him of the Being to whom he owed everything, and of the grief such disorders caused his respectable aunt, I perceived nothing in him but spleen and ill-humor and especially impatience at having to see, in such hands and for so long, riches which, he would say, already ought to belong to him; I saw nothing but the most inveterate hatred for that so gentle woman, nothing but the most determined revolt against every natural sentiment. It would then be true that when in one's tastes one has been able so formally to transgress that law's sacred instinct, the necessary consequence of this original crime is a frightful penchant to commit every other.

Sometimes I employed the means Religion provides; almost always comforted by it, I attempted to insinuate its sweetnesses into this perverse creature's soul, more or less certain he could be restrained by those bonds were I to succeed in having him strike at the lure; but the Count did not long tolerate my use of such weapons. A declared enemy of our most holy mysteries, a stubborn critic of the purity of our dogmas, an impassioned antagonist of the idea of a Supreme Being's existence, Monsieur de Bressac, instead of letting himself be converted by me, sought rather to work my corruption.

"All religions start from a false premise, Therese," he would say; "each supposes as necessary the worship of a Creator, but that creator never existed. In this connection, put yourself in mind of the sound precepts of that certain Coeur-de-fer who, you told me, used to labor over your mind as I do; nothing more just, nor more precise, than that man's principles, and the degradation in which we have the stupidity to keep him does not deprive him of the right to reason well.

"If all Nature's productions are the resultant effects of the laws whereof she is a captive; if her perpetual action and reaction suppose the motion necessary to her essence, what becomes of the sovereign master fools gratuitously give her? that is what your sagacious instructor said to you, dear girl. What, then, are religions if not the restraint wherewith the tyranny of the mightier sought to enslave the weaker? Motivated by that design, he dared say to him whom he claimed the right to dominate, that a God had forged the irons with which cruelty manacled him; and the latter, bestialized by his misery, indistinctly believed everything the former wished. Can religions, born of these rogueries, merit respect? Is there one of them, Therese, which does not bear the stamp of imposture and of stupidity? What do I descry in them all? Mysteries which cause reason to shudder, dogmas which outrage Nature, grotesque ceremonies which simply inspire derision and disgust. But if amongst them all there were one which most particularly deserves our scorn and hatred, O Therese, is it not that barbaric law of the Christianity into which both of us were born? Is there any more odious? one which so spurs both the heart and mind to revolt? How is it that rational men are still able to lend any credence to the obscure mutterings, to the alleged miracles of that appalling cult's vile originator? Has there ever existed a rowdy scoundrel more worthy of public indignation! What is he but a leprous Jew who, born of a slut and a soldier in the world's meanest stews, dared fob himself off for the spokesman of him who, they say, created the universe! With such lofty pretensions, you will have to admit, Therese, at least a few credentials are necessary. But what are those of this ridiculous Ambassador? What is he going to do to prove his mission? Is the earth's face going to be changed? are the plagues which beset it going to be annihilated? is the sun going to shine upon it by night as well as by day? vices will soil it no more? Are we going to see happiness reign at last?... Not at all; it is through hocus-pocus, antic capers, and puns...

(The Marquis de Bievre never made one quite as clever as the Nazarene's to his disciple: "Thou art Peter and upon this Rock I will build my Church"; and they tell Us that witty language is one of our century's innovations!)

... that God's envoy announces himself to the world; it is in the elegant society of manual laborers, artisans, and streetwalkers that Heaven's minister comes to manifest his grandeur; it is by drunken carousing with these, bedding with those, that God's friend, God himself, comes to bend the toughened sinner to his laws; it is by inventing nothing for his farces but what can satisfy either his lewdness or his gourmand's guts that the knavish fellow demonstrates his mission; however all that may be, he makes his fortune; a few beef-witted satellites gravitate toward the villain; a sect is formed; this crowd's dogmas manage to seduce some Jews; slaves of the Roman power, they joyfully embrace a religion which, ridding them of their shackles, makes them subject to none but a metaphysical tyranny. Their motives become evident, their indocility unveils itself, the seditious louts are arrested; their captain perishes, but of a death doubtless much too merciful for his species of crime, and through an unpardonable lapse of intelligence, this uncouth boor's disciples are allowed to disperse instead of being slaughtered cheek to jowl with their leader. Fanaticism gets minds in its grip, women shriek, fools scrape and scuffle, imbeciles believe, and lo! the most contemptible of beings, the most maladroit quacksalver, the clumsiest impostor ever to have made his entrance, there he is: behold! God, there's God's little boy, his papa's peer; and now all his dreams are consecrated I and now all his epigrams are become dogmas! and all his blunders mysteries! His fabulous father's breast opens to receive him and that Creator, once upon a time simple, of a sudden becomes compound, triple, to humor his son, this lad so worthy of his greatness; but does that sacred God stick at that? No, surely not, his celestial might is going to bestow many another and greater favor. At the beck and call of a priest, of, that is to say, an odd fellow foul with lies, the great God, creator of all we behold, is going to abase himself to the point of descending ten or twelve million times every morning in a morsel of wheat paste; this the faithful devour and assimilate, and God Almighty is lugged to the bottom of their intestines where he is speedily transmuted into the vilest excrements, and all that for the satisfaction of the tender son, odious inventor of this monstrous impiety which had its beginnings in a cabaret supper. He spake, and it was ordained. He said: this bread you see will be my flesh; you will digest it as such; now, I am God; hence, God will be digested by you; hence, the Creator of Heaven and Earth will be changed, because I have spoken, into the vilest stuff the body of man can exhale, and man will eat his God, because this God is good and because he is omnipotent. However, these blatherings increase; their growth is attributed to their authenticity, their greatness, their sublimity to the puissance of him who introduced them, while in truth the commonest causes double their existence, for the credit error acquires never proved anything but the presence of swindlers on the one side and of idiots on the other. This infamous religion finally arrives on the throne, and it is a weak, cruel, ignorant and fanatical emperor who, enveloping it in the royal mantle, soils the four corners of the earth with it. O Therese, what weight are these arguments to carry with an inquiring and philosophic mind? Is the sage able to see anything in this appalling heap of fables but the disgusting fruit of a few men's imposture and the diddled credulity of a vast number? had God willed it that we have some religion or other, and had he been truly powerful or, to frame it more suitably, had there truly been a God, would it have been by these absurd means he would have imparted his instructions to us? Would it have been through the voice of a contemptible bandit he would have shown how it were necessary to serve him? Were he supreme, were he mighty, were he just, were he good, this God you tell me about, would it be through enigmas and buffooneries he would wish to teach me to serve and know him? Sovereign mover of the stars and the heart of man, may he not instruct us by employing the one or convince us by graving himself in the other? Let him, one of these days, upon the Sun indite the law, writ out in letters of fire, the law as he wants us to understand it, in the version that pleases him; then from one end of the universe to the other, all mankind will read it, will behold it at once, and thereafter will be guilty if they obey it not. But to indicate his desires nowhere but in some unknown corner of Asia; to select for witnesses the craftiest and most visionary of people, for alter ego the meanest artisan, the most absurd, him of the greatest rascality; to frame his doctrine so confusedly it is impossible to make it out; to limit knowledge of it to a small group of individuals; to leave the others in error and to punish them for remaining there . . . . Why, no, Therese, no, these atrocities are not what we want for our guidance; I should prefer to die a thousand deaths rather than believe them. When atheism will wish for martyrs, let it designate them; my blood is ready to be shed. Let us detest these horrors, Therese; let the most steadfast outrages cement the scorn which is patently their due . . . . My eyes were barely open when I began to loathe these coarse reveries; very early I made it a law unto myself to trample them in the dust, I took oath to return to them never more; if you would be happy, imitate me; as do I, hate, abjure, profane the foul object of this dreadful cult; and this cult too, created for illusion, made like him to be reviled by everyone who pretends to wisdom."

13

"Oh! Monsieur," I responded, weeping, "you would deprive an unfortunate of her fondest hope were you to wither in her heart this religion which is her whole comfort. Firmly attached to its teachings, absolutely convinced that all the blows leveled against it are nothing but libertinage's effects and the passions', am I to sacrifice, to blasphemies, to sophistries horrible to me, my heart's sweetest sustenance?"

I added a thousand other arguments to this one, they merely caused the Count to laugh, and his captious principles, nourished by a more male eloquence, supported by readings and studies I, happily, had never performed, daily attacked my own principles, without shaking them. Madame de Bressac, that woman filled with piety and virtue, was not unaware her nephew justified his wild behavior with every one of the day's paradoxes; she too often shuddered upon hearing them; and as she condescended to attribute somewhat more good sense to me than to her other women, she would sometimes take me aside and speak of her chagrin.

Meanwhile, her nephew, champing at the bit, had reached the point where he no longer bothered to hide his malign intentions; not only had he surrounded his aunt with all of that dangerous canaille which served his pleasures, but he had even carried boldness so far as to declare to her, in my presence, that were she to take it into her head to frustrate his appetite, he would convince her of their charm by practicing them before her very eyes.

I trembled; I beheld this conduct with horror. I strove to rationalize my reactions by attributing their origin to personal motives, for I wished to stifle the unhappy passion which burned in my soul; but is love an illness to be cured? All I endeavored to oppose to it merely fanned its flames, and the perfidious Count never appeared more lovable to me than when I had assembled before me everything which ought to have induced me to hate him.

I had remained four years in this household unrelentingly persecuted by the same sorrows, forever consoled by the same sweetnesses, when this abominable man, finally believing himself sure of me, dared disclose his infamous schemes. We were in the country at the time, I alone attended upon the Marquise, her first maid-in-waiting had obtained leave to remain in Paris through the summer to look after some of her husband's business. One evening shortly after I had retired, and as I was taking some air upon the balcony of my room, being unable to bring myself to go to bed because of the extreme heat, I suddenly heard the Count knock; he wished to have a word or two with me. Alas! the moments that cruel author of my ills accorded me of his presence were too precious for me to dare refuse him one; he enters, carefully closes the door and flings himself into an armchair.

"Listen to me, Therese," and there is a note of embarrassment in his voice, "I have things of the greatest importance to say to you; swear to me you will never reveal any of them."

"Monsieur," I reply, "do you think me capable of abusing your confidence?"

"You have no idea what you would be risking - were you to prove to me I had made a mistake in trusting you!"

"The most frightful of all my woes should be to lose your trust, I have no need of greater menaces . . . ."

"Ah then, Therese, I have condemned my aunt to die . . . and it is your hand I must employ."

"My hand!" I cried, recoiling in fright, "have you been able, Monsieur, to conceive such projects?... no, dispose of my life if you must, but imagine not you will ever obtain from me the horror you propose."

"Hear me, Therese," says the Count, reasoning with me calmly, "I indeed foresaw your distaste for the idea but, as you have wit and verve, I flattered myself with the belief I could vanquish your feelings... could prove to you that this crime, which seems to you of such enormity, is, at bottom, a very banal affair.

"Two misdeeds present themselves, Therese, to your not very philosophic scrutiny: the destruction of a creature bearing a resemblance to us, and the evil with which this destruction is augmented when the said creature is one of our near kinsmen. With regard to the crime of destroying one's fellow, be persuaded, dear girl, it is purely hallucinatory; man has not been accorded the power to destroy; he has at best the capacity to alter forms, but lacks that required to annihilate them: well, every form is of equal worth in Nature's view; nothing is lost in the immense melting pot where variations are wrought: all the material masses which fall into it spring incessantly forth in other shapes, and whatsoever be our interventions in this process, not one of them, needless to say, outrages her, not one is capable of offending her. Our depredations revive her power; they stimulate her energy, but not one attenuates her; she is neither impeded nor thwarted by any . . . . Why! what difference does it make to her creative hand if this mass of flesh today wearing the conformation of a bipedal individual is reproduced tomorrow in the guise of a handful of centipedes? Dare one say that the construction of this two-legged animal costs her any more than that of an earthworm, and that she should take a greater interest in the one than in the other? If then the degree of attachment, or rather of indifference, is the same, what can it be. to her if, by one man's sword, another man is transspeciated into a fly or a blade of grass? When they will have convinced me of the sublimity of our species, when they will have demonstrated to me that it is really so important to Nature, that her laws are necessarily violated by this transmutation, then I will be able to believe that murder is a crime; but when the most thoughtful and sober study has proven to me that everything that vegetates upon this globe is of equal value in her eyes, I shall never concede that the alteration of one of these creatures into a thousand others can in any sense upset her intentions or sort ill with her desires. I say to myself: all men, all animals, all plants growing, feeding, destroying and reproducing themselves by the same means, never undergoing a real death, but a simple variation in what modifies them; all, I say, appearing today in one form and several years or hours later in another, all may, at the will of the being who wishes to move them, change a thousand thousand times in a single day, without one of Nature's directives being affected for one instant Ä what do I say? without this transmuter having done anything but good, since, by dismantling the individuals whose basic components again become necessary to Nature, he does naught by this action, improperly qualified as criminal, but render her the creative energy of which she is necessarily deprived by him who, through brutish indifference, dares not undertake any shuffling, as it were, of the deck . . . . O Therese, it is man's pride alone erects murder as a crime. This vain creature, imagining himself the most sublime of the globe's inhabitants, its most essential, takes his departure from this false principle in order to affirm that the deed which results in his undoing can be nothing but an infamy; but his vanity, his lunacy alter the laws of Nature not one jot; no person exists who in the depths of his heart does not feel the most vehement desire to be rid of those by whom he is hampered, troubled, or whose death may be of some advantage to him; and do you suppose, Therese, that the difference between this desire and its effect is very great? Now, if these impressions come to us from Nature, can it be presumed they irritate her? Would she inspire in us what would cause her downfall? Ah, be at ease, dear girl, we experience nothing that does not serve her; all the impulses she puts in us are the agents of her decrees; man's passions are but the means she employs to attain her ends. If she stands in need of more individuals, she inspires lust in us and behold! there are creations; when destructions become necessary to her, she inserts vengeance, avarice, lechery, ambition into our hearts and lo! you have murders; but she has not ceased to labor in her own behalf, and whatever we do, there can be no question of it, we are the unthinking instruments of her caprices.

"Ah, no, Therese, no! Nature does not leave in our hands the possibility of committing crimes which would conflict with her economy; has it ever been known to happen that the weakest were able to offend the mightiest? What are we in comparison to her? Can she, when she created us, have placed in us what would be capable of hurting her? Can that idiotic supposition consort with the sublime and sure manner in which we see her attain her ends? Ah! were murder not one of the human actions which best fulfilled her intentions, would she permit the doing of murder? May to imitate then be to injure her? Can she be incensed to see man do to his brethren what she herself does to him every day? Since it is proven that she cannot reproduce without destructions, is it not to act in harmony with her wishes to multiply them unceasingly? The man who moves in this direction, who plunges ahead with all possible zeal, will incontestably be the one who serves her best, since it will be he who most cooperates with the schemes she manifests constantly. The primary and most beautiful of Nature's qualities is motion, which agitates her at all times, but this motion is simply a perpetual consequence of crimes, she conserves it by means of crimes only; the person who most nearly resembles her, and therefore the most perfect being, necessarily will be the one whose most active agitation will become the cause of many crimes; whereas, I repeat, the inactive or indolent person, that is to say, the virtuous person, must be in her eyes - how may there be any doubt of it? Ä the least perfect since he tends only to apathy, to lethargy, to that inactivity which would immediately plunge everything back into chaos were his star to be in the ascendant. Equilibrium must be preserved; it can only be preserved by crimes; therefore, crimes serve Nature; if they serve her, if she demands them, if she desires them, can they offend her? And who else can be offended if she is not?

"But my aunt is the creature I am going to destroy . . . . Oh, Therese, in a philosopher's view how frivolous are these consanguinary ties! Forgive me, but I do not even wish to discuss them, so futile are they. These contemptible chains, fruit of our laws and our political institutions Ä can they mean anything to Nature?

"Desert your prejudices, Therese, leave them behind, and serve me; your fortune is made."

"Oh Monsieur !" I replied, terrified by the Comte de Bressac, "your mind invents this theory of an impassive, indifferent Nature; deign rather to heed your heart, and you will hear it condemn all libertinage's false reasonings. Is not that heart, to whose tribunal I recommend you, the sanctuary where this Nature you outrage wishes to be heard and respected? If she engraves upon it the extreme horror of the crime you meditate, will you grant me it is a damnable one? Passions, I know, are blinding you at the present moment, but once they subside, how will you not be torn by remorse? The greater your sensitivity, the more cruelly shall it sting you . . . . Oh Monsieur! preserve, respect this tender, invaluable friend's life;

sacrifice it not; you would perish of despair! Every day... at every instant you would be visited by the image of this cherished aunt, she whom your unthinking rage would have hurled into her tomb; you would hear her plaintive voice still pronouncing those sweet names that were your childhood's joy; she would be present during your waking hours and appear to torture you in your dreams; she would open with her bloodstained fingers the wounds wherewith you would have mutilated her; thereafter not one happy moment would shine for you while you dwelt upon this earth; you would become a stranger to pleasures; your every idea would be of trouble; a celestial arm, whose might you do not appreciate, would avenge the days you would have obliterated, by envenoming your own, and without having tasted happiness from your felonies, you would be slain by mortal sorrow for having dared accomplish them."

As I uttered these words tears returned to my eyes, I sank to my knees before the Count; by all that is most holy I did implore him to let fade into oblivion an infamous aberration I swore to him all my life I would conceal . . . . But I did not know the man with whom I was dealing; I knew not to what point passions had enthroned crime in that perverse soul. The Count rose and spoke in a voice of ice.

"I see very well I was mistaken, Therese," said he. "I regret it, perhaps as much on your account as on my own; no matter, I shall discover other means, and it will be much you shall have lost without your mistress gaining anything."

The threat changed all my ideas; by not accepting the criminal role proposed to me, I was exposing myself to great personal risk and my protectress was infallibly to perish; by consenting to be his accomplice, I would shield myself from the Count's wrath and would assuredly save his aunt; an instant's reflection convinced me I should agree to everything. But as so rapid a reversal would have appeared suspicious, I strove to delay my capitulation; I obliged the Count to repeat his sophistries often; little by little I took on an air of not knowing what to reply: Bressac believed me vanquished; I justified my weakness by the potency of his art and in the end I surrendered. The Count sprang into my arms. Ah, how I should have been overjoyed had his movement been inspired by another motive . . . . What is it I am saying? The time had passed: his horrible conduct, his barbarous designs had annihilated all the feelings my weakling heart had dared conceive, and I saw in him nothing but a monster . . . .

14

"You are the first woman I have ever held in my arms," said the Count, "and truly, it is with all my soul . . . . You are delicious, my child; a gleam of wisdom seems to have penetrated into your mind! That this charming mind has lain in darkness for so long! Incredible."

Next, we came to facts. In two or three days, as soon, that is, as an opportunity presented itself, I was to drop a dose of poison Ä Bressac gave me the package that contained it Ä into the cup of chocolate Madame customarily took in the morning. The Count assured my immunity against all consequences and directly I consummated the deed, handed me a contract providing me with an annuity of two thousand crowns; he signed these promises without characterizing the state in which I was to enjoy their benefits; we separated.

In the midst of all this, something most singular occurred, something all too able to reveal the atrocious soul of the monster with whom I had to deal; I must not interrupt myself for a moment for, no doubt, you are awaiting the denouement of the adventure in which I had become involved.

Two days following the conclusion of our criminal pact, the Count learned that an uncle, upon whose succession he had not in the least counted, had just left him an income of eighty thousand pounds . . . . "O Heaven!" I said to myself upon hearing the news, "is it then in thuswise celestial justice punishes the basest conspiracy!" And straightway repenting this blasphemy spoken against Providence, I cast myself upon my knees and implored the Almighty's forgiveness, and happily supposed that this unexpected development should at least change the Count's plans . . . . What was my error!

"Ah, my dear Therese," he said that same evening, having run to my room, "how prosperity does rain down upon me! Often I have told you so: the idea of a crime or an execution is the surest means to attract good fortune; none exists save for villains."

"What!" I responded, "this unhoped for bounty does not persuade you, Monsieur, patiently to await the death you wished to hasten?"

"Wait?" the Count replied sharply, "I do not intend to wait two minutes, Therese; are you not aware I am twenty-eight? Well, it is hard to wait at my age . . . . No, let this affect our scheme not in the slightest, give me the comfort of seeing everything brought to an end before the time comes for us to return to Paris . . . . Tomorrow, at the very latest the day after tomorrow, I beseech you. There has been delay enough: the hour approaches for the payment of the first quarter of your annuity... for performing the act which guarantees you the money . . . ."

As best I could, I disguised the fright this desperate eagerness inspired in me, and I renewed my resolution of the day before, well persuaded that if I were not to execute the horrible crime I had engaged to commit, the Count would soon notice I was playing a trick upon him and that, if I were to warn Madame de Bressac, whatever would be her reaction to the project's disclosure, the young Count, observing himself deceived one way or another, would promptly resort to more certain methods which, causing his aunt equally to perish, would also expose me to all her nephew's vengeance. There remained the alternative of consulting the law, but nothing in the world could have induced me to adopt it; I decided to forewarn the Marquise; of all possible measures, that seemed the best, and I elected it.

"Madame," I said to her on the morrow of my last interview with the Count, "Madame, I have something of the highest importance to reveal, but however vital its interest to you, I shall not broach it unless, beforehand, you give me your word of honor to bear no resentment against your nephew for what Monsieur has had the audacity to concert . . . . You will act, Madame, you will take the steps prudence enjoins, but you will say not a word. Deign to give me your promise; else I am silent."

Madame de Bressac, who thought it was but a question of some of her nephew's everyday extravagances, bound herself by the oath I demanded, and I disclosed everything. The unhappy woman burst into tears upon learning of the infamy . . . . "The monster!" she cried, "have I ever done anything that was not for his good? Had I wished to thwart his vices, or correct them, what other motive than his own happiness could have constrained me to severity! And is it not thanks to me he inherits this legacy his uncle has just left him? Ah, Therese, Therese, prove to me that it is true, this project... put me in a way that will prevent me from doubting; I need all that may aid in extinguishing the sentiments my unthinking heart dares yet preserve for the monster . . . ." And then I brought the package of poison into view; it were difficult to furnish better proof; yet the Marquise wished to experiment with it; we made a dog swallow a light dose, shut up the animal, and at the end of two hours it was dead after being seized by frightful convulsions. Any lingering doubt by now dispelled, Madame de Bressac came to a decision; she bade me give her the rest of the poison and immediately sent a courier with a letter to the Duc de Sonzeval, related to her, asking him to go directly, but in secrecy, to the Secretary of State, and to expose the atrocity of a nephew whose victim she might at any moment become; to provide himself with a lettre de cachet; to make all possible haste to come and deliver her from the wretch who had so cruelly plotted to take her life.

But the abominable crime was to be consummated; some inconceivable permission must have been granted by Heaven that virtue might be made to yield to villainy's oppressions: the animal upon which we had experimented revealed everything to the Count: he heard it howling; knowing of his aunt's fondness for the beast, he asked what had been done to it; those to whom he spoke knew nothing of the matter and made him no clear answer; from this moment, his suspicions began to take shape; he uttered not a word, but I saw that he was disquieted; I mentioned his state to the Marquise, she became further upset, but could think of nothing to do save urge the courier to make yet greater haste, and, if possible, still more carefully to hide the purpose of his mission. She advised her nephew that she was writing to Paris to beg the Duc de Sonzeval to waste not a moment to take up the matter of the recently deceased uncle's inheritance for if no one were to appear to claim it, there was litigation to be feared; she added that she had requested the Duke to come and give her a complete account of the affair, in order that she might learn whether or not she and her nephew would be obliged to make a journey to Paris. Too skillful a physiognomist to fail to notice the embarrassment in his aunt's face, to fail to observe, as well, some confusion written upon mine, the Count smiled at everything and was no less on his guard.

Under the pretext of taking a promenade, he leaves the chateau; he lies in wait for the courier at a place the man must inevitably pass. The messenger, far more a creature of the Count than his aunt's trustworthy minion, raises no objections when his master demands to see the dispatches he is carrying, and Bressac, once convinced of what no doubt he calls my treachery, gives the courier a hundred louis, together with instructions never to appear again at the Marquise's. He returns to the chateau, rage in his heart; however, he restrains himself; he encounters me, as usual he cajoles me, asks whether it shall not be tomorrow, points out it is essential the deed be performed before the Duke's arrival, then goes to bed with a tranquil air about which nothing is to be remarked. At the time I knew nothing, I was the dupe of everything. Were the appalling crime to be committed Ä as the Count's actions informed me later Ä he would of course have to commit it himself; but I did not know how; I conjectured much; what good would it do to tell you what I imagined? Rather, let us move ahead to the cruel manner in which I was punished for not having wished to undertake the thing. On the day after the messenger was intercepted, Madame drank her chocolate as she always did, dressed, seemed agitated, and sat down at table; scarcely was I out of the dining room when the Count accosted me.

"Therese," and nothing could have been more phlegmatic than his manner as he spoke, "I have found a more reliable method than the one I proposed to attain our objectives, but numerous details are involved, and I dare not come so often to your room; at precisely five o'clock be at the corner of the park, I'll join you, we will take a walk together in the woods; while on our promenade I'll explain it all."

I wish to affirm, Madame, that, whether because of the influence of Providence, whether owing to an excessive candor, whether to blindness, nothing gave me a hint of the terrible misery awaiting me; I believed myself so safe, thanks to the Marquise's secret arrangements, that I never for a moment imagined that the Count had been able to discover them; nevertheless I was not entirely at ease.

"Le parjure est vertu quand on promit le crime," one of our tragic poets has said; but perjury is always odious to a delicate and sensitive spirit which finds itself compelled to resort to it. My role embarrassed me.

However that may be, I came to the rendezvous; the Count was not late in getting there; he came up to me very gay and easy, and we set off into the forest; the while he but laughed banteringly and jested, as was his habit when we were together. When I sought to guide the conversation to the subject which he had desired to discuss, he told me to wait yet a little, he said he feared we might be observed, it did not seem to him we were in a safe enough place; very gradually, without my perceiving it, we approached the four trees to which I had been so cruelly bound long ago. Upon seeing the place, a quiver ran through me: all the horror of my fate rose up before my eyes, and fancy whether my terror was not doubled when I caught sight of the preparations which had been made in that horrible place. Ropes hung from one of the trees; huge mastiffs were leashed to each of the other three and seemed to be waiting for nothing but me in order to fall to sating the hunger announced by their gaping foam-flecked jaws; one of the Count's favorites guarded them.

Whereupon the perfidious creature ceased to employ all but the very foulest epithets.

"Scum," quoth he, "do you recognize that bush whence I dragged you like a wild beast only to spare a life you deserved to lose? Do you recognize these trees unto which I threatened to lash you were you ever to give me cause to repent my kindness? Why did you agree to perform the task I demanded, if you intended to betray me to my aunt? and how could you imagine it was virtue you served by imperiling the freedom of him to whom you owe all your happiness? By necessity placed between two crimes, why have you chosen the more abominable?"

"Alas ! I did not choose the less..."

"But you should have refused," the Count continued, in his rage seizing one of my arms and shaking me furiously, "yes, certainly, refused, and not consented to betray me."

Then Monsieur de Bressac told me how he had gone about the interception of Madame's messages, and how the suspicion had been born which had led him to decide to stop them.

"What has your duplicity done for you, unworthy creature? You have risked your life without having saved my aunt's: the die is cast, upon my return to the chateau I will find a fortune awaiting me, but you must perish; before you expire you must learn that the virtuous road is not always the safest, and that there are circumstances in this world when complicity in crime is preferable to informing." And without giving me time to reply, without giving evidence of the least pity for the frightful situation I was in, he dragged me toward the tree destined for me and by which his valet stood expectantly. "Here she is," he said, "the creature who wanted to poison my aunt and who may already have committed the terrible crime in spite of my efforts to prevent it; no doubt, it would have been better to have put her into the hands of justice, but the law would have taken away her life, and I prefer to leave it to her in order that she have longer to suffer."

The two villains then lay hands on me, in an instant they strip me naked. "Pretty buttocks," said the Count in a tone of cruelest irony, brutally handling those objects, "superb flesh... excellent lunch for the dogs." When no article of clothing is left upon me, I am secured to the tree by a rope attached around my waist; so that I may defend myself as best I can, my arms are left free, and enough slack is provided for me to advance or retreat about two yards. The arrangements completed, the Count, very much moved, steps up to have a look at my expression, he turns and passes around me; his savage way of handling me seems to say that his murderous fingers would like to dispute the rage of his mastiff's steel teeth . . . .

"Come," says he to his lieutenant, "free the animals, the time has arrived."

They are loosed, the Count excites them, all three fling themselves upon my poor body, one would think they were sharing it in such wise that not one of its parts would be exempt from assault; in vain I drive them back, they bite and tear me with renewed fury, and throughout this horrible scene, Bressac, the craven Bressac, as if my torments had ignited his perfidious lust... the beastly man gives himself up, while he regards me, to his companion's criminal caresses.

"Enough," said he after several minutes had gone by, "that will do. Tie up the dogs and let's abandon this creature to her sweet fate."

"Well indeed, Therese," says he as he severs my bonds, "virtue is not to be practiced at some expense; a pension of two thousand crowns, would that not have been worth more than the bites you are covered with?"

But in my state I can scarcely hear him; I slump to the foot of the tree and am about to lose consciousness.

"It is most generous of me to save your life," continues the traitor whom my sufferings inflame, "at least take good care how you make use of this favor . . . ."

Then he orders me to get up, dress, and quit the place at once. As my blood is flowing everywhere, in order that my few clothes, the only clothes I have, not be stained, I gather some grass to wipe myself; Bressac paces to and fro, much more preoccupied with his thoughts than concerned with me.

My swollen flesh, the blood that continues to stream from my multiple wounds, the atrocious pain I am enduring, everything makes the operation of dressing well nigh impossible; never once does the dishonest man who has just put me into this horrible state... him for whom I once would have sacrificed my life, never once does he deign to show me the least hint of sympathy. When at length I am ready:

"Go wherever you wish," says he; "you must have some money left, I will not take it from you, but beware of reappearing at any one of my houses in the city or the country: there are two excellent reasons for not doing so: you may just as well know, first of all, that the affair you thought finished is not at all over. They informed you that the law was done with you; they told you what is not true; the warrant for your arrest still holds, the case is still warm: you were left in this situation so that your conduct might be observed. In the second place, you are going to pass, insofar as the public is concerned, for the Marquise's murderer; if she yet breathes, I am going to see to it she carries this notion into the grave, the entire household will share it; and there you have two trials still to face instead of one: instead of a vile usurer, you have for an adversary a rich and powerful man who is determined to hound you into Hell itself if you misuse the life his compassion leaves to you."

15

"Oh Monsieur !" was my response, "whatever have been your severities with me, fear not that I will retaliate; I thought myself obliged to take steps against you when it was a question of your aunt's life; but where only the unhappy Therese is involved, I shall never do anything. Adieu, Monsieur, may your crimes render you as happy as your cruelties have made me to suffer; and no matter what the fate reserved to me by Heaven, while it shall prolong my deplorable life, I shall only employ my days in uttering prayers for you."

The Count raised his head; he could not avoid glancing at me upon hearing these words, and, as he beheld me quavering and covered with tears and doubtless was afraid lest he be moved by what he saw, the cruel one went away, and I saw him nevermore.

Entirely delivered unto my agony, I fell back again and lay by the tree; there, giving free reign to my hurt, I made the forest resound with my groans; I pressed my stricken frame against the earth, and shed upon the sward all my tears.

"O my God," I cried out, "Thou hast so willed it; it was grained in Thy eternal decrees that the innocent were to fall unto the guilty and were to be their prey: dispose of me, O Lord, I am yet far away from what Thou didst suffer for us; may those I endure, as I adore Thee, render me worthy someday of what rewards Thou keepeth for the lowly, when he hath Thee before him in his tribulations, and let his anguishes be unto Thy greater glorification!"

Night was closing: it was almost beyond my power to move; I was scarcely able to stand erect; I cast my eyes upon the thicket where four years earlier I had slept a night when I had been in circumstances almost as unhappy! I dragged myself along as best I could, and having reached the very same spot, tormented by my still bleeding wounds, overwhelmed by my mind's anxieties and the sorrows of my heart, I passed the cruelest night imaginable.

By dawn, thanks to my youth and my vigorous temperament, some of my strength was restored; greatly terrified by the proximity of that baneful chateau, I started away from it without delay; I left the forest, and resolved at any price to gain the first habitation which might catch my eye, I entered the town of Saint-Marcel, about five leagues distant from Paris; I demanded the address of a surgeon, one was given me; I presented myself and besought him to dress my wounds; I told him that, in connection with some affair at whose source lay love, I had fled my mother's house, quit Paris, and during the night had been overtaken in the forest by bandits who in revenge for my resistance to their desires, had set their dogs upon me. Rodin, as this artist was called, examined me with the greatest attention, found nothing dangerous about my injuries; had I come to him directly, he said, he would have been able to guarantee that in the space of a fortnight he would have me as fresh and whole as I had been before my adventure; however, the night passed in the open and my worry had infected my wounds, and I could not expect to be well in less than a month. Rodin found space in his own house to lodge me, took all possible care of me, and on the thirtieth day there no longer existed upon my body a single vestige of Monsieur de Bressac's cruelties.

As soon as I was fit to take a little air, my first concern was to find in the town some girl sufficiently adroit and intelligent to go to the Marquise's chateau and find out what had taken place there since my departure. This apparently very dangerous inquisitiveness would without the slightest doubt have been exceedingly misplaced; but here it was not a question of mere Curiosity. What I had earned while with the Marquise remained in my room; I had scarcely six louis about me, and I possessed above forty at the chateau. I did not suppose the Count would be unkind enough to refuse me what was so legitimately mine. Persuaded that, his first fury once passed, he would not wish to do me such an injustice, I wrote a letter calculated to touch him as deeply as possible. I was careful to conceal my address and I begged him to send back my old clothes together with the small sum that would be found in my chamber. A lively and spirited peasant girl of twenty-five undertook to deliver my letter and promised to do her best to bring me back all the information she could garner upon the various subjects about which I gave her to understand I needed to be enlightened. I insisted, that above all else, she hide the name of the place where I was, that she not breathe a word of me in whatever form or connection, and that she say she had taken the letter from a man who had brought it from somewhere fifteen leagues away. Jeannette left, and twenty-four hours later she came back with the reply; it still exists, I have it here, Madame, but before you read it, deign to learn what had transpired at the Count's chateau since I had been out of it.

Having fallen seriously ill the very day I left, the Marquise de Bressac had been seized by frightful pains and convulsions, and had died the next morning; the family had rushed to the chateau and the nephew, seemingly gripped in the greatest desolation, had declared that his aunt had been poisoned by a chambermaid who had taken flight the same day. Inquiries were made, and they had the intention to put the wretch to death were she to be found; as for the rest, the Count discovered that the inheritance had made him much wealthier than he had ever anticipated he would be; the Marquise's strongbox, pocketbook, and gems, all of them objects of which no one had known anything, put the nephew, apart from his revenues, in possession of more than six hundred thousand francs in chattels or cash. Behind his affected grief, the young man had, it was said, considerable trouble concealing his delight, and the relatives, convoked for the autopsy demanded by the Count, after having lamented the unhappy Marquise's fate and sworn to avenge her should the culprit fall into their hands, had left the young man in undisputed and peaceful possession of his villainy. Monsieur de Bressac himself had spoken to Jeannette, he had asked a number of questions to which the girl had replied with such frankness and decision that he had resolved to give her his response without pressing her further. There is the fatal letter, said Therese, handing it to Madame de Lorsange, yes, there it is, Madame, sometimes my heart has need of it and I will keep it until I die; read it, read it without shuddering, if you can.

Madame de Lorsange, having taken the note from our lovely adventuress' hands, read therein the following words:

The criminal capable of having poisoned my aunt is brazen indeed to dare thus write to me after her execrable deed; better still is the care with which she conceals her retreat; for she may be sure she will be discomfited if she is discovered. But what is it she has the temerity to demand? What are these references to money? Does what she left behind equal the thefts she committed, either during her sojourn in the house or while consummating her final crime? Let her avoid sending a second request similar to this, for she is advised her ambassador will be arrested and held until the law acquaints itself with the place where the guilty party is taking cover.

Madame de Lorsange returned the note to Therese; "Continue, my dear child," said she, "the man's behavior is horrifying; to be swimming in gold and to deny her legitimate earnings to a poor creature who merely did not want to commit a crime, that is a gratuitous infamy entirely without example."

Alas! Madame, Therese continued, resuming her story, I was in tears for two days over that dreadful letter; I was far more afflicted by the thought of the horrible deed it attested than by the refusal it contained. Then, I groaned, then I am guilty, here am I a second time denounced to justice for having been overly respectful of the law! So be it, I repent nothing, I shall never know the least remorse so long as my soul is pure, and may I never be responsible for any evil other than that of having too much heeded the equitable and virtuous sentiments which will never abandon me.

I was, however, simply unable to believe that the pursuits and inquiries the Count mentioned were really true, for they seemed highly implausible: it would be so dangerous for him to have me brought into court that I imagined there was far greater reason for him to be frightened at the prospect of having to confront me, than I had cause to tremble before his menaces. These reflections led me to decide to stay where I was and to remain, if possible, until the augmentation of my funds might allow me to move on; I communicated my plan to Rodin, who approved it, and even suggested I keep my chamber in his house; but first of all, before I speak of what I decided to do, it is necessary to give you an idea of this man and his entourage.

Rodin was forty years of age, dark-haired, with shaggy eye-brows, a sparkling bright eye; there was about him what bespoke strength and health but, at the same time, libertinage. In wealth he was risen far above his native station, possessing from ten to twelve thousand pounds a year; owing to which, if Rodin practiced his surgical art, it was not out of necessity, but out of taste; he had a very attractive house in Saint-Marcel which, since the death of his wife two years previously, he shared with two girls, who were his servants, and with another, who was his own daughter. This young person, Rosalie by name, had just reached her fourteenth year; in her were gathered all the charms most capable of exciting admiration: the figure of a nymph, an oval face, clear, lovely, extraordinarily animated, delicate pretty features, very piquant as well, the prettiest mouth possible, very large dark eyes, soulful and full of feeling, chestnut-brown hair falling to below her waist, skin of an incredible whiteness… aglow, smooth, already the most beautiful throat in all the world, and, furthermore, wit, vivacity, and one of the most beautiful souls Nature has yet created. With respect to the companions with whom I was to serve in this household, they were two peasant girls: one of them was a governess, the other the cook. She who held the first post could have been twenty-five, the other eighteen or twenty, and both were extremely attractive; their looks suggested a deliberate choice, and this in turn caused the birth of some suspicions as to why Rodin was pleased to accommodate me. What need has he of a third woman? I asked myself, and why does he wish them all to be pretty? Assuredly, I continued, there is something in all this that little conforms with the regular manners from which I wish never to stray; we'll see.

In consequence, I besought Monsieur Rodin to allow me to extend my convalescence at his home for yet another week, declaring that, at the end of this time, he would have my reply to what he had very kindly proposed.

I profited from this interval by attaching myself more closely to Rosalie, determined to establish myself in her father's house only if there should prove to be nothing about it whence I might be obliged to take umbrage. With these designs, I cast appraising glances in every direction, and, on the following day, I noticed that this man enjoyed an arrangement which straightway provoked in me furious doubts concerning his behavior.

16

Monsieur Rodin kept a school for children of both sexes; during his wife's lifetime he had obtained the required charter and they had not seen fit to deprive him of it after he had lost her. Monsieur Rodin's pupils were few but select: in all, there were but fourteen girls and fourteen boys: he never accepted them under twelve and they were always sent away upon reaching the age of sixteen; never had monarch prettier subjects than Rodin. If there were brought to him one who had some physical defect or a face that left something to be desired, he knew how to invent twenty excuses for rejecting him, all his arguments were very ingenious, they were always colored by sophistries to which no one seemed able to reply; thus, either his corps of little day students had incomplete ranks, or the children who filled them were always charming. These youngsters did not take their meals with him, but came twice a day, from seven to eleven in the morning, from four to eight in the afternoon. If until then I had not yet seen all of this little troupe it was because, having arrived at Rodin's during the holidays, his scholars were not attending classes; toward the end of my recovery they reappeared.

Rodin himself took charge of the boys' instruction, his governess looked after that of the girls, whom he would visit as soon as he had completed his own lessons; he taught his young pupils writing, arithmetic, a little history, drawing, music, and for all that no other master but himself was employed.

I early expressed to Rosalie my astonishment that her father, while performing his functions as a doctor, could at the same time act as a schoolmaster; it struck me as odd, said I, that being able to live comfortably without exercising either the one or the other of these professions, he devoted himself to both. Rosalie, who by now had become very fond of me, fell to laughing at my remark; the manner in which she reacted to what I said only made me the more curious, and I besought her to open herself entirely to me.

"Listen," said that charming girl, speaking with all the candor proper to her age, and all the naivete of her amiable character; "listen to me, Therese, I am going to tell you everything, for I see you are a well brought up girl... incapable of betraying the secret I am going to confide to you.

"Certainly, dear friend, my father could make ends meet without pursuing either of these two occupations; and if he pursues both at once, it is because of the two motives I am going to reveal to you. He practices medicine because he has a liking for it; he takes keen pleasure in using his skill to make new discoveries, he has made so many of them, he has written so many authoritative texts based upon his investigations that he is generally acknowledged the most accomplished man in France at the present time; he worked for twenty years in Paris, and for the sake of his amusements he retired to the country. The real surgeon at Saint-Marcel is someone named Rombeau whom he has taken under his tutelage and with whom he collaborates upon experiments; and now, Therese, would you know why he runs a school?... Libertinage, my child, libertinage alone, a passion he carries to its extremes. My father finds in his pupils of either sex objects whose dependence submits them to his inclinations, and he exploits them . . . . But wait a moment ... come with me," said Rosalie, "today is Friday, one of the three days during the week when he corrects those who have misbehaved; it is in this kind of punishment my father takes his pleasure; follow me, I tell you, you shall see how he behaves. Everything is visible from a closet in my room which adjoins the one where he concludes his business; let's go there without making any noise, and above all be careful not to say a word both about what I am telling you and about what you are going to witness."

It was a matter of such great importance to familiarize myself with the customs of this person who had offered me asylum, that I felt I could neglect nothing which might discover them to me; I follow hard upon Rosalie's heels, she situates me near a partition, through cracks between its ill-joined boards one can view everything going on in the neighboring room.

Hardly have we taken up our post when Rodin enters, leading a fourteen-year-old girl, blond and as pretty as Love; the poor creature is sobbing away, all too unhappily aware of what awaits her; she comes in with moans and cries; she throws herself down before her implacable instructor, she entreats him to spare her, but his very inexorability fires the first sparks of the unbending Rodin's pleasure, his heart is already aglow, and his savage glances spring alive with an inner light . . . .

"Why, no, no," he cries, "not for one minute, this happens far too frequently, Julie, I repent my forbearance and leniency, their sole result has been repeated misconduct on your part, but could the gravity of this most recent example of it possibly allow me to show clemency, even supposing I wished to? A note passed to a boy upon entering the classroom!"

"Sir, I protest to you, I did not -"

"Ah I but I saw it, my dear, I saw it."

"Don't believe a word of it," Rosalie whispered to me, "these are trifles he invents by way of pretext; that little creature is an angel, it is because she resists him he treats her harshly."

Meanwhile, Rodin, greatly aroused, had seized the little girl's hands, tied them to a ring fitted high upon a pillar standing in the middle of the punishment room. Julie is without any defense... any save the lovely face languishingly turned toward her executioner, her superb hair in disarray, and the tears which inundate the most beautiful face in the world, the sweetest... the most interesting. Rodin dwells upon the picture, is fired by it, he covers those supplicating eyes with a blindfold, approaches his mouth and dares kiss them, Julie sees nothing more, now able to proceed as he wishes, Rodin removes the veils of modesty, her blouse is unbuttoned, her stays untied, she is naked to the waist and yet further below . . . . What whiteness! What beauty! These are roses strewn upon lilies by the Graces' very hands... what being is so heartless, so cruel as to condemn to torture charms so fresh... so poignant? What is the monster that can seek pleasure in the depths of tears and suffering and woe? Rodin contemplates... his inflamed eye roves, his hands dare profane the flowers his cruelties are about to wither; all takes place directly before us, not a detail can escape us: now the libertine opens and peers into, now he closes up again those dainty features which enchant him; he offers them to us under every form, but he confines himself to these only: although the true temple of Love is within his reach, Rodin, faithful to his creed, casts not so much as a glance in that direction, to judge by his behavior, he fears even the sight of it; if the child's posture exposes those charms, he covers them over again; the slightest disturbance might upset his homage, he would have nothing distract him... finally, his mounting wrath exceeds all limits, at first he gives vent to it through invectives, with menaces and evil language he affrights this poor little wretch trembling before the blows wherewith she realizes she is about to be torn; Rodin is beside himself, he snatches up a cat-o'-nine-tails that has been soaking in a vat of vinegar to give the thongs tartness and sting. "Well there," says he, approaching his victim, "prepare yourself, you have got to suffer"; he swings a vigorous arm, the lashes are brought whistling down upon every inch of the body exposed to them; twenty-five strokes are applied; the tender pink rosiness of this matchless skin is in a trice run into scarlet.

Julie emits cries... piercing screams which rend me to the soul; tears run down from beneath her blindfold and like pearls shine upon her beautiful cheeks; whereby Rodin is made all the more furious . . . . He puts his hands upon the molested parts, touches, squeezes, worries them, seems to be readying them for further assaults; they follow fast upon the first, Rodin begins again, not a cut he bestows is unaccompanied by a curse, a menace, a reproach... blood appears...

Rodin is in an ecstasy; his delight is immense as he muses upon the eloquent proofs of his ferocity. He can contain himself no longer, the most indecent condition manifests his overwrought state; he fears not to bring everything out of hiding, Julie cannot see it... he moves to the breech and hovers there, he would greatly like to mount as a victor, he dares not, instead, he begins to tyrannize anew; Rodin whips with might and main and finally manages, thanks to the leathern stripes, to open this asylum of the Graces and of joy . . . . He no longer knows who he is or where; his delirium has attained to such a pitch the use of reason is no longer available to him; he swears, he blasphemes, he storms, nothing is exempt from his savage blows, all he can reach is treated with identical fury, but the villain pauses nevertheless, he senses the impossibility of going further without risking the loss of the powers which he must preserve for new operations.

"Dress yourself," he says to Julie, loosening her bonds and readjusting his own costume, "and if you are once again guilty of similar misconduct, bear it firmly in mind you will not get off quite so lightly."

Julie returns to her class, Rodin goes into the boys' and immediately brings back a young scholar of fifteen, lovely as the day; Rodin scolds him; doubtless more at his ease with the lad, he wheedles and kisses while lecturing him.

"You deserve to be punished," he observes, "and you are going to be."

Having uttered these words, he oversteps the last bounds of modesty with the child; for in this case, everything is of interest to him, nothing is excluded, the veils are drawn aside, everything is palpated indiscriminately; Rodin alternates threats, caresses, kisses, curses; his impious fingers attempt to generate voluptuous sentiments in the boy and, in his turn, Rodin demands identical ministrations.

"Very well," cries the satyr, spying his success, "there you are in the state I forbade . . . . I dare swear that with two more movements you'd have the impudence to spit at me . . . ."

But too sure of the titillations he has produced, the libertine advances to gather a homage, and his mouth is the temple offered to the sweet incense; his hands excite it to jet forth, he meets the spurts, devours them, and is himself ready to explode, but he wishes to persevere to the end.

"Ah, I am going to make you pay for this stupidity!" says he and gets to his feet.

He takes the youth's two hands, he clutches them tight, and offers himself entirely to the altar at which his fury would perform a sacrifice. He opens it, his kisses roam over it, his tongue drives deep into it, is lost in it. Drunk with love and ferocity, Rodin mingles the expressions and sentiments of each . . . .

"Ah, little weasel!" he cries, "I must avenge myself upon the illusion you create in me."

The whips are picked up, Rodin flogs; clearly more excited by the boy than he was by the vestal, his blows become both much more powerful and far more numerous: the child bursts into tears, Rodin is in seventh heaven, but new pleasures call, he releases the boy and flies to other sacrifices. A little girl of thirteen is the boy's successor, and she is followed by another youth who is in turn abandoned for a girl; Rodin whips nine: five boys, four girls; the last is a lad of fourteen, endowed with a delicious countenance: Rodin wishes to amuse himself, the pupil resists; out of his mind with lust, he beats him, and the villain, losing all control of himself, hurls his flame's scummy jets upon his young charge's injured parts, he wets him from waist to heels; enraged at not having had strength enough to hold himself in check until the end, our corrector releases the child very testily, and after warning him against such tricks in the future, he sends him back to the class: such are the words I heard, those the scenes which I witnessed.

"Dear Heaven!" I said to Rosalie when this appalling drama came to its end, "how is one able to surrender oneself to such excesses? How can one find pleasure in the torments one inflicts?"

"Ah," replied Rosalie, "you do not know everything. Listen," she said, leading me back into her room, "what you have seen has perhaps enabled you to understand that when my father discovers some aptitudes in his young pupils, he carries his horrors much further, he abuses the girls in the same manner he deals with the boys." Rosalie spoke of that criminal manner of conjugation whereof I myself had believed I might be the victim with the brigands' captain into whose hands I had fallen after my escape from the Conciergerie, and by which I had been soiled by the merchant from Lyon. "By this means," Rosalie continued, "the girls are not in the least dishonored, there are no pregnancies to fear, and nothing prevents them from finding a husband; not a year goes by without his corrupting nearly all the boys in this way, and at least half the other children. Of the fourteen girls you have seen, eight have already been spoiled by these methods, and he has taken his pleasure with nine of the boys; the two women who serve him are submitted to the same horrors . . . . O Therese! " Rosalie added, casting herself into my arms, "O dear girl, and I too, yes I, he seduced me in my earliest years; I was barely eleven when I became his victim... when, alas! I was unable to defend myself against him."

"But Mademoiselle," I interrupted, horrified, "at least Religion remained to you... were you unable to consult a confessor and avow everything?"

"Oh, you do not know that as he proceeds to pervert us he stifles in each of us the very seeds of belief, he forbids us all religious devotions, and, furthermore, could I have done so? he had instructed me scarcely at all. The little he had said pertaining to these matters had been motivated by the fear that my ignorance might betray his impiety. But I had never been to confession, I had not made my First Communion; so deftly did he cover all these things with ridicule and insinuate his poisonous self into even our smallest ideas, that he banished forever all their duties out of them whom he suborned; or if they are compelled by their families to fulfill their religious duties, they do so with such tepidness, with such complete indifference, that he has nothing to fear from their indiscretion; but convince yourself, Therese, let your own eyes persuade you," she continued, very quickly drawing me back into the closet whence we had emerged; "come hither: that room where he chastises his students is the same wherein he enjoys us; the lessons are over now, it is the hour when, warmed by the preliminaries, he is going to compensate himself for the restraint his prudence sometimes imposes upon him; go back to where you were, dear girl, and with your own eyes behold it all."

However slight my curiosity concerning these new abominations, it was by far the better course to leap back into the closet rather than have myself surprised with Rosalie during the classes; Rodin would without question have become suspicious. And so I took my place; scarcely was I at it when Rodin enters his daughter's room, he leads her into the other, the two women of the house arrive; and thereupon the impudicious Rodin, all restraints upon his behavior removed, free to indulge his fancies to the full, gives himself over in a leisurely fashion and undisguisedly to committing all the irregularities of debauchery. The two peasants, completely nude, are flogged with exceeding violence; while he plies his whip upon the one the other pays him back in kind, and during the intervals when he pauses for rest, he smothers with the most uninhibited, the most disgusting caresses, the same altar in Rosalie who, elevated upon an armchair, slightly bent over, presents it to him; at last, there comes this poor creature's turn: Rodin ties her to the stake as he tied his scholars, and while one after another and sometimes both at once his domestics flay him, he beats his daughter, lashes her from her ribs to her knees, utterly transported by pleasure. His agitation is extreme: he shouts, he blasphemes, he flagellates: his thongs bite deep everywhere, and wherever they fall, there immediately he presses his lips. Both the interior of the altar and his victim's mouth... everything, the before-end excepted, everything is devoured by his suckings; without changing the disposition of the others, contenting himself with rendering it more propitious, Rodin by and by penetrates into pleasure's narrow asylum; meanwhile, the same throne is offered by the governess to his kisses, the other girl beats him with all her remaining strength, Rodin is in seventh heaven, he thrusts, he splits, he tears, a thousand kisses, one more passionate than the other, express his ardor, he kisses whatever is presented to his lust: the bomb bursts and the libertine besotted dares taste the sweetest of delights in the sink of incest and infamy...

Rodin sat down to dine; after such exploits he was in need of restoratives. That afternoon there were more lessons and further corrections, I could have observed new scenes had I desired, but I had seen enough to convince myself and to settle upon a reply to make to this villain's offers. The time for giving it approached. Two days after the events I have described, he himself came to my room to ask for it. He surprised me in bed. By employing the excuse of looking to see whether any traces of my wounds remained, he obtained the right, which I was unable to dispute, of performing an examination upon me, naked, and as he had done the same thing twice a day for a month and had never given any offense to my modesty I did not think myself able to resist. But this time Rodin had other plans; when he reaches the object of his worship, he locks his thighs about my waist and squeezes with such force that I find myself, so to speak, quite defenseless.

"Therese," says he, the while moving his hands about in such a manner as to erase all doubt of his intents, "you are fully recovered, my dear, and now you can give me evidence of the gratitude with which I have beheld your heart overflowing; nothing simpler than the form your thanks would take; I need nothing beyond this," the traitor continued, binding me with all the strength at his command. "...Yes, this will do, merely this, here is my recompense, I never demand anything else from women... but," he continued, " 'tis one of the most splendid I have seen in all my life... What roundness, fullness!... unusual elasticity!... what exquisite quality in the skin!... Oh my! I absolutely must put this to use . . . ."

17

Whereupon Rodin, apparently already prepared to put his projects into execution, is obliged, in order to proceed to the next stage, to relax his grip for a moment; I seize my opportunity and extricating myself from his clutches,

"Monsieur," I say, "I beg you to be well persuaded that there is nothing in the entire world which could engage me to consent to the horrors you seem to wish to commit. My gratitude is due to you, indeed it is, but I will not pay my debt in a criminal coin. Needless to say, I am poor and most unfortunate; but no matter; here is the small sum of money I possess," I continue, producing my meager purse, "take what you esteem just and allow me to leave this house, I beg of you, as soon as I am in a fitting state to go."

Rodin, confounded by the opposition he little expected from a girl devoid of means and whom, according to an injustice very ordinary amongst men, he supposed dishonest by the simple fact she was sunk in poverty; Rodin, I say, gazed at me attentively.

"Therese," he resumed after a minute's silence, "Therese, it is hardly appropriate for you to play the virgin with me; I have, so it would seem to me, some right to your complaisance; but, however, it makes little difference: keep your silver but don't leave me. I am highly pleased to have a well-behaved girl in my house, the conduct of these others I have about me being far from impeccable... Since you show yourself so virtuous in this instance, you will be equally so, I trust, in every other. My interests would benefit therefrom; my daughter is fond of you, just a short while ago she came and begged me to persuade you not to go; and so rest with us, if you will, I invite you to remain."

"Monsieur," I replied, "I should not be happy here; the two women who serve you aspire to all the affection you are able to give them; they will not behold me without jealousy, and sooner or later I will be forced to leave you."

"Be not apprehensive," Rodin answered, "fear none of the effects of these women's envy, I shall be quite capable of keeping them in their place by maintaining you in yours, and you alone will possess my confidence without any resultant danger to yourself. But in order to continue to deserve it, I believe it would be well for you to know that the first quality, the foremost, I require in you, Therese, is an unassailable discretion. Many things take place here, many which do not sort with your virtuous principles; you must be able to witness everything, hear all and never speak a syllable of it . . . . Ah, Therese, remain with me, stay here, Therese, my child, it will be a joy to have you; in the midst of the many vices to which I am driven by a fiery temper, an unrestrainable imagination and a much rotted heart, at least I will have the comfort of a virtuous being dwelling close by, and upon whose breast I shall be able to cast myself as at the feet of a God when, glutted by my debauches, I..." "Oh Heaven!" I did think at this moment, "then Virtue is necessary, it is then indispensable to man, since even the vicious one is obliged to find reassurance in it and make use of it as of a shelter." And then, recollecting Rosalie's requests that I not leave her, and thinking to discern some good principles in Rodin, I resolved to stay with him.

"Therese," Rodin said to me several days later, "I am going to install you near my daughter; in this way, you will avoid all frictions with the other two women, and I intend to give you three hundred pounds wages."

Such a post was, in my situation, a kind of godsend; inflamed by the desire to restore Rosalie to righteousness, and perhaps even her father too Were I able to attain some influence over him, I repented not of what I had just done... Rodin, having had me dress myself, conducted me at once to where his daughter was; Rosalie received me with effusions of joy, and I was promptly established.

Ere a week was gone by I had begun to labor at the conversions after which I thirsted, but Rodin's intransigence defeated all my efforts.

"Do not believe," was the response he made to my wise counsels, "that the kind of deference I showed to the virtue in you proves that I either esteem virtue or have the desire to favor it over vice. Think nothing of the sort, Therese, 'twould be to deceive yourself; on the basis of what I have done in your regard, anyone who was to maintain, as consequential to my behavior, the importance or the necessity of virtue would fall into the very largest error, and sorry I would be were you to fancy that such is my fashion of thinking. The rustic hovel to which I repair for shelter when, during the hunt, the excessive heat of the sun's rays falls perpendicularly upon me, that hut is certainly not to be mistaken for a superior building: its worth is merely circumstantial: I am exposed to some sort of danger, I find something which affords protection, I use it, but is this something the grander on that account? can it be the less contemptible? In a totally vicious society, virtue would be totally worthless; our societies not being entirely of this species, one must absolutely either play with virtue or make use of it so as to have less to dread from its faithful followers. If no one adopts the virtuous way, it becomes useless; I am then not mistaken when I affirm that it owes its necessity to naught but opinion or circumstances; virtue is not some kind of mode whose value is incontestable, it is simply a scheme of conduct, a way of getting along, which varies according to accidents of geography and climate and which, consequently, has no reality, the which alone exhibits its futility. Only what is constant is really good; what changes perpetually cannot claim that characterization: that is why they have declared that immutability belongs to the ranks of the Eternal's perfections; but virtue is completely without this quality: there is not, upon the entire globe, two races which are virtuous in the same manner; hence, virtue is not in any sense real, nor in any wise intrinsically good and in no sort deserves our reverence. How is it to be employed? as a prop, as a device: it is politic to adopt the virtue of the country one inhabits, so that those who practice it, either because they have a taste for it or who have to cultivate it because of their station, will leave you in peace, and so that this virtue which happens to be respected in your area will guarantee you, by its conventional preponderance, against the assaults delivered by them who profess vice. But, once again, all that is at the dictation of variable circumstances, and nothing in all that assigns a real merit to virtue. There are, furthermore, such virtues as are impossible to certain men; now, how are you going to persuade me that a virtue in conflict or in contradiction with the passions is to be found in Nature? And if it is not in Nature and natural; how can it be good? In those men we are speaking of there will certainly be vices opposed to these virtues, and these vices will be preferred by these men, since they will be the only modes... the only schemes of being which will be thoroughly agreeable to their peculiar physical constitutions or to their uncommon organs; in this hypothesis, there would then be some very useful vices: well, how can virtue be useful if you demonstrate to me that what is contrary to virtue is useful? In reply to that, one hears that virtue is useful to others, and that in this sense it is good; for if it is posited that I must do only what is good to others, in my turn I will receive only good. And this argument is pure sophistry: in return for the small amount of good I receive at the hands of others thanks to the virtue they practice, my obligation to practice virtue in my turn causes me to make a million sacrifices for which I am in no wise compensated. Receiving less than I give, I hence conclude a very disadvantageous bargain, I experience much more ill from the privations I endure in order to be virtuous, than I experience good from those who do it to me; the arrangement being not at all equitable, I therefore must not submit to it, and certain, by being virtuous, not to cause others as much pleasure as I receive pain by compelling myself to be good, would it not be better to give up procuring them a happiness which must cost me so much distress? There now remains the harm I may do others by being vicious and the evil I myself would suffer were everyone to resemble me. Were we to acknowledge an efficient circulation of vices, I am certainly running a grave danger, I concede it; but the grief experienced by what I risk is offset by the pleasure I receive from causing others to be menaced: and there! you see, equality is re-established: and everyone is more or less equally happy: which is not the case and cannot be the case in a society where some are good and others are bad, because, from this mixture, perpetual pitfalls result! and no pitfalls exist in the other instance. In the heterogeneous society, all interests are unalike: there you have the source of an infinite number of miseries; in the contrary association, all interests are identical, each individual composing it is furnished with the same proclivities, the same penchants, each one marches together with all the others and to the same goal; they are all happy. But, idiots complain to you, evil does not make for happiness. No, not when everyone has agreed to idolise good; but merely cease to prize, instead deflate, heap abuse upon what you call good, and you will no longer revere anything but what formerly you had the idiocy to call evil; and every man will have the pleasure of committing it not at all because it will be permitted (that might be, upon occasion, a reason for the diminishment of its appeal), but because the law will no longer punish it, and it is the law, through the fear it inspires, which lessens the pleasure Nature has seen to it we take in crime. I visualize a society where it will be generally admitted that incest (let us include this offense together with all the others), that incest, I say, is criminal: those who commit incest will be unhappy, because opinion, laws, beliefs, everything will concert to chill their pleasure; those who desist from doing this evil, those who, because of these restraints, will not dare, will be equally unhappy: thus, the law that proscribes incest will have done nothing but cause wretchedness. Now, I visualize another society neighboring the first; in this one incest is no crime at all: those who do not desist will not be unhappy, and those who desire it will be happy. Hence, the society which permits this act will be better suited to mankind than the one in which the act is represented as a crime; the same pertains to all other deeds clumsily denominated criminal; regard them from this point of view, and you create crowds of unhappy persons; permit them, and not a complaint is to be heard; for he who cherishes this act, whatever it happens to be, goes about performing it in peace and quiet, and he who does not care for it either remains in a kind of neutral indifference toward it, which is certainly not painful, or finds restitution for the hurt he may have sustained by resorting to a host of other injuries wherewith in his turn he belabors whosoever has aggrieved him: thus everyone in a criminal society is either very happy indeed, or else in a paradise of unconcern; consequently, there's nothing good, nothing respectable, nothing that can bring about happiness in what they call virtue. Let those who follow the virtuous track be not boastingly proud of the concessions wrung from us by the structural peculiarities of our society; 'tis purely a matter of circumstance, an accident of convention that the homages demanded of us take a virtuous form; but in fact, this worship is a hallucination, and the virtue which obtains a little pious attention for a moment is not on that account the more noble."

Such was the infernal logic of Rodin's wretched passions; but Rosalie, gentle and less corrupt, Rosalie, detesting the horrors to which she was submitted, was a more docile auditor and more receptive to my opinions. I had the most ardent desire to bring her to discharge her primary religious duties; but we would have been obliged to confide in a priest, and Rodin would not have one in the house; he beheld them, and the beliefs they professed, with horror: nothing in the world would have induced him to suffer one to come near his daughter; to lead the girl to a confessor was equally impossible: Rodin never allowed Rosalie to go abroad unless he accompanied her. We were therefore constrained to bide our time until some occasion might present itself; and while we waited I instructed the young person; by giving her a taste for virtue, I inspired in her another for Religion, I revealed to her its sacred dogmas and its sublime mysteries, and I so intimately attached these two sentiments to her youthful heart that I rendered them indispensable to her life's happiness.

"O Mademoiselle," I said one day, my eyes welling with tears at her compunction, "can man blind himself to the point of believing that he is not destined to some better end? Is not the fact he has been endowed with the capacity of consciousness of his God sufficient evidence that this blessing has not been accorded him save to meet the responsibilities it imposes? Well, what may be the foundation of the veneration we owe the Eternal, if it is not that virtue of which He is the example? Can the Creator of so many wonders have other than good laws? And can our hearts be pleasing unto Him if their element is not good? It seems to me that, for sensitive spirits, the only valid motives for loving that Supreme Being must be those gratitude inspires. Is it not a favor thus to have caused us to enjoy the beauties of this Universe? and do we not owe Him some gratitude in return for such a blessing? But a yet stronger reason establishes, confirms the universal chain of our duties; why should we refuse to fulfill those required by His decrees, since they are the very same which consolidate our happiness amongst mortals? Is it not sweet to feel that one renders oneself worthy of the Supreme Being simply by practicing those virtues which must bring about our contentment on earth, and that the means which render us worthy to live amongst our brethren are the identical ones which give us the assurance of a rebirth, in the life still to come, close by the throne of God! Ah, Rosalie! how blind are they who would strive to ravish away this our hope! Mistaken, benighted, seduced by their wretched passions, they prefer to deny eternal verities rather than abandon what may render them deserving of them. They would rather say, 'These people deceive us,' than admit they deceive themselves; the lingering thought of what they are preparing themselves to lose troubles them in their low riot and sport; it seems to them less dreadful to annihilate hope of Heaven, than to be deprived of what would acquire it for them! But when those tyrannical passions finally weaken and fade in them, when the veil is torn away, when there is no longer anything left in their disease-eaten hearts to counter the imperious voice of that God their delirium disregardingly misprized, Oh Rosalie! what must it be, this cruel awakening I and how much its accompanying remorse must inflate the price to be paid for the instant's error that blinded them I Such is the condition wherein man has got to be in order to construe his proper conduct: 'tis neither when in drunkenness, nor when in the transport produced by a burning fever, he ought to be believed or his sayings marked, but when his reason is calmed and enjoys its full lucid energy he must seek after the truth, 'tis then he divines and sees it. 'Tis then with all our being we yearn after that Sacred One of Whom we were once so neglectful; we implore Him, He becomes our whole solace; we pray to Him, He hears our entreaties. Ah, why then should I deny Him, why should I be unheeding of this Object so necessary to happiness? Why should I prefer to say with the misguided man, There is no God, while the heart of the reasoning part of human- kind every instant offers me proofs of this Divine Being's existence? Is it then better to dream amongst the mad than rightly to think with the wise? All derives nevertheless from this initial principle: immediately there exists a God, this God deserves to be worshiped, and the primary basis of this worship indisputably is Virtue."

From these elementary truths I easily deduced the others and the deistic Rosalie was soon made a Christian. But by what means, I repeat, could I join a little practice to the morality? Rosalie, bound to obey her father, could at the very most do no more than display her disgust for him, and with a man like Rodin might that not become dangerous? He was intractable; not one of my doctrines prevailed against him; but although I did not win him over, he for his part at least did not shake me.

However, such an academy, dangers so permanent, so real, caused me to tremble for Rosalie, so much so in fact that I could not find myself in any wise guilty in engaging her to fly from this perverse household. It seemed to me that to snatch her from her incestuous father were a lesser evil than to leave her prey to all the risks she must run by staying with him. I had already delicately hinted at the idea and perhaps I was not so very far from success when all of a sudden Rosalie vanished from the house; all my efforts to find out where she was failed. When I interrogated his women or Rodin himself I was told she had gone to pass the summer months with a relative who lived ten leagues away. When I made inquiries around the neighborhood, they were at first astonished to hear such a question from a member of the household, then, as had Rodin and his domestics, they would answer that she had been seen, everyone had bade her farewell the day before, the day she had left; I received the same replies everywhere. I asked Rodin why this departure had been kept secret from me; why had I not been allowed to accompany my mistress? He assured me the unique reason had been to avoid a scene difficult for both Rosalie and me, and that I would certainly see the person I loved very soon. I had to be content with these answers, but it was more difficult to be convinced of their truth. Was it presumable that Rosalie Ä and how great was her affection for me I Ä could have consented to leave me without so much as one word? and according to what I knew of Rodin's character, was there not much to fear for the poor girl's fate? I resolved to employ every device to learn what had become of her, and in order to find out, every means seemed justifiable.

The following day, noticing I was alone in the house, I carefully investigated every corner of it; I thought I caught the sound of moans emanating from a very obscure cellar . . . . I approached; a pile of firewood seemed to be blocking a narrow door at the end of a passageway; by removing the obstructions I am able to advance... further noises are to be heard... I believe I detect a voice... I listen more carefully... I am in doubt no longer.

"Therese," I hear at last, "O Therese, is it you?"

"Yes, my dear, my most tender friend," I cry, recognizing Rosalie's accents . . . . "Yes, 'tis Therese Heaven sends to your rescue . . ."

And my numerous questions scarcely allow this interesting girl time to reply. At length I learn that several hours before her disappearance, Rombeau, Rodin's friend and colleague, had examined her naked and that she had received an order from her father to ready herself to undergo, at Rombeau's hands, the same horrors Rodin exposed her to every day; that she had resisted; that Rodin, furious, had seized her and himself presented her to his companion's frantic attacks; that, next, the two men had spoken together in whispers for a very long time, leaving her naked the while, and periodically renewing their probings, they had continued to amuse themselves with her in the same criminal fashion and had maltreated her in a hundred different ways; that, after this session, which had lasted four or five hours, Rodin had finally said he was going to send her to the country to visit one of her family, but that she must leave at once and without speaking to Therese, for reasons he would explain the day afterward, for he intended to join her immediately. He had given Rosalie to understand he meant to marry her and this accounted for the examination Rombeau had given her, which was to determine whether she were capable of becoming a mother. Rosalie had indeed left under an old woman's guardianship; she had crossed through the town, in passing said farewell to several acquaintances; but immediately night had fallen, her conductress had led her back to her father's house; she had entered at midnight. Rodin, who was waiting for her, had seized her, had clapped his hand over her mouth to stifle her voice and, without a word, had plunged her into this cellar where, in truth, she had been decently well fed and looked after.

"I have everything to fear," the poor thing added; "my father's conduct toward me since he put me here, his discourses, what preceded Rombeau's examination, everything, Therese, everything suggests that these monsters are going to use me in one of their experiments, and that your poor Rosalie is doomed."

After copious tears had flowed from my eyes, I asked the unhappy girl whether she knew where the key to the cellar was kept; she did not; but she did not believe their custom was to take it with them. I sought for it everywhere; in vain; and by the time the hour arrived œor me to return upstairs I had been able to give the dear child no more by way of aid than consoling words, a few hopes, and many tears. She made me swear to come back the next day; I promised, even assuring her that if by that time I had discovered nothing satisfactory regarding her, I would leave the house directly, fetch the police and extricate her, at no matter what price, from the terrible fate threatening her.

18

I went up; Rombeau was dining with Rodin that evening. Determined to stick at nothing to clarify my mistress' fate, I hid myself near the room where the two friends were at table, and their conversation was more than enough to convince me of the horror of the project wherewith both were occupied.

It was Rodin who was speaking: "Anatomy will never reach its ultimate state of perfection until an examination has been performed upon the vaginal canal of a fourteen- or fifteen-year-old child who has expired from a cruel death; it is only from the contingent contraction we can obtain a complete analysis of a so highly interesting part."

"The same holds true," Rombeau replied, "for the hymeneal membrane; we must, of course, find a young girl for the dissection. What the deuce is there to be seen after the age of puberty? nothing; the menstrual discharges rupture the hymen, and all research is necessarily inexact; your daughter is precisely what we need; although she is fifteen! she is not yet mature; the manner in which we have enjoyed her has done no damage to the membranous tissue, and we will be able to handle her with complete immunity from interference. I am delighted you have made up your mind at last."

"Oh, I certainly have," Rodin rejoined; "I find it odious that futile considerations check the progress of science; did great men ever allow themselves to be enslaved by such contemptible chains? And, when Michelangelo wished to render a Christ after Nature, did he make the crucifixion of a young man the occasion for a fit of remorse? Why no: he copied the boy in his death agonies. But where it is a question of the advance of our art, how absolutely essential such means become I And how the evil in permitting them dwindles to insignificance! Only think of it! you sacrifice one, but you save a million, perhaps; may one hesitate when the price is so modest? Is the murder operated by the law of a species different from the one we are going to perform? and is not the purpose of those laws, which are commonly found so wise, the sacrifice of one in order to save a thousand?"

"But what other way can one approach the problem?" Rombeau demanded; "there is certainly no other by which to obtain any information. In those hospitals where I worked as a young man I saw similar experiments by the thousand; but in view of the ties which attach you to this creature, I must confess I was afraid you would hesitate."

"What! because she is my daughter? A capital reason!" Rodin roared, "and what rank do you then fancy this title must allot her in my heart? I place roughly the same value (weighing the matter very nicely) upon a little semen which has hatched its chick, and upon that I am pleased to waste while enjoying myself. One has the power to take back what one has given; amongst no race that has ever dwelled upon earth has there been any disputing the right to dispose of one's children as one sees fit. The Persians, the Medes, the Armenians, the Greeks enjoyed this right in its fullest latitude. The constitution decreed by Lycurgus, that paragon of lawgivers, not only accorded fathers every right over their offspring, but even condemned to death those children parents did not care to feed, or those which were discovered malformed. A great proportion of savage peoples kill their young immediately they are born. Nearly all the women of Asia, Africa, and America practice abortions, and are not for that reason covered with discredit; Cook discovered the custom widespread in all the South Sea islands. Romulus permitted infanticide; the law of the twelve tables similarly tolerated it and until the era of Constantine the Romans exposed or killed their children with impunity. Aristotle recommended this pretended crime; the Stoic sect regarded it as praiseworthy; it is still very much in use in China. Every day one counts, lying in the streets and floating in the canals of Peking, more than ten thousand individuals immolated or abandoned by their parents, and in that wisely-governed empire whatever be the child's age, a father need but put it into the hands of a judge to be rid of it. According to the laws of the Parthians, one killed one's son, one's daughter, or one's brother, even at the age of nubility; Caesar discovered the custom universal amongst the Gauls; several passages in the Pentateuch prove that amongst the children of God one was allowed to kill one's children; and, finally, God Himself ordered Abraham to do just that. It was long believed, declares a celebrated modern author, that the prosperity of empires depends upon the slavery of children; this opinion is supported by the healthiest logic. Why! a monarch will fancy himself authorized to sacrifice twenty or thirty thousand of his subjects in a single day to achieve his own ends, and a father is not to be allowed, when he esteems it propitious, to become the master of his children's lives! What absurdity! O folly! Oh what is this inconsistency, this feebleness in them upon whom such chains are binding! A father's authority over his children, the only real one, the one that serves as basis to every other, that authority is dictated to us by the voice of Nature herself, and the intelligent study of her operations provides examples of it at every turn and instant. Czar Peter was in no doubt as to this right; he used it habitually and addressed a public declaration to all the orders of his empire, in which he said that, according to laws human and divine, a father had the entire and absolute right to sentence his children to death, without appeal and without consulting the opinion of anyone at all. It is nowhere but in our own barbarous France that a false and ludicrous pity has presumed to suppress this prerogative. No," Rodin pursued with great feeling, "no, my friend, I will never understand how a father, who had the kindness to provide it with life, may not be at liberty to bestow death upon his issue. 'Tis the ridiculous value we attach to this life which eternally makes us speak drivel about the kind of deed to which a man resorts in order to disencumber himself of a fellow creature. Believing that existence is the greatest of all goods, we stupidly fancy we are doing something criminal when we convey someone away from its enjoyment; but the cessation of this existence, or at least what follows it, is no more an evil than life is a good; or rather, if nothing dies, if nothing is destroyed, if nothing is lost to

Nature, if all the decomposed parts of any body whatsoever merely await.dissolution to reappear immediately under new forms, how indifferent is this act of murder! and how dare one find any evil in it? In this connection I ought to act according to nothing but my own whim; I ought to regard the thing as very simple indeed, especially so when it becomes necessary to an act of such vital importance to mankind... when it can furnish such a wealth of knowledge: henceforth it is an evil no longer, my friend, it is no longer a crime, no, not a petty misdemeanor, it is the best, the wisest, the most useful of all actions, and crime would exist only in refusing oneself the pleasure of committing it."

"Ha!" said Rombeau, full of enthusiasm for these appalling maxims, "I applaud you, my dear fellow, your wisdom enchants me, but your indifference is astonishing; I thought you were amorous -"

"I? in love with a girl?... Ah, Rombeau! I supposed you knew me better; I employ those creatures when I have nothing better to hand: the extreme penchant I have for pleasures of the variety you have watched me taste makes very precious to me all the temples at which this sort of incense can be offered, and to multiply my devotions, I sometimes assimilate a little girl into a pretty little boy; but should one of these female personages unhappily nourish my illusion for too long, my disgust becomes energetically manifest, and I have never found but one means to satisfy it deliciously... you understand me, Rombeau; Chilperic, the most voluptuous of France's kings, held the same views. His boisterous organ proclaimed aloud that in an emergency one could make use of a woman, but upon the express condition one exterminated her immediately one had done with her.

For five years this little wench has been serving my pleasures; the time has come for her to pay for my loss of interest by the loss of her existence."

The meal ended; from those two madmen's behavior, from their words, their actions, their preparations, from their very state, which bordered upon delirium, I was very well able to see that there was not a moment to be lost, and that the hour of the unhappy Rosalie's destruction had been fixed for that evening. I rushed to the cellar, resolved to deliver her or die.

"O dear friend," I cried, "there is not an instant to waste... the monsters ... it is to be tonight ... they are going to come . . . ."

And upon saying that, I make the most violent efforts to batter down the door. One of my blows dislodges something, I reach out my hand, it is the key, I seize it, I hasten to open the door... I embrace Rosalie, I urge her to fly, I promise to follow her, she springs forward... Just Heaven! It was again decreed that Virtue was to succumb, and that sentiments of the tenderest commiseration were going to be brutally punished; lit by the governess, Rodin and Rombeau appeared of a sudden, the former grasped his daughter the instant she crossed the threshold of the door beyond which, a few steps away, lay deliverance.

"Ah, wretch, where are you going?" Rodin shouts, bringing her to a halt while Rombeau lays hands upon me . . . . "Why," he continues, glancing at me, "here's the rascal who has encouraged your flight! Therese, now we behold the results of your great virtuous principles... the kidnapping of a daughter from her father!"

"Certainly," was my steadfast reply, "and I must do so when that father is so barbarous as to plot against his daughter's life."

"Well, well! Espionage and seduction," Rodin pursued; "all a servant's most dangerous vices; upstairs, up with you, I say, the case requires to be judged."

Dragged by the two villains, Rosalie and I are brought back to the apartments; the doors are bolted. The unlucky daughter of Rodin is tied to the posts of a bed, and those two demoniacs turn all their rage upon me, their language is of the most violent, the sentence pronounced upon me appalling: it is nothing less than a question of a vivisection in order to inspect the beating of my heart, and upon this organ to make observations which cannot practicably be made upon a cadaver. Meanwhile, I am undressed, and subjected to the most impudicious fondlings.

"Before all else," says Rombeau, "my opinion is a stout attack ought to be delivered upon the fortress your lenient proceedings have respected . . . . Why, 'tis superb! do you mark that velvet texture, the whiteness of those two half-moons defending the portal! never was there a virgin of such freshness."

"Virgin! but so she is, or nearly," says Rodin, "once raped, and then it was despite her wishes; since then, untouched. Here, let me take the wheel a moment..." and the cruel one added to Rombeau's his homage made up of those harsh and savage caresses which degrade rather than honor the idol. Had whips been available I should have been cruelly dealt with; whips were indeed mentioned, but none were found, they limited themselves to what the bare hand could achieve; they set me afire... the more I struggled, the more rigidly I was held; when however I saw them about to undertake more serious matters, I flung myself prostrate before my executioners and offered them my life.

"But when you are no longer a virgin," said Rombeau, "what is the difference? What are these qualms? we are only going to violate you as you have been already and not the least peccadillo will sit on your conscience; you will have been vanquished by force..." and comforting me in this manner, the infamous one placed me on a couch.

"No," spoke up Rodin, interrupting his colleague's effervescence, of which I was on the brink of becoming the victim, "no, let's not waste our powers with this creature; remember we cannot further postpone the operations scheduled for Rosalie, and our vigor is necessary to carry them out; let's punish this wretch in some other manner."

Upon saying which, Rodin put an iron in the fire. "Yes," he went on, "let's punish her a thousand times more than we would were we to take her life, let's brand her; this disgrace, joined to all the sorry business about her body, will get her hanged if she does not first die of hunger; until then she will suffer, and our more prolonged vengeance will become the more delicious."

Wherewith Rombeau seized me, and the abominable Rodin applied behind my shoulder the red-hot iron with which thieves are marked.

"Let her dare appear in public, the whore," the monster continued, exhibiting the ignominious letter, "and I'll sufficiently justify my reasons for sending her out of the door with such secrecy and promptitude."

They bandage me, dress me, and fortify me with a few drops of brandy, and under the cover of night the two scientists conduct me to the forest's edge and abandon me cruelly there after once again having sketched what dangers a recrimination would expose me to were I to dare bring complaint in my present state of disgrace.

Anyone else might have been little impressed by the menace; what would I have to fear as soon as I found the means to prove that what I had just suffered had been the work not of a tribunal but of criminals? But my weakness, my natural timidity, the frightful memory of what I had undergone at Paris and recollections of the chateau de Bressac Ä it all stunned me, terrified me; I thought only of flight, and was far more stirred by anguish at having to abandon an innocent victim to those two villains, who were without doubt ready to immolate her, than I was touched by my own ills. More irritated, more afflicted morally than in physical pain, I set off at once; but, completely unoriented, never stopping to ask my way, I did but swing in a circle around Paris and on the fourth day of traveling I found I had got no further than Lieursaint. Knowing this road would lead me to the southern provinces, I resolved to follow it and try to reach those distant regions, fancying to myself that the peace and calm so cruelly denied me in those parts of France where I had grown up were, perhaps, awaiting me in others more remote; fatal error! how much there remained of grief and pain yet to experience.

19

Whatever had been my trials until that time, at least I was in possession of my innocence. Merely the victim of a few monsters' attempts, I was still able to consider myself more or less in the category of an honest girl. The fact was I had never been truly soiled save by a rape operated five years earlier, and its traces had healed... a rape consummated at an instant when my numbed state had not even left me the faculty of sensation. Other than that, what was there with which I could reproach myself? Nothing, oh! nothing, doubtless; and my heart was chaste, I was overweeningly proud of it, my presumption was to be punished; the outrages awaiting me were to be such that in a short while it would no longer be possible, however slight had been my participation, for me to form the same comforting ideas in the depths of my heart.

This time I had my entire fortune about me; that is to say, about a hundred crowns, comprising the total of what I had saved from Bressac's clutches and earned from Rodin. In my extreme misery I was able to feel glad that this money, at least, had not been taken from me; I flattered myself with the notion that through the frugality, temperance, and economy to which I was accustomed, this sum would amply suffice until I was so situated as to be able to find a place of some sort. The execration they had just stamped upon my flesh did not show, I imagined I would always be able to disguise it and that this brand would be no bar to making my living. I was twenty-two years old, in good health, and had a face which, to my sorrow, was the object of eulogies all too frequent; I possessed some virtues which, although they had brought me unremitting injury, nevertheless, as I have just told you, were my whole consolation and caused me to hope that Heaven would finally grant me, if not rewards, at least some suspension of the evils they had drawn down upon me. Full of hope and courage, I kept my road until I gained Sens, where I rested several days. A week of this and I was entirely restored; I might perhaps have found work in that city but, penetrated by the necessity of getting further away, I resumed my journeying with the design of seeking my fortune in Dauphine; I had heard this province much spoken of, I fancied happiness attended me there, and we are going to see with what success I sought it out.

Never, not in a single one of my life's circumstances, had the sentiments of Religion deserted me. Despising the vain casuistries of strong-headed thinkers, believing them all to emanate from libertinage rather than consequent upon firm persuasion, I had dressed my conscience and my heart against them and, by means of the one and the other, I had found what was needed in order to make them stout reply. By my misfortunes often forced to neglect my pious duties, I would make reparation for these faults whenever I could find the opportunity.

I had just, on the 7th of August, left Auxerre; I shall never forget that date. I had walked about two leagues: the noonday heat beginning to incommode me, I climbed a little eminence crowned by a grove of trees; the place was not far removed from the road, I went there with the purpose of refreshing myself and obtaining a few hours of sleep without having to pay the expense of an inn, and up there I was in greater safety than upon the highway. I established myself at the foot of an oak and, after a frugal lunch, I drifted off into sweet sleep. Well did I rest, for a considerable time, and in a state of complete tranquillity; and then, opening my eyes, it was with great pleasure I mused upon the landscape which was visible for a long distance. From out of the middle of a forest that extended upon the right, I thought I could detect, some three or four leagues from where I was, a little bell tower rising modestly into the air . . . . "Beloved solitude," I murmured, "what a desire I have to dwell a time in thee; and thou afar," said I, addressing the abbey, "thou must be the asylum of a few gentle, virtuous recluses who are occupied with none but God... with naught but their pious duties; or a retreat unto some holy hermits devoted to Religion alone... men who, far removed from that pernicious society where incessant crime, brooding heavily, threatfully over innocence, degrades it, annihilates it... ah! there must all virtues dwell, of that I am certain, and when mankind's crimes exile them out of the world, 'tis thither they go in that isolated place to commune with the souls of those fortunate ones who cherish them and cultivate them every day."

I was absorbed in these thoughts when a girl of my age, keeper of a flock of sheep grazing upon the plateau, suddenly appeared before my eyes; I question her about that habitation, she tells me what I see is a Benedictine monastery occupied by four solitary monks of peerless devotion, whose continence and sobriety are without example. Once a year, says the girl, a pilgrimage is made to a miraculous Virgin who is there, and from Her pious folk obtain all their hearts' desire. Singularly eager immediately to go and implore aid at the feet of this holy Mother of God, I ask the girl whether she would like to come and pray with me; 'tis impossible, she replies, for her mother awaits her; but the road there is easy. She indicates it to me, she assures me the superior of the house, the most respectable, the most saintly of men, will receive me with perfect good grace and will offer me all the aid whereof I can possibly stand in need. "Dom Severino, so he is called," continues the girl, "is an Italian closely related to the Pope, who overwhelms him with kindnesses; he is gentle, honest, correct, obliging, fifty-five years old, and has spent above two-thirds of his life in France... you will be satisfied with him, Mademoiselle," the shepherdess concluded, "go and edify yourself in that sacred quiet, and you will only return from it improved."

This recital only inflamed my zeal the more, I became unable to resist the violent desire I felt to pay a visit to this hallowed church and there, by a few acts of piety, to make restitution for the neglect whereof I was guilty. However great was my own need of charities, I gave the girl a crown, and set off down the road leading to Saint Mary-in-the-Wood, as was called the monastery toward which I directed my steps.

When I had descended upon the plain I could see the spire no more; for guide I had nothing but the forest ahead of me, and before long I began to fear that the distance, of which I had forgotten to inform myself, was far greater than I had estimated at first; but was in nowise discouraged. I arrived at the edge of the forest and, some amount of daylight still remaining, I decided to forge on, considering I should be able to reach the monastery before nightfall. However, not a hint of human life presented itself to my gaze, not a house, and all I had for road was a beaten path I followed virtually at random; I had already walked at least five leagues without seeing a thing when, the Star having completely ceased to light the universe, it seemed I heard the tolling of a bell... I harken, I move toward the sound, I hasten, the path widens ever so little, at last I perceive several hedges and soon afterward the monastery; than this isolation nothing could be wilder, more rustic, there is no neighboring habitation, the nearest is six leagues removed, and dense tracts of forest surround the house on all sides; it was situated in a depression, I had a goodly distance to descend in order to get to it, and this was the reason I had lost sight of the tower; a gardener's cabin nestled against the monastery's walls; it was there one applied before entering. I demanded of this gate-keeper whether it were permitted to speak to the superior; he asked to be informed of my errand; I advised him that a religious duty had drawn me to this holy refuge and that I would be well repaid for all the trouble I had experienced to get to it were I able to kneel an instant before the feet of the miraculous Virgin and the saintly ecclesiastics in whose house the divine image was preserved. The gardener rings and I penetrate into the monastery; but as the hour is advanced and the fathers are at supper, he is some time in returning. At last he reappears with one of the monks:

"Mademoiselle," says he, "here is Dom Clement, steward to the house; he has come to see whether what you desire merits interrupting the superior."

Clement, whose name could not conceivably have been less descriptive of his physiognomy, was a man of forty-eight years, of an enormous bulk, of a giant's stature; somber was his expression, fierce his eye; the only words he spoke were harsh, and they were expelled by a raucous voice: here was a satyric personage indeed, a tyrant's exterior; he made me tremble . . . . And then despite all I could do to suppress it, the remembrance of my old miseries rose to smite my troubled memory in traits of blood . . . .

"What do you want?" the monk asked me; his air was surly, his mien grim; "is this the hour to come to a church?... Indeed, you have the air of an adventuress."

"Saintly man," said I, prostrating myself, "I believed it was always the hour to present oneself at God's door; I have hastened from far off to arrive here; full of fervor and devotion, I ask to confess, if it is possible, and when what my conscience contains is known to you, you will see whether or not I am worthy to humble myself at the feet of the holy image."

"But this is not the time for confession," said the monk, his manner softening; "where are you going to spend the night? We have no hospice... it would have been better to have come in the morning." I gave him the reasons which had prevented me from doing so and, without replying, Clement went to report to the superior. Several minutes later the church was opened, Don Severino himself approached me, and invited me to enter the temple with him.

Dom Severino, of whom it would be best to give you an idea at once, was, as I had been told, a man of fifty-five, but endowed with handsome features, a still youthful quality, a vigorous physique, herculean limbs, and all that without harshness; a certain elegance and pliancy reigned over the whole and suggested that in his young years he must have possessed all the traits which constitute a splendid man. There were in all the world no finer eyes than his; nobility shone in his features, and the most genteel, the most courteous tone was there throughout. An agreeable accent which colored every one of his words enabled one to identify his Italian origin and, I admit it, this monk's outward graces did much to dispel the alarm the other had caused me.

"My dear girl," said he very graciously, "although the hour is unseasonable and though it is not our usage to receive so late, I will however hear your confession, and afterward we will confer upon the means whereby you may pass the night in decency; tomorrow you will be able to bow down before the sacred image which brings you here."

We enter the church; the doors are closed; a lamp is lit near the confessional. Severino bids me assume my place, he sits down and requests me to tell him everything with complete confidence.

I was perfectly at ease with a man who seemed so mild-mannered, so full of gentle sympathy. I disguised nothing from him: I confessed all my sins; I related all my miseries; I even uncovered the shameful mark wherewith the barbaric Rodin had branded me. Severino listened to everything with keenest attention, he even had me repeat several details, wearing always a look of pity and of interest; but a few movements, a few words betrayed him nevertheless Ä alas! it was only afterward I pondered them thoroughly. Later, when able to reflect calmly upon this interview, it was impossible not to remember that the monk had several times permitted himself certain gestures which dramatized the emotion that had heavy entrance into many of the questions he put to me, and those inquiries not only halted complacently and lingered lovingly over obscene details, but had borne with noticeable insistence upon the following five points: 1. Whether it were really so that I were an orphan and had been born in Paris. 2. Whether it were a certainty I were bereft of kin and had neither friends, nor protection, nor, in a word, anyone to whom I could write. 3. Whether I had confided to anyone, other than to the shepherdess who had pointed out the monastery to me, my purpose in going there, and whether I had not arranged some rendezvous upon my return. 4. Whether it were certain that I had known no one since my rape, and whether I were fully sure the man who had abused me had done so on the side Nature condemns as well as on the side she permits. 5. Whether I thought I had not been followed and whether anyone, according to my belief, might have observed me enter the monastery.

After I had answered these questions in all modesty, with great sincerity, and most naively: "Very well," said the monk, rising and taking me by the hand, "come, my child, tomorrow I shall procure you the sweet satisfaction of communing at the feet of the image you have come to visit; let us begin by supplying your primary needs," and he led me toward the depths of the church . . . .

"Why!" said I, sensing a vague inquietude arise in me despite myself, "what is this, Father? Why are we going inside?"

"And where else, my charming pilgrim?" answered the monk, introducing me into the sacristy. "Do you really fear to spend the night with four saintly anchorites? Oh, we shall find the means to succor you, my dearest angel, and if we do not procure you very great pleasures, you will at least serve ours in their most extreme amplitude." These words sent a thrill of horror through me; I burst out in a cold sweat, I fell to shivering; it was night, no light guided our footsteps, my terrified imagination raised up the specter of death brandishing its scythe over my head; my knees were buckling... and at this point a sudden shift occurred in the monk's speech. He jerked me upright and hissed:

"Whore, pick up your feet and get along; no complaints, don't try resistance, not here, it would be useless."

These cruel words restore my strength, I sense that if I falter I am doomed, I straighten myself. "O Heaven!" I say to the traitor, "must I then be once again my good sentiments' victim, must the desire to approach what is most respectable in Religion be once again punished as a crime..."

We continue to walk, we enter obscure byways, I know not where I am, where I am going. I was advancing a pace ahead of Dom Severino; his breathing was labored, words flowed incoherently from his lips, one might have thought he was drunk; now and again he stopped me, twined his left arm about my waist while his right hand, sliding beneath my skirts from the rear, wandered impudently over that unseemly part of ourselves which, likening us to men, is the unique object of the homages of those who prefer that sex for their shameful pleasures. Several times the libertine even dared apply his mouth to these areas' most secluded lair; and then we recommenced our march. A stairway appears before us; we climb thirty steps or forty, a door opens, brightness dazzles my eyes, we emerge into a charmingly appointed, magnificently illuminated room; there, I see three monks and four girls grouped around a table served by four other women, completely naked. At the spectacle I recoil, trembling; Severino shoves me forward over the threshold and I am in the room with him.

"Gentlemen," says he as we enter, "allow me to present you with one of the veritable wonders of the world, a Lucretia who simultaneously carries upon her shoulder the mark stigmatizing girls who are of evil repute, and, in her conscience, all the candor, all the naivete of a virgin . . . . One lone violation, friends, and that six years ago; hence, practically a vestal... indeed, I do give her to you as such... the most beautiful, moreover... Oh Clement! how that cheerless countenance of yours will light up when you fall to work on those handsome masses... what elasticity, my good fellow! what rosiness!"

"Ah, fuck!" cried the half-intoxicated Clement, getting to his feet and lurching toward me: "we are pleasantly met, and let us verify the facts."

I will leave you for the briefest possible time in suspense about my situation, Madame, said Therese, but the necessity to portray these other persons in whose midst I discovered myself obliges me to interrupt the thread of my story. You have been made acquainted with Dom Severino, you suspect what may be his predilections; alas, in these affairs his depravation was such he had never tasted other pleasures Ä and what an inconsistency in Nature's operations was here! for with the bizarre fantasy of choosing none but the straiter path, this monster was outfitted with faculties so gigantic that even the broadest thoroughfares would still have appeared too narrow for him.

20

As for Clement, he has been drawn for you already. To the superficies I have delineated, join ferocity, a disposition to sarcasm, the most dangerous roguishness, intemperance in every point, a mordant, satirical mind, a corrupt heart, the cruel tastes Rodin displayed with his young charges, no feelings, no delicacy, no religion, the temperament of one who for five years had not been in a state to procure himself other joys than those for which savagery gave him an appetite Ä and you have there the most complete characterization of this horrid man.

Antonin, the third protagonist in these detestable orgies, was forty; small, slight of frame but very vigorous, as formidably organized as Severino and almost as wicked as Clement; an enthusiast of that colleague's pleasures, but giving himself over to them with a somewhat less malignant intention; for while Clement, when exercising this curious mania, had no objective but to vex, to tyrannize a woman, and could not enjoy her in any other way, Antonin using it with delight in all its natural purity, had recourse to the flagellative aspect only in order to give additional fire and further energy to her whom he was honoring with his favors. In a word, one was brutal by taste, the other by refinement.

Jerome, the eldest of the four recluses, was also the most debauched; every taste, every passion, every one of the most bestial irregularities were combined in this monk's soul; to the caprices rampant in the others, he joined that of loving to receive what his comrades distributed amongst the girls, and if he gave (which frequently happened), it was always upon condition of being treated likewise in his turn: all the temples of Venus were, what was more, as one to him, but his powers were beginning to decline and for several years he had preferred that which, requiring no effort of the agent, left to the patient the task of arousing the sensations and of producing the ecstasy. The mouth was his favorite temple, the shrine where he liked best to offer, and while he was in the pursuit of those choice pleasures, he would keep a second woman active: she warmed him with the lash. This man's character was quite as cunning, quite as wicked as that of the others; in whatever shape or aspect vice could exhibit itself, certain it was immediately to find a spectator in this infernal household. You will understand it more easily, Madame, if I explain how the society was organized. Prodigious funds had been poured by the Order into this obscene institution, it had been in existence for above a century, and had always been inhabited by the four richest monks, the most powerful in the Order's hierarchy, they of the highest birth and of a libertinage of sufficient moment to require burial in this obscure retreat, the disclosure of whose secret was well provided against as my further explanations will cause you to see in the sequel; but let us return to the portraits.

The eight girls who were present at the supper were so much separated by age I cannot describe them collectively, but only one by one; that they were so unlike with respect to their years astonished me I will speak first of the youngest and continue in order.

This youngest one of the girls was scarcely ten: pretty but irregular features, a look of humiliation because of her fate, an air of sorrow and trepidation.

The second was fifteen: the same trouble written over her countenance, a quality of modesty degraded, but a bewitching face, of considerable interest all in all.

The third was twenty: pretty as a picture, the loveliest blond hair; fine, regular, gentle features; she appeared less restive, more broken to the saddle.

The fourth was thirty: she was one of the most beautiful women imaginable; candor, quality, decency in her bearing, and all a gentle spirit's virtues.

The fifth was a girl of thirty-six, six months pregnant; dark-haired, very lively, with beautiful eyes, but having, so it seemed to me, lost all remorse, all decency, all restraint.

The sixth was of the same age: a tall creature of grandiose proportions, a true giantess, fair of face but whose figure was already ruined in excess flesh; when I first saw her she was naked, and I was readily able to notice that not one part of her body was unstamped by signs of the brutality of those villains whose pleasures her unlucky star had fated her to serve.

The seventh and eighth were two very lovely women of about forty.

Let us continue with the story of my arrival in this impure place.

I did tell you that no sooner had I entered than each one approached me: Clement was the most brazen, his foul lips were soon glued to my mouth; I twisted away in horror, but I was advised all resistance was pure affectation, pretense, and useless; I should do best by imitating my companions.

"You may without difficulty imagine," declared Dom Severino, "that a recalcitrant attitude will be to no purpose in this inaccessible retreat. You have, you say, undergone much suffering; but that greatest of all woes a virtuous girl can know is yet missing from the catalogue of your troubles. Is it not high time that lofty pride be humbled? and may one still expect to be nearly a virgin at twenty-two? You see about you companions who, upon entering here, like yourself thought to resist and who, as prudence will bid you to do, ended by submitting when they noticed that stubbornness could lead them to incur penalties; for I might just as well declare to you, Therese," the superior continued, showing me scourges, ferules, withes, cords, and a thousand other instruments of torture, "yes, you might just as well know it: there you see what we use upon unmanageable girls; decide whether you wish to be convinced. What do you expect to find here? Mercy? we know it not; humaneness? our sole pleasure is the violation of its laws. Religion? 'tis as naught to us, our contempt for it grows the better acquainted with it we become; allies... kin... friends... judges? there's none of that in this place, dear girl, you will discover nothing but cruelty, egoism, and the most sustained debauchery and impiety. The completest submissiveness is your lot, and that is all; cast a glance about the impenetrable asylum which shelters you: never has an outsider invaded these premises: the monastery could be taken, searched, sacked, and burned, and this retreat would still be perfectly safe from discovery: we are in an isolated outbuilding, as good as buried within the six walls of incredible thickness surrounding us entirely, and here you are, my child, in the midst of four libertines who surely have no inclination to spare you and whom your entreaties, your tears, your speeches, your genuflections, and your outcries will only further inflame. To whom then will you have recourse? to what? Will it be to that God you have just implored with such earnestness and who, by way of reward for your fervor, only precipitates you into further snares, each more fatal than the last? to that illusory God we ourselves outrage all day long by insulting his vain commandments?... And so, Therese, you conceive that there is no power, of whatever species you may suppose, which could possibly deliver you out of our hands, and there is neither in the category of things real nor in that of miracles, any sort of means which might permit you successfully to retain this virtue you yet glory in; which might, in fine, prevent you from becoming, in every sense and in every manner, the prey of the libidinous excesses to which we, all four of us, are going to abandon ourselves with you... Therefore, little slut, off with your clothes, offer your body to our lusts, let it be soiled by them instantly or the severest treatment will prove to you what risks a wretch like yourself runs by disobeying us."

This harangue... this terrible order, I felt, left me no shifts, but would I not have been guilty had I failed to employ the means my heart prompted in me? my situation left me this last resource: I fall at Dom Severino's feet, I employ all a despairing soul's eloquence to supplicate him not to take advantage of my state or abuse it; the bitterest tears spring from my eyes and inundate his knees, all I Imagine to be of the strongest, all I believe the most pathetic, I try everything with this man . . . . Great God! what was the use? could I have not known that tears merely enhance the object of a libertine's coveting? how was I able to doubt that everything I attempted in my efforts to sway those savages had the unique effect of arousing them . . . . "Take the bitch," said Severino in a rage, "seize her, Clement, let her be naked in a minute, and let her learn that it is not in persons like ourselves that compassion stifles Nature." My resistance had animated Clement, he was foaming at the mouth: he took hold of me, his arm shook nervously; interspersing his actions with appalling blasphemies, he had my clothing torn away in a trice.

"A lovely creature," came from the superior, who ran his fingers over my flanks, "may God blast me if I've ever seen one better made; friends," the monk pursued, "let's put order into our procedures; you know our formula for welcoming newcomers: she might be exposed to the entire ceremony, don't you think? Let's omit nothing; and let's have the eight other women stand around us to supply our wants and to excite them."

A circle is formed immediately, I am placed in its center and there, for more than two hours, I am inspected, considered, handled by those four monks, who, one after the other, pronounce either encomiums or criticisms.

You will permit me, Madame, our lovely prisoner said with a blush, to conceal a part of the obscene details of this odious ritual; allow your imagination to figure all that debauch can dictate to villains in such instances; allow it to see them move to and fro between my companions and me, comparing, confronting, contrasting, airing opinions, and indeed it still will not have but a faint idea of what was done in those initial orgies, very mild, to be sure, when matched against all the horrors I was soon to experience.

"Let's to it," says Severino, whose prodigiously exalted desires will brook no further restraint and who in this dreadful state gives the impression of a tiger about to devour its prey, "let each of us advance to take his favorite pleasure." And placing me upon a couch in the posture expected by his execrable projects and causing me to be held by two of his monks, the infamous man attempts to satisfy himself in that criminal and perverse fashion which makes us to resemble none but the sex we do not possess while degrading the one we have; but either the shameless creature is too strongly proportioned, or Nature revolts in me at the mere suspicion of these pleasures; Severino cannot overcome the obstacles; he presents himself, and he is repulsed immediately . . . . He spreads, he presses, thrusts, tears, all his efforts are in vain; in his fury the monster lashes out against the altar at which he cannot speak his prayers; he strikes it, he pinches it, he bites it; these brutalities are succeeded by renewed challenges; the chastened flesh yields, the gate cedes, the ram bursts through; terrible screams rise from my throat; the entire mass is swiftly engulfed, and darting its venom the next moment, robbed then of its strength, the snake gives ground before the movements I make to expel it, and Severino weeps with rage. Never in my life have I suffered so much.

Clement steps forward; he is armed with a cat-o'-nine-tails; his perfidious designs glitter in his eyes.

"'Tis I," says he to Severino, "'tis I who shall avenge you, Father, I shall correct this silly drab for having resisted your pleasures." He has no need of anyone else to hold me; with one arm he enlaces me and forces me, belly down, across his knees; what is going to serve his caprices is nicely discovered. At first, he tries a few blows, it seems they are merely intended as a prelude; soon inflamed by lust, the beast strikes with all his force; nothing is exempt from his ferocity; everything from the small of my back to the lower part of my thighs, the traitor lays cuts upon it all; daring to mix love with these moments of cruelty, he fastens his mouth to mine and wishes to inhale the sighs agony wrests from me... my tears flow, he laps them up, now he kisses, now he threatens, but the rain of blows continues; while he operates, one of the women excites him; kneeling before him, she works with each hand at diverse tasks; the greater her success, the more violent the strokes delivered me; I am nigh to being rent and nothing yet announces the end of my sufferings; he has exhausted every possibility, still he drives on; the end I await is to be the work of his delirium alone; a new cruelty stiffens him: my breasts are at the brute's mercy, he irritates them, uses his teeth upon them, the cannibal snaps, bites, this excess determines the Crisis, the incense escapes him. Frightful cries, terrifying blasphemies, shouts characterize its spurtings, and the monk, enervated, turns me over to Jerome.

"I will be no more of a threat to your virtue than Clement was," said this libertine as he caressed the blood-spattered altar at which Clement had just sacrificed, "but I should indeed like to kiss the furrows where the plow passed; I too am worthy to open them, and should like to pay them my modest respects; but I should like even more," went on the old satyr, inserting a finger where Severino had lodged himself, "I should like to have the hen lay, and 'twould be most agreeable to devour its egg... does one exist? Why, yes indeed, by God!... Oh, my dear, dear little girl! how very soft..."

His mouth takes the place of his finger... I am told what I have to do, full of disgust I do it. In my situation, alas, am I permitted to refuse? The infamous one is delighted... he swallows, then, forcing me to kneel before him, he glues himself to me in this position; his ignominious passion is appeased in a fashion that cannot justify any complaint on my part. While he acts thus, the fat woman flogs him, another puts herself directly above his mouth and acquits herself of the same task I have just been obliged to execute.

"'Tis not enough," says the monster, "each one of my hands has got to contain... for one cannot get one's fill of these goodies." The two prettiest girls approach; they obey: there you have the excesses to which satiety has led Jerome. At any rate, thanks to impurities he is happy, and at the end of half an hour, my mouth finally receives, with a loathing you must readily appreciate, this evil man's disgusting homage.

Antonin appears. "Well," says he, "let's have a look at this so very spotless virtue; I wonder whether, damaged by a single assault, it is really what the girl maintains." His weapon is raised and trained upon me; he would willingly employ Clement's devices: I have told you that active flagellation pleases him quite as much as it does the other monk but, as he is in a hurry, the state in which his colleague has put me suffices him: he examines this state, relishes it, and leaving me in that attitude of which they are all so fond, he spends an instant pawing the two hemispheres poised at the entrance; in a fury, he rattles the temple's porticos, he is soon at the sanctuary; although quite as violent as Severino's, Antonin's assault, launched against a less narrow passage, is not as painful to endure; the energetic athlete seizes my haunches and, supplying the movements I am unable to make, he shakes me, pulls me to him vivaciously; one might judge by this Hercules' redoubling efforts that, not content to be master of the place, he wishes to reduce it to a shambles. Such terrible attacks, so new to me, cause me to succumb; but unconcerned for my pain, the cruel victor thinks of nothing but increasing his pleasure; everything embraces, everything conspires to his voluptuousness; facing him, raised upon my flanks, the fifteen year-old girl, her legs spread open, offers his mouth the altar at which he sacrifices in me: leisurely, he pumps that precious natural juice whose emission Nature has only lately granted the young child; on her knees, one of the older women bends toward my vanquisher's loins, busies herself about them and with her impure tongue animating his desires, she procures them their ecstasy while, to inflame himself yet further, the debauchee excites a woman with either hand; there is not one of his senses which is not tickled, not one which does not concur in the perfection of his delirium; he attains it, but my unwavering horror for all these infamies inhibits me from sharing it . . . . He arrives there alone; his jets, his cries, everything proclaims it and, despite myself, I am flooded with the proofs of a fire I am but one of six to light; and thereupon I fall back upon the throne which has just been the scene of my immolation, no longer conscious of my existence save through my pain and my tears... my despair and my remorse.

21

However, Dom Severino orders the women to bring me food; but far from being quickened by these attentions, an access of furious grief assails my soul. I, who located all my glory, all my felicity in my virtue, I who thought that, provided I remained well-behaved at all times, I could be consoled for all fortune's ills, I cannot bear the horrible idea of seeing myself so cruelly sullied by those from whom I should have been able to expect the greatest comfort and aid: my tears flowed in abundance, my cries made the vault ring; I rolled upon the floor, I lacerated my breast, tore my hair, invoked my butchers, begged them to bestow death upon me... and, Madame, would you believe it? this terrible sight excited them all the more.

"Ah!" said Severino, "I've never enjoyed a finer spectacle: behold, good friends, see the state it puts me in; it is really unbelievable, what feminine anguish obtains from me."

"Let's go back to work," quoth Clement, "and in order to teach her to bellow at fate, let the bitch be more sharply handled in this second assault."

The project is no sooner conceived than put into execution; up steps Severino, but his speeches notwithstanding, his desires require a further degree of irritation and it is only after having used Clement's cruel measures that he succeeds in marshaling the forces necessary to accomplish his newest crime. Great God! What excess of ferocity! Could it be that those monsters would carry it to the point of selecting the instant of a crisis of moral agony as violent as that I was undergoing, in order to submit me to so barbarous a physical one! "'Twould be an injustice to this novice," said Clement, "were we not to employ in its major form what served us so well in its merely episodic dimension," and thereupon he began to act, adding: "My word upon it, I will treat her no better than did you." "One instant." said Antonin to the superior whom he saw about to lay hands upon me again; "while your zeal is exhaled into this pretty maiden's posterior parts, I might, it seems to me, make an offering to the contrary God; we will have her between us two."

The position was so arranged I could still provide Jerome with a mouth; Clement fitted himself between my hands, I was constrained to arouse him; all the priestesses surrounded this frightful group; each lent an actor what she knew was apt to stir him most profoundly; however, it was I supported them all, the entire weight bore down upon me alone; Severino gives the signal, the other three follow close after him and there I am a second time infamously defiled by the proofs of those blackguards' disgusting luxury.

"Well," cries the superior, "that should be adequate for the first day; we must now have her remark that her comrades are no better treated than she." I am placed upon an elevated armchair and from there I am compelled to witness those other horrors which are to terminate the orgies.

The monks stand in queue; all the sisters file before them and receive whiplashes from each; next, they are obliged to excite their torturers with their mouths while the latter torment and shower invectives upon them.

The youngest, she of ten, is placed upon a divan and each monk steps forward to expose her to the torture of his choice; near her is the girl of fifteen; it is with her each monk, after having meted out punishment, takes his pleasure; she is the butt; the eldest woman is obliged to stay in close attendance upon the monk presently performing, in order to be of service to him either in this operation or in the act which concludes it. Severino uses only his hands to molest what is offered him and speeds to engulf himself in the sanctuary of his whole delight and which she whom they have posted nearby presents to him; armed with a handful of nettles, the eldest woman retaliates upon him for what he has a moment ago done to the child; 'tis in the depths of painful titillations the libertine's transports are born . . . . Consult him; will he confess to cruelty? But he has done nothing he does not endure in his turn.

Clement lightly pinches the little girl's flesh; the enjoyment offered within is beyond his capabilities, but he is treated as he has dealt with the girl, and at the feet of the idol he leaves the incense he lacks the strength to fling into its sanctuary.

Antonin entertains himself by kneading the fleshier parts of the victim's body; fired by her convulsive struggling, he precipitates himself into the district offered to his chosen pleasures. In his turn he is mauled, beaten, and ecstasy is the fruit of his torments.

Old Jerome employs his teeth only, but each bite leaves a wound whence blood leaps instantly forth; after receiving a dozen, the target tenders him her open mouth; therein his fury is appeased while he is himself bitten quite as severely as he did bite.

The saintly fathers drink and recover their strength.

The thirty-six-year-old woman, six months pregnant, as I have told you, is perched upon a pedestal eight feet high; unable to pose but one leg, she is obliged to keep the other in the air; round about her, on the floor, are mattresses garnished three feet deep with thorns, splines, holly; a flexible rod is given to her that she may keep herself erect; it is easy to see, on the one hand, that it is to her interest not to tumble, and on the other, that she cannot possibly retain her balance; the alternatives divert the monks; all four of them cluster around her, during the spectacle each has one or two women to excite him in divers manners; great with child as she is, the luckless creature remains in this attitude for nearly a quarter of an hour; at last, strength deserts her, she falls upon the thorns, and our villains, wild with lust, one last time step forward to lavish upon her body their ferocity's abominable homage... the company retires.

The superior put me into the keeping of the thirty-year-old girl of whom I made mention; her name was Omphale; she was charged to instruct me, to settle me in my new domicile. But that night I neither saw nor heard anything. Annihilated, desperate, I thought of nothing but to capture a little rest. In the room where I had been installed I noticed other women who had not been at the supper; I postponed consideration of these new objects until the following day, and occupied myself with naught else but repose. Omphale left me to myself; she went to put herself to bed; scarcely had I stepped into mine when the full horror of my circumstances presented itself to me in yet more lively colors: I could not dispel the thought of the execrations I had suffered, nor of those to which I had been a witness. Alas! if at certain times those pleasures had occurred to my wandering imagination, I had thought them chaste, as is the God Who inspires them, given by Nature in order to comfort human beings; I had fancied them the product of love and delicacy. I had been very far from believing that man, after the example of savage beasts, could only relish them by causing his companion to shudder... then, returning to my own black fate... "O Just Heaven," I said to myself, "it is then absolutely certain that no virtuous act will emanate from my heart without being answered at once by an agonizing echo! And of what evil was I guilty, Great God! in desiring to come to accomplish some religious duties in this monastery? Do I offend Heaven by wanting to pray? Incomprehensible decrees of Providence, deign," I continued, "deign to open wide my eyes, cause me to see if you do not wish me to rebel against you!" Bitterest tears followed these musings, and I was still inundated with them when daylight appeared; then Omphale approached my bed.

"Dear companion," she said, "I come to exhort you to be courageous; I too wept during my first days, but now the thing has become a habit; as have I, you will become accustomed to it all; the beginnings are terrible: it is not simply the necessity to sate these debauchees' hungers which is our life's torture, it is the loss of our freedom, it is the cruel manner in which we are handled in this terrible house."

The wretched take comfort in seeing other sufferers about them. However trenchant were my anguishes, they were assuaged for an instant; I begged my companion to inform me of the ills I had to expect.

"In a moment," my instructress said, "but first get up and let me show you about our retreat, observe your new companions; then we'll hold our conversation."

Following Omphale's suggestion, I began by examining the chamber we were in. It was an exceedingly large chamber, containing eight little beds covered with clean calico spreads; by each bed was a partitioned dressing room; but all the windows which lit both these closets and the room itself were raised five feet above the floor and barred inside and out. In the middle of the room was a large table, secured to the floor, and it was intended for eating or work; three doors bound and braced with iron closed the room; on our side no fittings or keyholes were to be seen; on the other, enormous bolts.

"And this is our prison?"

"Alas! yes, my dear," Omphale replied; "such is our unique dwelling place; not far from here, the eight other girls have a similar room, and we never communicate with each other save when the monks are pleased to assemble us all at one time."

I peered into the alcove destined for me; it was eight feet square, daylight entered it, as in the great room, by a very high window fitted all over with iron. The only furniture was a bidet, a lavatory basin and a chaise perce'e. I re-emerged; my companions, eager to see me, gathered round in a circle: they were seven, I made the eighth. Omphale, inhabiting the other room, was only in this to indoctrinate me; were I to wish it, she would remain with me, and one of the others would take her place in her own chamber; I asked to have the arrangement made. But before coming to Omphale's story, it seems to me essential to describe the seven new companions fate had given me; I will proceed according to age, as I did with the others.

The youngest was twelve years old: a very animated, very spirited physiognomy, the loveliest hair, the prettiest mouth.

The second was sixteen: she was one of the most beautiful blondes imaginable, with truly delicious features and all the grace, all the sweetness of her age, mingled with a certain interesting quality, the product of her sadness, which rendered her yet a thousand times more beautiful.

The third was twenty-three; very pretty, but an excessive effrontery, too much impudence degraded, so I thought, the charms Nature had endowed her with.

The fourth was twenty-six: she had the figure of Venus; but perhaps her forms were rather too pronounced; a dazzling fair skin; a sweet, open, laughing countenance, beautiful eyes, a mouth a trifle large but admirably furnished, and superb blond hair.

The fifth was thirty-two; she was four months pregnant; with an oval, somewhat melancholic face, large soulful eyes; she was very pale, her health was delicate, she had a harmonious voice but the rest seemed somehow spoiled. She was naturally libertine: she was, I was told, exhausting herself.

The sixth was thirty-three; a tall strapping woman, the loveliest face in the world, the loveliest flesh.

The seventh was thirty-eight; a true model of figure and beauty: she was the superintendent of my room; Omphale forewarned me of her malicious temper and, principally, of her taste for women.

"To yield is the best way of pleasing her," my companion told me; "resist her, and you will bring down upon your head every misfortune that can befall you in this house. Bear it in mind."

Omphale asked permission of Ursule, which was the superintendent's name, to instruct me; Ursule consented upon condition I kiss her. I approached: her impure tongue sought to attach itself to mine, and meanwhile her fingers labored to determine sensations she was far indeed from obtaining. However, I had to lend myself to everything, my own feelings notwithstanding, and when she believed she had triumphed, she sent me back to my closet where Omphale spoke to me in the following manner:

"All the women you saw yesterday, my dear Therese, and those you have just seen, are divided into four classes, each containing four girls; the first is called the children's class: it includes girls ranging from the most tender age to those of sixteen; a white costume distinguishes them.

"The second class, whose color is green, is called the youthful class; it contains girls of from sixteen to twenty-one.

"The third is the class of the age of reason; its vestments are blue; its ages are from twenty-one to thirty, and both you and I belong to it.

"The fourth class, dressed in reddish brown, is intended for those of mature years; it is composed of anyone over thirty.

"These girls are either indiscriminately mingled at the Reverend Fathers' suppers, or they appear there by class: it all depends upon the whims of the monks but, when not at the meals, they are mixed in the two dormitories, as you are able to judge by those who are lodged in ours.

"The instruction I have to give you," said Omphale, "divides under the headings of four primary articles; in the first, we will treat of what pertains to the house; in the second we will place what regards the behavior of the girls, their punishment, their feeding habits, etc., etc., etc.; the third article will inform you of the arrangement of these monks' pleasures, of the manner in which the girls serve them; the fourth will contain observations on personnel changes.

"I will not, Therese, describe the environs of this frightful house, for you are as familiar with them as I; I will only discuss the interior; they have shown it all to me so that I can give a picture of it to newcomers, whose education is one of my chores, and in whom, by means of this account, I am expected to dash all hope of escape. Yesterday Severino explained some of its features and he did not deceive you, my dear. The church and the pavilion form what is properly called the monastery; but you do not know where the building we inhabit is situated and how one gets here; 'tis thus: in the depths of the sacristy, behind the altar, is a door hidden in the wainscoting and opened by a spring; this door is the entrance to a narrow passage, quite as dark as it is long, whose windings your terror, upon entering, prevented you from noticing; the tunnel descends at first, because it must pass beneath a moat thirty feet deep, then it mounts after the moat and, leveling out, continues at a depth of no more than six feet beneath the surface;

thus it arrives at the basements of our pavilion having traversed the quarter of a league from the church; six thick enclosures rise to baffle all attempts to see this building from the outside, even were one to climb into the church's tower; the reason for this invisibility is simple: the pavilion hugs the ground, its height does not attain twenty-five feet, and the compounded enclosures, some stone walls, others living palisades formed by trees growing in strait proximity to each other, are, all of them, at least fifty feet high: from whatever direction the place is observed it can only be taken for a dense clump of trees in the forest, never for a habitation; it is, hence, as I have said, by means of a trap door opening into the cellars one emerges from the obscure corridor of which I gave you some idea and of which you cannot possibly have any recollection in view of the state you must have been while walking through it. This pavilion, my dear, has, in all, nothing but basements, a ground floor, an entresol, and a first floor; above it there is a very thick roof covered with a large tray, lined with lead, filled with earth, and in which are planted evergreen shrubberies which, blending with the screens surrounding us, give to everything a yet more realistic look of solidity; the basements form a large hall in the middle, around it are distributed eight smaller rooms of which two serve as dungeons for girls who have merited incarceration, and the other six are reserved for provisions; above are located the dining room, the kitchens, pantries, and two cabinets the monks enter when they wish to isolate their pleasures and taste them with us out of their colleagues' sight; the intervening story is composed of eight chambers, whereof four have each a closet: these are the cells where the monks sleep and introduce us when their lubricity destines us to share their beds; the four other rooms are those of the serving friars, one of whom is our jailer, another the monks' valet, a third the doctor, who has in his cell all he needs for emergencies, and the fourth is the cook; these four friars are deaf and dumb; it would be difficult to expect, as you observe, any comfort or aid from them; furthermore, they never pass time in our company and it is forbidden to accost or attempt to communicate with them. Above the entresol are two seraglios; they are identical; as you see, each is a large chamber edged by eight cubicles; thus, you understand, dear girl, that, supposing one were to break through the bars in the casement and descend by the window, one would still be far from being able to escape, since there would remain five palisades, a stout wall, and a broad moat to get past: and were one even to overcome these obstacles, where would one be? In the monastery's courtyard which, itself securely shut, would not afford, at the first moment, a very safe egress. A perhaps less perilous means of escape would be, I admit, to find, somewhere in our basements, the opening to the tunnel that leads out; but how are we to explore these underground cellars, perpetually locked up as we are? were one even to be able to get down there, this opening would still not be found, for it enters the building in some hidden corner unknown to us and itself barricaded by grills to which they alone have the key. However, were all these difficulties vanquished, were one in the corridor, the route would still not be any the more certain for us, for it is strewn with traps with which only they are familiar and into which anyone who sought to traverse the passageways would inevitably fall without the guidance of the monks. And so you must renounce all thought of escape, for it is out of the question, Therese; believe me, were it thinkable, I should long have fled this detestable place, but that cannot be. They who come here never leave save upon their death; and thence is born this impudence, this cruelty, this tyranny these villains use with us; nothing inflames them, nothing stimulates their imagination like the impunity guaranteed them by this impregnable retreat; certain never to have other witnesses to their excesses than the very victims they feast upon, sure indeed their perversities will never be revealed, they carry them to the most abhorrent extremes; delivered of the law's restraints, having burst the checks Religion imposes, unconscious of those of remorse, there is no atrocity in which they do not indulge themselves, and by this criminal apathy their abominable passions are so much more agreeably pricked that nothing, they say, incenses them like solitude and silence, like helplessness on one hand and impunity on the other. The monks regularly sleep every night in this pavilion, they return here at five in the afternoon and go to the monastery the following morning at nine, except for one of the four, chosen daily, who spends the day here: he is known as the Officer of the Day. We will soon see what his duties are. As for the four subaltern friars, they never budge from here; in each chamber we have a bell which communicates with the jailer's cell; the superintendent alone has the right to ring for him but, when she does so in time of her need or ours, everyone comes running instantly; when they return each day, the fathers themselves bring the necessary victuals and give them to the cook, who prepares our meals in accordance with their instructions; there is an artesian well in the basements, abundant wines of every variety in the cellars. We pass on to the second article which relates to the girls' manners, bearing, nourishment, punishment, etc.

22

"Our number is always maintained constant; affairs are so managed that we are always sixteen, eight in either chamber, and, as you observe, always in the uniform of our particular class; before the day is over you will be given the habit appropriate to the one you are entering; during the day we wear a light costume of the color which belongs to us; in the evening, we wear gowns of the same color and dress our hair with all possible elegance. The superintendent of the chamber has complete authority over us, disobedience to her is a crime; her duty is to inspect us before we go to the orgies and if things are not in the desired state she is punished as well as we. The errors we may commit are of several kinds. Each has its particular punishment, and the rules, together with the list of what is to be expected when they are broken, are displayed in each chamber; the Officer of the Day, the person who comes, as I explained a moment ago, to give us orders, to designate the girls for the supper, to visit our living quarters, and to hear the superintendents' complaints, this monk, I say, is the one who, each evening, metes out punishment to whoever has merited it: here are the crimes together with the punishments exacted for them.

"Failure to rise in the morning at the prescribed hour, thirty strokes with the whip (for it is almost always with whipping we are punished; it were perfectly to be expected that an episode in these libertines' pleasures would have become their preferred mode of correction). The presentation during the pleasurable act, either through misunderstanding or for whatsoever may be the reason, of one part of the body instead of some other which was desired, fifty strokes; improper dress or an unsuitable coiffure, twenty strokes; failure to have given prior notice of incapacitation due to menstruation, sixty strokes; upon the day the surgeon confirms the existence of a pregnancy, one hundred strokes are administered; negligence, incompetence, or refusal in connection with luxurious proposals, two hundred strokes. And how often their infernal wickedness finds us wanting on that head, without our having made the least mistake! How frequently it happens that one of them will suddenly demand what he very well knows we have just accorded another and cannot immediately do again! One undergoes the punishment nonetheless; our remonstrances, our pleadings are never heeded; one must either comply or suffer the consequences. Imperfect behavior in the chamber, or disobedience shown the superintendent, sixty strokes; the appearance of tears, chagrin, sorrow, remorse, even the look of the slightest return to Religion, two hundred strokes. If a monk selects you as his partner when he wishes to taste the last crisis of pleasure and if he is unable to achieve it, whether the fault be his, which is most common, or whether it be yours, upon the spot, three hundred strokes; the least hint of revulsion at the monks' propositions, of whatever nature these propositions may be, two hundred strokes; an attempted or concerted escape or revolt, nine days' confinement in a dungeon, entirely naked, and three hundred lashes each day; caballing, the instigation of plots, the sowing of unrest, etc., immediately upon discovery, three hundred strokes; projected suicide, refusal to eat the stipulated food or the proper quantity, two hundred strokes; disrespect shown toward the monks, one hundred eighty strokes. Those only are crimes; beyond what is mentioned there, we can do whatever we please, sleep together, quarrel, fight, carry drunkenness, riot and gourmandizing to their furthest extremes, swear, blaspheme: none of that makes the faintest difference, we may commit those faults and never a word will be said to us; we are rated for none but those I have just mentioned. But if they wish, the superintendents can spare us many of these unpleasantnesses; however, this protection, unfortunately, can be purchased only by complacencies frequently more disagreeable than the sufferings for which they are substitutes; these women, in both chambers, have the same taste, and it is only by according them one's favors that one enters into their good graces. Spurn one of them, and she needs no additional motive to exaggerate her report of your misdeeds, the monks the superintendents serve double their powers, and far from reprimanding them for their injustice, unceasingly encourage it in them; they are themselves bound by all those regulations and are the more severely chastised if they are suspected of leniency: not that the libertines need all that in order to vent their fury upon us, but they welcome excuses; the look of legitimacy that may be given to a piece of viciousness renders it more agreeable in their eyes, adds to its piquancy, its charm. Upon arriving here each of us is provided with a little store of linen; we are given everything by the half-dozen, and our supplies are renewed every year, but we are obliged to surrender what we bring here with us; we are not permitted to keep the least thing. The complaints of the four friars I spoke of are heard just as are the superintendents'; their mere delation is sufficient to procure our punishment; but they at least ask nothing from us and there is less to be feared from that quarter than from the superintendents who, when vengeance informs their maneuvers, are very demanding and very dangerous. Our food is excellent and always copious; were it not that their lust derives benefits thence, this article might not be so satisfactory, but as their filthy debauches profit thereby, they spare themselves no pains to stuff us with food: those who have a bent for flogging seek to fatten us, and those, as Jerome phrased it yesterday, who like to see the hen lay, are assured by means of abundant feeding, of a greater yield of eggs. Consequently, we eat four times a day; at breakfast, between nine and ten o'clock we are regularly given volaille au riz, fresh fruit or compotes, tea, coffee, or chocolate; at one o'clock, dinner is served; each table of eight is served alike; a very good soup, four entrees, a roast of some kind, four second courses, dessert in every season. At five-thirty an afternoon lunch of pastries and fruit arrives. There can be no doubt of the evening meal's excellence if it is taken with the monks; when we do not join them at table, as often happens, since but four of us from each chamber are allowed to go, we are given three roast plates and four entremets; each of us has a daily ration of one bottle of white wine, one of red, and an half-bottle of brandy; they who do not drink that much are at liberty to distribute their quota to the others; among us are some great gourmands who drink astonishing amounts, who get regularly drunk, all of which they do without fear of reprimand; and there are, as well, some for whom these four meals still do not suffice; they have but to ring, and what they ask for will be brought them at once.

"The superintendents require that the food be consumed, and if someone persists in not wishing to eat, for whatever reason, upon the third infraction that person will be severely punished; the monks' supper is composed of three roast dishes, six entrees followed by a cold plate and eight entremets, fruit, three kinds of wine, coffee and liqueurs: sometimes all eight of us are at table with them, sometimes they oblige four of us to wait upon them, and these four dine afterward; it also happens from time to time that they take only four girls for supper; they are, ordinarily, an entire class; when our number is eight, there are always two from each class. I need hardly tell you that no one ever visits us; under no circumstances is any outsider ever admitted into this pavilion. If we fall ill, we are entrusted to the surgeon friar only, and if we die, we leave this world without any religious ministrations; our bodies are flung into one of the spaces between the circumvallations, and that's an end to it; but, and the cruelty is signal, if the sick one's condition becomes too grave or if there is fear of contagion, they do not wait until we are dead to dispose of us; though still alive, we are carried out and dropped in the place I mentioned; During the eighteen years I have been here I have seen more than ten instances of this unexampled ferocity; concerning which they declare it is better to lose one than endanger sixteen; the loss of a girl, they continue, is of very modest import, and it may be so easily repaired there is scant cause to regret it. Let us move on to the arrangements concerning the monks' pleasures and to all of what pertains to the subject.

"We rise at exactly nine every morning, and in every season; we retire at a later or an earlier hour, depending upon the monks' supper. Immediately we are up, the Officer of the Day comes on his rounds; he seats himself in a large armchair and each of us is obliged to advance, stand before him with our skirts raised upon the side he prefers; he touches, he kisses, he examines, and when everyone has carried out this duty, he identifies those who are to participate at the evening's exercises: he prescribes the state in which they must be, he listens to the superintendent's report, and the punishments are imposed. Rarely does the officer leave without a luxurious scene in which all eight usually find roles. The superintendent directs these libidinous activities, and the most entire submission on our part reigns during them. Before breakfast it often occurs that one of the Reverend Fathers has one of us called from bed; the jailer friar brings a card bearing the name of the person desired, the Officer of the Day sees to it she is sent, not even he has the right to withhold her, she leaves and returns when dismissed. This first ceremony concluded, we breakfast; from this moment till evening we have no more to do; but at seven o'clock in summer, at six in winter, they come for those who have been designated; the jailer friar himself escorts them, and after the supper they who have not been retained for the night come back to the seraglio. Often, all return; other girls have been selected for the night, and they are advised several hours in advance in what costume they must make their appearance; sometimes only the Girls of the Watch sleep out of the chamber."

"Girls of the Watch?" I interrupted. "What function this?" "I will tell you," my historian replied. "Upon the first day of every month each monk adopts a girl who must serve a term as his servant and as the target of his shameful desires; only the superintendents are exempted, for they have the task of governing their chambers. The monks can neither exchange girls during the month, nor make them serve two months in succession; there is nothing more cruel, more taxing than this drudgery, and I have no idea how you will bear up under it. When five o'clock strikes, the Girl of the Watch promptly descends to the monk she serves and does not leave his side until the next day, at the hour he sets off for the monastery. She rejoins him when he comes back; she employs these few hours to eat and rest, for she must remain awake all night throughout the whole of the term she spends with her master; I repeat to you, the wretch remains constantly on hand to serve as the object of every caprice which may enter the libertine's head; cuffs, slaps, beatings, whippings, hard language, amusements, she has got to endure all of it; she must remain standing all night long in her patron'.c bedroom, at any instant ready to offer herself to the passions which may stir that tyrant; but the cruelest, the most ignominious aspect of this servitude is the terrible obligation she is under to provide her mouth or her breast for the relief of the one and the other of the monster's needs: he never uses any other vase: she has got to be the willing recipient of everything and the least hesitation or recalcitrance is straightway punished by the most savage reprisals. During all the scenes of lust these are the girls who guarantee pleasure's success, who guide and manage the monks' joys, who tidy up whoever has become covered with filth: for example, a monk dirties himself while enjoying a woman: it is his aide's duty to repair the disorder; he wishes to be excited? the task of rousing him falls to the wretch who accompanies him everywhere, dresses him, undresses him, is ever at his elbow, who is always wrong, always at fault, always beaten; at the suppers her place is behind her master's chair or, like a dog, at his feet under the table, or upon her knees, between his thighs, exciting him with her mouth; sometimes she serves as his cushion, his seat, his torch; at other times all four of them will be grouped around the table in the most lecherous, but, at the same time, the most fatiguing attitudes. "If they lose their balance, they risk either falling upon the thorns placed near by, or breaking a limb, or being killed, such cases have been known; and meanwhile the villains make merry, enact debauches, peacefully get drunk upon meats, wines, lust, and upon cruelty."

"O Heaven!" said I to my companion, trembling with horror, "is it possible to be transported to such excesses! What infernal place is this!"

"Listen to me, Therese, listen, my child, you have not yet heard it all, not by any means," said Omphale. "Pregnancy, reverenced in the world, is the very certitude of reprobation amongst these villains; here, the pregnant woman is given no dispensations: brutalities, punishments, and watches continue; on the contrary, a gravid condition is the certain way to procure oneself troubles, sufferings, humiliations, sorrows; how often do they not by dint of blows cause abortions in them whose fruits they decide not to harvest, and when indeed they do allow the fruit to ripen, it is in order to sport with it: what I am telling you now should be enough to warn you to preserve yourself from this state as best you possibly can."

"But is one able to?"

"Of course, there are certain devices, sponges... But if Antonin perceives what you are up to, beware of his wrath; the safest way is to smother whatever might be the natural impression by striving to unhinge the imagination, which with monsters like these is not difficult.

"We have here as well," my instructress continued, "certain dependencies and alliances of which you probably know very little and of which it were well you had some idea; although this has more to do with the fourth article Ä with, that is to say, the one that treats of our recruitings, our retrenchments, and our exchanges Ä I am going to anticipate for a moment in order to insert the following details. "You are not unaware, Therese, that the four monks composing this brotherhood stand at the head of their Order; all belong to distinguished families, all four are themselves very rich: independently of the considerable funds allocated by the Benedictines for the maintenance of this bower of bliss into which everyone hopes to enter in his turn, they who do arrive here contribute a large proportion of their property and possessions to the foundation already established. These two sources combined yield more than a hundred thousand crowns annually which is devoted solely to finding recruits and meeting the house's expenses; they have a dozen discreet and reliable women whose sole task is to bring them every month a new subject, no younger than twelve nor older than thirty. The conscriptee must be free of all defects and endowed with the greatest possible number of qualities, but principally with that of eminent birth. These abductions, well paid for and always effected a great distance from here, bring no consequent discomfitures; I have never heard of any that resulted in legal action; their extreme caution protects them against everything. They do not absolutely confine themselves to virgins: a girl who has been seduced already or a married woman may prove equally pleasing, but a forcible abduction has got to take place, rape must be involved, and it must be definitely verified; this circumstance arouses them; they wish to be certain their crimes cost tears; they would send away any girl who was to come here voluntarily; had you not made a prodigious defense, had they not recognized a veritable fund of virtue in you, and, consequently, the possibility of crime, they would not have kept you twenty-four hours. Everyone here, Therese, comes of a distinguished line; my dear friend, you see before you the only daughter of the Comte de _____, carried off from Paris at the age of twelve and destined one day to have a dowry of a hundred thousand crowns: I was ravished from the arms of my governess who was taking me by carriage, unoccupied save for ourselves, from my father's country seat to the Abbey of Panthemont where I was brought up; my guardian disappeared; she was in all likelihood bought; I was fetched hither by post chaise. The same applies to all the others. The girl of twenty belongs to one of the noblest families of Poitou. The one sixteen years old is the daughter of the Baron de _____, one of the greatest of the Lorraine squires; Counts, Dukes, and Margraves are the fathers of the girls of twenty-three, twelve, and thirty-two; in a word, there is not one who cannot claim the loftiest titles, not one who is not treated with the greatest ignomiry. But these depraved men are not content to stop at these horrors; they have wished to bring dishonor into the very bosom of their own family. The young lady of twenty-six, without doubt one of the most beautiful amongst us, is Clement's daughter; she of thirty-six is the niece of Jerome.

"As soon as a new girl has arrived in this cloaca, as soon as she has been sealed in here forever to become a stranger to the world, another is immediately retrenched: such is our sufferings' complement; the cruelest of our afflictions is to be in ignorance of what happens to us during these terrible and disquieting dismissals. It is absolutely impossible to say what becomes of one upon leaving this place. From all the evidence we in our isolation are able to assemble, it seems as if the girls the monks retire from service never appear again; they themselves warn us, they do not conceal from us that this retreat is our tomb, but do they assassinate us? Great Heaven! Would murder, the most execrable of crimes, would murder be for them what it was for that celebrated Marechal de Retz,

a species of erotic entertainment whose cruelty, exalting their perfidious imaginations, were able to plunge their senses into a more intense drunkenness! Accustomed to extracting joy from suffering only, to know no delectation save what is derived from inflicting torment and anguish, would it be possible they were distracted to the point of believing that by redoubling, by ameliorating the delirium's primary cause, one would inevitably render it more perfect; and that, without principles as without faith, wanting manners as they are lacking in virtues, the scoundrels, exploiting the miseries into which their earlier crimes plunged us, were able to find satisfaction in the later ones which snatch our lives away from us . . . . I don't know . . . . If one questions them upon the matter, they mumble unintelligibilities, sometimes responding negatively, sometimes in the affirmative; what is certain is that not one of those who has left, despite the promises she made us to denounce these men to the authorities and to strive to procure our liberation, not one, I say, has ever kept her word . . . . Once again: do they placate us, dissuade us, or do they eliminate the possibility of our preferring charges? What we ask those who arrive for news of them who have gone, they never have any to communicate. What becomes of these wretches? That is what torments me, Therese, that is the fatal incertitude which makes for the great unhappiness of our existence. I have been in this house for eighteen years, I have seen more than two hundred girls depart from it . . . . Where are they? All of them having sworn to help us, why has not one kept her vow?

"Nothing, furthermore, justifies our retirement; age, loss of looks, this is not what counts: caprice is their single rule. They will dismiss today the girl they most caressed yesterday, and for ten years they will keep another of whom they are the most weary: such is the story of this chamber's superintendent; she has been twelve years in the house, and to preserve her I have seen them get rid of fifteen-year-old children whose beauty would have rendered the very Graces jealous. She who left a week ago was not yet sixteen; lovely as Venus herself, they had enjoyed her for less than a year, but she became pregnant and, as I told you Therese, that is a great sin in this establishment. Last month they retired one of sixteen, a year ago one of twenty, eight months pregnant; and, recently, another when she began to feel the first pangs of childbirth. Do not imagine that conduct has any bearing upon the matter: I have seen some who flew to do their every bidding and who were gone within six months' time; others sullen, peevish, fantastical whom they kept a great number of years; hence, it is useless to prescribe any kind of behavior to our newly arrived; those monsters' whimsy bursts all circumscriptions, and caprice forms the unique law by which their actions are determined.

23

"When one is going to be dismissed, one is notified the same morning, never earlier: as usual, the Officer of the Day makes his appearance at nine o'clock and says, let us suppose, 'Omphale, the monastery is sending you into retirement; I will come to take you this evening.' Then he continues about his business. But you do not present yourself for his inspection; he examines the others, then he leaves; the person about to be released embraces her comrades, she makes a thousand promises to strive in their behalf, to bring charges, to bruit abroad what transpires in the monastery: the hour strikes, the monk appears, the girl is led away, and not a word is heard of her. Supper takes place in the usual fashion; we have simply been able to remark that upon these days the monks rarely reach pleasure's ultimate episodes, one might say they proceed gingerly and with unwonted care. However, they drink a great deal more, sometimes even to inebriation; they send us to our chamber at a much earlier hour, they take no one to bed with them, even the Girls of the Watch are relegated to the seraglios."

"Very well," I say to my companion, "if no one has helped you it is because you have had to deal with frail, intimidated creatures, or women with children who dared not attempt anything for you. That they will kill us is not my fear; at least, I don't believe they do: that reasoning beings could carry crime to that point... it is unthinkable... I know that full well... After what I have seen and undergone I perhaps ought not defend mankind as I do, but, my dear, it is simply inconceivable that they can execute horrors the very idea of which defies the imagination. Oh dear companion!" I pursued with great emotion, "would you like to exchange that promise which for my part I swear I will fulfill!... Do you wish it?"

"Yes."

"Ah, I swear to you in the name of all I hold most holy, in the name of the God Who makes me to breathe and Whom only I adore... I vow to you I will either die in the undertaking or destroy these infamies... will you promise me the same?"

"Do not doubt it," Omphale replied, "but be certain of these promises' futility; others more embittered than you, stauncher, no less resolute and not so scrupulous, in a word, friends who would have shed their last drop of blood for us, have not kept identical vows; and so, dear Therese, and so allow my cruel experience to consider ours equally vain and to count upon them no more."

"And the monks," I said, "do they also vary, do new ones often come here?"

"No," answered Omphale, "Antonin has been here ten years, Clement eighteen, Jerome thirty, Severino twenty-five. The superior was born in Italy, he is closely allied to the Pope with whom he is in intimate contact; only since his arrival have the so-called miracles of the Virgin assured the monastery's reputation and prevented scandalmongers from observing too closely what takes place here; but when he came the house was already furnished as presently you see it to be; it has subsisted in the same style and upon this footing for above a century, and all the superiors who have governed it have perpetuated a system which so amicably smiles upon their pleasures. Severino, the most libertine man of our times, has only installed himself here in order to lead a life consonant with his tastes. He intends to maintain this abbey's secret privileges as long as he possibly can. We belong to the diocese of Auxerre, but whether or not the bishop is informed, we never see him, never does he set foot in the monastery: generally speaking, very few outsiders come here except toward the time of the festival which is that of Notre Dame d'Aout; according to the monks, ten persons do not arrive at this house over the period of a twelvemonth; however, it is very likely that when strangers do present themselves, the superior takes care to receive them with hospitality; by appearances of religion and austerity he imposes upon them, they go away content, the monastery is eulogized, and thus these villains' impunity is established upon the people's good faith and the credulity of the devout."

Omphale had scarcely concluded her instruction when nine o'clock tolled; the superintendent called us to come quickly, and the Officer of the Day did indeed enter. 'Twas Antonin; according to custom, we drew ourselves up in a line. He cast a rapid glance upon the group, counted us, and sat down; then, one by one, we went forward and lifted our skirts, on the one side as high as the navel, on the other up to the middle of the back. Antonin greeted the homage with the blasé unconcern of satiety; then, clapping an eye upon me, he asked how I liked this newest of my adventures. Getting no response but tears, "She'll manage," he said with a laugh; "in all of France there's not a single house where girls are finished as nicely as they are in this." From the superintendent's hands he took the list of girls who had misbehaved, then, addressing himself to me again, he caused me to shudder; each gesture, each movement which seemed to oblige me to submit myself to these libertines was for me as a sentence of death. Antonin commanded me to sit on the edge of a bed and when I was in this posture he bade the superintendent uncover my breast and raise my skirt to above my waist; he himself spread my legs as far apart as possible, he seats himself before this prospect, one of my companions comes and takes up the same pose on top of me in such a way that it is the altar of generation instead of my visage which is offered to Antonin; with these charms raised to the level of his mouth he readies himself for pleasure. A third girl, kneeling before him, begins to excite him with her hands, and a fourth, completely naked, with her fingers indicates where he must strike my body. Gradually, this girl begins to arouse me and what she does to me Antonin does as well, with both his hands, to two other girls on his left and right. One cannot imagine the language, the obscene speeches by which that debauchee stimulates himself; at last he is in the state he desires, he is led to me, but everyone follows him, moves with him, endeavors to inflame him yet further while he takes his pleasure; his naked hind parts are exposed, Omphale takes possession of them and neglects nothing in order to irritate him: rubbings, kisses, pollutions, she employs them all; completely afire, Antonin leaps toward me . . . . "I wish to stuff her this time," he says, beside himself . . . . These moral deviations determine the physical. Antonin, who has the habit of uttering terrible cries during the final instants of drunkenness, emits dreadful ones; everyone surrounds, everyone serves him, everyone labors to enrich his ecstasy, and the libertine attains it in the midst of the most bizarre episodes of luxury and depravation.

These groupings were frequent; for when a monk indulged in whatever form of pleasure, all the girls regularly surrounded him in order to fire all his parts' sensations, that voluptuousness might, if one may be forgiven the expression, more surely penetrate into him through every pore.

Antonin left, breakfast was brought in; my companions forced me to eat, I did so to please them. We had not quite finished when the superior entered: seeing us still at table, he dispensed us from ceremonies which were to have been identical with those we had just executed for Antonin. "We must give a thought to dressing her," said he, looking at me; and then he opened a wardrobe and threw upon my bed several garments of the color appropriate to my class, and several bundles of linen as well.

"Try that on," he said, "and give me what belongs to you."

I donned the new clothes and surrendered my old; but, in anticipation of having to give them up, I had, during the night, prudently removed my money from my pockets and had concealed it in my hair. With each article of clothing I took off, Severino's ardent stare fell upon the feature newly exposed, and his hands wandered to it at once. At length, when I was half-naked, the monk seized me, put me in the position favorable to his pleasure, that is to say, in the one exactly opposite to the attitude Antonin had made me assume; I wish to ask him to spare me, but spying the fury already kindled in his eyes, I decide the obedient is the safer way; I take my place, the others form a ring around me, Severino is able to see nothing but a multitude of those obscene altars in which he delights; his hands converge upon mine, his mouth fastens upon it, his eyes devour it... he is at the summit of pleasure.

With your approval, Madame, said the beautiful Therese, I shall limit myself to a foreshortened account of the first month I spent in that monastery, that is, I will confine myself to the period's principal anecdotes; the rest would be pure repetition; the monotony of that sojourn would make my recital tedious; immediately afterward, I should, it seems to me, move on to the events which finally produced my emergence from this ghastly sewer.

I did not attend supper that first day; I had simply been selected to pass the night with Dom Clement. In accordance with custom, I was outside his cell some few minutes before he was expected to return to it; the jailer opened the door, then locked it when I had gone in.

Clement arrives as warm with wine as lust, he is followed by the twenty-six year-old girl who, at the time was officiating as his watch; previously informed of what I am to do, I fall to my knees as soon as I hear him coming; he nears me, considers me in my humbled posture, then commands me to rise and kiss him upon the mouth; he savors the kiss for several moments and imparts to it all the expression... all the amplitude one could possibly conceive. Meanwhile, Armande, as his thrall was named, undresses me by stages; when the lower part of the loins, with which she had begun, is exposed, she bids me turn around and display to her uncle the area his tastes cherish. Clement examines it, feels it, then, reposing himself in an armchair, orders me to bring it close so that he can kiss it; Armande is upon her knees, rousing him with her mouth, Clement places his at the sanctuary of the temple I present to him and his tongue strays into the path situate at its center; his hands fasten upon the corresponding altar in Armande but, as the clothing the girl is still wearing impedes him, he commands her to be rid of it, this is soon done, and the docile creature returns to her uncle to take up a position in which, while exciting him with only the hand, she finds herself better within reach of Clement's. The impure monk uninterruptedly occupied with me in like fashion, then tells me to give the largest possible vent to whatever winds may be hovering in my bowels, and these I am to direct into his mouth; this eccentricity struck me as revolting, but I was at the time far from perfect acquaintance with all the irregularities of debauch: I obey and straightway feel the effect of this intemperance. More excited, the monk becomes more impassioned: he suddenly applies bites to six different places upon the fleshy globes I have put at his disposal; I emit a cry and start forward involuntarily, whereat he stands, advances toward me, rage blazing in his eyes, and demands whether I know what I am risking by unsettling him . . . . I make a thousand apologies, he grasps the corset still about my torso, rips it away, and my blouse too, in less time than it takes to tell . . . . Ferociously he seizes my breasts, spouting invectives as he squeezes, wrings, crushes them; Armande undresses him, and there we are, all three of us, naked. Upon Armande his attention comes to bear for a moment: he deals her savage blows with his fists; kisses her mouth; nibbles her tongue and lips, she screams; pain now and again sends the girl into uncontrollable gales of weeping; he has her stand upon a chair and extracts from her just what he desired from me. Armande satisfies him, with one hand I excite him, and, during this luxury, I whip him gently with the other, he also bites Armande, but she holds herself somehow in check, not daring to stir a hair. The monster's tooth-marks are soon printed upon the lovely girl's flesh; they are to be seen in a number of places; brusquely wheeling upon me: "Therese," he says, "you are going to suffer cruelly" Ä he had no need to tell me so, for his eyes declared it but too emphatically. "You are going to be lashed everywhere," he continues, "everywhere, without exception," and as he spoke he again laid hands upon my breasts and mauled them brutally, he bruised their extremities with his fingertips and occasioned me very sharp pain; I dared not say a word for fear of irritating him yet more, but sweat bathed my forehead and, willy-nilly, my eyes filled with tears; he turns me about, makes me kneel on the edge of a chair upon whose back I must keep my hands without removing them for a single instant; he promises to inflict the gravest penalties upon me if I lift them; seeing me ready and well within range, he orders Armande to fetch him some birch rods, she presents him with a handful, slender and long; Clement snatches them, and recommending that I not stir, he opens with a score of stripes upon my shoulders and the small of my back; he leaves me for an instant, returns to Armande, brings her back, she too is made to kneel upon a chair six feet from where I am; he declares he is going to flog us simultaneously and the first of the two to release her grip, utter a cry, or shed a tear will be exposed on the spot to whatever torture he is pleased to inflict: he bestows the same number of strokes upon Armande he has just given me, and positively upon the identical places, he returns to me, kisses everything he has just left off molesting, and raising his sticks, says to me, "Steady, little slut, you are going to be used like the last of the damned." Whereupon I receive fifty strokes, all of them directed between the region bordered by the shoulders and the small of the back. He dashes to my comrade and treats her likewise: we pronounce not a word; nothing may be heard but a few stifled groans, we have enough strength to hold back our tears. There was no indication as to what degree the monk's passions were inflamed; he periodically excited himself briskly, but nothing rose. Returning now to me, he spent a moment eyeing those two fatty globes then still intact but about to undergo torture in their turn; he handled them, he could not prevent himself from prying them apart, tickling them, kissing them another thousand times. "Well," said he, "be courageous…" and a hail of blows descended upon these masses, lacerating them to the thighs. Extremely animated by the starts, the leaps, the grinding of teeth, the contortions the pain drew from me, examining them, battening upon them rapturously, he comes and expresses, upon my mouth which he kisses with fervor, the sensations agitating him . . . . "This girl entertains me," he cries, "I have never flogged another with as much pleasure," and he goes back to his niece whom he treats with the same barbarity; there remained the space between the upper thigh and the calves and this he struck with identical vehemence: first the one of us, then the other. "Ha !" he said, now approaching me, "let's change hands and visit this place here"; now wielding a cat-o'-nine-tails he gives me twenty cuts from the middle of my belly to the bottom of my thighs; then wrenching them apart, he slashed at the interior of the lair my position bares to his whip. "There it is," says he, "the bird I am going to pluck": several thongs having, through the precautions he had taken, penetrated very deep, I could not suppress my screams. "Well, well!" said the villain, "I must have found the sensitive area at last; steady there, calm yourself, we'll visit it a little more thoroughly"; however, his niece is put in the same posture and treated in the same manner; once again he reaches the most delicate region of a woman's body; but whether through habit, or courage, or dread of incurring treatment yet worse, she has enough strength to master herself, and about her nothing is visible beyond a few shivers and spasmodic twitchings. However, there was by now a slight change in the libertine's physical aspect, and although things were still lacking in substance, thanks to strokings and shakings a gradual improvement was being registered.

"On your knees," the monk said to me, "I am going to whip your titties."

"My titties, oh my Father!"

"Yes, those two lubricious masses which never excite me but I wish to use them thus," and upon saying this, he squeezed them, he compressed them violently.

"Oh Father! They are so delicate! You will kill me!"

"No matter, my dear, provided I am satisfied," and he applied five or six blows which, happily, I parried with my hands. Upon observing that, he binds them behind my back; nothing remains with which to implore his mercy but my countenance and my tears, for he has harshly ordered me to be silent. I strive to melt him... but in vain, he strikes out savagely at my now unprotected bosom; terrible bruises are immediately writ out in black and blue; blood appears as his battering continues, my suffering wrings tears from me, they fall upon the vestiges left by the monster's rage, and render them, says he, yet a thousand times more interesting... he kisses those marks, he devours them and now and again returns to my mouth, to my eyes whose tears he licks up with lewd delight. Armande takes her place, her hands are tied, she presents breasts of alabaster and the most beautiful roundness; Clement pretends to kiss them, but to bite them is what he wishes . . . . And then he lays on and that lovely flesh, so white, so plump, is soon nothing more in its butcher's eyes but lacerations and bleeding. stripes. "Wait one moment," says the berserk monk, "I want to flog simultaneously the most beautiful of behinds and the softest of breasts." He leaves me on my knees and, bringing Armande toward me, makes her stand facing me with her legs spread, in such a way that my mouth touches her womb and my breasts are exposed between her thighs and below her behind; by this means the monk has what he wants before him: Armande's buttocks and my titties in close proximity: furiously he beats them both, but my companion, in order to spare me blows which are becoming far more dangerous for me than for her, has the goodness to lower herself and thus shield me by receiving upon her own person the lashes that would inevitably have wounded me. Clement detects the trick and separates us: "She'll gain nothing by that," he fumes, "and if today I have the graciousness to spare that part of her, 'twill only be so as to molest some other at least as delicate." As I rose I saw that all those infamies had not been in vain: the debauchee was in the most brilliant state; and it made him only the more furious; he changes weapons Ä opens a cabinet where several martinets are to be found and draws out one armed with iron tips. I fall to trembling. "There, Therese," says he showing me the martinet, "you'll see how delicious it is to be whipped with this... you'll feel it, you'll feel it, my rascal, but for the instant I prefer to use this other one..." It was composed of small knotted cords, twelve in all; at the end of each was a knot somewhat larger than the others, about the size of a plum pit. "Come there! Up!

The cavalcade!... the cavalcade!" says he to his niece; she, knowing what is meant, quickly gets down on all fours, her rump raised as high as possible, and tells me to imitate her; I do. Clement leaps upon my back, riding facing my rear; Armande, her own presented to him, finds herself directly ahead of Clement: the villain then discovering us both well within reach, furiously cuts at the charms we offer him; but, as this position obliges us to open as wide as possible that delicate part of ourselves which distinguishes our sex from men's, the barbarian aims stinging blows in this direction: the whip's long and supple strands, penetrating into the interior with much more facility than could withes or ferules, leave deep traces of his rage; now he strikes one, now his blows fly at the other; as skilled a horseman as he is an intrepid flagellator, he several times changes his mount; we are exhausted, and the pangs of pain are of such violence that it is almost impossible to bear them any longer. "Stand up," he tells us, catching up the martinet again, "yes, get up and stand in fear of me" Ä his eyes glitter, foam flecks his lips Ä like persons distracted, we run about the room, here, there, he follows after us, indiscriminately striking Armande, myself; the villain brings us to blood; at last he traps us both between the bed and the wall: the blows are redoubled: the unhappy Armande receives one upon the breast which staggers her, this last horror determines his ecstasy, and while my back is flailed by its cruel effects, my loins are flooded by the proofs of a delirium whose results are so dangerous.

24

"We are going to bed," Clement finally says to me; "that has perhaps been rather too much for you, Therese, and certainly not enough for me; one never tires of this mania notwithstanding the fact it is a very pale image of what one should really like to do; ah, dear girl! you have no idea to what lengths this depravity leads us, you cannot imagine the drunkenness into which it plunges us, the violent commotion in the electrical fluid which results from the irritation produced by the suffering of the object that serves our passions; how one is needled by its agonies! The desire to increase them... 'tis, I know, the reef upon which the fantasy is doomed to wreck, but is this peril to be dreaded by him who cares not a damn for anything?"

Although Clement's mind was still in the grip of enthusiasm, I observed that his senses were much more calm, and by way of reply to what he had just said, I dared reproach him his tastes' depravation, and the manner in which this libertine justified them merits inclusion, it seems to me, amidst the confessions you wish to have from me.

"Without question the silliest thing in the world, my dear Therese," Clement said to me, "is to wish to dispute a man's tastes, to wish to contradict, thwart, discredit, condemn, or punish them if they do not conform either with the laws of the country he inhabits on with the prejudices of social convention. Why indeed! Will it never be understood that there is no variety of taste, however bizarre, however outlandish, however criminal it may be supposed, which does not derive directly from and depend upon the kind of organization we have individually received from Nature? That posed, I ask with what right one man will dare require another either to curb or get rid of his tastes or model them upon those of the social order? With what right will the law itself, which is created for man's happiness only, dare pursue him who cannot mend his ways, or who would succeed in altering his behavior only at the price of forgoing that happiness whose protection the law is obliged to guarantee him? Even were one to desire to change those tastes could one do so? Have we the power to remake ourselves? Can we become other than what we are? Would you demand the same thing from someone born a cripple? and is this inconformity of our tastes anything in the moral sphere but what the ill-made man's imperfection is in the physical?

"Shall we enter into details? Why, very well. The keen mind I recognize in you, Therese, will enable you to appreciate them. I believe you have been arrested by two irregularities you have remarked in us: you are astonished at the piquant sensation experienced by some of our friends where it is a question of matters commonly beheld as fetid or impure, and you are similarly surprised that our voluptuous faculties are susceptible of powerful excitation by actions which, in your view, bear none but the emblem of ferocity; let us analyze both these tastes and attempt, if 'tis possible, to convince you that there is nothing simpler or more normal in this world than the pleasures which are their result.

"Extraordinary, you declare, that things decayed, noisome, and filthy are able to produce upon our senses the irritation essential to precipitate their complete delirium; but before allowing oneself to be startled by this, it would be better to realize, Therese, that objects have no value for us save that which our imagination imparts to them; it is therefore very possible, bearing this constant truth well in mind, that not only the most curious but even the vilest and most appalling things may affect us very appreciably. The human imagination is a faculty of man's mind whereupon, through the senses' agency, objects are painted, whereby they are modified, and wherein, next, ideas become formed, all in reason of the initial glimpsing of those external objects. But this imagination, itself the result of the peculiar organization a particular individual is endowed with, only adopts the received objects in such-and-such a manner and afterward only creates ideas according to the effects produced by perceived objects' impact: let me give you a comparison to help you grasp what I am exposing. Therese, have you not seen those differently formed mirrors, some of which diminish objects, others of which enlarge them; some give back frightful images of things, some beautify things; do you now imagine that were each of these types of mirrors to possess both a creative and an objective faculty, they would not each give a completely different portrait of the same man who stands before them, and would not that portrait be different thanks to the manner in which each mirror had perceived the object? If to the two faculties we have just ascribed to the mirror, there were added a third of sensation, would not this man, seen by it in such-and-such a manner, be the source of that one kind of feeling the mirror would be able, indeed would be obliged, to conceive for the sort of being the mirror had perceived? The mirror sees the man as beautiful, the mirror loves the man; another mirror sees the man as frightful and hates him, and it is always the same being who produces various impressions.

"Such is the human imagination, Therese; the same object is represented to it under as many forms as that imagination has various facets and moods, and according to the effect upon the imagination received from whatsoever be the object, the imagination is made to love or to hate it; if the perceived object's impact strikes it in an agreeable manner, the object is loved, preferred, even if this object has nothing really attractive about it; and if the object, though of a certain high value in the eyes of someone else, has only struck in a disagreeable manner the imagination we are discussing, hostility will be the result, because not one of our sentiments is formed save in reason of what various objects produce upon the imagination; these fundamentals once grasped, should not by any means be cause for astonishment that what distinctly pleases some is able to displease others, and, conversely, that the most extraordinary thing is able to find admirers . . . . The cripple also discovers certain mirrors which make him handsome.

"Now, if we admit that the senses' joy is always dependent upon the imagination, always regulated by the imagination, one must not be amazed by the numerous variations the imagination is apt to suggest during the pleasurable episode, by the infinite multitude of different tastes and passions the imagination's various extravagances will bring to light. Luxurious though these tastes may be, they are never intrinsically strange; there is no reason to find a mealtime eccentricity more or less extraordinary than a bed-room whim; and in the one and the other, it is not more astonishing to idolize what the common run of mankind holds detestable than it is to love something generally recognized as pleasant. To like what others like proves organic conformity, but demonstrates nothing in favor of the beloved object. Three-quarters of the universe may find the rose's scent delicious without that serving either as evidence upon which to condemn the remaining quarter which might find the smell offensive, or as proof that this odor is truly agreeable.

"If then in this world there exist persons whose tastes conflict with accepted prejudices, not only must one not be surprised by the fact, not only must one not scold these dissenters or punish them, but one must aid them, procure them contentment, remove obstacles which impede them, and afford them, if you wish to be just, all the means to satisfy themselves without risk; because they are no more responsible for having this curious taste than you are responsible for being live-spirited or dull-witted, prettily made or knock-kneed. It is in the mother's womb that there are fashioned the organs which must render us susceptible of such-and-such a fantasy; the first objects which we encounter, the first conversations we overhear determine the pattern; once tastes are formed nothing in the world can destroy them. Do what it will, education is incapable of altering the pattern, and he who has got to be a villain just as surely becomes a villain, the good education you give him notwithstanding; quite as he, however much he has lacked good example, flies unerringly toward virtue if his organs dispose him to the doing of good. Both have acted in accordance with their organic structure, in accordance with the impressions they have received from Nature, and the one is no more deserving of punishment than the other is of reward.

"Curiously enough, so long as it is merely a question of trifles, we are never in the least astonished by the differences existing among tastes; but let the subject take on an erotic tincture, and listen to the word spread about! rumors fly, women, always thoughtful of guarding their rights - women whose feebleness and inconsequence make them especially prone to seeing enemies everywhere aboutÄ, women, I say, are all constantly trembling and quivering lest something be snatched away from them and if, when taking one's pleasure, one unfortunately puts practices to use which conflict with woman-worship, lo! there you have crimes which merit the noose. And what an injustice! Must sensual pleasure render a man better than life's other pleasures? In one word, must our penchants be any more concentrated upon the temple of generation, must it necessarily more certainly awaken our desires, than some other part of the body either the most contrary to or at the furthest remove from it? than some emanation of the body either the most fetid or the most disgusting? It should not, in my opinion, appear any more astonishing to see a man introduce singularity into his libertine pleasures than it should appear strange to see him employ the uncommon in any other of life's activities. Once again, in either case, his singularity is the result of his organs: is it his fault if what affects you is naught to him, or if he is only moved by what repels you? What living man would not instantly revise his tastes, his affections, his penchants and bring them into harmony with the general scheme, what man, rather than continue a freak, would not prefer to be like everyone else, were it in his power to do so? It is the most barbarous and most stupid intolerance to wish to fly at such a man's throat; he is no more guilty toward society, regardless of what may be his extravagances, than is, as I have just said, the person who came blind and lame into the world. And it would be quite as unjust to punish or deride the latter as to afflict or berate the other. The man endowed with uncommon tastes is sick; if you prefer, he is like a woman subject to hysterical vapors. Has the idea to punish such a person ever occurred to us? Let us be equally fair when dealing with the man whose caprices startle us; perfectly like unto the ill man or the woman suffering from vapors, he is deserving of sympathy and not of blame; that is the moral apology for the persons whom we are discussing; a physical explanation will without doubt be found as easily, and when the study of anatomy reaches perfection they will without any trouble be able to demonstrate the relationship of the human constitution to the tastes which it affects. Ah, you pedants, hangmen, turnkeys, lawmakers, you shavepate rabble, what will you do when we have arrived there? what is to become of your laws, your ethics, your religion, your gallows, your Gods and your Heavens and your Hell when it shall

be proven that such a flow of liquids, this variety of fibers, that degree of pungency
in the blood or in the animal spirits are sufficient to make a man the object of your
givings and your takings away? We continue. Cruel tastes astonish you.

"What is the aim of the man who seeks his joy? is it not to give his senses all the
irritation of which they are susceptible in order, by this means, better and more
warmly to reach the ultimate crisis... the precious crisis which characterizes the
enjoyment as good or bad, depending upon the greater or lesser activity which
occurs during the crisis? Well, is one not guilty of an untenable sophistry when
one dares affirm it is necessary, in order to ameliorate it, that it be shared with the
woman? Is it not plain enough that the woman can share nothing with us without
taking something from us? and that all she makes away with must necessarily be
had by her at our expense? And what then is this necessity, I ask, that a woman
enjoy herself when we are enjoying ourselves? in this arrangement is there any
sentiment but pride which may be flattered? and does one not savor this proud
feeling in a far more piquant manner when, on the contrary, one harshly
constrains this woman to abandon her quest for pleasure and to devote herself to
making you alone feel it? Does not tyranny flatter the pride in a far more lively
way than does beneficence? In one word, is not he who imposes much more surely
the master than he who shares? But how could it ever have entered a reasonable
man's head that delicacy is of any value during enjoyment? 'Tis absurd, to
maintain it is necessary at such a time; it never adds anything to the pleasure of
the senses, why, I contend that it detracts therefrom. To love and to enjoy are two
very different things: the proof whereof is that one loves every day without
enjoying, and that even more often one enjoys without loving. Anything by way
of consideration for the woman one stirs into the broth has got to dilute its
strength and impair its flavor for the man; so long as the latter spends his time
giving enjoyment, he assuredly does not himself do any enjoying, or his enjoyment
is merely intellectual, that is to say, chimerical and far inferior to sensual
enjoyment. No, Therese, no, I will not cease repeating it, there is absolutely no
necessity that, in order to be keen, an enjoyment must be shared; and in order
that this kind of pleasure may be rendered piquant to the utmost, it is, on the
contrary, very essential that the man never take his pleasure save at the expense
of the woman, that he take from her (without regard for the sensation she may
experience thereby) everything which may in any way improve or increase the
voluptuous exercise he wants to relish, and this without the slightest concern for
whatever may be the effects of all this upon the woman, for preoccupation of that
sort will prove bothersome to him; he either wants the woman to partake of
pleasure, and thereupon his joys are at an end; or he fears lest she will suffer, and
he is hurled into confusion, all's brought to a stop. If egoism is Nature's
fundamental commandment, it is very surely most of all during our lubricious
delights that this celestial Mother desires us to be most absolutely under its rule;
why, it's a very small evil, is it not, that, in the interests of the augmentation of the
man's lecherous delights he has got either to neglect or upset the woman's; for if

this upsetting of her pleasure causes him to gain any, what is lost to the object which serves him affects him in no wise, save profitably: it must be a matter of indifference to him whether that object is happy or unhappy, provided it be delectable to him; in truth, there is no relation at all between that object and himself. He would hence be a fool to trouble himself about the object's sensations and forget his own; he would be entirely mad if, in order to modify those sensations foreign to him, he were to renounce improvement of his. That much established, if the individual in question is, unhappily, organized in such a fashion he cannot be stirred save by producing painful sensations in the object employed, you will admit he is forced to go ruthlessly to work, since the point of it all is to have the best possible time, the consequences for the object being entirely excluded from consideration . . . . We will return to the problem; let us continue in an orderly fashion.

"Isolated enjoyment therefore has its charms, it may therefore have more of them than all other kinds; why I if it were not so, how should the aged and so many deformed or defective persons be able to enjoy themselves? for they know full well they are not loved nor lovable; perfectly certain it is impossible to share what they experience, is their joy any the less powerful on that account? Do they desire even the illusion? Behaving with utter selfishness in their riots, you will observe them seeking pleasure, you will see them sacrifice everything to obtain it, and in the object they put to use never other than passive properties. Therefore, it is in no wise necessary to give pleasures in order to receive them; the happy or unhappy situation of the victim of our debauch is, therefore, absolutely as one from the point of view of our senses, there is never any question of the state in which his heart or mind may be; it matters not one whit, the object may be pleased by what you do to it, the object may suffer, it may love or detest you: all these considerations are nullified immediately it is only a question of your sensation. Women, I concede, may establish contrary theories, but women, who are nothing but machines designed for voluptuousness, who ought to be nothing but the targets of lust, are untrustworthy authorities whenever one has got to construct an authentic doctrine upon this kind of pleasure. Is there a single reasonable man who is eager to have a whore partake of his joy? And, however, are there not millions of men who amuse themselves hugely with these creatures? Well, there you have that many individuals convinced of what I am urging, who unhesitatingly put it into practice, and who scorn those who use good principles to legitimate their deeds, those ridiculous fools, the world is stuffed to overflowing with them, who go and come, who do this and that, who eat, who digest, without ever sensing a thing.

"Having proven that solitary pleasures are as delicious as any others and much more likely to delight, it becomes perfectly clear that this enjoyment, taken in independence of the object we employ, is not merely of a nature very remote from what could be pleasurable to that object, but is even found to be inimical to that object's pleasure: what is more, it may become an imposed suffering, a vexation, or a torture, and the only thing that results from this abuse is a very certain increase of pleasure for the despot who does the tormenting or vexing; let us attempt to demonstrate this.

"Voluptuous emotion is nothing but a kind of vibration produced in our soul by shocks which the imagination, inflamed by the remembrance of a lubricious object, registers upon our senses, either through this object's presence, or better still by this object's being exposed to that particular kind of irritation which most profoundly stirs us; thus, our voluptuous transport Ä this indescribable convulsive needling which drives us wild, which lifts us to the highest pitch of happiness at which man is able to arrive Ä is never ignited save by two causes: either by the perception in the object we use of a real or imaginary beauty, the beauty in which we delight the most, or by the sight of that object undergoing the strongest possible sensation; now, there is no more lively sensation than that of pain; its impressions are certain and dependable, they never deceive as may those of the pleasure women perpetually feign and almost never experience; and, furthermore, how much self-confidence, youth, vigor, health are not needed in order to be sure of producing this dubious and hardly very satisfying impression of pleasure in a woman. To produce the painful impression, on the contrary, requires no virtues at all: the more defects a man may have, the older he is, the less lovable, the more resounding his success. With what regards the objective, it will be far more certainly attained since we are establishing the fact that one never better touches, I wish to say, that one never better irritates one's senses than when the greatest possible impression has been produced in the employed object, by no matter what devices; therefore, he who will cause the most tumultuous impression to be born in a woman, he who will most thoroughly convulse this woman's entire frame, very decidedly will have managed to procure himself the heaviest possible dose of voluptuousness, because the shock resultant upon us by the impressions others experience, which shock in turn is necessitated by the impression we have of those others, will necessarily be more vigorous if the impression these others receive be painful, than if the impression they receive be sweet and mild; and it follows that the voluptuous egoist, who is persuaded his pleasures will be keen only insofar as they are entire, will therefore impose, when he has it in his power to do so, the strongest possible dose of pain upon the employed object, fully certain that what by way of voluptuous pleasure he extracts will be his only by dint of the very lively impression he has produced."

"Oh, Father," I said to Clement, "these doctrines are dreadful, they lead to the cultivation of cruel tastes, horrible tastes."

"Why, what does it matter?" demanded the barbarian; "and, once again, have we any control over our tastes? Must we not yield to the dominion of those Nature has inserted in us as when before the tempest's force the proud oak bends its head? Were Nature offended by these proclivities, she would not have inspired them in us; that we can receive from her hands a sentiment such as would outrage her is impossible, and, extremely certain of this, we can give ourselves up to our passions, whatever their sort and of whatever their violence, wholly sure that all the discomfitures their shock may occasion are naught but the designs of Nature, of whom we are the involuntary instruments. And what to us are these passions' consequences? When one wishes to delight in any action whatsoever, there is never any question of consequences."

"I am not speaking to you of consequences," I put in abruptly, "but of the thing itself; if indeed you are the stronger and if through atrocious principles of cruelty you love to take your pleasure only by means of causing suffering with the intention of augmenting your sensations, you will gradually come to the point of producing them with such a degree of violence that you will certainly risk killing the employed object."

"So be it; that is to say that, by means of tastes given me by Nature, I shall have carried out the intentions of Nature who, never affecting her creations save through destructions, never inspires the thought of the latter in me save when she is in need of the former; that is to say that from an oblong portion of matter I shall have formed three or four thousand round or square ones. Oh Therese, is there any crime here? Is this the name with which to designate what serves Nature? Is it in man's power to commit crimes? And when, preferring his own happiness to that of others, he overthrows or destroys whatever he finds in his path, has he done anything but serve Nature whose primary and most imperious inspirations enjoin him to pursue his happiness at no matter whose expense? The doctrine of brotherly love is a fiction we owe to Christianity and not to Nature; the exponent of the Nazarene's cult, tormented, wretched and consequently in an enfeebled state which prompted him to cry out for tolerance and compassion, had no choice but to allege this fabulous relationship between one person and another; by gaining acceptance for the notion he was able to save his life. But the philosopher does not acknowledge these gigantic rapports; to his consideration, he is alone in the universe, he judges everything subjectively, he only is of importance. If he is thoughtful of or caresses another for one instant, it is never but in strait connection with what profit he thinks to draw from the business; when he is no longer in need of others, when he can forcefully assert his empire, he then abjures forever those pretty humanitarian doctrines of doing good deeds to which he only submitted himself for reasons of policy; he no longer fears to be selfish, to reduce everyone about him, and he sates his appetites without inquiring to know what his enjoyments may cost others, and without remorse."

"But the man you describe is a monster."

"The man I describe is in tune with Nature."

"He is a savage beast."

"Why, is not the tiger or the leopard, of whom this man is, if you wish, a replica, like man created by Nature and created to prosecute Nature's intentions? The wolf who devours the lamb accomplishes what this common mother designs, just as does the malefactor who destroys the object of his revenge or his lubricity."

"Oh, Father, say what you will, I shall never accept this destructive lubricity."

"Because you are afraid of becoming its object Ä there you have it: egoism. Let's exchange our roles and you will fancy it very nicely. Ask the lamb, and you will find he does not understand why the wolf is allowed to devour him; ask the wolf what the lamb is for: to feed me, he will reply. Wolves which batten upon lambs, lambs consumed by wolves, the strong who immolate the weak, the weak victims of the strong: there you have Nature, there you have her intentions, there you have her scheme: a perpetual action and reaction, a host of vices, a host of virtues, in one word, a perfect equilibrium resulting from the equality of good and evil on earth; the equilibrium essential to the maintenance of the stars, of vegetation and, lacking which, everything would be instantly in ruins. O Therese, mightily astonished she would be, this Nature, were she to be able to converse with us for a moment and were we to tell her that these crimes which serve her, these atrocities she demands and inspires in us are punished by laws they assure us are made in imitation of hers. 'Idiots' she would reply to us, 'sleep, eat, and fearlessly commit whatever crimes you like whenever you like: every one of those alleged infamies pleases me, and I would have them all, since it is I who inspire them in you. It is within your province to regulate what annoys me and what delights, indeed! be advised that there is nothing in you which is not my own, nothing I did not place in you for reasons it is not fitting you be acquainted with; know that the most abominable of your deeds is, like the most virtuous of some other, but one of the manners of serving me. So do not restrain yourself, flout your laws, a fig for your social conventions and your Gods; listen to me and to none other, and believe that if there exists a crime to be committed against me it is the resistance you oppose, in the forms of stubbornness or casuistries, to what I inspire in you.'"

"Oh, Just Heaven!" I cried, "you make me shudder! Were there no crimes against Nature, whence would come that insurmountable loathing we experience for certain misdeeds?"

"That loathing is not dictated by Nature," the villain replied with feeling, "its one source is in the total lack of habit; does not the same hold true for certain foods? Although they are excellent, is not our repugnance merely caused by our being unaccustomed to them? would you dare say, upon the basis of your prejudices or ignorance, that they are good or bad? If we make the effort, we will soon become convinced and will find they suit our palate; we have a hostility toward medicaments, do we not, although they are salutary; in the same fashion, let us accustom ourselves to evil and it will not be long before we find it charming; this momentary revulsion is certainly a shrewdness, a kind of coquetry on the part of Nature, rather than a warning that the thing outrages her: thus she prepares the pleasures of our triumph; she even manages thus to augment those of the deed itself: better still, Therese, better still: the more the deed seems appalling to us, the more it is in contradiction with our manners and customs, the more it runs headlong against restraints and shatters them, the more it conflicts with social conventions and affronts them, the more it clashes with what we mistake for

Nature's laws, then the more, on the contrary, it is useful to this same Nature. It is never but by way of crimes that she regains possession of the rights Virtue incessantly steals away from her. If the crime is slight, if it is at no great variance with Virtue, its weight will be less in re- establishing the balance indispensable to Nature; but the more capital the crime, the more deadly, the more it dresses the scales and the better it offsets the influence of Virtue which, without this, would destroy everything. Let him then cease to be in a fright, he who meditates a crime or he who has just committed one: the vaster his crime, the better it will serve Nature."

25

These frightful theories soon led me to think of Omphale's doubts upon the manner in which we left the terrible house we were in. And it was then I conceived the plans you will see me execute in the sequel. However, to complete my enlightenment I could not prevent myself from putting yet a few more questions to Father Clement.

"But surely," I said, "you do not keep your passions' unhappy victims forever; you surely send them away when you are wearied of them?"

"Certainly, Therese," the monk replied; "you only entered this establishment in order to leave it when the four of us agree to grant your retirement. Which will most certainly be granted."

"But do you not fear," I continued, "lest the younger and less discreet girls sometimes go and reveal what is done here?"

"'Tis impossible."

"Impossible?"

"Absolutely."

"Could you explain..."

"No, that's our secret, but I can assure you of this much: that whether you are discreet or indiscreet, you will find it perfectly impossible ever to say a word about what is done here when you are here no longer. And thus you see, Therese, I recommend no discretion to you, just as my own desires are governed by no restraining policy . . . ."

And, having utter'd these words, the monk fell asleep. From that moment onward, I could no longer avoid realizing that the most violent measures were used with those unhappy ones of us who were retrenched and that this terrible security they boasted of was only the fruit of our death. I was only the more confirmed in my resolve; we will soon see its effect.

As soon as Clement was asleep, Armande came near to me.

"He will awake shortly," she said; "he will behave like a madman: Nature only puts his senses to sleep in order to give them, after a little rest, a much greater energy; one more scene and we will have peace until tomorrow."

"But you," I said to my companion, "aren't you going to sleep a little while?"

"How can I?" Armande replied, "when, were I not to remain awake and standing by his side, and were my negligence to be perceived, he would be the man to stab me to death."

"O Heaven!" I sighed, "why! even as he sleeps the villain would that those around him remain in a state of suffering !"

"Yes," my companion responded, "it is the very barbarity of the idea which procures the furious awakening you are going to witness; upon this he is like unto those perverse writers whose corruption is so dangerous, so active, that their single aim is, by causing their appalling doctrines to be printed, to immortalize the sum of their crimes after their own lives are at an end; they themselves can do no more, but their accursed writings will instigate the commission of crimes, and they carry this sweet idea with them to their graves: it comforts them for the obligation, enjoined by death, to relinquish the doing of evil."

"The monsters!" I cried . . . .

Armande, who was a very gentle creature, kissed me as she shed a few tears, then went back to pacing about the roue's bed.

Two hours passed and then the monk did indeed awake in a prodigious agitation and seized me with such force I thought he was going to strangle me; his respiration was quick and labored, his eyes glittered, he uttered incoherent words which were exclusively blasphemous or libertine expressions; he summoned Armande, called for whips, and started in again with his flogging of us both, but in a yet more vigorous manner than before having gone to sleep. It seemed as if he wished to end matters with me; shrill cries burst from his mouth; to abridge my sufferings, Armande excited him violently, he lost his head entirely, and finally made rigid by the most violent sensations, the monster lost both his ardor and his desires together with smoking floods of semen.

Nothing transpired during the rest of the night; upon getting up, the monk was content to touch and examine each of us; and as he was going to say Mass, we returned to the seraglio. The superintendent could not be prevented from desiring me in. the inflamed state she swore I must be in; exhausted I indeed was and, thus weakened, how could I defend myself? She did all she wished, enough to convince me that even a woman, in such a school, soon losing all the delicacy and restraint native to her sex, could only, after those tyrants' example, become obscene and cruel.

Two nights later, I slept with Jerome; I will not describe his horrors to you; they were still more terrifying. What an academy, great God! by week's end I had finally made the circuit, and then Omphale asked me whether it were not true that of them all, Clement was the one about whom I had the most to complain.

"Alas!" was my response, "in the midst of a crowd of horrors and messes of filth which now disgust and now revolt, it is very difficult to pronounce upon these villains' individual odiousness; I am mortally weary of them all and would that I were gone from here, whatever be the fate that awaits me."

"It might be possible that you will soon be satisfied," my companion answered; "we are nearing the period of the festival: this circumstance rarely takes place without bringing them victims; they either seduce girls by means of the confessional, or, if they can, they cause them to disappear: which means so many new recruits, each of whom always supposes a retrenchment."

The famous holiday arrived... will you be able to believe, Madame, what monstrous impieties the monks were guilty of during this event! They fancied a visible miracle would double the brilliance of their reputation; and so they dressed Florette, the youngest of the girls, in all the Virgin's attire and adornments; by means of concealed strings they tied her against the wall of the niche and ordered her to elevate her arms very suddenly and with compunction toward heaven simultaneously the host was raised. As the little creature was threatened with the cruelest chastising if she were to speak a single word or mismanage in her role, she carried it off marvelously well, and the fraud enjoyed all the success that could possibly have been expected. The people cried aloud the miracle, left rich offerings to the Virgin, and went home more convinced than ever of the efficacity of the celestial Mother's mercies. In order to increase their impiety, our libertines wanted to have Florette appear at the orgies that evening, dressed in the same costume that had attracted so many homages, and each one inflamed his odious desires to submit her, in this guise, to the irregularity of his caprices. Aroused by this initial crime, the sacrilegious ones go considerably further: they have the child stripped naked, they have her lie on her stomach upon a large table; they light candles, they place the image of our Saviour squarely upon the little girl's back and upon her buttocks they dare consummate the most redoubtable of our mysteries. I swooned away at this horrible spectacle, 'twas impossible to bear the sight. Severino, seeing me unconscious, says that, to bring me to heel, I must serve as the altar in my turn. I am seized; I am placed where Florette was lying; the sacrifice is consummated, and the host... that sacred symbol of our august Religion... Severino catches it up and thrusts it deep into the obscene locale of his sodomistic pleasures... crushes it with oaths and insults... ignominiously drives it further with the intensified blows of his monstrous dart and as he blasphemes, spurts, upon our Saviour's very Body, the impure floods of his lubricity's torrents . . . .

I was insensible when they drew me from his hands; I had to be carried to my room, where for a week I shed uninterrupted tears over the hideous crime for which, against my will, I had been employed. The memory still gnaws at my soul, I never think back upon that scene without shuddering . . . . In me, Religion is the effect of sentiment; all that offends or outrages it makes my very heart bleed.

The end of the month was close at hand when one morning toward nine Severino entered our chamber; he appeared greatly aroused; a certain crazed look hovered in his eyes; he examines us, one after the other, places us in his cherished attitude, and especially lingers over Omphale; for several minutes he stands, contemplating her in the posture she has assumed, he excites himself, mutters dully, secretly, kisses what is offered him, allows everyone to see he is in a state to consummate, and consummates nothing; next, he has her straighten up, casts upon her glances filled with rage and wickedness; then, swinging his foot, with all his strength he kicks her in the belly, she reels backward and falls six yards away.

"The company is retrenching you, whore," he says, "we are tired of you, be ready by this afternoon. I will come to fetch you myself." And he leaves.

When he is gone Omphale gets up and, weeping, casts herself into my arms.

"Ah!" she says, "by the infamy, by the cruelty of the preliminaries... can you still blind yourself as to what follows? Great God! what is to become of me?"

"Be easy," I say to the miserable girl, "I have made up my mind about everything; I only await the opportunity; it may perhaps present itself sooner than you think; I will divulge these horrors; if it is true the measures they take are as cruel as we have reason to believe, strive to obtain some delays, postpone it, and I will wrest you from their clutches."

In the event Omphale were to be released, she swore in the same way to aid me, and both of us fell to weeping. The day passed, nothing happened during it; at five o'clock Severino returned.

"Well," he asked Omphale, "are you ready?"

"Yes, Father," she answered between sobs, "permit me to embrace my friends."

" 'Tis useless," replied the monk; "we have no time for lachrymose scenes; they are waiting for us; come." Then she asked whether she were obliged to take her belongings with her.

"No," said the superior; "does not everything belong to the house? You have no further need of any of it"; then, checking himself, as might one who has said too much:

"Those old clothes have become useless; you will have some cut to fit your size, they will be more becoming to you; be content to take along only what you are wearing."

I asked the monk whether I might be allowed to accompany Omphale to the door of the house; his reply was a glance that made me recoil in terror . . . . Omphale goes out, she turns toward us eyes filled with uneasiness and tears, and the minute she is gone I fling myself down upon the bed, desperate.

26

Accustomed to these occurrences or blind to their significance, my companions were less affected by Omphale's departure than I; the superior returned an hour later to lead away the supper's girls of whom I was one Ä we were only four: the girl of twelve, she of sixteen, she of twenty-three, and me. Everything went more or less as upon other days; I only noticed that the Girls of the Watch were not on hand, that the monks often whispered in each other's ears, that they drank much, that they limited themselves violently to exciting desires they did not once consummate, and that they sent us away at an early hour without retaining any of us for their own beds . . . . I deduced what I could from what I observed, because, under such circumstances, one keeps a sharp eye upon everything, but what did this evidence augur? Ah, such was my perplexity that no clear idea presented itself to my mind but it was not immediately offset by another; recollecting Clement's words, I felt there was everything to fear... of course; but then, hope... that treacherous hope which comforts us, which blinds us, and which thus does us almost as much ill as good... hope finally surged up to reassure me . . . . Such a quantity of horrors were so alien to me that I was simply unable to conceive of them. In this terrible state of confusion, I lay down in bed; now I was persuaded Omphale would not fail to keep her word; and the next instant I was convinced the cruel devices they would use against her would deprive her of all power to help us, and that was my final opinion when I saw an end come to the third day of having heard nothing at all.

Upon the fourth I found myself again called to supper; the company was numerous and select: the eight most beautiful women were there that evening, I had been paid the honor of being included amongst them; the Girls of the Watch attended too. Immediately we entered we caught sight of our new companion.

"Here is the young lady the corporation has destined to replace Omphale, Mesdemoiselles," said Severino.

And as the words escaped his lips he tore away the mantlets and lawn which covered the girl's bust, and we beheld a maiden of fifteen, with the most agreeable and delicate face: she raised her lovely eyes and graciously regarded each of us; those eyes were still moist with tears, but they contained the liveliest expression; her figure was supple and light, her skin of a dazzling whiteness, she had the world's most beautiful hair, and there was something so seductive about the whole that it was impossible not to feel oneself automatically drawn to her. Her name was Octavie; we were soon informed she was a girl of the highest quality, born in Paris, and had just emerged from a convent in order to wed the Comte de_____: she had been kidnaped while en route in the company of two governesses and three lackeys; she did not know what had become of her retinue; it had been toward nightfall and she alone had been taken; after having been blindfolded, she had been brought to where we were and it had not been possible to know more of the matter.

As yet no one had spoken a word to her. Our libertine quartet, confronted by so much charm, knew an instant of ecstasy; they had only the strength to admire her. Beauty's dominion commands respect; despite his heartlessness, the most corrupt villain must bow before it or else suffer the stings of an obscure remorse; but monsters of the breed with which we had to cope do not long languish under such restraints.

"Come, pretty child," quoth the superior, impudently drawing her toward the chair in which he was settled, "come hither and let's have a look to see whether the rest of your charms match those Nature has so profusely distributed in your countenance."

And as the lovely girl was sore troubled, as she flushed crimson and strove to fend him off, Severino grasped her rudely round the waist.

"Understand, my artless one," he said, "understand that what I want to tell you is simply this: get undressed. Strip. Instantly."

And thereupon the libertine slid one hand beneath her skirts while he grasped her with the other. Clement approached, he raised Octavie's clothes to above her waist and by this maneuver exposed the softest, the most appetizing features it is possible anywhere to find; Severino touches, perceives nothing, bends to scrutinize more narrowly, and all four agree they have never seen anything as beautiful. However, the modest Octavie, little accustomed to usage of this sort, gushes tears, and struggles.

"Undress, undress," cries Antonin, "we can't see a thing this way."

He assists Severino and in a trice we have displayed to us all the maiden's unadorned charms. Never, without any doubt, was there a fairer skin, never were there more happily modeled forms . . . . God! the crime of it!... So many beauties, such chaste freshness, so much innocence and daintiness Ä all to become prey to these barbarians! Covered with shame, Octavie knows not where to fly to hide her charms, she finds naught but hungering eyes everywhere about, nothing but brutal hands which sully those treasures; the circle closes around her, and, as did I, she rushes hither and thither; the savage Antonin lacks the strength to resist; a cruel attack determines the homage, and the incense smokes at the goddess' feet. Jerome compares her to our young colleague of sixteen, doubtless the seraglio's prettiest; he places the two altars of his devotion one next to the other.

"Ha! what whiteness! what grace!" says he as he fingers Octavie, "but what gentility and freshness may be discerned in this other one: indeed," continues the monk all afire, "I am uncertain"; then imprinting his mouth upon the charms his eyes behold, "Octavie," he cries, "to you the apple, it belongs to none but you, give me the precious fruit of this tree my heart adores . . . . Ah, yes! yes! one of you, give it me, and I will forever assure beauty's prize to who serves me sooner."

Severino observes the time has come to meditate on more serious matters; absolutely in no condition to be kept waiting, he lays hands upon the unlucky child, places her as he desires her to be; not yet being able to have full confidence in Octavie's aid, he calls for Clement to lend him a hand. Octavie weeps and weeps unheeded; fire gleams in the impudicious monk's glance; master of the terrain, one might say he casts about a roving eye only to consider the avenues whereby he may launch the fiercest assault; no ruses, no preparations are employed; will he be able to gather these so charming roses? will he be able to battle past the thorns? Whatever the enormous disproportion between the conquest and the assailant, the latter is not the less in a sweat to give fight; a piercing cry announces victory, but nothing mollifies the enemy's chilly heart; the more the captive implores mercy, the less quarter is granted her, the more vigorously she is pressed; the ill-starred one fences in vain: she is soon transpierced.

"Never was laurel with greater difficulty won," says Severino, retreating, "I thought indeed that for the first time in my life I would fall before the gate... ah! 'twas never so narrow, that way, nor so hot; 'tis the God's own Ganymede."

"I had better bring her round to the sex you have just soiled," cries Antonin, seizing Octavie where she is, and not wishing to let her stand up; "there's more than one breach to a rampart," says he, and proudly, boldly marching up, he carries the day and is within the sanctuary in no time at all. Further screams are heard.

"Praise be to God," quoth the indecent man, "I thought I was alone; and would have doubted of my success without a groan or two from the victim; but my triumph is sealed. Do you observe? Blood and tears."

"In truth," says Clement, who steps up with whip in hand, "I'll not disturb her sweet posture either, it is too favorable to my desires." Jerome's Girl of the Watch and the twenty-year-old girl hold Octavie: Clement considers, fingers; terrified, the little girl beseeches him, and is not listened to.

"Ah, my friends!" says the exalted monk, "how are we to avoid flogging a schoolgirl who exhibits an ass of such splendor !"

The air immediately resounds to the whistle of lashes and the thud of stripes sinking into lovely flesh; Octavie's screams mingle with the sounds of leather, the monk's curses reply: what a scene for these libertines surrendering themselves to a thousand obscenities in the midst of us all I They applaud him, they cheer him on; however, Octavie's skin changes color, the brightest tints incarnadine join the lily sparkle; but what might perhaps divert Love for an instant, were moderation to have direction of the sacrifice, becomes, thanks to severity, a frightful crime against Love's laws; nothing stops or slows the perfidious monk, the more the young student complains, the more the professor's harshness explodes; from the back to the knee, everything is treated in the same way, and it is at last upon his barbaric pleasures' blood-drenched vestiges the savage quenches his flames.

"I shall be less impolite, I think," says Jerome, laying hands upon the lovely thing and adjusting himself between her coral lips; "where is the temple where I would sacrifice? Why, in this enchanting mouth . . . ."

I fall silent . . . . 'Tis the impure reptile withering the rose Ä my figure of speech relates it all.

The rest of the soiree would have resembled all the others had it not been for the beauty and the touching age of this young maiden who more than usually inflamed those villains and caused them to multiply their infamies; it was satiety rather than commiseration that sent the unhappy child back to her room and gave her, for a few hours at least, the rest and quiet she needed.

I should indeed have liked to have been able to comfort her that first night, but, obliged to spend it with Severino, it may well have been I on the contrary who stood in the greater need of help, for I had the misfortune, no, not to please, the word would not be suitable, no, but in a most lively manner to excite that sodomite's infamous passions; at this period he desired me almost every night; being exhausted on this particular one, he conducted some researches; doubtless afraid the appalling sword with which he was endowed would not cause me an adequate amount of pain, he fancied, this time, he might perforate me with one of those articles of furniture usually found in nunneries, which decency forbids me from naming and which was of an exorbitant thickness; here, one was obliged to be ready for anything. He himself made the weapon penetrate into his beloved shrine; thanks to powerful blows, it was driven very deep; I screamed; the monk was amused, after a few backward and forward passes, he suddenly snapped the instrument free and plunged his own into the gulf he had just dug open... what whimsy! Is that not positively the contrary of everything men are able to desire! But who can define the spirit of libertinage? For a long time we have realized this to be an enigma of Nature; she has not yet pronounced the magic word.

In the morning, feeling somewhat renewed, he wanted to try out another torture: he produced a far more massy machine: this one was hollow and fitted with a high-pressure pump that squirted an incredibly powerful stream of water through an orifice which gave the jet a circumference of over three inches; the enormous instrument itself was nine inches around by twelve long. Severino loaded it with steaming hot water and prepared to bury it in my front end; terrified by such a project, I throw myself at his knees to ask for mercy, but he is in one of those accursed situations where pity cannot be heard, where far more eloquent passions stifle it and substitute an often exceedingly dangerous cruelty. The monk threatens me with all his rage if I do not acquiesce; I have to obey. The perfidious machine penetrates to the two-thirds mark and the tearing it causes combined with its extreme heat are about to deprive me of the use of my senses; meanwhile, the superior, showering an uninterrupted stream of invectives upon the parts he is molesting, has himself excited by his follower; after fifteen minutes of rubbing which lacerates me, he releases the spring, a quart of nearly boiling water is fired into the last depths of my womb... I fall into a faint. Severino was in an ecstasy... he was in a delirium at least the equal of my agony.

"Why," said the traitor, "that's nothing at all. When I recover my wits, we'll treat those charms much more harshly... a salad of thorns, by Jesus! well peppered, a copious admixture of vinegar, all that tamped in with the point of a knife, that's what they need to buck them up; the next mistake you make, I condemn you to the treatment," said the villain while he continued to handle the object of his worship; but two or three homages after the preceeding night's debauches had near worked him to death, and I was sent packing.

Upon returning to my chamber I found my new companion in tears; I did what I could to soothe her, but it is not easy to adjust to so frightful a change of situation; this girl had, furthermore, a great fund of religious feeling, of virtue, and of sensitivity; owing to it, her state only appeared to her the more terrible. Omphale had been right when she told me seniority in no way influenced retirement; that, simply by the monks' caprice, or by their fear of ulterior inquiries, one could undergo dismissal at the end of a week as easily as at the end of twenty years. Octavie had not been with us four months when Jerome came to announce her departure; although 'twas he who had most enjoyed her during her sojourn at the monastery, he who had seemed to cherish her and seek her more than any other, the poor child left, making us the same promises Omphale had given; she kept them just as poorly.

From that moment on, my every thought was bent upon the plan I had been devising since Omphale's departure; determined to do everything possible to escape from this den of savages, nothing that might help me succeed held any terrors for me. What was there to dread by putting my scheme into execution? Death. And were I to remain, of what could I be certain? Of death. And successful flight would save me; there could be no hesitation for there was no alternative; but it were necessary that, before I launched my enterprise, fatal examples of vice rewarded be yet again reproduced before my eyes; it was inscribed in the great book of fate, in that obscure tome whereof no mortal has intelligence, 'twas set down there, I say, that upon all those who had tormented me, humiliated me, bound me in iron chains, there were to be heaped unceasing bounties and rewards for what they had done with regard to me, as if Providence had assumed the task of demonstrating to me the inutility of virtue . . . . Baleful lessons which however did not correct me, no, I wavered not; lessons which, should I once again escape from the blade poised above my head, will not prevent me from forever remaining the slave of my heart's Divinity.

27

One morning, quite unexpectedly, Antonin appeared in our chamber and announced that the Reverend Father Severino, allied to the Pope and his protege, had just been named General of the Benedictine Order by His Holiness. The next day that monk did in effect depart, without taking his leave of us; 'twas said another was expected to replace him, and he would be far superior in debauch to all who remained; additional reasons to hasten ahead with my plans.

The day following Severino's departure, the monks decided to retrench one more of my companions; I chose for my escape the very day when sentence was pronounced against the wretched girl, so that the monks, preoccupied with her, would pay less attention to me.

It was the beginning of spring; the length of the nights still somewhat favored my designs: for two months I had been preparing them, they were completely unsuspected; little by little I sawed through the bars over my window, using a dull pair of scissors I had found; my head could already pass through the hole; with sheets and linen I had made a cord of more than sufficient length to carry me down the twenty or twenty-five feet Omphale had told me was the building's height. When they had taken my old belongings, I had been careful, as I told you, to remove my little fortune which came to about six louis, and these I had always kept hidden with extreme caution; as I left, I put them into my hair, and nearly all of our chamber having left for that night's supper, finding no one about but one of my companions who had gone to bed as soon as the others had descended, I entered my cabinet; there, clearing the hole I had scrupulously kept covered at all times, I knotted my cord to one of the undamaged bars, then, sliding down outside, I soon touched the ground Ä 'twas not this part which troubled me: the six enclosures of stone and trees my companion had mentioned were what intrigued me far more.

Once there, I discovered that each concentric space between one barrier and the next was no more than eight feet wide, and it was this proximity which assured a casual glance that there was nothing in the area but a dense cluster of trees. The night was very dark; as I turned round the first alley to discover where I might not find a gap in the palisade, I passed beneath the dining hall, which seemed deserted; my inquietude increased; however, I continued my search and thus at last came abreast the window to the main underground room, located directly below that in which the orgies were staged. Much light flooded from the basement, I was bold enough to approach the window and had a perfect view of the interior. My poor companion was stretched out upon a trestle table, her hair in disarray; she was doubtless destined for some terrible torture by which she was going to find freedom, the eternal end of her miseries . . . . I shuddered, but what my glances fell upon soon astonished me more: Omphale had either not known everything, or had not told all she knew; I spied four naked girls in the basement, and they certainly did not belong to our group; and so there were other victims of these monsters' lechery in this horrible asylum... other wretches unknown to us . . . . I fled away and continued my circuit until I was on the side opposite the basement window; not yet having found a breach, I resolved to make one; all unobserved, I had furnished myself with a long knife; I set to work; despite my gloves, my hands were soon scratched and torn; but nothing daunted me; the hedge was two feet thick, I opened a passage, went through, and entered the second ring; there, I was surprised to find nothing but soft earth underfoot; with each step I sank in ankle-deep: the further I advanced into these copses, the more profound the darkness became. Curious to know whence came the change of terrain, I felt about with my hands... O Just Heaven! my fingers seized the head of a cadaver! Great God! I thought, whelmed with horror, this must then be the cemetery, as indeed I was told, into which those murderers fling their victims; they have scarcely gone to the bother of covering them with earth!... this skull perhaps belongs to my dear Omphale, perhaps it is that of the unhappy Octavie, so lovely, so sweet, so good, and who while she lived was like unto the rose of which her charms were the image. And I, alas! might that this have been my resting place! Wouldst that I had submitted to my fate! What had I to gain by going on in pursuit of new pitfalls? Had I not committed evil enough? Had I not been the occasion of a number of crimes sufficiently vast? Ah! fulfill my destiny!

O Earth, gape wide and swallow me up I Ah, 'tis madness, when one is so forsaken, so poor, so utterly abandoned, madness to go to such pains in order to vegetate yet a few more instants amongst monsters!... But no! I must avenge Virtue in irons . . . . She expects it of my courage . . . . Let her not be struck down... let us advance: it is essential that the universe be ridded of villains as dangerous as these. Ought I fear causing the doom of three or four men in order to save the millions of individuals their policy or their ferocity sacrifice?

And therewith I pierce the next hedge; this one was thicker than the first: the further I progressed, the stouter they became. The hole was made, however, but there was firm ground beyond... nothing more betrayed the same horrors I had just encountered; and thus I arrived at the brink of the moat without having met with the wall Omphale had spoken of; indeed, there turned out to be none at all, and it is likely that the monks mentioned it merely to add to our fear. Less shut in when beyond the sextuple enclosure, I was better able to distinguish objects: my eyes at once beheld the church and the bulk of the adjacent building; the moat bordered each of them; I was careful not to attempt to cross it at this point; I moved along the edge and finally discovering myself opposite one of the forest roads, I resolved to make my crossing there and to dash down that road as soon as I had climbed up the other side of the ditch; it was very deep but, to my good fortune, dry and lined with brick, which eliminated all possibilities of slipping; then leapt: a little dazed by my fall, it was a few moments before I got to my feet... I went ahead, got to the further side without meeting any obstacle, but how was I to climb it! I spent some time seeking a means and at last found one where several broken bricks at once gave me the opportunity to use the others as steps and to dig foot-holds in order to mount; I had almost reached the top.when something gave way beneath my weight and I fell back into the moat under the debris I dragged with me; I thought myself dead; this involuntary fall had been more severe than the other; I was, as well, entirely covered with the material which had followed me; some had struck my head... it was cut and bleeding. O God! I cried out in despair, go no further; stay there; 'tis a warning sent from Heaven; God does not want me to go on: perhaps I am deceived in my ideas, perhaps evil is useful on earth, and when God's hand desires it, perhaps it is a sin to resist it! But, soon revolted by that doctrine, the too wretched fruit of the corruption which had surrounded me, I extricated myself from the pile of rubble on top of me and finding it easier to climb by the breach I had just made, for now there were new holes, I try once again, I take courage, a moment later I find myself at the crest. Because of all this I had strayed away from the path I had seen, but having taken careful note of its position, I found it again, and began to run. Before day-break I reached the forest's edge and was soon upon that little hill from which, six long months before, I had, to my sorrow, espied that frightful monastery; I rest a few minutes, I am bathed in perspiration; my first thought is to fall upon my knees and beg God to forgive the sins I unwillingly committed in that odious asylum of crime and impurity; tears of regret soon flowed from my eyes. Alas! I said, I was far less a criminal when last year I left this same road, guided by a devout principle so fatally deceived! O God! In what state may I now behold myself! These lugubrious reflections were in some wise mitigated by the pleasure of discovering I was free; I continued along the road toward Dijon, supposing it would only be in that capital my complaints could be legitimately lodged . . . .

At this point Madame de Lorsange persuaded Therese to catch her breath for a few minutes at least; she needed the rest; the emotion she put into her narrative, the wounds these dreadful recitals reopened in her soul, everything, in short, obliged her to resort to a brief respite. Monsieur de Corville had refreshments brought in, and after collecting her forces, our heroine set out again to pursue her deplorable adventures in great detail, as you shall see.

By the second day all my initial fears of pursuit had dissipated; the weather was extremely warm and, following my thrifty habit, I left the road to find a sheltered place where I could eat a light meal that would fortify me till evening. Off the road to the right stood a little grove of trees through which wound a limpid stream; this seemed a good spot for my lunch. My thirst quenched by this pure cool water, nourished by a little bread, my back leaning against a tree trunk, I breathed deep draughts of clear, serene air which relaxed me and was soothing. Resting there, my thoughts dwelled upon the almost unexampled fatality which, despite the thorns strewn thick along the career of Virtue, repeatedly brought me back, whatever might happen, to the worship of that Divinity and to acts of love and resignation toward the Supreme Being from Whom Virtue emanates and of Whom it is the image. A kind of enthusiasm came and took possession of me; alas! I said to myself, He abandons me not, this God I adore, for even at this instant I find the means to recover my strength. Is it not to Him I owe this merciful favor? And are there not persons in the world to whom it is refused? I am then not completely unfortunate because there are some who have more to complain of than I . . . . Ah! am I not much less so than the unlucky ones I left in that den of iniquity and vice from which God's kindness caused me to emerge as if by some sort of miracle?... And full of gratitude I threw myself upon my knees, raised my eyes, and fixing the sun, for it seemed to me the Divinity's most splendid achievement, the one which best manifests His greatness, I was drawing from that Star's sublimity new motives for prayer and good works when all of a sudden I felt myself seized by two men who, having cast something over my head to prevent me from seeing and crying out, bound me like a criminal and dragged me away without uttering a word.

And thus had we walked for nearly two hours during which I knew not whither my escorts were taking me when one of them, hearing me gasp for air, proposed to his comrade that I be freed of the sack covering my head; he agreed, I drank in fresh air and observed that we were in the midst of a forest through which we were traveling along a fairly broad although little frequented road. A thousand dark ideas rushed straightway into my mind. I feared I was being led back to their odious monastery.

"Ah," I say to one of my guides, "ah Monsieur, will you tell me where I am being conducted? May I not ask what you intend to do with me?"

"Be at ease, my child," the man replied, "and do not let the precautions we are obliged to take cause you any fright; we are leading you to a good master; weighty considerations engage him to procure a maid for his wife by means of this mysterious process, but never fear, you will find yourself well off."

"Alas! Messieurs," I answered, "if 'tis my welfare for which you labor it is to no purpose I am constrained; I am a poor orphan, no doubt much to be commiserated; I ask for nothing but a place and since you are giving me one, I have no cause to run away, do I?"

"She's right," said one of my escorts, "let's make her more comfortable; untie everything but her hands."

They do so and we resume our march. Seeing me calmed, they even respond to my questions, and I finally learn that I am destined to have for master one Comte de Gernande, a native of Paris, but owning considerable property in this country and rich to the tune of five hundred thousand pounds a year, all of which he consumes alone Ä so said one of my guides.

"Alone?"

"Yes, he is a solitary man, a philosopher: he never sees a soul; but on the other hand he is one of Europe's greatest epicures; there is not an eater in all the world who can hold a candle to him. But I'll say no more about it; you'll see."

"But what do these cautious measures signify, Monsieur?"

"Well, simply this. Our master has the misfortune to have a wife who has become insane; a strict watch must be kept over her, she never leaves her room, no one wishes to be her servant; it would have done no good to propose the work to you, for had you been forewarned you'd never have accepted it. We are obliged to carry girls off by force in order to have someone to exercise this unpleasant function."

"What? I will be made this lady's captive?"

"Why, forsooth, yes, you will, and that's why we have you tied this way; but you'll get on... don't fret, you'll get on perfectly; apart from this annoyance, you'll lack nothing."

"Ah! Merciful Heaven! what thralldom!"

"Come, come, my child, courage, you'll get out of it someday and you'll have made your fortune."

28

My guide had no sooner finished speaking than we caught sight of the chateau. It was a superb and vast building isolated in the middle of the forest, but this great edifice which could have accommodated hundreds of persons, seemed to be inhabited hardly at all. I only noticed a few signs of life coming from kitchens situated in the vaults below the central part of the structure; all the rest was as deserted as the chateau's site was lonely. No one was there to greet us when we entered; one of my guides went off in the direction of the kitchens, the other presented me to the Count. He was at the far end of a spacious and superb apartment, his body enveloped in an oriental satin dressing gown, reclining upon an ottoman, and having hard by him two young men so indecently, or rather so ridiculously, costumed, their hair dressed with such elegance and skill, that at first I took them for girls; a closer inspection allowed me to recognize them for two youths, one of about fifteen, the other perhaps sixteen. Their faces struck me as charming, but in such a state of dissipated softness and weariness, that at the outset I thought they were ill.

"My Lord, here is a girl," said my guide, "she seems to us to be what might suit you: she is properly bred and gentle and asks only to find a situation; we hope you will be content with her."

" 'Tis well," the Count said with scarcely a glance in my direction; "you, Saint-Louis, will close the doors when you go out and you will say that no one is to enter unless I ring."

Then the Count rose to his feet and came up to examine me. While he makes a detailed investigation I can describe him to you: the portrait's singularity merits an instant's attention. Monsieur de Gernande was at that time a man of fifty, almost six feet tall and monstrously fat. Nothing could be more terrifying than his face, the length of his nose, his wicked black eyes, his large ill-furnished mouth, his formidable high forehead, the sound of his fearful raucous voice, his enormous hands; all combined to make a gigantic individual whose presence inspired much more fear than reassurance. We will soon be able to decide whether the morals and actions of this species of centaur were in keeping with his awesome looks. After the most abrupt and cavalier scrutiny, the Count demanded to Know my age.

"I am twenty-three, Monsieur," I replied.

And to this first question he added some others of a personal nature. I made him privy to everything that concerned me; I did not even omit the brand I had received from Rodin, and when I had represented my misery to him, when I had proven to him that unhappiness had constantly dogged my footsteps:

"So much the better," the dreadful man replied, "so much the better, it will have made you more pliable Ä adaptability counts heavily toward success in this household Ä I see nothing to regret in the wretchedness that hounds an abject race of plebeians Nature has doomed to grovel at our feet throughout the period allotted them to live on the same earth as we. Your sort is more energetic and less insolent, the pressures of adversity help you fulfill your duties toward us."

"But, Monsieur, I told you that I am not of mean birth."

"Yes, yes, I have heard that before, they always pass themselves off for all kinds of things when in fact they are nothing or miserable. Oh indeed, pride's illusions are of the highest usefulness to console fortune's ills, and then, you see, it is up to us to believe what we please about these lofty estates beaten down by the blows of destiny. Pish, d'ye know, it's all the same to me if you fancy yourself a princess. To my consideration you have the look and more or less the costume of a servant, and as such you may enter my hire, if it suits you. However," the hard-hearted man continued, "your welfare, your happiness Ä they are your concern, they depend on your performance: a little patience, some discretion, and in a few years you will be sent forth in a way to avoid further service."

Then he took one after the other of my arms, rolled my sleeves to the elbows, and examined them attentively while asking me how many times I had been bled.

"Twice, Monsieur," I told him, rather surprised at the question, and I mentioned when and under what circumstances it had happened. He pressed his fingers against the veins as one does when one wishes to inflate them, and when they were swollen to the desired point, he fastened his lips to them and sucked. From that instant I ceased to doubt libertinage was involved in this dreadful person's habits, and tormenting anxieties were awakened in my heart.

"I have got to know how you are made," continued the Count, staring at me in a way that set me to trembling; "the post you are to occupy precludes any corporeal defects; show me what you have about you."

I recoiled; but the Count, all his facial muscles beginning to twitch with anger, brutally informed me that I should be ill-advised to play the prude with him, for, said he, there are infallible methods of bringing women to their senses.

"What you have related to me does not betoken a virtue of the highest order; and so your resistance would be quite as misplaced as ludicrous."

Whereupon he made a sign to his young boys who, approaching immediately, fell to undressing me. Against persons as enfeebled, as enervated as those who surrounded me, it is certainly not difficult to defend oneself; but what good would it have done? The cannibal who had cast me into their hands could have pulverized me, had he wished to, with one blow of his fist. I therefore understood I had to yield: an instant later I was unclothed; 'twas scarcely done when I perceived I was exciting those two Ganymedes to gales of laughter.

"Look ye, friend," said the younger, "a girl's a pretty thing, eh? But what a shame there's that cavity there."

"Oh!" cried the other, "nothing nastier than that hole, I'd not touch a woman even were my fortune at stake."

And while my fore end was the subject of their sarcasms, the Count, an intimate partisan of the behind (unhappily, alas! like every libertine), examined mine with the keenest interest: he handled it brutally, he browsed about with avidity; taking handfuls of flesh between his fingers, he rubbed and kneaded them to the point of drawing blood. Then he made me walk away from him, halt, walk backward in his direction, keeping my behind turned toward him while he dwelled upon the sight of it. When I had returned to him, he made me bend, stoop, squat, stand erect, squeeze and spread. Now and again he slipped to his knees before that part which was his sole concern. He applied kisses to several different areas of it, even a few upon that most secret orifice; but all his kisses were distinguished by suction, his lips felt like leeches. While he was applying them here and there and everywhere he solicited numerous details concerning what had been done to me at the monastery of Saint Mary-in-the-Wood, and without noticing that my recitations doubled his warmth, I was candid enough to give them all with naivete. He summoned up one of his youths and placing him beside me, he untied the bow securing a great red ribbon which gathered in white gauze pantaloons, and brought to light all the charms this garment concealed. After some deft caresses bestowed upon the same altar at which, in me, the Count had signaled his devotion, he suddenly exchanged the object and fell to sucking that part which characterized the child's sex. He continued to finger me: whether because of habit in the youth, whether because of the satyr's dexterity, in a very brief space Nature, vanquished, caused there to flow into the mouth of the one what was ejected from the member of the other. That was how the libertine exhausted the unfortunate children he kept in his house, whose number we will shortly see; 'twas thus he sapped their strength, and that was what caused the languor in which I beheld them to be. And now let us see how he managed to keep women in the same state of prostration and what was the true cause of his own vigor's preservation.

The homage the Count rendered me had been protracted, but during it not a trace of infidelity to his chosen temple had he revealed; neither his glances, nor his kisses, nor his hands, nor his desires strayed away from it for an instant; after having sucked the other lad and having in likewise gathered and devoured his sperm:

"Come," he said to me, drawing me into an adjacent room before I could gather up my clothes, "come, I am going to show you how we manage."

I was unable to dissimulate my anxiety, it was terrible; but there was no other way to put a different aspect upon my fate, I had to quaff to the lees the potion in the chalice tendered to me.

Two other boys of sixteen, quite as handsome, quite as peaked as the first two we had left in the salon, were working upon a tapestry when we entered the room. Upon our entrance they rose.

"Narcisse," said the Count to one of them, "here is the Countess' new chambermaid; I must test her; hand me the lancets."

Narcisse opens a cupboard and immediately produces all a surgeon's gear. I allow your imagination to fancy my state; my executioner spied my embarrassment, and it merely excited his mirth.

"Put her in place, Zephire," Monsieur de Gernande said to another of the youths, and this boy approached me with a smile.

"Don't be afraid, Mademoiselle," said he, "it can only do you the greatest good. Take your place here."

It was a question of kneeling lightly upon the edge of a tabouret located in the middle of the room; one's arms were elevated and attached to two black straps which descended from the ceiling.

No sooner have I assumed the posture than the Count steps up scalpel in hand: he can scarcely breathe, his eyes are alive with sparks, his face smites me with terror; he ties bands about both my arms, and in a flash he has lanced each of them. A cry bursts from between his teeth, it is accompanied by two or three blasphemies when he catches sight of my blood; he retires to a distance of six feet and sits down. The light garment covering him is soon deployed; Zephire kneels between his thighs and sucks him; Narcisse, his feet planted on his master's armchair, presents the same object to him to suckle he is himself having drained by Zephire. Gernande gets his hands upon the boy's loins, squeezes them, presses them to him, but quits them long enough to cast his inflamed eyes toward me. My blood is escaping in floods and is falling into two white basins situated underneath my arms. I soon feel myself growing faint.

"Monsieur, Monsieur," I cry, "have pity on me, I am about to collapse." I sway, totter, am held up by the straps, am unable to fall; but my arms having shifted, and my head slumping upon my shoulder, my face is now washed with blood. The Count is drunk with joy... however, I see nothing like the end of his operation approaching, I swoon before he reaches his goal; he was perhaps only able to attain it upon seeing me in this state, perhaps his supreme ecstasy depended upon this morbid picture . . . . At any rate, when I returned to my senses I found myself in an excellent bed, with two old women standing near me; as soon as they saw me open my eyes, they brought me a cup of bouillon and, at three-hour intervals, rich broths; this continued for two days, at the end of which Monsieur de Gernande sent to have me get up and come for a conversation in the same salon where I had been received upon my arrival. I was led to him; I was still a little weak and giddy, but otherwise well; I arrived.

"Therese," said the Count, bidding me be seated, "I shall not very often repeat such exercises with you, your person is useful for other purposes; but it was of the highest importance I acquaint you with my tastes and the manner in which you will expire in this house should you betray me one of these days, should you be unlucky enough to let yourself be suborned by the woman in whose society you are going to be placed.

"That woman belongs to me, Therese, she is my wife and that title is doubtless the most baleful she could have, since it obliges her to lend herself to the bizarre passion whereof you have been a recent victim; do not suppose it is vengeance that prompts me to treat her thus, scorn, or any sentiment of hostility or hatred; it is merely a question of passion. Nothing equals the pleasure I experience upon shedding her blood... I go mad when it flows; I have never enjoyed this woman in any other fashion. Three years have gone by since I married her, and for three years she has been regularly exposed every four days to the treatment you have undergone. Her youth (she is not yet twenty), the special care given her, all this keeps her aright; and as the reservoir is replenished at the same rate it is tapped, she has been in fairly good health since the regime began. Our relations being what they are, you perfectly well appreciate why I can neither allow her to go out nor to receive visitors. And so I represent her as insane and her mother, the only living member of her family, who resides in a chateau six leagues from here, is so firmly convinced of her derangement that she dares not even come to see her. Not infrequently the Countess implores my mercy, there is nothing she omits to do in order to soften me; but I doubt whether she shall ever succeed. My lust decreed her fate, it is immutable, she will go on in this fashion so long as she is able; while she lives she will want nothing and as I am incredibly fond of what can be drained from her living body, I will keep her alive as long as possible; when finally she can stand it no more, well, tush, Nature will take its course. She's my fourth; I'll soon have a fifth. Nothing disturbs me less than to lose a wife. There are so many women about, and it is so pleasant to change.

29

"In any event, Therese, your task is to look after her. Her blood is let once every ninety-six hours; she loses two bowls of it each time and nowadays no longer faints, having got accustomed to it. Her prostration lasts twenty-four hours; she is bedridden one day out of every four, but during the remaining three she gets on tolerably well. But you may easily understand this life displeases her; at the outset there was nothing she would not try to deliver herself from it, nothing she did not undertake to acquaint her mother with her real situation: she seduced two of her maid-servants whose maneuvers were detected early enough to defeat their success: she was the cause of these two unhappy creatures' ruin, today she repents what she did and, recognizing the irremediable character of her destiny, she is co-operating cheerfully and has promised not to make confederates of the help I hire to care for her. But this secret and what becomes of those who conspire to betray me, these matters, Therese, oblige me to put no one in her neighborhood but persons who, like yourself, have been impressed; and thus inquiries are avoided. Not having carried you off from anyone's house, not having to render an account of you to anyone at all, nothing stands in the way of my punishing you, if you deserve to be, in a manner which, although you will be deprived of mortal breath, cannot nevertheless expose me to interrogations or embroil me in any unpleasantnesses. As of the present moment you inhabit the world no longer, since the least impulse of my will can cause you to disappear from it. What can you expect at my hands? Happiness if you behave properly, death if you seek to play me false. Were these alternatives not so clear, were they not so few, I would ask for your response; but in your present situation we can dispense with questions and answers. I have you, Therese, and hence you must obey me . . . . Let us go to my wife's apartment."

Having nothing to object to a discourse as precise as this, I followed my master: we traversed a long gallery, as dark, as solitary as the rest of the chateau; a door opens, we enter an antechamber where I recognize the two elderly women who waited upon me during my coma and recovery. They got up and introduced us into a superb apartment where we found the unlucky Countess doing tambour brocade as she reclined upon a chaise longue; she rose when she saw her husband.

"Be seated," the Count said to her, "I permit you to listen to me thus. Here at last we have a maid for you, Madame," he continued, "and I trust you will remember what has befallen the others Ä and that you will not try to plunge this one into an identical misfortune."

"It would be useless," I said, full eager to be of help to this poor woman and wishing to disguise my designs, "yes, Madame, I dare certify in your presence that it would be to no purpose, you will not speak one word to me I shall not report immediately to his Lordship, and I shall certainly not jeopardize my life in order to serve you."

"I will undertake nothing, Mademoiselle, which might force you into that position," said this poor woman who did not yet grasp my motives for speaking in this wise; "rest assured: I solicit nothing but your care."

"It will be entirely yours, Madame," I answered, "but beyond that, nothing."

And the Count, enchanted with me, squeezed my hand as he whispered: "Nicely done, Therese, your prosperity is guaranteed if you conduct yourself as you say you will." The Count then showed me to my room which adjoined the Countess' and he showed me as well that the entirety of this apartment, closed by stout doors and double grilled at every window, left no hope of escape.

"And here you have a terrace," Monsieur de Gernande went on, leading me out into a little garden on a level with the apartment, "but its elevation above the ground ought not, I believe, give you the idea of measuring the walls; the Countess is permitted to take fresh air out here whenever she wishes, you will keep her company... adieu."

I returned to my mistress and, as at first we spent a few moments examining one another without speaking, I obtained a good picture of her Ä but let me paint it for you.

Madame de Gernande, aged nineteen and a half, had the most lovely, the most noble, the most majestic figure one could hope to see, not one of her gestures, not a single movement was without gracefulness, not one of her glances lacked depth of sentiment: nothing could equal the expression of her eyes, which were a beautiful dark brown although her hair was blond; but a certain languor, a lassitude entailed by her misfortunes, dimmed their e'clat, and thereby rendered them a thousand times more interesting; her skin was very fair, her hair very rich; her mouth was very small, perhaps too small, and I was little surprised to find this defect in her: 'twas a pretty rose not yet in full bloom; but teeth so white... lips of a vermillion... one might have said Love had colored them with tints borrowed from the goddess of flowers; her nose was aquiline, straight, delicately modeled;

upon her brow curved two ebony eyebrows; a perfectly lovely chin; a visage, in one word, of the finest oval shape, over whose entirety reigned a kind of attractiveness, a naivete, an openness which might well have made one take this adorable face for an angelic rather than mortal physiognomy. Her arms, her breasts, her flanks were of a splendor... of a round fullness fit to serve as models to an artist; a black silken fleece covered her mons veneris, which was sustained by two superbly cast thighs; and what astonished me was that, despite the slenderness of the Countess' figure, despite her sufferings, nothing had impaired the firm quality of her flesh: her round, plump buttocks were as smooth, as ripe, as firm as if her figure were heavier and as if she had always dwelled in the depths of happiness. However, frightful traces of her husband's libertinage were scattered thickly about; but, I repeat, nothing spoiled, nothing damaged... the very image of a beautiful lily upon which the honeybee has inflicted some scratches. To so many gifts Madame de Gernande added a gentle nature, a romantic and tender mind, a heart of such sensibility!... well-educated, with talents... a native art for seduction which no one but her infamous husband could resist, a charming timbre in her voice and much piety: such was the unhappy wife of the Comte de Gernande, such was the heavenly creature against whom he had plotted; it seemed that the more she inspired ideas, the more she inflamed his ferocity, and that the abundant gifts she had received from Nature only became further motives for that villain's cruelties.

"When were you last bled, Madame?" I asked in order to have her understand I was acquainted with everything.

"Three days ago," she said, "and it is to be tomorrow . . . ." Then, with a sigh: "... yes, tomorrow... Mademoiselle, tomorrow you will witness the pretty scene."

"And Madame is not growing weak?"

"Oh, Great Heaven! I am not twenty and am sure I shall be no weaker at seventy. But it will come to an end, I flatter myself in the belief, for it is perfectly impossible for me to live much longer this way: I will go to my Father, in the arms of the Supreme Being I will seek a place of rest men have so cruelly denied me on earth."

These words clove my heart; wishing to maintain my role, I disguised my trouble, but upon the instant I made an inward promise to lay down my life a thousand times, if necessary, rather than leave this ill-starred victim in the clutches of this monstrous debauchee.

The Countess was on the point of taking her dinner. The two old women came to tell me to conduct her into her cabinet; I transmitted the message; she was accustomed to it all, she went out at once, and the two women, aided by the two valets who had carried me off, served a sumptuous meal upon a table at which my place was set opposite my mistress. The valets retired and the women informed me that they would not stir from the antechamber so as to be near at hand to receive whatever might be Madame's orders. I relayed this to the Countess, she took her place and, with an air of friendliness and affability which entirely won my heart, invited me to join her. There were at least twenty dishes upon the table.

"With what regards this aspect of things, Mademoiselle, you see that they treat me well."

"Yes, Madame," I replied, "and I know it is the wish of Monsieur le Comte that you lack nothing." "Oh yes! But as these attentions are motivated only by cruelty, my feelings are scarcely of gratitude."

Her constant state of debilitation and perpetual need of what would revive her strength obliged Madame de Gernande to eat copiously. She desired partridge and Rouen duckling; they were brought to her in a trice. After the meal, she went for some air on the terrace, but upon rising she took my arm, for she was quite unable to take ten steps without someone to lean upon. It was at this moment she showed me all those parts of her body I have just described to you; she exhibited her arms: they were covered with small scars.

"Ah, he does not confine himself to that," she said, "there is not a single spot on my wretched person whence he does not love to see blood flow."

And she allowed me to see her feet, her neck, the lower part of her breasts and several other fleshy areas equally speckled with healed punctures. That first day I limited myself to murmuring a few sympathetic words and we retired for the night.

The morrow was the Countess' fatal day. Monsieur de Gernande, who only performed the operation after his dinner Ä which he always took before his wife ate hers Ä had me join him at table; it was then, Madame, I beheld that ogre fall to in a manner so terrifying that I could hardly believe my eyes. Four domestics, amongst them the pair who had led me to the chateau, served this amazing feast. It deserves a thorough description: I shall give it you without exaggeration. The meal was certainly not intended simply to overawe me. What I witnessed then was an everyday affair.

Two soups were brought on, one a consomme flavored with saffron, the other a ham bisque; then a sirloin of English roast beef, eight hors d'oeuvres, five substantial entrees, five others only apparently lighter, a boar's head in the midst of eight braised dishes which were relieved by two services of entremets, then sixteen plates of fruit; ices, six brands of wine, four varieties of liqueur and coffee. Monsieur de Gernande attacked every dish, and several were polished off to the last scrap; he drank a round dozen bottles of wine, four, to begin with, of Burgundy, four of Champagne with the roasts; Tokay, Mulseau, Hermitage and Madeira were downed with the fruit. He finished with two bottles of West Indies rum and ten cups of coffee.

As fresh after this performance as he might have been had he just waked from sleep, Monsieur de Gernande said:

"Off we go to bleed your mistress; I trust you will let me know if I manage as nicely with her as I did with you."

Two young boys I had not hitherto seen, and who were of the same age as the others, were awaiting at the door of the Countess' apartment; it was then the Count informed me he had twelve minions and renewed them every year. These seemed yet prettier than the ones I had seen hitherto; they were livelier... we went in . . . . All the ceremonies I am going to describe now, Madame, were part of a ritual from which the Count never deviated, they were scrupulously observed upon each occasion, and nothing ever changed except the place where the incisions were made.

The Countess, dressed only in a loose-floating muslin robe, fell to her knees instantly the Count entered.

"Are you ready?" her husband inquired.

"For everything, Monsieur," was the humble reply; "you know full well I am your victim and you have but to command me. '

Monsieur de Gernande thereupon told me to undress his wife and lead her to him. Whatever the loathing I sensed for all these horrors, you understand, Madame, I had no choice but to submit with the most entire resignation. In all I have still to tell you, do not, I beseech you, do not at any time regard me as anything but a slave; I complied simply because I could not do otherwise, but never did I act willingly in anything whatsoever.

I removed my mistress' simar, and when she was naked conducted her to her husband who had already taken his place in a large armchair: as part of the ritual she perched upon this armchair and herself presented to his kisses that favorite part over which he had made such a to-do with me and which, regardless of person or sex, seemed to affect him in the same way.

"And now spread them, Madame," the Count said brutally.

And for a long time he rollicked about with what he enjoyed the sight of; he had it assume various positions, he opened it, he snapped it shut; with tongue and fingertip he tickled the narrow aperture; and soon carried away by his passions' ferocity, he plucked up a pinch of flesh, squeezed it, scratched it. Immediately he produced a small wound he fastened his mouth to the spot. I held his unhappy victim during these preliminaries, the two boys, completely naked, toiled upon him in relays; now one, now the other knelt between Gernande's thighs and employed his mouth to excite him. It was then I noticed, not without astonishment, that this giant, this species of monster whose aspect alone was enough to strike terror, was howbeit barely a man; the most meager, the most minuscule excrescence of flesh or, to make a juster comparison, what one might find in a child of three was all one discovered upon this so very enormous and otherwise so corpulent individual; but its sensations were not for that the less keen and each pleasurable vibration was as a spasmodic attack. After this prologue he stretched out upon a couch and wanted his wife, seated astride his chest, to keep her behind poised over his visage while with her mouth she rendered him, by means of suckings, the same service he had just received from the youthful Ganymedes who were simultaneously, one to the left, one to the right, being excited by him; my hands meanwhile worked upon his behind: I titillated it, I polluted it in every sense; this phase of activities lasted more than a quarter of an hour but, producing no results, had to be given up for another; upon her husband's instructions I stretched the Countess upon a chaise longue: she lay on her back, her legs spread as wide as possible. The sight of what she exposed put her husband in a kind of rage, he dwelt upon the perspective... his eyes blaze, he curses; like one crazed he leaps upon his wife, with his scalpel pricks her in several places, but these were all superficial gashes, a drop or two of blood, no more, seeped from each. These minor cruelties came to an end at last; others began. The Count sits down again, he allows his wife a moment's respite, and, turning his attention to his two little followers, he now obliges them to suck each other, and now he arranges them in such a way that while he sucks one, the other sucks him, and now again the one he sucked first brings round his mouth to render the same service to him by whom he was sucked: the Count received much but gave little. Such was his satiety, such his impotence that the extremest efforts availed not at all, and he remained in his torpor: he did indeed seem to experience some very violent reverberations, but nothing manifested itself; he several times ordered me to suck his little friends and immediately to convey to his mouth whatever incense I drained from them; finally he flung them one after the other at the miserable Countess. These young men accosted her, insulted her, carried insolence to the point of beating her, slapping her, and the more they molested her, the more loudly the Count praised and egged them on.

30

Then Gernande turned to me; I was in front of him, my buttocks at the level of his face, and he paid his respects to his God; but he did not abuse me; nor do I know why he did not torment his Ganymedes; he chose to reserve all his unkindness for the Countess. Perhaps the honor of being allied to him established one's right to suffer mistreatment at his hands; perhaps he was moved to cruelty only by attachments which contributed energy to his outrages. One can imagine anything about such minds, and almost always safely wager that what seems most apt to be criminal is what will inflame them most. At last he places his young friends and me beside his wife and enlaces our bodies; here a man, there a woman, etc., all four dressing their behinds; he takes his stand some distance away and muses upon the panorama, then he comes near, touches, feels, compares, caresses; the youths and I were not persecuted, but each time he came to his wife, he fussed and bothered and vexed her in some way or other. Again the scene changes: he has the Countess lie belly down upon a divan and taking each boy in turn, he introduces each of them into the narrow avenue Madame's posture exposes: he allows them to become aroused, but it is nowhere but in his mouth the sacrifice is to be consummated; as one after another they emerge he sucks each. While one acts, he has himself sucked by the other, and his tongue wanders to the throne of voluptuousness the agent presents to him. This activity continues a long time, it irritates the Count, he gets to his feet and wishes me to take the Countess' place; I instantly beg him not to require it of me, but he insists. He lays his wife upon her back, has me superimpose myself upon her with my flanks raised in his direction and thereupon he orders his aides to plumb me by the forbidden passage: he brings them up, his hands guide their introduction; meanwhile, I have got to stimulate the Countess with my fingers and kiss her mouth; as for the Count, his offertory is still the same; as each of the boys cannot act without exhibiting to him one of the sweetest objects of his veneration, he turns it all to his profit and, as with the Countess, he who has just perforated me is obliged to go, after a few lunges and retreats, and spill into his mouth the incense I have warmed. When the boys are finished, seemingly inclined to replace them, the Count glues himself to my buttocks.

"Superfluous efforts," he cries, "this is not what I must have... to the business... the business... however pitiable my state... I can hold back no longer... come, Countess, your arms!"

He seizes her ferociously, places her as I was placed, arms suspended by two black straps; mine is the task of securing the bands; he inspects the knots: finding them too loose, he tightens them, "So that," he says, "the blood will spurt out under greater pressure"; he feels the veins, and lances them, on each arm, at almost the same moment. Blood leaps far: he is in an ecstasy; and adjusting himself so that he has a clear view of these two fountains, he has me kneel between his legs so I can suck him; he does as much for first one and then the other of his little friends, incessantly eyeing the jets of blood which inflame him. For my part, certain the instant at which the hoped for crisis occurs will bring a conclusion to the Countess' torments, I bring all my efforts to bear upon precipitating this denouement, and I become, as, Madame, you observe, I become a whore from kindness, a libertine through virtue. The much awaited moment arrives at last; I am not familiar with its dangers or violence, for the last time it had taken place I had been unconscious... Oh, Madame! what extravagance! Gernande remained delirious for ten minutes, flailing his arms, staggering, reeling like one falling in a fit of epilepsy, and uttering screams which must have been audible for a league around; his oaths were excessive; lashing out at everyone at hand, his strugglings were dreadful. The two little ones are sent tumbling head over heels; he wishes to fly at his wife, I restrain him: I pump the last drop from him, his need of me makes him respect me; at last I bring him to his senses by ridding him of that fiery liquid, whose heat, whose viscosity, and above all whose abundance puts him in such a frenzy I believe he is going to expire; seven or eight tablespoons would scarcely have contained the discharge, and the thickest gruel would hardly give a notion of its consistency; and with all that, no appearance of an erection at all, rather, the limp look and feel of exhaustion: there you have the contrarieties which, better than might I, explain artists of the Count's breed. The Count ate excessively and only dissipated each time he bled his wife, every four days, that is to say. Would this be the cause of the phenomenon? I have no idea, and not daring to ascribe a reason to what I do not understand, I will be content to relate what I saw.

However, I rush to the Countess, I stanch her blood, untie her, and deposit her upon a couch in a state of extreme weakness; but the Count, totally indifferent to her, without condescending to cast even a glance at this victim stricken by his rage, abruptly goes out with his aides, leaving me to put things in whatever order I please. Such is the fatal apathy which better than all else characterizes the true libertine soul: if he is merely carried away by passion's heat, limned with remorse will be his face when, calmed again, he beholds the baleful effects of delirium; but if his soul is utterly corrupt? then such consequences will affright him not: he will observe them with as little trouble as regret, perhaps even with some of the emotion of those infamous lusts which produced them.

I put Madame de Gernande to bed. She had, so she said, lost much more this time than she ordinarily did; but such good care and so many restoratives were lavished upon her, that she appeared well two days later. That same evening, when I had completed all my chores in the Countess' apartment, word arrived that the Count desired to speak to me; Gernande was taking supper; I was obliged to wait upon him while he fed with a much greater intemperance than at dinner; four of his pretty little friends were seated round the table with him and there, every evening, he regularly drank himself into drunkenness; but to that end, twenty bottles of the most excellent wine were scarcely sufficient and I often saw him empty thirty. And every evening, propped up by his minions, the debauchee went to bed, and took one or two of the boys with him; these were nothing but vehicles which disposed him for the great scene.

But I had discovered the secret of winning this man's very highest esteem: he frankly avowed to me that few women had pleased him so much; and thereby I acquired the right to his confidence, which I only exploited in order to serve my mistress.

One morning Gernande called me to his room to inform me of some new libertine schemes; after having listened closely and approved enthusiastically, and seeing him in a relatively calm state, I undertook to persuade him to mitigate his poor wife's fate. "Is it possible, Monsieur," I said to him, "that one may treat a woman in this manner, even setting aside all the ties which bind you to her? Condescend to reflect upon her sex's touching graces."

"Oh Therese!" the Count answered with alacrity, "why in order to pacify me do you bring me arguments which could not more positively arouse me? Listen to me, my dear girl," he continued, having me take a place beside him, "and whatever the invectives you may hear me utter against your sex, don't lose your temper; no, a reasoned discussion; I'll yield to your arguments if they're logically sound.

"How are you justified, pray tell me, Therese, in asserting that a husband lies under the obligation to make his wife happy? and what titles dares this woman cite in order to extort this happiness from her husband? The necessity mutually to render one another happy cannot legitimately exist save between two persons equally furnished with the capacity to do one another hurt and, consequently, between two persons of commensurate strength: such an association can never come into being unless a contract is immediately formed between these two persons, which obligates each to employ against the other no kind of force but what will not be injurious to either; but this ridiculous convention assuredly can never obtain between two persons one of whom is strong and the other weak. What entitles the latter to require the former to treat kindly with him? and what sort of a fool would the stronger have to be in order to subscribe to such an agreement? I can agree not to employ force against him whose own strength makes him to be feared; but what could motivate me to moderate the effects of my strength upon the being Nature subordinates to me? Pity, do you say? That sentiment is fitting for no one but the person who resembles me and as he is an egoist too, pity's effects only occur under the tacit circumstances in which the individual who inspires my commiseration has sympathy for me in his turn; but if my superiority assures me a constant ascendancy over him, his sympathy becoming valueless to me, I need never, in order to excite it, consent to any sacrifice. Would I not be a fool to feel pity for the chicken they slaughtered for my dinner? That object, too inferior to me, lacking any relation to me, can never excite any feelings in me; well, the relationships of a wife to her husband and that of the chicken to myself are of identical consequence, the one and the other are household chattels which one must use, which one must employ for the purpose indicated by Nature, without any differentiation whatsoever. But, I ask, had it been Nature's intention to create your sex for the happiness of ours and vice versa, would this blind Nature have caused the existence of so many ineptitudes in the construction of the one and the other of those sexes? Would she have implanted faults so grave in each that mutual estrangement and antipathy were bound infallibly to be their result? Without going any further in search of examples, be so good as to tell me, Therese, knowing my organization to be what it is, what woman could I render happy? and, reversibly, to what man can the enjoyment of a woman be sweet when he is not endowed with the gigantic proportions necessary to satisfy her? In your opinion, will they be moral qualities which will compensate his physical shortcomings? And what thinking being, upon knowing a woman to her depths, will not cry with Euripides: 'That one amongst the Gods who brought women into the world may boast of having produced the worst of all creatures and the most afflicting to man.' If then it is demonstrated that the two sexes do not at all sort agreeably with each other and that there is not one well-founded grievance of the one which could not equally and immediately be voiced by the other, it is therefore false, from this moment, to say that Nature created them for their reciprocal happiness. She may have permitted them the desire to attain each other's vicinity in order to conjugate in the interests of propagation, but in no wise in order to form attachments with the design of discovering a mutual felicity. The weaker therefore having no right to mouth complaints with the object of wresting pity from the stronger and no longer being able to raise the objection that the stronger depends for his happiness upon her, the weaker, I say, has no alternative but to submit; and as, despite the difficulty of achieving that bilateral happiness, it is natural that individuals of both sexes labor at nothing but to procure it for themselves, the weaker must reconcile herself to distilling from her submissiveness the only dose of happiness she can possibly hope to cull, and the stronger must strive after his by whatever oppressive methods he is pleased to employ, since it is proven that the mighty's sole happiness is yielded him by the exercise of his strong faculties, by, that is to say, the most thorough-going tyranny; thus, that happiness the two sexes cannot find with each other they will find, one in blind obedience, the other in the most energetic expression of his domination. Why! were it not Nature's intention that one of the sexes tyrannize the other, would she not have created them equally strong? By rendering one in every particular inferior to the other, has she not adequately indicated that she wills the mightier to exploit the rights she has given him? the more the latter broadens his authority, the more, by means of his preponderance, he worsens the misery of the woman enthralled by her destiny, the better he answers Nature's intentions; the frail being's complaints do not provide a correct basis for analyzing the process; judgments thus come by would be nothing if not vicious, since, to reach them, you would have to appropriate none but the feeble's ideas: the suit must be judged upon the stronger party's power, upon the scope he has given to his power, and when this power's effects are brought to bear upon a woman, one must examine the question, What is a woman? and how has this contemptible sex been viewed in ancient times and in our own by seventy-five per cent of the peoples of this earth?

"Now, what do I observe upon coolly proceeding to this investigation? A puny creature, always inferior to man, infinitely less attractive than he, less ingenious, less wise, constructed in a disgusting manner entirely opposite to what is capable of pleasing a man, to what is able to delight him... a being three-quarters of her life untouchable, unwholesome, unable to satisfy her mate throughout the entire period Nature constrains her to childbearing, of a sharp turn of humor, shrill, shrewish, bitter, and thwart; a tyrant if you allow her privileges, mean, vile, and a sneak in bondage; always false, forever mischievous, constantly dangerous; in short, a being so perverse that during several convocations the question was very soberly agitated at the Council of Macon whether or not this peculiar creature, as distinct from man as is man from the ape, had any reasonably legitimate pretensions to classification as a human; but this quandary might be merely an error of the times; were women more favorably viewed in earlier ages? Did the Persians, the Medes, the Babylonians, the Greeks, the Romans honor this odious sex we are able to dare make our idol today? Alas! I see it oppressed everywhere, everywhere rigorously banished from affairs, condemned everywhere, vilified, sequestered, locked up; women treated, in a word, like beasts one stables in the barn and puts to use when the need arises. Do I pause a moment at Rome? then I hear the wise Cato exclaim from the heart of the ancient world's capital: 'Were women lacking to men, they would yet hold conversation with the Gods.' I hear a Roman censor begin his harangue with these words: 'Gentlemen, were we ever to find a means to live without women, thereupon unto us should true happiness be known.' I hear the Greek theater resound to these lines intoned: 'O Zeus! what reason was it obliged thee to create women? couldst not have given being to humankind by better devices and wiser, by schemes which in a word would have spared us this female pestilence?' I see this same Greek race hold that sex in such high contempt legislation was needed to oblige a Spartan to reproduce, and one of the penalties decreed in those enlightened republics was to compel a malefactor to garb himself in a woman's attire, that is to say, to wear the raiments of the vilest and most scorned creature of which man had acquaintance.

"But without inquiring for examples in ages at such a great remove from ours, with what sort of an eye is this wretched sex still viewed upon the earth's surface? How is it dealt with? I behold it imprisoned throughout Asia and serving there as slave to the barbarous whims of a despot who molests it, torments it, and turns its sufferings into a game. In America I find a naturally humane race, the Eskimos, practicing all possible acts of beneficence amongst men and treating women with all imaginable severity: I see them humiliated, prostituted to strangers in one part of the world, used as currency in another. In Africa, where without doubt their station is yet further degraded, I notice them toiling in the manner of beasts of burden, tilling the soil, fertilizing it and sowing seed, and serving their husbands on their knees only. Will I follow Captain Cook in his newest discoveries? Is the charming isle of Tahiti, where pregnancy is a crime sometimes meriting death for the mother and almost always for the child, to offer me women enjoying a happier lot? In the other islands this same mariner charted, I find them beaten, harassed by their own offspring, and bullied by the husband himself who collaborates with his family to torment them with additional rigor.

"Oh, Therese I let not all this astonish you, nor be more surprised by the general pre-eminence accorded men over their wives in all epochs: the more a people is in harmony with Nature, the better will be its use of her laws; the wife can have no relation to her husband but that of a slave to his master; very decidedly she has no right to pretend to more cherished titles. One must not mistake for a prerogative the ridiculous abuses which, by degrading our sex, momentarily elevates yours: the cause for these travesties must be sought out, enunciated, and afterward one must only the more constantly return to reason's sagacious counsels. Well, Therese, here is the cause of the temporary respect your sex once upon a time enjoyed and which it still misuses today while they who perpetuate it are unaware of what they are doing.

"In the Gaul of long ago, that is to say, in that one part of the world where women were not totally treated as slaves, women had the habit of prophesying, of predicting the happy event: the people fancied they plied their trade successfully only because of the intimate commerce they doubtless had with the Gods; whence they were, so to speak, associated with the sacerdotal and enjoyed a measure of the consideration lavished upon priests. French chivalry was founded upon these inanities and finding them favorable to its spirit, adopted them: but what happened next was what happens always: the causes became extinct, the effects were preserved; chivalry vanished, the prejudices it nourished persevered. This ancient veneration accorded for no sound reason could not itself be annihilated when what founded the illusion had dissipated: we no longer stand in awe of witches, but we reverence whores and, what is worse, we continue to kill each other for them. May such platitudes cease to influence these our philosophers' minds, and restoring women to their true position, may the intelligent spirit conceive them, as Nature indicates, as the wisest peoples acknowledge, to be nothing but individuals created for their pleasures, submitted to their caprices, objects whose frailty and wickedness make them deserving of naught but contempt.

"But not only, Therese, did all the peoples of the earth enjoy the most extensive rights over their women, there were even to be found certain races which condemned women to death immediately they were born into the world, and of their numbers retained only those few necessary to the race's reproduction. The Arabs known as Koreish interred their daughters at the age of seven upon a mountain near Mecca, because, said they, so vile a sex appeared to them unworthy of seeing the light; in the seraglio of the King of Achem, the most appalling tortures are applied as punishment for the mere suspicion of infidelity, for the slightest disobedience in the service of the prince's lusts, or as soon as his women inspire his distaste; upon the banks of the River Ganges they are obliged to immolate themselves over their husbands' ashes, for they are esteemed of no further purpose in the world once their lords are able to enjoy them no more; in other regions they are hunted like wild beasts, 'tis an honor to kill a quantity of them; in Egypt they are sacrificed to the Gods; they are trampled under foot in Formosa if they become pregnant; German law condemned the man who killed a foreign woman to pay a fine of about ten crowns, nothing at all if the woman was his own or a courtesan; everywhere, to be brief, everywhere, I repeat, I see women humiliated, molested, everywhere sacrificed to the superstition of priests, to the savagery of husbands, to the playfulness of libertines. And because I have the misfortune to live amidst a people still so uncouth as not to dare abolish the most ludicrous of prejudices, I should deprive myself of the rights Nature has granted me! I should forgo all the pleasures to which these privileges give birth... Come, come, Therese, that's not just, no, 'tis unfair: I will conceal my behavior because I must, but I will be compensated, in the retreat where I have exiled myself, and silently, for the absurd chains to which I am condemned by legislation, and here I will treat my wife as I like, for I find my right to do so lettered in all the universe's codes, graved in my heart, and sealed in Nature."

"Oh Monsieur," said I, "your conversion is impossible."

"And I advise you not to attempt it, Therese," Gernande answered; "the tree is too long out of the nursery; at my age one can advance a few steps in the career of evil, but not one toward good. My principles and my tastes have brought me joy since childhood, they have always been the unique bases of my conduct and actions: I will, who knows? go further, I have the feeling it could be done, but return? never; I have too great a horror for mankind's prejudices, I too sincerely hate their civilization, their virtue and their Gods ever to sacrifice my penchants to them." From this moment I saw very clearly that nothing remained for me, in order either to extricate myself from this house or to save the Countess, but the employment of strategems and joint action with her.

31

During the year I had spent in the house, what I had allowed her to read in my heart was more than sufficient to dispel any doubts she might have of my desire to serve her, and now she could not fail to divine what had at first prompted me to act differently. I became less guarded, then spoke; she assented; we settled upon a plan: it was to inform her mother, to expose the Count's infamies to her eyes. Madame de Gernande was certain that unfortunate lady would hasten with all expedition to sever her daughter's bonds; but how were we to approach her? for we were so securely imprisoned, so closely watched! Accustomed to coping with ramparts, I gauged those upon which the terrace was raised: their height was scarcely thirty feet; there was no other enclosure in sight; once at the foot of the wall I thought one would find oneself already on the road through the forest; but the Countess, having been brought to this apartment at night and never having left it since, was unable to confirm my ideas. I agreed to attempt the descent; the letter Madame de Gernande wrote to her mother could not have been better phrased to melt and persuade her to come to the rescue of her most unhappy daughter; I slipped the letter into my bosom, I embraced that dear and attractive woman, then, as soon as night had fallen, aided by our bed linen, I slid to the ground outside the fortress. What had become of me, O Heaven? I discovered that instead of being outside the enclosure I was simply in a park, and in a park girt by walls which the quantity and dense foliage of trees had camouflaged from sight: these battlements were more than forty feet high, all of them garnished at the top with broken glass, and of a prodigious thickness... what was to become of me? Dawn was not far off: what would they think when I was found in a place into which I could not have come without a certain plan of escape? Would I be able to keep the Count's fury at bay? Was it not very likely that ogre would drink my blood to punish such an offense? To return was out of the question, the Countess had drawn back the sheets; to knock at the door would be still more certainly to betray myself; a little more and I would have lost my head altogether and ceded to the violent effects of my despair. Had I been able to recognize some pity in the Count's soul, I might perhaps have been lulled into hopefulness, but a tyrant, a barbarian, a man who detested women and who, he said, had long been seeking the occasion to immolate one by draining away her blood drop by drop in order to find out how many hours she would be able to last... No doubt about it, he was going to put me to the test. Knowing not what would happen or what to do, discovering dangers everywhere, I threw myself down beside a tree, determined to await my fate and silently resigning myself to the Eternal's will . . . . The sun rose at last; merciful Heaven! the first object to present itself to me... is the Count himself: it had been frightfully warm during the night, he had stepped out to take a breath of air. He believes he is in error, he supposes this a specter, he recoils, rarely is courage a traitor's virtue: I get trembling to my feet, I fling myself at his knees.

"Therese! What are you doing here?" he demands.

"Oh, Monsieur, punish me," I reply, "I am guilty and have nothing to answer you."

Unhappily, in my fright I had forgotten to destroy the Countess' letter: he suspects its existence, asks for it, I wish to deny I have it; but Gernande sees the fatal letter protruding above my kerchief, snatches, it, reads it, and orders me to follow him.

We enter the chateau, descend a hidden stairway leading down to the vaults: the most profound stillness reigns there below ground; after several detours, the Count opens a dungeon and casts me into it.

"Impudent girl," says he, "I gave you warning that the crime you have just committed is punished here by death: therefore prepare yourself to undergo the penalty you have been pleased to incur. When tomorrow I rise from dinner I am going to dispatch you."

Once again I fall prostrate before him but, seizing me by the hair, he drags me along the ground, pulls me several times around my prison, and ends by hurling me against the wall in such a manner I am nigh to having my brains dashed out.

"You deserve to have me open your four veins this instant," says he as he closes the door, "and if I postpone your death, be very sure it is only in order to render it the more horrible."

He has left; I am in a state of the most violent agitation; I shall not describe the night I passed: my tormented imagination together with the physical hurt done me by the monster's initial cruelties made it one of the most dreadful I had ever gone through. One has no conception of what anguish is suffered by the wretch who from hour to hour awaits his ordeal, from whom hope has fled, and who knows not whether this breath he draws may not be his last. Uncertain of the torture, he pictures it in a thousand forms, one more frightful than the other; the least noise he hears may be that of his approaching assassins; the blood freezes in his veins, his heart grows faint, and the blade which is to put a period to his days is less cruel than those terrible instants swollen with the menace of death.

In all likelihood the Count began by revenging himself upon his wife: you will be as convinced of it as I by the event which saved me. For thirty-six hours I lingered in the critical condition I have just described; during that time I was brought no relief; and then my door was opened and the Count appeared: he was alone, fury glittered in his eyes.

"You must be fully cognizant of the death you are going to undergo: this perverse blood has got to be made to seep out of you: you will be bled three times a day, I want to see how long you can survive the treatment. 'Tis an experiment I have been all afire to make, you know; my thanks to you for furnishing me the means."

And, for the time being occupying himself with no passion but his vengeance, the monster made me stretch forth an arm, pricked it and stopped the wound after he had drawn two bowls of blood. He had scarcely finished when cries were heard.

"Oh, my Lord, my Lord !" exclaimed one of the servants who came running up to him, "come as quick as ever you can, Madame is dying, she wishes to speak to you before she gives up her soul."

And the old woman turned and flew back to her mistress.

However habituated one may be to crime, it is rarely that news of its accomplishment does not strike terror into him who has committed it; this fear avenges Virtue: Virtue resumes possession of its rights: Gernande goes out in alarm, he forgets to secure the dungeon's doors; although enfeebled by a forty hours' fast and the blood I have lost, I exploit my opportunity, leap from my cell, find my way unimpeded, traverse the court, the park, and reach the forest without having been perceived. Walk, I say to myself, walk, walk, be courageous; if the mighty scorn the weak, there is an omnipotent God Who shields the latter and Who never abandons them. My head crowded with these ideas, I advance with a stout heart and before night closes I find myself in a cottage four leagues from the chateau. Some money remained to me, my needs were attended to, in a few hours I was rested. I left at daybreak and, renouncing all plans to register old or new complaints with the authorities, I asked to be directed toward Lyon; the road was pointed out to me and on the eighth day I reached that city, very weak, suffering much, but happy and unpursued; once arrived, I turned all my thoughts to recovery before striking out for Grenoble where, according to one of my persistent notions, happiness awaited me.

One day my eye fell upon a gazette printed in some distant place; what was my surprise to behold crime crowned once again and to see one of the principal authors of my miseries arrived at the pinnacle of success. Rodin, the surgeon of Saint-Michel, that infamous wretch who had punished me with such cruelty for having wished to spare him the murder of his daughter, had just, the news-paper declared, been named First Surgeon to the Empress of Russia with the considerable emoluments accompanying that post. May he prosper, the villain, I muttered to myself, may he be so whilst Providence so wills it; and thou, unhappy creature, suffer, suffer uncomplainingly, since it is decreed that tribulations and pain must be Virtue's frightful share; no matter, I shall never lose my taste for it.

But I was far from done with these striking examples of the triumph of vice, examples so disheartening for Virtue, and the flourishing condition of the personage whose acquaintance I was about to renew was surely to exasperate and amaze me more than any other, since it was that of one of the men at whose hands I had endured the bloodiest outrages. I was exclusively busied with preparing my departure when one evening a lackey clad in gray and completely unknown to me brought me a note; upon presenting it, he said his master had charged him to obtain my response without fail. The missive was worded this way: "A man who has somewhat wronged you, who believes he recognized you in the Place de Belle-cour, is most desirous to see you and to make amends for his conduct: hasten to come to meet him; he has things to tell you which may help liquidate his entire indebtedness to you."

The message carried no signature and the lackey offered no explanations. Having declared I was resolved to make no answer at all lest I was informed of who his master was:

"He is Monsieur de Saint-Florent, Mademoiselle," the lackey said; "he has had the honor to know you formerly in the neighbor-hood of Paris; you rendered him, he maintains, services for which he burns to attest his gratitude. Presently risen to a position of undisputed eminence in this city's commercial circles, he at once enjoys the consideration and the means which put him in a position to prove his regard for you. He awaits you."

My deliberations were soon completed. If this man had other than good intentions, I said to myself, would he be apt to write to me, to have me spoken to in this fashion? He repented his past infamies, was covered with remorse, it was with horror he remembered having torn from me what I cherished most and, by inaugurating a sequence of nightmares, having reduced me to the cruelest circumstances a woman may know... yes, yes, no doubt of it, this is repentance, I should be culpable before the Supreme Being were I not to consent to assuage his sufferings. Am I in a position, furthermore, to spurn the support that is proposed here? Rather, ought I not eagerly snatch at all that is offered to relieve me? This man wishes to see me in his town house: his prosperity must surround him with servants before whom he will have to act with enough dignity to prevent him from daring to fail me again, and in my state, Great God! can I inspire anything but sympathy in him? Therefore I assured Saint-Florent's lackey that upon the morrow at eleven o'clock I would take the privilege of going to salute his master; that I congratulated him upon his good fortune, and added that luck had treated me in nothing approaching the same manner.

I returned to my room, but I was so preoccupied with what this man might wish to say to me that I slept not a wink all night; the next day I arrived at the indicated address: a superb mansion, a throng of domestics, that insolent canaille's contemptuous glances at the poverty it scorned, everything afflicts me and I am about ready to retreat when up comes the same liveryman who had spoken to me the previous evening, and, reassuring me, he conducts me into a sumptuous drawing room where, although it is nine years since I have set eyes on him, I perfectly recognize my butcher who has now reached the age of forty-five. He does not rise upon my entrance, but gives the order we be left alone, and gestures me to come and seat myself near the vast armchair where he is enthroned.

"I wanted to see you again, my child," says he with a humiliating tone of superiority, "not that I thought I had much wronged you, not that a troublesome recollection bids me make restitutions from which I believe my position exempts me; but I remember that, however brief was our acquaintance, you exhibited some parts during it: wit and character are needed for what I have to propose to you and if you accept, the need I will then have of you will insure your discovery of the resources which are necessary to you, and upon which it should be in vain you were to count without signifying your agreement."

I wished to reply with some reproaches for the levity of this beginning, but Saint-Florent imposed silence upon me.

" 'Tis water under the bridge," says he, "a purely emotional episode, and my principles support the belief I have, that no brake should be applied to passion; when the appetites speak, they must be heard: that's my law. When I was captured by the thieves with whom you were, did you see me burst into tears? Swallow the bitter pill and act with diligence if one is weak, enjoy all one's rights if powerful: that's my doctrine. You were young and pretty, Therese, we found ourselves in the middle of a forest, nothing so arouses me sensually as the rape of a young virgin girl; such you were, I raped you; I might perhaps have done worse had what I attempted not met with success and had you put up any resistance. But I raped you, then left you naked and robbed in the middle of the night, upon a perilous road: two motives gave rise to that further villainy: I needed money and had none; as for the other reason which drove me to do this, 'twould be in vain were I to explain it, Therese, it would surpass your understanding. Only those spirits who are deep-learned in the heart of man, who have studied its innermost recesses, gained access to the most impenetrable nooks of this dim-lit labyrinth, they alone might be able to account for this consequence of an aberration."

"What, Monsieur! the money I gave you... the service I had just rendered you... to be paid for what I did in your behalf by the blackest treachery... that may, you think, be understood, justified?"

"Why yes, Therese! yes indeed! the proof an explanation exists for all I did is that, having just pillaged you, molested you... (for, Therese, I did beat you, you know), why! having taken twenty steps, I stopped and, meditating upon the state in which I had left you, I at once found strength in these ideas, enough to perpetrate additional outrages I might not have committed had it not been for that: you had lost but one maidenhead . . . . I turned, retraced my steps, and made short work of the other . . . . And so it is true that in certain souls lust may be born from the womb of crime! What do I say? it is thus true that only crime awakes and stiffens lust and that there is not a single voluptuous pleasure it does not inflame and improve . . . ."

"Oh Monsieur! what horror is this?"

"Could I not have acquitted myself of a still greater? I was close enough to it, I confess, but I was amply sure you were going to be reduced to the last extremities: the thought satisfied me, I left you. Well, Therese, let's leave the subject and continue to my reason for desiring to see you. "My incredible appetite for both of a little girl's maidenheads has not deserted me, Therese," Saint-Florent pursued; "with this it is as with all libertinage's other extravagances: the older you grow, the more deeply they take root; from former misdeeds fresh desires are born, and new crimes from these desires. There would be nothing to the matter, my dear, were not the means one employs to succeed exceedingly culpable. But as the desire of evil is the primum mobile of our caprices, the more criminal the thing we are led to do, the better our irritation. When one arrives at this stage, one merely complains of the mediocrity of the means: the more encompassing their atrociousness, the more piquant our joy becomes, and thus one sinks in the quagmire without the slightest desire to emerge.

"That, Therese, is my own history: two young children are necessary for my daily sacrifices; having once enjoyed them, - not only do I never again set eyes upon these objects, but it even becomes essential to my fantasies' entire satisfaction that they instantly leave the city: I should not at all savor the following day's pleasures were I to imagine that yesterday's victims still breathed the same air I inhale; the method for being rid of them is not complicated. Would you believe it, Therese? They are my debauches which populate Languedoc and Provence with the multitude of objects of libertinage with which those regions are teeming:

(Let this not be mistaken for a fable: this wretched figure existed in this same Lyon. What is herein related of his maneuvers is exact and authentic: he cost the honor of between fifteen and twenty thousand unhappy little creatures: upon the completion of each operation, the victim was embarked on the Rhone, and for thirty years the above-mentioned cities were peopled with the objects of this villain's debauchery, with girls undone by him. There is nothing fictitious about this episode but the gentleman's name.)

...one hour after these little girls have served me, reliable emissaries pack them off and sell them to the matchmakers of Montpellier, Toulouse, Nimes, Aix, and Marseilles: this trade, two-thirds of whose net profits go to me, amply recompenses the outlay required to procure my subjects, and thus I satisfy two of my most cherished passions, lust and greed; but reconnoitering and seduction are bothersome. Furthermore, the kind of subject is of infinite importance to my lubricity: I must have them all procured from those asylums of misery where the need to live and the impossibility of managing to do so eat away courage, pride, delicacy, finally rot the soul, and, in the hope of an indispensable subsistence, steel a person to undertake whatever appears likely to provide it. I have all these nests

ransacked, all these dungheaps combed pitilessly: you've no idea what they yield;
I would even go further, Therese: I say that civil activity, industry, a little social
ease would defeat my subornations and divest me of a great proportion of my
subjects: I combat these perils with the influence I enjoy in this city, I promote
commercial and economic fluctuations or instigate the rise of prices which,
enlarging the poverty-stricken class, depriving it, on the one hand, of possibilities
of work and on the other rendering difficult those of survival, increases according
to a predictable ratio the total number of the subjects misery puts into my
clutches. The strategy is a familiar one, Therese: these scarcities of firewood,
dearths of wheat and of other edibles where-from Paris has been trembling for so
many years, have been created for the identical purposes which animate me:
avarice, libertinage: such are the passions which, from the gilded halls of the rich,
extend a multitude of nets to ensnare the poor in their humble dwellings. But
whatever skill I employ to press hard in this sector, if dexterous hands do not
pluck nimbly in another, I get nothing for my troubles, and the machine goes
quite as badly as if I were to cease to exhaust my imagination in devising and my
credit in operating. And so I need a clever woman, young and intelligent, who,
having herself found her way through misery's thorny pathways, is more familiar
than anyone else with the methods for debauching those who are in the toils; a
woman whose keen eyes will descry adversity in its darkest caves and attics, whose
suborning intelligence will determine destitution's victims to extricate themselves
from oppression by the means I make available; a spirited woman, in a word,
unscrupulous and ruthless, who will stop at nothing in order to succeed, who will
even go to the point of cutting away the scanty reserves which, still bolstering up
those wretches' hopes, inhibit them from taking the final step. I had an excellent
woman and trustworthy, she has just died: it cannot be imagined to what lengths
that brilliant creature carried effrontery; not only did she use to isolate these
wretches until they would be forced to come begging on their knees, but if these
devices did not succeed in accelerating their fall, the impatient villain would
hasten matters by kidnaping them. She was a treasure; I need but two subjects a
day, she would have got me ten had I wanted them. The result was I used to be
able to make better selections, and the superabundance of raw material consumed
by my operations reimbursed me for inflated labor costs. That's the woman I have
got to replace, my dear, you'll have four people under your command and ten
thousand crowns wages for your trouble; I have had my say, Therese; give me your
answer, and above all do not let your illusions prevent you from accepting
happiness when chance and my hand offer it to you."

32

    "Oh Monsieur," I say to this dishonest man, shuddering at his speech, "is it
possible you have been able to conceive such joys and that you dare propose that
I serve them? What horrors you have just uttered in my hearing! Cruel man, were

you to be miserable for but two days, you would see these doctrines upon humanity swiftly obliterated from your heart: it is prosperity blinds and hardens you: mightily blase you are before the spectacle of the evils whence you suppose yourself sheltered, and because you hope never to suffer them, you consider you have the right to inflict them; may happiness never come nigh unto me if it can produce this degree of corruption! O Just Heaven! not merely to be content to abuse the misfortunate! To drive audacity and ferocity to the point of increasing it, of prolonging it for the unique gratification of one's desires! What cruelty, Monsieur! the wildest animals do not give us the example of a comparable barbarity."

"You are mistaken, Therese, there is no roguery the wolf will not invent to draw the lamb into his clutches: these are natural ruses, while benevolence has nothing to do with Nature: charity is but an appurtenance of the weakness recommended by the slave who would propitiate his master and dispose him to leniency; it never proclaimed itself in man save in two cases: in the event he is weak, or in the event he fears he will become weak; that this alleged virtue is not natural is proven by the fact it is unknown to the man who lives in a state of Nature. The savage expresses his contempt for charity when pitilessly he massacres his brethren from motives of either revenge or cupidity... would he not respect that virtue were it etched in his heart? but never does it appear there, never will it be found wherever men are equal. Civilization, by weeding certain individuals out of society, by establishing rank and class, by giving the rich man a glimpse of the poor, by making the former dread any change of circumstances which might precipitate him into the latter's misery, civilization immediately puts the desire into his head to relieve the poor in order that he may be helped in his turn should he chance to lose his wealth; and thus was benevolence born, the fruit of civilization and fear: hence it is merely a circumstantial virtue, but nowise a sentiment originating in Nature, who never inserted any other desire in us but that of satisfying ourselves at no matter what the price. It is thus by confounding every sentiment, it is by continually refusing to analyze a single one of them that these people are able to linger in total darkness about them all and deprive themselves of every pleasurable enjoyment."

"Ah, Monsieur," I interrupted with great emotion, "may there be one any sweeter than the succoring of misfortune? Leaving aside the dread lest someday one have to endure suffering oneself, is there any more substantial satisfaction than that to be had from obliging others?... from relishing gratitude's tearful thanks, from partaking of the well-being you have just distributed like manna to the downtrodden who, your own fellow creatures, nevertheless want those things which you take airily for granted; oh! to hear them sing your praise and call you their father, to restore serenity to brows clouded by failure, destitution, and despair; no, Monsieur, not one of this world's lewd pleasures can equal this: it is that of the Divinity Himself, and the happiness He promises to those who on earth will serve Him, is naught other than the possibility to behold or make happy creatures in Heaven. All virtues stem directly from that one, Monsieur; one is a better father, a better son, a better husband when one knows the charm of alleviating misfortune's lot. One might say that like unto the sun's rays, the charitable man's presence sheds fertility, sweetness, and joy everywhere about and upon all, and the miracle of Nature, after this source of celestial light, is the honest, delicate, and sensitive soul whose supreme felicity consists in laboring in behalf of that of others."

"Feeble Phoebus stuff, Therese," Saint-Florent smiled; "the character of man's enjoyment is determined by the kind of organs he has received from Nature; a weak individual's, and hence every woman's, incline in the direction of procuring moral ecstasies which are more keenly felt than any other by these persons whose physical constitution happens to be entirely devoid of energy; quite the opposite is the case for vigorous spirits who are far more delighted by powerful shocks imparted to what surround them than they would be by the delicate impressions the feeble creatures by whom they are surrounded inevitably prefer, as befits their constitution; similarly the vigorous spirits delight more in what affects others painfully than in what affects them agreeably: such is the only difference between the cruel and the meek; both groups are endowed with sensibility, but each is endowed with it in a special manner. I do not deny that each class knows its pleasures, but I, together with a host of philosophers, maintain of course that those of the individual constructed in the more vigorous fashion are incontestably more lively than all his adversary's; and, these axioms established, there may and

there must be men of one sort who take as much joy in everything cruelty suggests, as the other category of persons tastes delight in benevolence; but the pleasures of the latter will be mild, those of the former keen and strong: these will be the most sure, the most reliable, and doubtless the most authentic, since they characterize the penchants of every man who is still a creature of Nature, and indeed of all children before they have fallen under the sway of civilization; the others will merely be the eff civilization and, consequently, of deceiving and vapid delights. Well, my child, since we are met not so much in order to philosophize as to conclude a bargain, be so kind as to give me your final decision... do you or do you not accept the post I propose to you?"

"I very decidedly reject it, Monsieur," I replied, getting to my feet, "... indeed I am poor... oh yes! very poor, Monsieur; but richer in my heart's sentiments than I could be in all fortune's blessings; never will I sacrifice the one in order to possess the other; I may die in indigence, but I will not betray Virtue."

"Get out," the detestable man said to me, "and, above all, should I have anything to fear from your indiscretion, you will be promptly conveyed to a place where I need dread it no longer."

Nothing heartens Virtue like the fear of vice; a good deal less timorous than I should have thought, I dared, upon promising he would have nothing to dread at my hands, remind him of what he had from me in the forest of Bondy and apprise him of my present circumstances which, I said, made this money indispensable to me. The monster gave me harsh answer, declaring it was up to me to earn it and that I had refused.

"No Monsieur, no," I replied firmly, "no, I repeat, I would rather perish a thousand times over than preserve my life at that price."

"And as for myself," Saint-Florent rejoined, "there is in the same way nothing I would not prefer to the chagrin of disbursing unearned money: despite the refusal you have the insolence to give me, I should relish passing another fifteen minutes in your company; and so if you please, we will move into my boudoir and a few moments of obedience will go far to straighten out your pecuniary difficulties."

"I am no more eager to serve your debauches in one sense than in another, Monsieur," I proudly retorted; "it is not charity I ask, cruel man; no, I should not procure you the pleasure of it; what I demand is simply most infamous manner . . . . Keep it, cruel wretch, keep it if you see fit: unpityingly observe my tears; hear, if you are able, hear without emotion need's sorrowing accents, but bear in mind that if you commit this newest outrage, I will have bought, for the price it costs me, the right to scorn you forever."

Furious, Saint-Florent ordered me to leave and I was able to read in his dreadful countenance that, had it not been for what he had confided in me and were he not afraid lest it get abroad, my bold plain speaking might perhaps have been repaid by some brutality . . . . I left. At the same instant they were bringing the debauchee one of the luckless victims of his sordid profligacy. One of those women whose horrible state he had suggested I share was leading into the house a poor little girl of about nine who displayed every attribute of wretchedness and dereliction: she scarcely seemed to have enough strength to keep er is it conceivable that such objects can inspire any feelings but those of pity? Woe unto the depraved one who will be able to suspect pleasures in the womb want consumes, who will seek to gather kisses from lips withered by hunger and which open only to curse him!

Tears spilled from my eyes; I should have liked to snatch that victim from the tiger awaiting her; I dared not. Could I have done it? I returned directly to my hotel, quite as humiliated by the misfortune which attracted such proposals as revolted by the opulence which ventured to make them.

The following day I left Lyon by way of the road to Dauphine, still filled with the mad faith which allowed me to believe happiness awaited me in that province. Traveling afoot as usual, with a pair of blouses and some handkerchiefs in my pockets, I had not proceeded two leagues when I met an old woman; she approached me with a look of suffering and implored alms. Far from I had just received such cruel examples, and knowing no greater worldly happiness than what comes of obliging a poor person, I instantly drew forth my purse with the intention of selecting a crown and giving it to this woman; but the unworthy creature, much quicker than I, although I had at first judged her aged and crippled, leaps nimbly at my purse, seizes it, aims a powerful blow of her fist at my stomach, topples me, and the next I see of her, she has put a hundred yards betwixt us; there she is, surrounded by four rascals who gesture threateningly and warn me not to come near.

"Great God!" I cried with much bitterness, "then it is Impossible for my soul to give vent to any virtuous impulse without my being instantly and very severely punished for it!" At this fatal moment all my courage deserted me; today I beg Heaven's forgiveness in all sincerity, for I faltered; but I was blinded by despair. I felt myself ready to give up a career bese two alternatives: that of going to join the scoundrels who had just robbed me, or that of returning to Lyon to accept Saint-Florent's offer. God had mercy upon me; I did not succumb, and though the fresh hope He quickened in me was misleading, since so many adversities yet lay in store for me, I nevertheless thank Him for having held me upright: the unlucky star which guides me, although innocent, to the gallows, will never lead me to worse than death; other supervision might have brought me to infamy, and the one is far less cruel than the other.

I continue to direct my steps toward Vienne, having decided to sell what remains to me in order to get on to Grenoble: I was walking along sadly when, at a quarter league's distance from this city, I spied a plain to the right of the highway, and in the fields were two riders busily trampling a man beneath their horses' hooves; after having left him for dead, the pair rode off at a gallop. Th an unluckier person than I; health and strength at least remain to me, I can earn my living, and if that poor fellow is not rich, what is to become of him?"

However much I ought to have forbidden myself the self-indulgence of sympathy, however perilous it was for me to surrender to the impulse, I could not vanquish my extreme desire to approach the man and to lavish upon him what care I could offer. I rush to his side, I aid him to inhale some spirits I had kept about me: at last he opens his eyes and his first accents are those of gratitude. Still more eager to be of use to him, I tear up one of my blouses in order to bandage his wounds, to stanch his blood: I sacrificed for this wretched man one of the few belongings I still owned. These first attentions completed, I give him a little wine to drink: the unlucky one has completely come back to his senses, I cast an eye upon him a him more closely. Although traveling on foot and without baggage, he had some valuable effects Ä rings, a watch, a snuff box Ä but the latter two have been badly damaged during his encounter. As soon as he is able to speak he asks me what angel of charity has come to his rescue and what he can do to express his gratitude. Still having the simplicity to believe that a soul enchained by indebtedness ought to be eternally beholden to me, I judge it safe to enjoy the sweet pleasure of sharing my tears with him who has just shed some in my arms: I instruct him of my numerous reverses, he listens with interest, and when I have concluded with the latest catastrophe that has befallen me, the recital provides him with a glimpse of my poverty.

"How happy I am," he exclaims, "to be able at least to acknowledge all you have just done for me; my name is Roland," the adventurer continues, "I am the owner of an exceedingly fine chateau in the mountains fifteen leagues hence, I that this proposal cause your delicacy no alarm, I am going to explain immediately in what way you will be of service to me. I am unwedded, but I have a sister I love passionately: she has dedicated herself to sharing my solitude; I need someone to wait upon her; we have recently lost the person who held that office until now, I offer her post to you."

I thanked my protector and took the liberty to ask him how it chanced that a man such as he exposed himself to the dangers of journeying alone, and, as had just occurred, to being molested by bandits.

"A stout, youthful, and vigorous fellow, for several years," said Roland, "I have been in the habit of traveling this way between the place where I reside and Vienne. My health and pocketbook benefit from walking. It is not that I need avoid the expense of a coach, for I am wealthy, and you will soon see proof of it if you are good enough to return home with me; but thriftiness never hurts. men who insulted me a short while ago, they are two would-be gentlemen of this canton from whom I won a hundred louis last week in a gaming house at Vienne; I was content to accept their word of honor, then I met them today, asked for what they owe me, and you witnessed in what coin they paid me."

Together with this man I was deploring the double misfortune of which he was the victim when he proposed we continue our way.

"Thanks to your attentions I feel a little better," said Roland; "night is approaching, let's get on to a house which should be two leagues away; by means of the horses we will secure tomorrow, we might be able to arrive at my chateau the same afternoon."

Absolutely resolved to profit from the aid Heaven seemed to have sent me, I help Roland to get up, I give him my arm while we walk, and indeed, after progressing two leagues we find the inn he had mentioned. We take supper together, 'tis very proper and nice; after our meal Roland en following day we set off on two mules we have rented and which are led by a boy from the inn; we reach the frontier of Dauphine, ever heading into the highlands. We were not yet at our destination when the day ended, so we stopped at Virieu, where my patron showed me the same consideration and provided me with the same care; the next morning we resumed our way toward the mountains. We arrived at their foot toward four in the afternoon; there, the road becoming almost impassable, Roland requested my muleteer not to leave me for fear of an accident, and we penetrated into the gorges. We did but turn, wind, climb for the space of more than four leagues, and by then we had left all habitations and all traveled roads so far behind us I thought myself come to the end of the world; despite myself, I was seized by a twinge of uneasiness; Roland could not avoid seeing it, but he said nothing, and I was made yet more uncomfortable by his to a castle perched upon the crest of a mountain; it beetled over a dreadful precipice into which it seemed ready to plunge: no road seemed to lead up to it; the one we had followed, frequently by goats only, strewn with pebbles and stones, however did at last take us to this awful eyrie which much more resembled the hideaway of thieves than the dwelling place of virtuous folk.

"That is where I live," said Roland, noticing I was gazing up at his castle.

I confessed my astonishment to see that he lived in such isolation.

"It suits me," was his abrupt reply.

This response redoubled my forebodings. Not a syllable is lost upon the miserable; a word, a shift of inflection and, when 'tis a question of the speech of the person upon whom one depends, 'tis enough to stifle hope or revive it; but, being completely unable to do anything, I held my tongue and waited. We mounted by zigzags; the strange pile suddenly loomed up before us: roughly a quart separated it from us: Roland dismounted and having told me to do likewise, he returned both mules to the boy, paid him and ordered him to return. This latest maneuver was even more displeasing to me; Roland observed my anxiety.

"What is the trouble, Therese?" he demanded, urging me on toward his fortress; "you are not out of France; we are on the Dauphine border and within the bishopric of Grenoble."

"Very well, Monsieur," I answered; "but why did it ever occur to you to take up your abode in a place befitting brigands and robbers?"

"Because they who inhabit it are not very honest people," said Roland; "it might be altogether possible you will not be edified by their conduct."

"Ah, Monsieur I" said I with a shudder, "you make me tremble; where then are you leading me?"

"I am leading you into the service of the counterfeiters of whom I am the chief," said Roland, grasping my arm and driving me over a little drawbridge that was lowered at our immediately we had traversed it; "do you see that well?" he continued when we had entered; he was pointing to a large and deep grotto situated toward the back of the courtyard, where four women, nude and manacled, were turning a wheel; "there are your companions and there your task, which involves the rotation of that wheel for ten hours each day, and which also involves the satisfaction of all the caprices I am pleased to submit you and the other ladies to; for which you will be granted six ounces of black bread and a plate of kidney beans without fail each day; as for your freedom, forget it; you will never recover it. When you are dead from overwork, you will be flung into that hole you notice beside the well, where the remains of between sixty and eighty other rascals of your breed await yours, and your place will be taken by somebody else."

"Oh, Great God!" I exclaimed, casting myself at Roland's feet, "deign to remember, Monsieur, that I saved you gratitude for an instant, you seemed to offer me happiness and that it is by precipitating me into an eternal abyss of evils you reward my services. Is what you are doing just? and has not remorse already begun to avenge me in the depths of your heart?"

"What, pray tell, do you mean by this feeling of gratitude with which you fancy you have captivated me?" Roland inquired. "Be more reasonable, wretched creature; what were you doing when you came to my rescue? Between the two possibilities, of continuing on your way and of coming up to me, did you not choose the latter as an impulse dictated by your heart? You therefore gave yourself up to a pleasure? How in the devil's name can you maintain I am obliged to recompense you for the joys in which you indulge yourself? And how did you ever get it into your head that a man like myself, who is swimming in gold and opulence, should condescend to lower himself to owing something to a wretch of your species? you nothing immediately it were plain you had acted out of selfishness only: to work, slave, to work; learn that though civilization may overthrow the principles of Nature, it cannot however divest her of her rights; in the beginning she wrought strong beings and weak and intended that the lowly should be forever subordinated to the great; human skill and intelligence made various the positions of individuals, it was no longer physical force alone that determined rank, 'twas gold; the richest became the mightiest man, the most penurious the weakest; if the causes which establish power are not to be found in Nature's ordinations, the priority of the mighty has always been inscribed therein, and to Nature it made no difference whether the weak danced at the end of a leash held by the richest or the most energetic, and little she cared whether the yoke crushed the poorest or the most enfeebled; but these grateful impulses out of which you them not; it has never been one of her laws that the pleasure whereunto someone surrenders when he acts obligingly must become a cause for the recipient of his gratuitous kindness to renounce his rights over the donor; do you detect these sentiments you demand in the animals which serve us as examples? When I dominate you by my wealth or might is it natural for me to abandon my rights to you, either because you have enjoyed yourself while obliging me or because, being unhappy, you fancied you had something to gain from your action? Even were service to be rendered by one equal to another, never would a lofty spirit's pride allow him to stoop to acknowledge it; is not he who receives always humiliated? And is this humiliation not sufficient payment for the benefactor who, by this alone, finds himself superior to the other? Is it not pride's delight to be raised above one's fellow? Is any other necessary to the person wh obligation, by causing humiliation to him who receives, becomes a burden to him, by what right is he to be forced to continue to shoulder it? Why must I consent to let myself be humiliated every time my eyes fall upon him who has obliged me? Instead of being a vice, ingratitude is as certainly a virtue in proud spirits as gratitude is one in humble; let them do what they will for me if doing it gives them pleasure, but let them expect nothing from me simply because they have enjoyed themselves."

33

Having uttered these words, to which Roland gave me no opportunity to reply, he summoned two valets who upon his instructions seized me, despoiled me, and shackled me next to my companions, so was I set to work at once, without a moment's rest after the fatiguing journey I had just made. Then Roland approaches me, he brutally handles all those parts of me designation of which modesty forbids, heaps sarcasms upon me, makes impertinent reference to the damning a brand Rodin printed upon me, then, catching up a bull's pizzle always kept in readiness nearby, he applies twenty cuts to my behind.

"That is how you will be treated, bitch," says he, "when you lag at the job; I'm not giving you this for anything you've already done, but only to show you how I cope with those who make mistakes."

I screamed, struggled against my manacles; my contortions, my cries, my tears, the cruel expressions of my pain merely entertained my executioner . . . .

"Oh, little whore, you'll see other things," says Roland, "you're not by a long shot at the end of your troubles - and I want you to make the acquaintance of even the most barbaric refinements of misery."

He leaves me.

Located in a cave on the edge of that vast well were six dark kennels; they were barred like dungeons, and they served us as shelters for the night, which arrived not long after I was enlisted in this dreadful chain gang. They came to remove my fetters and my

and dry bread Roland had mentioned, we were locked up.

I was no sooner alone than, undistracted, I abandoned myself to contemplating my situation in all its horror. Is it possible, I wondered, can it be that there are men so hardened as to have stifled in themselves their capacity for gratitude? This virtue to which I surrender myself with such charm whenever an upright spirit gives me the chance to feel it... can this virtue be unknown to certain beings, can they be utter strangers to it? and may they who have suppressed it so inhumanly in themselves be anything but monsters?

I was absorbed in these musings when suddenly I heard the door to my cell open; 'tis Roland: the villain has come to complete his outraging of me by making me serve his odious eccentricities: you may well imagine, Madame, that they were to be as ferocious as his other proceedings and that such a man's love-makings are necessarily by his abhorrent character. But how can I abuse your patience by relating these new horrors? Have I not already more than soiled your imagination with infamous recitations? Dare I hazard additional ones?

"Yes, Therese," Monsieur de Corville put in, "yes, we insist upon these details, you veil them with a decency that removes all their edge of horror; there remains only what is useful to whoever seeks to perfect his understanding of enigmatic man. You may not fully apprehend how these tableaux help toward the development of the human spirit; our backwardness in this branch of learning may very well be due to the stupid restraint of those who venture to write upon such matters. Inhibited by absurd fears, they only discuss the puerilities with which every fool is familiar, and dare not, by addressing themselves boldly to the investigation of the human heart, offer its gigantic idiosyncrasies to our view."

"Very well, Monsieur, I shall proceed," Therese resumed, affected, "and proceeding as I have done until this point, I will strive to offer my sketches in the least revolting colors."

Roland, with whose portrait I ought to begin, was a short, heavy-set man, thirty-five years old, incredibly vigorous and as hirsute as a bear, with a glowering mien and fierce eye; very dark, with masculine features, a long nose, bearded to the eyes, black, shaggy brows; and in him that part which differentiates men from our sex was of such length and exorbitant circumference, that not only had I never laid eyes upon anything comparable, but was even absolutely convinced Nature had never fashioned another as prodigious; I could scarcely surround it with both hands, and its length matched that of my forearm. To this physique Roland joined all the vices which may be the issue of a fiery temperament, of considerable imagination, and of a luxurious life undisturbed by anything likely to distract from one's leisure pursuits. From his father Roland very early on in life he had become surfeited by ordinary pleasures, and begun to resort to nothing but horrors; these alone were able to revive desires in a person jaded by excessive pleasure; the women who served him were all employed in his secret debauches and to satisfy appetites only slightly less dishonest within which, nevertheless, this libertine was able to find the criminal spice wherein above all his taste delighted; Roland kept his own sister as a mistress, and it was with her he brought to a climax the passions he ignited in our company.

He was virtually naked when he entered; his inflamed visage was evidence simultaneously of the epicurean intemperance to which he had just given himself over, and the abominable lust which consumed him; for an instant he considers me with eyes that unstring my limbs.

"Get out of those clothes," says he, himself tearing off what I was wearing to cover me during the night... "yes, get rid of all that an follow me; a little while ago I made you sense what you risk by laziness; but should you desire to betray us, as that crime would be of greater magnitude, its punishment would have to be proportionally heavier; come along and see of what sort it would be."

I was in a state difficult to describe, but Roland, affording my spirit no time in which to burst forth, immediately grasped my arm and dragged me out; he pulls me along with his right hand, in his left he holds a little lantern that emits a feeble light; after winding this way and that, we reach a cellar door; he opens it, thrusts me ahead of him, tells me to descend while he closes this first barrier; I obey; a hundred paces further, a second door; he opens and shuts it in the same way; but after this one there is no stairway, only a narrow passage hewn in the rock, filled with sinuosities, whose downward slope is extremely abrupt. Not a word from Roland; the silence affrights me still more; he lights us along with his travel for about fifteen minutes; my frame of mind makes me yet more sensitive to these subterranean passages' terrible humidity. At last, we had descended to such a depth that it is without fear of exaggeration I assure you the place at which we were to arrive must have been more than a furlong below the surface of the earth;

on either side of the path we followed were occasional niches where I saw coffers containing those criminals' wealth: one last bronze door appeared, Roland unlocked it, and I nearly fell backward upon perceiving the dreadful place to which this evil man had brought me. Seeing me falter, he pushed me rudely ahead, and thus, without wishing to be there, I found myself in the middle of that appalling sepulcher. Imagine, Madame, a circular cavern, twenty-five feet in diameter, whose walls, hung in black, were decorated by none but the most lugubrious objects, skeletons of all sizes, crossed bones, several heads, bundles of whips and collecti cutlasses, poignards, firearms: such were the horrors one spied on the walls illuminated by a three-wicked oil lamp suspended in one corner of the vault; from a transverse beam dangled a rope which fell to within eight or ten feet of the ground in the center of this dungeon and which, as very soon you will see, was there for no other purpose than to facilitate dreadful expeditions: to the right was an open coffin wherein glinted an effigy of death brandishing a threatful scythe; a prayer stool was beside it; above it was visible a crucifix bracketed by candles of jet; to the left, the waxen dummy of a naked woman, so lifelike I was for a long time deceived by it; she was attached to a cross, posed with her chest facing it so that one had a full view of her posterior and cruelly molested parts; blood seemed to ooze from several wounds and to flow down her thighs; she had the most beautiful hair in all the world, her lovely head was turned toward us and plainly wrought upon her lovely face, and there were even tears flowing down her cheeks: the sight of this terrible image was again enough to make me think I would collapse; the further part of the cavern was filled by a vast black divan which eloquently bespoke all the atrocities which occurred in this infernal place.

"And here is where you will perish, Therese," quoth Roland, "if ever you conceive the fatal notion of leaving my establishment; yes, it is here I will myself put you to death, here I will make you reverberate to the anguishes inflicted by everything of the most appalling I can possibly devise."

As he gave vent to this threat Roland became aroused; his agitation, his disorder made him resemble a tiger about to spring upon its prey: 'twas then he brought to light the formidable member wherewith he was outfitted; he had me touch it, asked me whether I had ever beheld its peer.

"Such as you see has, however, got to be introduced into the narrowest part of your body even if I must split you in half; my sister, considerably your junior, manages it in the same sector; never do I enjoy women in any other fashion," and so as to leave me in no doubt of the locale he had in mind, he inserted into it three fingers armed with exceedingly long nails, the while saying:

"Yes, 'tis there, Therese, it will be shortly into this hole I will drive this member which affrights you; it will be run every inch of the way in, it will tear you, you'll bleed and I will be beside myself."

Foam flecked his lips as he spoke these words interspersed with revolting oaths and blasphemies. The hand, which had been prying open the shrine he seemed to want to attack, now strayed over all the adjacent parts; he scratched them, he did as much to my breast, he clawed me so badly I was not to get over the pain for a fortnight. Next, he placed me on t mossy tonsure with which Nature ornaments the altar wherein our species finds regeneration; he set it afire and burned it. His fingers closed upon the fleshy protuberance which surmounts this same altar, he snatched at it and scraped roughly, then he inserted his fingers within and his nails ripped the membrane which lines it. Losing all control over himself, he told me that, since he had me in his lair, I might just as well not leave it, for that would spare him the nuisance of bringing me back down again; I fell to my knees and dared remind him again of what I had done in his behalf . . . . I observed I but further excited him by harping again upon the rights to his pity I fancied were mine; he told me to be silent, bringing up his knee and giving me a tremendous blow in the pit of the stomach which sent me sprawling on the flagstones. He seized a handful of my hair and jerked me erect.

"Very well!" he said, "come now! prepare yourself; it is a certainty, I am going to kill you . . . ."

"Oh, Monsieur!"

"No, no, you've got to die; I do not want to hear you reproach me with your good little deeds; I don't like owing anything to anybody, others have got to rely upon me for everything . . . . You're going to perish, I tell you, get into that coffin, let's see if it fits."

He lifts me, thrusts me into it and shuts it, then quits the cavern and gives me the impression I have been left there. Never had I thought myself so near to death; alas! it was nonetheless to be presented to me under a yet more real aspect. Roland returns, he fetches me out of the coffin.

"You'll be well off in there," says he, "one would say 'twas made for you; but to let you finish peacefully in that box would be a death too sweet; I'm going to expose you to one of a different variety which, all the same, will have its agreeable qualities; so implore your God, whore, pray to him to come posthaste and avenge you if h really has it in him . . . ."

I cast myself down upon the prie-dieu, and while aloud I open my heart to the Eternal, Roland in a still crueler manner intensifies, upon the hindquarters I expose to him, his vexations and his torments; with all his strength he flogs those parts with a steel-tipped martinet, each blow draws a gush of blood which springs to the walls.

"Why," he continued with a curse, "he doesn't much aid you, your God, does he? and thus he allows unhappy virtue to suffer, he abandons it to villainy's hands; ah! what a bloody fine God you've got there, Therese, what a superb God he is! Come," he says, "come here, whore, your prayer should be done," and at the same time he places me upon the divan at the back of that cell; "I told you Therese, you have got to die!"

He seizes my arms, binds them to my side, then he slips a black silken noose about my neck; he holds both ends of the cord and, by tightening, he can strangle and dispatch me to the other world ei quickly or slowly, depending upon his pleasure.

"This torture is sweeter than you may imagine, Therese," says Roland; "you will only approach death by way of unspeakably pleasurable sensations; the pressure this noose will bring to bear upon your nervous system will set fire to the organs of voluptuousness; the effect is certain; were all the people who are condemned to this torture to know in what an intoxication of joy it makes one die, less terrified by this retribution for their crimes, they would commit them more often and with much greater self-assurance; this delicious operation, Therese, by causing, as well, the contraction of the locale in which I am going to fit myself," he added as he presented himself to a criminal avenue so worthy of such a villain, "is also going to double my pleasure."

He thrusts, he sweats, 'tis in vain; he prepares the road, 'tis futile; he is too monstrously proportioned, his enterprises are repeatedly frustrated; and then his wrath nails, his hands, his feet fly to revenge him upon the opposition Nature puts up against him; he returns to the assault, the glowing blade slides to the edge of the neighboring canal and smiting vigorously, penetrates to nigh the midway mark; I utter a cry; Roland, enraged by his mistake, withdraws petulantly, and this time hammers at the other gate with such force the moistened dart plunges in, rending me. Roland exploits this first sally's success; his efforts become more violent; he gains ground; as he advances, he gradually tightens the fatal cord he has passed round my neck, hideous screams burst from my lips; amused by them, the ferocious Roland urges me to redouble my howlings, - for he is but too confident of their insufficiency, he is perfectly able to put a stop to them when he wishes; their shrill sharp notes inflame him, the noose's pressure is modulated by his degrees of delight; little by little my voice waxes faint; the tightenings now become so intense that my senses weaken although I do not lose the power to feel; brutally shaken by the enormous instrument with which Roland is rending my entrails, despite my frightful circumstances, I feel myself flooded by his lust's jetted outpourings; I still hear the cries he mouths as he discharges; an instant of stupor followed, I knew not what had happened to me, but soon my eyes open again to the light, I find myself free, untied, and my sensory organs seem to come back to life.

"Well, Therese," says my butcher, "I dare swear that if you'll tell the truth you'll say you felt pleasure only?"

"Only horror, Monsieur, only disgust, only anguish and despair."

"You are Lying, I am fully acquainted with the effects you have just experienced, but what does it matter what they were? I fancy you already know me well enough to be damned certain that when I undertake something with you, the joy you reap from it concerns me infinitely less than my own, and this voluptuousness I seek has been so keen that in an instant I am going to procure some more of it. It is now upon yourself, Therese," declares this signal libertine, "it is upon you alone your life is going to depend."

Whereupon he hitches about my neck the rope that hangs from the ceiling; he has me stand upon a stool, pulls the rope taut, secures it, and to the stool he attaches a string whose end he keeps in his hand as he sits down in an armchair facing me; I am given a sickle which I am to use to sever the rope at the moment when, by means of the string, he jerks the stool from beneath my feet.

"Notice, Therese," he says when all is ready, "that though you may miss your blow, I'll not miss mine; and so I am not mistaken when I say your life depends upon you."

He excites himself; it is at his intoxication's critical moment he is to snatch away the stool which, removed, will leave me dangling from the beam; he does everything possible to pretend the instant has come; he would be beside himself were I to miss my cue; but do what he will, I divine the crisis, the violence of his ecstasy betrays him, I see him make the telltale movement, the stool flies away, I cut the rope and fall to the ground; there I am, completely detached, and although five yards divide us, would you believe it, Madame? I feel my entire body drenched with the evidence of his delirium and his frenzy.

Anyone but I, taking advantage of the weapon she clutched in her hand, would doubtless have leapt upon that monster; but what might I have gained by this brave feat? for I did not have the keys to those subterranean passages, I was ignorant of their scheme, I should have perished before being able to emerge from them; Roland, furthermore, was armed; and so I got up, leaving the sickle on the ground so that he might not conceive the slightest suspicion of my intentions, and indeed he had none, for he had savored the full extent of pleasure and, far more content with my tractability, with my resignation, than with my agility, he signaled to me and we left.

34

The next day I cast an appraising eye upon my companions: those four girls ranged from twenty-five to thirty years of age; although bestialized and besotted by misery and warped by excessive drudgery, they still had the remnants of beauty; their figures were handsome, and the youngest, called Suzanne, still had, together with charming eyes, very fine hair; Roland had seized her in Lyon, he had deflowered her, and after having sworn to her family he would marry her, he had brought her to this frightful chateau, where she had been three years his slave, and during that period she had been especially singled out to be the object of the monster's ferocities: by dint of blows from the bull's pizzle, her buttocks had become as calloused and toughened as would be cow's hide dried in the sun; she had a cancer upon her left breast and an abscess in her matrix which caused her unspeakable suffering; all that was the perfidious Roland's achievement; each of those horrors was the fruit of his lecheries.

It was she who informed me Roland was on the eve of departing for Venice if the considerable sums he had very recently shipped to Spain could be converted into letters of credit he needed for Italy, for he did not want to transport his gold east across the Alps; never did he send any in that direction: it was in a different country from the one he had decided to inhabit that he circulated his false coins; by this device, rich to be sure but only in the bank-notes of another kingdom, his rascalities could never be detected in the land where he planned to take up his next abode. But everything could be overthrown within the space of an instant and the retirement he envisioned wholly depended upon this latest transaction in which the bulk of his treasure was compromised. Were Cadiz to accept his false piasters, sequins, and louis, and against them send him letters negotiable in Venice, Roland would be established for the rest of his days; were the fraud to be detected, one single day would suffice to demolish the fragile edifice of his fortune.

"Alas!" I remarked upon learning these details, "Providence will be just for once. It will not countenance the success of such a monster, and all of us will be revenged . . . ."

Great God I in view of the experience I had acquired, how was I able thus to reason!

Toward noon we were given a two-hour respite, which we always used to good advantage to go for a little individual rest and food in our cells; at two o'clock we were reattached to the wheel and were made to work till nightfall; never were we allowed to enter the chateau; if we were naked, 'twas not only because of the heat, but so as better to be able to receive the bull's pizzle beatings our savage master periodically came to inflict upon us; in winter we were given pantaloons and a light sweater which so closely hugged the skin that our bodies were not the less exposed to the blows of a villain whose unique pleasure was to beat us half-senseless.

A week passed during which I saw no sign of Roland; on the ninth day he visited us at work and maintained Suzanne and I were improperly applying ourselves to our task; he distributed thirty cuts with the pizzle upon each of us, slashing us from back to calf.

At midnight on that same day, the evil man came to get me in my kennel and, warmed by the sight of what his cruelties had produced, he once again introduced his terrible bludgeon into the shadowy lair I exposed by the posture he made me assume in order to inspect the vestiges of his rage. When his hungers were appeased I thought to profit from his momentary calm to supplicate him to mitigate my lot. Alas! I was unaware that in such a genius, whereas the delirious interlude stimulates the penchant for cruelty into greater activity, the subsequent reflux does not by any means restore the honest man's pacific virtues to it; 'tis a fire more or less quickened by the fuel wherewith it is fed, but one whose embers, though covered with cinder, burn nonetheless.

"And what right have you," Roland replied to me, "to expect me to sweeten your circumstances? Because of the fantasies I am pleased to put into execution with you? But am I to throw myself at your feet and implore you to accord favors for the granting of which you can implore some recompense? I ask nothing from you, I take, and I simply do not see that, because I exercise one right over you, it must result that I have to abstain from demanding a second; there is no love in what I do: love is a chivalric sentiment I hold in sovereign contempt and to whose assaults my heart is always impervious; I employ a woman out of necessity, as one employs a round and hollow vessel for a different purpose but an analogous need; but never according this individual, which my money and authority make subject to me, either esteem or tenderness, owing to myself what I get from her and never exacting from her anything but submission, I cannot be constrained, in the light of all this, to acknowledge any gratitude toward her. I ask them who would like to compel me to be thankful whether a thief who snatches a man's purse in the woods because he, the thief, is the stronger of the two, owes this man any gratitude for the wrong he has just done him; the same holds true for an outrage committed against a woman: it may justify a repetition of the abuse, but never is it a sufficient reason to grant her compensation."

"Oh, Monsieur," I said to him, "to what limits you do carry your villainy!"

"To the ultimate periods," Roland answered; "there is not a single extravagance in the world in which I have not indulged, not a crime I have not committed, and not one that my doctrines do not excuse or legitimate; unceasingly, I have found in evil a kind of attractiveness which always redounds to my lust's advantage; crime ignites my appetites; the more frightful it is, the more it stimulates; in committing it, I enjoy the same sort of pleasure ordinary folk taste in naught but lubricity, and a hundred times I have discovered myself, while thinking of crime, while surrendering to it, or just after having executed it, in precisely the same state in which one is when confronted by a beautiful naked woman; it irritates my senses in the same way, and I have committed it in order to arouse myself as, when one is filled with impudicious designs, one approaches a beautiful object."

"Oh, Monsieur! 'tis frightful, what you say, but I have beheld examples of it."

"There are a thousand, Therese. It must not be supposed that it is a woman's beauty which best stirs a libertine mind, it is rather the species of crime that the law has associated with possession of her: the proof of which is that the more criminal this possession the more one is inflamed by it; the man who enjoys a woman he steals from her husband, a daughter he snatches from her parents, knows a far greater delectation, no doubt of it, than does the husband who enjoys no one but his wife, and the more the ties one breaks appear to be respected, the more the voluptuousness is compounded. If 'tis one's mother, or one's daughter, so many additional charms to the pleasures experienced; when you've savored all this, then you truly would have interdictions further increase in order to give the violation of them added difficulty and greater charm; now, if pleasure-taking is seasoned by a criminal flavoring, crime, dissociated from this pleasure, may become a joy in itself; there will then be a certain delight in naked crime. Well, it is impossible that what contributes the saline tang not itself be very salty. Thus, let me imagine, the abduction of a girl on one's own account will give a very lively pleasure, but abduction in the interests of someone else will give all that pleasure with which the enjoyment of this girl is improved by rape; the theft of a watch, the rape of a purse will also give the same pleasure, and if I have accustomed my senses to being moved by the rape of some girl qua rape, that same pleasure, that same delight will be found again in the seizing of the watch or of the purse, etc.; and that explains the eccentricity in so many honest folk who steal without needing to steal. Nothing more common; from this moment on, one both tastes the greatest pleasure in everything criminal, and, by every imaginable device, one renders simple enjoyments as criminal as they can possibly be rendered; by conducting oneself in this style, one but adds to enjoyment the dash of salt which was wanting and which became indispensable to happiness' perfection. These doctrines lead far, I know; perhaps, Therese, I shall even show you how far before too long, but what matter? enjoyment's the thing. Was there, for example, dear girl, anything more ordinary or more natural than for me to enjoy you? But you oppose it, you ask that it stop; it would seem that, in the light of my obligations toward you, I ought to grant what you request; however, I surrender to nothing, I listen to nothing, I slash through all the knots that bind fools, I submit you to my desires, and out of the most elementary, the most monotonous enjoyment I evolve one that is really delicious; therefore submit, Therese, submit, and if ever you are reincarnated and return to the world in the guise of the mighty, exploit your privileges in the same way and you will know every one of the most lively and most piquant pleasures."

These words gone out of his mouth, Roland went away and left me to ponder thoughts which, as you may well believe, presented him in no favorable aspect.

I had been six months in this household, from time to time serving the villain's disgraceful debauches, when one night I beheld him enter my prison with Suzanne.

"Come, Therese," said he, " 'tis already a long time, I find, since I took you down to that cavern which impressed you so deeply; both of you are going to accompany me there, but don't expect to climb back together, for I absolutely must leave one of you behind; well, we'll see which one fate designates."

I get to my feet, cast alarmed glances at my companion, I see tears rolling from her eyes... and we set off.

When we were locked into the underground vault, Roland examined each of us with ferocious eyes, he amused himself by reiterating our sentence and persuading us both that one of the two would certainly remain there below.

"Well," said he, seating himself and having us stand directly before him, "each of you take your turn and set to work exorcising this disabled object; there's a devil in it keeps it limp, and woe unto the one of you who restores its energy."

" 'Tis an injustice," quoth Suzanne; "she who arouses you most should be the one to obtain your mercy."

"Not at all," Roland retorted, "once it is manifest which of you arouses me most, it is established which one's death will give me the greater pleasure... and

I'm aiming at pleasure, nothing else. Moreover, by sparing her who inflames me the more rapidly, you would both proceed with such industry that you might perhaps plunge my senses into their ecstasy before the sacrifice were consummated, and that must not happen."

" 'Tis to want evil for evil's sake, Monsieur," I said to Roland, "the completion of your ecstasy ought to be the only thing you desire, and if you attain it without crime, why do you want to commit one?"

"Because I only deliciously reach the critical stage in this way, and because I only came down here in order to commit one. I know perfectly well I might succeed without it, but I want it in order to succeed."

And, during this dialogue, having chosen me to begin, I start exciting his behind with one hand, his front with the other, while he touches at his leisure every part of my body offered him by my nakedness.

"You've still a long way to go, Therese," said he, fingering my buttocks, "before this fine flesh is in the state of petrified callosity and mortification apparent in Suzanne's; one might light a fire under that dear girl's cheeks without her feeling a thing; but you, Therese, you... these are yet roses bound in lilies: we'll get to them in good time, in good time."

You simply have no idea, Madame, how much that threat set me at ease; Roland doubtless did not suspect, as he uttered it, the peace it sent flooding through me, for was it not clear that, since he planned to expose me to further cruelties, he was not yet eager to immolate me? I have told you, Madame, that everything the wretched hear drives home, and thenceforth I was reassured. Another increase of happiness! I was performing in vain, and that enormous mass telescoped into itself resisted all my shakings; Suzanne was in the same posture, she was palpated in the same areas, but as her flesh was toughened in a very different way, Roland treated it with much less consideration; however, Suzanne was younger.

"I am convinced," our persecutor was saying, "that the most awesome whips would now fail to draw a drop of blood from that ass."

He made each of us bend over and, our angle of inclination providing him with the four avenues of pleasure, his tongue danced wriggling into the two narrowest; the villain spat into the others; he turned us about, had us kneel between his thighs in such a manner our breasts found themselves at a level with what of him we were stimulating.

"Oh! as regards breasts," said Roland, "you've got to yield to Suzanne; never had you such fine teats; now then, let's take a look at this noble endowment."

And with those words he pressed the poor girl's breasts till, beneath his fingers, they were covered with bruises. At this point it was no longer I who was exciting him, Suzanne had replaced me; scarcely had she fallen into his clutches when his dart, springing from its quiver, began to menace everything surrounding it.

"Suzanne," said Roland, "behold an appalling triumph . . . . 'tis your death decreed, Suzanne; I feared as much," added that ferocious man as he nipped and clawed her breasts.

As for mine, he only sucked and chewed them. At length, he placed Suzanne on her knees at the edge of the sofa, he made her bend her head and in this attitude he enjoyed her according to the frightful manner natural to him; awakened by new pains, Suzanne struggles and Roland, who simply wishes to skirmish, is content with a brisk passage of arms, and comes to take refuge in me at the same shrine at which he has sacrificed in my companion whom he does not cease to vex and molest the while.

"There's a whore who excites me cruelly," he says to me, "I don't know what to do with her."

"Oh, Monsieur," say I, "have pity upon her; her sufferings could not be more intense."

"Oh, but you're wrong!" the villain replies, "one might . . . ah I if only I had with me that celebrated Emperor Kie, one of the greatest scoundrels ever to have sat on the Chinese throne,'

(Kie, the Emperor of China, had a wife as cruel and debauched as he; bloodshed was as naught to them, and for their exclusive pleasure they spilled rivers of it every day; Within their palace they had a secret chamber where victims were put to death before their eyes and while they enjoyed themselves. Theo, one of this Prince's successors had, like him, a very bloodthirsty wife; they invented a brass column and this great cylinder they would heat red hot; unlucky persons were bound to it while the royal couple looked on: "The Princess," writes the historian from whom we have borrowed these touches, "was infinitely entertained by these melancholy victims' contortions and screams; she was not content unless her husband gave her this spectacle frequently." Hist. des Conj. vol. 7, page 43.)

...with Kie we'd really be able to perform wonders. Both he and his wife, they say, immolated victims daily and would have them live twenty-four hours in death's cruelest agonies, and in such a state of suffering that they were constantly on the verge of expiring but never quite able to die, for those monsters administered that kind of aid which made them flutter between relief and torture and only brought them back to life for one minute in order to kill them the next . . . . I, Therese, I am too gentle, I know nothing of those arts, I'm a mere apprentice."

Roland retires without completing the sacrifice and hurts me almost as much by this precipitous withdrawal as he had upon inserting himself. He throws himself into Suzanne's arms, and joining sarcasm to outrage:

"Amiable creature," he apostrophizes, "with such delight I remember the first instants of our union; never had woman given me such thrilling pleasures, never had I loved one as I did you... let us embrace, Suzanne, for we're going to part, perhaps the season of our separation will be long."

"Monster!" my companion retorts, thrusting him away with horror, "begone; to the torments you inflict upon me, join not the despair of hearing your terrible remarks; sate your rage, tigerish one, but at least respect my sufferings."

Roland laid hands on her, stretched her upon the couch, her legs widespread, and the workshop of generation ideally within range.

"Temple of my ancient pleasures," the infamous creature intoned, "you who procured me delights so sweet when I plucked your first roses, I must indeed address to you my farewells . . . ."

The villain! he drove his fingernails into it and, rummaging about inside for a few minutes while screams burst from Suzanne's mouth, he did not withdraw them until they were covered with blood. Glutted and wearied by these horrors, and feeling, indeed, he could restrain himself no longer:

"Come, Therese, come," he said, "let's conclude all this with a little scene of funambulism: it'll be cut-the-cord, dear girl."

(This game, described above, was in great use amongst the Celts from whom we are descended (see Monsieur Peloutier's 'Histoire d'u Celts'); virtually all these extravagances of debauchery, these extraordinary libertine passions some part of which are described in this book and which, - how ridiculously! today awaken the law's attention, were, in days bygone, either our ancestors' sports, games far superior to our contemporary amusement, or legalized customs, or again, religious ceremonies; currently, they are transformed into crimes. In how many pious rituals did not the pagans employ flagellation! Several people used these identical tortures, or passions, to initiate their warriors; this was known as huscanaver (viz., the religious ceremonies of every race on earth). These pleasantries, whose maximum inconvenience may be at the very most the death of a slut, are capital crimes at the moment. Three cheers for the progress of civilization! How it conspires to the happiness of man, and how much more fortunate than our forebears we are!)

...that was the name he gave that deadly legerdemain of which I gave you a description when I mentioned Roland's cavern for the first time. I mount the three-legged stool, the evil fellow fits the halter about my neck, he takes his place opposite me; although in a frightful state, Suzanne excites him manually; an instant passes, then he snaps the stool from beneath me, but equipped with the sickle, I sever the cord immediately and fall uninjured to the ground.

"Nicely done, very neat!" says Roland, "your turn, Suzanne, there it is, and I'll spare you, if you manage as cleverly."

Suzanne takes my place. Oh, Madame, allow me to pass over that dreadful scene's details . . . . The poor thing did not recover from it.

"And now off we go, Therese," says Roland, "you'll not return to this place until your time has come."

"Whenever you like, Monsieur, whenever you like," I reply; "I prefer death to the frightful life you have me lead. Are there wretches such as we for whom life can be valuable?..."

35

And Roland locked me into my cell. The next day my companions asked what had become of Suzanne and I told them; they were hardly surprised; all were awaiting the same fate and each, like me, seeing therein a term to their suffering, passionately longed for it.

And thus two years went by, Roland indulging in his customary debauchery, I lingering on with the prospect of a cruel death, when one day the news went about the chateau that not only were our master's expectations satisfied, not only had he received the immense quantity of Venetian funds he had wished, but that he had even obtained a further order for another six millions in counterfeit coin for which he would be reimbursed in Italy when he arrived to claim payment; the scoundrel could not possibly have enjoyed better luck; he was going to leave with an income of two millions, not to mention his hopes of getting more: this was the new piece of evidence Providence had prepared for me. This was the latest manner in which it wished to convince me that prosperity belongs to Crime only and indigence to Virtue.

Matters were at this stage when Roland came to take me to his cavern a third time. I recollect what he threatened me with on my previous visit, I shudder . . . .

"Rest assured," he says, "you've nothing to fear, 'tis a question of something which concerns me alone... an uncommon joy I'd like to taste and from which you will incur no risks."

I follow him. When the doors are shut:

"Therese," says Roland, "there's no one in the house but you to whom I dare confide the problem; I've got to have a woman of impeccable honesty . . . . I've no one about but you, I confess that I prefer you to my sister . . . .

Taken aback, I entreat him to clarify himself.

"Then listen," says he; "my fortune is made, but whatever be the favors I have received from fate, it can desert me at any instant; I may be trapped, I could be caught while transporting my bullion, and if that misfortune occurs, Therese, it's the rope that's waiting for me: 'tis the same delight I am pleased to have women savor: that's the one will serve as my undoing; I am as firmly persuaded as I can possibly be that this death is infinitely sweeter than cruel; but as the women upon whom I have tested its initial anguishes have never really wished to tell me the truth, it is in person I wish to be made acquainted with the sensation. By way of the experience itself I want to find out whether it is not very certain this asphyxiation impels, in the individual who undergoes it, the erectory nerve to produce an ejaculation; once convinced this death is but a game, I'll brave it with far greater courage, for it is not my existence's cessation terrifies me: my principles are determined upon that head and well persuaded matter can never become anything but matter again, I have no greater dread of Hell than I have expectation of Paradise; but a cruel death's torments make me apprehensive; I don't wish to suffer when I perish; so let's have a try. You will do to me everything I did to you; I'll strip; I'll mount the stool, you'll adjust the rope, I'll excite myself for a moment, then, as soon as you see things assume a certain consistency, you'll jerk the stool free and I'll remain hanging; you'll leave me there until you either discern my semen's emission or symptoms of death's throes; in the latter case, you'll cut me down at once; in the other, you'll allow Nature to take her course and you'll not detach me until afterward. You observe, Therese, I'm putting my life in your hands; your freedom, your fortune will be your good conduct's reward."

"Ah, Monsieur, there's folly in the proposition."

"No, Therese, I insist the thing be done," he answered, undressing himself, "but behave yourself well; behold what proof I give you of my confidence and high regard !"

What possibility of hesitation had I? Was he not my master? Furthermore, it seemed to me the evil I was going to do him would be immediately offset by the extreme care I would take to save his life: I was going to be mistress of that life, but whatever might be his intentions with respect to me, it would certainly only be in order to restore it to him.

We take our stations; Roland is stimulated by a few of his usual caresses; he climbs upon the stool, I put the halter round his neck; he tells me he wants me to curse him during the process, I am to reproach him with all his life's horrors, I do so; his dart soon rises to menace Heaven, he himself gives me the sign to remove the stool, I obey; would you believe it, Madame? nothing more true than what Roland had conjectured: nothing but symptoms of pleasure ornament his countenance and at practically the same instant rapid jets of semen spring nigh to the vault. When 'tis all shot out without any assistance whatsoever from me, I rush to cut him down, he falls, unconscious, but thanks to my ministrations he quickly recovers his senses.

"Oh Therese !" he exclaims upon opening his eyes, "oh, those sensations are not to be described; they transcend all one can possibly say: let them now do what they wish with me, I stand unflinching before Themis' sword! "You're going to find me guilty yet another time, Therese," Roland went on, tying my hands behind my back, "no thanks for you, but, dear girl, what can one expect? a man doesn't correct himself at my age . . . . Beloved creature, you have just saved my life and never have I so powerfully conspired against yours; you lamented Suzanne's fate; ah well, I'll arrange for you to meet again; I'm going to plunge you alive into the dungeon where she expired."

I will not describe my state of mind, Madame, you fancy what it was; in vain did I weep, groan, I was not heeded. Roland opened the fatal dungeon, he hangs out a lamp so that I can still better discern the multitude of corpses wherewith it is filled; next, he passes a cord under my arms which, as you know, are bound behind my back, and by means of this cord he lowers me thirty feet: I am twenty more from the bottom of the pit: in this position I suffer hideously, it is as if my arms are being torn from their sockets. With what terror was I not seized I what a prospect confronted my eyes! Heaps of bodies in the midst of which I was going to finish my life and whose stench was already infecting me. Roland cinches the rope about a stick fitted above the hole then, brandishing a knife, I hear him exciting himself.

"Well, Therese," he cries, "recommend your soul to God, the instant my delirium supervenes will be that when I plunge you into the eternal abyss awaiting you; ah... ah... Therese, ah..." and I feel my head covered with proof of his ecstasy; but, happily, he has not parted the rope: he lifts me out.

"Ha," says he, "were you afraid?"

"Oh, Monsieur -"

" 'Tis thus you'll die, be sure of it, Therese, be sure of it, and 'twas pleasant to familiarize you with your egress."

We climb back to the light . . . . Was I to complain? or be thankful? What a reward for what I had just done for him! But had the monster not been in a position to do more? Could he not have killed me? Oh, what a man!

Roland prepared his departure; on the eve of setting out he pays me a visit; I fall before his feet, most urgently I beg him to free me and to give me whatever little sum of money he would like, that I might be able to reach Grenoble.

"Grenoble! Certainly not, Therese, you'd denounce us when you got there."

"Very well, Monsieur," I say, sprinkling his knees with my tears, "I swear to you I'll never go there and, to be sure of me, condescend to take me to Venice with you; I will perhaps find gentler hearts there than in my native land, and once you are so kind as to set me free, I swear to you by all that is holy I will never importune you."

"I'll not aid you, not a pennyworth of aid will you get from me," that peerless rogue answered; "everything connected with pity, commiseration, gratitude is so alien to my heart that were I three times as rich as I am, they'd not see me give one crown to the poor; the spectacle of misery irritates me, amuses me, and when I am unable to do evil myself, I have a delicious time enjoying that accomplished by the hand of destiny. Upon all this I have principles to which, Therese, I adhere faithfully; poverty is part of the natural order; by creating men of dissimilar strength, Nature has convinced us of her desire that inequality be preserved even in those modifications our culture might bring to Nature's laws. To relieve indigence is to violate the established order, to imperil it, it is to enter into revolt against that which Nature has decreed, it is to undermine the equilibrium that is fundamental to her sublimest arrangements; it is to strive to erect an equality very perilous to society, it is to encourage indolence and flatter drones, it is to teach the poor to rob the rich man when the latter is pleased to refuse the former alms, for it's a dangerous habit, and gratuities encourage it."

"Oh, Monsieur, how harsh these principles are! Would you speak thus had you not always been wealthy?"

"Who knows, Therese? everyone has a right to his opinion, that's mine, and I'll not change it. They complain about beggars in France: if they wished to be rid of them, the thing could soon be done; hang seven or eight thousand of 'em and the infamous breed will vanish overnight. The Body Politic should be governed by the same rules that apply to the Body Physical. Would a man devoured by vermin allow them to feed upon him out of sympathy? In our gardens do we not uproot the parasitic plant which harms useful vegetation? Why then should one choose to act otherwise in this case?"

"But Religion," I expostulated, "benevolence, Monsieur, humanity..."

"... are the chopping blocks of all who pretend to happiness," said Roland; "if I have consolidated my own, it is only upon the debris of all those infamous prejudices of mankind; 'tis by mocking laws human and divine; 'tis by constantly sacrificing the weak when I find them in my path, 'tis by abusing the public's good faith; 'tis by ruining the poor and stealing from the rich I have arrived at the summit of that precipice whereupon sits the temple sacred to the divinity I adore; why not imitate me? The narrow road leading to that shrine is as plainly offered to your eyes as mine; the hallucinatory virtues you have preferred to it, have they consoled you for your sacrifices? 'Tis too late, luckless one, 'tis too late, weep for your sins, suffer, and strive to find in the depths of the phantoms you worship, if any finding there is to be done, what the reverence you have shown them has caused you to lose."

With these words, the cruel Roland leaps upon me and I am again forced to serve the unworthy pleasures of a monster I had such good reason to abhor; this time I thought he would strangle me; when his passions were satisfied, he caught up the bull's pizzle and with it smote me above a hundred blows all over my body, the while assuring me I was fortunate he lacked the time to do more.

36

On the morrow, before setting out, the wretch presented us with a new scene of cruelty and of barbarity whereof no example is furnished by the annals of Andronicus, Nero, Tiberius, or Wenceslaus. Everyone at the chateau supposed Roland's sister would leave with him, and he had indeed told her to dress and ready herself for the journey; at the moment of mounting his horse, he leads her toward us. "There's your post, vile creature," says he, ordering her to take off her clothes, "I want my comrades to remember me by leaving them as a token the woman for whom they thought I had a fancy; but as we need only a certain number and as I am going to follow a dangerous road upon which my weapons will perhaps be useful, I must try my pistols upon one of these rascals." Whereupon he loads one of his guns, aims it at each of our breasts, and comes at last to his sister. "Off you go, whore," says he, blasting out her brains, "go advise the devil that Roland, the richest villain on earth, is he who most insolently taunts the hand of Heaven and challenges Satan's own!" The poor girl did not expire at once: she writhed in her death throes for a considerable period: 'twas a hideous spectacle:

that infamous scoundrel calmly considered it and did not tear his eyes away until he had left us forever.

Everything changed the day after Roland went away. His successor, a gentle and very reasonable man, had us released at once .

"That is hardly fit work for a frail and delicate sex," he said to us with kindness; "animals should be employed at this machine; our trade is criminal enough without further offending the Supreme Being with gratuitous atrocities."

He installed us in the chateau and, without requiring me to do so, suggested I assume possession of the duties Roland's sister had performed; the other women were busied cutting out counterfeit coins, a much less fatiguing task, no doubt, and one for which they were rewarded, as was I, with good lodgings and excellent food.

At the end of two months, Dalville, Roland's successor, informed us of his colleague's happy arrival at Venice; there he had established himself and there realized his fortune and there he enjoyed it in peace and quiet, wholly content, full of the felicity he had anticipated. The fate of the man who replaced him was of a distinctly different character. The unfortunate Dalville was honest in his profession, indeed, even more honest than was necessary in order to be destroyed.

One day, while all was calm at the chateau, while, under the direction of that good master, the work, although criminal, was however being carried on with gaiety, one day the gates were stormed, the moats bridged and the house, before our men had a moment's opportunity to look to their defense, found itself invaded by soldiers of the constabulary, sixty strong. Surrender was our sole alternative; we were shackled like beasts; we were attached to the horses and marches down to Grenoble. "O Heaven!" I said to myself as we entered, "'tis then the scaffold destiny holds for me in this city wherein I wildly fancied my happiness was to be born . . . . Oh! how deceived is man by his intuitions!"

The court was not long tarrying over the counterfeiters' case; they were all sentenced to the gallows; when the mark that branded me was detected, they scarcely gave themselves the trouble of interrogating me and I was about to be hanged along with the others when I made a last effort to obtain some pity from that famous magistrate who proved to be an honor to his tribunal, a judge of integrity, a beloved citizen, an enlightened philosopher whose wisdom and benevolence will grave his name for all time in letters of gold upon Themis' temple. He listened to me; convinced of my good faith and the authenticity of my wretched plight, he deigned to give my case a little more attention than his cohorts saw fit to lavish upon it . . . . O great man, 'tis to thee I owe an homage: a miserable creature's gratitude would not sit onerously with thee and the tribute she offers thee, by publishing abroad thy goodness of heart, will always be her sweetest joy.

Monsieur S_____ himself became my advocate; my testimony was heard, and his male eloquence illumined the mind of the court. The general depositions of the false coiners they were going to execute fortified the zeal of the man who had the kindness to take an interest in me: I was declared an unwilling party to crime, innocent, and fully acquitted of all charges, was set at complete liberty to become what I wished; to those services my protector added a collection he had taken for my relief, and it totaled more than fifty louis; I began to see a dawning of happiness at last; my presentiments seemed finally about to be realized and I thought I had reached an end of my tribulations when it pleased Providence to convince me they were still far from their definitive cessation.

Upon emerging from jail I took up lodgings at an inn facing the Isere bridge on the side of the faubourgs where, I had been assured, I might find proper quarters. My plan, suggested by the advice of Monsieur S____, was to stay there awhile in order to try to find a situation in the town; in the event the letters of recommendation Monsieur S____ had so kindly given me produced no results, I was to return to Lyon. On the second day I was dining at my inn - -'twas what is called table d'hote Ä when I noticed I was being closely scrutinized by a tall, very handsomely attired woman who went under a baroness' title; upon examining her in my turn, I believed I recognized her; we both rose and approached each other, we embraced like two people who once knew each other but cannot remember under what circumstances.

Then the baroness drew me aside.

"Therese," says she, "am I in error? are you not the person I saved from the Conciergerie ten years ago? have you entirely forgotten your Dubois?"

Little flattered by this discovery, I however replied to it with politeness, but I was dealing with the most subtle, the most adroit woman in contemporary France; there was no way of eluding her. Dubois overwhelmed me with attentions, she said that she, like the entire town, had taken an interest in my fate but that had she known who I really was, she would have resorted to all sorts of measures and made many a representation to the magistrates, amongst whom, she declared, she had several friends. As usual, I was weak, I permitted myself to be led to this woman's room and there I related my sufferings to her.

"My dear friend," said she, renewing her embraces, "if I have desired to see you more intimately, it is to tell you I have made my fortune and that all I possess is at your disposal; look here," she said, opening some caskets brimming with gold and diamonds, "these are the fruits of my industry; had I worshiped Virtue like you, I should be in prison today, or hanged."

"O Madame," I cried, "if you owe all that to naught but crime, Providence, which eventually is always just, will not suffer you to enjoy it for long."

"An error," said Dubois; "do not imagine that Providence invariably favors Virtue; do not let a brief interlude of prosperity blind you to this point. It is as one to the maintenance of Providence's scheme whether 'tis Peter or Paul who follows the evil career while the other surrenders himself to good; Nature must have an equal quantity of each, and the exercise of crime rather than the commission of good is a matter of you've no idea what indifference to her; listen Therese, pay a little attention to me," continued that corruptor, seating herself and bidding me take a nearby chair; "you have some wit, my child, and your intelligence will be speedily convinced.

"'Tis not man's election of Virtue which brings him happiness, dear girl, for Virtue, like vice, is nothing beyond a scheme of getting along in the world; 'tis not, hence, a question of adopting one course rather than another; 'tis merely a matter of following the road generally taken; he who wanders away from it is always wrong; in an entirely virtuous world, I would recommend virtue to you, because worldly rewards being associated therewith, happiness would infallibly be connected with it too; in a totally corrupt world, I would never advise anything but vice. He who does not walk along with others has inevitably to perish; everyone he encounters he collides with, and, as he is weak, he has necessarily to be crushed. It is in vain the law wishes to re-establish order and restore men to righteousness; too unjust to undertake the task, too insufficient to succeed in it, those laws will lure you away from the beaten path, but only temporarily; never will they make man abandon it. While the general interest of mankind drives it to corruption, he who does not wish to be corrupted with the rest will therefore be fighting against the general interest; well, what happiness can he expect who is in perpetual conflict with the interest of everyone else? Are you going to tell me it is vice which is at odds with mankind's welfare? I would grant this true in a world composed of equal proportions of good and bad people, because in this instance, the interest of the one category would be in clear contradiction with that of the other; however, that does not hold true in a completely corrupt society; in it, my vices outrage the vicious only and provoke in them other vices which they use to square matters: and thus all of us are happy: the vibration becomes general: we have a multitude of conflicts and mutual injuries whereby everyone, immediately recovering what he has just lost, incessantly discovers himself in a happy position. Vice is dangerous to naught but Virtue which, frail and timorous, dares undertake nothing; but when it shall no longer exist on earth, when its wearisome reign shall reach its end, vice thereafter outraging no one but the vicious, will cause other vices to burgeon but will cause no further damage to the virtuous. How could you help but have foundered a thousand times over in the course of your life, Therese? for have you not continually driven up the one-way street all the world has crowded down? Had you turned and abandoned yourself to the tide you would have made a safe port as well as I. Will he who wishes to climb upstream cover as much distance in a day as he who moves with the current? You constantly talk about Providence; ha! what proves to you this Providence is a friend of order and consequently enamored of Virtue? Does It not give you uninterrupted examples of Its injustices and Its irregularities? Is it by sending mankind war, plagues, and famine, is it by having formed a universe vicious in every one of its particulars It manifests to your view Its extreme fondness of good? Why would you have it that vicious individuals displease It since Providence Itself acts only through the intermediary of vices? since all is vice and corruption in Its works? since all is crime and disorder in what It wills?

Moreover, whence do we derive those impulses which lead us to do evil? is it not Providence's hand which gives them to us? is there a single one of our sensations which does not come from It? one of our desires which is not Its artifact? is it then reasonable to say that It would allow us or give us penchants for something which might be harmful to It or useless? if then vices serve Providence, why should we wish to disown them, disclaim them, resist them? what would justify our labors to destroy them? and whence comes the right to stifle their voice? A little more philosophy in the world would soon restore all to order and would cause magistrates and legislators to see that the crimes they condemn and punish with such rigor sometimes have a far greater degree of utility than those virtues they preach without practicing and without ever rewarding."

"But when I become sufficiently enfeebled, Madame," I replied, "to be able to embrace your appalling doctrines, how will you manage to suppress the feelings of guilt in my heart whose birth they will cause at every instant?"

"Guilt is an illusion," Dubois answered; "my dear Therese, it it naught but the idiotic murmuring of a soul too debilitated to dare annihilate it."

"Annihilate it! May one?"

"Nothing simpler; one repents only of what one is not in the habit of doing; frequently repeat what makes you remorseful and you'll quickly have done with the business; against your qualms oppose the torch of your passions and self-interest's potent laws: they'll be put to rout in a trice. Remorse is no index of criminality; it merely denotes an easily subjugated spirit; let some absurd command be given you, which forbids you to leave this room, and you'll not depart without guilty feelings however certain it is your departure will cause no one any harm. And so it is not true that it is exclusively crime which excites remorse. By convincing yourself of crime's nullity, of its necessity with what regards Nature's universal scheme, it would therefore be as possible to vanquish the guilt one would sense after having committed it as it would be to throttle that which would be born from your leaving this room after having received the illegal order to stay here. One must begin with a precise analysis of everything mankind denominates as criminal; by convincing oneself that it is merely the infraction of its laws and national manners they characterize thus, that what is called crime in France ceases to be crime two hundred leagues away, that there is no act really considered criminal everywhere upon earth, none which, vicious or criminal here, is not praiseworthy and virtuous a few miles hence, that it is all a matter of opinion and of geography and that it is therefore absurd to tie oneself down to practicing virtues which are only vices somewhere else, and to flying from crimes which are excellent deeds in another climate - I ask you now if, after these reflections, I can still retain any feelings of guilt for having committed, either for the sake of pleasure or of self-interest, a crime in France which is nothing but a virtue in China? or if I ought to make myself very miserable or be prodigiously troubled about practicing actions in France which would have me burned in Siam? Now, if remorse exists only in reason of prohibition, if it is never but born of the wreckage of the inhibitory check and in no wise of the committed act, is it so very wise to allow the impulse in itself to subsist? is it not stupid not to extirpate it at once? Let one become accustomed to considering as inconsequential the act which has just excited remorse; let the scrupulously meditated study of the manners and customs of all the world's nations culminate in one's judging the act indifferent; as a result of this research, let one repeat this act, whatever it is, as often as possible; or, better still, let one commit more powerful versions of the act one is concerting so as better to habituate oneself to it, do this, and familiarity together with reason will soon destroy remorse for it; they will rapidly annihilate this shadowy, furtive impulse, issue of naught but ignorance and education. One will straightway feel that there being nothing really criminal in anything whatsoever, there is stupidity in repentance and pusillanimity in not daring to do everything that may be useful or agreeable to us, whatever be the dikes one must breach, the fences one must topple in order to do it. I am forty-five, Therese; I committed my first crime at fourteen. That one emancipated me from all the bonds that hampered me; since then I have not ceased to chase fortune throughout a career sown with crimes, there's not a single one I've not done or had done... and never have I known any remorse. However that may be, I am reaching my term, yet another two or three neat strokes and I pass from the mediocre condition wherein I was to have spent my life, to an income of above fifty thousand a year. I repeat, my dear, never upon this happily traveled road has remorse made me feel its stings; a catastrophic miscarriage might this instant plunge me from the pinnacle into the abyss, I'd not feel remorse, no: I would lament my want of skill or accuse men, but I should always be at peace with my conscience."

37

"Very well," I replied, "very well, Madame, but let's spend a moment reasoning in terms of your own principles: what right have you to require that my conscience be as impregnable as yours when since childhood it has not been accustomed to vanquishing the same prejudices? By what title do you require that my mind, which is not constituted like your own, be able to adopt the same systems? You acknowledge sums of good and evil in Nature, you admit that, in consequence, there must be a certain quantity of beings who practice good and another group which devotes itself to evil; the course I elect is hence natural; therefore, how would you be able to demand that I take leave of the rules Nature prescribes to me? You say you find happiness in the career you pursue; very well, Madame, why should it be that I do not also find it in the career I pursue? Do not suppose, furthermore, that the law's vigilance long leaves in peace him who violates its codes, you have just had a striking example of the contrary; of the fifteen scoundrels with whom I was living, fourteen perish ignominiously . . . ."

"And is that what you call a misfortune?" Dubois asked. "But what does this ignominy mean to him who has principles no longer? When one has trespassed every frontier, when in our eyes honor is no more than a hallucination, reputation of perfect indifference, religion an illusion, death a total annihilation; is it then not the same thing, to die on the scaffold or in bed? There are two varieties of rascals in the world, Therese: the one a powerful fortune or prodigious influence shelters from this tragic end; the other one who is unable to avoid it when taken. The latter, born unprovided with possessions, must have but one desire if he has any esprit: to become rich at no matter what price; if he succeeds, he obtains what he wanted and should be content; if he is put on the rack, what's he to regret since he has nothing to lose? Those laws decreed against banditry are null if they are not extended to apply to the powerful bandit; that the law inspire any dread in the miserable is impossible, for the sword is the miserable man's only resource."

"And do you believe," I broke in, "that in another world Celestial Justice does not await him whom crime has not affrighted in this one?"

"I believe," this dangerous woman answered, "that if there were a God there would be less evil on earth; I believe that since evil exists, these disorders are either expressly ordained by this God, and there you have a barbarous fellow, or he is incapable of preventing them and right away you have a feeble God; in either case, an abominable being, a being whose lightning I should defy and whose laws contemn. Ah, Therese I is not atheism preferable to the one and the other of these extremes? that's my doctrine, dear lass, it's been mine since childhood and I'll surely not renounce it while I live."

"You make me shudder, Madame," I said, getting to my feet; "will you pardon me? for I am unable to listen any longer to your sophistries and blasphemies."

"One moment, Therese," said Dubois, holding me back, "if I cannot conquer your reason, I may at least captivate your heart. I have need of you, do not refuse me your aid; here are a thousand louis: they will be yours as soon as the blow is struck."

Heedless of all but my penchant for doing good, I immediately asked Dubois what was involved so as to forestall, if 'twere possible, the crime she was getting ready to commit.

"Here it is," she said: "have you noticed that young tradesman from Lyon who has been taking his meals here for the past four or five days?"

"Who? Dubreuil?"

"Precisely."

"Well?"

"He is in love with you, he told me so in confidence, your modest and gentle air pleases him infinitely, he adores your candor, your virtue enchants him; this romantic fellow has eight hundred thousand francs in gold or paper, it's all in a little coffer he keeps near his bed; let me give the man to understand you consent to hear him, whether that be true or not; for, does it matter? I'll get him to propose you a drive, you'll take a carriage out of the town, I'll persuade him he will advance matters with you during your promenade; you'll amuse him, you'll keep him away as long as possible, meanwhile I'll rob him, but I'll not flee; his belongings will reach Turin before I quit Grenoble, we will employ all imaginable art to dissuade him from settling his eyes upon us, we'll pretend to assist his searches; however, my departure will be announced, he'll not be surprised thereby, you'll follow me, and the thousand louis will be counted out to you immediately we get to the Piedmont."

"Agreed, Madame," I said to Dubois, fully determined to warn Dubreuil of the concerted theft, "but consider," I added in order more thoroughly to deceive this villain, "that if Dubreuil is fond of me, by revealing the business or by giving myself to him, I might get much more from him than you offer me to betray him."

"Bravo," replied Dubois, "that's what I call an adept scholar, I'm beginning to believe Heaven gave you a greater talent for crime than you pretend: ah well," she continued, picking up a quill, "here's my note for twenty thousand crowns, now dare say no to me."

"Not for the world, Madame," quoth I, taking her note, "but, at least, my weakness and my wrong in surrendering to your seductions are to be attributed only to my impecunious circumstances."

"I'd prefer to interpret it as a meritorious act of your intelligence," said Dubois, "but if you prefer me to blame your poverty, why then, as you like; serve me and you will always be content."

Everything was arranged; the same evening I began in earnest to play my game with Dubreuil, and indeed I discovered he had some taste for me.

Nothing could have been more embarrassing than my situation: I was without any doubt far from lending myself to the proposed crime even had it been worth ten thousand times as much gold; but the idea of denouncing this woman was also painful for me; I was exceedingly loath to expose to death a creature to whom I had owed my freedom ten years before. I should have liked to have been able to find a way of preventing the crime without having it punished, and with anyone else but a consummate villain like Dubois I should have succeeded; here then is what I resolved to do, all the while unaware that this horrible woman's base maneuvers would not only topple the entire edifice of my honorable schemes but even punish me for having dreamt of them.

Upon the day fixed for the projected outing, Dubois invites us both to dine in her room, we accept, and the meal over, Dubreuil and I descend to summon the carriage that has been prepared for us; Dubois does not accompany us, I find myself alone with Dubreuil the moment before we set out.

"Monsieur," I say, speaking very rapidly, "listen closely to me, don't be alarmed, no noise, and above all pay strict attention to what I am going to recommend; have you a reliable friend at this hotel?"

"Yes, I have a young associate upon whom I can count with absolute confidence."

"Then, Monsieur, go promptly and order him not to leave your room for a second while we are on our drive."

"But I have the key to the room; what does this excess of precaution signify?"

"It is more essential than you believe, Monsieur, I beg you to employ it, or else I shall not go out with you; the woman with whom we dined is a bandit, she only arranged our outing in order more easily to rob you while we are gone; make haste, Monsieur, she is watching us, she is dangerous; quickly, turn your key over to your friend, have him go and install himself in your room and let him not budge until we're back. I'll explain the rest as soon as we are in the carriage."

Dubreuil heeds me, presses my hand in token of thanks, flies to give orders relative to the warning he has received, and returns; we leave; when en route, I disclose the entire adventure to him, I recite mine and inform him of the unhappy circumstances in my life which have caused me to make the acquaintance of such a woman. This correct and sensible young man expresses the deepest gratitude for the service I have just so kindly rendered him, he takes an interest in my misfortunes, and proposes to alleviate them with the bestowal of his hand.

"I am only too happy to be able to make you restitution for the wrongs fortune has done you, Mademoiselle," says he; "I am my own master, dependent upon no one, I am going on to Geneva to make a considerable investment with the funds your timely warning has saved me from losing; accompany me to Switzerland; when we arrive there I shall become your husband and you will not appear in Lyon under any other title, or, if you prefer, Mademoiselle, if you have any misgivings, it will only be in my own country I will give you my name."

Such an offer, so very flattering, was one I dared not refuse; but it did not on the other hand become me to accept it without making Dubreuil aware of all that might cause him to repent it; he was grateful for my delicacy and only insisted the more urgently... unhappy creature that I was! 'twas necessary that happiness be offered me only in order that I be more deeply penetrated with grief at never being able to seize it! it was then ordained that no virtue could be born in my heart without preparing torments for me!

Our conversation had already taken us two leagues from the city, and we were about to dismount in order to enjoy the fresh air along the bank of the Isere, when all of a sudden Dubreuil told me he felt very ill . . . . He got down, he was seized by dreadful vomitings; I had him climb into the carriage at once and we flew back posthaste to Grenoble. Dubreuil is so sick he has to be borne to his room; his condition startles his associate whom we find there and who, in accordance with instructions, has not stirred from the chamber; a doctor comes, Just Heaven! Dubreuil has been poisoned! I no sooner learn the fatal news than I dash to Dubois' apartment; the infamous creature! she's gone; I rush to my room, my armoire has been forced open, the little money and odds and ends I possess have been removed; Dubois, they tell me, left three hours ago in the direction of Turin. There was no doubt she was the author of this multitude of crimes; she had gone to Dubreuil's door; annoyed to find his room occupied, she revenged herself upon

me and had envenomed Dubreuil at dinner so that upon our return, if she had
succeeded with her theft, that unhappy young man would be more busied with his
own failing life than concerned to pursue her who had made off with his fortune
and would let her fly in safety; the accident of his death, occurring, so to speak,
while he was in my arms, would make me appear more suspect than herself;
nothing directly informed us of the scheme she had contrived, but could it have
been different?

And then I rush back to Dubreuil's room; I am not allowed to approach his
bedside. "But why?" I demand and am given the reason: the poor man is expiring
and is no longer occupied with anyone save his God. However, he exonerates me,
he gives assurance of my innocence; he expressly forbids that I be pursued; he
dies. Hardly has he closed his eyes when his associate hastens to bring me the
news and begs me to be easy. Alas! how could I be? how was I not to weep
bitterly for the loss of a man who had so generously offered to extricate me from
misery! how was I not to deplore a theft which forced me back into the
wretchedness whence I had only a moment before emerged! Frightful creature!
I cried; if 'tis to this your principles lead you, is it any wonder they are abhorred
and that honest folk punish them! But I was arguing from the injured party's
viewpoint and Dubois, who had only reaped happiness therefrom and saw nothing
but her interest in what she had undertaken, Dubois, I say, had doubtless reached
a very different conclusion.

To Dubreuil's associate, whose name was Valbois, I divulged everything, both
what had been concerted against the man we had lost and what had happened
to me. He sympathized with me, most sincerely regretted Dubreuil and blamed
the overly nice scruples which had prevented me from lodging a complaint
instantly I had been advised of Dubois' schemes; we agreed that this monster who
needed but four hours to get to another country and security would arrive there
before we would be able to organize her pursuit, that to follow her would involve
considerable expense, that the inn-keeper, heavily compromised by the
proceedings we would launch, by defending himself with vehemence might
perhaps end by having me crushed, I... who seemed to be living in Grenoble as
one who had missed the gallows by a hairsbreadth. These reasons convinced me
and even terrified me to the point I resolved to leave the town without even
saying farewell to my protector, Monsieur S_____. Dubreuil's friend approved the
idea; he did not conceal from me that if the entire adventure were to be revealed
he would be obliged to make depositions which, his precautions notwithstanding,
would involve me as much by my intimacy with Dubreuil as in reason of my last
outing with his friend; in the light of which he urged me to leave at once without
a word to anyone, and I could be perfectly sure that, on his side, he would never
take steps against me, whom he believed innocent, and, in all that had just
occurred, whom he could only accuse of weakness.

38

Upon pondering Valbois' opinions, I recognized they were that much better the more certain it appeared I would be beheld with suspicion; the less my guilt, the wiser his suggestions; the one thing that spoke in my behalf, the recommendation I had made to Dubreuil at the outset of our promenade, which had, so they told me, been unsatisfactorily explained by the article of his death, would not appear so conclusive as I might hope; whereupon I promptly made my decision; I imparted it to Valbois.

"Would," said he, "that my friend had charged me with some dispositions favorable to you, I should carry out such requests with the greatest pleasure; I am sorry indeed he did not tell me 'twas to you he owed the advice to guard his room; but he said nothing of the sort, not a word did I have from him, and consequently I am obliged to limit myself to merely complying with his orders. What you have suffered by his loss would persuade me to do something in my own name were I able to, Mademoiselle, but I am just setting up in business, I am young, my fortune is not boundless, I am compelled to render an account of Dubreuil to his family and without delay; allow me then to confine myself to the one little service I beg you to accept: here are five louis and I have here as well an honest merchant from Chalon-sur-Saone, my native city; she is going to return there after a day and a night's stop at Lyon where she is called by business matters; I put you into her keeping."

"Madame Bertrand," Valbois continued, "here is the young lady I spoke of; I recommend her to you, she wishes to procure herself a situation. With the same earnestness which would apply were she my own sister, I beg you to take all possible steps to find something in our city which will be suitable to her person, her birth, and her upbringing; that until she is properly installed she incur no expense; do see to her requirements and I shall reimburse you immediately I am home."

Valbois besought me leave to embrace me. "Adieu, Mademoiselle," he continued, "Madame Bertrand sets off tomorrow at daybreak; accompany her and may a little more happiness attend you in a city where I shall perhaps soon have the satisfaction of seeing you again."

The courtesy of this young man, who was in no sort indebted to me, brought tears to my eyes. Kind treatment is sweet indeed when for so long one has experienced naught but the most odious. I accepted his gifts, at the same time swearing I was going to work at nothing but to put myself in a way to be able someday to reciprocate. Alas! I thought as I retired, though the exercise of yet another virtue has just flung me into destitution, at least, for the first time in my life, the hope of consolation looms out of this appalling pit of evil into which Virtue has cast me again.

The hour was not advanced; I needed a breath of air and so went down to the Isere embankment, desiring to stroll there for several instants; and, as almost always happens under similar circumstances, my thoughts, absorbing me entirely, led me far. Finding myself, at length, in an isolated place, I sat down, more leisurely to ponder. However, night descended before I thought to return; of a sudden I felt myself seized by three men: one clapped a hand over my mouth, the other two precipitated me into a carriage, climbed in, and for three full hours we sped along, during which time not one of these brigands deigned either to say a word to me or respond to any of my questions. The blinds were drawn down, I saw nothing; the carriage came to a halt before a house, gates swung wide, we entered, the gates clanged to immediately. My abductors pick me up, lead me through several unlit apartments, and finally leave me in one near which is a room wherein I perceive a light.

"Stay here," says one of my ravishers as he withdraws with his companions, "you're soon going to see an old acquaintance."

And they disappear, carefully shutting all the doors. At almost the same time, that leading into the room where I had spied illumination is opened, and carrying a candle in her hand, I see emerge... oh, Madame, fancy who it was... Dubois... Dubois herself, that frightful monster, devoured, no question of it, by the most ardent desire to be revenged.

"Hither, charming girl," said she in an arrogant tone, "come here and receive the reward for the virtues in which you indulged yourself at my expense..." And angrily clutching my hand: "...ah, you wretch I I'll teach you to betray me!"

"No, Madame, no," I say in great haste, " I betrayed you not at all: inform yourself: I uttered not one word which could cause you any inquietude, no, I spoke not the least word which might compromise you."

"But did you not offer resistance to the crime I meditated? have you not thwarted its execution, worthless creature! You've got to be chastened . . . ."

And, as we were entering, she had no time to say more. The apartment into which I was made to pass was lit with equal sumptuousness and magnificence; at the further end, reclining upon an ottoman, was a man of about forty, wearing a billowing taffeta dressing robe.

"Monseigneur," said Dubois, presenting me to him, "here is the young lady you wanted, she in whom all Grenoble has become interested... the celebrated Therese, to be brief, condemned to hang with the counterfeiters, then delivered thanks to her innocence and her virtue. Acknowledge that I serve you with skill, Monseigneur; not four days ago you evinced your extreme desire to immolate her to your passions; and today I put her into your hands; you will perhaps prefer her to that pretty little pensionnaire from the Benedictine convent at Lyon you also desired and who should be arriving any minute: the latter has her physical and moral integrity this one here has nothing but a sentimental chastity; but it is deep-grained in her being and nowhere will you find a creature more heavily ballasted with candor and honesty. They are both at your disposition, Monseigneur: you'll either dispatch each this evening, or one today and the other tomorrow. As for myself, I am leaving you: your kindnesses in my regard engaged me to make you privy to my Grenoble adventure. One man dead, Monseigneur, one dead man; I must fly Ä"

"Ah no, no, charming woman!" cried the master of the place; "no, stay, and fear nothing while you have my protection! You are as a soul unto my pleasures; you alone possess the art of exciting and satisfying them, and the more you multiply your crimes, the more the thought of you inflames my mind . . . . But this Therese is a pretty thing . . . ." and addressing himself to me: "what is your age, my child?"

"Twenty-six, Monseigneur," I replied, "and much grief."

"Ha, yes, grief indeed, lots of distress, excellent, I'm familiar with all that, hugely amusing, just what I like; we're going to straighten everything out, we'll put a stop to these tumbles; I guarantee you that in twenty-four hours you'll be unhappy no longer, ha!..." and, with that, dreadful flights of laughter... " 'tis true, eh, Dubois? I've a sure method for ending a young girl's misfortunes, haven't I?"

"Indeed you do," the odious creature replied; "and if Therese weren't a friend of mine, I'd never have brought her to you; but it is only fair I reward her for what she did for me. You'd never imagine how useful this dear thing was to me during my latest enterprise at Grenoble; you, Monseigneur, have had the kindness to accept my expression of gratitude, and, I pray you, repay what I owe her with interest."

The opaque ambiguity of these phrases, what Dubois had said to me upon entering, the species of gentleman with whom I had to do, this other girl whose forthcoming appearance had been announced, all this instantly troubled my imagination to a degree it would be difficult to describe. A cold sweat seeped from my pores and I was about to fall in a swoon Ä 'twas at that instant this man's projects finally became clear to me. He calls me to him, begins with two or three kisses whereby our mouths are obliged to unite; he seeks my tongue, finds and sucks it and his, running deep into my throat, seems to be pumping the very breath from my lungs. He has me bend my head upon his chest, he lifts my hair and closely observes the nape of my neck.

"Oh, 'tis delicious!" he cries, squeezing it vigorously; "I've never seen one so nicely attached; 'twill be divine to make it jump free."

This last remark confirmed all my intimations; I saw very clearly I was once again in the clutches of one of those libertines moved by cruel passions, whose most cherished delights consist in enjoying the agonies or the death of the luckless victims procured them by money; I observed I was in danger of losing my life.

And then a knock at the door; Dubois leaves and an instant later ushers in the young Lyonnaise she had mentioned shortly before. I'll now try to sketch the two personages in whose company you are going to see me for a while. The Monseigneur, whose name and estate T never discovered, was, as I told you, a man of forty years, slender, indeed slight of frame, but vigorously constituted, sinewy, with his muscles almost constantly tensed, powerful biceps showing upon arms that were covered with a growth of thick black hair; everything about him proclaimed strength and good health; his face was animated, his gaze ardent, his eyes small, black, and wicked, there were splendid white teeth in his mouth, and liveliness in his every feature; his height was above average, and this man's amatory goad, which I was to have but too frequent occasion to see and feel, was roughly a foot long and above eight inches around. This incisive, nervous, constantly alerted and oozing instrument, ribboned with great purple veins that rendered its aspect still more formidable, was levitated throughout the seance, which lasted five or six hours; never once did it sink or falter. I had never before or since found a more hirsute man: he resembled those fauns described in fables. His powerful hands ended in fingers whose strength was that of a vice; as for his character, it seemed to me harsh, abrupt, cruel, his mind was inclined to that sarcasm and teasing of a sort calculated to redouble the sufferings one was perfectly well able to see one had to expect such a man would strive to inflict.

The little Lyonnaise was called Eulalie. A glimpse of her was enough to convince one of her distinguished birth and virtue: she was the daughter of one of the City's foremost families from whose house Dubois' criminal hirelings had abducted her under the pretext of conveying her to a rendezvous with the lover she idolized; together with an enchanting forthrightness and naivete, she possessed one of the most delightful countenances imaginable. Barely sixteen years old, Eulalie had the face of a genuine Madonna; her features were embellished by an enviable innocence and modesty; she had little color but was only the more fetching for that; and the sparkle in her superb eyes endowed her pretty face with all the fire and warmth whereof, at first glance, this pallor seemed to deprive her; her rather generous mouth was filled with the prettiest teeth, her already fully matured breasts seemed yet whiter than her complexion; but she was no sense lacking in plumpness: her form was round and well furnished, all her flesh was firm, sweet, and succulent. Dubois asserted it were impossible to behold a more beautiful ass: little expert in these matters, you will permit me to abstain from judging here. A fine mossy growth shadowed her fore end; majestic blond hair floated about all those charms, rendering them still more piquant; and to complete the masterpiece, Nature, who seemed to have created it for pleasure, had endowed her with the sweetest and most lovable temperament. Tender and delicate flower, thus were you to grace the world for but an instant in order more swiftly to be withered!

"Oh, Madame!" she said upon recognizing Dubois, "is it in this way you have deceived me !... Just Heaven! where have you brought me?"

"You shall see, my child," put in the master of the house, abruptly seizing Eulalie, drawing her to him and forthwith beginning his kisses while, upon his orders, I excited him with one hand.

Eulalie sought to protect herself, but, thrusting the girl toward the libertine, Dubois eliminated all possibility of her escape. The sitting was long; for very fresh, new-blown was that flower, and the hornet's desire to drain its pollen was commensurately great. His iterated suckings were succeeded by an inspection of

Eulalie's neck; betimes, I palpated his member and felt it throb with growing insistence.

"Well," said Monseigneur, "here are two victims who shall fill my cup of joy to overflowing: Dubois, you shall be well paid, for I am well served. Let's move into my boudoir; follow us, dear woman, come," he continued as he led us away; "you'll leave tonight, but I need you for the party."

Dubois resigns herself, and we pass into the debauchee's pleasure chamber, where we are stripped naked.

Oh, Madame, I shall not attempt to represent the infamies of which I was at once victim and witness. This monster's pleasures were those of the executioner; his unique joy consisted in decapitating. My luckless companion... oh, no! Madame... no! do not require me to finish... I was about to share her fate; spurred on by Dubois, the villain had decided to render my torture yet more horrible when both experienced a need to revive their strength; whereupon they sat down to eat . . . . What a debauch! But ought I complain? for did it not save my life? Besotted with wine, exhausted by overeating, both fell dead drunk and slumbered amidst the litter that remained from their feast. No sooner do I see them collapse than I leap to the skirt and mantle Dubois had just removed in order to appear more immodest in her patron's view; I snatch up a candle and spring toward the stairway: this house, divested, or nearly so, of servants, contains nothing to frustrate my escape, I do encounter someone, I put on a terrified air and cry to him to make all haste to relieve his master who is dying, and I reach the door without meeting further obstacles. I have no acquaintance with the roads, I'd not been allowed to see the one whereby we had come, I take the first I see... 'tis the one leading to Grenoble; there is nothing denied us when fortune deigns momentarily to smile upon us; at the inn everyone was still abed, I enter secretly and fly to Valbois' room, knock, Valbois wakes and scarcely recognizes me in my disordered state; he demands to know what has befallen me, I relate the horrors whereof I was simultaneously an observer and object.

"You can have Dubois arrested," I tell him, "she's not far from here, I might even be able to point out the way . . . . Quite apart from all her other crimes, the wretch has taken both my clothing and the five louis you gave me."

"O Therese," says Valbois, "there's no denying it, you are without doubt the unluckiest girl on earth, but, nevertheless, my honest creature, do you not perceive, amidst all these afflictions which beset you, a celestial arm that saves you? may that be unto you as one additional motive for perpetual virtuousness, for never do good deeds go unrewarded. We will not chase after Dubois, my reasons for letting her go in peace are the same you expounded yesterday, let us simply repair the harm she has done you: here, first of all, is the money she stole from you. In an hour's time I'll have a seamstress bring two complete outfits for you, and some linen.

"But you have got to leave, Therese, you must leave this very day, Bertrand expects you, I've persuaded her to delay her departure a few hours more, join her . . . ."

"O virtuous young man," I cried, falling into my benefactor's arms, "may Heaven someday repay you for the kindness you have done me."

"Ah, Therese," said Valbois, embracing me, "the happiness you wish me... I've enjoyed it already, 'tis presently mine, since your own is my doing... fare thee well."

And thus it was I left Grenoble, Madame, and though I had not found in that city all the felicity I had imagined was awaiting me there, at least I had never met in another so many kindly and goodhearted people assembled to sympathize with or assuage my woes.

My conductress and I were in a small covered carriage drawn by one horse we drove from within; we had with us, beside Madame Bertrand's baggage, her baby girl of fifteen months whom she was still suckling and for whom I straightway, to my vast misfortune, formed an attachment quite as deep as was that of the mother who had brought the infant into the world.

She was, this Bertrand, an unattractive person, suspicious, gossipy, noisy, monotonous, and dull-witted. Every night we regularly emptied the carriage and transported everything into our inn and then went to sleep in the same room. Until Lyon, everything went along very smoothly, but during the three days this woman needed for her business dealings, I fell upon someone I was far from expecting to encounter in that city.

Together with girls from the hotel whom I had got to accompany me, I would take walks on the Rhone quay; one day I all of a sudden espied the Reverend Father Antonin formerly of Saint Mary-in-the-Wood, now superior in charge of his order's establishment located in that city. That monk accosted me and after rebuking me in a very low and still sharper tone for my flight, and having given me to understand I would be running great risks of recapture were he to relay information to the Burgundian monastery, he added, softening his manner, that he would not breathe a word if I should be willing that very instant to come to visit him in his new quarters and to bring with me the girl I was with, who struck him as worth having; then repeating his proposal aloud, and to this other creature: "We shall reward you handsomely, both of you," quoth the monster; "there are ten of us in our house, and I promise you a minimum of one louis from each if your complacency is unlimited." I flush crimson upon hearing these words; I spend a moment trying to convince the monk he has made a mistake; failing at that, I attempt to use signs to induce him to be silent, but nothing prevails with this insolent fellow, and his solicitations become only the more heated; at last having received repeated refusals, he demands to know our address; in order to get rid of him, I immediately give a fictitious one, he writes it down, and leaves us with the assurance we will soon meet again.

39

Upon returning to our inn I explained as best I could the history of this unfortunate acquaintance; but whether my companion was not at all satisfied by what I told her, or whether she may perhaps have been exceedingly annoyed by my virtuous performance which deprived her of an adventure wherefrom she might have earned much, she waggled her tongue, the effects of which were only too plainly revealed by Bertrand's remarks upon the occasion of the deplorable catastrophe I am going to relate to you in a moment; however, the monk never did reappear, and we left Lyon.

Having quit the city late, we could get no further than Villefranche that day, and there we stopped for the night; 'twas in that town, Madame, there took place the horrible event which today causes me to appear before you in a criminal guise, although I was no more a malefactor in that one of my life's fateful circumstances than in any other of those where you have observed me so unjustly assaulted by the blows of fate; and as in many another instance, so this time I was flung into the abyss by nothing other than the goodness of my heart and the wickedness of men.

Having made Villefranche toward six o'clock in the evening, we supped in haste and retired directly, that we might be able to undertake a longer stage on the morrow; we had not been two hours in bed when a dreadful smell of smoke roused us from sleep; convinced the flames are near at hand, we get instantly from bed. Just Heaven! the havoc wrought by the fire was already but too frightful; half-naked, we open our door and all around us hear nothing but the fracas of collapsing walls, the noise of burning timbers and woodwork and the shrieks of those who had fallen into the blaze; surrounded by devouring flames we have no idea in which direction to run; to escape their violence, we rush past them and soon find ourselves lost in a milling crush of wretches who, like ourselves, are seeking salvation in flight; at this point I remember that my conductress, more concerned for her own than for her child's safety, has not thought of preserving it from death; without a word to the woman, I fly to our chamber, having to pass through the conflagration and to sustain burns in several places: I snatch up the poor little creature, spring forward to restore her to her mother: I advance along a half-consumed beam, miss my footing, instinctively thrust out my hands, this natural reflex forces me to release the precious burden in my arms... it slips from my grasp and the unlucky child falls into the inferno before its own mother's eyes; at this instant I am myself seized... carried away; too upset to be able to distinguish anything, I am unaware whether 'tis aid or peril which surrounds me but, to my grief, I am but too fully enlightened when, flung into a post chaise, I discover myself beside Dubois who, clapping a pistol to my head, threatens to blow out my brains if I utter a syllable...

"Ah, little villain," says she, "I've got you now and this time for good."

"Oh, Madame! you?" I exclaim. "Here?"

"Everything that has just transpired is my doing," the monster replies, " 'twas by arson I saved your life; and by a fire you're going to lose it: in order to catch you I'd have followed you to Hell had it been necessary. Monseigneur was furious, believe me, when he found out you had escaped; I get two hundred louis for every girl I procure him, and not only did he not want to pay me for Eulalie, but he menaced me with all his anger could produce were I to fail to bring you back. I discovered I'd missed you by two hours at Lyon; yesterday I reached Villefranche an hour after your arrival, I had the hotel burned by the henchmen I always have in my employ, I wanted to incinerate you or get you back; I've got you, I m returning you to a house your flight has plunged into trouble and unquiet, and I'm taking you there, Therese, to be treated in a cruel manner. Monseigneur swore he'd not have tortures terrible enough for you, and we'll not step from this carriage until we are at his seat. Well, Therese, what is your present opinion of Virtue?"

"Oh, Madame! that it is very frequently crime's prey; that it is happy when triumphant; but that it ought to be the unique object of the Heavenly God's rewards even though human atrocities bring about its downfall upon earth."

"You've not long to wait before you know, Therese, whether there is really a God who punishes or recompenses the deeds of mortals . . . . Ah! if, in the eternal inexistence you are shortly going to enter, if 'twere possible to cogitate in that state of annihilation, how much you would regret the fruitless sacrifices your inflexible stubbornness has forced you to make to phantoms who have never doled out any but the wages of sorrow . . . . Therese, there is yet time left to you: if you wish to be my accomplice I'll save you, for, I avow, 'tis more than I can bear to see you break down ever and ever again upon Virtue's routes all beset by perils. What? are you not yet sufficiently punished for your good behavior and false principles? What kind of misery do you have to know in order to be persuaded to mend your ways? What then are the examples you require in order to be convinced the attitude you have adopted is the worst of all and that, as I have told you a hundred times over, one must expect nothing but calamity when, breasting the crowd's headlong stampede, one wishes to be virtuous and alone in a completely corrupt society. You count upon an avenging God; cease to be a gull, Therese, disabuse yourself, the God you fabricate for yourself is but a fiction whose stupid existence is never found elsewhere but in the heads of the crazed; 'tis a phantom invented by human wickedness; the solitary purpose of this illusion is to deceive mankind or to create armed divisions among men. The service it were possible to render humankind would have been instantly to cut the throat of the first impostor who took it into his head to speak of God to men. How much blood that one murder would have spared the universe! Get on, get on with you, Therese, perpetually active Nature, Nature acting always, has no need of a master for her government. And if indeed this master did exist, after all the faults and sins with which he has stuffed creation, would he, think you, would he merit anything from us but scorn and outrage? Ah, if he exists, your God, how I do hate him!

Therese, how I abhor him! Yes, were this existence authentic, I affirm that the mere pleasure of perpetually irritating whatever I found that bore his impress or bespoke his touch would become for me the most precious compensation for the necessity in which I would find myself to acknowledge some belief in him . . . . Once again, Therese, do you wish to become my confederate? A superb possibility presents itself, with courage we can execute the thing; I'll save your life if you'll undertake it. This Monseigneur to whose house we are going, and whom you know, lives alone in the country house where he gives his parties; their species, with which you are familiar, requires isolation; a single valet lives with him when he takes up residence there for the sake of his pleasures: the man riding ahead of the coach, you and I, dear girl, that's three of us against two; when that libertine is inflamed by his lecheries, I'll snatch away the saber with which he decapitates his victims, you'll hold him, we'll kill him, and meanwhile my man will have done in the valet. There's money hidden in that house; more than eight hundred thousand francs, Therese, I'm sure of it, the thing's well worth the trouble... Choose, clever creature, decide: death or an alliance; if you betray me, if you expose my plan to him, I'll accuse you of having contrived it alone, and don't doubt for a moment that the confidence he has always had in me will tip the balance my way... think carefully before you give me your answer: this man is a villain; hence, by assassinating him we merely aid the law whose rigorous treatment he deserves. A day does not go by, Therese, without this rascal murdering a girl; is it then to outrage Virtue by punishing Crime? And does the reasonable proposition I make you still alarm your wild principles?"

"Be certain of it, Madame," I answered; "it is not with object of chastening crime you propose this deed, it is rather with the sole intention of committing one yourself; consequently there cannot be but great evil in doing what you suggest, and no semblance of legitimacy can appear thereupon; better still, even were you to intend to avenge humanity for this man's horrors, you would still be committing evil by doing so, for this is not a problem which concerns you: there are laws decreed to punish the guilty; let those laws take their course, it is not unto our feeble hands the Supreme Being has entrusted their sword, never might we wield that blade without affronting justice."

"Well, then you'll have to die, worthless creature," retorted the furious Dubois, "you'll die; don't tease yourself with hopes of escaping your fate."

"What matters it to me?" I calmly answered, "I shall be delivered of all the ills that assail me; death holds no terrors for me, 'tis life's last sleep, 'tis the downtrodden's haven of repose . . . ."

And, upon these words, that savage beast sprang at me, I thought she was going to strangle me; she struck several blows upon my breast, but released me, however, immediately I cried out, for she feared lest the postilion hear me.

We were moving along at a brisk pace; the man who was riding ahead arranged for new horses and we stopped only long enough to change teams. As the new pair was being harnessed, Dubois suddenly raised her weapon and clapped it to my heart... what was she about to do?... Indeed, my exhaustion and my situation had beaten me down to the point of preferring death to the ordeal of keeping it at bay.

We were then preparing to enter Dauphine, of a sudden six horsemen, galloping at top speed behind our coach, overtook it and, with drawn cutlasses, forced our driver to halt. Thirty feet off the highway was a cottage to which these cavaliers, whom we soon identified as constables, ordered the driver to lead the carriage; when we were alongside it, we were told to get out, and all three of us entered the peasant's dwelling. With an effrontery unthinkable in a woman soiled with unnumbered crimes, Dubois who found herself arrested, archly demanded of these officers whether she were known to them, and with what right they comported themselves thus with a woman of her rank.

"We have not the honor of your acquaintance, Madame," replied the officer in charge of the squadron; "but we are certain you have in your carriage the wretch who yesterday set fire to the principal hotel in Villefranche"; then, eyeing me closely: "she answers the description, Madame, we are not in error - ; have the kindness to surrender her to us and to inform us how a person as respectable as you appear to be could have such a woman in your keeping."

"Why, 'tis very readily accounted for," replied Dubois with yet greater insolence, "and, I declare, I'll neither hide her from you nor take her side in the matter if 'tis certain she is guilty of the horrible crime you speak of. I too was staying at that hotel in Villefranche, I left in the midst of all the commotion and as I am getting into my coach, this girl runs up, begs my compassion, says she has just lost everything in the fire, and implores me to take her with me to Lyon where she hopes to be able to find a place. Far less attentive to my reason than to my heart's promptings, I acquiesced, consented to fetch her along; once in the carriage she offered herself as my servant; once again imprudence led me to agree to everything and I have been taking her to Dauphine where I have my properties and family: 'tis a lesson, assuredly, I presently recognize with utmost clarity all of pity's shortcomings; I shall not again be guilty of them. There she is, gentlemen, there she is; God forbid that I should be interested in such a monster, I abandon her to the law's severest penalties, and, I beseech you, take every step to prevent it from being known that I committed the unfortunate mistake of lending an instant's credence to a single word she uttered."

I wished to defend myself, I wanted to denounce the true villain; my speeches were interpreted as calumniatory recriminations to which Dubois opposed nothing but a contemptuous smile. O fatal effects of misery and biased prepossession, of wealth and of insolence! Were it thinkable that a woman who had herself called Madame la Baronne de Fulconis, who proclaimed a high degree and displayed opulence, who asserted she owned extensive holdings and arrogated a family to herself; were it to be conceived that such a personage could be guilty of a crime wherefrom she did not appear to have the slightest thing to gain? And, on the other hand, did not everything condemn me? I was unprotected, I was poor, 'twas a very sure thing I'd done a fell deed.

The squadron officer read me the catalogue of Bertrand's deposed charges. 'Twas she had accused me; I'd set the inn afire to pillage her with greater ease, and she'd been robbed indeed to her last penny; I'd flung her infant into the flames in order that, blinded by the despair with which this event would overwhelm her, she'd forget all else and give not a thought to my maneuvers; and, furthermore, Bertrand had added, I was a girl of suspect virtue and bad habits who had escaped the gallows at Grenoble and whom she had only taken in charge, very foolishly, thanks to the excessive kindness she had shown a young man from her own district, my lover, no doubt. I had publicly and in broad daylight solicited monks in Lyon: in one word, there was nothing the unworthy creature had not exploited in order to seal my doom, nothing that calumny whetted by despair had not invented in order to besmirch me. Upon the woman's insistence, a juridical examination had been conducted on the premises. The fire had begun in a hayloft into which several persons had taken oath I had entered the evening of that fatal day, and that was true. Searching for a water closet to which I had not been very clearly directed by a maid I had consulted, I had entered this loft having failed to locate the sought after place, and there I had remained long enough to make what I was accused of plausible, or at least to furnish probabilities of its truth; and 'tis well known: in this day and age those are proofs. And so, do what I could to defend myself, the officer's single response was to ready his manacles.

"But, Monsieur," I expostulated before allowing him to put me in irons, "if I robbed my traveling companion at Villefranche, the money ought to be found upon my person; search me."

This ingenuous defense merely excited laughter; I was assured I'd not been alone, that they were certain I had accomplices to whom, as I fled, I had transferred the stolen funds. Then the malicious Dubois, who knew of the brand which to my misfortune Rodin had burned upon my flesh long ago, in one instant Dubois put all sympathy to rout.

"Monsieur," said she to the officer, "so many mistakes are committed every day in affairs of this sort that you will forgive me for the idea that occurs to me: if this girl is guilty of the atrocity she is accused of it is surely not her first; the character required to execute crimes of this variety is not attained in a night: and so I beg you to examine this girl, Monsieur... were you to find, by chance, something upon her wretched body... but if nothing denounces her, allow me to defend and protect her."

The officer agreed to the verification... it was about to be carried out...

"One moment, Monsieur," said I, "stay; this search is to no purpose; Madame knows full well I bear the frightful mark; she also knows very well what misfortune caused it to be put on me: this subterfuge of hers is the crowning horror which will, together with all the rest, be revealed at Themis' own temple. Lead me away, Messieurs: here are my hands, load them with chains; only Crime blushes to carry them, stricken Virtue is made to groan thereby, but is not terrified."

"Truth to tell," quoth Dubois, "I'd never have dreamt my idea would have such success; but as this creature repays my kindness by insidious inculpations, I am willing to return with her if you deem it necessary."

"There's no need whatsoever to do so, Madame la Baronne," rejoined the officer, "this girl is our quarry: her avowals, the mark branded on her body, it all condemns her; we need no one else, and we beg your pardon a thousand times over for having caused you this protracted inconvenience."

I was handcuffed immediately, flung upon the crupper of one of the constables' mounts, and Dubois went off, not before she had completed her insults by giving a few crowns to my guards, which generously bestowed silver was to aid me during my melancholy sojourn while awaiting trial.

O Virtue! I cried when I perceived myself brought to this dreadful humiliation; couldst thou suffer a more penetrating outrage? Were it possible that Crime might dare affront thee and vanquish thee with so much insolence and impunity!

We were soon come to Lyon; upon arrival I was cast into the keep reserved for criminals and there I was inscribed as an arsonist, harlot, child-murderer, and thief.

Seven persons had been burned to death in the hotel; I had myself thought I might be; I had been on the verge of perishing; but she who had been the cause of this horror was eluding the law's vigilance and Heaven's justice: she was triumphant, she was flying on to new crimes whereas, innocent and unlucky, I had naught for prospect but dishonor, castigation, and death.

For such a long time habituated to calumny, injustice, and wretchedness; destined, since childhood, to acquit myself of not a single virtuous deed or feel a single righteous sentiment without suffering instant retribution therefor, my anguish was rather mute and blunted than rending, and I shed fewer tears than I might have supposed... however, as 'tis instinctive in the distressed creature to seek after every possible device to extricate himself from the chasm into which his ill-fortune has plunged him, Father Antonin came to my mind; whatever the mediocre relief I could hope from him, I did not deny to myself I was anxious to see him: I asked for him, he appeared. He had not been informed of by whom he was desired; he affected not to recognize me; whereupon I told the turn-key that it was indeed possible he had forgotten me, having been my confessor only when I was very young, but, I continued, it was as my soul's director I solicited a private interview with him. 'Twas agreed by both parties. As soon as I was alone with this holy man I cast myself at his knees, rained tears upon them and besought him to save me from my cruel situation; I proved my innocence to him; I did not conceal that the culpable proposals he had made me some days before had provoked my young companion's enmity, and presently, said I, she accused me out of spite. The monk listened attentively.

"Therese," said he when I was done, "don't lose control of yourself as you customarily do when someone contradicts your damnable prejudices; you notice to what a pass they've brought you, and you can at present readily convince yourself that it's a hundred times better to be a rascal and happy than well-behaved and unprosperous; your case is as bad as it possibly could be, dear girl, there's nothing to be gained by hiding the fact from you: this Dubois you speak of, having the largest benefits to reap from your doom, will unquestionably labor behind the scene to ruin you: Bertrand will accuse you, all appearances stand against you, and, these days, appearances are sufficient grounds for decreeing the death sentence: you are, hence, lost, 'tis plain: one single means might save you: I get on well with the bailiff, he has considerable influence with this city's magistrature; I'm going to tell him you are my niece, and that by this title I am claiming you: he'll dismiss the entire business: I'll ask to send you back to my family; I'll have you taken away, but 'twill be to our monastery and incarceration there, whence you'll never emerge... and there, why conceal it? you, Therese, will be the bounden slave of my caprices, you'll sate them all without a murmur; as well, you will submit yourself to my colleagues: in a word, you will be as utterly mine as the most subordinated of victims... you heed me: the task is hard; you know what are the passions of libertines of our variety; so make up your mind, and make me prompt answer."

"Begone, Father," I replied, horror-struck, "begone, you are a monster to dare so cruelly take advantage of my circumstances in order to force upon me the alternatives of death or infamy; I shall know how to die, if die I must, but 'twill be to die sinless."

"As you like," quoth the cruel man as he prepared to withdraw; "I have never been one to impose happiness upon reluctant people . . . . Virtue has so handsomely served you until the present, Therese, you are quite right to worship at its altar... good-bye: above all, let it not occur to you to ask for me again."

He was leaving; an unconquerable impulse drew me to his knees yet another time.

"Tiger!" I exclaimed through my tears, "open your granite heart, let my appalling misadventures melt it, and do not, in order to conclude them, do not impose conditions more dreadful to me than death itself . . . ."

The violence of my movements had disturbed what veiled my breast, it was naked, my disheveled hair fell in cascades upon it, it was wetted thoroughly by my tears; I quicken desires in the dishonest man... desires he wants to satisfy on the spot; he dares discover to me to what point my state arouses them; he dares dream of pleasures lying in the middle of the chains binding me and beneath the sword which is poised to smite me... I was upon my knees... he flings me backward, leaps upon me, there we lie upon the wretched straw I use for a bed; I wish to cry out, he stuffs his handkerchief into my mouth; he ties my arms; master of me, the infamous creature examines me everywhere... everything becomes prey to his gaze, his fingerings, his perfidious caresses; at last, he appeases his desires.

"Listen to me," says he, untying me and readjusting his costume, "you do not want me to be helpful, all very well; I am leaving you; I'll neither aid nor harm you, but if it enters your head to breathe a word of what has just happened, I will, by charging you with yet more enormous crimes, instantly deprive you of all means of defending yourself; reflect carefully before jabbering... I am taken for your confessor... now hark: we are permitted to reveal anything and all when 'tis a question of a criminal; fully approve what I am going to say to your warden, or else I'll crush you like a fly."

He knocks, the jailer appears.

"Monsieur," says the traitor, "the nice young lady is in error; she wished to speak to a Father Antonin who is now in Bordeaux; I have no acquaintance of her, never have I even set eyes upon her: she besought me to hear her confession, I did so, I salute you and her and shall always be ready to present myself when my ministry is esteemed important."

Upon uttering these words, Antonin departs and leaves me as much bewildered by his fraudulence as revolted by his libertinage and insolence.

My situation was so dreadful that, whatever it might be, I could ill afford not to employ every means at my disposal; I recollected Monsieur de Saint-Florent: in the light of my behavior toward him, I was incapable of believing this man could underestimate my character; once long ago I had rendered him a most important service, he had dealt most cruelly with me, and therefore I imagined he could not, in my presently critical plight, very well refuse to make reparation for the wrongs he had done me; no, I was sure he would at least have to acknowledge, as best he were able, what I had so generously done in his behalf; passions' heat might have blinded him upon the two occasions I had held commerce with him; there had been some sort of excuse for his former horrors, but in this instance, it seemed to me, no feeling should prevent him from coming to my aid . . . . Would he renew his last proposals? to the assistance I was going to request from him would he attach the condition I must agree to the frightful employments he had outlined to me before? ah, very well! I'd accept and, once free, I should easily discover the means to extricate myself from the abominable kind of existence into which he might have the baseness to lure me. Full of these ideas, I write a letter to him, I describe my miseries, I beg him to visit me; but I had not devoted adequate thought to analyzing this man's soul when I supposed it susceptible of infiltration by beneficence; I either did not sufficiently remember his appalling theories, or my wretched weakness constantly forcing me to use my own heart as the standard by which to judge others, fancied this man was bound to comport himself toward me as I should certainly have done toward him.

He arrives; and, as I have asked to see him alone, he is freely introduced into my cell. From the marks of respect showered profusely upon him it was easy to determine the eminent position he held in Lyon.

"Why, it's you!" said he, casting scornful eyes upon me, "I was deceived by the letter; I thought it written by a woman more honest than you and whom I would have helped with all my heart; but what would you have me do for an imbecile of your breed? What! you're guilty of a hundred crimes one more shocking than the other, and when someone suggests a way for you to earn your livelihood you stubbornly reject the proposal? Never has stupidity been carried to these lengths."

"Oh, Monsieur I" I cried, "I am not in the least guilty."

"Then what the devil must one do in order to be?" the harsh creature sharply rejoined. "The first time in my life I clapped eyes on you, there you were, in the thick of a pack of bandits who wanted to assassinate me; and now it is in the municipal prison I discover you, accused of three or four new crimes and wearing, so they tell me, a mark on your shoulder which proclaims your former misdeeds. If that is what you designate by the word honest, do inform me of what it would require not to be."

"Just Heaven, Monsieur!" I replied, "can you excoriate that period in my life when I knew you, and should it not rather be for me to make you blush at the memory of what passed then? You know very well, Monsieur, the bandits who captured you, and amongst whom you found me, kept me with them by force; they wanted to kill you, I saved your life by facilitating your escape while making mine; and what, cruel man, did you do to thank me for my aid? is it possible you can recall your actions without horror? You yourself wanted to murder me; you dazed me by terrible blows and, profiting from my half-unconscious state, you snatched from me what I prized most highly; through an unexampled refinement of cruelty, you plundered me of the little money I possessed quite as if you had desired to summon humiliation and misery to complete your victim's obliteration! And great was your success, barbaric one! indeed, it has been entire; 'tis you who precipitated me into desolation; 'tis you who made the abyss to yawn, and 'tis thanks to you I fell into it and have not ceased to fall since that accursed moment. "Nevertheless, Monsieur, I would forget it all, yes, everything is effaced from my memory, I even ask your pardon for daring to upbraid you for what is past, but can you hide from yourself the fact that some recompense, some gratitude is owing to me? Ah, deign not to seal up your heart when the wing of death brushes its shadow over my unhappy days; 'tis not death I fear, but disgrace; save me from the dread horror of a criminal's end: all I demand from you comes to that single mercy, refuse me it not, and both Heaven and my heart will reward you someday."

I was weeping, I was upon my knees before this ferocious man and, far from reading upon his face the effect I thought I should be able to expect from the disturbances I flattered myself I was producing in his soul, I distinguished nothing but a muscular alteration caused by that sort of lust whose germinal origins are in cruelty. Saint-Florent was seated opposite me; his wicked dark eyes considered me in a dreadful manner, and I noticed his hand glide to a certain sector and his fingers begin to perform those certain motions which indicated I was putting him in a state which was by no means that of pity; he concealed himself withal, and, getting to his feet:

"Look here," he said, "your case rests entirely in the hands of Monsieur de Cardoville; I need not tell you what official post he occupies; it suffices that you know your fate depends absolutely upon him; he and I have been intimate friends since childhood; I shall speak to him; if he agrees to a few arrangements, you will be called for at sunset and in order that he may see you, you'll be brought to either his home or mine; such an interrogation, wrapped in secrecy, will make it much simpler to turn matters in your favor, which could not possibly be done here. If he consents to bestow the favor, justify yourself when you have your interview with him, prove your innocence to him in a persuasive manner; that is all I can do for you. Adieu, Therese, keep yourself ready for any eventuality and above all do not have me waste my time taking futile measures." Saint-Florent left.

Nothing could have equaled my perplexity; there had been so little harmony between that man's remarks, the character I knew him to have, and his actual conduct, that I dreaded yet further pitfalls; but, Madame, pause a moment and decide whether I was right or wrong; was I in a position to hesitate? for my position was desperate; and was I not obliged to leap at everything which had the semblance of assistance? Hence I decided to accompany the persons who would come to fetch me; should I be compelled to prostitute myself, I would put up what defense I could; was it to death I was to be led? too bad; it would not, at least, be ignominious, and I would be rid of all my sufferings. Nine o'clock strikes, the jailer appears, I tremble.

"Follow me," that Cerberus says; "you are wanted by Messieurs Saint-Florent and de Cardoville; consider well and take advantage, as it befits you, of the favor Heaven offers you; there are many here who might desire such a blessing and who will never obtain it."

Arrayed as best I am able, I follow the warden who puts me into the keeping of two strange tall fellows whose savage aspect doubles my fright; not a word do they utter; the carriage rolls off and we halt before an immense mansion I soon recognize as Saint-Florent's. Silence enshrouds everything; it augments my dread, however, my guides grasp my arms, hustle me along, and we climb to the fourth floor; there we discover a number of small decorated apartments; they seem to me very mysterious indeed. As we progress through them every door closes shut behind us, and thus we advance till we reach a remote room in which, I notice, there are no windows; Saint-Florent awaits me, and also the man I am told is Monsieur de Cardoville, in whose hands my case rests; this heavy-set, fleshy personage, provided with a somber and feral countenance, could have been about fifty years of age; although he was in lounging costume, 'twas readily to be seen he was a gentleman of the bar. An air of severity seemed to distinguish his entire aspect; it made a deep impression upon me. O cruel injustice of Providence! 'tis then possible Virtue may be overawed by Crime. The two men who had led me hither, and whom I was better able to make out by the gleam of the twenty candles which lit this room, were not above twenty-five and thirty years old. The first, referred to as La Rose, was a dark handsome chap with Hercules' own figure; he seemed to me the elder; the other had more effeminate features, the loveliest chestnut locks and large brown eyes; he was at least five feet ten inches tall, a very Adonis, had the finest skin to be seen, and was called Julien. As for Saint-Florent, you are acquainted with him; as much of coarseness in his traits as in his character, yet, nevertheless, certain splendid features.

"Everything is secured fast?" Saint-Florent asked Julien.

"We're well shut in, yes, Monsieur," the young man replied; "your servants are off for the night in accordance with your orders and the gatekeeper, who alone is on watch, will follow his instructions to admit no one under any circumstances." These few words enlightened me, I shivered, but what could I have done, confronted as I was by four men?

"Sit down over there, my friends," said Cardoville, kissing the two men, "we'll call for your co-operation when the need arises."

Whereupon Saint-Florent spoke up: "Therese," said he, presenting me to Cardoville, "here is your judge, this is the man upon whom your fate depends; we have discussed your problem; but it appears to me that your crimes are of such a nature we will have much to do to come to terms about them."

"She has exactly forty-two witnesses against her," remarks Cardoville, who takes a seat upon Julien's knees, who kisses him upon the lips, and who permits his fingers to stray over the young man's body in the most immodest fashion; "it's a perfect age since we condemned anyone to die for crimes more conclusively established."

"I? Conclusively established crimes?"

"Conclusively established or inconclusively established," quoth Cardoville, getting to his feet and coming up to shout, with much effrontery, at my very nose, "you're going to burn pissing if you do not, with an entire resignation and the blindest obedience, instantly lend yourself to everything we are going to require of you."

"Yet further horrors!" I cried; "ah indeed! 'tis then only by yielding to infamies innocence can escape the snares set for it by the wicked!"

"That's it; 'tis ordained," Saint-Florent broke in; "you know, my dear: the weak yield to the strong's desires, or fall victims to their wickedness: that's all: that's your whole story, Therese, therefore obey."

And while he spoke the libertine nimbly pulled up my skirts. I recoiled, fended him off, horrified, but, having reeled backward into Cardoville's arms, the latter grasped my hands and thereupon exposed me, defenseless, to his colleague's assaults. The ribbons holding up my skirts were cut, my bodice torn away, my kerchief, my blouse, all were removed, and in no time I found myself before those monsters' eyes as naked as the day I came into the world.

"Resistance..." said one. "Resistance," chimed in the other, both proceeding to despoil me, "the whore fancies she can resist us . . . ." and not a garment was ripped from my body without my receiving a few blows.

When I was in the state they wished, they drew up their chairs, which were provided with protruding armrests; thus a narrow space between the chairs was left and into it I was deposited; and thus they were able to study me at their leisure: while one regarded my fore end, the other mused upon my behind; then they turned me round, and turned me again. In this way I was stared at, handled, kissed for thirty minutes and more; during this examination not one lubricious episode was neglected, and I thought it safe to conjecture, upon the basis of those preliminaries, that each had roughly the same Idiosyncrasies.

"Well, now," Saint-Florent said to his friend, "did I not tell you she had a splendid ass!"

"Yes, by God! her behind is sublime," said the jurist who thereupon kissed it; "I've seen damned few buttocks molded like these: why! look ye! solid and fresh at the same time!... how d'ye suppose that fits with such a tempestuous career?"

"Why, it's simply that she's never given herself of her own accord; I told you there's nothing as whimsical as this girl's exploits! She's never been had but by rape" Ä and then he drives his five fingers simultaneously into the peristyle of Love's temple Ä "but she's been had... unfortunately, for it's much too capacious for me: accustomed to virgins, I could never put up with this."

Then, swinging me around, he repeated the same ceremony with my behind wherein he found the same flaws.

"Ah well, you know our secret," said Cardoville.

"And I'll employ it too," replied Saint-Florent; "and you who have no need of the same resource, you, who are content with a factitious activity which, although painful for the woman, nevertheless brings enjoyment of her to perfection, you, I hope, will not have her till I'm done."

"Fair enough," Cardoville answered, "while watching you, I'll busy myself with those preludes so cherished by my lechery; I'll play the girl with Julien and La Rose while you masculinize Therese, and, so I think, the one's as good as the other."

"Doubtless a thousand times better; for you've no idea how fed up I am with women !... do you suppose I would be capable of enjoying those whores without the help of the auxiliary episodes we both use to add a tart flavor to the business?"

40

With these words, having afforded me clear evidence their state called for more substantial pleasures, the impudicious creatures rose and made me mount upon a large chair, my forearms leaning upon its back, my knees propped upon its arms, and my behind arched so that it was prominently thrust toward them. I was no sooner placed in this attitude than they stepped out of their breeches, tucked up their shirts, and save for their shoes, they thus discovered themselves completely naked from the waist down; they exhibited themselves to me, passed several times to and fro before my eyes, making boastful display of their behinds of which they were overweeningly proud, for, they declared, they had parts far superior to anything I could offer; indeed, each was womanishly made in this region: 'twas especially Cardoville who was possessed of elegant lines and majestic form, snowy white color and enviable plumpness; they whiled away a minute or two polluting themselves in full view of me, but did not ejaculate: about Cardoville, nothing that was not of the most ordinary; as for Saint-Florent, 'twas monstrous: I shuddered to think that such was the dart which had immolated me. Oh Just Heaven! what need of maidenheads had a man of those dimensions? Could it be anything other than ferocity which governed such caprices? But what, alas I were the other weapons I was going to be confronted by! Julien and La Rose, plainly aroused by these exhibitions, also ridded themselves of their clothes and advanced pike in hand . . . . Oh, Madame! never had anything similar soiled my gaze, and whatever may have been my previous representations, what now I beheld surpassed everything I have been able to describe until the present: 'tis like unto the ascendancy the imperious eagle enjoys over the dove. Our two debauchees soon laid hands upon those menacing spears: they caressed them, polluted them, drew them to their mouths, and the combat straightway became more in earnest. Saint-Florent crouches upon the armchair supporting me; he is so adjusted my widespread buttocks are on an exact level with his mouth; he kisses them, his tongue penetrates into first one then the other temple. Saint-Florent provided Cardoville with amusement, the latter offers himself to the pleasures of La Rose whose terrific member instantly vanishes into the redoubt dressed before him, and Julien, situated beneath Saint-Florent, excites him with his mouth the while grasping his haunches and modulating them before the resolute blows of Cardoville who, treating his friend with intransigent rudeness, does not quit him before having wetted the sanctuary with his incense. Nothing could equal Cardoville's transports when the crisis deprives him of his senses; softly abandoning himself to the man who is serving as husband to him, but pressing hard after him of whom he is making a wife, this dastardly libertine, with hoarse gasps like unto those of a dying man, thereupon pronounces indescribable blasphemies; as for Saint-Florent, measure governs his evolutions, he restrains himself, and the tableau is dissolved without his having performed his beau geste.

"Truly," Cardoville says to his comrade, "you still give me as much pleasure as you did when you were fifteen . . . . Indeed," he continues, turning and kissing La Rose, " 'tis true this fine lad knows how to arouse me too . . . . Have you not found me rather gulfy this evening, angelic boy?... would you believe it, Saint-Florent? 'tis the thirty-sixth time I've had it today... only natural that the thing be somewhat dilated; I'm all yours, dear friend," the abominable man pursues, fitting himself into Julien's mouth, his nose glued to my behind, and his own offered to Saint-Florent, "I'm yours for the thirty-seventh." Saint-Florent takes his pleasure with Cardoville, La Rose his with Saint-Florent, and after a quick skirmish the latter burns in his friend the same offering his friend had burned in him. If Saint-Florent's ecstasy was of briefer duration, it was no less intense, less noisy, less criminal than Cardoville's; the one shouted, roared out everything that came to his mouth, the other restricted his transports' scope without their being the less energetic for that; Saint-Florent chose his words with care, but they were simply yet filthier and more impure: distraction and rage, to select precise terms, seemed to characterize the delirium of the one, wickedness and ferocity were the eminent qualities announced in the other's.

"To work, Therese, revive us," says Cardoville; "you see the lamps are extinguished, they've got to be lit again."

While Julien enjoyed Cardoville and La Rose Saint-Florent, the two libertines inclined over me and one after the other inserted their languishing instruments into my mouth; while I pumped one, I was obliged to go to the rescue of the other and pollute it with my hands, then I had to anoint the member itself and the adjacent parts with an alcoholic liquid I had been given; but I was not to limit myself to sucking, I had to revolve my tongue about the heads and I was required to nibble them with my teeth while my lips squeezed tightly about them. However, our two patients were being vigorously thumped and jolted; Julien and La Rose shifted in order to increase the sensations produced by entrances and exits. When at length two or three homages had flowed into those impure temples I began to perceive a degree of firmness; although the elder of the two, Cardoville's was the first to manifest solidity; he swung his hand and with all the strength at his command slapped one of my titties: that was my reward. Saint-Florent was not far behind him; he repaid my efforts by nearly tearing one of my ears from my head. They backed away, reviewed the situation, and then warned me to prepare to receive the treatment I richly deserved. An analysis of these libertines' appalling language allowed to me to conclude that vexations were about to descend like a hailstorm upon me. To have besought mercy in the state to which they had just reduced me would have been to have further aroused them: and so they placed me, completely naked as I was, in the center of the circle they formed by all four drawing up chairs. I was obliged to parade from one to the next and to receive the penance each in his turn chose to order me to do; I had no more compassion from the youths than from the older men, but 'twas above all Cardoville who distinguished himself by refined teasings which Saint-Florent, cruel as he was, was unable to duplicate without an effort.

A brief respite succeeded these vicious orgies, I was given a few instants to catch my breath; I had been beaten black and blue, but what surprised me was that they doctored and healed the damage done me in less time than it had taken to inflict it, whereof not the slightest trace remained. The lubricities were resumed.

There were moments when all those bodies seemed to form but one and when Saint-Florent, lover and mistress, received copious quantities of what the impotent Cardoville doled out with sparing economy: the next instant, no longer active but lending himself in every manner, both his mouth and hindquarters served as altars to frightful homages. Cardoville cannot resist such a profusion of libertine scenes. Seeing his friend brilliantly elevated, he comes up to offer himself to Saint-Florent's lust, and the tradesman enjoys him; I sharpen the spears, I steer them in the direction they are to thrust, and my exposed buttocks provide a perspective to the lubricity of some, a target for the bestiality of others. As all this wears on our two libertines become more circumspect, for considerable efforts are the price of reanimation; they emerge unscathed from their joustings and their new state is such to terrify me even more.

"Very well, La Rose," says Saint-Florent, "take the bitch; we'll tighten her up: it's time for the stricturing."

I am not familiar with the expression: a cruel experiment soon reveals its meaning. La Rose seizes me, he places my flanks upon a small circular repentance stool not a foot in diameter: once there, lacking any other support, my legs fall on one side, my head and arms on the other; my four limbs, stretched as far apart as possible, are tied to the floor; the executioner who is going to perform the stricturing catches up a long needle through whose eye he passes a stout waxed thread, and with complete unconcern for either the blood he is to shed or the sufferings he is going to cause me, the monster, directly before the two colleagues whom the spectacle amuses, sews shut the entrance to the temple of Love; when finished, he turns me over, now my belly rests upon the repentance stool; my limbs hang free, they are attached as before, and the indecent shrine of Sodom is barricaded in the same manner: I do not speak of my agonies, Madame, you must yourself fancy what they were, I was on the verge of losing consciousness.

"Splendid, that's how I must have them," quoth Saint-Florent when I had been turned over again and was lying on my buttocks, and when, in this posture, he spied well within striking range the fortress he wanted to invade. "Accustomed to reaping nothing but the first fruits, how, without this ceremony, should I be able to harvest any pleasures from this creature?"

Saint-Florent had the most violent erection, they were currying and drubbing his device to keep it rampant; grasping that pike, he advances: in order to excite him further, Julien enjoys Cardoville before his eyes; Saint-Florent opens the attack, maddened by the resistance he encounters, he presses ahead with incredible vigor, the threads are strained, some snap. Hell's tortures are as naught to mine; the keener my agonies, the more piquant seem to be my tormenter's delights. At length, everything capitulates before his efforts, I am ripped asunder, the glittering dart sinks to the ultimate depths, but Saint-Florent, anxious to husband his strength, merely touches bottom and withdraws; I am turned over; the same obstacles: the savage one scouts them as he stands heating his engine and with his ferocious hands he molests the environs in order to put the place in fit condition for assault. He presents himself, the natural smallness of the locale renders his campaign more arduous to wage, my redoubtable vanquisher soon storms the gates, clears the entry; I am bleeding; but what does it matter to the conquering hero? Two vigorous heaves carry him into the sanctuary and there the villain consummates a dreadful sacrifice whose racking pains I should not have been able to endure another second.

"My turn," cries up Cardoville, causing me to be untied, "I'll have no tailoring done, but I'm going to place the dear girl upon a camping bed which should restore her circulation, and bring out all the warmth and mobility her temperament or her virtue refuse us."

Upon the spot La Rose opens a closet and draws out a cross made of gnarled, thorny, spiny wood. 'Tis thereon the infamous debauchee wishes to place me, but by means of what episode will he improve his cruel enjoyment? Before attaching me, Cardoville inserts into my behind a silver-colored ball the size of an egg; he lubricates it and drives it home: it disappears. Immediately it is in my body I feel it enlarge and begin to burn; without heeding my complaints, I am lashed securely to this thorn-studded frame; Cardoville penetrates as he fastens himself to me: he presses my back, my flanks, my buttocks on the protuberances upon which they are suspended. Julien fits himself into Cardoville; obliged to bear the weight of these two bodies, and having nothing to support myself upon but these accursed knots and knurs which gouge into my flesh, you may easily conceive what I suffered; the more I thrust up against those who press down upon me, the more I am driven upon the irregularities which stab and lacerate me. Meanwhile the terrible globe has worked its way deep into my bowels and is cramping them, burning them, tearing them; I scream again and again: no words exist which can describe what I am undergoing; all the same and all the while, my murderer frolics joyfully, his mouth glued to mine, he seems to inhale my pain in order that it may magnify his pleasures: his intoxication is not to be rendered; but, as in his friend's instance, he feels his forces about to desert him, and like Saint-Florent wants to taste everything before they are gone entirely. I am turned over again, am made to eject the ardent sphere, and it is set to producing in the vagina itself, the same conflagration it ignited in the place whence it has just been flushed; the ball enters, sears, scorches the matrix to its depths; I am not spared, they fasten me belly-down upon the perfidious cross, and far more delicate parts of me are exposed to molestation by the thorny excrescences awaiting them. Cardoville penetrates into the forbidden passage; he perforates it while another enjoys him in similar wise: and at last delirium holds my persecutor in its grasp, his appalling shrieks announce the crime's completion; I am inundated, then untied.

"Off you go, dear friends," Cardoville says to the pair of young men, "get your hands on this whore and amuse yourselves in whatever way your whims advise: she's yours, we're done with her." The two youthful libertines seize me. While one entertains himself with the front, the other buries himself in the rear; they change places and change again; I am more gravely torn by their prodigious thickness than I have been by Saint-Florent's artificial barricadings; both he and Cardoville toy with the young men while they occupy themselves with me. Saint-Florent sodomizes La Rose who deals in like manner with me, and Cardoville does as much to Julien who employs a more decent place to excite himself in me. I am the focal point of these execrable orgies, their absolute center and mainspring; La Rose and Julien have each four times done reverence at my altars, whilst Cardoville and Saint-Florent, less vigorous or more enervated, are content with one sacrifice offered to each of my lovers. And then the last measure of seed is sown by La Rose Ä 'twas high time, for I was ready to swoon.

"My comrade has certainly hurt you, Therese," says Julien, "and I am going to repair all the damage." He picks up a flask of spirits and several times rubs all my wounds. The traces of my executioners' atrocities vanish, but nothing assuages my pain, and never had I experienced any as sharp.

"What with our skill at making the evidence of our cruelties disappear, the ladies who would like to lodge complaints against us must have the devil's own time getting themselves believed, eh, Therese?" says Cardoville. "What proofs do you fancy could be presented to support an accusation?"

"Oh," Saint-Florent interrupts, "the charming Therese is in no condition to level charges; on the eve of being immolated herself, we ought to expect nothing but prayers from her."

"Well, she'd be ill-advised to undertake the one or the other," Cardoville replies; "she might inculpate us; but would she be heard? I doubt it; our consequence and eminent stations in this city would scarcely allow anyone to notice suits which, anyhow, always come before us and whereof we are at all times the masters. Her final torture would simply be made crueler and more prolonged. Therese must surely sense we have amused ourselves with her person for the natural, common, and uncomplex reason which engages might to abuse feebleness; she must surely sense she can-not escape her sentence, that it must be undergone, that she will undergo it, that it would be in vain she might divulge this evening's absence from jail; she'd not be believed; the jailer Ä for he's ours Ä would deny it at once. And so may this lovely and gentle girl, so penetrated with the grandeur of Providence, peacefully offer up to Heaven all she has just suffered and all that yet awaits her; these will be as so many expiations for the frightful crimes which deliver her into the hands of the law; put on your clothes, Therese, day is not yet come, the two men who brought you hither are going to conduct you back to your prison."

I wanted to say a word, I wanted to cast myself a suppliant at these ogres' feet, either to unbend their hearts, or ask that their hands smite away my life. But I am dragged off, pitched into a cab, and my two guides climb in after me; we had hardly started off when infamous desires inflamed them again.

"Hold her for me," quoth Julien to La Rose, "I simply must sodomize her; I have never laid eyes on a behind which could squeeze me so voluptuously; I'll render you the same service."

There is nothing I can do to defend myself, the project is executed, Julien triumphs, and it is not without atrocious agonies I sustain this newest attack: the assailant's exorbitant bulk, the lacerated condition of those parts, the fire with which that accursed ball had devoured my intestines, everything combined to make me suffer tortures which La Rose renewed immediately his companion was finished. Before arriving I was thus yet another time victim of those wretched valets' criminal libertinage; we reached our destination at last. The jailer greeted us, he was alone, it was still night, no one saw me enter.

"Go to sleep, Therese," said he, restoring me to my cell, "and if ever you wish to tell, it makes no difference whom, that on this night you left prison, remember that I will contradict you, and that this useless accusation will get you nowhere . . . ."

And, said I to myself when I was left alone, I should regret departing this world! I should dread to leave a universe freighted with such monsters! Ah! were the hand of God to snatch me from their clutches at whatever instant and in whatever manner He sees fit! why! I'd complain no more; the unique consolation which may remain to the luckless one bred up in this den of savage beasts, his one comfort is the hope of leaving it soon.

The next day I heard nothing and resolved to abandon myself to Providence, I languished and would touch no food. The day after that, Cardoville came to question me; I could not repress a shudder upon beholding the nonchalance wherewith that scoundrel walked in to execute his judiciary duties Ä he, Cardoville, the most villainous of mortals, he who, contrary to every article of the justice in which he was cloaked, had just so cruelly abused my innocence and exploited my misery; it was in vain I pled my cause, the dishonest man's artfulness devised more crimes than I could invent defenses; when all the charges had been well established in the view of this iniquitous judge, and when the case was made, he had the impudence to ask me whether I knew in Lyon one Monsieur de Saint-Florent, a wealthy and estimable citizen; I answered that I knew him, yes.

"Excellent," said Cardoville, "no more is needed. This Monsieur de Saint-Florent, whom you declare you know, also has a perfect knowledge of you; he has deposed that he saw you in a band of thieves, that you were the first to steal his money and his pocket- book. He further deposes that your comrades wished to spare his life, that you recommended they take it from him; nevertheless, he managed to escape. Saint-Florent adds that, several years later, having recognized you in Lyon, he yielded to your importunings and permitted you to come to pay him a call at his home upon condition you would give him your word to behave well in future and that, while he was delivering a lecture on manners to you, while he was seeking to persuade you to persist along the paths of righteousness, you carried insolence and crime to the point of choosing these moments of kindness to steal a watch and one hundred louis he had left lying upon the mantel . . . ."

And, profiting from the resentment and anger such atrocious calumnies provoked in me, Cardoville ordered the court clerk to write that my silence and my facial expressions were ample acknowledgment of my guilt and were tantamount to a confession.

I threw myself upon the ground, I made the walls resound with my cries, I struck my head against the stone floor, hoping to obtain a speedier death, unable to find vehicles to give expression to my rage: "Villain!" I screamed, "I put my faith in the God of Justice who will revenge me for your crimes; He shall cry out innocence, He shall make you repent your disgraceful abuse of the authority vested in you!" Cardoville rings and tells the jailer to take me away, I appear, says he, to be unsettled by despair and remorse and, at any rate, in no state to follow the interrogation; "But, on the other hand, what remains to be asked or said? The dossier is complete; she has confessed to all her crimes." And the villain leaves peacefully I And divine lightning strikes him not!

The case was tried in short order; motivated and directed by hatred, vengeance, and lust, the court promptly condemned me and I was dispatched to Paris for the confirmation of my sentence. While on this fatal journey, which, though guiltless, I made in the character of the last of criminals, the most bitter and the most dolorous thoughts gathered in my head and completed the desolation of my heart. Under what doom-spelling star must I have been born, I wondered, in order that I be utterly incapable of conceiving a single generous sentiment without immediately being drowned in a sea of misfortunes! And why is it that this enlightened Providence whose justice I am pleased to worship, the while punishing me for my virtues, simultaneously shows me those who crush me with their crimes carried to the pinnacle of happiness!

During my childhood I meet a usurer; he seeks to induce me to commit a theft, I refuse, he becomes rich. I fall amongst a band of thieves, I escape from them with a man whose life I save; by way of thanks, he rapes me. I reach the property of an aristocratic debauchee who has me set upon and devoured by his dogs for not having wanted to poison his aunt. From there I go to the home of a murderous and incestuous surgeon whom I strive to spare from doing a horrible deed: the butcher brands me for a criminal; he doubtless consummates his atrocities, makes his fortune, whilst I am obliged to beg for my bread. I wish to have the sacraments made available to me, I wish fervently to implore the Supreme Being whence howbeit I receive so many ills, and the august tribunal, at which I hope to find purification in our most holy mysteries, becomes the bloody theater of my ignominy: the monster who abuses and plunders me is elevated to his order's highest honors and I fall back into the appalling abyss of misery. I attempt to preserve a woman from her husband's fury, the cruel one wishes to put me to death by draining away my blood drop by drop. I wish to relieve a poor woman, she robs me. I give aid to a man whom adversaries have struck down and left unconscious, the thankless creature makes me turn a wheel like an animal; he hangs me for his pleasure's sake; all fortune's blessings accrue to him, and I come within an ace of dying on the gallows for having been compelled to work for him. An unworthy woman seeks to seduce me for a new crime, a second time I lose the little I own in order to rescue her victim's treasure. A gentleman, a kind spirit wishes to compensate me for all my sufferings by the offer of his hand, he dies in my arms before being able to do anything for me. I risk my life in a fire in order to snatch a child, who does not belong to me, from the flames; the infant's mother accuses and launches legal proceedings against me. I fall into my most mortal enemy's hands; she wishes to carry me off by force and take me to a man whose passion is to cut off heads: if I avoid that villain's sword it is so that I can trip and fall under Themis'. I implore the protection of a man whose life and fortune I once saved; I dare expect gratitude from him, he lures me to his house, he submits me to horrors, and there I find the iniquitous judge upon whom my case depends; both abuse me, both outrage me, both accelerate my doom; fortune overwhelms them with favors, I hasten on to death.

That is what I have received from mankind, that is what I have learned of the danger of trafficking with men; is it any wonder that my soul, stung, whipsawed by unhappiness, revolted by outrage and injustice, aspires to nothing more than bursting from its mortal confines?

A thousand pardons, Madame, said this unlucky girl, terminating her adventures at this point; a thousand times over I ask to be forgiven for having sullied your spirit with such a host of obscenities, for having, in a word, so long abused your patience. I have, perhaps, offended Heaven with impure recitals, I have laid open my old wounds, I have disturbed your ease and rest; farewell, Madame, Godspeed; the Star rises above the horizon, I hear my guards summon me to come, let me run on to meet my destiny, I fear it no more, 'twill abridge my torment: this last mortal instant is dreaded only by the favored being whose days have passed un-clouded; but the wretched creature who has breathed naught but the venomous effluvia of reptiles, whose tottering feet have trod only upon nettles, who has never beheld the torch of dawn save with feelings like unto those of the lost traveler who, trembling, perceives the thunderbolt's forked track; she from whom cruel accident has snatched away parents, all kin, friends, fortune, protection, aid; she who in all this world has nothing more than tears to quench her thirst and for sustenance her tribulations; she, I say, undismayed sees death advance, she even yearns for it as for a safe haven, a port wherein tranquillity will be born again unto her when she is clasped to the breast of a God too just to permit that innocence, defiled and ground under the heel on earth, may not find recompense for so many evils in another world.

The honest Monsieur de Corville had not heard this tale without profound emotion; as for Madame de Lorsange in whom, as we have said, the monstrous errors of her youth had not by any means extinguished sensibility, as for Madame de Lorsange, she was ready to swoon.

"Mademoiselle," said she to Justine, "it is difficult to listen to you without taking the keenest interest in you; but, and I must avow it! an inexplicable sentiment, one far more tender than this I describe, draws me invincibly toward you and does make of your ills my very own. You have disguised your name, you have concealed your birth, I beg you to disclose your secret to me; think not that it is a vain curiosity which bids me speak thus to you... Great God! may what I suspect be true?... O Therese! were you Justine?... were it that you would be my sister !"

"Justine ! Madame ! 'tis a strange name."

"She would have been your age -"

"Juliette! is it you I hear?" cried the unhappy prisoner, casting herself into Madame de Lorsange's arms; "... you... my sister!.... ah, I shall die far less miserable, for I have been able to embrace you again!...."

And the two sisters, clasped in each other's arms, were prevented by their sobs from hearing one another, and found expression in naught but tears.

Monsieur de Corville was unable to hold back his own; aware of the overpowering significance of this affair and sensing his involvement in it, he moves into an adjoining room, sits down and writes a letter to the Lord Chancellor, with fiery strokes, in ardent ciphers he paints in all its horror the fate of poor Justine, whom we shall continue to call Therese; he takes upon himself responsibility for her innocence, he will guarantee it under oath; he asks that, until the time her case has been finally clarified, the allegedly guilty party be confined to no other prison but his chateau, and Corville gives his word he will produce her in court the instant the Chief Justice signals his desire to have her appear there; he makes himself known unto Therese's two guards, entrusts his correspondence to them, makes himself answerable for their prisoner; he is obeyed, Therese is confided to him; a carriage is called for.

"Come, my too unfortunate creature," Monsieur de Corville says to Madame de Lorsange's interesting sister, "come hither; all is going to be changed; it shall not be said your virtues ever remained unrewarded and that the beautiful soul you had from Nature ever encountered but steel; follow us, 'tis upon me you depend henceforth . . . ."

And Monsieur de Corville gave a brief account of what he had just done.

"Dearly beloved and respectable man," said Madame de Lorsange, casting herself down before her lover, "this is the most splendid gesture you have performed in your life, it is such as comes from one who has true acquaintance with the human heart and the spirit of the law which is the avenger of oppressed innocence. There she stands, Monsieur, behold, there is your captive; go, Therese, go, run, fly at once and kneel down before this equitable protector who will not, as have all others, abandon you. O, Monsieur, if those attachments of love which have bound me to you have been cherished, how much more so are they to become now that they are strengthened by the most tender esteem . . . ."

And one after the other the two women embraced the knees of a so generous friend, and upon him they did shed their tears.

A few hours later they arrived at the chateau; once there, Monsieur de Corville and Madame de Lorsange both strove with might and main to raise Therese from the ultimate deeps of unhappiness to the pure sunshine of contentment and well-being. They took greatest joy in giving her to eat of the most succulent foods, they laid her to sleep in the finest of beds, they did urge her to command and they made her will to be done, and into their hospitable proceedings they introduced all the gentility and understanding it were possible to expect from two sensitive souls. She was given medicines for several days, she was bathed, dressed, arrayed in elegant attire, embellished, the two lovers worshiped her, each labored at nothing but to make her forget her sorrows as quickly as might be. An excellent surgeon was fetched; he undertook to make the ignominious mark disappear, and soon the cruel result of Rodin's villainy was effectively gone; and everything responded to the cares her benefactors lavished upon Therese: the shadowed memories of misery were already effaced from that amiable girl's brow; already the Graces had re-established their empire thereupon. For the livid tints on her cheeks of alabaster were substituted the rosy hue appropriate to her years; what had been withered by such a multitude of griefs was called back to fresh new life. Laughter, for so many years banished from her lips, reappeared again under the wings of Pleasure. The very best news came from the Court; Monsieur de Corville had put all of France in action, he had reanimated the zeal of Monsieur S_____, who collaborated with him to publicize Therese's ill-treatment and to restore her to a tranquillity to which she was so heavily entitled. At length letters came from the King, they nullified all the legal proceedings unjustly initiated against her, they gave her back the name of an honest citizen, imposed silence upon all the realm's tribunals before which efforts had been made to defame her, and accorded her a thousand crowns a year, interest realized upon the gold seized in the counterfeiters' Dauphine work-shop. They wished to make Cardoville and Saint-Florent answer for their misdeeds but, in accordance with the fatality of the star intending upon all of Therese's persecutors, one of them, Cardoville, had just, before his crimes were made known, been named to the administration of the Province of _____, and the other to general supervision of Colonial Trade; each had already reached his destination, the edicts affected no one but the powerful families who soon found means to quiet the storm and, pacifically installed in Fortune's sanctuary, those monsters' depredations were quickly forgotten.

(As for the monks of Saint Mary-in-the-Wood, suppression of the religious orders will expose the atrocious crimes of that horrible crew.)

With what regards Therese, as soon as she learned of so many agreeable developments she came well-nigh to expiring from joy; for several days on end the sweetest tears flowed from her eyes and she rejoiced upon her guardians' breasts, and then, all of a sudden, her humor altered, and 'twas impossible to ferret out the cause. She became somber, uneasy, troubled, was given to dreaming, sometimes she burst into weeping before her friends, and was not herself able to explain what was the subject of her woe. "I was not born for such felicity," said she to Madame de Lorsange, "... oh, dear sister, 'tis impossible it last much longer." She was assured all her troubles were over, none remained, said they, no more inquietude for her; 'twas all in vain, nothing would quiet her; one might have said that this melancholy creature, uniquely destined for sorrow, and feeling the hand of misery forever raised above her head, already foresaw the final blow whereby she was going to be smitten down.

Monsieur de Corville was still residing on his country estate; 'twas toward summer's end, they had planned an outing when the approach of a dreadful storm obliged them to postpone their promenade; the excessive heat had constrained them to leave all the windows open. Lightning glitters, shakes, hail slashes down, winds blow wrathfully, heaven's fire convulses the clouds, in the most hideous manner makes them to seethe; it seems as if Nature were wearied out of patience with what she has wrought, as if she were ready to confound all the elements that she might wrench new forms from them. Terrified, Madame de Lorsange begs her sister to make all haste and close the shutters; anxious to calm her, Therese dashes to the windows which are already being broken; she would do battle with the wind, she gives a minute's fight, is driven back and at that instant a blazing thunderbolt reaches her where she stands in the middle of the room... transfixes her.

Madame de Lorsange emits a terrible cry and falls in a faint; Monsieur de Corville calls for help, attentions are given each woman, Madame de Lorsange is revived, but the unhappy Therese has been struck in such wise hope itself can no longer subsist for her; the lightning entered her right breast, found the heart, and after having consumed her chest and face, burst out through her belly. The miserable thing was hideous to look upon; Monsieur de Corville orders that she be borne away . . . .

"No," says Madame de Lorsange, getting to her feet with the utmost calm; "no, leave her here before my eyes, Monsieur, I have got to contemplate her in order to be confirmed in the resolves I have just taken. Listen to me, Corville, and above all do not oppose the decision I am adopting; for the present, nothing in the world could swerve my designs.

"The unheard of sufferings this luckless creature has experienced although she has always respected her duties, have something about them which is too extraordinary for me not to open my eyes upon my own self; think not I am blinded by that false-gleaming felicity which, in the course of Therese's adventures, we have seen enjoyed by the villains who battened upon her. These caprices of Heaven's hand are enigmas it is not for us to sound, but which ought never seduce us. O thou my friend! The prosperity of Crime is but an ordeal to which Providence would expose Virtue, it is like unto the lightning, whose traitorous brilliancies but for an instant embellish the atmosphere, in order to hurl into death's very deeps the luckless one they have dazzled. And there, before our eyes, is the example of it; that charming girl's incredible calamities, her terrifying reversals and uninterrupted disasters are a warning issued me by the Eternal, Who would that I heed the voice of mine guilt and cast myself into His arms. Ah, what must be the punishment I have got to fear from Him, I, whose libertinage, irreligion, and abandon of every principle have stamped every instant of my life I What must I not expect if 'tis thus He has treated her who in all her days had not a single sin whereof to repent I Let us separate, Corville, the time has come, no chain binds us one to the other, forget me, and approve that I go and by an eternal penance abjure, at the Supreme Being's feet, the infamies wherewith I am soiled absolutely. That appalling stroke was necessary to my conversion in this life, it was needed for the happiness I dare hope for in another. Farewell, Monsieur; the last mark of your friendship I ask is that you institute no perquisitions to discover what shall have become of me. Oh, Corville! I await you in a better world, your virtues should lead you unto it; may the atonements I make, to expiate my crimes, in this place where I go to spend the unhappy years that remain to me, permit me to encounter you again someday."

Madame de Lorsange leaves the house immediately; she takes some money with her, leaps into a carriage, to Monsieur de Corville abandons the rest of her ownings after having recommended that they be turned into a pious legacy, and flies to Paris, where she takes a Carmelite's veil; not many years go by before she becomes the example of her order and the edification, as much by her great piety as by the wisdom of her mind and the regularity of her manners.

Monsieur de Corville, worthy of his country's highest posts, attained to them, and, whatever were his honors, he employed them for no end but to bring happiness to the people, glory to his master, whom, "although a minister," he served well, and fortune to his friends.

O you who have wept tears upon hearing of Virtue's miseries; you who have been moved to sympathy for the woe-ridden Justine; the while forgiving the perhaps too heavy brushstrokes we have found ourselves compelled to employ, may you at least extract from this story the same moral which determined Madame de Lorsange! May you be convinced, with her, that true happiness is to be found nowhere but in Virtue's womb, and that if, in keeping with designs it is not for us to fathom, God permits that it be persecuted on Earth, it is so that Virtue may be compensated by Heaven's most dazzling rewards.

The 120 Days of Sodom

Introdction

The extensive wars wherewith Louis XIV was burdened during his reign, while draining the State's treasury and exhausting the substance of the people, none the less contained the secret that led to the prosperity of a swarm of those bloodsuckers who are always on the watch for public calamities, which, instead of appeasing, they promote or invent so as, precisely, to be able to profit from them the more advantageously. The end of this so very sublime reign was perhaps one of the periods in the history of the French Empire when one saw the emergence of the greatest number of these mysterious fortunes whose origins are as obscure as the lust and debauchery that accompany them. It was toward the close of this period, and not long before the Regent sought, by means of the famous tribunal which goes under the name of the Chambre de Justice, to flush this multitude of traffickers, that four of them conceived the idea for the singular revels whereof we are going to give an account. One must not suppose that it was exclusively the low-born and vulgar sort which did this swindling; gentlemen of the highest note led the pack. The Duc de Blangis and his brother the Bishop of X_____, each of whom had thuswise amassed immense fortunes, are in themselves solid proof that, like the others, the nobility neglected no opportunities to take this road to wealth. These two illustrious figures, through their pleasures and business closely associated with the celebrated Durcet and the Président de Curval, were the first to hit upon the debauch we propose to chronicle, and having communicated the scheme to their two friends, all four agreed to assume the major roles in these unusual orgies.

For above six years these four libertines, kindred through their wealth and tastes, had thought to strengthen their ties by means of alliances in which debauchery had by far a heavier part than any of the other motives that ordinarily serve as a basis for such bonds. What they arranged was as follows: the Duc de Blangis, thrice a widower and sire of two daughters one wife had given him, having noticed that the Président de Curval appeared interested in marrying the elder of these girls, despite the familiarities he knew perfectly well her father had indulged in with her, the Duc, I say, suddenly conceived the idea of a triple alliance.

"You want Julie for your wife," said he to Curval, "I give her to you unhesitatingly and put but one condition to the match: that you'll not be jealous when, although your wife, she continues to show me the same complaisance she always has in the past; what is more, I'd have you lend your voice to mine in persuading our good Durcet to give me his daughter Constance, for whom, I must confess, I have developed roughly the same feelings you have formed for Julie."

"But," said Curval, "you are surely aware that Durcet, just as libertine as you..."

"I know all that's to be known," the Duc rejoined. "In this age, and with our manner of thinking, is one halted by such things? do you think I seek a wife in order to have a mistress? I want a wife that my whims may be served, I want her to veil, to cover an infinite number of little secret debauches the cloak of marriage wonderfully conceals. In a word, I want her for the reasons you want my daughter - do you fancy I am ignorant of your object and desires? We libertines wed women to hold slaves: as wives they are rendered more submissive than mistresse, and you know the value we set upon despotism in the joys we pursue."

It was at this point Durcet entered. His two friends related their conversation and, delighted by an overture which promptly induced him to avow the sentiments he too had conceived for Adelaide, the Président's, Durcet accepted the Duc as his son-in-law, provided he might become Curval's. The three marriages were speedily concluded, the dowries were immense, the wedding contracts identical.

No less culpable than his two colleagues, the Président had admitted to Durcet, who betrayed no displeasure upon learning it, that he maintained a little clandestine commerce with his own daughter; the three fathers, each wishing not only to preserve his rights, but noticing here the possibility of extending them, commonly agreed that the three young ladies, bound to their husbands by goods and homes only, would not in body belong more to one than to any of them, and the severest punishments were prescribed for her who should take it into her head not to comply with any of the conditions whereunto she was subject.

They were on the eve of realizing their plan when the Bishop of X____, already closebound through pleasure shared with his brother's two friends, proposed contributing a fourth element to the alliance should the other three gentlemen consent to his participation in the affair. This element, the Duc's second daughter and hence the Bishop's niece, was already more thoroughly his property than was generally imagined. He had effected connections with his sister-in-law and the two brothers knew beyond all shadow of doubt that the existence of this maiden, who was called Aline, was far more accurately to be ascribed to the Bishop than to the Duc; the former who, from the time she left the cradle, had taken the girl into his keeping, had not, as one may well suppose, stood idle as the years brought her charms to flower. And so, upon this head, he was his colleagues' equal, and the article he offered to put on the market was in an equal degree damaged or degraded; but as Aline's attractions and tender youth outshone even those of her three companions, she was unhesitatingly made a part of the bargain. As had the other three, the Bishop yielded her up, but retained the rights to her use; and so each of our four characters thus found himself husband to four wives. Thus there resulted an arrangement which, for the reader's convenience, we shall recapitulate:

The Duc, Julie's father, became the husband of Constance, Durcet's daughter;

Durcet, Constance's father, became the husband of Adelaide, the Président's daughter;

The Président, Adelaide's father, became the husband of Julie, the Duc's elder daughter;

And the Bishop, Aline's uncle and father, became the husband of the other three females by ceding this same Aline to his friends, the while retaining the same rights over her.

It was at a superb estate of the Duc, situated in the Bourbonnais, that these happy matches were made, and I leave to the reader to fancy how they were consummated and in what orgies; obliged as we are to describe others, we shall forego the pleasure of picturing these.

Upon their return to Paris, our four friends' association became only the firmer; and as our next task is to make the reader familiar with them, before proceeding to individual and more searching developments, a few details of their lubricious arrangements will serve, it seems to me, to shed a preliminary light upon the character of these debauchees.

The society had created a common fund, which each of its members took his turn administering for six months; the sums, allocated for nothing but expenses in the interests of pleasure, were vast. Their excessive wealth put the most unusual things within their reach, and the reader ought not be surprised to hear that two million were annually disbursed to obtain good cheer and lust's satisfaction.

Four accomplished procuresses to recruit women, and a similar number of pimps to scout out men, had the sole duty to range both the capital and the provinces and bring back everything, in the one gender and in the other, that could best satisfy their sensuality's demands. Four supper parties were held regularly every week in four different country houses located at four extremities of Paris. At the first of these gatherings, the one exclusively given over to the pleasures of sodomy, only men were present; there would always be at hand sixteen young men, ranging in age from twenty to thirty, whose immense faculties permitted our four heroes, in feminine guise, to taste the most agreeable delights. The youths were selected solely upon the basis of the size of their member, and it almost became necessary that this superb limb be of such magnificence that it could never have penetrated any woman; this was an essential clause, and as naught was spared by way of expense, only very rarely would it fail to be fulfilled. But simultaneously to sample every pleasure, to these sixteen husbands was joined the same quantity of boys, much younger, whose purpose was to assume the office of women. These lads were from twelve to eighteen years old, and to be chosen for service each had to possess a freshness, a face, graces, charms, an air, an innocence, a candor which are far beyond what our brush could possibly paint. No woman was admitted to these masculine orgies, in the course of which everything of the lewdest invented in Sodom and Gomorrah was executed.

At the second supper were girls of superior class who, upon these occasions forced to give up their proud ostentation and the customary insolence of their bearing, were constrained, in return for their hire, to abandon themselves to the most irregular caprices, and often even to the outrages our libertines were pleased to inflict upon them. Twelve of these girls would appear, and as Paris could not have furnished a fresh supply of them as often as would have been necessary, these evenings were inters- persed with others at which were admitted, only in the same number as the well-bred ladies, women ranging from procuresses up through the class of officers' wives. There are above four or five thousand in Paris who belong to one or the other of the two latter classes and whom need or lust obliges to attend soirees of this kind; one has but to have good agents to find them, and our libertines, who were splendidly represented, would frequently come across miraculous specimens. But it was in vain one was honest or a decent woman, one had to submit everything: our Lordships' libertinage, of a variety that never brooks limits, would overwhelm with horrors and infamies whatever, whether by Nature or social convention, ought to have been exempt from such ordeals. Once one was there, one had to be ready for anything, and as our four villains had every taste that accompanies the lowest, most crapulous debauch, this fundamental acquiescence to their desires was not by any means a matter of inconsequence.

The guests at the third supper were the vilest, foulest creatures that can possibly be met with. To him who has some acquaintance with debauchery's extravagances, this refinement will appear wholly understandable; 'tis most voluptuous to wallow, so to speak, in filth with persons of this category; these exercises offer the completest abandon, the most monstrous intemperance, the most total abasement, and these pleasures, compared with those tasted the evening before, or with the distinguished individuals in whose company we have tasted them, have a way of lending a sharp spice to earlier activities. At these third suppers, debauch being more thorough, nothing was omitted that might render it complex and piquant. A hundred whores would appear in the course of six hours, and only too often something less than the full hundred would leave the games. But there is nothing to be gained by hurrying our story or by broaching subjects which can only receive adequate treatment in the sequel.

As for the fourth supper, it was reserved for young maids; only those between the ages of seven and fifteen were permitted. Their condition in life was of no importance, what counted was their looks: they had to be charming; as for their virginity, authentic evidence was required. Oh, incredible refinement of libertinage! It was not, assuredly, that they wished to pluck all those roses, and how indeed could they have done so? for those untouched flowers were always a score in number, and of our four libertines only two were capable of proceeding to the act, one of the remaining two, the financier, being absolutely incapable of an erection, and the Bishop being absolutely unable to take his pleasure save in a fashion which, yes, I agree, may dishonor a virgin but which, however, always leaves her perfectly intact. No matter; the twenty maiden-heads had to be there, and those which were not impaired by our quartet of masters became, before their eyes, the prey of certain of their valets just as depraved as they, whom they kept constantly at beck and call for more than one reason.

Apart from these four supper parties there was another, a secret and private one held every Friday, involving many fewer persons but surely costing a great deal more. The participants were restricted to four young and high-born damsels who, by means of strategy and money, had been abducted from their parents' homes. Our libertines' wives nearly always had a share in this debauch, and their extreme submissiveness, their docile attentions, their services made it more of a success each time. As for the genial atmosphere at these suppers, it goes without saying that even greater profusion than delicacy reigned there; not one of these meals cost less than ten thousand francs, and neighboring countries as well as all France were ransacked so that what was of the rarest and most exquisite might be assembled together. Fine and abundant wines and liqueurs were there, and even during the winter they had fruits of every season; in a word, one may be certain that the table of the world's greatest monarch was not dressed with as much luxury nor served with equal magnificence.

But now let us retrace our steps and do our best to portray one by one each of our four heroes - to describe each not in terms of the beautiful, not in a manner that would seduce or captivate the reader, but simply with the brush strokes of Nature which, despite all her disorder, is often sublime, indeed even when she is at her most depraved. For - and why not say so in passing - if crime lacks the kind of delicacy one finds in virtue, is not the former always more sublime, does it not unfailingly have a character of grandeur and sublimity which surpasses, and will always make it preferable to, the monotonous and lackluster charms of virtue? Will you protest the greater usefulness of this or of that, is it for us to scan Nature's laws, ours to determine whether, vice being just as necessary to Nature as is virtue, she perhaps does not implant in us, in equal quantity, the penchant for one or the other, depending upon her respective needs? But let us proceed.

The Duc de Blangis, at eighteen the master of an already colossal fortune which his later speculations much increased, experienced all the difficulties which descend like a cloud of locusts upon a rich and influental young man who need not deny himself anything; it almost always happens in such cases that the extent of one's vices, and one stints oneself that much less the more one has the means to procure oneself everything. Had the Duc received a few elementary qualities from Nature, they might possibly have counter-balanced the dangers which beset him in his position, but this curious mother, who sometimes seems to collaborate with chance in order that the latter may favor every vice she gives to those certain beings of whom she expects attentions very different from those virtue supposes, and this because she has just as much need of the one as of the other, Nature, I say, in destining Blangis for immense wealth, had meticulously endowed him with every impulse, every inspiration required for its abuse. Together with a tenebrous and very evil mind, she had accorded him a heart of flint and an utterly criminal soul, and these were accompanied by the disorders in tastes and irregularity of whim whence were born the dreadful libertinage to which the Duc was in no common measure addicted. Born treacherous, harsh, imperious, barbaric, selfish as lavish in the pursuit of pleasure as miserly when it were a question of useful spending, a liar, a gourmand, a drunk, a dastard, a sodomite, fond of incest, given to murdering, to arson, to theft, no, not a single virtue compensated that host of vices. Why, what am I saying! not only did he never so much as dream of a single virtue, he beheld them all with horror, and he was frequently heard to say that to be truly happy in this world a man ought not merely fling himself into every vice, but should never permit himself one virtue, and that it was not simply a matter of always doing evil, but also and above all of never doing good. "Oh, there are plenty of people," the Duc used to observe, "who never misbehave save when passion spurs them to ill; later, the fire gone out of them, their now calm spirit peacefully returns to the path of virtue and, thus passing their life going from strife to error and from error to remorse, they end their days in such a way there is no telling just what roles they have enacted on earth. Such persons," he would continue, "must surely be miserable: forever drifting, continually undecided, their entire life is spent detesting in the morning what they did the evening before. Certain to repent of the pleasures they taste, they take their delight in quaking, in such sort they become at once virtuous in crime and criminal in virtue. However," our hero would add, "my more solid character is a stranger to these contradictions; I do my choosing without hesitation, and as I am always sure to find pleasure in the choice I make, never does regret arise to dull its charm. Firm in my principles because those I formed are sound and were formed very early, I always act in accordance with them; they have made me understand the emptiness and nullity of virtue; I hate virtue, and never will I be seen resorting to it. They have persuaded me that through vice alone is man capable of experiencing this moral and physical vibration which is the source of the most delicious voluptuousness; so I give myself over to vice. I was still very young when I learned to hold religion's fantasies in contempt, being perfectly convinced that the existence of a creator is a revolting absurdity in which not even children continue to believe. I have no need to thwart my inclinations in order to flatter some god; these instincts were given me by Nature, and it would be to irritate her were I to resist them; if she gave me bad ones, that is because they were necessary to her designs. I am in her hands but a machine which she runs as she likes, and not one of my crimes does not serve her: the more she urges me to commit them, the more of them she needs; I should be a fool to disobey her. Thus, nothing but the law stands in my way, but I defy the law, my gold and my prestige keep me well beyond reach of those vulgar instruments of repression which should be employed only upon the common sort." If one were to raise the objection that, nevertheless, all men possess ideas of the just and the unjust which can only be the product of Nature, since these notions are found in every people and even amongst the uncivilized, the Duc would reply affirmatively, saying that yes, those ideas have never been anything if not relative, that the stronger has always considered exceedingly just what the weaker regarded as flagrantly unjust, and that it takes no more than the mere reversal of their positions for each to be able to change his way of thinking too; whence the Duc would conclude that nothing is really just but what makes for pleasure, and what is unjust is the cause of pain;

that in taking a hundred louis from a man's pocket, he was doing something very just for himself, although the victim of the robbery might have to regard the action with another eye; that all these notions therefore being very arbitrary, a fool he who would allow himself to become their thrall. It was by means of arguments in this kind the Duc used to justify his trans-gressions, and as he was a man of greatest possible wit, his arguments had a decisive ring. And so, modeling his conduct upon his philosophy, the Duc had, from his most tender youth, abandoned himself unrestrainedly to the most shameful extravagances, and to the most extraordinary ones. His father, having died young and, as I indicated, left him in control of a huge fortune, had however stipulated in his will that the young man's mother should, while she lived, be allowed to enjoy a large share of this legacy. Such a condition was not in displeasing Blangis: poison appearing to be the only way to avoid having to subscribe to this article, the knave straightway decided to make use of it. But this was the period when he was only making his first steps in a vicious career; not daring to act himself, he brought one of his sisters, with whom he was carrying on a criminal intrigue, to take charge of the execution, assuring her that if she were to succeed, he would see to it that she would be the beneficiary of that part of the fortune whereof death would deprive their mother. However, the young lady was horrified by this proposal, and the Duc, observing that this ill-confided secret was perhaps going to betray him, decided on the spot to extend his plans to include the sister he had hoped to have for an accomplice; he conducted both women to one of his properties whence the two unfortunate ones never returned. Nothing quite encourages as does one's first unpunished crime. This hurdle once cleared, an open field seemed to beckon to the Duc. Immediately any person whomsoever showed opposition to his desires, poison was employed forthwith. From necessary murders he soon passed to those of pure pleasure; he was captivated by that regrettable folly which causes us to find delight in the sufferings of others; he noticed that a violent commotion inflicted upon any kind of an adversary is answered by a vibrant thrill in our own nervous system; the effect of this vibration, arousing the animal spirits which flow within these nerves' con-cavities, obliges them to exert pressure on the erector nerves and to produce in accordance with this perturbation what is termed a lubricious sensation. Consequently, he set about committing thefts and murders in the name of debauchery and libertinage, just as someone else would be content, in order to inflame these same passions, to chase a whore or two. At the age of twenty-three, he and three of his companions in vice, whom he had indoctrinated with his philosophy, made up a party whose aim was to go out and stop a public coach on the highway, to rape the men among the travelers along with the women, to assassinate them afterward, to make off with their victims' money (the conspirators certainly had no need of this), and to be back that same night, all three of them, at the Opera Ball in order to have a sound alibi. This crime took place, ah, yes: two charming maids were violated and massacred in their mother's arms; to this was joined an endless list of other horrors, and no one dared suspect the Duc. Weary of the delightful wife his father had bestowed upon him before dying, the young Blangis wasted no time uniting her shade to his mother's, to his sister's, and to those of all his other victims. Why all this? to be able to marry a girl, wealthy, to be sure, but publicly dishonored and whom he knew full well was her brother's mistress. The person in question was the mother of Aline, one of the figures in our novel we mentioned above. This second wife, soon sacrificed like the first, gave way to a third, who followed hard on the heels of the second. It was rumored abroad that the Duc's huge construction was responsible for the undoing of all his wives, and as this gigantic tale corresponded in every point to its gigantic inspiration, the Duc let the opinion take root and veil the truth. That dreadful colossus did indeed make one think of Hercules or a centaur: Blangis stood five foot eleven inches tall, had limbs of great strength and energy, powerful sinews, elastic nerves, in addition to that a proud and masculine visage, great dark eyes, handsome black eyelashes, an aquiline nose, fine teeth, a quality of health and exuberance, broad shoulders, a heavy chest but a well-proportioned figure withal, splendid hips, superb buttocks, the handsomest leg in the world, an iron temperament, the strength of a horse, the member of a veritable mule, wondrously hirsute, blessed with the ability to eject its sperm any number of times within a given day and at will, even at the age of fifty, which was his age at the time, a virtually constant erection in this member whose dimensions were an exact eight inches for circumference and twelve for length over-all, and there you have the portrait of the Duc de Blangis, drawn as accurately as if you'd wielded the pencil yourself. But if this masterpiece of Nature was violent in its desires, what was it like, Great God! when crowned by drunken voluptuousness? 'Twas a man no longer, 'twas a raging tiger. Woe unto him who happened then to be serving its passions; frightful cries, atrocious blasphemies sprang from the Duc's swollen breast, flames seemed to dart from his eyes, he foamed at the mouth, he whinnied like a stallion, you'd have taken him for the very god of lust. Whatever then was his manner of having his pleasure, his hands necessarily strayed, roamed continually, and he had been more than once seen to strangle woman to death at the instant of his perfidious discharge. His presence of mind once restored, his frenzy was immediately replaced by the most complete indifference to the infamies wherewith he had just indulged himself, and of this indifference, of this kind of apathy, further sparks of lechery would be born almost at once.

In his youth, the Duc had been known to discharge as often as eighteen times a day, and that without appearing one jot more fatigued after the final than after the initial ejaculation. Seven or eight crises within the same interval still held no terrors for him, his half a century of years notwithstanding. For roughly twenty-five years he had accustomed himself to passive sodomy, and he withstood its assaults with the identical vigor characterized his manner of delivering them actively when, the very next moment, it pleased him to exchange roles. He had once wagered he could sustain fifty-five attacks in a day, and so he had. Furnished, as we have pointed out, with prodigious strength, he needed only one hand to violate a girl, and he had proved it upon several occasions. One day he boasted he could squeeze the life out of a horse with his legs; he mounted the beast, it collapsed at the instant he had predicted. His prowess at the table outshone, if that is possible, what he demonstrated upon the bed. There's no imagining what had come to be the quantity of the food he consumed. He regularly ate three meals a day, and they were all three exceedingly prolonged and exceedingly copious, and it was as nothing to him to toss down his usual ten bottles of Burgundy; he had drunk up to thirty, and needed but to be challenged and he would set out for the mark of fifty; but his intoxication taking on the tinge of his passions, and liqueurs or wines having heated his brain, he would wax furious, and they would be obliged to tie him down. And despite all that, would you believe it? a steadfast child might have hurled this giant into a panic; true indeed it is that the spirit often poorly corresponds with the fleshy sheath enveloping it: as soon as Blangis discovered he could no longer use his treachery or his deceit to make away with his enemy, he would become timid and cowardly, and the mere thought of even the mildest combat, but fought on equal terms, would have sent him fleeing to the ends of the earth. He had nevertheless, in keeping with custom, been in one or two campaigns, but had acquitted himself so disgracefully he had retired from the service at once. Justifying his turpitude with equal amounts of cleverness and effrontery, he loudly proclaimed that his poltroonery being nothing other than the desire to preserve himself, it were perfectly impossible for anyone in his right senses to condemn it for a fault.

Keep in mind the identical moral traits; next, adapt them to an entity from the physical point of view infinitely inferior to the one we just described; there you have the portrait of the Bishop of X____, the Duc de Blangis' brother. The same black soul, the same penchant for crime, the same contempt for religion, the same atheism, the same deception and cunning, a yet more supple and adroit mind, however, and more art in guiding his victims to their doom, but a slender figure, not heavy, no, a little thin body, wavering health, very delicate nerves, a greater fastidiousness in the pursuit of pleasure, mediocre prowess, a most ordinary member, even small, but deft, profoundly skilled in management, each time yielding so little that his incessantly inflamed imagination would render him capable of tasting delight quite as frequently as his brother; his sensations were of a remarkable acuteness, he would experience an irritation so prodigious he would often fall into a deep swoon upon discharging, and he almost always temporarily lost consciousness when doing so.

He was forty-five, had delicate features, rather attractive eyes but a foul mouth and ugly teeth, a hairless pallid body, a small but well-shaped ass, and a prick five inches around and six in length. An idolater of active and passive sodomy, but eminently of the latter, he spent his life having himself buggered, and this pleasure, which never requires much expense of energy, was best suited to the modesty of his means. We will speak of his other tastes in good time. With what regards those of the table, he carried them nearly as far as the Duc, but went about the matter with somewhat more sensuality. Monseigneur, no less a criminal than his elder brother, possessed characteristics which had doubtless permitted him to match the celebrated feats of the hero we painted a moment ago; we will content ourselves with citing one of them, 'twill be enough to make the reader see of what such a man may be capable, and what he was prepared and disposed to do, having done the following:

One of his friends, a man powerful and rich, had formerly had an intrigue with a young noblewoman who had borne him two children, a girl and a boy. He had, however, never been able to wed her, and the maiden had become another's wife. The unlucky girl's lover died while still young, but the owner howbeit of a tremendous fortune; having no kin to provide for, it occurred to him to bequeath all he had to the two ill-fated children his affair had produced.

On his deathbed, he made the Bishop privy to his intentions and entrusted him with these two immense endowments: he divided the sum, put them in two purses, and gave them to the Bishop, confiding the two orphans' education to this man of God and enlisting him to pass on to each what was to be his when they attained their majority. At the same time he enjoined the prelate to invest his wards' funds, so that in the meantime they would double in size. He also affirmed that it was his design to leave his offsprings' mother in eternal ignorance of what he was doing for them, and he absolutely insisted that none of this should ever be mentioned to her. These arrangements concluded, the dying man closed his eyes, and Monseigneur found himself master of about a million in banknotes, and of two children. The scoundrel was not long deliberating his next step: the dying man had spoken to no one but him, the mother was to know nothing, the children were only four or five years old. He circulated the intelligence that his friend, upon expiring, had left his fortune to the poor; the rascal acquired it the same day. But to ruin those wretched children did not suffice; furnished with authority by their father, the Bishop - who never committed one crime without instantly conceiving another - had the children removed from the remote pension in which they were being brought up, and placed them under the roof of certain people in his hire, from the outset having resolved soon to make them serve his perfidious lust. He waited until they were thirteen; the little boy was the first to arrive at that age: the Bishop put him to use, bent him to all his debauches, and as he was extremely pretty, sported with him for a week. But the little girl fared less well: she reached the prescribed age, but was very ugly, a fact which had no mitigating effect upon the good Bishop's lubricious fury. His desires appeased, he feared lest these children, left alive, would someday discover something of the secret of their interests. Therefore, he conducted them to an estate belonging to his brother and, sure of recapturing, by means of a new crime, the sparks of lechery enjoyment had just caused him to lose, he immolated both of them to his ferocious passions, and accompanied their death with episodes so piquant and so cruel that his voluptuousness was reborn in the midst of the torments wherewith he beset them. The thing is, unhappily, only too well known: there is no libertine at least a little steeped in vice who is not aware of the great sway murder exerts over the senses, and how voluptuously it determines a discharge. And that is a general truth whereof it were well the reader be early advised before undertaking the perusal of a work which will surely attempt an ample development of this system.

Henceforth at ease in the face of whatever might transpire, Monseigneur returned to Paris to enjoy the fruit of his misdeeds, and without the least qualms about having counteracted the intentions of a man who, in his present situation, was in no state to derive either pain or pleasure therefrom.

The Président de Curval was a pillar of society; almost sixty years of age, and worn by debauchery to a singular degree, he offered the eye not much more than a skeleton. He was tall, he was dry, thin, had two blue lusterless eyes, a livid and unwholesome mouth, a prominent chin, a long nose. Hairy as a satyr, flat-backed, with slack, drooping buttocks that rather resembled a pair of dirty rags flapping upon his upper thighs; the skin of those buttocks was, thanks to whipstrokes, so deadened and toughened that you could seize up a handful and knead it without his feeling a thing. In the center of it all there was displayed - no need to spread those cheeks - an immense orifice whose enormous diameter, odor, and color bore a closer resemblance to the depths of a well-freighted privy than to an asshole; and, crowning touch to these allurements, there was numbered among this sodomizing pig's little idiosyncrasies that of always leaving this particular part of himself in such a state of uncleanliness that one was at all times able to observe there a rim or pad a good two inches thick. Below a belly as wrinkled as it was livid and gummy, one perceived, within a forest of hairs, a tool which, in its erectile condition, might have been about eight inches long and seven around; but this condition had come to be the most rare and to procure it a furious sequence of things was the necessary preliminary. Nevertheless, the event occurred at least two or three times each week, and upon these occasions the Président would glide into every hole to be found, indiscriminately, although that of a young lad's behind was infinitely the most precious to him. The head of the Président's device was now at all times exposed, for he had had himself circumcised, a ceremony which largely facilitates enjoyment and to which all pleasure-loving persons ought to submit. But one of the purposes of the same operation is to keep this privity cleaner; nothing of the sort in Curval's case: this part of him was just as filthy as the other: this uncapped head, naturally quite thick to begin with, was thus made at least an inch ampler in circumference. Similarly untidy about all the rest of his person, the Président, who furthermore had tastes at the very least as nasty as his appearance, had become a figure whose rather malodorous vicinity might not have succeeded in pleasing everyone. However, his colleagues were not at all of the sort to be scandalized by such trifles, and they simply avoided discussing the matter with him. Few mortals had been as free in their behavior or as debauches as the Président; but, entirely jaded, absolutely besotted, all that remained to him was the depravation and lewd profligacy of libertinage. Above three hours of excess, and of the most outrageous excess, were needed before one could hope to inspire a voluptous reaction in him. As for his emission, although in Curval the phenomenon was far more frequent than erection, and could be observed once every day, it was, all the same, so difficult to obtain, or it never occurred save as an aftermath to things so strange and often so cruel or so unclean, that the agents of his pleasure not uncommonly renounced the struggle, fainting by the wayside, the which would give birth in him to a kind of lubricious anger and this, through its effects, would now and again triumph where his efforts had failed. Curval was to such a point mired down in the morass of vice and libertinage that it had become virtually impossible for him to think or speak of anything else. He unendingly had the most appalling expressions in his mouth, just as he had the vilest designs in his heart, and these with surpassing energy he mingled with blasphemies and imprecations supplied him by his true horror, a sentiment he shared with his companions, for everything that smacked of religion. This disorder of mind, yet further augmented by the almost continual intoxication in which he was fond of keeping himself, had during the past few years given him an air of imbecility and prostration which, he would declare, made for his most cherished delight.

Born as great a gourmand as a drunk, he alone was fit to keep abreast of the Duc, and in the course of this tale we will behold him to perform wonders which will no doubt astonish the most veteran eaters.

It had been ten years since Curval had ceased to discharge his judicial duties; it was not simply that he was no longer fit to carry them out, but I even believe that while he had been, he may have been asked to leave these matters alone for the rest of his life.

Curval had led a very libertine life, every sort of perversion was familiar to him, and those who knew him personally had the strong suspicion he owed his vast fortune to nothing other than two or three murders. However that may be, it is, in the light of the following story, highly probable that this variety of extravagance had the power to stir him deeply, and it is this adventure, which attracted some unfortunate publicity, that was responsible for his exclusion from the Court. We are going to relate the episode in order to give the reader an idea of his character.

There dwelled in the neighborhood of Curval's town house a miserable street porter who, the father of a charming little girl, was ridiculous enough to be a person of sensibility. Twenty messages of every kind had already arrived containing proposals relating to the poor fellow's daughter; he and his wife had remained unshaken despite this barrage aimed at their corruption, and Curval, the source of these embassies, only irritated by the growing number of refusals they had evoked, knew not what tack to take in order to get his hands upon the girl and to subject her to his libidinous caprices, until it struck to him that by simply having the father broken he would lead the daughter to his bed. The thing was as nicely conceived as executed. Two or three bullies in the Président's pay intervened in the suit, and before the month was out, the wretched porter was enmeshed in an imaginary crime which seemed to have been committed at his door and which got him speedily lodged in one of the Conciergerie's dungeons. The Président, as one would expect, soon took charge of the case, and, having no desire to permit it to drag on, arranged in the space of three days, thanks to his knavery and his gold, to have the unlucky porter condemned to be broken on the wheel, without the culprit ever having committed any crime but that of wishing to preserve his honor and safeguard his daughter's.

Meanwhile, the solicitations were renewed. The mother was brought in, it was explained to her that she alone had it in her power to save her husband, that if she were to satisfy the Président, what could be clearer than that he would thereupon snatch her husband from the dreadful fate awaiting him. Further hesitation was impossible; the woman made inquiries; Curval knew perfectly well to whom she addressed herself, the counsels were his creatures, and they gave her unambiguous replies: she ought not waste a moment. The poor woman herself brought her daughter weeping to her judge's feet; the latter could not have been more liberal with his promises, nor have been less eager to keep his word. Not only did he fear lest, were he to deal honorably and spare the husband, the man might go and raise an uproar upon discovering the price that had been paid to save his life, but the scoundrel even found a further delight, a yet keener one, in arranging to have himself given what he wished without being obliged to make any return.

This thought led to others; numerous criminal possibilities entered his head, and their effect was to increase his perfidious lubricity. And this is how he set about the matter so as to put the maximum of infamy and piquancy into the scene:

His mansion stood facing a spot where criminals are sometimes executed in Paris, and as this particular offense had been committed in that quarter of the city, he won assurance the punishment would be meted out on this particular square. The wretch's wife and daughter arrived at the Président's home at the appointed hour; all windows overlooking the square were well shuttered, so that, from the apartments where he amused himself with his victims, nothing at all could be seen of what was going on outside. Apprised of the exact minute of the execution, the rascal selected it for the deflowering of the little girl who was held in her mother's arms, and everything was so happily arranged that Curval discharged into the child's ass the moment her father expired. Instantly he'd completed his business, "Come have a look," quoth he, opening a window looking upon the square, "come see how well I've kept my bargain," and one of his two princesses saw her father, the other her husband, delivering up his soul to the headsman's steel.

Both collapsed in a faint, but Curval had provided for everything: this swoon was their agony, they'd both been poisoned, and nevermore opened their eyes. Notwithstanding the precautions he had taken to swathe the whole of this exploit in the most profound mystery, something did indeed transpire: nothing was known of the women's death, but there existed a lively suspicion he had been untruthful in connection with the husband's case. His motive was half-known, and his eventual retirement from the bench was the outcome. As of this moment, no longer having to maintain appearances, Curval flung himself into a new ocean of errors and crimes. He sent everywhere for victims to sacrifice to the perversity of his tastes. Through an atrocious refinement of cruelty, but one, however, very easily understood, the downtrodden classes were those upon which he most enjoyed hurling the effects of his raging perfidy. He had several minions who were abroad night and day, scouring attics and hovels, tracking down whatever of the most destitute misery might be able to provide, and under the pretext of dispensing aid, either he envenomed his catch - to give poison was one of his most delectable pastimes - or he lured it to his house and slew it upon the altar of his perverse preferences. Men, women, children: anything was fuel to his rage, and at its bidding he performed excesses which would have got his head between block and blade a thousand times over were it not for the silver he distributed and the esteem he enjoyed, factors whereby he was a thousand times protected. One may well imagine such a being had no more religion than his two confreres; he without doubt detested it as sovereignly as they, but in years past had done more to wither it in others, for, in the days when his mind had been sound, it had also been clever, and he had put it to good use writing against religion; he was the author of a several works whose influence had been prodigious, and these successes, always present in his memory, still constituted one of his dearest delights.

The more we multiply the objects of our enjoyments...(the portrait of Durcet) (a) ...the years of a sickly childhood.

Durcet is fifty-three; he is small, short, broad, thickset; an agreeable, hearty face; a very white skin; his entire body, and principally his hips and buttocks, absolutely like a woman's; his ass is cool and fresh, chubby, firm, and dimpled, but excessively agape, owing to the habit of sodomy; his prick is extraordinarily small, 'tis scarcely two inches around, no more than four inches long; it has entirely ceased to stiffen; his discharges are rare and uneasy, far from abundant and always preceded by spasms which hurl him into a kind of furor which, in turn, conducts him to crime; he has a chest like a woman's, a sweet, pleasant voice and, when in society, the best-bred manners, although his mind is without question as depraved as his colleagues' a schoolmate of the Duc, they still sport together every day, and one of Durcet's loftiest pleasures is to have his anus tickled by the Duc's enormous member.

And such, dear reader, are the four villains in whose company I am going to have you pass a few months. I have done my best to describe them; if, as I have wished, I have made you familiar with even their most secret depths, nothing in the tale of their various follies will astonish you. I have not been able to enter into minute detail with what regards their tastes - to have done so now would have been to impair the value and to harm the main scheme of this work. But as we move progressively along, you will have but to keep an attentive eye upon our heroes, and you'll have no trouble discerning their characteristic peccadillos and the particular type of voluptuous mania which best suits each of them. Roughly all we can say at the present time is that they were generally susceptible of an enthusiasm for sodomy, that the four of them had themselves buggered regularly, and that they all four worshiped behinds.

The Duc, however, relative to the immensity of his weapon and, doubtless, more through cruelty than from taste, still fucked cunts with the greatest pleasure.

So also did the Président, but less frequently.

As for the Bishop, such was his supreme loathing for them the mere sight of one might have kept him limp for six months. He had never in all his life fucked but one, that belonging to his sister-in-law, and expressly to beget a child wherewith some day to procure himself the pleasures of incest; we have seen how well he succeeded.

As regards Durcet, he certainly idolized the ass with as much fervor as the Bishop, but his enjoyment of it was more accessory; his favorite attacks were directed toward a third sanctuary - this mystery will be unveiled in the sequel. But on with the portraits essential to the intelligence of this work, and let us now give our reader an idea of these worthy husbands' four wives.

What a contrast! Constance, the Duc's wife and the daughter of Durcet, was a tall woman, slender, lovely as a picture, and modeled as if the Graces had taken pleasure in embellishing her, but the elegance of her figure in no way detracted from her freshness, she was not for that the less plumpy fleshed, and the most delicious forms graced by a skin fairer than the lily, often induced one to suppose that, no, it had been Love itself who had undertaken her formation. Her face was a trifle long, her features wonderfully noble, more majesty than gentleness was in her look, more grandeur than subtlety. Her eyes were large, black, and full of fire; her mouth extremely small and ornamented by the finest teeth imaginable, she had a narrow, supple tongue, of the loveliest pink, and her breath was sweeter still than the scent of a rose. She was full-breasted, her bosom was buxom, fair as alabaster and as firm. Her back was turned in an extraordinary way, its lines sweeping deliciously down to the most artistically and the most precisely cleft ass Nature has produced in a long time. Nothing could have been more perfectly round, not very large, but firm, white, dimpled; and when it was opened, what used to peep out but the cleanest, most winsome, most delicate hole. A nuance of tenderest pink had shaded this ass, charming asylum of lubricity's sweetest pleasures, but, great God! it was not for long to preserve so many charms! Four or five attacks, and the Duc had spoiled all those graces, how quickly had they gone, and soon after her marriage Constance was become no more than the image of a beautiful lily wherefrom the tempest has of late stripped the petals away. Two round and perfectly molded thighs supported another temple, in all likelihood less delicious, but, to inclined to worship there, offering so many allurements it would be in vain were my pen to strive to describe them. Constance was almost a virgin when the Duc married her, and her father, the only man who had known her, had, as they say, left that side of her perfectly intact. The most beautiful black hair - falling in natural curls to below her shoulders and, when one wished it thus, reaching down to the pretty fur, of the same color, which shaded that voluptuous little cunt - made for a further adornment I might have been guilty of omitting, and lent this angelic creature, aged about twenty-two, all the charms Nature is able to lavish upon a woman. To all these amenities Constance joined a fair and agreeable wit, a spirit somewhat more elevated than it ought to have been, considering the melancholy situation fate had awarded her, for thereby she was enabled to sense all its horrors and, doubtless, she would have been happier if furnished with less delicate perceptions.

Durcet, who had raised her more as if she were a courtesan than his daughter, and who had been much more concerned to give her talents than manners, had all the same never been able totally to destroy the principles of rectitude and of virtue it seemed Nature had been pleased to engrave in her heart. She had no formal religion, no one had ever mentioned such a thing to her, the exercise of a belief was not to be tolerated in her father's household, but all that had not blotted out this modesty, this natural humility which has nothing to do with theological chimeras, and which, when it dwells in an upright, decent, and sensitive soul, is very difficult to obliterate. Never had she stepped out of her father's house, and the scoundrel had forced her, beginning at the age of twelve, to serve his crapulous pleasures. She found a world of difference in those the Duc imbided with her, her body was noticeably altered by those formidable dimensions, and the day after the Duc had despoiled her of her maidenhead, sodomistically speaking, she had fallen dangerously ill. They believed her rectum had been irreparably damaged; but her youth, her health, and some salutary local remedies soon restored the use of that forbidden avenue to the Duc, and the luckless Constance, forced to accustom herself to this daily torture, and it was but one amongst others, entirely recovered and became adjusted to everything.

Adelaide, Durcet's wife and the daughter of the Président, had a beauty which was perhaps superior to Constance's, but of an entirely different sort. She was twenty, small and slender, of an extremely slight and delicate build, of classic loveliness, had the finest blond hair to be seen. An interesting air, a look of sensibility distributed everywhere about her, and above all in her features, gave her the quality of a heroine in a romance. Her exceptionally large eyes were blue, they expressed at once tenderness and decency; two long but narrow and remarkably drawn eyebrows adorned a forehead not very high but of such noble charm one might have thought this were modesty's very temple. Her nose, thin, a little pinched at the top, descended to assume a semi-aquiline contour; her lips inclined toward the thin, were of a bright, ripe red; a little large, her mouth was the unique flaw in this celestial physiognomy, but when it opened, there shone thirty-two pearls Nature seemed to have sown amidst roses. Her neck was a shade long, attached in a singular way, through what one judged a natural habit, her head was ever so faintly bent toward her right shoulder, especially when she was listening; but with what grace did not this interesting attitude endow her! Her breasts were small, very round, very firm, well-elevated, but there was barely enough there to fill the hand. They were like two little apples a frolicking Cupid had fetched hither from his mother's garden. Her chest was a bit narrow, it was also a very delicate chest, her belly was satin smooth, a little blond mound not much garnished with hair served as peristyle to the temple in which Venus seemed to call out for an homage. This temple was narrow to such a point you could not insert a finger therein without eliciting a cry from Adelaide; nevertheless, two lustrums had revolved since the time when, thanks to the Président, the poor child had ceased to be a virgin, either in that place or in the delicious part it remains for us to sketch. Oh, what were the attractions this second sanctuary possessed, what a flow in the line of her back, how magnificently were those buttocks cut, what whiteness there, and what dazzling rose blush! But all on all, it was on the small side. Delicate in all her lines, she was rather the sketch than the model of beauty, it seemed as though Nature had only wished to indicate in Adelaide what she had so majestically articulated in Constance. Peer into that appetizing behind, and lo! a rosebud would offer itself to your gaze, and it was in all its bloom and in the most tender pink Nature wished you to behold it; but narrow? tiny? it had only been at the price of infinite labors the Président had navigated through those straits, and he had only renewed these assaults successfully two or three times.

Durcet, less exacting, gave her little affliction in this point, but, since becoming his wife, in exchange for how many other cruel complaisances, with what a quantity of other perilous submissions had she not been obliged to purchase this little kindness? And, furthermore, turned over to the four libertines, as by their mutual consent she was, how many other cruel ordeals had she not to undergo, both of the species Durcet spared her, and of every other.

Adelaide had the mind her face suggested, that is to say, an extremely romantic mind, solitary places were the ones she preferred, and once there, she would shed involuntary tears - tears to which we do not pay sufficient heed - tears apparently torn from Nature by foreboding. She was recently bereft of a friend, a girl she idolized, and this frightful loss constantly haunted her imagination. As she was thoroughly acquainted with her father, as she knew to what extents he carried his wild behavior, she was persuaded her young friend had fallen prey to the Président's villainies, for he had never managed to induce the missing person to accord him certain privileges. The thing was not unlikely. Adelaide imagined the same would someday befall her; nor was that improbable. The Président, in her regard, had not paid the same attention to the problem of religion Durcet had in the interests of Constance, no, he had allowed all that nonsense to be born, to be fomented, supposing that his writings and his discourses would easily destroy it. He was mistaken: religion is the nourishment upon which a soul such as Adelaide's feeds. In vain the Président had preached, in vain he had made her read books, the young lady had remained a believer, and all these extravagances, which she did not share, which she hated, of which she was the victim, fell far short of disabusing her about illusions which continued to make for her life's happiness. She would go and hide herself to pray to God, she'd perform Christian duties on the sly, and was unfailingly and very severely punished, either by her father or her husband, when surprised in the act by the one or the other.

Adelaide patiently endured it all, fully convinced Heaven would someday reward her. Her character was as gentle as her spirit, and her benevolence, one of the virtues for which her father most detested her, went to the point of extreme. Curval, whom that vile class of the poverty-stricken irritated, sought only to humiliate it, to further depress it, or to wring victims from it; his generous daughter, on the other hand, would have foregone her own necessities to procure them for the poor, and she had often been espied stealing off to take to the needy sums which were intended for her pleasures. Durcet and the Président finally succeeded in scolding and pounding good manners into her, and in ridding her of this corrupt practice by withholding absolutely all means whereby she could resume it. Adelaide, having nothing left but her tears to bestow upon the poor, went none the less to sprinkle them upon their woes, and her powerless howbeit staunchly sensitive spirit was incapable of ceasing to be virtuous. One day she learned that some poor woman was to come to prostitute her daughter to the Président because extreme need bade her do so; the enchanted old rake was already preparing himself for the kind of pleasure-taking he liked best. Adelaide had one of her dresses sold and immediately got the money put it in the mother's hands; by means of this small assistance and some sort of a sermon, she diverted the woman from the she was about to commit. Hearing of what she had done, the Président proceeded to such violences with her - his daughter was not yet married at the time - that she was a fortnight abed; but all that was to no avail: nothing could put a stop to this gentle soul's tender impulses.

Julie, the Président's wife, the Duc's elder daughter, would have eclipsed the two preceding women were it not for something which many behold as a capital defect, but which had perhaps in itself aroused Curval's passion for her, so true it is that the effects of passion are unpredictable, nay, inconceivable, and that their disorder, the outcome of disgust and satiety, can only be matched by their irregular flights. Julie was tall, well made although quite fat and fleshy, had the most lovely brown eyes in the world, a charming nose, striking and gracious features, the most beautiful chestnut brown hair, a fair body of the most appetizing fullness, an ass which might easily have served as model to the one Praxiteles sculpted, her cunt was hot, strait, and yielded as agreeable a sensation as such a locale ever may; her legs were handsome, her feet charming, but she had the worst-decked mouth, the foulest teeth, and was by habit so dirty in every other part of her body, and principally at the two temples of lubricity, that no other being, let me repeat it, no other being but the Président, himself subject to the same shortcomings and unquestionably fond of them, nay, no one else, despite her allurements, could have put up with Julie. Curval, however, was mad about her;

his most divine pleasures were gathered upon that stinking mouth, to kiss it plunged him into delirium, and as for her natural uncleanliness, far from rebuking her for it, to the contrary he encouraged her in it, and had finally got her accustomed to a perfect divorce from water. To these faults Julie added a few others, but they were surely less disagreeable: she was a vast eater, she had a leaning toward drunkenness, little virtue, and I believe that had she dared try it, whoredom would have held little by way of terror for her. Brought up by the Duc in a total abandon of principles and manners, she adopted a whore's philosophy, and she was probably an apt student of all its tenets; but, through yet another very curious effect of libertinage, it often happens that a woman who shares our faults pleases us a great deal less in our pleasures than one who is full of naught but virtues: the first resembles us, we scandalize her not; the other is terrified, and there is one very certain charm more.

Despite his proportions, the Duc had sported with his daughter, but he had had to wait until she was fifteen, and even so had not been able to prevent Julie from being considerably damaged by the adventure, indeed, so much so that, eager to marry her off, he had been forced to put a term to pleasure-taking of this variety and to be content with delights less dangerous for her, but at least as fatiguing. Julie gained little by gaining the Président, whose prick, as we know, was exceedingly thick and, furthermore, however much she was dirty from neglect of herself, she could not in any wise keep up with a filthiness in debauch such as the one that distinguished the Président, her beloved spouse.

Aline, Julie's younger sister and really the daughter of the Bishop, possessed habits and defects and a character very unlike her sister's.

She was the most youthful of the four, she had just become eighteen; she had a fetching, exuberantly healthy, and almost pert little countenance; a little turned-up nose; brown eyes full of expression and vivacity; a delicious mouth; a most shapely though somewhat tall figure, well-fleshed; the skin a bit dark but soft and fine; ass rather on the ample side but well-molded, a pair of the most voluptuous buttocks that ever a libertine eye may behold, the love mound brown-haired and pretty, the cunt a trifle low or, as they say, à l'anglaise, but as tight as one might wish, and when she was presented to the assembly she was thoroughly a maid. And she still was at the time the party we are to chronicle got under way, and we shall see in what manner her maidenhead was annihilated. As for the first fruits of her ass, the Bishop had been peacefully plucking them every day for the past eight years, but without, however, arousing in his dear daughter much of a taste for these exercises: she, despite her mischievous and randy air, only cooperated out of obedience and had never hinted that she shared the slightest pleasure in the infamies whose daily victim she was. The Bishop had left her in the most profound ignorance, scarcely did she know how to read or write, and she had absolutely no idea of religion's existence; her mind was natural, it was that of a child, she would give droll replies, she liked to play, she loved her sister a great deal, detested the Bishop out of all measure, and feared the Duc as she dreaded fire. On the wedding day, when she discovered herself naked and surrounded by the four men, she wept, and moreover did all that was asked of her, acting without pleasure as without ill-temper. She was sober, very clean, and having no other fault but that of laziness, nonchalance reigned in all her movements and doings and everywhere about her person, despite the liveliness announced by her bright eyes. She abhorred the Président almost as much as she hated her uncle, and Durcet, who treated her with no excess of consideration, nevertheless seemed to be the only one for whom she appeared to have no repugnance.

These were the eight principal characters in whose company we are going to enable you to live, good reader. It is now time to divulge the object of singular pleasures that were proposed.

It is commonly accepted amongst authentic libertines that the sensations communicated by the organs of hearing are the most flattering and those impressions are the liveliest; as a consequence, our four villains, who were of a mind to have voluptuousness implant itself in the very core of their beings as deeply and as overwhelmingly as ever it could penetrate, had, to this end, devised something quite clever indeed.

It was this: after having immured themselves within everything that was best able to satisfy the senses through lust, after having established this situation, the plan was to have described to them, in the greatest detail and in due order, every one of debauchery's extravagances, all its divagations, all its ramifications, all its contingencies, all of what is termed in libertine language its passions. There is simply no conceiving the degree to which man varies them when his imagination grows inflamed; excessive may be the differences between men that is created by all their other manias, by all their other tastes, but in this case it is even more so, and he who should succeed in isolating and categorizing and detailing these follies would perhaps perform one of the most splendid labors which might be undertaken in the study of manners, and perhaps one of the most interesting. It would thus be a question of finding some individuals capable of providing an account of all these excesses, then of analyzing them, of extending them, of itemizing them, of graduating them, and of running a story through it all, to provide coherence and amusement. Such was the decision adopted. After innumerable inquiries and investigations, they located four women who had attained their prime - that was necessary, experience was the fundamental thing here - four women, I say, who, having spent their lives in the most furious debauchery, had reached the state where they could provide an exact account of all these matters; and, as care had been taken to select four endowed with a certain eloquence and a fitting turn of mind, after much discussion, recording, and arranging, all four were ready to insert, each into the adventures of her life, all the most extraordinary vagaries of debauch, and to do so in such an order and at such a pace that the first, for example, would work into the tale of her life's activities the one hundred and fifty simple passions and the least esoteric or most ordinary deviations; the second, within the same framework, an equal number of more unusual passions involving one or more men with one or several women; the third was also to introduce into her narration one hundred and fifty of the most criminal whimsies and those which most outrage the laws of both Nature and religion; and as all these excesses lead to murder and as these murders committed through libertinage are infinitely various and are just as numerous as the occasions upon which the libertine's inflamed imagination adopts different tortures, the fourth was to adorn the events of her life with a meticulous report upon one hundred and fifty assorted examples of them. In the meantime, our libertines, surrounded, as at the outset I indicated, by their wives and also by other objects in every kind, were to pay close heed, were to be mentally heated, and were to end by extinguishing, by means of either their wives or those various objects, the conflagration the storytellers were to have lit. There is surely nothing more voluptuous in this project than the luxurious manner whereby it was carried out, and they are both this manner and these several recitations which are to compose this work; wherewith, having said this much, I advise the overmodest to lay my book aside at once if he would not be scandalized, for 'tis already clear there's not much of the chaste in our plan, and we dare hold ourselves answerable in advance that there'll be still less in its execution. Insomuch as the four actresses we have been speaking of play a most essential role in these memoirs, we believe, even were we to have to beg the reader's forgiveness therefor, we should still feel obliged to describe them; they will narrate, they will act: such being the case, is it possible that they remain unknown? Banish all expectation of beauties portrayed, although there were doubtless in the plans provisions for employing these four creatures physically as well as morally; be that as it may, neither their charms nor their years were the deciding factors, but rather their minds and their experience only that counted, and with what regards the latter, our friends could not possibly have made better choices.

Madame Duclos was she to whom they entrusted the relating of the one hundred and fifty simple passions; the woman who went by this name was forty-eight years of age, still in fairly good condition and preserving the vestiges of beauty; she had very handsome eyes, an exceedingly fair skin, and one of the most splendid and plumpest asses that could ever favor your gaze; a mouth both clean and fresh, superb breasts, and pretty brown hair, a heavy figure but a noble one, and all the looks and tone of a brilliant whore. She had spent her life, as shall be observed, in places and under circumstances where indeed she had been obliged to study what she is going to relate, and to see her was to realize she must have gone to the task with wit and verve, with ease and interest.

Madame Champville was a tall woman about fifty, slender, well made, having the most voluptuous quality in her look and bearing; a faithful devotee of Sappho, she had that kind of expression even in her slightest movements, in her simplest gestures, in her least words. She had ruined herself for the sake of keeping girls and, had it not been for this predilection to which she generally sacrified everything she was able to earn abroad, she might have been comfortably well to do. For a long time she had been in public service, and during recent years had been making her way as an outfitter in her turn, but had confined herself to a limited practice, her clients being reliable rakehells of a certain age; never did she receive young men, and this prudent conduct was lucrative and did something to improve her affairs. She had been blond, but a more venerable tint, and that of wisdom, was beginning to color her hair; her eyes were still exceedingly attractive, blue, and they contained a most agreeable expressiveness. Her mouth was lovely, still fresh, missing no teeth as yet, she was flat-chested but had a belly which was good, but had never aroused envy, her mound was rather prominent, and her clitoris protruded three inches when well warmed; tickle this part of her and one was certain to see her fly into an ecstasy in no time, and especially if the service was rendered by a female. Her ass was very flabby and worn from use, entirely soft, wrinkled, withered, and so toughened by the libidinous customs she in recounting her history will explain to us, that one could do everything one wished without her feeling anything there. One strange and assuredly very rare thing, above all in Paris: she was as much a maid on this side as a girl emerging from a convent, and perhaps, had it not been for the accursed part she put to use with people who cared for nothing but the extraordinary and whom, consequently, that side pleased, perhaps, I say, had it not been for that part, this singular virginity might have perished with her.

Madame Martaine, a portly matron of fifty-two, very well preserved and very healthy and blessed with the biggest and most beautiful rump one could wish for, boasted the precise opposite by way of adventure. She had devoted her life to sodomitical debauch, and was so well familiarized therewith she tasted absolutely no joy save therefrom. A natural deformity (she had also been blessed with an obstruction) having prevented her from knowing any other, she had given herself over to this kind of pleasure, led to it both by her inability to do anything else and by early habit, in consideration of which she clung fast to this lubricity wherein 'twas declared she was yet delicious, ready to brave come what might, dreading nothing. The most monstrous engines were as naught to her, in fact such were the ones she preferred, and the sequel to these papers will perhaps reveal her still giving valorious fight beneath the standards of Sodom, as the most intrepid of buggresses. Her features were gracious enough, but signs of languor and of decline were beginning to mar her attractions, and but for the plumpness sustaining her yet, she might have been thought timeworn and frayed.

As for Madame Desgranges, she was vice and lust personified; tall, thin, fifty-six, ghostly pale and emaciated, dead dull eyes, dead lips, she offered an image of crime about to perish for lack of strength. She had once upon a time been brunette, there were some who even maintained she'd had a beautiful body; not long thereafter it had become a mere skeleton capable of inspiring nothing but disgust. Her ass, withered, worn, marked, torn, more resembled marbled paper than human skin, and its hole was so gaping, sprung, and rugose that the bulkiest machines could, without her knowing a thing, penetrate it dry. By way of crowning graces, this generous Cytherean athlete, wounded in several combats, was missing one nipple and three fingers. She limped, and was without six teeth and an eye. We may perhaps learn by what order of attacks she had been so mistreated; but one thing is certain: nothing she had suffered had induced her to mend her ways, and if her body was the picture of ugliness, her was the depository of all the most unheard of vices and crimes: an arsonist, a parricade, a sodomite, a tribade, a murderess, a poisoner, guilty of incest, of rape, of theft, of abortions, and of sacrileges, one might truthfully affirm that there is not a single crime in the world this villain had not committed herself, or had others commit for her. Her present calling was procuring; she was one of society's most heavily titled furnishers, and as to much experience she joined a more or less agreeable prattle, she had been chosen to fill the role of fourth storyteller, that is to say, the one in whose story the greatest number of infamies and horrors were to be combined. Who better than a creature who had performed them all could have played this part?

These women once found, and found in every article to be such as was desired, the friends turned their attentions to accessories. They had from the outset planned to surround themselves with a large number of lust-inspiring objects of either sex, but when it was brought to their attention that the only setting in which this lubricious roister could conveniently be held was that same château in Switzerland belonging to Durcet, the one in which he had dispatched little Elvire, when, I say, it was remarked that this château of only moderate size would not be able to lodge so great a throng of inhabitants, and that, what was more, it might well prove unwise or dangerous to bring along such a host, the list of subjects was trimmed to thirty-two in all, the storytellers included: to wit: four of that class, eight young girls, eight young boys, eight men endowed with monstrous members, for the delights of passive sodomy, and four female servants. But thoroughness went into the recruiting of all that; a year was devoted to these details, an enormous amount of money too, and these are the measures they employed to obtain the most delicious specimens of all France could offer in the way of eight little girls: sixteen intelligent procuresses, each accompanied by two lieutenants, were sent into the sixteen major provinces of France, while a seventeeth was occupied with the same work in Paris only. Each of these outfitters was given a rendezvous at one of the Duc's estates on the outskirts of Paris, and all of them were to appear there, during the same week, exactly ten months after the date of their departure - this was the period they were given for searching. Each was to bring back nine subjects, which came to a total of one hundred and fifty-three girls, from which one hundred and fifty-three a choice of only eight was to be made.

The procuresses were instructed to emphasize high birth, virtuousness, and the most delicious visage possible; they were to conduct their researches so as to draw material chiefly from eminent families, and were not to hand over any girl without being able to prove that she had been forcibly abducted from either a convent housing pensionnaires of quality, or from the home of a family, and that a family of distinction. Whatever was not superior to the class of bourgeoisie, and what from these upper classes was not both very virtuous and wholly virgin and impeccably beautiful, would be refused without mercy; spies were posted to survey these women's proceedings and to supply the society with exhaustive and prompt reports of what they were doing.

For each suitable subject found, they were paid thirty thousand francs, the agents assuming all expenses. The costs were incredible. With respect to age, it was fixed at from twelve to fifteen; anything above or between was pitilessly rejected. At the same time, under identical circumstances, with the same means, at the same expense, seventeen ages of sodomy likewise scoured the capital and the provinces in search of little boys, and their rendezvous was set for a month after the selection of the girls. As for the young men whom we propose henceforth to designate as fuckers, the size of the member was the sole criterion: nothing under ten or eleven inches long by seven or eight around was acceptable. Eight men labored throughout the kingdom to supply this demand, and their rendezvous was scheduled to fall a month after the little boys'. While the story of how these selections were made and received is not our foremost concern, it might not be inappropriate at this point to insert a word on the subject in order to bring out yet a little more of our four heroes' genius; it seems to me that nothing which serves to enlarge the reader's understanding of these figures and to shed light upon a party as extraordinary as the one we are going to describe, can be judged irrelevant.

The time for the assembling of the little girls having arrived, everyone converged upon the Duc's estate. Some few procuresses having been unable to fill their quota of nine, some others having lost their charges en route, either by illness or flight, only one hundred and thirty of them were present at the rendezvous, but what charms, great God! never, I believe, have so many charms been seen gathered together in one place. Thirteen days were given over to this examination, and each day ten of them were inspected. The four friends gathered in a circle, and in its middle was placed the little girl, dressed as she had been seized; the procuress responsible for her capture recited her history. If something of the conditions of high birth or virtue were wanting, the inquiry went no deeper, the child was forthwith rejected, without appeal, and sent on her way, and the purveyor lost all that she had spent in connection with her. Next, having provided all the vital particulars, the procuress was asked to retire, and the child was interrogated in order to determine whether what had just been alleged were true. If all seemed well, the procuress was called in again, and she lifted the girl's skirts from behind, so as to expose her buttocks to the group; this was the first thing it wished to examine. The slightest defect in this part was grounds for immediate rejection; if on the contrary naught were amiss here, she was ordered to strip, or was stripped, and, naked, she passed and passed again, five or six times over, from one of our libertines to the other, she was turned about, she was turned the other way, she was fingered, she was handled, they sniffed, they spread, they peeped, they examined the state of the goods, was it new, was it used, but did all this coolly and without permitting the senses' illusion to upset any aspect of the examination. This done, the child was led away, and beside her name inscribed upon a ballot, the examiners wrote passed or failed and signed their names; these ballots were then dropped into a box, the voters refraining from communicating their opinions to one another; all the girls examined, the box was opened: in order to be accepted, a girl had to have our four friend's names in her favor. The absence of one name was enough to exclude her instantly and, in every instance, inexorably, as I have said: the unsuitable ones were kicked directly out, set at large, alone and without a guide, save when, as happened with perhaps a dozen, our liberines frolicked with them after the choices had been made and before turning them over to their procuresses.

This round resulted in the exclusion of fifty candidates, the other eighty were gone over afresh, but with much greater exactitude and severity; the least defect warranted instantaneous dismissal. One, lovely as the day, was weeded out because one of her teeth grew a shade higher from the gum than the rest; more than twenty others were refused because they were daughters of nothing better than bourgeois. Thirty were eliminated during this second round, hence only fifty were left. The friends resolved not to continue to the third round until having first being relieved of some fuck through these fifty aspirants' own ministry, this in order that the senses' perfect calm could insure saner and sounder choice. Each of the quartet encompassed himself by a team of twelve or thirteen children; members of each team adopted varying attitudes, teams were shifted, everything was brought off with such dexterity, there was, in a word, so much lubricity in the doing that sperm flow, temperatures subsided, and another thirty disappeared from the race. Twenty remained; that was still a dozen too many. Further expedients to procure calm were resorted to, every means wherefrom one would suppose disgust could be born was employed, but the twenty still remained, and how might one have subtracted from a number of creatures so wonderfully celestial you would have declared they were the very work of a divinity? Equal in beauty, something else had to discovered which could at least award eight of them some kind of superiority over the twelve others, and what the Président then proposed was worthy indeed of all the disorder of his mind. That made no difference; the suggestion was accepted: it had to do with finding out which of them would best do something the chosen eight would be often called upon to do. Four days sufficed amply to decide this question, and at last twelve were given their leave, but not blankly as in the case of the others; they provided a week's complete and exhaustive amusement, then were put into the keeping of the procuresses who soon made a pretty penny from the prostitution of creatures as distinguished as these. As for the successful eight, they were installed in a convent to keep until the day of departure, and in order to reserve until the designated period the pleasure of enjoying them, the four colleagues did not touch them before then.

I'll not be so foolhardy as to attempt to describe these beauties: they were all of them superior in an equal degree: my brush strokes would necessarily be monotonous; I shall be content to give their names and to affirm that upon my word it is perfectly impossible to obtain an idea of such an assemblage of graces, of attractions, of perfections, and that had Nature wished to give Man an idea of what her greatest and wisest art can create, she would not have presented him with other models.

The first was named Augustine: she was fifteen, the daughter of a Languedoc baron, and had been kidnaped from a convent in Montpellier.

The second was named Fanny: she was the daughter of a counselor to the parliament of Brittany and had been abducted from her father's own château.

The third was named Zelmire: she was fifteen years old, she was the Comte de Terville's daughter, and he idolized her. He had taken her hunting with him on one of his estates in Beauce and, having left her alone in the forest for a moment, she had been pounced upon at once. She was only a child and, with a dowry of four hundred thousand francs, was the following year to have married a very great lord. It was she who most wept and grieved at the horror of her fate.

The fourth was named Sophie: she was fourteen and was the daughter of a rather well-to-do gentleman who lived on his estate in Berry. She had been seized while on a walk with her mother, who, seeking to defend her, was flung into a river, where she expired before her daughter's eyes.

The fifth was named Colombe: she was from Paris, the child of a counselor to Parliament; she was thirteen and had been kidnaped while returning in the evening to her convent with a governess, after leaving a children's ball. The governess had been stabbed to death.

The sixth was named Hébé: she was just twelve, the daughter of a cavalry captain, a nobleman who lived in Orléans. The youngster had been enticed and carried away from the convent where she was being brought up; two nuns had been bought. You could not hope to find anything more seductive or sweeter.

The seventh was named Rosette: she was thirteen and was the child of the Lieutenant-General of Chalon-sur-Saône. Her father had just died, she was with her mother in the countryside near the city, and was captured within sight of her relatives by agents disguised as thieves.

The last was named Mimi or Michette: she was twelve, she was the daughter of the Marquis de Sénanges and had been kidnaped on her father's estate in the Bourbonnais while on a carriage drive which she had been allowed to take with two or three women from the château. The women were murdered. It will be remarked that the preparations for these revels cost much money and many crimes; to such people, treasure means exceedingly little, and as for crime, one was then living in an age when it was not by any means probed and punished the way it is nowadays. Hence everything succeeded, and so prettily that, the inquests amounting to virtually nothing at all, our libertines were never troubled by consequences.

The time drew nigh for the examination of the little boys. Easier to obtain, their number was greater. The pimps produced one hundred and fifty of them, and it will surely be no exaggeration if I affirm that they at least equaled the little girls, as much in their innocence, and their elevated rank. Thirty thousand francs were paid for each of them, the same sum given for the girls, but the entrepreneurs risked nothing, because this game being more delicate and far more to the taste of our epicures, it had been decided that no one would be put in danger of losing his expenses, that while the lads with whom it was impossible to come to terms would be rejected, as they would be put to some use they would also be paid for.

Their examination was conducted like that of the girls, ten were verified each day, but with the very wise precaution which had been a little too much neglected with the girls, with the precaution, I say, of always preceding the examination by a discharge arranged with the aid of the ten who were under present scrutiny. The others were half of a mind to bar the Président from the ceremony, they were wary of the depravation of his tastes; they had feared, in the selection of the girls, being made the dupes of his accursed predilection for infamy and degradation: he promised to keep himself in check, and if he kept his word, it is unlikely he did so without difficulty, for when once a damaged or diseased imagination becomes accustomed to these species of outrages against good taste and Nature, outrages which so deliciously flatter it, it is no easy matter to restore such a person to the path of righteousness: it seems as if the desire to satisfy his longing displaces reason in his judgements. Scorning what is truly beautiful, no longer cherishing but what is frightful, desire's pronouncements correspond to its criteria, and the return to truer sentiments would appear to him to be a wrong done those principles whence he should be most sorry to stray. One hundred hopefuls were found unanimously approved when the initial séances were over, and these decisions had to be five times reconsidered in order to arrive at the small group alone to be accepted. Thrice in succession fifty survived the balloting, and then, to reduce that number to the stipulated eight, the jurors were compelled to resort to unusual measures in order somehow to lessen the appeal of idols still glamorous despite everything they had been able to do to them. The idea occurred to them to dress the boys as girls: twenty-five were eliminated by this trick which, lending to a sex they worshiped the garb of one to which they had become indifferent, depreciated their value and ruined almost all the illusion. But nothing could alter the voting on the twenty-five that were left. 'Twas all in vain, in vain they spattered their fuck about, in vain they wrote their names upon the ballots at the same moment they discharged, in vain they put to use the expedient adopted with the little girls, the twenty-five proved irreducible every time, and at last they agreed to have them draw lots. Here are the names they gave the lucky ones who remained, their age, their birth, and a word or two about their adventures; their portraits? I cry off: Cupid's own features were surely no more delicate, and the models Albani sought from which to choose traits for his divine angels must certainly have been inferior by far.

Zélamir was thirteen years old: he was the only son of a gentleman out of Poitou who had been bringing him up with the greatest care. Escorted by a single domestic, he had been sent to Poitiers to visit a kinsman; our rogues ambushed them, slew the domestic, and made off with the child.

Cupidon was the same age: he had been a pupil in a school at La Flèche, and was the son of a gentleman dwelling in the vicinity of that town. A trap was laid for the boy, he was kidnaped while on an outing the students used to take on Sundays. He was the prettiest pupil in the entire collège.

Narcisse was twelve; he was a Knight of Malta. He had been abducted in Rouen, where his father filled an honorable post compatible with his nobility; the boy was en route to the Collège de Louis-le-Grand at Paris, he was waylaid and seized while on the road.

Zéphyr, the most delicious of the eight, it being supposed that their excessive beauty might allow the possibility of a choice, was from Paris; he was pursuing his studies there, in a famous pension. His father, a ranking officer, did all in his power to get his son back, and failed; money had seduced the headmaster of the school, who delivered seven specimens, of whom six were refused. Zéphyr had set the Duc's head to spinning, and the latter protested that were it to have cost a million to bugger the boy he would have paid it in cash on the spot. He reserved to himself the lad's initiation, and it was generally granted him. O tender and delicate child, what disproportion and what a dreadful fate were in store for you!

Céladon was the son of a magistrate of Nancy; he was captured at Lunéville, whither he had gone to visit his aunt. He had just attained his fourteenth year. In this case a girl was used to bait the trap. Céladon and she were introduced, the little wench drew him into the snare by feigning love for him; he was negligently chaperoned, the stroke was successful.

Adonis was fifteen; he was ravished at Plessis, where he was enrolled in school. He was the son of a judge of the assize courts who raised a great hue and cry, but all to no avail, the capture had been so nicely planned no one knew a thing about it. Curval, who had been mad about the child for two years, had made his acquaintance at his father's house, and it was he who had supplied the means and information necessary to debauch him. The others were greatly surprised to find such sensible good taste in a head so depraved as Curval's, and he, most proud, profited from the event to show his colleagues that, as was plainly to be seen, he still could boast a sometimes fine palate. The child recognized him and fell to weeping, but the Président consoled him with the assurance it would be to him would befall the deflowering, and while uttering these comforting words, he wobbled his enormous engine against those frail little buttocks. Curval asked the assembly for the boy; his request was unopposed.

Hyacinthe was fourteen years old; he was the son of a retired officer living in a small city in Champagne. He adored hunting and was taken while afield, his father having been so imprudent as to allow him to set out alone.

Giton was twelve; he was kidnaped at Versailles from amidst of the page boys at the King's stables. He was the son of a man of consequence from the Nivernais, who not six months prior had brought him to Versailles. He was very simply abducted while walking alone on the avenue de Saint-Cloud. He became the Bishop's passion, and to the Bishop was the prize decreed.

Those, thus, were the masculine deities our libertines prepared for their lubricity; we will see in due time and place the use to which they were put. One hundred and forty-two subjects remained, but whereas there had been much trifling over the eight, there was none with this game: not one of the defeated candidates was dismissed until he had served some purpose.

Our libertines spent a month with them at the Duc's château. As they were on the eve of setting forth, as all the practical arrangements were completed, the company had little else to do but amuse itself until the day of departure. When at last they were thoroughly fed up with their sport, they fell upon a pleasant means for disposing of what had provided it: that was to sell the boys to a Turkish pirate, a scheme whereby no trace of them would be left and a part of the costs would be recovered. They were sent in small groups to a place near Monaco, the Turk came to get them and lead them off into slavery, doubtless a dreadful fate, but one whereby, none the less, our four villains were hugely entertained.

And now came the moment of choosing the fuckers. Those of this class who failed to meet the standards were the cause of no embarrasment; being mature and reasonable men, it was enough to pay them for their trouble, their traveling expenses, and send them home. The eight experts who had contracted to furnish the fuckers had, furthermore, many fewer obstacles to surmount, since the specifications were by and large concrete and the conditions made no difference at all. Thus it was fifty came to the rendezvous; from amongst the twenty biggest, the eight youngest and most attractive were singled out, and since in the sequel mention will almost never be made save of the four biggest of the eight, I shall restrict myself to naming these.

Hercule, with a body hewn in the image of the god whose name he had been given, was twenty-six years of age and was endowed with a member eight and one-quarter inches around by thirteen long. Nothing more beautiful nor more majestic has ever been seen; this tool was almost always upright, and with only eight discharges, so tests revealed, it could fill a pint measure to the brim. Hercule was also very gentle, very sweet, and had an interesting countenance.

Antinoüs, so named because, like Hadrian's favourite, he had, together with the world's prettiest prick, its most voluptuous ass, and that exceedingly rare. Antinoüs wielded a device measuring eight inches in circumference and twelve in length. He was thirty and had a face worthy of his other features.

Bum-Cleaver lugged a club so amusingly shaped it was nearly impossible for him to perform an embuggery without splitting the ass, whence came the name he bore. The head of his prick resembled the heart of an ox, it was eight and three-eights inches around; behind it, the shaft measured only eight, but was crooked and had such a curve it neatly tore the anus when penetrating it, and this quality, very precious to libertines as jaded as ours, had made him singularly sought after.

Invictus, so named because, no matter what he did, his erection was perpetual, was furnished with an engine eleven inches long and seven and fifteen-sixteenths inches around. Greater ones, who had difficulty stiffening, had been turned away to make room for him who, regardless of the quantity of discharges he produced in a day, rose heavenward at the slightest touch.

The other four were of about the same dimensions and the same shape. The forty-two rejected candidates provided a fortnight's entertainment and, after the friends had put them through their paces and worn them to the bone, they were well rewarded and bidden adieu.

Nothing now remained but the choice of the four ladies-in-waiting, and this final stage was without doubt the most picturesque. The Président was not the only one whose tastes were depraved; his three friends, and especially Durcet, were indeed a little tainted by his accursed, crapulous, and debauched mania which causes one to find a greater, more piquant attraction in an old, disgusting, and filthy object than in what Nature has fashioned most divinely. Explaining this fancy would probably be difficult, but it exists in many people; Nature's disorder carries with it a kind of sting which operates upon the high-keyed sort with perhaps as much and even more force than do her most regular beauties; it has been proven, moreover, that when one's prick is aloft, it is horror, villainy, the appalling, that pleases; well, where are they more emphatically present than in a vitiated object? If 'tis the filthy thing which pleases in the lubricious act, then certainly the more filthy the thing, the more it should please, and it is surely much filthier in the corrupted than in the intact and perfect object.

No, as to that there's no doubt. Furthermore, beauty belongs to the sphere of the simple, the ordinary, whilst ugliness is something extraordinary, and there is no question but that every ardent imagination prefers in lubricity the extraordinary to the commonplace. Beauty, health never strike one save in a simple way; ugliness, degradation deal a far stouter blow, the commotion they create is much stronger, the resultant agitation must hence be more lively; in the light of all this, there should be no cause for astonishment in the fact that an immense crowd of people prefer to take their pleasure with an aged, ugly, and even stinking crone and will refuse a fresh and pretty girl, no more reason to be astonished by that, I say, than at a man who for his promenades prefers the mountains' arid and rugged terrain to the monotonous pathways of the plains. All these matters depend upon our tastes in this connection than it is in our power to alter the form of our bodies.

Be that as it may, such, as I have said, was the dominating taste of the Président and, to tell the truth, the taste which came near to predominating in his three confreres, for when it came to choosing female servants, their views were identical, and we are about to see from this choice that its making bespoke the constitutional disorder and depravation to which we have just alluded.

The most painstaking search was initiated in Paris; the four creatures needed were finally located; however loathsome may be their portraits, the reader will none the less permit me to draw them: that I do so is essential to that aspect of manners the elucidation of which is one of the principal aims of this work.

Marie was the name of the first one; she had been servant of a notorious brigand quite recently put to death on the wheel, whipping and branding had been her penalty. She was fifty-eight years old, had almost no hair left, her nose stood askew, her eyes were dull and rheumy, her mouth large and filled with her thirty-two teeth, yes, they were all there, but all were yellow as sulphur; she was tall, raw-boned, having whelped fourteen children, all fourteen of whom, said she, she'd strangled from fear they'd turn out ne'er-do-wells. Her belly rippled like the waves of the sea, and one of her buttocks was devoured by an abscess.

The second was known as Louison; she was sixty, stunted, hunchbacked, blind in one eye, and lame, but she had a fine ass for her age and her skin was still in fairly good repair. She was as wicked as the devil and forever ready to commit any horror and every extravagance one could possibly demand of her.

Thérèse was sixty-two; she was tall, thin, looked like a skeleton, not a hair was left on her head, not a tooth in her mouth, and from this opening in her body she exhaled an odor capable of flooring any bystander. Her ass was peppered with wounds, and her buttocks were so prodigiously slack one could have furled the skin around a walking stick; the hole in this splendid ass resembled the crater of a volcano what for width, and for aroma the pit of a privy; in all her life, Thérèse declared, she had never once wiped her ass, whence we have proof positive that the shit of her infancy yet clung there. As for her vagina, it was the receptacle of everything ungodly, of every horror, a veritable sepulcher whose fetidity was enough to make you faint away. She had one twisted arm and limped in one leg.

The fourth was called Fanchon; six times she had been hanged in effigy, and not a crime exists in this world she had not committed. She was sixty-nine, she was flat-nosed, short, and heavy; she squinted, had almost no forehead, had nothing but two old teeth in her stinking maw, and they were ready to fall out, an erysipelas blazed all over her ass and hemorrhoids the size of your fist hung from her anus, a frightful chancre consumed her vagina, and one of her thighs had been entirely burned. She was dead drunk three-quarters of the year, and in that condition, her stomach being very weak, she vomited over everything. Despite the batch fo hemorrhoids adorning it, her asshole was naturally so large that all unawares she blew driblets and farts and often more besides. Apart from acting as servants in the luxurious recreation palace the four friends had in mind, these women were also to lend a hand at all the convocations and render all the lubricious services and ministrations that might be required of them.

As soon as all these matters had been decided and the summer having already begun, they turned their thoughts to the transporting of the various objects which were, during the four months' sojourn on Durcet's estate, to render its inhabitation comfortable and agreeable. A vast store of furniture and mirrors, of viands and wines and liqueurs of all kinds were ordered borne thither, workmen were sent there, and little by little the numerous subjects were conducted to the château where Durcet, who had gone ahead, received, lodged, and established them as they arrived.

But the moment has come to give the reader a description of the renowned temple appointed for so many luxurious sacrifices throughout the projected four-month season. He will observe with what great care they had chosen a remote and isolated retreat, as if silence, distance, and stillness were libertinage's potent vehicles, and as if everything which through these qualities instills a religious terror in the senses had necessarily and evidently to bestow additional charm upon lust. We are going to picture this retreat not as once it was, but in the state of embellishment and yet more perfect solitude that resulted from our four friends' efforts.

To reach the place one had first to get to Basel; at that city you crossed the Rhine, beyond which the road became steadily narrower until you had to abandon your carriage. Soon afterward you entered the Black Forest, you plunged about fifteen leagues into it, ascended a difficult, tortuous road that, without a guide, would be absolutely impracticable. By and by you caught sight of a sinister and mean hamlet of charcoal burners and gamekeepers; there began the territory Durcet owned, and the hamlet was his; as this little village's population was composed almost entirely of thieves or smugglers, Durcet easily befriended it, and his first order to the inhabitants was expressly to enjoin them under no circumstances to allow anyone whomsoever to pass on toward the château after the 1st of November, the date by which the entire society was to be assembled in it. He distributed weapons to his faithful vassals, granted them certain privileges they had been long soliciting, and the barrier was lowered. That done, and the gates tightly sealed, one will see by the following description how difficult of access was Silling, the name Durcet's châteu bore.

Having passed the village, you begin to scale a mountain almost as high as the Saint-Bernard and infinitely more difficult to ascend, for the only way to reach the summit is by foot; not that the route is forbidden to pack mules, but such are the precipices which everywhere border the one so very narrow path that must be followed, that you run the greatest danger if you ride; six of the mules used to transport supplies and food perished, taking with them two laborers who had though to mount astride them. Five full hours are required to reach the top of the mountain, and there you come upon another extraordinary feature which, owing to the precautions that had been taken, became a new barrier so insurmountable that none but birds might have overcome it: the topographical accident we refer to is a crevice above sixty yards wide which splits the crest into northern and southern parts, with the result that, after having climbed up the mountain, it is impossible, without great skill, to go back down it. Durcet had united these two parts, between which a precipice fell to the depth of a thousand feet and more, by a fine wooden bridge which was destroyed immediately the last of the crew had arrived, and from this moment on, all possibility of communicating with the Château of Silling ceased. For, cross the bridge and you come down into a little plain about four acres in area; the plain is surrounded on all sides by sheer crags rising to the clouds, crags which envelop the plain within a faultless screen. The passage known as the bridge path is hence the only one by which you may descend into or communicate with the little plain; the bridge removed or destroyed, there is not on this earth a single being, of no matter what species you may imagine, capable of gaining this small plot of level land.

And it is in the center of this flat space so well surrounded, so solidly protected, that one finds Durcet's château. Yet another wall, thirty feet high, girds it; beyond the wall a moat filled with water and exceedingly deep defends a last tall and winding enclosure; a low and strait postern finally leads into the great inner court around which all the living quarters are built, and they are very capacious, very well furnished thanks to the arrangements latterly concluded; one discovers a long gallery on the first floor. I would have it remarked that the description I am about to give of the apartments corresponds not to what in former times they may have been, but to the manner in which they had just been rearranged and distributed in accordance with our libertines' common conception. From the gallery you moved into a very attractive dining hall provided with buffets shaped like towers which, communicating with the kitchen, made it possible to serve the company its food hot, promptly, and without the help of any waiters. From this dining hall, hung in tapestries, warmed by heating devices, furnished with ottomans, with excellent armchairs, and with everything which could make it both comfortable and pleasing to the eye, you passed into a large living room or salon, simple, plain, but exceedingly warm and equipped with the very best furniture; adjacent to this room was an assembly chamber intended for the storytellers' narrations. This was, so to speak, the lists for the projected jousts, the seat of the lubricious conclaves, and as it had been decorated accordingly, it merits something by way of a special description.

Its shape was semicircular; set into the curving wall were four niches whose surfaces were faced with large mirrors, and each was provided with an excellent ottoman; these four recesses were so constructed that each faced the center of the circle; the diameter was formed by a throne, raised four feet above the floor and with its back to the flat wall, and it was intended for the storyteller; in this position she was not only well before the four niches intended for her auditors, but, the circle being small, was close enough to them to insure their hearing every word she said, for she was placed like an actor in a theater, and the audience in their niches found themselves situated as if observing a spectacle in an amphitheater. Steps led down from the throne, upon them were to sit the objects of debauchery brought in to soothe any sensory irritation provoked by the recitals; these several tiers, like the throne, were upholstered in black velvet edged with gold fringe, and the niches were furnished with similar and likewise enriched material, but in color dark blue. At the back of each niche was a little door leading into an adjoining closet which was to be used at times when, having summoned the desired subject from the steps, one preferred not to execute before everyone the delight for whose execution one had summoned that subject. These closets were provided with couches and with all the other furnishing required for every kind of impurity. On either side of the central throne an isolated column rose to the ceiling; these two columns were designed to support the subject in whom some misconduct might merit correction. All the instruments necessary to meting it out hung from hooks attached to the columns, and this imposing sight served to maintain the subordination so indispensable to parties of this nature, a subordination whence is born almost all the charm of the voluptuousness in persecutors' souls.

One could walk from this semicircular room directly to a chamber which formed the end of this part of the living quarters. This chamber was a kind of boudoir, it was soundproof and secluded, but very warm within, very dark during the day, and its purpose was for private interviews and secluded contests, or for certain other secret delights which will be unveiled in the sequel. To reach the other wing, one had to retrace one's footsteps, and once in the gallery, at the end of which an exceedingly handsome chapel was visible, one entered the opposite wing which completed the circuit of the inner courtyard. You discovered a splendid antechamber adjoined by four superb apartments, each having a boudoir and wash cabinets; splendid Turkish beds canopied in three-colored damask with matching furniture adorned these suites whose boudoirs offered everything and more of the most sensual that lubricity might fancy. These four units, exceptionally well-heated and comfortable, were intended for the four colleagues, who were perfectly lodged therein. In that the protocols stipulated that their wives were to occupy the same quarters, no separate space was set aside for them.

Upstairs, the second story contained about the same number of apartments, but they were otherwise divided; you first came upon, to one side, a vast room bordered by eight niches, each having a little bed - these were the girls' quarters, and beside them were two small chambers for the old women who were to have charge of them. Further along, a pair of pretty rooms had been set aside for two of the storytellers. Now turning about and going in the other direction, you found a similar eight-niched room for the little boys; by it were two rooms for the duennas appointed to supervise them; and beyond these were two more rooms, also alike, for the two storytellers. Eight cheerful rooms, as fine as anything you have yet seen, formed the eight fuckers' quarter, although these individuals were destined to do very little sleeping in their own beds. Below, on the ground floor, were the kitchens and, near them, six small chambers for the six persons to whom the preparation of food had been confided; amongst them were three cooks renowned for their art; they were all females, women having been preferred for a pleasure outing like this one, and I believe the decision was just. The cooks were assisted by three robust young scullery maids, but none of the kitchen staff was to appear at the revels, that was not its purpose, and if the rules imposed in this connection were violated, 'tis merely because libertinage stops at nothing, and the true way of extending and multiplying one's desires is to attempt to impose checks upon them. One of these three underlings was to look after the numerous livestock which had been fetched to the château - with the exception of the four aged ladies who were meant for household duties, there were no domestics save for these three cooks and their seconds. But depravity, cruelty, disgust, infamy, all those passions anticipated or experienced, had erected another locality whereof it is a matter of urgency that we give the sketch, for the laws essential to the proper unfolding of our tale demand that we depict it with thoroughness now.

A fatal stone there was which, cunningly made, could be raised from below the step of the altar in the little Christian temple we discerned from the gallery; beneath that stone one beheld a spiral stairway, very narrow and very steep, whose three hundred steps could convey you down into the bowels of the earth, to a kind of vaulted dungeon, closed by triple doors of iron, and in which was displayed everything the cruelest art and the most refined barbarity could invent of the most atrocious, as much for gripping one with terror as for proceeding to horrors. And there below, what tranquillity! to what degree might not the villain be reassured who brought his victim there! What had he to fear? He was out of France, in a safe province, in the depths of an uninhabitable forest, within this forest in a redoubt which, owing to the measures he had taken, only the birds of the air could approach, and he was in the depth of the earth's entrails. Woe, a hundred times woe to the unlucky creature who in the midst of such abandonment were to find himself at the mercy of a villain lawless and without religion, whom crime amused, and whose only interest lay in his passions, who heeded naught, had nothing to obey but the imperious decrees of his perfidious lusts. I know not what will transpire in that nether place, but this I may say without doing our tale a disservice, that when a description of the dungeon was given the Duc, he reacted by discharging three times in succession.

Everything being ready at last, everything perfectly disposed, the subjects installed, the Duc, the Bishop, Curval, and their wives, with the four second-ranking fuckers in their train, set off (Durcet and his wife, together with all the rest, having arrived beforehand, as we have previously noted), and not without infinite difficulty, finally reached the château on the evening of the 29th of October. Immediately they crossed it, Durcet had the bridge cut. But that was not all: having inspected the place, the Duc decided that, since all the provisions were within the fortress, and since therefore they had no need to leave it, it were necessary, in order to forestall external attack, which was little dreaded, and escapes from within, the possibilities of which were less unlikely, it were necessary,

I say, to have walled shut all the gates, all the passages whereby the château might be penetrated, and absolutely to enclose themselves inside their retreat as within a besieged citadel, without leaving the least entrance to an enemy, the least egress to a deserter. The recommendation was put into effect, they barricaded themselves to such an extent there was no longer any trace left of where the exits had been; and then they settled down comfortably inside.

After the provisions we have just cited had been taken, the two days still remaining before the 1st of November were devoted to resting the subjects, that they might make a fresh appearance at the scenes of debauchery soon to begin, and during this interval the four friends labored over a code of laws which, as soon as it was brought to perfection and signed, was promulgated to those concerned. Before advancing to the matter, it is essential that these articles of government be made known to the reader who, after the exact description we have given him of everything, will now have no more to do than follow the story, lightly and voluptuously, his mind impeded by nothing, his memory embarrassed by no unexpected intrusions.

STATUTES

The company shall rise every day at ten o'clock in the morning, at which time the four fuckers who have not been in duty during the night shall come to pay the friends a visit and shall each bring a little boy; they shall pass from one bedchamber to another, successively. They shall perform as bidden by the friends' likings and desires, but during the preliminaries the little boys shall serve only as a tempting prospect, for it has been decided and planned that the eight maidenheads of the little girls' cunts shall remain intact until the month of December, and their asses shall likewise remain in bond, as shall the asses of the eight little boys, until the month of January, at which times the respective seals shall be broken, and this in order to allow voluptuousness to become irritated by the augmentation of a desire incessantly inflamed and never satisfied, a state which must necessarily lead to that certain lascivious fury the friends shall strive to provoke, considering it one of lubricity's most highly delectable situations.

At eleven o'clock, the friends shall repair to the quarters appointed for the little girls. In that place will be served breakfast consisting of chocolate, or of roasts cooked in Spanish wine, or of other appropriate restoratives. This breakfast shall be served by the eight little girls, naked, aided by the two elders, Marie and Louison, assigned to the seraglio of girls, the other two elders being assigned to that of the boys. If, during this breakfast, the friends are moved to commit impudicities with the little girls, before or after, the latter shall lend themselves thereunto with the resignation prescribed to them, and wherein they shall not be found wanting without severe punishment being the consequence. But it is agreed that at this hour there shall be undertaken no secret or private exercises, and that if a moment's wantonizing be desired, it shall be conducted openly and before the public present at the morning meal.

These little girls shall adopt the general custom of kneeling at all times whenever they see or meet a friend, and they shall remain thus until told to stand; they, the wives, and the elders shall alone be subject to these regulations, wherefrom the others are dispensed, but everyone shall be bound never to address the friends save as my Lord.

Before leaving the girls' apartments, that one of the friends who is invested with the month's stewardship (it being intended that for the space of a month one friend shall be in general supervision of everything, each friend acceding to the office in his turn and in the following order: Durcet during November, the Bishop during December, the Président during January, the Duc during February), he, then, who is the month's presiding officer, before leaving the girls' quarters, shall inspect them all, to determine whether they are in the state wherein they have been instructed to maintain themselves, whereof the elders shall be each morning apprised and which will be determined by the need that exists for them to keep in such and such a state.

As it is strictly forbidden to relieve oneself anywhere save in the chapel, which has been outfitted and intended for this purpose, and forbidden to go there without individial and special permission, the which shall be often refused, and for good reason, the month's presiding officer shall scrupulously examine, immediately after breakfast, all the girls' water closets, and in the case of a contravention discovered in the one above-designated place or in the other, the delinquent shall be condemned to suffer the penalty of death.

The friends shall move from there into the little boys' apartments in order to perform the same inspections and similarly to pronounce capital punishment against offenders. The four little boys who have not been that morning with the friends, shall now receive them when they enter their chamber and shall untrouser themselves before them, the other four shall remain standing in attention, awaiting the orders which are given them. Messieurs may or may not indulge in lewd byplay with the four they have not until now seen during the day, but whatever they do shall be done publicly; no intimate commerce shall be held at this hour.

At one o'clock, those of the girls or the boys, of mature and of young years, who have obtained permission to satisfy urgent needs, that is to say, the heavier sort, and this permission shall never be put most sparingly accorded, and at the most to a third of the subjects, those, we repeat, shall betake themselves to the chapel where everything has been artistically arranged for the voluptuous delights falling under this head. In this place they will find the four friends who shall wait for them until two o'clock and never any longer, and who shall distribute and adjust them as they judge proper to the delights of this order which they may be moved to taste.

From two to three the first two tables shall be served: they shall dine simultaneously, one in the girls' large apartment, the other in that of the young boys: the three kitchen servants shall serve these two tables. At the first shall sit the eight little girls and the four elders; at the second the four wives, the eight little boys, and the four storytellers. During their meal, Messieurs will be pleased to gather in the living room where they will chat together until three o'clock. Just before this hour, the eight fuckers shall make their appearance here, as well clothed and as well adorned as it is in their power to be.

At three shall be served the masters' dinner, and the honor to be present there shall be enjoyed by none but the eight fuckers; this meal shall be served by the four wives, entirely naked, aided by the four elders, clad as sorceresses; to the latter shall fall the task of bringing the plates from the towers into which the servants, on the other side, shall have put them, and the plates shall be handed to wives, who shall deposit them on the table. The eight fuckers, in the course of the dinner, will be at liberty to handle and touch the unclothed bodies of the wives in whatever manner and to whatever extent they please, without the said wives being permitted to refuse or defend themselves; the fuckers will even be able to go to the point of employing insults and of thickening their sticks by apostrophizing them with all the invectives they may see fit to pronounce.

The friends shall rise from the table at five, at which time these Messieurs only (the fuckers shall retire until the hour of general assembly), these Messieurs only, I say, shall pass into the salon, where two little boys and two little girls, who shall be changed daily, shall, in a state of nudity, serve them coffee and liqueur; nor shall it be at this point in the day's activities Messieurs shall permit themselves diversions which might enervate them; conversation shall be limited to simple jesting.

Shortly before six o'clock, the four children who have been serving, shall withdraw and go promptly to dress themselves. At exactly six, Messieurs shall pass into the assembly chamber heretofore described. They shall each of them repair to their respective alcoves, and the following distribution shall be observed by the others: upon the throne shall be the storyteller, the tiers below the throne shall be occupied by the sixteen children, so arranged that four of them, that is to say, two girls and two boys, shall be situated directly opposite each niche; each niche shall have before it a like quatrain; this quatrain shall be specially allocated to the niche before which it is placed, the niches alongside being excluded from making any claims upon it, and these quatrains shall be diversified each day, never shall the same niche have the same quatrain. Each child in each quatrain shall have one end of a chain of artificial flowers secured to his arm, the other end of the chain leading to the niche, so that when the niche's proprietor wishes any given child in his quatrain, he has but to tug the garland, and the child shall come running and fling himself at the master's feet.

Above the quatrain shall be situate an elder, attached to the quatrain, and responsive to the orders of the chief of that quatrain's niche.

The three storytellers who are not on active service as raconteurs during the month shall be seated upon a bench at the foot of the throne, assigned to no one but yet ready to do anyone's bidding. The four fuckers appointed to spend the night with the friends may be absent from the assembly; they shall be in their rooms, busy grooming themselves for the coming night, at which time great feats shall be regularly expected of them. With respect to the four others, they shall be each one at the feet of one of the friends, who shall be in his niche and upon his couch beside that one of the wives whose turn it is to be with any given husband. This wife shall be at all times naked, the fucker shall wear a closefitting singlet and shorts of taffeta, pink in color, the month's storyteller shall be attired as an elegant courtesan, as shall be her three companions, the little boys and the little girls of the quatrains shall always be differently and splendidly costumed, one quatrain in Asiatic style, one in Spanish, another in Turkish garb, a fourth in Greek, and on the following day otherwise; but all these costumes shall be of taffeta or of lawn; at no time shall the lower half of the body be discomfited by any raiment, and the removal of a pin shall suffice to bare it completely.

As for the elders, they shall alternately interpret the Graeae, nuns, fairies, sorceresses, and upon occasion, widows. The doors to the closets contiguous to the niches shall be kept at a warm temperature by stoves, and shall be garnished with all the appurtenances required for various debauches. Four candles shall burn in each of the closets, and fifty in the auditorium.

Punctually at six o'clock, the storyteller shall begin her story, which the friends may interrupt at any point and as frequently as they please; this narration shall last until ten o'clock in the evening, and during this time, as its object is to inflame the imagination, every lubricity will be permitted, save however for those which might be prejudicial to the approved schedule of deflowerings, which shall be at all times rigorously observed; apart from this, Messieurs may do what they like with their fucker, wife, quatrain, quatrain elder, and even with the storytellers if this whim move them, and that either in their niche or in the adjacent closet. The narration shall be suspended for as long as the pleasures of him whose needs interrupt it continue, and when he shall have done and be sated, the tale shall be resumed.

The evening meal shall be served at ten. The wives, the storytellers, and the eight little girls shall without delay proceed to dine by themselves, women never being admitted to the men's supper, and the friends shall sup with the four fuckers not scheduled for night duty, and with four little boys. Aided by the elders, the four other boys shall serve.

The evening meal concluded, Messieurs shall pass into the salon for the celebration of what are to be called the orgies. Everyone shall convene there, both those who have supped apart and those who have supped with the friends, the four fuckers chosen for the night's service being excepted.

The salon shall be heated to an unusual temperature, and illuminated by chandeliers. All present shall be naked: storytellers, wives, little girls, little boys, elders, fuckers, friends, everything shall be pell-mell, everyone shall be sprawled on the floor and, after the example of animals, shall change, shall commingle, entwine, couple incestuously, adulterously, sodomistically, deflowerings being at all times banned, the company shall give itself over to every excess and to every debauch which may best warm the mind. When 'tis time for these deflowerings, it shall be at this moment and in these circumstances that those operations shall be performed, and once a child shall be initiate, it shall be available for every enjoyment, in all manners and at all times.

The orgies shall cease at precisely two in the morning, the four fuckers designated for nocturnal exercise shall come, in elegant undress, to lead away each of them the friend wherewith he is to bed, each friend shall be provided also with one of the wives or with a deflowered subject, when deflowered subjects there be, or with a storyteller, or with an elder to pass the night 'twixt her and his fucker, and all this according to his disposition, whereunto but one clause is put, that he submit himself to prudent arrangements whence it may result that each friend varies his companions every night, or is able so to do.

Such shall be the daily order of procedure. In addition, each week of the seventeen prescribed as the period of the sojourn at the château shall be marked by a festival. There shall be, first of all, marriages, full particulars relating to which shall be made available in due time and place. But as the first of these matches shall be made between the youngest of the children, who are not able to consummate them, they will in no wise disturb the schedule established for the deflorations. Marriages between adults being all post-defloratory, their consummation will damage nothing since, in acting, the friends shall be enjoying only what has been enjoyed already.

The four elders, to be held answerable for the behavior of their four children, shall, when it is faulty, report it to the month's presiding officer, and each Saturday there shall take place a common meting out of punishments, at the time of the orgies. An exact list of accumulating delinquencies shall be kept until then.

With what regards misbehavior on the part of the storytellers, their punishments shall be one-half that of the children, because their talents are to some purpose, and talent must always be respected. As for errors in the conduct of the wives, they shall always be rewarded by punishment double that given the children.

Should any subject in some way refuse anything demanded of him, even when incapacitated or when that thing is impossible, he shall be punished with utmost severity; 'tis for him to provide, for him to discover ways and means.

The least display of mirth, or the least evidence given of disrespect or lack of submission during the debauch activities, shall be esteemed one of the gravest of faults and shall be one of the most cruelly punished.

Any man taken flagrante delicto with a woman shall punished by the loss of a limb when authorization to enjoy this woman has not hitherto been granted him.

The slightest religious act on the part of any subject, whomsoever he be, whatsoever be that act, shall be punished by death.

Messieurs are expressly enjoined at all gatherings to employ none but the most lascivious language, remarks indicative of the greatest debauchery, expressions of the filthiest, the most harsh, and the most blasphemous.

The name of God shall never be uttered save when accompanied by invectives or imprecations, and thus qualified it shall be repeated as often as possible.

With respect to their tone, it shall at all times be exceedingly brutal, exceedingly harsh, and exceedingly imperious when addressing the wives and the little girls, but wheedling, whorish, and depraved when addressing the men whom the friends, by adopting with them the role of women, should regard as their husbands.

Any friend who fails to comply with any one of these articles, or who may take it into his head to act in accordance with a single glimmer of common sense or moderation and above all to spend a single day without retiring dead drunk to bed, shall be fined ten thousand francs.

Whenever a friend experiences the need to relieve himself heavily, a woman from that class he considers fitting shall be obliged to accompany him, to attend to those duties he shall during this activity indicate to her.

No subject, whether male or female, shall be allowed to fulfill duties of cleanliness whatsoever they may be, and above all those consequent upon the heavy need relieved, without express permission from the month's presiding officer, and if it be refused him, and if despite that refusal he surrender to this need, his punishment shall be of the very rudest.

The four wives shall have no prerogatives of any kind over the other women; on the contrary, they shall at all times be treated with a maximum of rigor and inhumanity, and they shall be frequently employed upon the vilest and most painful enterprises, such as for example the cleaning of the private and common privies established in the chapel. These privies shall be emptied only once every week, but always by them, and they shall be severely punished if they resist the work or accomplish it poorly.

Should a subject attempt evasion while the assembly is sitting, he shall be punished by death instantly, whomsoever he be.

The cooks and their assistants shall be respected, and those of the friends who violate this article shall pay a fine of one thousand gold louis. With regard to these fines, they shall all be specially employed, upon the return to France, for the initial expenses incidental to a new party, either in this same kind, or in another.

These affairs being settled and these regulations published on the 30th, the Duc spent the morning of the 31st inspecting everything, having the statutes repeated aloud, and scrupulously examining the premises to see whether they were susceptible to assault or favorable to escape.

Having concluded that one would have to have wings or the devil's powers to get out or in, he reported his findings to the society and devoted the evening to haranguing the women. By his order they were all convoked in the auditorium, and having mounted that kind of tribune or throne intended for the storyteller, here more or less is the speech he delivered to them:

"Feeble, enfettered creatures destined solely for our pleasures, I trust you have not deluded yourselves into supposing that the equally absolute and ridiculous ascendancy given you in the outside world would be accorded you in this place; a thousand times more subjugated than would be slaves, you must expect naught but humiliation, and obedience is that one virtue whose use I recommend to you: it and no other befits your present state. Above all, do not take it into your heads to rely in the least upon your charms; we are utterly indifferent to those snares and, you may depend on it, such bait will fail with us. Ceaselessly bear in mind that we will make use of you all, but that not a single one of you need beguile herself into imagining that she is able to inspire any feeling of pity in us. Roused in fury against the altars that have been able to snatch from us some few grains of incense, our pride and our libertinage shatter them as soon as the illusion has satisfied our senses, and contempt almost always followed by hatred instantly assumes the pre-eminence hitherto occupied by our imagination. What, furthermore, might you offer that we do not know by heart already? what will you tender us that we shall not grind beneath our heels, often at the very moment delirium transports us?

"Useless to conceal it from you: your service will be arduous, it will be painful and rigorous, and the slightest delinquencies will be requited immediately with corporal and afflicting punishments; hence, I must recommend to you prompt exactness, submissiveness, and a total self-abnegation that you be enabled to heed naught but our desires; let them be your only laws, fly to do their bidding, anticipate them, cause them to be born. Not that you have much to gain by this conduct, but simply because, by not observing it, you will have a great deal to lose.

"Give a thought to your circumstances, think what you are, what we are, and may these reflections cause you to quake - you are beyond the borders of France in the depths of an uninhabitable forest, high amongst naked mountains; the paths that brought you here were destroyed behind you as you advanced along them. You are enclosed in an impregnable citadel; no one on earth knows you are here; you are beyond the reach of your friends, of your kin: insofar as the world is concerned, you are already dead, and if yet you breathe, 'tis by our pleasure, and for it only. And what are the persons to whom you are now subordinated? Beings of a profound and recognized criminality, who have no god but their lubricity, no laws but their depravity, no care but for their debauch, godless, unprincipled, unbelieving profligates, of whom the least criminal is soiled by more infamies than you could number, and in whose eyes the life of a woman - what do I say, the life of a woman? the lives of all women who dwell on the face of the earth, are as insignificant as the crushing of a fly. There will, doubtless, be few you, without the flutter of an eyelash lend yourselves to them all, and faced with whatever it may be, show patience, submission, and courage. If unhappily, some amongst you succumb to our passions' intemperance, let her adjust bravely to her fate: we are not going to exist forever in this world, and the most fortunate thing that can befall a woman is to die young. Our ordinances have been read to you: they are very wise and well-designed for your safety and for our pleasures; obey them blindly, and expect the worst from us should we be irritated by your misbehavior.

Several amongst you have ties with us, I know, and perhaps they embolden you, and perhaps you hope for indulgence on this account; you would be most gravely mistaken were you to put much store by them: no blood attachment is sacred in the view of people like ourselves, and the more they seem so to you, the more their rupture will stimulate the perversity in our spirits. Daughters, wives, it is to you, then, I address myself at present: expect us to grant you no prerogative, you are herewith advised that you will be treated with an even greater severity than the others, and that specifically to point out to you with what scorn we view the bonds whereby you perhaps think us constrained.

"Moreover, do not simply wait for us to specify the orders we would have you execute: a gesture, a glance, often simply one of our internal feelings will announce our desire, and you will be as harshly punished for not having divined it as you would be were you, after having been notified, to ignore that desire or flout it. It is up to you to interpret our movements, our glances, our gestures, to interpret our expressions, and above all not to be mistaken as to our desires. Let us suppose, for example, this desire were to see a particular part of your body and that, through clumsiness, you were to exhibit some other - you appreciate to what extent such contempt would be upsetting to our imaginations, and you are aware of all that one risks by chilling the mind of a libertine who, let us presume, is expecting an ass for his discharge, and to whom some fool presents a cunt.

"By and large, offer your fronts very little to our sight; remember that this loathsome part, which only the alienation of her wits could have permitted Nature to create, is always the one we find most repugnant. And relative to your ass itself, there are precautions to observe: not only would you be well-advised, upon presenting it, to hide the odious lair which accompanies it, but it behooves you to avoid the display, at certain moments, of an ass in that certain state wherein other folk desire always to find it; you probably understand me; and furthermore, the four duennas will furnish you later on with instructions which will complete the explanation of everything.

"In short: shudder, tremble, anticipate, obey - and with all that, if you are not very fortunate, perhaps you will not be completely miserable. No intrigues amongst you, no alliances, none of that ridiculous friendship between the girls which, by softening the heart in one sense, in another renders it both more ill-tempered and less well-disposed to the one and simple humiliation to which you are fated by us; consider that it is not at all as human beings we behold you, but exclusively as animals one feeds in return for their services, and which one withers with blows when they refuse to be put to use.

"You have seen with what stringency you are forbidden anything resembling any act of religion whatsoever. I warn you: few crimes will be more severely punished than this one. It is only too well known that in your midst there are yet a few fools unable to bring themselves to abjure this infamous God and abhor his worship; I would have you know that these imbeciles will be scrupulously examined, and there is no extremity they will not suffer who are so unlucky as to be taken in the act. Let them be persuaded, these stupid creatures, let them henceforth be convinced that in all the world there are not twenty persons today who cling to this mad notion of God's existence, and that the religion he invokes is nothing but a fable ludicrously invented by cheats and impostors, whose interest in deceiving us is only too clear at the present time. In fine, decide for yourselves: were there a God and were this God to have any power, would he permit the virtue which honors him, and which you profess, to be sacrified to vice and libertinage as it is going to be? Would this all-powerful God permit a feeble creature like myself, who would, face to face with him, be as a mite in the eyes of an elephant, would he, I say, permit this feeble creature to insult him, to flout him, to defy him, to challenge him, to offend him as I do, wantonly, at my own sweet will, at every instant of the day?"

This little sermon concluded, the Duc descended from the chair and, with the exception of the four elders and the four narrators, who knew very well they were there as sacrificers and priestesses rather than as victims, except for those eight individuals, I say, everyone burst into tears, and the Duc, not much touched by the scene, left those enacting it to conjecture, jabber, and complain to each other, in perfect certainty the eight spies would render a thorough report of everything: and off he went to spend the night with Hercule, the member of the troupe of fuckers who had become his most intimate favorite in the capacity of a lover, little Zéphyr still having, as a mistress, the first place in his heart. In that upon the following morning everything was to begin, the mechanism was to start functioning, everyone accordingly completed final arrangements, went soundly to sleep, and on the morrow at the stroke of ten, the curtain rose upon a scene of libertinage which was to continue unimpeded, in strict compliance with prescription, until and including the 28th day of February.

And now, friend-reader, you must prepare your heart and your mind for the most impure tale that has ever been told since our world began, a book the likes of which are met with neither amongst the ancients nor amongst us moderns. Fancy, now, that all pleasure-taking either sanctioned by good manners or enjoyned by that fool you speak of incessantly, of whom you know nothing and whom you call Nature; fancy, I say, that all these modes of taking pleasure will be expressly excluded from this anthology, of that whenever peradventure you do indeed encounter them here, they will always be accompanied by some crime or colored by some infamy.

Many of the extravagances you are about to see illustrated will doubtless displease you, yes, I am well aware of it, but there are amongst them a few which will warm you to the point of costing you some fuck, and that, reader, is all we ask of you; if we have not said everything, analyzed everything, tax us not with partiality, for you cannot expect us to have guessed what suits you best. Rather, it is up to you to take what you please and leave the rest alone, another reader will do the same, and little by little, everyone will find himself satisfied. It is the story of the magnificent banquet: six hundred different plates offer themselves to your appetite; are you going to eat them all? No, surely not, but this prodigious variety enlarges the bounds of your choice and, delighted by this increase of possibilities, it surely never occurs to you to scold the Amphitryon who regales you. Do likewise here: choose and let lie the rest without declaiming against that rest simply because it does not have the power to please you. Consider that it will enchant someone else, and be a philosopher.

As for the diversity, it is authentic, you may be sure of it; study closely that passion which to your first consideration seems perfectly to resemble another, and you will see that a difference does exist and that, however slightly it may be, it possesses precisely that refinement, that touch which distinguishes and characterizes the kind of libertinage wherewith we are here involved.

We have, moreover, blended these six hundred passions into the storytellers' narratives. That is one more thing whereof the reader were well to have foreknowledge: it would have been too monotonous to catalogue them one by one outside the body of the story. But as some reader not much learned in these matters might perhaps confuse the designated passions with the adventure or simple event in the narrator's life, each of these passions has been carefully distinguished by a marginal notation: a line, above which is the title that may be given the passion. This mark indicates the exact place where the account of the passions begins, and the end of the paragraph always indicates where it finishes.

But as numerous personages participate in a drama of this kind, notwithstanding the care we have taken in this introduction to describe and designate each one... we shall provide an index which will contain the name and age of every actor, together with a brief sketch of them all; so that should the reader, as he moves along, encounter what seems to him an unfamiliar figure, he will have merely to turn back to this index, and if this little aid to his memory suffice not, to the more thorough portraits given earlier.

The Romance of the School for Libertinage
Dramatis Personae

The Duc de Blangis, fifty, built like a satyr, endowed with a monstrous member and prodigious strength; he may be regarded as the depository of every vice and every crime. He has killed his mother, his sister, and three of his wives.

The Bishop of X____ is his brother; forty-five years old, more slender and more delicate than the Duc; a nasty mouth. He is deceitful, adroit, a faithful sectary of sodomy, active and passive, he has an absolute contempt for all other kinds of pleasure, he has brought about the cruel deaths of the two children whose sizable fortune was left in trust with him; he is a nervous type, so sensitive he nearly swoons upon discharging.

The Président de Curval, sixty; a tall, thin, lank man, with sunken, dead eyes, an unhealthy mouth, the walking image of low license and libertinage, frightfully dirty about his body and attaching voluptuousness thereto. He has been circumcised, his erection is rare and difficult, it does take place however, and he ejaculates almost every day. His tastes induce him to prefer men; all the same, he has no scorn for a maid. For singularities in his tastes, he has a fondness for old age and whatever is kin to him in filthiness. He is endowed with a member practically as thick as the Duc's. In late years he has seemed as though unstrung by debauchery, and he drinks a great deal. He owes his fortune solely to murders and is nominally guilty of one, a dreadful one, whose details are contained in his biography previously given. When discharging, he experiences a sort of lubricious rage; it drives him to cruel deeds.

Durcet, banker, fifty-three, a great friend of the Duc, and his schoolmate; he is short, squat, and chubby, but his body looks healthy, pretty, and lair. He has the figure of a woman and all a woman's tastes: by his little firmness deprived from giving women pleasure, he has imitated that sex and has himself fucked at any time of day or night. He is also rather fond of a good mouthing, 'tis the only expedient which is able to afford him an agent's pleasures. His pleasures are his only gods, and he is constantly prepared to sacrify everything to them. He is clever, adroit, and has committed a profusion of crimes; he poisoned his mother, his wife, and her niece in order to assure his inheritance. His spirit is stoical, stalwart his heart, and absolutely insensible to pity. He no longer stiffens, his ejaculations are most rare; his instants of crisis are preceded by a kind of spasm which hurls him into a lubricious fury dangerous for those who are serving his passions.

Constance, the Duc's wife, Durcet's daughter; twenty-two years of age, she is a Roman beauty, with more majesty than finesse, plump, but well-constructed, a superb body, a unique ass, a model ass, hair and eyes very dark. She is not without brains or wit, and but too well senses the horror of her fate. A great fund of native virtue nothing has been able to destroy.

Adelaide, Durcet's wife, the Président's daughter; a pretty little object, she is twenty, blond, very tender eyes of a lovely, animated blue, she has about her everything of the romantic heroine. A long, well-attached neck, her one defect is her mouth, which is a shade large. Small breasts and a little ass, but all that, though delicate, is fair and well-molded. A mind given to fantasy, a tender heart, excessively virtuous and believing; she secretly performs her Christian duties.

Julie, the Président's wife, elder daughter of the Duc; she is twenty-four, fat, fleshy, with fine brown eyes, a pretty nose, striking and agreeable features, but an appalling mouth. She has little virtue and even pronounced tendencies to uncleanliness, alcoholism, gluttony, and whoredom. Her husband loves her for her defective mouth; this singularity appeals to the Président's tastes. She has never been given either principles or religion.

Aline, her younger sister, supposed daughter of the Duc, really one of the Duc's wives and the Bishop's child; she is eighteen, has a very agreeable and fetching countenance, abounding health, brown eyes, an upturned nose, a mischievous air although she is profoundly indolent and lazy. She seems as yet to have no temperament and most sincerely detests all the infamies she is victim of. The Bishop baptized her behind at the age of ten. She has been left in crass ignorance, knows neither how to read nor write, she abhors the Bishop and greatly fears the Duc. She is much attached to her sister, is sober and tidy, speaks oddly and like a child; her ass is charming.

Duclos, the first storyteller; forty-eight, preserves her looks, is in good physical health, has the finest ass to be seen. Brunette, full figure, very well fleshed.

Champville is fifty; she is slender, well made, has lascivious eyes, she is a tribade, and everything about her proclaims it. Her present trade is pimping. She was once fair-haired, has pretty eyes, is long in the clitoris and ticklish in that part, has an ass much worn from service, but is none the less untupped in that place.

Martaine is fifty-two; she's a procuress too, a matronly dame, hale and hearty; inner obstructions have prevented her from ever knowing any but Sodom's delights, for which indeed she seems to have been specially created, for, her age notwithstanding, she has the world's noblest ass; it is both broad and big and so habituated to introductions that she can accommodate the weightiest engines without the flutter of an eyelash. She has pretty features still, but they are beginning to fade.

Desgranges is fifty-six; she is even now the greatest villain who has ever lived; she is tall, slender, pale, and was once dark-haired, she is crime's personification. Her withered ass resembles marbled paper, or parchment, and its orifice is immense. She is one-dugged, is missing three fingers and six teeth, fructus belli. There exists not a single crime she has not perpetrated or engineered, her prattle is pleasing to the ear, she has wit, and is currently one of the outfitters most highly respected by society.

Marie, the first of the duennas, is the youngest at fifty-eight; she has been whipped and branded, and was a servant to thieves. Her eyes are lackluster and running, her nose crooked, her teeth yellow, one buttock's gnawed by an abscess. She has borne and killed fourteen children.

Louison, the second duenna, is sixty; she is small, lame, one-eyed, and hunchbacked, but for all that she has yet a very pretty ass. She is always ready for crime and is extremely wicked. She and Marie are appointed as governesses to the girls, and the two following to the boys.

Thérèse, aged sixty-two, looks like a skeleton, has no hair, no teeth, a stinking mouth, an ass seamed with scars, its hole is of excessively generous diameter. Filthy and fetid to an atrocious degree; she has a twisted arm, and she limps.

Fanchon, sixty-nine years old, has been six times hanged in effigy and has perpetrated every crime under the sun; she squints, is flat-nosed, short, heavy, has no forehead, two teeth only. An erysipelas covers her ass, a bunch of hemorrhoids hangs from her hole, a chancre is eating her womb, she has a burnt thigh, and a cancer gnaws her breast. She is constantly drunk and vomits, farts, and shits here, there, and everywhere all the time, and all unawares she is doing it.

Harem of Little Girls

Augustine, daughter of a Languedoc baron, fifteen years old, alert and pretty little face.

Fanny, daughter of a Breton counselor, fourteen, a sweet and tender air.

Zelmire, daughter of the Comte de Terville, seigneur of Beauce, fifteen, a noble look and a very sensitive soul.

Sophie, daughter of a gentleman from Berry, charming features, fourteen years.

Colombe, daughter of a counselor to the Parliament of Paris, thirteen years old, exuberant health.

Hébé, daughter of an Orléans officer, a very libertine air, charming eyes, she is twelve.

Rosette and **Michette,** both look like lovely virgins. The first is thirteen and is the daughter of a Chalon-sur-Saône officer, the other is twelve and is a daughter of the Marquis de Sénanges; she was abducted from her father's estate in Bourbonnais.

Their figures, the rest of their features and chiefly their asses are beyond all description. They were chosen from amongst one hundred and fifty.

Harem of Little Boys

Zélamir, thirteen, son of a Poitou squire.

Cupidon, same age, son of a gentleman from near La Flèche.

Narcisse, twelve, son of a nobleman situated in Rouen, Knight of Malta.

Zéphyr, fifteen, son of a general living in Paris. He is destined for the Duc.

Céladon, son of a Nancy magistrate. He is fourteen.

Adonis, son of a judge of a Paris assize court; fifteen, destined for Curval.

Hyacinthe, fourteen, son of a retired officer dwelling in Champagne.

Giton, page to the King, twelve, son of a gentleman from the Nivernais.

No pen is capable of representing the graces, the features, and the charms of these eight children superior also to all the tongue is empowered to say, and chosen, as you know, from amongst a very large number.

Eight Fuckers

Hercule, twenty-six, very pretty, but also a very mean character, the Duc's favorite; his prick measures eight and one-quarter inches around and thirteen in length. Plentiful discharge.

Antinoüs is thirty. A fine specimen of a man, his prick is eight inches around and twelve inches long.

Bum-Cleaver, twenty-eight years old, has the look of a satyr; his majestic prick is bent saber fashion, its head, or glans, is enormous, it is eight and three-eighths inches in circumference and the shaft eight in length. A fine curve to this majestic prick.

Invictus is twenty-five, he is exceedingly ugly, but healthy and vigorous; the great favorite of Curval, he is continually aroused, and his prick is seven and fifteen-sixteenths inches around by eleven inches long.

The four others measure from nine to ten and fifteen-sixteenths inches long, by from seven and a half and five-eights inches around, and they are from twenty-five to thirty years of age.

Part the First

The 150 Simple Passions, or Those Belonging to the First Class, Composing the Thirty Days of November Passed in Hearing the Narration of Madame Duclos; Interspersed Amongst Which Are the Scandalous Doings at the Château During That Month; All Being Set down in the Form of a Journal.

The First Day

The company rose the 1st of November at ten o'clock in the morning, as was specified in the statutes which Messieurs had mutually sworn faithfully to observe in every particular. The four fuckers who had not shared the friends' couches, at their waking hour brought Zéphyr to the Duc, Adonis to Curval, Narcisse to Durcet, and Zélamir to the Bishop. All four children were very timid, even more awkward, but, encouraged by their guides, they very nicely carried out their tasks, and the Duc discharged. His three colleagues, more reserved and less prodigal with their fuck, had as much of it deposited in them as did the Duc, but distributed none of their own.

At eleven o'clock they passed into the women's quarters where the eight young sultanas appeared naked, and in this state served chocolate, aided and directed by Marie and Louison, who presided over this seraglio. There was a great deal of handling and colling, and the eight poor girls, wretched little victims of the most blatant lubricity, blushed, hid behind their hands, sought to protect their charms, and immediately displayed everything as soon as they observed that their modesty irritated and annoyed their masters. The Duc rose up like a shot and measured his engine's circumference against Michette's slender little waist: their difference did not exceed three inches. Durcet, the month's preseding officer, conducted the prescribed examinations and made the necessary searches; Hébé and Colombe were found to have lapsed, their punishment was pronounced at once and fixed for the following Saturday at orgy hour. They wept. No one was moved.

They proceeded to the boys' apartments. The four who had not appeared that morning, namely Cupidon, Céladon, Hyacinthe and Giton, bared their behinds in accordance with orders, and the sight provided an instant's amusement. Curval kissed them all on the mouth, and the Bishop spent a moment frigging their pricks while the Duc and Durcet were doing something else. The inspections were completed, no misconduct was discovered.

At one o'clock Messieurs betook themselves to the chapel where, as you know, the sanitary conveniences were installed. The calculation of requirements for the coming soiree having led to the refusal of a good number of requests, only Constance, Duclos, Augustine, Sophie, Zélamir, Cupidon, and Louison appeared; all the others had asked permission and had been instructed to hold back until evening. Our four friends, ranged around the same specially constructed seat, had these seven subjects take their seat one after another, and then retired when they had enough of this spectacle. They descended to the salon where, while the women dined, they gossiped and tattled until the time came for them to be served their meal. Each of the four friends placed himself between two fuckers, pursuant to the imposed rule that barred all women from their table, and the four naked wives, aided by the elders costumed as the Graeae, served them the most magnificent and the most succulent dinner it were possible to concoct. No one more delicate, more skilled than the cooks they had brought with them, and they were so well paid and so lavishly provided that everything could not fail to be a brilliant success. As the midday fare was to be less heavy than the evening meal, they were restricted to four superb courses, each composed of twelve plates. Burgundy wine arrived with the hors d'ouvres, Bordeaux was served with the entrees, champagne with the roasts, Hermitage accompanied the entrements, Tokay and madeira were served with dessert.

Spirits rose little by little; the fuckers, whom the friends had granted every liberty with their wives, treated them somewhat untenderly. Constance was even a bit knocked about, rather beaten for having dawdled over bringing a dish to Hercule who, seeing himself well advanced in the Duc's good graces, fancied he might carry insolence to the point of drubbing and molesting his wife; the Duc thought this very amusing. Curval, in an ugly humor by the time dessert arrived, flung a plate at his wife's face, and it might have clove her head in two had she not ducked. Spying one of his neighbors stiffen, Durcet, though they were still at table, promptly unbuttoned his breeches and presented his ass. The neighbor drove his weapon home; the operation once concluded, they fell to drinking again as if nothing had happened. The Duc soon imitated his old friend's little infamy and wagered that, enormous as Invictus' prick might be, he could calmly down three bottles of wine while lying embuggered upon it. What effortlessness, what ease, what detachment in libertinage! He won what he had staked, and as they were not drunk on an empty stomach, as those three bottles fell upon at least fifteen others, the Duc's head began gently to swim. The first object upon which his eye alighted was his wife, weeping over the abuse she had sustained from Hercule, and this sight so inspired the Duc he lost not an instant doing to her things too excessive for us to describe as yet. The reader will notice how hampered we are in these beginnings, and how stumbling are our efforts to give a coherent account of these matters; we trust he will forgive us for leaving the curtain drawn over a considerable number of little details. We promise it will be raised later on.

Our champions finally made their way into the salon, where new pleasures and further delights were awaiting them. Coffee and liqueurs were distributed by a charming quartet made up of Adonis and Hyacinthe, two appealing little boys, and two pretty maids, Zelmire and Fanny. Thérèse, one of the duennas, supervised them, for it was decreed that wherever two or more children were gathered, a duenna was to be on hand. Our four libertines, half-drunk but none the less resolved to abide their laws, contended themselves with kisses, fingerings, but their libertine intelligence knew how to season these mild activities with all the refinements of debauch and lubricity. It was thought for a moment that the Bishop was going to have to surrender his fuck in exchange for the extraordinary things he was wringing from Hyacinthe, while Zelmire frigged him. His nerves were already aquiver, an impending crisis was beginning to take possession of his entire being, but he checked himself, the tempting objects ready to triumph over his senses were sent spinning and, knowing there was yet a full day's work ahead of him, the Bishop saved his best for the evening. Six different kinds of liqueur were drunk, three kinds of coffee, and the hour sounding at last, the two couples withdrew to dress.

Our friends took a fifteen minute nap, then moved into the throne room, the place where the auditors were to listen to the narrations. The friends took their places upon their couches, the Duc having his beloved Hercule at his feet, near him, naked, Adelaide, Durcet's wife and the Président's daughter, and for quatrain opposite him, and linked to his niche by a chain of flowers, as has been explained, Zéphyr, Giton, Augustine, and Sophie costumed as shepherds, supervised by Louison as an old peasant woman playing the role of their mother.

At Curval's feet was Invictus, upon his couch lay Constance, the Duc's wife and Durcet's daughter, and for quatrain four little Spaniards, each sex dressed in its costume and as elegantly as possible: they were Adonis, Céladon, Fanny, and Zelmire; Fanchon clad as a duenna, watched over them.

The Bishop had Antinoüs at his feet, his niece Julie on his couch, and four little almost naked savages for quatrain. The boys: Cupidon and Narcisse; the girls: Hébé and Rosette; an old Amazon, interpreted by Thérèse, was in charge of them.

Durcet had Bum-Cleaver for fucker, near him reclined Aline, daughter of the Bishop, and in front of him were four little sultanas, the boys being dressed as girls, and this refinement to the last degree emphasized the enchanting visages of Zélamir, Hyacinthe, Colombe, and Michette. An old Arab slave, portrayed by Marie, presided over this quatrain.

The three storytellers, magnificently dressed as upper-class Parisian courtesans, were seated below the throne upon a couch, and Madame Duclos, the month's narrator, in very scanty and very elegant attire, well rouged and heavily bejeweled, having taken her place on the stage, thus began the story of what had occurred in her life, into which account she was, with all pertinent details, to insert the first one hundred and fifty passions designated by the title of simple passions:

'Tis no slight undertaking, Messieurs, to attempt to express oneself before a circle such as yours. Accustomed to all of the most subtle and most delicate that letters produce, how, one may wonder, will you be able to bear the ill-shaped periods and uncouth images of a humble creature like myself who has received no other education than the one supplied her by libertinage. But your indulgence reassures me; you ask for naught but the natural and true, and I dare say what of these I shall provide you will merit your attention.

My mother was twenty-five when she brought me into the world, and I was her second child; the first was also a daughter, by six years my elder. My mother's birth was not distinguished. She had been early bereft of both her father and mother, and as her parents had dwelled near the Récollet monastery in Paris, when she found herself an orphan, abandoned and without any resources, she obtained permission from these good fathers to come and ask for alms in their church. But as she had some youth and health, she soon attracted their notice, and gradually mounted from the church below to the rooms above, whence she soon descended with child. It was as a consequence of one such adventure my sister saw the light, and it is more likely that my own birth might rightly be ascribed to no other cause.

However, content with my mother's docility and seeing how she did make the community to prosper and flourish, the good fathers rewarded her works by granting her what might be earned from the rental of seats in their church; my mother no sooner obtained this post than, with her superior's leave, she married one of the house's water carriers who straightway, without the least repugnance, adopted my sister and me.

Born into the Church, I dwelled so to speak more in the House of God than in our own; I helped my mother arrange the chairs, I seconded the sacristans in their various operations, I would have said Mass had that been necessary, although I had not yet attained my fifth year.

One day, returning from my holy occupations, my sister asked me whether I had yet encountered Father Laurent . . . .

I said I had not.

"Well, look out," said she, "he's on the watch for you, I know he is, he wants to show you what he showed me. Don't run away, look him straight in the eye without being afraid, he won't touch you, but he'll show you something very funny, and if you let him do it he'll pay you a lot. There are more than fifteen of us around here whom he's shown it to. That's what he likes best, and he's given a present to us all."

You may well imagine, Messieurs, that nothing more was needed, not only to keep me from fleeing Father Laurent, but to induce me to seek him out; at that age the voice of modesty is a whisper at best, and its silence until the time one has left the tutelage of Nature is certain proof, is it not, that this factitious sentiment is far less the product of that original mother's training than it is the fruit of education? I flew instantly to the church, and as I was crossing a little court located between the entrance of the churchyard and the monastery, I bumped squarely into Father Laurent. He was a monk about forty, with a very handsome face. He stopped me.

"Whither are you going, Francon?" he asked.

"To arrange the chairs, Father."

"Never fear, never fear, your mother will attend to them," said he. "Come, come along with me," and he drew me toward a sequestered chamber hard by the place. "I am going to show you something you have never seen."

I follow him, we enter, he shuts the door and, having posted me directly opposite him:

"Well, Francon," says he, pulling a monstrous prick from his drawers, an instrument which nearly toppled me with fright; "tell me," he continues, frigging himself, "have you ever seen anything to equal it?... that's what they call a prick, my little one, yes, a prick... it's used for fucking, and what you're going to see, what's going to flow out of it in a moment or two, is the seed wherefrom you were created. I've shown it to your sister, I've shown it to all the little girls of your age, lend a hand, help it along, help get it out, do as your sister does, she's got it out of me twenty times or more . . . . I show them my prick, and then what do you suppose I do? I squirt the fuck in their face . . . . That's my passion, my child, I have no other... and you're about to behold it."

And at the same time I felt myself completely drenched in a white spray, it soaked me from head to foot, some drops of it had leapt even into my eyes, for my little head just came to the height of his fly. However, Laurent was gesticulating. "Ah! the pretty fuck, the dear fuck I am losing," he cried, "why, look at you! You're covered with it." And gradually regaining control of himself, he calmly put his tool away and decamped, slipping twenty sous into my hand and suggesting that I bring him any little companions I might happen to have.

As you may readily fancy, I could not have been more eager to run and tell everything to my sister; she wiped me dry, taking the greatest care to overlook none of the spots, and she who had enabled me to earn my little fortune did not fail to demand half of my wages. Instructed by this example, I did not fail, in the hope of a similar division of the spoils, to round up as many little girls for Father Laurent as I could find. But having brought him one with whom he was already familiar, he turned her away, the while giving me three sous by way of encouragement.

"I never see the same one twice, my child," he told me, "bring me some I don't know, never any of those who say they've already had dealings with me."

I managed more successfully; in the space of three months, I introduced Father Laurent to more than twenty new girls, with whom, for the sake of his pleasure, he employed the identical proceedings he had with me. Together with the stipulation that they be strangers to him, there was another relative for age, and it appeared to be of infinite importance: he had no use for anything younger than four or older than seven. And my little fortune could not have been faring better when my sister, noticing that I was encroaching upon her domain, threatened to divulge everything to my mother if I did not put a stop to this splendid commerce; I had to give up Father Laurent.

However, my functions continued to keep me in the neighborhood of the monastery; the same day I reached the age of seven I encountered a new lover whose preferred caprice, although very childish, was nevertheless somewhat more serious. This one was named Father Louis, he was older than Laurent, and had some unidentifiable quality in his bearing that was a great deal more libertine. He sidled up to me at the door of the church as I was entering it, and made me promise to come up to his room. At first I advanced a few objections, but once he had assured me that three years ago my sister had come for a visit and that he received little girls of my age every day, I went with him. Scarcely were we in his cell when he closed and bolted the door and, having poured some elixir into a goblet, made me swallow it and then two more copious measures too. This preparatory step taken, the reverend, more affectionate than his confrere, fell to kissing me and, chattering all the while, he untied my apron and, raising my skirt to my bodice, he laid hands, despite my faint strugglings, upon all the anterior parts he had just brought to light; and after having thoroughly fingered and considered them, he inquired of me whether I did not desire to piss. Singularly driven to this need by the strong dose he had a few moments earlier had me drink, I assured him the urge to do so was as powerful as ever it could be, but that I did not want to satisfy it in front of him.

"Oh, my goodness, do! Why yes, my little rascal," quoth the bawdy fellow, "by God yes, you'll piss in my presence and, what's worse, you'll piss upon me. Here it is," he went on, plucking his prick from his breeches, "here's the tool you're going to moisten, just piss on it a little."

And thereupon he lifted me up and set me on two chairs, one foot on one chair, the other foot on the other, he moved the chairs apart as far as was possible, then bade me squat. Holding me in this posture, he placed a container beneath me, established himself on a little stool about as high as the pot; his engine was in his hand, directly under my cunt. One of his hands supporting my haunches, he frigged himself with the other, and my mouth being at a level with his, he kissed it.

"Off you go, my little one, piss," cried he, "flood my prick with that enchanting liquid whose hot outpouring exerts such a sway over my senses. Piss, my heart, care not but to piss and try to inundate my fuck."

Louis became animated, excited himself, it was easy to see that this unusual operation was the one which all his senses most cherished; the sweetest, gentlest ecstasy crowned that very moment when the liquids wherewith he had swollen my stomach, gushed most abundantly out of me, and we simultaneously filled the same pot, he with fuck, I with urine. The exercise concluded, Louis delivered roughly the same speech to me I had heard from Laurent, he wished to make a procuress of his little whore, and this time, caring precious little for my sister's threats, I boldly guided every child I knew to dear Louis. He had every one of them do the same thing, and as he experienced no compunction upon seeing any one of them a second or third time, and as he always gave me separate payment, which had nothing to do with the additional fee I extracted from my little comrades, before six months had passed I found myself with a tidy little sum which was entirely my own; I had only to conceal knowledge of it from my sister.

"Duclos," the Président interrupted at this point, "we have, I believe, advised you that your narrations must be decorated with the most numerous and searching details; the precise way and extent to which we may judge how the passion you describe relates to human manners and man's character is determined by your willingness to disguise no circumstance; and, what is more, the least circumstance is apt to have an immense influence upon the procuring of that kind of sensory irritation we expect from your stories."

"Yes, my Lord," Duclos replied, "I have been advised to omit no detail and to enter into the most minute particulars whenever they serve to shed light upon the human personality, or upon the species of passion; have I neglected something in connection with this one?"

"You have," said the Président; "I have not the faintest notion of your second monk's prick, nor any idea of its discharge. In addition, did he frig your cunt, pray tell, and did he have you dandle his device? You see what I mean by neglected details."

"Your pardon, my Lord," said Duclos, "I shall repair these present mistakes and avoid them in the future. Father Louis possessed a very ordinary member, greater in its length than it was around and in general of a most common shape and turn; indeed, I do recall that he stiffened rather poorly and that it was not until the crisis arrived he took on a little firmness. No, he did not frig my cunt, he was content to enlarge it with his fingers as much as possible, so as to give free issue to the urine. He brought his prick very close two or three times, and his discharge was rapid, intense, and brief; nothing came from his mouth but the words: 'Ah, fuck! piss, my child, piss the pretty fountain, piss, d'ye hear, piss away, don't you see me come?' And, while saying that, he intermittently sprinkled kisses on my mouth. They were not excessively libertine."

"That's it, Duclos," said Durcet, "the Président was right; I could not visualize a thing on the basis of your first telling, but now I have your man well in view."

"One moment, Duclos," said the Bishop, upon seeing that she was about to proceed. "I have on my own account a need rather more pressing than to piss, it's had me in its grip for an age and I have the feeling it's got to go."

So saying he drew Narcisse to his alcove. Fire leapt from the prelate's eyes, his prick stood up against his belly, foam flecked his lips, it was confined fuck that wished absolutely to escape and which could not be liberated save by violent means. He dragged his niece and the little boy into his closet. Everything came to a pause; a discharge was regarded as something far too portentous not to suspend everything the moment someone was about to produce one; all was to concur to make it delicious. But upon this occasion Nature's will did not correspond with the Bishop's wishes, and several minutes after having retired to the closet, he emerged from it, furious, in the same state of erection and, addressing himself to Durcet, presiding officer for November:

"Put that odd little fellow down for some punishment on Saturday," he said, flinging the child ten feet away from him, "and make it severe, if you please."

It was apparent that the boy had not been able to satisfy Monseigneur, and Julie whispered in her father's ear what had happened.

"Well, by God, then take another," cried the Duc, "choose something from one of our quatrains if nothing in yours suits you."

"Ah, my satisfaction now would be far beyond the damned little that would have been sufficient a moment ago," said the prelate. "You know to what we are led by a thwarted desire; I'd prefer to restrain myself, but no undue leniency with that poor little fool ," he continued, "that's what I recommend..."

"But be at ease, my dear Bishop," said Durcet, "I promise you he'll get a good scolding, 'tis a fine idea to provide the others with an example. I'm sorry to see you in such a state; try something else; have yourself fucked."

"Monseigneur," spoke up Martaine, "I feel myself greatly disposed to satisfy you, were Your Excellency to wish it..."

"No, no, Christ, no!" the Bishop cried, "don't you know that there are a thousand occasions when one does not want a woman's asshole? I'll wait...let Duclos continue, I'll get rid of it tonight, I'll have to find the one I want. Proceed, Duclos."

And the friends having laughed right heartily at the Bishop's libertine frankness- "there are a thousand occasions when one does not want a woman's asshole"- the storyteller resumed in these terms:

It was not long after I had attained the age of seven that one day, following my custom of bringing one of my little comrades to Louis, I found another monk with him in his cell. As that had never happened before, I was surprised and wanted to leave, but Louis having reassured us, my little friend and I went boldly in.

"Well there, Geoffrey," Louis said to his companion, pushing me toward him, "did I not tell you that she was nice?"

"Why yes indeed, she is," said Geoffrey, taking me upon his knees and giving me a kiss. "How old are you, my little one?"

"Seven, Father."

"Just fifty years younger than I," said the good father, kissing me anew.

And during this little dialogue, the sirup was being prepared and, as it was customary, each of us swallowed three big glasses of it, but, as it was not customary for me to drink when I brought Louis a toy, because he only expected a sprinkling from the girl I brought, because I did not usually stay for the ceremony but used to leave at once, for all these reasons I was astonished by their actions, and in a tone of the most naive innocence I inquired:

"And why do you have me drink, good Father? do you want me to piss?"

"To be sure, we do, my child," quoth Geoffrey, who still had me squeezed between his thighs and whose hands were already straying over my front, "yes, you're to piss, and the adventure is to take place with me; it will be, perhaps, a little different from the other one you experienced here. Come into my cell, let's leave Father Louis with your little friend, and let's get to business ourselves; we'll return when all our needs are satisfied."

We left; before going, Louis told me in a whisper to be very obliging with his friend, and said I'd not regret it if I were. Geoffrey's cell was not far from Louis', and we reached it without being seen. No sooner inside than Geoffrey, having barricaded the door, told me to get rid of my skirts. I obeyed, he himself pulled my shift above my navel and, having seated me on the edge of his bed, he spread my thighs as wide as it were possible, at the same time thrusting me back in such a way my belly came into full view and my weight rested entirely upon the base of my spine. He besought me to keep in that position and to begin to piss immediately he gave one of my thighs a little slap with his hand. Then, scrutinizing me for a moment in this attitude, with one hand he separated the lips of my cunt, with the other he unbuttoned his breeches and with quick and energetic movements began to shake a dark, stunted little member which seemed not much inclined to respond to what was required of it. To give it some encouragement, our man set about doing his duty and proceeded to his chosen custom, the one which procured him the greatest possible titillation - down he went on his knees, I say, between my legs, spent another instant peering into the little orifice I presented to his eye, several times applied his mouth to it, between his teeth muttering certain luxurious phrases I cannot remember because at the time I did not understand them, and continued to agitate that sullen little member, which, though fearfully bullied, did not budge. Finally, he sealed his lips to those of my cunt, I received the signal, and instantly draining what my bladder contained into the gentleman's mouth, I flooded him with a stream of urine he swallowed as fast as I launched it into his gullet. Whereupon his member unfurled, and its proudly lifted head throbbed against one of my thighs: I felt it bravely spray his debilitated manhood's sterile issue. Everything had been so well managed he swallowed the final drops at the same moment his prick, confused by his victory, wept bloody tears over it. Trembling in every limbs, Geoffrey got to his feet, and I observed that he no longer had for his idol, once the incense had been extinguished, the same religious fervor he had while delirium, inflaming his homage, still sustained its glory: he rather abruptly gave me twelve sous, opened the door without asking me, as had the others, to bring him girls (he was evidently furnished by someone else) and, pointing the way to his friend's cell, told me to go there, said that he was in a hurry, that he had his offices to perform, that he could not conduct me himself, and then shut his door without affording me the chance to answer him.

"Oh yes indeed!" said the Duc, "unnumbered are they who absolutely cannot bear the instant when the illusion is shattered. It seems as if one's pride suffers when one lets a woman see one in such a state of feebleness, and disgust would appear to be the result of the discomfiture one experiences at such moments."

"No," said Curval, whom Adonis, kneeling, was frigging, and whose hands were wandering over Zelmire, "no, my friend, pride has nothing to do with it, but the object which is in the profoundest sense devoid of all value save the one our lust endows it with, that object, I say, shows itself for what in truth it is once our lubricity has subsided. The more violent has been the irritation the more this object is stripped of its attraction when this irritation ceases to sustain it, just as we are more or less fatigued after greater or lesser exertion, and this aversion we thereupon sense is nothing but the sentiment of a glutted soul whereunto happiness is displeasing because happiness has just wearied it."

"But from this aversion, all the same," spoke up Durcet, "is often born a plan for revenge, whose fatal consequences have often been observed."

"Yes, but that's another matter," Curval replied, "and as the aftermath of these recitals will perhaps afford us examples of what you're saying, let's not anticipate through dissertations what will be naturally produced of itself."

"Président, be frank," said Durcet: "on the verge of running amuck yourself, I believe that at the present moment you prefer to prepare yourself to feel how one enjoys than to discuss how one becomes disgusted."

"Why, not at all, not a bit of it," said Curval, "I am as cool as ice... To be sure, yes," he continued, kissing Adonis' lips, "this child is charming... but he's not to be fucked; I know of nothing worse than your damnable regulations... one must reduce oneself to things... to things... Go on, Duclos, go on, continue, for I have the feeling I might perpetrate something foolish, and I want my illusion to remain intact at least until I go to bed."

The Président, perceiving his engine beginning to rebel, sent the two children back to their posts and, lying down beside Constance, who, pretty as she was, doubtless failed to stimulate him as much, he a second time besought Duclos to resume her story; she did at once, as follows:

I rejoined my little comrade. Louis had been serviced; not very well pleased, we both left the monastery, I almost resolved not to return again. Geoffrey's tone had wounded my little pride, and without probing further to determine the origins of my displeasure, I liked neither its apparent cause nor its consequences. However, it had been written in my destiny that I was to have yet a few more adventures in that pious retreat, and the example of my sister, who had, so she told me, done business with fourteen of its inhabitants, was to convince me that I was still far from the end of my tour. Three months after this last episode, I became aware of overtures being made to me by another one of these reverend fathers, this one a man of about sixty. He invented every kind of ruse to lure me to his room; one of them succeeded, so well in fact that one fine Sunday morning I found myself there, without knowing why or how it had happened. The old rascal, known as Father Henri, shut and locked the door as soon as I had crossed the threshold, and embraced me with exceeding warmth.

"Ah, little imp!" cried he, transported with joy, "I've got you now, you'll not escape me this time, ha!"

The weather was extremely cold at the time, my little nose was running as children's usually do in the winter; I drew out a handkerchief.

"What's this? What's this? Be careful there," warned Henri, "I'm the one who'll attend to that operation, my sweet."

And having stretched me out upon his bed with my head a little to one side, he sat down next to me and raised my head upon his lap. He peered avidly at me, his eyes seemed ready to devour the secretion oozing from my nose. "Oh, the pretty little snotface," said he, beginning to pant, "how I'm going to suck her." Therewith bending down over me, and taking my nose in his mouth, not only did he devour all the mucus between my nose and mouth, but he even lewdly darted the tip of his tongue into each of my nostrils, one after the other, and with such cleverness he provoked two or three sneezes which redoubled the flow he desired and was consuming so hungrily. But ask me for no details bearing upon this fellow, Messieurs, nothing appeared, and whether because he did nothing, or because he did it all in his drawers, there was nothing to be seen, and amidst the multitude of his kisses and lecherous lickings there was nothing outstanding which might have denoted an ecstasy, and consequently it is my opinion that he did not discharge. All my clothes were in place, even his hands stayed still, and I give you my word that this old libertine's fantasy might be performed upon the world's most respectable and least initiated girl without her being able to suppose there was anything lewd in it at all.

But the same could not be said of the one that chance presented to my consideration the same day I turned nine years old. Father Etienne, that was the libertine's name, had several times asked my sister to bring me to him, and she had got me to promise to go alone, for she was unwilling to accompany me, fearing lest my mother, who already scented something in the wind, might find out; well, I was planning to pay him a visit when, one day, I ran directly into him in a corner of the church, near the sacristy. His manner was so gracious, he argued so persuasively that he had no need to drag me away by main force. Father Etienne was about forty, a healthy, robust, strapping fellow. We were no sooner closeted together than he asked whether I knew how to frig a prick.

"Alas!" said I, blushing to the ears, "I don't even know what you're talking about."

"Well then I'll explain, my chit," said he, bestowing heartfelt kisses upon my mouth and eyes, "my unique pleasure in this world is to educate little girls, and the lessons I give are so excellent they prove unforgettable. Begin by removing your skirts, for if I am to teach you how you must proceed in order to give me pleasure, 'tis only fair that at the same time I teach you what to do in order to receive it, and that lesson cannot be a success if anything hinders us. Here we go. We shall begin with you. What you behold down here," said he, placing his hand on my mound, "is called a cunt, and this is what you must do in order to awaken very felicitous sensations in it. With one finger - one will do - lightly rub this little protuberance you feel here. It, by the way, is called the clitoris."

I followed instructions.

"There, you see, that way, my little one, while one hand is busy there, let one finger of your other hand gradually work its way into this delicious crack . . . ."

He adjusted my hands.

"That's the way, yes... Well! Don't you feel anything?" he asked, keeping me to my task.

"No, Father, I truly don't," I answered most naively.

"Ah, that's because you are still too young, but two years from now you'll see the pleasures it gives."

"Wait," I interrupted, "I think something's happening."

And with all imaginable vigor I rubbed the places he had pointed out . . . . Yes, sure enough, a few faint titillations convinced me that what I'd begun was worth continuing, and the extensive use I have made ever since of this relief-providing exercise has more than once persuaded me of my master's competence.

"And now 'tis my turn," said Etienne, "for your pleasures arouse my desires, and I simply must share them, my angel. Here we are; take this," he said, inviting me to grip a tool so monstrous my two little hands were scarce able to close around it, "take this, my child, 'tis called a prick, and this movement here," he went on, guiding my wrists in rapid jerks, "this action is called frigging. Thus, by means of this action you frig my prick. Go to it, my child, put all your strength to it. The more rapid and persistent your movements, the more you will hasten a moment which, believe me, I cherish. But bear one essential thing in mind," he added, all the while directing my flying hands, "be careful at all times to keep the tip uncovered. Never allow this skin, we call it the prepuce, to cover it over; were this prepuce to happen to cover this part, which we call the glans, all my pleasure would vanish. That's it; we're shortly going to see something, my little one," my teacher continued, "watch me do on you what you did on me."

And pressing himself against my chest as he spoke and as I kept in motion, he placed his hands so adroitly, he wriggled his fingers with such high art that pleasure rose at last to grip me, and it is without a shadow of a doubt to him I owe my initiation. And then, my head reeling, I abandoned my task, and the reverend, not yet ready to complete it, consented to forget his pleasure for a moment in order to devote himself exclusively to cultivating mine; and when he had caused me to taste it all, he had me resume the work my ecstasy had obliged me to interrupt, and very expressly enjoined me to keep my mind strictly on what I was about and to care for naught but him. I did so with all my soul. It was only just: I surely owed him my thanks. I went so merrily to work, and I observed all his instructions so faithfully that the monster, vanquished by such rapid vibrations, finally spewed forth all its rage and covered me with its venom. Thereupon Etienne seemed to go out of his mind, borne aloft in the most voluptuous delirium; ardently he kissed my mouth, he fondled and frigged my cunt, and the wildness in his speech still more emphatically declared his disorder. Gross expressions, mingling with others of the most endearing sort, characterized this transport, which lasted quite a while, and whence at last the gallant Etienne, so unlike his piss-swallowing colleague, emerged to tell me that I was charming, that he greatly hoped I would come back to see him, and that he would treat me every time as he was going to now: pressing a silver coin into my hand, he conducted me back to the place he had brought me from and left me wonderstruck, thrilled and enchanted with this latest good fortune. Feeling much better about the monastery, I decided to return to it often in the future, persuaded that the more I advanced in age, the more agreeable adventures I would meet with there. But destiny called me elsewhere; more important events awaited me in a new world, and upon returning to my house I learned news which was soon to sober the elation produced in me by the happy outcome of my latest experience.

Here a bell was heard struck in the salon; it announced supper. Whereupon Duclos, generally applauded for the auspicious little beginnings she had made, descended from the stage, and, after having made a few adjustments to repair the disorder all four of them seemed to be in, the friends turned their thoughts to new pleasures and hastened to find out what Comus held in store for them.

This meal was to be served by the eight little girls, naked. Having been wise enough to leave the auditorium a few minutes early, they stood ready the moment the masters entered these fresh surroundings. The table companions were to be twenty in number: the libertine quartet, the eight fuckers, the eight little boys. But, still furious with Narcisse, the Bishop wished to veto his presence at the banquet, and as it was perfectly natural that they make allowances for one another's whims and observe a mutual tolerance, no one raised his voice to contest the sentence, and the poor little simpleton was confined alone in a dark closet to await that stage in the orgies when perhaps Monseigneur might be inclined to make friends with him again. The wives and the storytellers, dining apart, had concluded their meal in great haste in order to be ready for the orgies, the elders directed the movements of the eight little girls, and dinner was begun.

This meal, much heavier than the one which had been eaten earlier in the day, was served with far greater opulence and splendor. I began with a shellfish soup and hors d'oeuvres composed of twenty dishes; twenty entrees came on next, and soon gave way to another twenty lighter entrees made up entirely of breasts of chicken, of assorted game prepared in every possible way. This was offset by a serving of roasts; everything of the rarest imaginable was brought on. Next arrived some cold pastry, soon afterward twenty-six entremets of every description and form. The table was cleared, and what had just been removed was replaced by a whole array of cold and hot sugared pastries. Dessert finally appeared: a prodigious number and variety of fruits, though the season was winter, then ices, chocolate, and the liqueurs which were taken at table. As for the wines, they varied with each service: Burgundy accompanied the first; two kinds of Italian wine came with the second and third; Rhine wine with the fourth; with the fifth, Rhône wines; sparkling champagne with the sixth; two kinds of Greek wine with the other two courses. Spirits were prodigiously roused, for, as distinct from lunch, one was not granted permission during dinner to take the waitresses to task, or with that same severity; these creatures, being the very quintessence of what the company had to offer, had to be treated rather more sparingly but, on the other hand, the friends indulged in a furious round of impurities with them.

Half-drunk, the Duc said he would not touch another drop, from now it was Zelmire's urine or nothing, and he drained two large glasses of it which he obtained by having the child climb upon the table and squat over his plate. "Why, there's nothing to drinking weak young piss," said Curval and, calling Fanchon to him: "Come hither, venerable bitch, I'd slake my thirst at the very source." And thrusting his head between the old crone's legs, he greedily sucked up the impure floods of poisonous urine she darted into his stomach. And now their words grew heated, they argued various philosophical problems and considered several questions relating to manners; I leave it to the reader to imagine the purity of those discourses and the loftiness of their moralizing. The Duc undertook an encomium of libertinage, and proved that it was natural, and that the more numerous were its extravagances, the better they served the creator of us all. His opinion was generally acclaimed, enthusiastically applauded, and they rose to go and put into practice the doctrines which had just been established. Everything was ready in the orgy salon: the women were there, already naked, lying upon piles of pillows on the floor, strewn promiscuously amongst the young catamites who had hastened away from table a little after dessert. Our friends reeled in; two elders undressed them, and they fell upon the flock like wolves assailing a sheepfold. The Bishop, whose passions had been cruelly irritated by the obstacles they had encountered of late, laid hands on Antinoüs' sublime ass while Hercule skewered him, and vanquished by this latest sensation and by the important and doubtless so much desired service Antinoüs was rendering him, he finally spat out streams of semen so hard driven and so pungent he swooned in ecstasy. Bacchus' wiles had spellbound senses glutted from excess, numbed from luxury; our hero passed from his faint to a sleep so profound he had to be carried to his bed. The Duc was having a marvelous time. Curval, recollecting what Martaine had offered the Bishop, stuffed her while he got his own ass stoppered. A thousand other horrors, a thousand other infamies accompanied and succeeded those, and our three indomitable champions - for the Bishop no longer was of this world - our valorous athletes, I say, escorted by the four night-toiling fuckers who had not been at the revels but who now came to fetch them, retired with the same wives who had shared their couches during the story time. Luckless victims of their brutality, upon whom it is only too likely they showered more outrages than caresses and who, it is equally probable, inspired in them more disgust than pleasure. . . .

Such were the events that transpired on the first day.

The Second Day

The company rose at the customary hour. The Bishop, entirely recovered from his excess, and who, waking at four in the morning, was deeply shocked to find they had let him go to bed unaccompanied, had summoned Julie and his fucker for the night to come and occupy their posts. They answered the call instantly, and in their arms the libertine plunged back into the thick of new impurities.

When, in keeping with regulations, breakfast had been taken in the girls' quarters, Durcet went on his rounds, and, notwithstanding all the arguments he heard, further delinquencies appeared to his eyes. Michette was guilty of one kind of fault and Augustine, whom Curval had ordered to keep herself throughout the day in a certain state, was found in the absolutely opposite state; she declared she had forgotten, made a hundred apologies, and promised it would not happen again, but the quadrumvirate was inexorable, and both names were inscribed on the list of punishments to be executed come the first Saturday.

Highly dissatisfied with all these little girls' ineptness in the art of masturbation, annoyed by the effects of this awkwardness with which he had been obliged to put up the previous evening, Durcet proposed that one hour in the morning be set aside for giving them lessons, and that the friends take turns rising an hour early, the exercise period being set from nine until ten - one friend would rise at nine every morning, I say, to participate in the training. It was decided that the supervisor would be seated comfortably in a chair in the middle of the harem and that each little girl, led forth and guided by Duclos, the best frigger in the castle, would demonstrate upon the friend, would direct the little girl's hand, her motion, would explain the intricacies of tempo, how much and how little speed was required and how that depended on the patient's condition, would also explain what attitudes and postures were most conducive to the operation's success; furthermore, punishments were fixed for her who at the end of a fortnight, despite the lessons, should fail of perfect proficiency in this art. It was emphasized to the little girls that, pursuant to the good ecclesiastic's doctrines, the glans was to be kept uncovered at all times, and that the hand not in action was meanwhile continually to be employed exciting the adjacent areas, this in keeping with the particular fancy of the patient.

The financier's proposal pleased everyone; Duclos was informed, she accepted her appointment, and that same day she set up a frigging dummy upon which, in their spare time, the little girls could exercise their wrists and maintain the necessary degrees of agility and suppleness. Hercule was given the same instructorship in the boys' chamber; they being, as always, more skilled in this technique than the girls, because in the case of boys it is merely a question of doing for others what they do unto themselves, a week was ample time to turn them into the most delicious corps of friggers you could ever hope to meet with. On this particular morning, not one of them was found at fault, and Narcisse's behavior of the previous day having brought about the refusal of all permissions, the chapel was empty save for Duclos, a pair of fuckers, Julie, Thérèse, Cupidon, and Zelmire. Curval was stiff as a ramrod, Adonis had inspired an astonishingly high temperature in him when, that morning, he had visited the boys, and it was generally thought he would erupt while watching Thérèse and the two fuckers manage their affairs; but he kept a grip upon himself.

The midday meal was the usual affair, but the Président, having drunk a singular amount and frolicked about even more while eating, became inflamed all over again when coffee was served by Augustine and Michette, Zélamir and Cupidon, directed by old Fanchon, whom out of whimsy they had commanded to be as naked as the children. From this contrast Curval's new lubricious furor was born, and he gave himself over to some choice extravagances at the expense of Zélamir and the duenna; this riotous conduct finally cost him his fuck.

The Duc, pike aloft, closed in upon Augustine; he brayed, he swore, he waxed unreasonable, and the poor little thing, all atremble, retreated like a dove before the bird of prey ready to pounce upon it. He limited himself, however, to a few libertine kisses, and was content to give her an introductory lesson in advance of the ones she was to begin the following morning. The two others, less animated, having already started their naps, our two champions imitated them, and the quartet did not wake until six o'clock, the hour when the storytelling began in the throne room.

All the previous day's quatrains had been altered with respect to both subjects and dress, and our friends had these couch companions: the Duc shared his niche with Aline, the Bishop's daughter and consequently his own niece; beside the Bishop lay his sister-in-law, Constance, the Duc's wife and Durcet's daughter; Durcet was with Julie, the Duc's daughter, the Président's wife; that he might be roused from sleep and roused to more, Curval had with him Adelaide, Durcet's wife, one of the creatures in this world it gave him the greatest pleasure to tease because of her virtue and her piety. He opened up with a few scurrile jests and low pranks, and having ordered her throughout the séance to maintain a posture that sorted well with his tastes, but which the poor woman found very tiresome to maintain, he threatened her with all his anger might produce were she to budge or give him a moment's inconvenience. Everything being ready, Duclos ascended the platform and resumed her narration in this wise:

Three days having elapsed since my mother had appeared at the house, her husband, far more uneasy about his belongings and his money than about her, took it into his head to enter her room, where it was their custom to hide their most precious possessions; and what was his astonishment when, instead of what he was seeking, he found nothing but a note, written by my mother, advising him to make the best of his loss because, having decided to leave him forever, and having no money of her own, she had been forced to take all she had been able to make off with. As for the rest, he was to blame himself and his hard use of her for her departure and for her having left him with two daughters who were, however, certainly worth as much as and possibly more than what she had removed. But the old gaffer was far from judging equal what now he had and what he had just lost, and the dismissal he graciously gave us, together with the request we not even sleep in the house that night, was convincing evidence some discrepancy existed between his way of reckoning and my mother's.

Not much afflicted by a compliment which gave us full liberty to launch forth unimpeded into the little mode of life that was beginning to please us so much, my sister and I thought only to collect our few belongings and to bid as swift a farewell to our dear stepfather as he had seen fit to bid us. Without the loss of a minute, we withdrew, and while waiting to decide how best to come to grips with our new destinies, we took lodgings in a small room in the neighborhood. Our first thoughts turned to what might be our mother's fate and whereabouts; we had not the least doubt but that she had gone to the monastery, having decided to live secretly with some father, or that she was being kept somewhere in the vicinity, and this was the opinion we held, without being unduly concerned, when a friar from the monastery brought us a note that bore out our conjectures. The substance of the note was that we would be very well advised, immediately night had fallen, to come to the monastery and speak to the Father Superior, who was the note's author; he would wait for us in the church until ten o'clock and would lead us to the place presently occupied by our mother, whose actual happiness and peace he would gladly have us share. He very energetically urged us not to fail to come, and above all to conceal our movements with all possible care; for it was essential our stepfather know nothing of what was being done in behalf of both our mother and ourselves. My sister, fifteen years old at the time and hence more clever and more reasonable than I, who was but nine, after having dismissed the bearer of the letter and given him the reply that she would ponder its contents, admitted she found all these maneuvers very peculiar indeed.

"Francon," says she, "let's not go. There's something wrong with it. If this were an honest proposal, why wouldn't Mother have either added a few words or made some kind of sign. Father Adrien, her best friend, left there almost three years ago, and since then she's only dropped in at the monastery while passing by, and hasn't had any other regular intrigue there. What would have led her to choose this place for hiding? The Father Superior isn't her lover and never has been. I know, it's true she has amused him two or three times, but he's not the man to lose his head over a woman for that slender reason: he's even more inconstant and brutal to women once his caprice is satisfied. And so why would he have taken such an interest in our mother? There's something queer about it, I tell you. I never liked that old Superior; he's wicked and harsh, and he's a brute. Once he got me into his room, there were three more of them there, and after what happened to me then I swore I'd never set foot in the place again. If you take my advice, you'll leave all those nasty monks alone. There's no reason why I shouldn't tell you so now, Francon, I have an acquaintance, a good friend, I dare say; her name is Madame Guérin, I've been going to her place for the past two years, and in all that time not one week has gone by without her arranging something nice for me. But none of those six-penny fucks like the ones at the monastery; I get at least three crowns from every one. Here, there's proof of it," my sister continued, showing me a purse containing more than ten louis, "you can see I'm able to make my own way in the world. Well, my advice to you is to do what I do. Guérin will take you on, I'm sure of it, she got a glimpse of you a week ago when she came to fetch me for a party, and she told me to make you a proposal, and she said that, young as you are, she'd always find some way of placing you. Do like me, I tell you, and we'll be well off in no time. Now, that's all I've got to say to you; I'll pay your expenses for tonight, but from then on don't count on me, little sister. Each for himself in this world. That's what I say. I've earned that money with my body and my fingers, do the same yourself. And if you have any qualms, go talk it over with the devil, but don't come looking for me; well, I've told what I think, and I'll tell you now that I'd sooner stick my tongue two feet out than give you even a glass of water for nothing. As for Mother, I don't care what's happened to her, as a matter of fact, even if it's the worst I'm perfectly delighted, and all I hope is that the whore is far enough away so I'll never see her again for the rest of my life. I know all the things she did to prevent me from getting anywhere in the trade, and all the while she was giving me that fine advice, the bitch was doing things three times worse. So, may the devil take her and above all not bring her back, that's all I care."

Not having, to tell you the truth, a heart more tender, nor a soul much more generous than my sister's, it was in all good faith I echoed the invectives wherewith she pilloried that excellent mother, and thanking my sister for the helpful words she promised to speak in my behalf, I in my turn promised to follow her to this woman's house and, once I had been adopted, to put an end to my reliance on her. As for refusing to go to the monastery, we were fully agreed.

"If indeed she is happy, so much the better for her," I commented, "and in that case we can look out for our own welfare without having to go and submit to the same fate. And if it is a trap they're setting for us, we've got to avoid it."

Whereupon my sister embraced me.

"Splendid," said she, "I see you're a good girl. Don't worry, we're going to make a fortune. I'm pretty, so are you; we'll earn as much as we want, my chit, but don't become attached to anyone, remember that. One today, another tomorrow, you've got to be a whore, a whore in body and soul. As for myself," she went on, "I'm one now, such as you see me, and there isn't any confessional, or priest, or counsel, or threat that could ruin things for me. By Jesus, I'd go show my ass on the sidewalk as calmly and coolly as I'd drink a glass of wine. Imitate me, Francon, be amenable and you can get anything out of men; the trade's a little hard in the beginning, but you'll get along and things get better. So many men, so many tastes. At first you've got to expect it, one of them wants one thing, another wants something else. But that doesn't matter, you're there to please and give them service; the customer is always right. It doesn't take long, and then the money's in your pocket."

I admit I was amazed to hear such wild remarks from a girl so young, who had always seemed to me so decent. But as my heart beat in harmony with the spirits of what she said, I let her know at once that I was not only disposed to duplicate all her actions, but even prepared to go a great deal further if necessary. Delighted with me, she fell to embracing me again, and as it was growing late, we sent out for a chicken and some good wine and supped and slept together, having decided to present ourselves the very next morning at the establishment of Madame Guérin and to ask her to include us amongst her pensionnaires.

It was during that supper my sister taught me all I still did not know about libertinage. She showed herself naked to me, and I can warrant that she was one of the prettiest creatures there was in Paris at the time: the fairest of skin, the most agreeable plumpness, yet the most supple and intriguing figure, the loveliest blue eyes, and all the rest correspondingly fine. I also learned for how long Guérin had been promoting her interests, and with what great pleasure she procured her clients who, never tired of her, asked for her constantly. No sooner were we in bed than it occurred to us we had managed very badly in failing to give the Father Superior a reply, for our negligence might annoy him, and while we remained in this quarter of town it was important to humor him at least. But what was to be done? Eleven o'clock had struck; we resolved to let things take their course.

The adventure probably meant a great deal to the Superior, we supposed, and hence it was not difficult to surmise that he was laboring more in his own behalf than in that of the alleged happiness he had mentioned in his communication; at any rate, midnight had just sounded when we heard a soft knocking at our door. It was the Superior himself; he had been waiting for us, said he, since two in the afternoon, we should at least have given him a response, and, seating himself at our bedside, he informed us that our mother had decided to spend the rest of her days in a little secret apartment they had at the monastery and in which she was having the world's most cheerful time, improved by the company of all the house's bigwigs who would drop in to spend half the day with her and with another young woman, our mother's companion; it was simply up to us to come and increase the number, but, in that we were a little too young to stay on permanently, he would only contract us to a three-year's stint, at the end of which he swore we would be granted our freedom and a thousand crowns apiece; he added that he had been charged by our mother to assure us that we would be doing her a great kindness were we to come to share her solitude.

"Father," my sister said most imprudently, "we thank you for your proposal. But at our age we have no inclination to have ourselves locked up in a cloister in order to be whores for priests, we've had enough of that already."

The Superior renewed his arguments, he spoke with a heat and energy which illustrated his powerful desire to have the thing succeed; finally observing that it was destined to fail, he hurled himself almost in a fury upon my sister.

"Very well, little whore," he cried, "at least satisfy me once again before I take my leave."

And unbuttoning his breeches, he got astride her; she offered no resistance, persuaded that by allowing him to have his way she'd be rid of him all the sooner. And the smutty fellow, pinning her between his knees, began to brandish and then to abuse a tough and rather stout engine, advancing it to within a quarter of an inch of my sister's face.

"Pretty face," he gasped, "pretty little whore's face, how I'll soak it in my fuck, by sweet Jesus!"

And therewith the sluices opened, the sperm flew out, and the entirety of my sister's face, especially her nose and mouth, were covered with evidence of our visitor's libertinage, whose passion might not have been so cheaply satisfied had his design in coming to us met with success. More complacent now, the man of God's only thoughts were of escape; after having flung a crown upon the table and relit his lantern:

"You little fools, you are little tramps," he told us. "You are ruining your chances in this world; may Heaven punish your folly by causing you to fall on evil days, and may I have the pleasure of seeing you in misery; that would be my revenge, that is what I wish you."

My sister, busy wiping her face, paid him back his stupidities in kind, and, our door shutting behind the Superior, we spent the remainder of the night in peace.

"You've just seen one of his favorite stunts," said my sister. "He's mad about discharging in girls' faces. If he only confined himself to that... but the scoundrel has a good many other eccentricities, and some of them are so dangerous that I do indeed fear..."

But my sister was sleepy, she dozed off without completing her sentence, and the morrow bringing fresh adventures with it, we gave no more thought to that one.

We were up early; having prettied ourselves as much as possible, we set out for Madame Guérin's. That heroine lived in the rue Soli, in a very neat ground-floor apartment she shared with six tall young ladies between the ages of sixteen and twenty-two, all in splendid health, all very pretty. But, Messieurs, you will be so kind as to allow me to postpone giving their descriptions until the proper moment in my story arrives. Delighted by the project which brought my sister to her for a long stay, Madame Guérin greeted us cordially and with the greatest pleasure showed us our rooms.

"Young as you may find this child to be," my sister said as she introduced me, "she will serve you well, I guarantee it. She is mild-tempered, thoughtful, has a very good character, and the soul of a thoroughgoing whore. You must have a number of old lechers amongst your acquaintances who are fond of children; well this is just what they're looking for... put her to work."

Turning in my direction, Guérin asked me if I was willing to undertake anything.

"Yes, Madame," I answered with something of an indignant air, and it pleased her, "anything provided it pays."

We were introduced to our new companions, who already knew my sister very well and our of friendship for her promised to look after me. We all sat down to dine together, and such, in a few words, Messieurs, was how I became installed in my first brothel.

I was not to remain long unemployed; that same evening, an old businessman arrived wrapped up in a cloak; Guérin selected him for my first customer and arranged the match.

"Ah, this time," said she to the old libertine, leading me forth, "if it's still hairless you like them, Monsieur Duclos, you'll be delighted with the article, or your money back. Not a hair on her body."

"Indeed," said the old original, peering down at me, "it looks like a child, yes indeed. How old are you, little one?"

"Nine, Monsieur."

"Nine years old! ... Well, well! that's how I like them, Madame Guérin, that's how I like them, you know. I'd take them even younger if you had any around. Why, bless my soul, they're ready as soon as they're weaned."

And laughing good-naturedly at his remarks, Guérin withdrew, leaving us alone together. Then the old libertine came up and kissed me upon the mouth two or three times. With one of his hands guiding mine, he had me pull from his fly a little device that could not have been more limp; continuing to act more or less in silence, he untied my skirts, lay me upon the couch with my blouse raised high upon my chest, mounted astride my thighs which he had separated as far as possible; with one hand he pried open my little cunt while the other put all his strength into manipulating his meager machine. "Ah, pretty little bird," he said as he agitated himself and emitted sighs of pleasure, "ah, how I'd tame you if I were still able to, but I can't anymore. There's no remedy for it, in four year's time this bugger of a prick will have ceased to get stiff. Open up, open up, my dearest, spread your legs." And finally after fifteen minutes of struggle, I observed my man to sigh and pant with greater energy. A few oaths lent strength to his expression, and I felt the area surrounding my cunt inundated with the hot, scummy seed which the rascal, unable to shoot it inside, was attempting to tamp down with his fingertips.

He had no sooner done so than he was gone like a flash of lightning, and I was still cleaning myself when my gallant passed out on the door and into the street. And so it was I came, Messieurs, to be named Duclos; the tradition in this house was for each girl to adopt the name of her firstcomer. I obeyed the custom.

"One moment there," said the Duc. "I delayed interrupting you until you came to a pause; you are at one now. Would you provide further information upon two matters: first, have you ever had any news of your mother, have you ever discovered what became of her? Secondly, was there any cause for the antipathy you and your sister had for her, or would you say these feelings were naturally inculcate in you both? This relates to the problem of the human heart, and 'tis upon that we are concentrating our major efforts."

"My Lord," Duclos replied, "neither my sister nor I have ever heard the slightest word from that woman."

"Excellent," said the Duc, "in that case it's all very clear, wouldn't you say so, Durcet?"

"Incontestably," answered the banker. "Not a shadow of a doubt, and you are very fortunate you did not put your foot in that one. Neither of you would ever have got out."

"'Tis incredible," Curval commented, "what headway that mania has made with public."

"Why, no; after all, there's nothing more delicious," the Bishop replied.

"And the second point?" asked the Duc, addressing the storyteller.

"As for the second point, my Lord, that is to say, as for the reason for our antipathy, I'm afraid I should be hard pressed to account for it, but it was so violent in our two hearts that we both made the avowal that we would in all probability and very easily have poisoned her had we not managed, as it turned out, to be rid of her by other means. Our aversion had reached the ultimate degree of intensity, and as nothing overt occurred to give rise to it, I should judge it most likely that this sentiment was inspired in us by Nature."

"What doubt of it can there be?" said the Duc. "It happens every day that she implants the most violent inclination to commit what mortals call crimes, and had you poisoned her twenty times over, this act would never have been anything but the result of the penchant for crime Nature put in you, a penchant she wishes to draw your attention by endowing you with such a powerful hostility. It is madness to suppose one owes something to one's mother. And upon what, then, would gratitude be based? is one to be thankful that she discharged when someone once fucked her? That would suffice, to be sure. As for myself, I see therein naught but grounds for hatred and scorn. Does that mother of ours give us happiness in giving us life? ...Hardly. She casts us into a world beset with dangers, and once in it, 'tis for us to manage as best we can. I distinctly recall that, long ago, I had a mother who aroused in me much the same sentiments Duclos felt for hers: I abhorred her. As soon as I was in a position to do so, I dispatched her into the next world; may she roast there; never in my life have I tasted a keener delight than the one I knew when she closed her eyes for the last time."

At this point dreadful sobs were heard to come from one of the quatrains. It proved to be the Duc's; upon closer examination it was discovered that young Sophie had burst into tears. Provided with a heart unlike those villains', their conversation had brought to mind the cherished memory of her who had given her life, and who had perished in an effort to protect her while she was being abducted; this cruel vision offered itself to her tender imagination, a flood of tears ensued.

"Ah, by God, now!" said the Duc, "that's splendid. It's for mama you're crying, is it, my little snotface? Come here, come along, let me comfort you."

And the libertine, warmed by what had been happening, by these words of his, and by the effects they produced, displayed a thunderous prick which was apparently speeding toward a discharge. Marie, the quatrain's duenna, led the child forward all the same. Her tears flowed abundantly down her cheeks, the novice's dress she was wearing that day seemed to lend yet more charm to the sorrow which embellished herlooks: it was impossible for a creature to be lovelier.

"By the Holy Bugger," quoth the Duc, springing up like one gone out of his mind, "what a pretty mouthful we have here. I'm going to do what Duclos has just described... smear some fuck on her cunt... Undress her."

And everyone silently awaited the issue of this little skirmish.

"Oh! my Lord, my Lord!" cried Sophie, casting herself at the Duc's feet, "at least respect my sorrow, I groan for my mother's fate, she was dear to me, she died defending me, I shall never see her again. Have pity upon my tears, grant me this one evening of respite."

"Why, fuck my eyes!" the Duc exclaimed, fondling his heaventhreatening prick, "I'd never have believed this scene could be so voluptuous. Off with her clothes, I tell you to take them off," he roared at Marie, "she should already be naked."

And Aline, lying upon the Duc's couch, shed warm tears, so did Adelaide, who was heard to utter a moan in Curval's alcove; the latter, in no wise partaking of that lovely creature's grief, violently scolded his playmate for having shifted from the position he had commanded her to keep, and, that done, turned an appreciative gaze upon the delicious scene whose outcome interested him exceedingly.

Sophie's clothes are removed without the faintest regard for her feelings, she is placed in the posture Duclos has just described, the Duc announces that he is about to discharge. But how is the thing to be done? What Duclos has just related had been performed by a man virtually incapable of an erection, and he had been able to direct his flabby prick's discharge wherever he wished. Such was not the case here: the threatful head of the Duc's engine had not the least inclination to lower the awful stare whereby it seemed bent on cowing heaven; it appeared necessary, so to speak, to place the child on high. No one knew what to do, and the more obstacles were encountered, the more the enraged Duc fumed and blasphemed. Desgranges finally came to the rescue; nothing that pertained to libertinage was unknown to that sage old dame. She caught up the child and set her so skillfully upon her knees that, whatever the stance the Duc might adopt, the end of his prick was sure to nudge her vagina. Two servants came up to hold

Sophie's legs, and had it been her deflowering hour, never might she have displayed the merchandise to better advantage. But there was yet more to attend to: a clever hand was needed to cause the torrent to leap its banks and to direct the flood fairly to its destination. Blangis had no desire to entrust so important a matter to an untutored child.

"Take Julie," Durcet suggested, "she'll suit you; she's beginning to frig like an angel."

"Bah," muttered the Duc, "I know the clumsy bitch. And she knows her father. No, she'd be panic-stricken, she'd fumble it."

"Upon my soul, I do recommend a boy for the job," said Curval; "why not Hercule? His wrist is like a whip."

"I won't have anyone but Duclos," the Duc answered, "she's the best of our friggers, allow her to quit her post for a moment or two."

Duclos steps forward, beaming with pride to have been accorded so distinguished a preference. She rolls her sleeve to the elbow and grasps the nobleman's enormous instrument, she sets to rattling that spear, keeps the foreskin snapped broadly back, she moves it with such art, she agitates it by means of strokes so swift and simultaneously so perfectly attuned to the state she observes her patient to be in, that the bomb finally explodes upon the very hole it is to cover, inundating it. The Duc shrieks, swears, storms. Duclos is disconcerted not in the least, she gauges her movements by the degree of pleasure they produce. Antinoüs, properly situated for this function, delicately works the sperm into the vagina as proportionally it flows from the spigot, and the Duc, vanquished by the most delicious sensations, dying from joy, sees grow gradually slack, between his frigger's fingers, that high-spirited, mettlesome member whose ardor has just been so powerfully communicated to the rest of himself. He flings himself back upon his sofa, Duclos strides back to her throne, the child wipes herself, is consoled, and regains her quatrain, and the recital continues, leaving the spectators convinced of a truth wherewith, I believe, they have already been penetrated for a long time: that the idea of crime is able always to ignite the senses and lead us to lubricity.

I was greatly surprised, said Duclos, taking up the thread of her narrative, to see all my companions laugh when I returned, and ask me if I had wiped myself, and say a thousand other things which proved they knew perfectly well what had just happened. I was not long left in my quandary; leading me into a room adjacent to the one in which the parties ordinarily took place and in which a short while before I had been at work, my sister showed me a hole to see everything that transpired there. She told me that the young ladies found it diverting to watch what men did to their colleagues; I could come and do some spying whenever I wished, provided there was not someone already at the hole. For it not infrequently occurred, said she, that this respectable hole had a part in mysteries which would be disclosed to me later on. The week was not out before I took advantage of my opportunities: one morning someone came and asked for a girl named Rosalie, one of the most lovely blondes it were possible to behold; I was curious to see what was to be done to her. I hid myself and witnessed the following scene.

The man with whom she had to cope was no older than twenty-six or thirty. Immediately she entered, he had her sit down on a very high stool used especially for this ceremony. As soon as she was settled, he removed all her combs and hairpins and down all the way to the floor floated in a cloud the superb golden hair that adorned Rosalie's head. He drew a comb from his pocket, combed her hair, took handfuls of it, tangled it, kissed it, everything he did was accompanied by remarks praising the beauty of that hair in which he took such a keen and exclusive interest. At last, from out of his trousers he pulled a smart little prick, already quite stiff, and he promptly enveloped it in his Dulcinea's hair; once well wrapped, he began to fondle his dart and discharged, at the same time passing his other arm around Rosalie's neck and applying his lips to her mouth. He extricated his defunct engine, I saw that my companion's hair was matted with glistening fuck; she cleaned it, put it up again, and our lovers separated.

A month later, someone came in quest of my sister; this personage, I was told by the others, merited observing, for he had a most baroque specialty. He was a man of about fifty. Straightway he entered, without any preamble, without a caress, he exhibited his behind to my sister, who knew her part to perfection; he has her take her place on the bed, he backs toward her, she seizes that flaccid and wrinkled old ass, drives her five fingers into the orifice, and begins to struggle and battle and worry it with such force the bed creaks. Be that as it may, without bringing anything else to light, our man wriggles, twitches, follows my sister's movements, lends himself luxuriously to this fearful abuse, cries he is coming, comes, and affirms this is the greatest of all pleasures. He had indeed taken a furious buffeting, my sister was in a sweat; but what mild stuff! what lack of imagination!

Although the gentleman with whom I had to do not long afterward was hardly more difficult to satisfy, he at least seemed more voluptuous and, in my view, his mania had more of the libertine tincture. He was a heavy-set man of about forty-five, short, sturdy, but energetic and hearty. Never having met a person with his predilection, my first act, as soon as we were alone together, was to hoist my skirts to the navel: a dog confronted by a hickory stick could not have looked more unhappy: "Good God, dearie, let's not have any of your cunt, please put it away." So saying, he snatched down my skirts even more hastily than I had raised them. "These poor little whores," he mumbled, screwing up his face in a pout, "never have anything but cunts to show you. I may not be able to discharge this evening, thanks to that exhibition... unless I can succeed in getting the accursed image of that cunt out of my head." Whereupon he turned me about and methodically raised my petticoats from behind. Guiding me himself, and keeping my skirts raised at all times, he moved me about in order to observe how my buttocks bounced when I walked, and then he had me approach the bed, upon which he had me lie belly down. Next, with the most scrupulous attention he examined my ass, with one hand screening his eyes to avoid any glimpse of my cunt whereof, it appeared, he was in mortal terror. At last, having warned me to do all in my power to conceal that unworthy (I employ his expression) part from his sight, he brought both hands to bear on my ass and manipulated it lewdly and at length: he opened it, he closed it again, spread and squeezed it, sometimes he applied his mouth to it, and once or twice I even felt him press his lips to the hole; but he still had not touched himself, nothing could be discerned. None the less, he must have felt hidden pressures mount and readied himself for the denouement of his little ritual. "Lie down," he told me, tossing a few pillows on the floor, "yes, down there, that's it, that will do... with your legs well spread, the ass a shade higher, and the hole stretched as wide open as it will go; come now, wider still," he continued, noticing my docility. And then, taking a stool and placing it between my legs, he sat down in such a way that his prick, which he now dragged from his breeches and began to vibrate, was as it were at a level with the hole upon which he was to offer a libation. His movements now grew more rapid, with one hand he frigged himself, with the other he separated my buttocks, and a few adulatory commendations seasoned with a quantity of hard language constituted his speech. "Ah, bugger the Almighty, here 'tis, the lovely ass," he cried, "the sweet little hole, and how I'm going to wet it." He kept his word. I felt myself soaked; his ecstasy seemed to annihilate the libertine. Ah, how true it is that the homage rendered at this temple is always more ardent than the incense which is burned at the other; and my worshipper left after promising to return to see me again, for he averred I satisfied his desires very well. He did indeed come back the next day, but was untrue to me, his inconstancy led him to my sister's asshole; I observed them, saw everything: every aspect of the rite was absolutely the same, and my sister lent herself to it with the same good will.

"Did your sister have a handsome ass?" Durcet inquired.

"You may judge by one fact, my Lord," Duclos replied. "A famous painter commissioned to do a Venus with a magnificent behind asked her the following year to be his model after having, he said, consulted every procuress in Paris without finding anything to equal her."

"Well now, since she was fifteen and since we have a few girls of the same age here, compare her ass," the financier continued, "with some of the asses you see in this room."

Duclos' eyes came to rest upon Zelmire, and she told Durcet that it would be impossible, not only with respect to the ass, but even with respect to the face, to find anyone who bore a closer resemblance to her sister.

"In that case," said Durcet, "come here, Zelmire, present your cheeks."

She did indeed belong to his quatrain; the charming girl approached all atremble. She was placed at the foot of the couch, made to lie upon her belly, her rump was raised by means of cushions, the little hole was in plain sight. The lecher's prick begins to rise, he falls to kissing and fondling what lies under his nose. He orders Julie to frig him, she sets to work, his hands stray hither and yon, snatching at divers objects, lust heats his brain, under Julie's voluptuous treatment his little prick looks as if it were about to stiffen, the lecher swears, the fuck flows, and the bell sounds for dinner.

As the same profusion reigned at every meal, to have described one is to have described them all; but as almost everyone had discharged, there was a general need to recuperate strength, and therefore the friends drank a great deal at this supper. Zelmire, to whom they gave the sobriquet of Duclos' sister, was to an uncommon degree regaled during the subsequent orgies, and everyone simply had to kiss her ass. The Bishop left a puddle of fuck thereon, the three others restiffened over it, and they went to bed as they had the night before, that is to say, each with the wife he had had upon his couch, and with one of the four fuckers who had not appeared since the midday meal.

The Third Day

The Duc was abroad at nine o'clock. 'Twas he who volunteered to be the first to lend a hand in the lessons Duclos was to administer to the little girls. He installed himself in an armchair and for one long hour submitted to various fondlings, masturbations, pollutions, and to a wide variety of tricks performed by each of those little ones who, throughout it all, were guided and supervised by their mistress; and as may be readily imagined, his spirited temperament was furiously aroused by the ceremony. He was obliged to make unbelievable efforts to preserve his fuck from loss, but, more or less in control of himself, he managed to contain himself and returned to his friends in triumph, boasting that he'd just weathered an assault he defied any one of them to beat off as phlegmatically. That brought on considerable wagering, the stakes were high, a fine of fifty louis was ultimately imposed upon whoever discharged during the lessons.

Instead of taking breakfast and conducting searches, this morning was employed in drawing up a program for the seventeen orgies planned for the end of each week, in this way definitively to fix the dates of the deflowerings now that, after having become better acquainted with the subjects than they had been previously, they were able to pass legislation. In that this timetable in the most decisive manner regulated all the operations to be executed during the campaign, we have deemed it necessary to provide the reader with a copy: it seems to us that, once he has perused it and familiarized himself with the subjects' several destinies, he will be able to take a keener interest in their individual persons.

Schedule of Works to Be Accomplished During the Remainder of the Party

On the 7th of November, at which time the first week will have drawn a close, Messieurs shall proceed in the morning to the marriage of Michette and Giton, and those two wedded individuals, whose age forbids them from conjoining, as is true in the cases of three following couples, shall be separated on their marriage night, for to closet them together would be as futile as this ridiculous ceremony which will serve only to create diversion during the day. That same evening, punishments which have accumulated and been entered on the list kept by the month's presiding officer shall be meted out.

On the 14th, Messieurs shall in the same way effect the marriage of Narcisse and Hébé, with the same clauses as those cited above.

On the 21st, in the same way, Colombe and Zélamir shall be married.

On the 28th, Cupidon and Rosette.

On the 4th of December, Champville's narrations having prepared the way for the following enterprises, the Duc shall deflower Fanny.

On the 5th, the said Fanny shall be wedded to Hyacinthe who, in the presence of the company assembled, shall take his pleasure with his young wife. In such will consist the fifth week's festival, and the corrections shall take place in the evening as usual, because the marriages shall be celebrated in the morning.

On the 8th, Curval shall deflower Michette.

On the 11th, the Duc shall deflower Sophie.

On the 12th, to celebrate the sixth week's festival, Sophie shall be married to Céladon, and the clauses cited for the above-mentioned marriage shall be made to apply to this one; this shall not be repeated for those to follow.

On the 15th, Curval shall deflower Hébé.

On the 18th, the Duc shall deflower Zelmire, and on the 19th, in order to celebrate the seventh week's festival, Adonis shall marry Zelmire.

On the 20th, Curval shall deflower Colombe.

On the 25th, Christmas Day, the Duc shall deflower Augustine, and on the 26th, for the eighth week's festival, Zéphyr shall marry Augustine.

On the 29th, Curval shall deflower Rosette, and all the foregoing arrangements have been made to insure that Curval, less well membered than the Duc, be provided with more youthful girls.

On the 1st of January, the first day of the year and one upon which Martaine's newly begun narration will influence imaginations to consider new pleasures, the sodomistic deflorations shall be inaugurated, and shall proceed in the following order:

On the 1st of January, the Duc shall sound Hébé's ass.

On the 2nd, in celebration of the ninth week, Hébé, having been plumbed fore by Curval, from behind by the Duc, shall be turned over to Hercule, who, before the company assembled, shall employ her for purposes to be specified upon the occasion.

On the 4th, Curval shall embugger Zélamir.

On the 6th, the Duc shall embugger Michette; on the 9th, in celebration of the tenth week's festival, the said Michette, who will have been deflowered fore by Curval, and whose ass will have been tried by the Duc, shall be turned over to Bum-Cleaver, that he may enjoy her, etc., etc.

On the 11th, the Bishop shall sodomize Cupidon.

On the 13th, Curval shall sodomize Zelmire.

On the 15th, the Bishop shall sodomize Colombe.

On the 16th, for the eleventh week's festival, Colombe, whose cunt will have been deflowered by Curval, her ass by the Bishop, shall be turned over to Antinoüs, who shall enjoy her, etc.

On the 17th, the Duc shall embugger Giton.

On the 19th, Curval shall embugger Sophie.

On the 21st, the Bishop shall embugger Narcisse.

On the 22nd, the Duc shall embugger Rosette.

On the 23rd, for the twelfth week's festival, Rosette shall be turned over to Invictus.

On the 25th, Curval shall march into Augustine's behind.

On the 28th, the Bishop shall enter Fanny's.

On the 30th, for the thirteenth week's festival, the Duc shall take Hercule for his husband and Zéphyr for his wife, and the marriage shall be both accomplished and consummated before the eyes of everyone, as shall be the three others which follow.

On the 6th of February, for the fourteenth week's festival, Bum-Cleaver shall become Curval's husband, Adonis his wife.

On the 13th of February, for the fifteenth week's festival, Antinoüs shall be made husband to the Bishop, to him shall Céladon be made a wife.

On the 20th of February, for the sixteenth week's festival, Invictus shall as a husband be wedded to Durcet, Hyacinthe as a wife.

As for the festival of the seventeeth week, due to fall on the 27th of February, upon the eve of the narrations' conclusion, it shall be celebrated by sacrifices for which Messieurs reserve themselves in petto the choice of victims.

These arrangements provide for the obliteration of all maidenheads by the 30th of January, with the exception of those of the four young boys whom Messieurs are to marry as wives, and whom they are eager to preserve intact until their weddings, in order that their amusement be made to last until the end of the party.

As the objects are progressively depucelated, they shall the place of the wives upon the couches at storytelling time, and, at nighttime, they shall lie with Messieurs, alternately, and at Messieurs' choice, together with the last four fairies Messieurs will take to themselves as wives during the final month.

From the moment a girl or a depucelated boy shall have replaced a wife upon the couch, the said wife shall be repudiated. From this moment onward, she shall be in general discredit, and shall be ranked lower than the servants.

With regard to Hébé, aged twelve, Michette, aged twelve, Colombe, aged thirteen, and Rosette, aged thirteen, as progressively they are surrendered to the fuckers and exercised by the latter, they too shall fall into discredit, shall henceforth be used for none but harsh and brutal purposes, shall rank with the repudiated wives, and shall be treated with utmost rigor. And as of the 24th of January, all four of them will have descended to the same inferior level.

This schedule affirms that unto the Duc shall fall nine celages: the first encuntments of Fanny, Sophie, Zelmire, Augustine, the original embuggeries of Hébé, Michette, Giton, Rosette, and Zéphyr.

Unto Curval shall fall the cunt-pucelages of Michette, Hébé, Colombe, Rosette, the ass-pucelages of Zélamir, Zelmire, Sophie, Augustine, and Adonis, being in all nine deflorations.

Unto Durcet, who does not fuck at all, is reserved the ass-pucelage of Hyacinthe, who in the capacity of a wife shall be wedded to him.

And unto the Bishop, who fucks naught but asses, are reserved the sodomistical depucelations of Cupidon, of Colombe, of Narcisse, of Fanny, and of Céladon.

The entire day having been spent preparing this program and chatting about it, and no one having been found at fault, all went uneventfully ahead, the storytelling hour arrived; everyone took his place, the illustrious Duclos mounted the stage. She proceeded in this wise:

A young man, whose mania, although not in my opinion very libertine, is none the less curious enough, appeared at Madame Guérin's shortly after the adventure I spoke of yesterday. He had to have a young and healthy wet nurse; he suckled the good woman's teat and leaked his seed over her thighs while gorging himself on her milk. His prick struck me as paltry and mean, all his person rather puny, and his discharge was as mild as his proceedings were benign.

Another one appeared in the same room the next day; his mania will doubtless prove more entertaining to you. He insisted upon having his woman enveloped in a sheet so that her face and breast would be entirely hidden from him, the single part of her body he wanted to see, and which had to be of the highest degree of excellence, was her ass, all the rest meant nothing to him, and he assured Madame Guérin that a glimpse of anything else would anger him exceedingly. Guérin had a woman brought in from the outside: she was ugly to the point of bitterness and almost fifty years old, but her buttocks were molded like those of Venus, nothing more beautiful could ever bewitch one's gaze.

I was eager to see this operation; the old duenna, well wrapped up, was told at once to lie belly down on the edge of the bed. Our libertine, a man of about thirty and who seemed to me a gentleman of the cloth, lifts her skirts above her loins, is thrilled by what greets his eyes and flatters his tastes. He touches, he spreads this superb breech, showers passionate kisses upon it, and, his imagination fired by what he supposes rather than by what he would actually have seen had the woman been unveiled and even had she been attractive, he fancies he is holding commerce with Aphrodite herself, and at the end of a fairly brief career, his engine hardens thanks to the jerks and jolts, and unlooses a warm rain over the ensemble of the sublime ass exposed to his view. His discharge was sharp and impetuous. He was seated facing the adored idol; one of his hands opened it while with the other he polluted it, and he cried ten times in succession: "Ah, what a beautiful ass! Ah, what a delight to drown such an ass in fuck!" He rose when done, and left without indicating the least desire to find out with whom he had been dealing.

A young abbot called for my sister a short time afterward. He was youthful and handsome, but one could scarcely discern his prick, so minute and soft it was. He stretched his almost naked partner on a couch, knelt down between her thighs, supporting her buttocks with both hands, with one of them tickling the pretty little hole in her behind. Meanwhile, he conveyed his mouth to my sister's cunt. He tickled its clitoris with his tongue, and managed so cunningly, so harmoniously synchronized the two activities, that within the space of three minutes he had plunged her into a delirium; I saw her head toss about, her eyes begin to roll, and heard the rascal cry: "Ah, my dear Reverend Father, you're slaying me with pleasure!"

The abbot's custom was simply to swallow the liquid his libertine dexterity made flow; and this he did not now fail to do, shaking himself the while, agitating himself as he bore down upon my sister: I saw him spatter indubitable evidence of his virility upon the floor. My turn came the next day, and I believe I can assure you, Messieurs, that it was one of the sweetest operations to which in all my life I have ever been exposed: that scoundrel of an abbot had my first fruits, and it was into his mouth I shed my first fuck. More eager than my sister to give him pleasure in return for what he had caused me, I unthinkingly seized his drooping prick, and my little hand replied to what his mouth had made me feel with such delight.

The Duc could not prevent himself from interrupting at this point. To a remarkable degree excited by the pollutions he had undergone that same morning, he had an idea that this species of lubric sport executed with the fascinating Augustine, whose sparkling, roguish eyes announced the most precocious temperament, would deliver him of a charge of fuck that was stinging his balls in a dreadful way. She was a member of his quatrain, he found her likeable, she was destined to be deflowered by him, he summoned her. On this particular evening she had a kerchief tied round her head, was clad in peasant guise, and seemed charming beneath that costume. The duenna hoisted her skirts and established her in the posture Duclos had represented. The Duc first of all lay hands on her buttocks, knelt, brought a finger to the anus and lightly titillated its rim, seized up the clitoris this amiable child already had in considerable growth, and sucked it. The people of Languedoc are high-spirited, they say, and Augustine proved them right; fire leapt into her pretty eyes, she sighed and panted and moaned, her thighs rose mechanically, and the Duc was pleased to sip a gush of young fuck which in all likelihood had never flowed before.

But joy is seldom succeeded by joy. There are libertines so hardened in vice that the simpler, the more delicate and banal be the thing they do, the less effect it has upon their execrable minds. Of their number our beloved Duc was one, he swallowed that delicious child's sperm without his own contriving to flow; all present beheld the moment arrive, for no one is more illogical than a libertine, the moment appeared at hand, I say, when he would blame his unresponse upon the poor little wretch who, all a dither at having yielded to Nature, was hiding her face in her hands and struggling to get free and return to her place.

"Get me another one," thundered the Duc, casting furious glances at Augustine, "I'll suck every last one of them if that's required to lose my fuck."

Zelmire, the second girl in his quatrain, was brought to the fore, she too was the Duc's by escheat. Though equal in years to Augustine, the grief for her plight robbed her of the power to taste a pleasure which, who knows, had it not been for that, Nature might have allowed her to relish. Up rose her skirts, up above two little thighs whiter than alabaster, a chubby little mons veneris hove into view, it was upholstered by a fluffy down just beginning to appear. She is adjusted, obliged to yield, she obeys automatically, but sweat, strain, suck though he does, nothing happens to the Duc. Fifteen minutes of this and he rises in a fury, and, flinging himself into his closet with Hercule and Narcisse:

"Ah, by fuck!" he roars. "It's very clear to me that's not the game I'm hunting" - 'tis to the two little girls he alludes - "and that I'll only have a fair shot at this."

It is not known to what excesses he surrendered himself, but ere an instant had passed screams and shouts declared he had carried the day, and proved that boys are always the far more certain implements to a discharge than the most adorable girls. In the meantime, the Bishop had likewise enchambered himself with Giton, Zélamir, and Invictus, and the outbursts which accompanied his discharge having struck the assembly's ears, the two brothers, who had probably resorted to similar expedients, returned, more calmly to listen to the rest of the story our heroine took up again in these terms:

Nigh unto two years passed by during which time no one of particular interest arrived at Madame Guérin's; the gentleman who called either had tastes too ordinary to warrant description, or had tastes analogous to those I have already described; and then one day I was told to prepare myself, and above all to wash out my mouth. A heavy, thickset man of about fifty stood beside the mistress of the house.

"Well, there she is," said Madame. "She's only twelve, Monsieur, just as clean and tidy as if she'd come this morning out of her mother's belly, and you can take my word for that."

The customer inspects me, has me open my mouth, he examines my teeth, sniffs my breath, and evidently satisfied that all is in order, he goes with me into the sanctuary intended for pleasure. We sit down face to face and very near to one another. No one could be more solemn than my gallant nor more phlegmatic. He stares coldly at me, then appraises me with narrowed eyes, I have no idea where all this is leading when, finally breaking his silence, he bids me collect a mouthful of saliva. I obey, and as soon as he fancies my mouth must be full, he throws himself upon my neck, passionately puts his arm around my head, thereby immobilizing it, and gluing his lips to my mouth, he pumps, sucks, eagerly swallows all the bewitching fluid I have collected, and it seems enough to put him in an overwhelming ecstasy. He sucks my tongue into his mouth with identical fervor, and when he senses it is dry, perceives my mouth is empty, he commands me to repeat the operation. He reiterates his, then I do, then he does, and so on eight or ten times over.

He sucked up my saliva with such furious avidity it discomfited my chest and lungs. I thought that at least a few sparks of pleasure were going to climax his transports; I was mistaken. His apathy, whence he emerged only brief instants during his most intense suckings, compassed him again immediately he had drained me, and when at last I told him I could do no more, he fell to eyeing me distantly, to staring at me as he had at the beginning, then got up without a word, paid Guérin, and left.

"Ah, God's prick and balls!" cried Curval, "I'm happier than he, for I'm coming."

Everyone raised his head, everyone saw the dear Président doing to Julie, his wife, whom that day he had for couch companion, the same thing Duclos had just been relating. That this passion appealed admirably to his tastes was generally well known; Julie by and large procured him abundant pleasure in this manner, Duclos had no doubt done less well by her gallant. But that was in all likelihood his own fault; failing to appreciate what certain mouths, in certain conditions, may offer, he got nothing from Duclos', whereas the Président obtained satisfaction from Julie's.

A month later, said Duclos, who had been invited to continue, I had dealings with a sucker who assailed what one might term the same fort but from an entirely different angle. This latter was an elderly abbot who, after having previously kissed and caressed my bum for above half an hour, introduced his tongue into its hole, made it penetrate deep, dart to left and right, turn this way, turn that way, all with such surpassing art I thought I felt it drive nigh to the depths of my entrails. But this abbot of mine, much less phlegmatic, as he used one hand to spread my buttocks, used the other to frig himself very voluptuously, and as he discharged he drew my anus to his face with such violence and tickled it so lubriciously that my ecstasy coincided with his. When he was finished, he spent another moment scrutinizing my buttocks, staring at that hole he'd just reamed wider, and couldn't prevent himself from gluing his mouth to it one last time; then he hastened off, assuring me he would be back frequently, would ask for me, and that he was most content with my ass. He kept his promise, and for six months he came to visit me three or four times a week, regularly performing the same operation to which I became so thoroughly accustomed that each time he executed his little project, I all but expired with delight - an aspect of the rite about which he appeared to care very little, for, as best I could judge, he had no inclination to find out whether or no my work pleased me; that did not seem to matter to him. And indeed, who can tell? Men are extraordinary indeed; had he known of it, my pleasure might even have displeased him.

And now Durcet, whom the story had inflamed, like the old priest was moved to suck some asshole or other, but would not have a girl's. He called for Hyacinthe, who of them all pleased him the most. He placed the little chap, kissed his ass, frigged his prick and sucked it. By the nervous shuddering of his body, by the spasm which ordinarily heralded his discharge, it was thought the evil little anchovy that Aline was thumping and pulling as best she could, was finally going to disgorge its seed, but no, the financier was penurious when it came to parting with his fuck, he simply could not, or would not, stiffen. It occurs to them all that his object ought to be changed, Céladon is substituted for Hyacinthe, but all's at a standstill, not the least improvement is apparent. The opportune tolling of a bell announcing supper saves the banker's honor.

"Why," says he, laughing with his confreres, "it's not my fault, you saw I was about to win a victory; this damned supper will have to delay it. Well, by God, let's go and have a fling at the table, I'll return all the more ardent to Cupid's tourney after having been crowned by Bacchus."

The evening meal was equally succulent and gay, quite as lubricious as ever, and was followed by orgies in the course of which an abundance of little infamies were perpetrated. Many were the mouths sucked and the asses, but one of the most engaging drolleries of all was the game in which they hid the face and chest of each little girl and gambled upon recognizing her on the basis of a study of her ass. The Duc was occasionally misled, but not so the others, for they were too well accustomed to the use of the bum. The friends retired for the night, and the morrow brought further and new pleasures, and a few reflections.

The Fourth Day

Being full eager to be able to distinguish immediately which of the youngsters in either sex was, in a depucelatory sense, to belong to each of their number, the friends decided to have them wear, regardless of their costume and, in that other extreme, even when undressed, a hair ribbon, which would indicate of whom the individual child was the property. Colors were thereupon chosen: the Duc adopted pink and green: whosoever should wear a pink ribbon to the fore, would be his by the cunt; similarly, whosoever wore a green ribbon to the rear, would be his by the ass. And so Fanny, Zelmire, Sophie, and Augustine straightway affixed a pink ribbon on one side of their coiffures; Rosette, Hébé, Michette, Giton, and Zéphyr attached a green favor to their hair where it fell toward the neck, this clue attesting the rights of the Duc enjoyed to their asses.

Curval chose black for the front, yellow for the rear; thus Michette, Hébé, Colombe, and Rosette were in future constantly to wear a black ribbon forward; Sophie, Zelmire, Augustine, Zélamir, and Adonis pinned a yellow one above their nape.

Durcet identified his Hyacinthe with a lilac ribbon hanging to the rear, and the Bishop, who owned title to but five assholes to be deflowered sodomistically, ordered Cupidon, Narcisse, Céladon, Colombe, and Fanny to wear a violet one in the rear.

Never, regardless of the subject's posture, chore, or dress, were these ribbons to be neglected or improperly worn, and so it was that by this simple arrangement each friend was always able to tell at a glance what property was his, and in what way.

Curval, who had passed the night with Constance, had bitter complaints to lodge against her in the morning. It was not entirely clear what lay at the root of the trouble, nor what precisely the trouble was; so little is needed to displease a libertine. But there was more than enough to the thing to cause him to have her listed for Saturday punishment, and he was formulating charges when that lovely creature declared that she was pregnant; Curval, apart from her husband the only one whom it was possible to suspect as the agent in this affair, had effected no carnal juncture with her save at the beginning of this party, that is to say, four days previously. Our libertines were gladdened by these tidings, seeing in the event much possibility of clandestine delight, and the Duc exulted over this stroke of fortune. In any event, the declaration earned her exemption from the punishment she would otherwise have had to undergo in return for having displeased Curval. She was to be spared: they preferred to leave the fruits on the branch to ripen, a gravid woman diverted them, and what they promised themselves for later on even more lewdly entertained their perfidious imaginations. Constance was dispensed from service at table, from chastisements, and from a few other little odds and ends the accomplishment of which her state no longer rendered voluptuous to observe, but she was still obliged to appear upon the couches and until further orders to share bed of whoever wished to choose her for the night.

It was Durcet who, that morning, contributed his presence to the pollution exercises, and as his prick was extraordinarily small, he gave the pupils rather more a problem than had been posed by the Duc's massive construction. However, they fell earnestly to work. But the little banker, who had been plying a woman's trade all night long, could never bear a man's. He was adamant, intractable, and the skill of these eight charming students combined with that of their deft instructress was unable, when all was said and done, even to get him to raise his nose. He left the classroom in triumph, and as impotence always provokes that kind of mood called a teasing one in the idiom of libertinage, his inspections were astonishingly severe. Rosette amongst the girls, Zélamir amongst the boys were the victims of his thoroughness: one was not as she had been told to be - this enigma will be explained - the other, unfortunately, had rid himself of what he had been ordered to keep.

Those present at the public latrines were only seven in number: Duclos, Marie, Aline, and Fanny, two second-class fuckers, and Giton, Curval, who did considerable stiffening that day, grew very excited over Duclos. Dinner, at which his conduct and remarks were very libertine indeed, calmed him not one whit, and the coffee served by Colombe, Sophie, Zéphyr, and his dear friend Adonis, set his brain all afire. He laid hands on this selfsame Adonis, tumbled him onto a sofa, and while spewing forth oaths slid his enormous member between the lad's thighs (approaching him from behind), and as that outsized tool protruded a fair six inches beyond, he commanded Adonis vigorously to frig what emerged, and himself set to frigging the boy above the morsel of flesh upon which Adonis was spitted. Meanwhile, he presented the assembly with an ass no less filthy than broad, whose impure orifice began to exert a potent attraction upon the Duc. Seeing this ass within reach, he trained his vivacious prick on the hole while continuing to suck Zéphyr's mouth, an operation he had begun before this new idea had occurred to him.

Curval, who had not been expecting such an attack, emitted blasphemous paeans of joy. He danced with delight, spread himself wider, braced himself; at the same instant, the fresh young fuck of the charming boy he was frigging started to drip out upon the enormous head of his own aroused instrument. That warm fuck he feels wetting him, the reiterated blows of the Duc who is also beginning to discharge, it all quickens his warrior's soul, the weapon is primed, off goes the gun, floods of foamy sperm splash against Durcet's ass, for the banker has just posted himself there within easy range lest, says he, something be wasted, and Durcet's plump white buttocks are submerged beneath a spellbinding liquor he would have by far preferred as a rinse for his bowels.

Nor was the Bishop idle; he was one after the other sucking clean the divine assholes of Colombe and Sophie. But doubtless fatigued by some nocturnal exercise, he showed not one spark of life, and like all other libertines rendered unjust by caprice and disgust, he lashed out furiously against these two delicious children, blaming them for the only too well merited shortcomings of his debilitated frame. Messieurs nap for a few minutes; then 'tis story-telling time, and in they troop to listen to the amiable Duclos, who resumes her tale in the following manner:

There had been a few changes in Madame Guérin's house, said our heroine. Two very pretty girls had just found dupes who were only too willing to keep them and whom they deceived just the way we all do. To fill the gaps in the ranks, our dear mother had scouted around and set her sights upon a rue Saint-Denis tavern-keeper's daughter, thirteen years old and one of the most fetching creatures in all the wide world. But the little lady, quite as well-behaved as she was pious, was successfully resisting all enticements when Guérin, having one day employed the cleverest stratagem to lure her to her house, immediately put her in the hands of the unusual person whose mania I propose to describe next. He was an ecclesiastic of fifty-five or fifty-six, but so youthful and vigorous you'd have thought him under forty. No man in Europe had such a singular talent for drawing young girls into vice, and as it was his one art, developed to a sublime degree, he had turned it into his one and only pleasure. The whole of his fleshy delight consisted in extirpating childhood prejudices and unnatural terrors, in cultivating scorn for virtue, in decking vice in the most dazzling colors. He neglected nothing: seductive images, flattering promises, delicious examples, he would press everything into service, everything would be brilliantly manipulated, his artistry being faultlessly attuned to the child's age and cast of mind, and never did he miss the mark. Granted a mere two hours of conversation, he was sure to make a whore of the best-behaved and most reasonable little girl; for thirty years he had been conducting his missionary labors in Paris, and, he had once assured Madame Guérin, who counted herself one of his best friends, he had to his credit more than ten thousand girls whom he had personally seduced and plunged into libertinage. He rendered similar services to at least fifteen procuresses, and whenever he was not coping with a particular problem at someone else's behest, he was busy doing research for its own sake and for his professional pleasure, energetically corrupting whatever he came across and then packing it off to his outfitters. Now, the most extraordinary aspect of the entire thing, and the one which, Messieurs, prompts me to cite the example of this uncommon idividual, was that he never enjoyed the fruit of his labors. He would encloset himself alone with the child, but, despite his vast understanding, his mind's agility, his eloquent persuasiveness, he used always to emerge from conference greatly inflamed. One could be perfectly certain the operation irritated his senses, but it was impossible to discover where or when or how he satisfied them. Closest scrutiny had never revealed anything but a prodigious blaze in his stare when once he had concluded his speeches, a few twitching movements of his hand upon the front of his breeches, within which one could tell there was a definite erection, produced by the diabolic work he was doing; but that was all.

He came to the house, was accorded a private interview with the young barmaid, I watched the proceedings: the consultation was prolonged, the seducer's language was amazingly pathetic, the child wept, got hot, seemed to enter into a kind of enthusiastic fit; it was at this moment the orator's eyes flamed brightest, and it was now we remarked the gestures in the neighborhood of his fly. Not long afterward, he rose, the child stretched forth her arms as if seeking to embrace him, he kissed her in a grave and fatherly manner, without any trace of lechery. He left, and three hours later the little girl arrived with her baggage at Madame Guérin's.

"And the man?" asked the Duc.

"He disappeared once his sermon was over," Duclos replied.

"Without coming back to see the results of his work?"

"No, my Lord, there was no doubt in his mind. He had never once failed."

"Now there is a most extraordinary personage," Curval admitted. "What does your Grace make of it?"

"I suspect," the Duc answered, "that the seduction provided all the heat necessary and that he discharged in his breeches."

"No," quoth the Bishop, "I think you underestimate the man: all this was simply by way of preparation for his debauches, and upon leaving I wager he went off to consummate greater ones."

"Greater ones?" cried Durcet. "And what more delicious, more voluptuous delight could one hope to procure oneself, than that of enjoying the objest one creates?" "I have it!" spoke up the Duc, "I dare say I've found him out: all this, just as you say, was merely preparatory in character, corrupting girls would heat his imagination, the off he'd go to dip his tool in boys. . . . I'll wager he was a bugger, yes, 'tis plain."

Duclos was asked whether she had any evidence to support that conjecture, and did he or did he not also seduce little boys? Our narrator replied that she had no proof of the thing, and despite the Duc's exceedingly likely allegation, everyone remained more or less in suspense as to the character of that strange preacher; after it had been unanimously agreed that his mania was truly delicious, but that one had either to consummate the work or do worse afterward, Duclos went on with her story:

The day after the arrival of our young novice, who was named Henriette, there came to the establishment an eccentric old lecher who put us both, Henriette and I, to work at the same time. This latest libertine had no other pleasure than that of observing through a hole all the voluptuous activities transpiring in an adjoining room, he adored spying on them, thus found in others' pleasures the divine aliment of his own lubricity. He was installed in the room I mentioned to you, the same one to which I and my companions often repaired for the diversion of watching libertines in action. I was assigned the task of amusing him while he looked through the hole, and young Henriette entered the arena together with the asshole-sucker I described you yesterday. The management considered that rascal's very voluptuous antics just the kind of spectacle my onlooker would relish, and in order better to arouse the actor, and in order that he render the scene yet more lascivious and more agreeable to see, he was told he was being given an apprentice and that it was with him she was to make her debut. The little barmaid's air of modesty and childishness speedily convinced him of it; and so he was as hot and as lewd in his nasty stunts as 'twere possible to be; nothing could have been further from his mind than that he was being observed. As for my old buck, his eye glued to the hole, one hand on my bum, the other on his prick, which he gently agitated, he seemed to be keeping the progress of his ecstasy abreast the one he was watching. "Ah, what a sight!" he said now and again; "what a fine ass that little girl has, and how well that bugger in there is tonguing it." At last, Henriette's lover having discharged, mine folded me in his arms and, after a moment's kissing, he turned me over, fondled, kissed, lewdly licked my behind, and squirted evidence of his virility over my cheeks.

"While frigging himself?" the Duc asked.

"Yes, my Lord," answered Duclos, "and frigging a prick whose incredible littleness, I assure you, isn't worth the bother describing."

The gentleman with whom I had to do next, Duclos continued, would not perhaps deserve to be included in my report were it not for one element, a rather unusual one, I should say, which distinguished his otherwise quite routine pleasures, and this little circumstance will illustrate to what point libertinage is able to degrade all a man's feelings of modesty, virtue and decorum. This person did not want to see; he wished to be seen. Knowing that men exist whose whim it is to spy upon the pleasure-takings of others, he bade Guérin find him one such fellow, conceal him, and said he would enact a drama for him. Guérin at once got in touch with the man I had entertained a few days previously behind the partition, and without telling him that the performer he was about to see knew that he was going to be seen - this would have interfered with his passion's fulfillment - she gave him to believe he was to observe a very arcane mystery indeed.

The inspector and my sister were put in the room with the hole, the actor and I went into the other one. He was a young man about twenty-eight years old, handsome and strong. Informed of the hole's location, he not too pointedly moved to where he could be perfectly viewed and had me take my place beside him. I frigged him. When his prick held a good slope, he got to his feet, exhibited his tool to the inspector, turned around, displayed his ass, raised my skirts and showed my mine, knelt before me, teased my anus with the tip of his nose, spread heartily, displayed everything with as much thoroughness as delight, and discharged by frigging himself, the while keeping my hinder skirts high and my ass squarely opposite the spy hole, in such wise that he who stood posted on the other side of the wall simultaneously beheld, at this decisive moment, both my bum and my lover's wrathful device. If the latter was in seventh heaven, God knows what was going on in the next room; my sister later told me she had had a madman on her back who had sworn he'd never had as fine a time as this, and after that her buttocks had been washed by a tide no less fierce than the one that had burst over mine.

"If that young man of yours truly had a good prick and pretty ass," Durcet opinioned, "there was ample in the situation to provoke a generous discharge."

"It must then have been delicious," returned Duclos, "for his engine was very long, quite thick, and his ass as soft, as sweetly plump, as attractively formed as the god of love's."

"Did you spread his cheeks?" the Bishop inquired. "Did you show his vent to the inspector?"

"Yes, your Lordship," said Duclos, "he displayed mine, I displayed his, he presented it with incomparable suggestiveness."

"I've been witness to a dozen such scenes," Durcet announced, "which have cost me a fortune in fuck; there is nothing more delicious to see or do. I refer to both: for it is just as pleasant to spy upon someone as to want to be observed."

Another individual, with approximately the same tastes, Duclos went on, took me to the Tuileries some few months later. He wanted me to accost men and frig them six inches from his face while he hid under a pile of folding chairs; and after I had frigged seven or eight passers-by, he settled himself upon a bench by one of the most frequented of the paths, lifted my skirts from behind, and displayed my ass to all and sundry, put his prick in the air and ordered me to frig it well within view of half of Paris, the which, although it was night, created such a scandal that by the time he most cynically unleashed his fuck, more than ten people had gathered around us, and we were obliged to dash away to avoid being publicly covered with shame.

When I related this adventure to Guérin, she laughed approvingly and said she had once known a man in Lyon (where panders enter into the trade at an early age), a man, I say, whose mania was certainly just as unusual. He would disguise himself as a public mercury, himself fetch in visitors to dally with the two girls he paid and maintained for no other purpose, then he would conceal himself in a corner to watch his client go to work; the girl, whose hire depended upon her skill in these moments, would guide the libertine she had in her arms and unfailingly give her employer a view of his prick and ass, the sight of which constituted the one pleasure that agreed with our false pimp's palate, the one that was able to loosen his fuck.

Duclos having brought her recital to an early conclusion that evening, the time that remained until supper was devoted to a few choice lubricities, and as the example of the cynic had fired their four daring brains, the friends did not isolate themselves in their closets, but disported within clear view each of the other. The Duc had Duclos strip off her clothes, had her bend and lean upon the back of a chair and commanded Desgranges to frig him upon her comrade's buttocks, in such wise that the head of his prick might graze Duclos' asshole with each stroke. To that one was added a number of other episodes which the proper presentation of our material forbids us from disclosing at this stage; but the fact remains that the chronicler's inferior vent was completely sprayed and that the Duc, handsomely served and entirely surrounded, discharged to the tune of bellowings and shouts which indicated to what a point his mind has been stimulated. Curval had himself fucked, the Bishop and Durcet for their part did passing strange things with both sexes; then supper was served.

After it, dances were held: the sixteen youngsters, the four fuckers, and the four wives were able to perform three quadrilles, but all the participants at the ball were naked, and our roués, indolently reclining upon sofas, were deliciously amused by all the different beauties one after another offered them by the divers attitudes the dancers were obliged to strike. Messieurs had the storytellers at their side, and these ladies manualized them rapidly or slowly, depending upon the pleasure they were experiencing; but, somewhat fatigued by the day's frolickings, no one discharged, and each went to bed to acquire the strength needed for all the following day's new infamies.

The Fifth Day

That morning it was Curval's duty to lend his presence at the academy of masturbation, and as the little girls were beginning to make tangible progress, he was hard put to resist the multiplying thumps and jerks and the variegated but universally lubricious postures of these eight charming little maids. Wishing to keep his weapon charged, he withdrew without firing it, lunch was announced, and at table the friends decreed that Messieurs' four young lovers, to wit: Zéphyr, the Duc's favorite; Adonis, beloved of Curval; Hyacinthe, friend to Durcet; and Céladon, unto whom the Bishop was plighted, were henceforth to be admitted to all meals, would dine beside their lovers in whose bedchambers they were, as well, regularly to sleep, a favor they would share with the wives and the fuckers; the which eliminated a ceremony customarily performed, as the reader is aware, every morning, this ceremony consisting in the fetching of the four lads by the four off-duty fuckers. They were now to come of their own accord, and when from now on Messieurs were to pass into the little boys' chambers, they were to be received, in accordance with prescribed regulation, by the remaining four only.

The Duc, who for the past two or three days had been head over heels in love with Duclos, whose ass he found superb and language pleasing, demanded that she also sleep in his bedroom, and this precedent having been established, Curval similarly introduced Fanchon, of whom he was passionately fond, into his. The two others decided to wait yet a little longer before deciding who was to fill this fourth post of privilege in their chambers.

It was that same morning ruled that the four young lovers who had just been chosen would have by way of ordinary dress, whenever they were not obliged to wear characterizing costumes, as when formed in quatrains, would have, I say, the clothing and style I am going to describe: it was a little jerkin, tight-fitting, of light cloth, tailored like a Prussian uniform with a slit tail, but much shorter, scarcely reaching to halfway down the thigh; this jacket, like all uniforms buttoned across the chest and at the vent, was of pink satin lined with white taffeta, the cuffs and trim were white satin, underneath was to be worn a kind of short vest or waistcoat, also of white satin, and the breeches were to match; but these breeches were provided with a heart-shaped rear flap under which one could slip one's hand and grasp the ass without the slightest difficulty; the flap was held up by a ribbon tied in a big bow, and when one wished to have the child completely exposed in this part, one had merely to undo the bow, which was of the color selected by the friend to whom the pucelage belonged. Their hair, carelessly arranged so that a few curls fell to either side, floated absolutely free behind, and was simply knotted by a ribbon of the appropriate color. A highly-scented powder, in color between gray and pink, tinted their hairdress, their eyebrows were carefully plucked and emphasized by black pencil, a light touch of rouge applied to the cheeks, all this heightened their natural beauty; their heads were never covered, black silk stockings brocaded in rose covered their legs, they were agreeably shod in gray slippers attached by a pink bow. A cream-colored gauze cravat, very voluptuously tied, blended prettily with a little lace ruffle; when the four of them were clad in this style, you may rest assured that nothing in all the world was as charming to behold as these little fellows.

Immediately they were granted their new privileges, a few others were abolished: all permissions, of the kind they had upon occasion been accorded in the morning, were absolutely refused now, but they were given all the rights over the wives the fuckers enjoyed: they could maltreat the women as they saw fit and not only at mealtime, no, but at any time of the day, all the time, if they chose, and they could be confident that in any dispute arising 'twixt the wives and themselves, their side would be heard with sympathy.

These matters attended to, the usual searches were conducted; the lovely Fanny, whom Curval had ordered to be in such and such a state, was found in the contrary one (the sequel will provide elucidation of this obscure point) : her name was set down in the punishment ledger. Amongst the young gentlemen, Giton had done what he had been forbidden to do; down went his name. After the chapel functions had been completed by the very few subjects who were on hand to execute them, the friends went to dinner.

This was the first meal at which the four lovers joined the friends at table. They took their places, each sitting to the right of the friend who doted upon him, the friend's favorite fucker being seated to the friend's left. These four additional guests lent a further charm to the meal; they were all four very gentle, very sweet, and were beginning to accommodate themselves very well to the general tone of the household. The Bishop, in the liveliest spirits that day, kissed Céladon virtually without interruption throughout the course of the meal, and as that child was a member of the quartet chosen to hand around the coffee, he left table a little before dessert. When Monseigneur, who had worked himself into a splendid sweat over the boy, saw him entirely naked in the salon, he lost all self-control.

"By Jesus!" he cried, his face purple, "since I cannot tup his ass, I can at least do what Curval did to his bardash yesterday."

And so saying he seized the good-natured little rascal, laid him on his belly, and slipped his prick between his thighs. The libertine was lost in the clouds, his weapon's hair rubbed the cute little hole he would fain have perforated: one of his hands fondled this delicious little cupid's buttocks, with the other he frigged Céladon's prick. What was more, he glued his mouth to the lovely child's, pumped the air from his lungs, swallowed his saliva. In order to excite his brother, the Duc created a libertine spectacle by placing himself in front of the Bishop and proceeding to lick out the asshole of Cupidon, the other of the two boys serving coffee that day. Curval moved to within close range and had himself frigged by Michette, and Durcet offered the prelate the sight of Rosette's widespread buttocks. Everyone toiled to procure him the ecstasy to which he plainly asprired; it occurred, his nerves trembled, his teeth chattered, his eyes shone, he would have been a terrifying object for anyone save those three who knew full well the terrible effects joy had upon that man of God. The fuck finally broke forth and flowed over Cupidon's buttocks, for that quick-witted little aide had at the last moment wriggled his way beneath his comrade so as to receive the treasure which might otherwise have gone entirely to waste.

The storytelling hour came, they readied themselves. By an unusual stroke of circumstance, all the fathers found their daughters beside them on their couches. But Messieurs were not alarmed. Duclos began to speak.

In that you have not required me, Messieurs, to give you an exact day by day account of everything that happened to me at Madame Guérin's establishment, but simply to relate the more out of the ordinary events which highlighted some of those days, I shall omit mention of several not very interesting episodes dating from my childhood, for they would be naught but tedious repetitions of what you have heard already. And so I shall tell you that I had just reached the age of sixteen, not without having acquired a wealth of experience in my métier, when it fell to my lot to have a libertine whose daily caprice merits to be cited. He was a sober, very grave judge of nearly fifty years, a man who, if one is to believe Madame Guérin, who told me she had known him for many years, regularly exercised every morning the whimsicality wherewith I shall entertain you. His ordinary pimp had reached the age of retirement and recommended that the judge put himself in our dear mother's hands; this was his first call at the house, and he began with me.

He stationed himself, alone, in the room with the spy hole, I entered the other with a hod carrier, a Savoyard, I believe; well, he was a common fellow, but a healthy strapping one: those qualifications were enough for the judge, who cared nothing for age or looks. I was, within clear view and as near as possible to the hole, to frig my honest churl, who knew what was expected of him and reckoned this a very pretty way indeed to earn his supper. After having unreservedly complied with all the instructions the good judge had given me, after having done all my sweet country buck could desire of me, I had him discharge into a porcelain dish, and having wrung the last drop from his prick, I dashed into the adjoining room. My man is awaiting me in an ecstasy, he pounces upon the dish, swallows the hot fuck, his own erupts; with one hand I encourage his ejaculation, with the other I collect in my hand every precious dram that falls and, between jets, quickly raising my hand to the old prankster's mouth, with great dexterity and nimbleness I see to it that he swallows his own fuck quite as fast as he squirts it out.

That was all there was to it; no fingerings, no kisses, he didn't even lift my skirts, and rising from his chair with just as much aplomb as a moment before he had been aroused, he took his cane and left, saying that I frigged very skillfully, so he considered, and that I had very well grasped his character. A new workman was brought in the next day, for they had to be changed daily, as had the women. My sister operated for him, he left content, returned again on the morrow, and during my entire stay at Madame Guérin's I never saw a single day go by without him arriving punctually at nine, and never did he raise a single skirt, although he was ministered by some charming girls.

"Had he any inclination to see the commoner's ass?" Curval wanted to know.

"He had indeed, Monsieur le Président," Duclos replied. "While amusing the man whose fuck he ate, one had to take great care to turn him this way and that, and the man had also to turn the girl around in every direction."

"Well, now," said Curval, "that makes sense. But for that I'd not have understood a thing."

Shortly afterward, continued Duclos, the harem's strength was increased by the arrival of a girl of about thirty, attractive enough, but with hair as red as Judas'. At first we though she was a new recruit, but no, she quickly disabused us by explaining that she had come for only one party. The man for whom this latest heroine was intended soon arrived also: he was an important financier of prepossessing appearance, and his singularity of taste, since the girl set aside for him would doubtless not have been wanted by anyone else, this singularity, I say, gave me the greatest desire to observe them come to grips. No sooner had they entered the room than the girl removed every stitch of her clothing and displayed a very fair and very plump body.

"Very well, be off, jump about, skip," said the financier, "you know perfectly well I like them in a sweat."

And thereupon the redhead falls to cutting capers, running around the room, leaping like a young goat, and our man keeps his eye fixed on her while he frigs himself; these activities continued a great while and there was no telling to what they were leading. When the girl was swimming in perspiration, she approached the libertine, raised an arm, and had him smell her armpit where the sweat was dripping from every hair.

"Ah, that's it, that's it!" cried the tycoon, staring with furious approval at that sticky arm she held a centimeter from his nose, "what an odor! ravishing!"

Then slipping to his knees before her, he sniffed the interior of her vagina, inhaling deeply, and then breathed in the scent emergent from her asshole, but he returned constantly to her armpits, whether because those parts flattered him the most, or because he found the bouquet superior, it was always there his mouth and nose betook themselves with the greatest fervor. At last a rather lengthy but not very thick device, a device he had been buffeting in vain for about an hour, decided to wake and have a look about. The girl takes her place, the financier comes up from behind and lodges his anchovy under her armpit, she squeezes her arm, exerting what I judged must have been a powerful grip; meanwhile, her posture enables the gentleman to enjoy the sight and odor of her other armpit, he lays hands on it, buries his snout under it and discharges while licking, while devouring this part which affords him such delight.

"And the creature had to have red hair?" asked the Bishop. "That was a sine qua non?"

"Absolutely," Duclos replied. "Those women, as you are not unaware, Monseigneur, exude an infinitely more violent underarm aroma, and his sense of smell once stung, no question of it, by ripe odors, his pleasure organs would be aroused at once."

"Of course," the Bishop agreed. "But, by God, it seems to me I'd have preferred smelling that woman's asshole to sniffing under her arms."

"Ah, ha!" spoke up Curval, "there is much to be said in favor of the one and the other, and let me assure you that if you'll but give the arms a try, you'll find them perfectly delicious."

"Which is to say, I take it," said the Bishop, "that Monsieur le Président finds that stew to his taste?"

"Why yes, I've sampled it," Curval replied, "and apart from a few occasions when I added other episodes to that one, I protest to you that all by itself it has always been able to get some fuck out of me."

"Oh yes, those episodes, I fancy what they were," the Bishop broke in, "you smelled the ass . . ."

"One moment there," interrupted the Duc. "Don't oblige him to make his confession, Monseigneur, he'd tell us things we are not yet to hear; go on, Duclos, don't let these chatterers encroach upon your domain."

I recall the period, our narrator resumed, when for more than six weeks Guérin absolutely forbade my sister to wash, requiring her, on the contrary, to keep herself in the rankest and most impure state she could contrive to be in; we had no inkling of the Madame's designs until one day there arrived a grog-blossomed old rake who, in a half-drunken and most uncouth tone, asked Guérin whether the whore was ready. "Oh, my goodness, you may be sure she is," Guérin replied. They are brought together, put in the room, I fly to the hole; scarcely am I there than I see my naked sister astride a capacious bidet filled with champagne and there is our man, armed with a great sponge, busily washing her and carefully recovering every bit of dirt that rolls from her body.

It had been so long since she had cleaned any part of herself, for she had been strictly ordered not to wipe her behind, that the wine immediately took on a brown and dirty hue, and probably an odor which could not have been very agreeable. But the more the wine became corrupted by the filth streaming into it, the more delighted our libertine grew. He sipped a little, found it exquisite, provided himself with a glass and, filling it to the brim six or seven times, he downed the putrid and disgusting wine in which he'd just finished washing a body laden for so long with impurities. When he had drunk his fill, he seized my sister, laid her down flat upon the bed, and upon her buttocks and well-opened hole, spewed floods of immodest semen brought to a boil by the unclean details of his unpleasant mania.

But another visitor, a far nastier one, was time and again to attract my regard. We had in the house one of those women who are called street scouts or trotters, to employ the bordello term, and whose function is to run abroad night and day and dig up new recruits. Over forty years old, this creature had, as well as very faded charms which had never been very winning, the dreadful defect that consists in stinking feet. And such, no other, was the fair sort whereof the Marquis de L_____ was enamored. He arrives, Dame Louise - for such was her name - is introduced to him, he finds her superb, and once he has conducted her into the pleasure sanctuary, "Pray remove your shoes," says he. Louise, who had been explicitly enjoined to wear the same stockings and slippers for a month, offers the Marquis a foot that would have made a man of less fine discrimination puke straight off; but, as I say, that foot's very filth and nauseous quality was precisely what our nobleman cherished most. He catches it up, kisses it with fervor, with his mouth he spreads each toe, one after the other, with his tongue he gathers from each space, and gathers with incomparable enthusiasm, the blackish and fetid scum Nature deposits there and which, with a little encouragement, easily increases by itself. Not only does he draw this unmentionable stuff into his mouth, but he swallows it, savors it, and the fuck he loses while frigging himself stands as unequivocal proof of the excessive pleasure he takes in this fare.

" 'Tis beyond me," was the Bishop's simple comment.

"Then I suppose I'd best explain it to you," Curval said.

"What? You've a taste for that?"

"Observe," the Président replied.

The others rose, came from their niches, surrounded him, and beheld that peerless libertine, in whom were met all the tastes of the most crapulous lewdness, embrace the indescribable foot tendered him by Fanchon, that aged and foul servant we described earlier. Curval was in half a swoon as he sucked.

"There's nothing to be wondered at there," said Durcet, "one need but be mildly jaded, and all these infamies assume a richer meaning: satiety inspires them in the libertinage which executes them unhesitatingly. One grows tired of the commonplace, the imagination becomes vexed, and the slenderness of our means, the weakness of our faculties, the corruption of our souls leads us to these abominations."

Such must surely have been the case, Duclos went on, with the elderly General C_____, one of Guérin's most reliable clients. The women he required had to be damaged either by Nature, by libertinage, or by the effects of the law; in a word, he accepted none who were not one-eyed or blind, lame, hunchbacked, legless cripples, or missing an arm or two, or toothless, or mutilated in their limbs, or whipped and branded or clearly marked by some other act of justice, and they always had to be of the ripest old age.

At the scene I witnessed he had been given a woman of about fifty, bearing the brand of a public thief, and who was, in addition, missing an eye. That double degradation figured as a treasure in his view. He closeted himself with her, had her strip away her clothes, ecstatically kissed the indubitable signs of crime on her shoulders, ardently sucked each ridge and furrow of those scars he called honorably won. That accomplished, he transferred his avid attentions to her asshole, he spread open her buttocks, appreciatively kissed the withered hole they defended, sucked it for what seemed an age, and then planting himself astride the old girl's back, he rubbed his prick on the wounds that attested the triumph of justice, and as he rubbed, he praised her for having gone down in exemplary defeat; and then, bending over her bum, he showered further kisses upon the altar at which he had rendered such a lengthy homage, and squirted an abundance of fuck upon the inspiring marks which had so fired his own warrior's spirit.

"Oh, by God!" cried Curval, whose brain was in a lubricious ferment that day, "look my friends, behold by the sign of this risen prick what a flame that passion described ignites in me."

And calling out to Desgranges:

"Hither, impure buggress," he continued in the same strain, "come, you who so resemble what we have just heard described; come, beget me the same pleasure the general got by her."

Desgranges approaches. Durcet, his friend in these excesses, helps the Président strip her. She raises a few objections at first; they are the more certain and pursue their way, scolding her for wishing to hide something whereby she may be cherished all the more by the society. Her branded back comes to light at last, and there are a "T" and a "P" which affirm that she has twice undergone the dishonoring ordeal whose vestiges nevertheless completely ignite our libertines' impudicious urges.

The rest of that worn and wasted body - that ass of parchment or ancient leather, that ample, noxious hole glistening in its center, this mutilated tit, those three vanished fingers, this short leg that causes her limp, that mouth destitute of teeth - everything combines to stimulate our libertine pair. Durcet sucks her from in front, Curval posteriorly, and even though objects of the greatest beauty and in the best condition are there before their eyes and ready to brave anything in order to satisfy the least of their desires, even so it is with what Nature and villainy have dishonored, have withered, it is with the filthiest and least appetizing object our two rakes, presently beside themselves, are about to taste the most delicious pleasures. . . . Ah, now give me your explanation of man - here are two men who seem as if they were disputing what is nigh to a cadaver, like two savage mastiffs wrangling over a corpse; here, I say, we have two eminent citizens who, after having given themselves over to the foulest excesses, finally erupt their fuck, and notwithstanding the exhaustion caused by these feats, would very possibly go on to perform other ones of the same crapulous and infamous kind, and perform them without an instant's delay, were it not for the supper bell announcing other pleasures well worth their consideration.

The Président, made desperate by his loss of fuck, and who in such cases could never be revived save by excessive feeding and swilling, flew to work and stuffed himself like a pig. Adonis frigged Invictus and gave him some fuck to drink, but hardly content with this latest outrage, which had been executed at once, Curval rose, said his imagination proposed a few rather more delicious stunts, and without further explanation, led Fanchon, Adonis, and Hercule away with him to the further boudoir and did not reappear until the orgies; but then conducted himself so brilliantly that he was again able to commit a thousand fresh horrors, each more extraordinary than the other, but not, we regret, to be described to the reader, or rather not yet, for the structure of our tale obliges us to defer them.

And then to bed. Curval, the unfathomable Curval to whom that night the divine Adelaide, his daughter, befell, Curval, who could have spent a most delightful night with her, was found the next morning squirming over the body of the disgusting Fanchon, with whom he had performed additional abominations all night long, whilst Adonis and Adelaide, driven from his couch, were, one of them, in a little bed far away, and the other lying on a mattress upon the floor.

The Sixth Day

It was Monseigneur's turn to assist at the masturbations; he presented himself. Had Duclos' disciples been males, Monseigneur would probably not have been able to resist them. But a little crack below the navel was a frightful blemish in his eyes, and had the Graces themselves encircled him, once he had caught sight of that imperfection nothing more would have been needed to calm him. And so he put up an indomitable defense, I even believe his prick remained limp, and the operations were continued.

Nothing could be plainer than that Messieurs were extremely eager to find fault with the eight little girls so as to procure themselves the following day, which was the fatal Saturday of retribution, so as, I say, at this time to procure themselves the pleasure of punishing all eight. They had six already on the list; the sweet and beautiful Zelmire made the seventh; did she in all good faith really merit correction? or was it simply that the pleasure of inflicting the proposed penalty won out in a struggle with strict equity? we leave the question to be decided by the wise Durcet's conscience; our task is simply to record events. One very fair dame further swelled the miscreants' ranks: 'twas the gentle Adelaide. Durcet, her husband, appeared anxious to set an example by pardoning less in her than in the others, and it was he himself she happened to disappoint. He had led her to a certain place where the services she had been forced to render him, after certain of his functions, were something less than absolutely clean or palatable; not everyone is as depraved as Curval, and although Adelaide was his daughter, she had none of his tastes. She may have balked. Or she may have managed poorly. Or, again, it might only have been some teasing on Durcet's part. Whatever the cause, she was inscribed upon the punishment list, to the vast satisfaction of nearly all concerned.

The examination of the boys' quarters having unearthed nothing, the friends moved on to the arcane pleasures of the chapel, pleasures all the more piquant and all the more extraordinary in that even those who besought permission to come and procure them, were usually refused admittance. Constance, two subaltern fuckers, and Michette were the only ones to attend that morning's party.

At dinner, Zéphyr, of whom they were becoming prouder every day, what for the charms which seemed more and more to embellish him and the voluntary libertinage wherein he was making great strides, Zéphyr, I say, insulted Constance who, although no longer a waitress, nevertheless always appeared at the midday meal. He called her a baby-maker and struck her several blows in the belly to teach her, said he, to lay eggs with her lover, then he kissed the Duc, caressed him, gave his prick a few affectionate tugs, and managed so successfully to fire that hero's brain that Blangis swore the afternoon would not pass without his moistening Zéphyr with fuck; and the little rascal nagged the Duc, daring him to do it at once. As Zéphyr was to serve coffee, he left at dessert time and reappeared naked with the Duc's cup. Instantly they were settled in the salon, the Duc, very animated, began with one or two smutty remarks; then sucked the child's mouth and prick, set him on a chair, his ass at the level of his mouth, and earnestly pumped at his hole for fifteen minutes. His prick rebelled at last, dressed its lofty head, and the Duc saw very clearly that the homage required some incense after all. However, their contract forbade everything save the expedient employed the day before; the Duc resolved therefore to emulate his associates. He had Zéphyr crouch on a sofa, drove his engine between the lad's thighs, but what had befallen Curval happened also to the Duc: his device protruded half a foot beyond.

"You'd best do as I did," Curval advised, "frig the child against your prick, water your glans with his fuck."

But the Duc found it more pleasant to impale two at the same time. He besought his brother to fit Augustine in place, her buttocks were pressed flush against Zéphyr's thighs and the Duc, thus simultaneously fucking a boy and a girl, as it were, to put yet a little more of the lubricious into the thing, frigged Zéphyr's prick on the pretty, round and fair buttocks of Augustine, and soaked them with that child-fuck which, as may easily be imagined, was mightily warmed by such treatment and soon spattered abundantly out.

Curval, who found the general perspective very inviting, and who spied the Duc's ass, open wide and fairly yawning for a prick - as does the ass of every bugger at those instants his prick is up - Curval, I say, drew up to repay him in kind for what he had received the previous evening, and the dear Duc no sooner felt the voluptuous joltings occasioned by this intromission, than his fuck, taking wing at almost the same time Zéphyr's departed him, splashed the lower edges of the temple whose columns Zéphyr was wetting. But Curval did not discharge, and withdrawing his proud and mettlesome engine from the Duc's bum, he menaced the Bishop, who was likewise frigging himself between Giton's thighs, threatening to make him undergo the fate the Duc had just experienced. The Bishop hurls a challenge, 'tis accepted, battle is joined, the Bishop is embuggered and, between the thighs of the pretty child he is caressing, goes on deliciously to lose a draught of libertine fuck most deliciously wheedled out of him. However, a benevolent spectator to it all, Durcet, having no one but Hébé and the duenna to attend to his needs, and although nearly dead drunk, was by no means wasting his opportunities and was quietly perpetrating infamies the proper time has not yet come to disclose. But calm finally descended over the field, the warriors slumbered, and woke again at six, the hour when Duclos' gifted tongue was to lay the foundation for new pleasures.

The quatrains that evening featured certain sexual changes: that is to say, all the girls were costumed as sailors, the little boys as tarts; the effect was ravishing, nothing quickens lust like this voluptuous little reversal; adorable to find in a little boy what causes him to resemble a girl, and the girl is far more interesting when for the sake of pleasing she borrows the sex one would like her to have. Each friend had his wife on his couch that day; they exchanged congratulations upon that very religious arrangement, and everyone being ready to listen, Duclos resumed her lewd stories.

There was, at Madame Guérin's, a certain girl of about thirty, blond, rather heavy-set, but unusually fair and healthy; her name was Aurore, she had a charming mouth, fine teeth, and a voluptuous tongue, but - and who would believe such a thing? - whether because of a faulty education, or owing to a weak stomach, from that adorable mouth there used constantly, incessantly to erupt prodigious quantities of wind, and above all after she had eaten a heartly meal, she was capable, for the space of an hour, of blowing a stream of belches powerful enought to turn a windmill. But they are right who declare no fault exists that is not a little appreciated by someone, and our fine lass, thanks to this one, had one of the most ardent suitors: he was a learned and grave professor of Scholasticism at the Sorbonne who, tired of wasting his time proving the existence of God in his school, would sometimes come to our brothel to convince himself of the existence of his dear God's creatures. He would send prior notice of his intended arrival, and Aurore would feed like one dying of hunger. Curious to see that pious colloquy, I fly to the spy hole: my lovers greet one another, I observe a few preliminary caresses all directed upon the mouth, then most delicately our rhetor seats his companion in a chair, seats himself opposite her and, taking her hands, deposits his relics between them, sad old vestiges they were, in the most deplorable state.

"Act," he enjoins her, "act, my lovely one. Act; you know by what means I may be drawn from this languid condition, I beg you to adopt them with all dispatch, for I feel myself pressed mightily to proceed."

With one hand she fondles the doctor's flabby tool, with the other she draws his head to hers, glues her lips to his mouth and in no time at all she has, one after another, shot sixty great belches down his gullet. Impossible to represent the ecstasy of this servant of God; he was in the clouds, he inhaled, he swallowed everything that came his way, you'd have thought the very idea of losing the least puff of air would have distressed him, and whilst all this was going on, his hands roamed inquiringly over my colleague's breasts and under her petticoat, but these fingerings were no more than episodic; the unique and capital object was that mouth overwhelming him with sighs and digestive rumblings. His prick finally enlarged by the voluptuous vibrations the ceremony caused to be born in him, he discharged into my companion's hand, and ran off to deliver a lecture, protesting as he went that never had he enjoyed himself more.

Some time after this, a rather more extraordinary man came to the house with a particular problem in mind, and it well deserves to be mentioned in this catalogue of natural wonders. Guérin had, that day, urged me to eat, had all but forced me to eat as copiously as, not long before, I had seen Aurora dine. Guérin took care to have me served everything she knew I liked best, and having forewarned me, as we rose from table, of everything I should have to do for the elderly libertine with whom she intended to match me, she had me swallow down three grains of emetic dissolved in a glass of warm water. The old sinner arrived, he was a brothel-hound I had seen dozens of times before without bothering to find out what he came to do. He embraces me, drives a dirty and disgusting tongue into my mouth, and the action of the emetic I'd drunk is complemented by his stinking breath. He sees my stomach's about to rise, he's in ecstasy. "Courage, dearie," he cries, "be brave, never fear, I don't propose to lose a drop of it." Being foreadvised of all he expects of me, I seat him on the couch, lay his head to rest on the edge of it; his thighs are separated, I unbutton his breeches, drag out a slack, stunted instrument that betrays no sign of stiffening, I shake, squeeze, pull it, he opens his mouth: all the while frigging him, all the while receiving the touches of his impudicious hands which stray over my buttocks, at point-blank I launch into his mouth the imperfectly digested dinner that vomitive has fetched up from my stomach. Our man is beside himself, he rolls his eyes, pants, bolts down the spew, goes to my lips to seek more of the impure ejaculation that intoxicates him, he does not indeed miss a drop, and when it seems to him the operation is in danger of ending, he provokes a repetition of it by dexterously inserting his appalling tongue into my mouth, and his prick, that prick I've scarcely been able to touch because of my convulsive retchings, that prick doubtless warmed by nothing but such infamies, grows purple, rises up of itself, and weeps into my fingers the unsuspected proof of the impressions these foul activities have made upon it.

"Ah, by God's balls," said Curval, "that's a very delicious passion indeed, but none the less susceptible of improvement."

"And how?" asked Durcet in a voice broken by signs of lubricity.

"How?" Curval repeated, "why, by the choice of food and of partner."

"Partner? Oh, but of course. You'd prefer a Fanchon."

"To be sure!"

"And the food?" Durcet continued, while Adelaide frigged him.

"Food?" the Président murmured, "why, I think I'd force her to give me back, and in the same manner, what I'd just introduced into her."

"That is to say," stammered the financier, beginning to lose all control of himself, "you'd spew into her mouth, she'd swallow and then have to blow it back at you?"

"Precisely."

And each rushing into his closet, the Président with Fanchon, Augustine, and Zélamir; Durcet with Desgranges, Rosette, and Invictus: proceedings were halted for roughly thirty minutes. Then the two lechers returned.

"Ah," the Duc said chidingly to Curval, the first to reappear, "you've been up to some nastiness or other?"

"Ah, a little of this, a little of that," the Président replied, "it's my life's happiness, you know. I've not much patience with mild or tidy pleasures."

"But I trust you were also purged of a little fuck?"

"Enough of that nonsense," the Président said, "do you suppose everyone is like you, flinging fuck this way and that every six minutes? Why no, I leave those efforts and that unconscionable prodigality to you and to vigorous champions like Durcet," he went on, watching the financier stagger weakly from his closet.

"Yes," said Durcet, "yes, it's true, there was no resisting the girl. Desgranges is so filthy in word, deed, and body, she is so adroit, so suitable in every way . . ."

"Well, Duclos," the Duc said, "go on with your story, for if we don't quiet him down, the indiscreet little fellow will tell us everything he did, and never once consider what a dreadful breach of good manners it is to boast of the favors one has received from a pretty woman."

And Duclos obediently returned to her tale.

Since, said our chronicler, these gentlemen are so fond of that kind of drollery, I greatly regret they were unable to restrain their enthusiasm yet another minute, for the effects of what I have still to relate this evening might, it seems to me, have better found their mark. Precisely that which Monsieur le Président declared to be lacking to the perfection of the passion I have just described was entirely present in the one that follows; what a pity, I repeat, that I was unable to get to it in time. The example of the elderly Président de Saclanges affords, in every particular and word for word, all the singularity Monsieur de Curval appeared to desire. By way of a partner for him, Guérin had chosen the dean of our chapter: a tall, sturdy lass of about thirty-six, a great and chronic drunk, loutish, foul-mouthed, rather a fishmonger's wife, although by no means unattractive; the good Président arrives, they are served supper, both get blind drunk, both become unreasonable, one vomits in the other's mouth, the one swallows the stuff, then the other vomits into the mouth of the first, now he swallows, and so forth and so on, and they finally collapse into the supper's debris, that is to say, into the filth they've just splashed all over the floor. And then I am sent into the fray, for my co-worker has not an ounce of strength left, indeed she has lost consciousness. But this, however, is the crucial moment from the libertine's point of view: I find him prone, his prick straight and hard as a crowbar; I seize his instrument, the

Président stammers, swears, draws me to him, sucks my mouth, and discharges like a bull, the while twisting and turning and continuing to wallow in his ordure.

The same girl, somewhat later, participated in a drama which was surely not much less filthy; a monk of some consequence, who paid her very liberally, threw himself astride her belly after having spread and immobilized my companion's thighs by tying them to heavy articles of furniture. Several kinds of food were brought in and served the monk, who had the dainties placed on the girl's naked belly. The merry fellow then picks up the morsels he is to eat, and dips them one by one in his Dulcinea's open cunt, and only consumes them after they have been completely impregnated with the spices the vagina secretes.

"Ha!" cried the Bishop, "an entirely novel manner of dining."

"And one which wouldn't suit you, eh, my Lord?" said Duclos.

"By God's belly, no!" replied the man of the Church, "I'm not that fond of the cunt."

Very well, our storyteller replied, lend an ear to the item with which I am going to close this evening's narrations, I am persuaded it will amuse you more.

I had been with Madame Guérin for eight years - had just reached the age of seventeen - and during this period not a day had passed without my seeing a certain farmer-general arrive at the house every morning and be received with the warmest welcome. He was thought very highly of by the management; a man of roughly sixty, rotund, short, he resembled Monsieur Durcet in a good many points. Like Monsieur, he had an air of freshness and youth, and was also plump; he required a different girl every day, and those of the house were never used save in emergencies or when someone contracted abroad failed to meet her appointment. Monsieur Dupont, so was our financier called, was just as discriminating in his choice of girls as he was fastidious in his tastes, he simply would not have a whore to attend to his needs except in the rare and extreme cases I mentioned; he had to have, on the contrary, working women, shopgirls, especially milliners or seamstresses. Their age and coloring also had to meet specification: they had to be between fifteen and eighteen, neither more or less, and, most important of all, they needed to have a sweetly moldered ass, an ass so absolutely clean that the least blemish, a mere grain of matter clinging at the hole was sufficient grounds for rejection. When they were maids, he paid twice as much.

They had made plans for, and were that day actually expecting the arrival of, a young lacemaker of sixteen whose ass was generally acclaimed by connoisseurs as a true model of what an ass should be; Monsieur Dupont did not know the treasure that was to be offered him, and as it turned out the young lady had word sent that on this particular morning she was unable to leave her parents' house and that matters would have to proceed without her. Guérin, knowing Dupont had never set eyes on me, ordered me to dress in a shopgirl's costume at once, to go out, take a cab at the end of the street, and alight again at the brothel, all this fifteen minutes after Dupont entered the house; I was to play my role with care and pass myself for a milliner's apprentice. But the most important consideration of all was the anise water: I was to fill my stomach at once with half a quart of it, and directly afterward I was to drink the large glass of balsamic liqueur she gave me; you shall shortly learn for what its effect was intended. Everything went forward very smoothly; fortunately, we had been given several hours' notice, and in this time were able to make thorough preparations. I arrived at the house with a very silly air, I was presented to the financier who directly scrutinized me very closely, but as I was keeping a sharp eye on my conduct, he could discover nothing about my person which might contradict the story that had been invented for him.

"Is she a maid?" Dupont asks.

"Not in that place," says Guérin, pointing to my belly, "but I will answer for the other side."

And it was a most impudent lie she told. Little does it matter; our man believed her, and that alone was necessary.

"Lift your skirts, hurry it up," says Dupont.

And Guérin raises my skirts from behind, drawing me toward her as she does so and thus entirely exposing the temple at which the libertine performed his worship. He stares, for a moment he fingers my buttocks, he spreads them with both hands, and evidently satisfied, he announces that the ass is suitable for his purposes. Next, he asks me several questions relating to my age, my trade, and content with my feigned innocence and the look of having been born yesterday that I affect, he has me accompany him to his apartment, for there was one reserved exclusively for him at Guérin's: he did not like being observed while at work, he was certain not to be in this place. Both of us having entered, he carefully shuts and secures the door, considers me for a moment, then in a rather brutal fashion - brutality characterized him throughout the scene - he inquired me whether it were indeed true that I had never been fucked in the ass. As my role called for total ignorance of the meaning of such an expression, I had him repeat it, declared I still understood nothing, and when by means of the most unambigious gestures he conveyed what he wished to say, I replied, with a stimulated look fo fright and modesty, that I should be a very unhappy girl indeed if ever I had lent myself to such infamies. Whereupon he told me to remove my skirts, but only my skirts, and once I had obeyed him, leaving my blouse down to hide my front, he raised it above my buttocks to the height of my bodice; but while he was undressing me my neckerchief slipped down, revealing my breasts. He became incensed.

"Devil take those damned tits of yours," he cried; "who asked you for tits? That's what I can't bear about these creatures, every single impudent one of them is wild to show you her miserable bubs."

Hastening to cover them over, I approached him to beg his pardon, but observing that I was going to exhibit my cunt thanks to the posture I was about to assume, he lost his temper a second time:

"But, sweet Jesus! Can't you stay put?" he demanded, seizing my haunches and turning me so that there was no danger he would catch a glimpse of anything but my ass, "stay that way, fuck your eyes, I don't care any more of your cunt than I do for your chest, your ass is all you need with me."

So saying, he stood up and guided me to the edge of the bed upon which he installed me in such wise the upper half of my body rested on the bed, then, seating himself on a very low stool, he found himself situated between my wide-flung legs and his head on a level with my ass. He peers at me for another instant, then, deciding I am not yet adjusted as I ought to be, up he gets, fetches a cushion, fits it under my belly, thus arching my ass more sharply; he sits down again, examines, and goes about everything with the sangfroid and confidence of the seasoned and mature libertine. A moment passes, then he grasps my two buttocks, spreads them, poses his open mouth upon the hole, fastens his lips hermetically to it, and immediately, pursuant to the signal he gives me and in obedience to the considerable pressure that has built up within me, I unleash a booming fart, possibly the most explosive one he has received in all his life; it shoots down his gullet and he backs away, furious.

"What the devil!" he cries, "so you are so bold as to fart into my mouth, are you?"

And he straightway claps his mouth to my asshole again.

"Yes, Monsieur," I say as I release a second stifler, "that's how I deal with gentlemen who kiss my ass."

"Very well then! fart, if you must, you little rascal, since you can't help it, fart, I say, fart as hard as you like and as often as you can."

From this moment onward I cast off all restraint, nothing can express the urgency of my desire to give vent to the boisterous winds produced by the potion I had drunk earlier; our man is thrilled by them, he receives some in his mouth, the others in his nostrils. After fifteen minutes of this exercise, he lies down upon the couch, draws me to him, his nose still wedged between my buttocks, orders me to frig him and meanwhile to continue a ceremony which gives rise in him to such exquisite pleasures. I fart, I frig, I manipulate a slack little prick neither much longer nor much thicker than my finger, but by dint of buffets, jerks, and farts the instrument finally stiffens. The augmentation of our gentleman's pleasure, the critical instant's approach is announced by a new iniquity: it is now his tongue that provokes my farts, 'tis his tongue that, like a flail, darts deep into my anus in order to stir up the winds, 'tis against his tongue he wants me to blow those zephyrs, he becomes unreasonable, he is no longer in possession of his wits, 'tis clear, and his wretched little engine sadly sprinkles seven or eight drops of watery, brownish sperm upon my fingers; and now he is restored to his senses. But as his native brutality fomented his distraction, so now it replaces it at once, and he barely gives me enough time to readjust myself. He scolds, he mutters and swears, in one word he offers me the abhorrent image of vice that has slaked its thirst, and I am made the butt of that unthinking indelicacy which, once its glitter has paled, seeks to find revenge in scorn for the worshiped object that latterly captivated the senses.

"Now that's a man I prefer to all the others," said the Bishop. "And do you know if he had his little sixteen-year-old apprentice the next day?"

"Yes, Monseigneur, he did indeed, and the day after that a maid of fifteen far prettier yet. As few men used to pay as much, few were better served."

This passion having stimulated heads so well acquainted with that species of disorder, and having put them in mind of a taste they all relished. Messieurs simply could not bear waiting any longer to make use of it. Each of them plucked what windy fruits there were to be had, neglecting no likely sources, then supper arrived, with their gourmandizing pleasures they blended nearly all the infamies they had just heard described, the Duc got Fanchon tipsy and had the befuddled old thing vomit into his mouth, Durcet had the whole harem fart, and in the course of the evening swallowed at least threescore mouthfuls of unwholesome air. As for Curval, in whose brain all kinds of extravagances danced gaily, he declared he was moved to perform some solitary orgies and went off to the remote boudoir, accompanied by Fanchon, Marie, Desgranges, and thirty bottles of Champagne wine. Later on, all four had to be carried back into society, for they were discovered floating in a very tide of their own ordures, and the Président was found asleep, his mouth fastened to that of Desgranges, who was still wearily retching into it. The three other friends aquitted themselves no less brilliantly, performing feats in like kind or somewhat different; they too had spent their orgy period drinking, they had got the little girls to fart, I truly haven't space to tell you all they did, and had it not been for Duclos, who coolly kept her wits about her, who when it was abandoned by the others assumed the government of the revels, preserved order, and put the merrymakers to bed, I repeat that had it not been for Duclos, it is very probable indeed that rosy-fingered Dawn, opening the gates of Apollo's palace, would have found them lying still plunged in their excrements, rather more after the example of swine than like heroes.

Needful only of rest, each lay by himself that night, and cradled in Morpheus' arms, recovered a little strength for the strenuous new day ahead.

The Seventh Day

The friends had ceased to participate in Duclos' nine o'clock lessons. Wearied from the night's riot, fearing, furthermore, lest some operation might result in loss of fuck at that very early hour, and esteeming, finally, that this ceremony was accelerating their indifference to joys and to objects whose interest and integrity it was surely to their advantage to preserve for a while, they agreed that instead of one of themselves, one of the fuckers would hereafter take his turn at the morning exercises.

The inspection and searches were conducted, only one little girl was wanting to make all eight of them eligible for correction, and she was the lovely and intriguing Sophie, a child accustomed to fulfilling all her duties; however ridiculous they may have seemed to her, she respected them none the less, but Durcet, who had earlier conferred with Louison, her governess, so artfully caused her to tumble into the snare that she was declared to be at fault and was as a consequence added to the fatal register. The sweet Aline, equally subjected to close scrutiny, was also judged guilty, and so it was that the evening's list contained mention of the eight little girls, four of the little boys, and two from among the wives.

These tasks accomplished, Messieurs concentrated their thoughts upon the marriage highlighting the festival that marked the end of the first week. No chapel permissions were granted that day, Monseigneur clad himself pontifically, they betook themselves to the altar. The Duc, representing the bride's father, and Curval, who represented the young groom's, led forth Michette and Giton. Both were extraordinarily arrayed in the most formal dress, but also reversedly, that is to say, the little boy was costumed as a girl, the little girl wore boy's clothes. We regret to say that the sequence we originally established for the treatment of our matter obliges us to postpone yet a little longer the pleasure the reader will doubtless take in learning the details of this religious ceremony; but the appropriate moment for disclosing them will surely arrive, and probably fairly soon.

Messieurs passed into the salon. It was while awaiting the hour of dinner our four libertines, encloseted with that charming little couple, had them remove their clothing, and obliged them mutually to perform everything in the sphere of matrimonial ritual their age permitted, with the single exception of the introduction of the virile member into the little girl's vagina, which introduction could perfectly well have been effected, for the boy stiffened very satisfactorily, but he was held in check in order that nothing might happen to spoil a flower destined for plucking by others. But, apart from that, they were allowed to finger and caress one another; young Michette polluted her little husband and Giton, aided by his masters, frigged his little wife as nicely as you please. However, they were both beginning to realize full well the bondage they were in, and this recognition prevented voluptuous joy, even that joy their young years permitted them to experience, from being born in their little hearts.

They dined, the bride and the groom assisted at the wedding feast, but at coffee, heads having waxed hot over them, they were stripped naked, as were Zélamir, Cupidon, Rosette, and Colombe, who were serving coffee. Thigh-fuckery having become fashionable at this time of day, Curval laid hands on the husband, the Duc captured his bride, and the two men enthighed the couple on the spot. The Bishop, who since coffee had been brought in had taken a liking to him, now fell ravenously upon the charming Zélamir's behind, which he tongued, sucked, and whence he elicited farts, and he soon managed to transpierce the little fellow in the same way, while Durcet committed his preferred little villainies upon Cupidon's charming behind. Our two principal athletes did not discharge; one of them soon had Rosette in his clutches, the other Colombe, they slipped their pricks between the children's legs and, just as they had with Michette and Giton, ordered them to frig, with their pretty little hands and in accordance with the instruction they had been receiving, those monstrous prick ends thrusting beyond their crotches and out into space; and while the youngsters toiled away, the libertines comfortably fingered their helpers' delicious, fresh little assholes. And still no fuck shed; Messieurs knew full well what delicious chores lay ahead that evening, they proceeded circumspectly. The young couple's privileges were abrogated, their marriage, although made in keeping with every formality, became no more than a jest; they each of them returned to their quatrains, and the company established itself in the auditorium. Duclos took up her story.

A man with more or less the same predilections as the financier whose exploits terminated yesterday evening's recital shall be the athlete whom, may it please your Lordships, today's shall begin. He was a crown attorney of some sixty years and not only were his eccentricities unusual, but for practicing them he would have none but women older than he. Guérin gave him one of her friends, an aged procuress whose withered buttocks bore a powerful likeness to a crumple of old parchment being used to keep tobacco moist. Such, notwithstanding, was to be the object employed for our libertine's offerings. He knelt down before that decrepit bum and kissed it lovingly; farts were blown up his nose, he waxed ecstatic, opened his mouth, the lady opened her vent, his tongue went enthusiastically in quest of the mellow winds soughing in that tunnel. He could not resist the delirium into which the operation was plunging him. From his breeches he has brought out an ancient, pale, shriveled little device, an object as ill-favored as the one he deifies. "Ah! Fart, my old sweetie, fart thoughtlessly, fart abundantly," he cries, frigging himself with all his strength. "Fart, my love, for only thy little farts will break the spell binding this slumbering prince." The procuress redoubles her efforts, and, drunk with joy, the libertine surrenders his burden: between his goddess' legs fall two or three unhappy droplets of the sperm responsible for the whole of his delight.

O terrible effect of example! Who would have believed it? At the very same instant, and quite as if they had received a signal, all four of our libertines individually summon the duennas of their quadrilles. They lay eager hands upon those foul and rammy asses, solicit farts, obtain them, and are fully prepared to be just as happy as the crown attorney, but restrain themselves, for they remember the pleasures awaiting them at the orgies; whereupon they dismiss each his Venus, and Duclos continues:

I shall lay little emphasis upon the following passions, said that amiable creature, for I realize that there are not many in your midst, Messieurs, who are its votaries; however, you have commanded me to tell everything, and I obey. A very young man, a young man with a very handsome face, used to find it vastly amusing to lick out my cunt once a month, and at a certain period. I would be lying on my back, my legs flung wide, he used to kneel in front of me and suck, with both hands lifting my flanks so as to bring my cunt to within easy reach. He swallowed both fuck and blood, for he managed so adroitly, worked with such good will, and was such a pretty lad I used to discharge. He would frig himself, would be in seventh heaven, nothing evidently could afford him so much pleasure, and the hottest, the most ardent discharge, performed while in action, used always to convince me of his high humor. The following day he would usually see Aurore, not long afterward it would be my sister, and in the course of the month he would pass us all in review, and he doubtless made the rounds of every other whorehouse in Paris at the same time.

But, Messieurs, I believe you will concur in my judgment when I say that the aforementioned caprice is no more singular than that of another gentleman, an old friend of Guérin, who had been furnishing him for years. She assured us that all his joy consisted in eating expelled ovulations and in lapping up miscarriages; he would be notified whenever a girl found herself in that case, he would rush to the house and swallow the embryo, half swooning with satisfaction.

"I knew that particular man," said Curval. "His existence and his tastes are as authentic as anything else in the world."

"Perhaps," said the Bishop. "And I know something just as certain as your man, and that is I'd not imitate him."

"And why, pray tell?" asked the Président. "I am convinced it would produce a lively discharge, and were Constance to grant me her kind permission, for I hear she's gravid now, why, I can promise her I'll fetch Monsieur her son along before he's fully done, and I'll toss him off like a sardine."

"Oh, all the world knows your horror of pregnant women," cried Constance, "and everyone also knows you only got rid of Adelaide's mother because she conceived a second time, and if Julie were to take my advice, she'd be careful."

"Why yes, 'tis perfectly true that I am not fond of progeny," quoth Curval, "and that when the beast is laden it quickens a furious loathing in me, but to imagine I killed my wife on that account is to be gravely mistaken. Bitch that you are, get it into your head that I have no need of reasons in order to kill a woman, above all a bitch that, were she mine, I'd very surely keep from whelping."

Constance and Adelaide fell to weeping, and this brief dialogue revealed something of the secret hatred the Président bore for the charming wife of the Duc who, for his part, very far from supporting her in discussion, replied to Curval, saying that he ought perfectly well to know that he, Blangis, was equally illdisposed to offspring, and that although Constance was pregnant, she had not yet given birth. And at this point Constance's tears flowed all the faster; she was on her father's couch, and Durcet, not taxing himself to comfort her, advised her daughter that if she did not cease her blubbering that instant, her state notwithstanding, he was going to boot her ass out of the auditorium. The hapless creature shed inwardly upon her heart the tears wherewith she was reproached, and was content to say: "Alas, Great God! very wretched am I, but 'tis my fate, I must endure it." Adelaide, who had also been weeping away on the Duc's couch and whose distress the Duc had been moving heaven and earth to increase, also managed to dry her tears, and this scene, somewhat tragical although very mirthful to our four libertines' villainous souls, ground to an end, and Duclos resumed her tale:

In Guérin's establishment there was a room most curiously constructed, and it was always used by one man. It had a double floor, and this narrow between-stories area, where there was only space enough to lie down, served to lodge the uncommon breed of libertine in the interests of whose passion I had regular employment. He would take a girl and, descending through a trap door, would lie down and arrange himself in such a manner his head was directly below a hole that had been bored in the floor above; the girl accompanying him had the single chore of frigging him, and I, located above, had simply to do the same thing for a second man. The hole, obscure and seemingly a natural flaw in the planks, remained uncovered as if through negligence, and I, acting at the behest of tidiness, eager to avoid spotting the floor, would while manualizing my man direct his fuck so that it fell through the hole and, consequently, upon the face of the gentleman below. It was all managed with such skill nothing seemed out of place, and the operation would be a success each time: at the moment the fuck frigged from the person above splashed upon the nose of the person being frigged below, the latter would unleash his own, and that was all there was to it.

However, the elderly dame I mentioned not long ago reappeared, but she was to be pitted against a different champion. This new one, a man of about fifty, had her remove her clothes and then licked out every orifice in her old corpse: ass, cunt, mouth, nostrils, armpits, ears, he omitted nothing, and with each sucking the rascal swallowed whatever he obtained. And he went further still, he had her chew slices of pastry which he would then have out of her mouth and into his, and swallow. He would have her keep mouthfuls of wine she had gargled or swished about, he would have them from her, and drink them too; and all the while his prick would be so furiously erected that the fuck seemed ready to fly all unaided. Finally he would sense the crucial instant's arrival and, hurling himself upon the crone, he would thrust his tongue at least six inches into her asshole and discharge like a madman.

"Ah, by God!" said Curval, "will you now say that youth and pretty looks are indispensable to an elicitation of fuck? Why, once again 'tis the filthy act that causes the greatest pleasure: and the filthier it be, the more voluptuously fuck is shed."

"Those are the piquant salts," Durcet concurred, "which as they are exhaled from the object serving our lust, enter us and irritate our animal spirits, put them in a commotion; well now, who is it doubts that everything derelict, maculate, or stinking secretes a greater quantity of these salts and hence has a greater capacity for stimulating and determining our discharge?" This thesis was soberly discussed for a little while; as there was a quantity of work to be done after supper, it was served earlier than was customary, and at dessert the little girls, every one of them condemned to do penance, departed for the salon where they were to be corrected together with the four boys and the two wives who also lay under sentence. That made fourteen victims: the eight girls, whose names the reader knows, Adelaide and Aline, and four youths: Narcisse, Cupidon, Zélamir, and Giton. Already drunk with anticipation of the particular delight that was awaiting them and of which they were incredibly fond, they completed their intoxication by imbibing a prodigious amount of wine and liqueurs, and then removed to the salon where the patients were awaiting them, and such was Messieurs' common state, so besotted were they, in such lecherous fury did they enter, that there is surely no one in the wide world who would have wished to exchange places with those unlucky culprits.

Attendance at the orgies was that day confined to the delinquents and the four elders who were there as servants; everyone was naked, everyone trembled, everyone was weeping and wondering what to expect when the Président, taking his seat in a tall armchair, bade Durcet announce the name of each criminal, and cite his offense. Durcet's face was as wrathful as his colleague's, he took up the register and undertook to read from it, but encountered difficulties and was unable to proceed; the Bishop came to his rescue, and although quite as drunk as the banker, held his wine with greater success and in a loud voice read one after the other the names of the guilty and their faults; and after each citation the Président pronounced sentence in keeping with the physical faculties and age of the criminal, but the punishment decreed was in every instance severe all the same. This ceremony concluded, punishment was inflicted. We are in despair, for here we are once again forced by the design or our history to make a little detour: yes, we must for the time being omit describing those lubricious corrections, but our readers will not hold it against us; they appreciate our inability to give them complete satisfaction at the present moment; but they can be sure of it, their time will come.

The ceremony lasted a very long time. There were fourteen subjects to punish, and some very pleasant episodes interrupted the proceedings. No doubt of it, everything was delicious, for our scoundrels discharged, all four of them, and retired so weary, so drunk with wine and pleasure, that had it not been for the four fuckers who came to fetch them, they might not have reached their chambers where, despite all they had just accomplished, further lewd exploits were performed.

The Duc, who had Adelaide for his bed companion that night, did not want her. She had been one of the delinquents punished, and punished so well by him that he, having poured out every drop of his fuck in her honor, had no more need of her that evening and, relegating her to a mattress on the floor, he gave her place to Duclos, more firmly installed in his good graces than ever.

The Eighth Day

The previous day's examples having made a deep impression, no one was found, no one could be found wanting the next day. The lessons continued, they were executed upon the fuckers, and as the day produced no outstanding event until coffee, we will begin our account with that little rite. Coffee was served by Augustine, Zelmire, Narcisse, and Zéphyr. The thigh-fuckeries began again, Curval laid hands on Zelmire, the Duc on Augustine, and after having admired and kissed their pretty buttocks which, I truly don't know why, that day possessed a charm, an attraction, a blush of vermilion the friends had not hitherto remarked, after, I say, our libertines had thoroughly kissed and caressed those exquisite little asses, farts were elicited from them; the Bishop, who had Narcisse in his grip, had already procured himself some, Zéphyr's could be heard spluttering into Durcet's mouth - why not imitate them? Zelmire succeeded, but Augustine had striven with might and main, the Duc had threatened her with another Saturday martyrdom, with punishment as severe as what she had just suffered the day before, but strains and struggles, menaces and imprecations were all in vain, nothing emerged from the poor little creature, she was already in tears when a driblet at length appeared and satisfied the Duc who inhaled the aroma and, highly pleased with this mark of docility in the pretty child of whom he was so fond, he camped his enormous engine between her thighs, then withdrew it as he was about to discharge, and totally inundated her two buttocks. Curval had done the same to Zelmire, but the Bishop and Durcet contented themselves with what is known as the little goosing; later, their nap over, they passed into the auditorium, where the splendid Duclos, arrayed that day in everything that could most successfully cause an observer to forget her age, appeared even lovelier under the candlelight, and our libertines, grown very hot with much looking at her, were loath to allow her to ascend to the platform without first having her exhibit her buttocks to the assembly.

"A magnificent ass, upon my soul," said Curval.

"Oh, indeed, my friend," said Durcet, "I warrant there are few better to be seen."

These encomiums heard, our heroine lowered her skirts, took her seat, and resumed her story in such wise as the reader shall observe, if he be pleased to continue, which we advise that he do for the sake of his pleasure.

A reflection and an event were responsible, Messieurs, for the shift in battlefields; the digladiations I shall from now on relate were performed in other surroundings. The reflection was a most simple one: I remarked the lamentable condition of my purse, and straightway was set to thinking. I had been nine years at Madame Guérin's, and although, during that time, I had disbursed very little, I now found myself without even a hundred louis; that woman, extremely clever and never once deaf to the pleading of her own welfare, always found a way to pocket two-thirds of the house's receipts and to impose additional deductions upon the remainder. These practices displeased me and, subject to repeated solicitations from another procuress, Madame Fournier, who wanted nothing more than to have me settle down with her, and knowing that this Fournier received elderly debauchees of a higher tone and greater means than Guérin's clientele, I decided to take my leave of the one and throw in my lot with the other. As for the event which lent support to my ideas, it was the loss of my sister: I had grown very attached to her, and I could no longer remain in a house where everything reminded me of her but whence she was absent.

For nearly six months that dear sister had been receiving visits from a tall, dark, and silent man whose face I found exceedingly disagreeable. They would retire together, and I do not know how they passed their time, for never did my sister want to discuss what they did, and never did they cavort in a place where I could view their commerce. In any event, she came into my room one fine morning, embraced me, and said that her fortune was made, she was to be the mistress of the tall man I disliked, and I learned only that the deciding factor in her conquest was the beauty of her buttocks. And with that she gave me her address, settled her accounts with Guérin, gave each of us a farewell kiss, and left. You may be sure that I did not fail to go the indicated address, for I wished to see her. It was two days after her departure; I arrived, asked for my sister, and my request was answered by shrugs and blank expressions. I saw perfectly clear that my sister had been duped, for I could not imagine she would have deprived me of the pleasure of her company. When I related the thing to Guérin and complained of what had happened, a malign smile crept over her face. She refused to explain herself; hence I concluded she was embroiled in this mysterious adventure but did not want me to become involved in it. It all had a deep effect upon me and brought a swift end to my unresolve; as, Messieurs, I shall have no occasion to speak of that beloved sister in future, I may say now that, notwithstanding the inquiries I had made and the lengths to which I went to find her, I was never able to discover what had become of her.

"I dare say not," Desgranges observed, "for, twenty-four hours after having left you, she was no longer alive. No, she did not deceive you; rather, she was herself deceived. But, as you surmised, Guérin knew what was afoot."

"Merciful Heavens! what are you telling me?" cried Duclos. "Alas! though deprived of the sight of her, I still imagined she was alive."

"Most erroneously," Desgranges replied. "She told you the strict truth: it was indeed the beauty of her buttocks, the astonishing superiority of that memorable ass that procured her the adventure in which she flattered herself a fortune was to be earned, but wherein she gained death only."

"And the tall silent man?" Duclos asked.

"He was no more than the courtier in the story, he was working for another."

"Yet, I tell you, he saw her assiduously for six months."

"In order to deceive her," Desgranges answered; "but go on with your tale, these clarifications might prove tedious to their Lordships, and should they wish to hear more of the matter, they may rest assured the anecdote will figure in my depositions."

"And spare us any emotional demonstrations, Duclos," said the Duc dryly, upon noticing that it was all she could do to keep back a few involuntary tears, "we don't much care for regrets and grievings, you know; as a matter of fact, all the works of Nature could be blown to hell and we'd not emit so much as a sigh. Leave tears to idiots and children, and may they never soil the cheeks of a clearheaded, clear-thinking woman, the sort we esteem."

With these words, our heroine took herself in hand and resumed her narrative at once.

Owing to the two reasons I have just presented to your Lordships, I made up my mind to leave; Fournier offered me better accommodations, a far more interesting table, much more remunerative although more arduous work, an equal share in the receipts, and service charges. I went to her at once. At that time she occupied an entire house, and five pretty young girls composed her seraglio; I made the sixth. You will allow me to proceed again as earlier I did when describing Guérin's establishment: I will not portray my companions-at-arms until one by one they step into the arena.

On the morrow of my arrival, I was given a project, for Fournier ran a bustling house, people came and went all the time, each of us would often receive five or six clients in the space of a day; but I shall continue, as I have until now, to select none but those who, by dint of singularity or piquancy, are apt to arrest your attention.

The first man I welcomed in my new habitation was a disbursing official, aged about fifty. He had me kneel by the bed with my chin resting on its edge; he established himself on the bed, kneeling also, and above me. He frigged his prick squarely into my mouth, commanding me to keep it wide open; I lost not a drop, and the bawdy fellow was prodigiously amused by the contortions and efforts to vomit this disgusting mouthwash caused in me.

You will perhaps prefer me to group the four other adventures in this category I had at Madame Fournier´s, although you understand, Messieurs, that these encounters were separated in time. I am certain the telling will be far from displeasing to Monsieur Durcet, and perhaps very opportune, and for the rest of the evening he will most kindly permit me to entertain him with accounts of a passion for which he has enthusiasm, and which procured me the honor of making his acquaintance.

"What's this?" exclaimed Durcet; "you are going to have me play a role in your story?"

"With your gracious leave, my Lord," Duclos replied. "I shall simply advise Messieurs when I reach the point where you make your entrance."

"But my modesty . . . oh dear, oh dear! Before these little girls, do you mean you intend to disclose all my turpitudes to their innocent hearing?"

And everyone having chuckled over the financier's whimsical fears, Duclos resumed her narrative.

Another libertine, much older and in a different way digusting, succeeded the one I mentioned a moment ago, and came to give me a second representation of the same mania; he had me stretch out naked upon a bed, stretched out himself, his head to my toe, popped his prick in my mouth and his tongue in my cunt, and having adopted this attitude, bade me make return for the voluptuous titillations he declared his tongue was very certainly going to procure for me. I sucked as best I could; he had my pucelage, he licked, bubbled, splashed about and, without doubt, in all these maneuvers, labored infinitely more in his own behalf than in mine. Whatever may have been the truth, I felt nothing, and was exceedingly happy not to be horribly revolted by the whole affair; there ensued the roué's discharge, an operation which, in accordance with Fournier's earnest wishes, for she had given me foreknowledge of everything, an operation, I say, which I strove to make as lubricious as possible by sucking, by wringing the juice from his prick with my lips, by swishing it about in my mouth, and by running my hand over his buttocks and tickling his anus, which last detail, he indicated, pleased him very much, and which he performed on me in turn as best he could. . . . The business completed, our man beat his retreat, assuring Madame Fournier that never yet had he been outfitted with a girl who gave him more satisfaction than I.

Shortly after this latest of my exploits, an old witch of about seventy came to our house; I was curious to know what brought her to us, she seemed to have an expectant air, and, yes, I was told that she was awaiting a customer. Extremely eager to see to what purpose the old bag of bones was going to be put, I asked my companions whether there were not a room from which one might have a view of the bouts, as had been possible at Guérin's. One of my friends replied that indeed such facilities were available and led me to a chamber equipped with not one, but two holes; we took our posts, and this is what we saw and heard, for the wall was no more than a thin partition, and sound traversed it so easily we lost not a word. The old dame arrived first. She looked at herself in a mirror, primped, made adjustments, as if she fancied her charms were yet capable of conquering. A few minutes later, in walked this Chloë's Daphnis; he was sixty at the most, a tax commissioner, a man who was very comfortably well off and who preferred spending his money upon worn-out sluts, old trash like this, rather than upon pretty girls; and why? 'Twas a singularity of taste you say that you understand, Messieurs, and indeed you explain the thing admirably. He advances, surveying his Dulcinea; she makes him a bow of deepest respect.

"No nonsense, you old bitch," says the rake, "I don't care for elegant manners. Get out of your clothes. . . . But wait just one moment. Have you any teeth?"

"No, Sire, not a one is left in my head," quoth the lady, opening her foul old mouth. "See for yourself, may it please your Lordship."

Whereupon up steps his Lordship and, grasping her head, he deposits upon her lips one of the most passionate kisses I have seen in all my life; not merely did he kiss, but he sucked, he devoured, most amorously he darted his tongue far, far into that putrid gullet, and the dear old grandmother, of whom not so much had been made in many a long year, replied with a tenderness which . . . I should have much difficulty describing to you.

"Very well," said the official, "that will do. Off with your clothes."

Meanwhile, he too undoes his breeches and brings out a little dark and wrinkled member about which there is nothing at all that promises an early erection. However, the old girl is naked, and with unimaginable effrontery comes up to offer her lover the sight of an ancient, yellow, and shriveled body, dry, shapeless, and unfleshed, the full description whereof, irrespective of your particular fancies in such matters, would so fill you with horror it were better for me to say no more; but far from being disgusted, repelled, upset by what greets his eye, our libertine is positively enchanted; ecstatic, he seizes her, draws her to where he is seated in a chair, manualizes her while waiting for her to remove a last stitch of clothing, again darts his tongue into her mouth and, turning her around, for a moment pays his respects to the other side of the coin. I very distinctly saw him fondle her buttocks - but what am I saying? buttocks? rather, I saw him manipulate the two wrinkled rags which fell in waves and little ripples from her haunches and lay flapping on her thighs. Well, such as they were he drew them apart, voluptuously fastened his lips upon the infamous cloaca they enclosed, drove his tongue repeatedly thereinto, and while he sweated happily over this ruin, she struggled to give some firmness to the moribund device she was rattling.

"Let's get to the heart of the matter," said her beloved; "without my favorite stunts, all your attempts will be useless. You've been told?"

"Yes, Monsieur, I have been told."

"And you know you've got to swallow?"

"Yes, my dearie, I'll swallow, oh yes, my little cabbage, my pet, down it'll go, I'll devour every little drop my duckling makes."

And therewith the libertine deposits her on the bed, her head lying toward its foot, he straightway pops his limp engine between her gums, drives doughtily in up to the balls, wriggles about until, seizing his delight's legs and perching them upon his shoulders, his snout is nicely lodged between the old creature's buttocks. His tongue wanders deep into that exquisite hole; the honeybee going in quest of the rose's nectar sucks not more voluptuously; the lady sucks too, our hero begins to stir. "Ah, fuck!" he cries after a quarter of an hour of this libidinous calisthenic, "suck me, suck me, suck and swallow it, you filthy buggress, swallow, for it's coming, by Jesus' sweet face, it's coming, don't you feel it?" And flinging kisses here and there, scattering kisses upon everything in sight, thighs, vagina, buttocks, anus, everything gets licked, everything is sucked, the old bitch gulps, and the poor old wreck, who withdraws as slack a device as the one he inserted, and who has apparently discharged unerected, goes tottering out all ashamed of his transports, and as promptly as ever he can gains the door in order to avoid the sobering sight of the appalling object which has just seduced him in his weakness.

"And the old bitch?" inquired the Duc.

The old bitch coughed, spat, blew her nose, dressed with all possible dispatch, and left.

A few days later, the same companion thanks to whom I had been able to enjoy witnessing this scene had her turn. She was a blond girl of about sixteen, with the world's most interesting physiognomy; I eagerly seized the opportunity to see her at work. The man with whom she was to hold conference was at least as old as the tax commissioner. He had her kneel between his legs, immobilized her head by catching hold of her ears, and snapped into her startled mouth a prick which looked to me to be dirtier and more unappetizing than a rag left to soak in the gutter. Observing that frightful morsel approaching her clean healthy lips, my poor colleague was moved to back away, but it was not for nothing our gentleman held her like a spaniel by the ears.

"What the devil's this?" he muttered. "Are you going to be difficult?"

And threatening to summon Fournier, who had doubtless recommended the most conciliatory attitude to her, he triumphed over her hesitations. She opens her lips, retreats, opens them again and finally, gagging and spluttering, accepts into that sweetest of mouths that most infamous of relics; from this point onward, the villain's speech was exceedingly rude.

"Ah, you little slut!" he shouted in a rage, "you've got scruples, have you, about sucking the finest prick in France? You suppose, do you, that one's got to wash one's balls just for your sake? Well, fuck you, bitch: suck, do you hear? suck the sweetmeat."

Waxing very hot thanks to these sarcasms and the revulsion he noticed he was inspiring my companion, for true it is, Messieurs, that the loathing you quicken in us becomes the gadfly that arouses your pleasure, stings your lust; waxing most ardent, I say, the libertine plunged into an ecstasy and left in the poor girl's mouth the most definite evidence of his virility. Less complaisant than the old woman, she swallowed nothing, and far more revolted, a moment later she retched her stomach empty, and our libertine, readjusting himself without paying much attention to what she was about, laughed sneeringly between his teeth, amused by his libertinage's cruel consequences.

My turn came next. But more fortunate than my two predecessors, it was Cupid himself I was turned over, and after having satisfied him I was left with nothing but wonder to find tastes so peculiar in a young man so well framed to please. He arrives, he has me take off what I am wearing and lies down upon the bed, orders me to squat above his face and with my mouth proceed to try to wring a discharge from a very mediocre prick, for which however he has words of praise and whose fuck he entreats me to swallow as soon as I feel it flow.

"But don't waste the occasion to idleness," the little libertine added, "meanwhile, I'd have that cunt of yours flood urine into my mouth, I promise you I'll swallow it as you shall my fuck, and I'd be delighted to sniff a few farts from that splendid ass."

I fell to the task and simultaneously executed my three chores with such skill and grace that the little anchovy soon vomited all its fury into my mouth; I swallowed heartily, my Adonis likewise made short shrift of the piss that poured out of my crack and, while he drank, he inhaled the fragrance that a continual stream of farts bore to his nostrils.

"Forsooth, Mademoiselle," murmured Durcet, "you could surely have dispensed with disclosures that portray all my youthful childishness."

"Ha!" said the Duc with a merry laugh, "well indeed! You who scarcely dare look at a cunt today, do you mean to say you used to have 'em piss in the old days?"

"'Tis true," said Durcet, "I blush to admit it, for what could be more dreadful than to have such turpitudes upon one's conscience? Oh, I presently feel the heavy weight of remorse, my friend. . . . O delicious asses!" he exclaimed, in his enthusiasm kissing Sophie's which he had drawn close for a minute's fondling, "O divine asses! how I reproach myself for the incense I deprived you of! O delicious fundaments, I promise you an expiatory sacrifice, I swear upon your altars never again while I live to stray from the paths of rectitude."

And that splendid behind having heated him somewhat, the libertine placed the novice in what was doubtless an exceedingly indecent posture but one in which he was able, as has been seen above, to give his little anchovy to be sucked while sucking the tidiest, freshest, most voluptuous of asses. But Durcet, become now too blasé, too surfeited with that pleasure, only very rarely found it invigorating; one could suck all one wished, he could do the same till his lips cracked, 'twas always the same: he would withdraw in the same collapsed state and, cursing and swearing at the girl, would regularly postpone until some happier moment the pleasures Nature denied him then.

Not everyone was so unfortunate; the Duc, who had passed into his closet with Zélamir, Bum-Cleaver, and Thérèse, emitted shouts and bellows which attested to his happiness, and Colombe, hawking and spitting in great earnestness, left precious little doubt about the temple at which he had done his worshiping. As for the Bishop, reclining upon his couch in the most natural manner, Adelaide's buttocks pinching his nose and his prick in her mouth, he was in seventh heaven, for he was having a wealth of farts out of the young woman; Curval, in an extremely upright state, plugged Hébé's little mouth with his outsized stopper, and yielded up his fuck as he resorted to other stunts.

Mealtime arrived. The Duc wished to advance the thesis that if happiness consisted in the entire satisfaction of all the senses, it were difficult to be happier than were they.

"The remark is not a libertine's," said Durcet. "How can you be happy if you are able constantly to satisfy yourself? It is not in desire's consummation happiness consists, but in the desire itself, in hurdling the obstacles placed before what one wishes. Well, what is the perspective here? One needs but wish and one has. I swear to you," he continued, "that since my arrival here my fuck has not once flowed because of the objects I find about me in this castle. Every time, I have discharged over what is not here, what is absent from this place, and so it is," the financier declared, "that, according to my belief, there is one essential thing lacking to our happiness. It is the pleasure of comparison, a pleasure which can only be born of the sight of wretched persons, and here one sees none at all. It is from the sight of him who does not in the least enjoy what I enjoy, and who suffers, that comes the charm of being able to say to oneself: 'I am therefore happier than he.' Wherever men may be found equal, and where these differences do not exist, happiness shall never exist either: it is the story of the man who only knows full well what health is worth after he has been ill."

"In that case," said the Bishop, "you would maintain as a real source of pleasure the act of going and contemplating the tears of persons stricken by misery?"

"Most assuredly," Durcet replied. "In all the world there is perhaps no voluptuousness that more flatters the senses than the one you cite."

"What? You would not succor the lowly and wretched?" exclaimed the Bishop who took the most genuine delight in engaging Durcet to expetiate upon a question whose examination was so much to the taste of them all and upon which, they knew, the financier was able to deliver some very sound opinions.

"What is it you term succor?" Durcet responded. "For the voluptuousness I sense and which is the result of this sweet comparison of their condition with mine, would cease to exist were I to succor them: by extricating them from a state of wretchedness, I should cause them to taste an instant's happiness, thus destroying the distinction between them and myself, thus destroying all the pleasure afforded by comparison."

"Well then, following that," reasoned the Duc, "one should in one way or another, so as the better to establish that distinction indispensable to happiness, one should, I say, rather aggravate their plight."

"There is no doubting it," said Durcet, "and that explains the infamies of which I have been accused all my life. Those who are in perfect ignorance of my motives," the banker continued, "call me harsh, ferocious, barbaric, but, laughing at these divers denominations, I go merrily on; I cause, I dare say, what fools describe as atrocities, but thereby I have created pleasure-giving distinctions and have made many a delectable comparison."

"Come now," said the Duc, "confess, my dear fellow: admit that upon more than a score of occasions you have engineered the ruin of some poor folk, simply by that means to serve the perverse tastes you have just acknowledged."

"More than a score?" said Durcet. "More than ten score, my friend, and, without the slightest exaggeration, I could enumerate above four hundred families reduced to beggardom, a state in which they'd not now be languishing had it not been for me."

"And," said Curval, "I fancy you have profited from their ruin?"

"Why yes, that has very frequently been the case, but I must also confess that often enough I have acted not to gain, but purely to undo, at the behest of that

Marquis de Sade

certain wickedness which almost always awakens the organs of lubricity in me; my prick positively jumps when I do evil, in evil I discover precisely what is needed to stimulate in me all of pleasure's sensations, and I perform evil for that reason, for it alone, without any ulterior motive."

"Upon my soul," declared the Président, "I own I fancy nothing better than that taste. When I was in Parliament I must have voted at least a hundred times to have some poor devil hanged; they were all innocent, you know, and I would never indulge in that little injustice without experiencing, deep within me, a most voluptuous titillation: no more was needed to inflame my balls, nothing used to heat them more certainly. You can imagine what I felt when I did worse."

"It is certain," said the Duc, whose brain was beginning to warm as he fingered Zéphyr, "that crime has sufficient charm of itself to ignite all the senses, without one having to resort to any other expedient; no one understands better than I that enormities and malpractices, even those at the most extreme remove from libertine misbehavior, are quite as capable of inciting an erection as those which lie directly within the sphere of libertinage. The man who is addressing you at this very instant has owed spasms to stealing, murdering, committing arson, and he is perfectly sure that it is not the object of libertine intentions which fire us, but the idea of evil, and that consequently it is thanks only to evil and only in the name of evil one stiffens, not thanks to the object, and were this object to be divested of the power to cause us to do evil, our prick would droop, 'twould interet us no more."

"What could be more certain than that?" the Bishop demanded. "And thence is born another certitude: the greatest pleasure is derived from the most infamous source. The doctrine which must perpetually govern our conduct is this: the more pleasure you seek in the depths of crime, the more frightful the crime must be; as for myself, Messieurs," added the Bishop, "if I may be permitted to speak personally, I affirm that I have reached the point of no longer being susceptible of this sensation you have been discussing, of no longer experiencing it, I say, as a result of lesser or minor crimes, and if the one I perpetrate does not combine as much of the atrocious, of the base, of the vicious, of the deceitful, of the treacherous as may be possibly imagined, the sensation is not merely faint, there is no sensation at all."

"Very well," said Durcet, "is it possible to commit crimes such as these our minds yearn after, crimes like those you mention? For my part, I must declare that my imagination has always outdistanced my faculties; I lack the means to do what I would do, I have conceived of a thousand times more and better than I have done, and I have ever had complaint against Nature who, while giving me the desire to outrage her, has always deprived me of the means."

"There are," said Curval, "but two or three crimes to perform in this world, and they, once done, there's no more to be said; all the rest is inferior, you cease any longer to feel. Ah, how many times, by God, have I not longed to be able to assail the sun, snatch it out of the universe, make a general darkness, or use that star to burn the world! oh, that would be a crime, oh yes, and not a little misdemeanor such as are all the ones we perform who are limited in a whole year's time to metamorphosing a dozen creatures into lumps of clay."

Whereupon, their minds having waxed gay and hot, as two or three young girls had already had cause to remark, and their pricks beginning to rise, they left the table and went in search of pretty mouths, thereinto to pour the floods of that liquor whose too insistent throbbings promoted the utterance of so many horrors. That evening they confined themselves to mouth pleasures, but invented a hundred manners of varying them, and when they had run, all four of them, each a magnificent race, in a few hours of repose they sought to find the strength necessary to starting out afresh.

The Ninth Day

That morning Duclos expressed her opinion, saying she held it prudent either to offer the little girls new patients to replace the fuckers then being employed in the masturbation exercises, or to terminate their lessons, for she believed their education sufficiently advanced. Duclos very astutely pointed out that by continued use of the young men known by their title of fucker, there might result that species of intrigue Messieurs wished especially to prevent; moreover, she added, for such exercises these young men were worth nothing at all; since they were prone to discharge immediately after they were touched, their skittishness or incontinence ought certainly be better exploited, Messieurs' asses had only to lose if the program remained unchanged. It was therefore decided that the lessons would cease; they had generally succeeded, there were already amongst the little girls a few who frigged masterfully: Augustine, Sophie, and Colombe could easily have been matched, what for skill and nimbleness of wrist, against the capital's most famous friggers. Of them all, Zelmire was least adept: not that she lacked agility or that considerable science was not conspicious in all her motions, no, but it was her tender and melancholic character which stood in her way, she seemed unable to forget her sorrows, she was sad and pensive at all times. At that morning's breakfast inspection tour, her duenna affirmed she had the previous evening caught the child in a prayerful attitude, flagrantly on her knees before retiring; Zelmire was summoned, questioned, she was asked the subject of her prayers; she at first refused to answer, then, threats having been employed, she fell to weeping and admitted she had besought God to deliver her from the perils wherewith she was beset, and had above all prayed that help would come before her virginity were lost. The Duc thereupon declared she deserved to die, and made her read the articles which dealt specifically with this subject.

"Very well," she sighed, "kill me, at least the God I invoke shall have pity upon me, kill me before you dishonor me, and that soul I have devoted to Him will at least fly in purity to His breast. I shall be delivered of the torment of seeing and hearing so many horrors every day."

A reply wherein reigned such a quantity of virtue, of candid innocence, and of gracious amenity caused our libertines prodigiuosly to stiffen. There were voices that called out for her instantaneous depucelation, but the Duc, reminding his cohorts of the inviolable contract they had subscribed to, was content to propose - and his suggestion was unanimously approved - that she be condemned to punished very violently the following Saturday and that, in the meantime, she kneel and for fifteen minutes take into her mouth and suck each friend's prick, and that she be given by way of warning the assurance that, were she to repeat her error, it would decidedly cost her her life, for she would be judged and punished to the fullest extent of the law. The poor little thing crawled up to accomplish the first part of her penance, but the Duc, whom the ceremony had aroused, and who after having pronounced sentence had prodigiously fondled her ass, like the villain he was, shot all his boiling seed into that pretty little mouth, in so doing threatening to strangle her if she spat out a drop, and the poor little wretch swallowed it all, not without furious repugnances. The three others were similarly sucked one after the other, but yielded nothing, and after the usual visit to the boys' quarters and the excursion to the chapel, which that morning produced little because almost everyone had been refused permission to join the party, the meal was served, and then Messieurs entered the salon for coffee.

It was served by Fanny, Sophie, Hyacinthe, and Zélamir; Curval fancied he might thigh-fuck Hyacinthe, and obliged Sophie to post herself in such a way as to be able to suck that length of his prick which protruded beyond Hyacinthe's tightly squeezed legs. The scene was pleasant and inspiriting, he frigged the little chap he held hugged to his belly, and Hyacinthe discharged upon Sophie's face; the Duc, who owing to the dimensions of his prick was the only other one who could imitate this performance, likewise arranged himself with Zélamir and Fanny, but the lad had not yet reached the discharging age, and thus the nobleman had to do without the very agreeable episode Curval considered so enjoyable. After they had finished, Durcet and the Bishop took charge of the four children and had themselves sucked, but no one discharged, and after a brief nap, the company moved into the auditorium where, everyone having assumed his place, Duclos went on with her disclosures.

Before any other audience, said that amiable girl, I might shrink at broaching the subject of the narratives wherewith this entire week we shall be occupied, but however crapulous that subject, I am too well acquainted with your tastes, Messieurs, to be in any wise apprehensive. No, I believe you'll not be displeased; quite the contrary, I am convinced you will find my anecdotes agreeable. I ought however to advise you that you are about to hear of abominable, filthy goings on; but whose ears could be better made to appreciate them? your hearts love and desire them, hence I enter into the matter without further delay or ambages.

At Madame Fournier's we had a trusty old client who was known as Chevalier, I don't know why, or whence the title came; his custom was to pay us a visit every evening, and the little rite that we regularly performed with him was equally simple and bizarre: he would unbutton his breeches, and we were required to form a queue and one by one drop a turd in them. Once we had all done our duty, he would button up again and go off in great haste, taking that freight with him. While he was being supplied he would frig himself for an instant or two, but he was never seen to discharge, and no one knew where he went or what he did with his breechload of shit.

"Oh, by Jesus!" muttered Curval, who never heard anything he had not a desire to do on the spot, "I'll have someone shit in my breeches, and I'll keep the treasure the whole evening."

And ordering Louison to come render him that service, the old libertine provided the assembly with a full-blown dramatization of the whimsy whereof account had just been delivered.

"Well, go on," he said phlegmatically, nodding to Duclos and settling down on his couch again, "there's nothing to it, and I expect it will only be the lovely Aline, my charming companion for the afternoon, who'll find something inconvenient about it. As for myself, a pound of shit in the vicinity suits me perfectly."

And Duclos resumed her story.

Forewarned, said she, of all that was destined to take place at the home of the libertine to whom I was being sent, I dressed myself as a boy, and as I was only twenty, with pretty hair and a pretty face, that costume very well became me. Before leaving, I took care to do in my breeches what Monsieur le Président has just had done for him in his. My man was awaiting me in bed, I approach him, he kisses me very lewdly two or three times, he tells me I'm the prettiest little boy he's ever set eyes upon, and while praising me he undertakes to unbutton my breeches. I put up a faint resistance with the single purpose of inflaming his desires all the more, he entreats me, urges me, he has his way, but how am I to describe to you the ecstasy that possesses him whe perceives the package I have brought along, and the colorful mess it has made of my two buttocks.

"Why, what's this?" cries he. "You've shit in your breeches, have you? But, my little rascal, 'tis very nasty, you know. How could you have done such a thing?"

And quick as a shot, holding me with my back turned to him and my breeches pulled down, he sets to frigging and rattling himself, presses against me, and spurts his fuck upon my beshitted behind, the while driving his tongue into my mouth.

"Do you mean to say," exclaimed the Duc, "he refrained from touching anything? Didn't he handle it?"

"No, your Lordship," Duclos made him answer, "I recount all that transpired, I conceal no detail; but have a little patience, Sire, and we will gradually reach more entertaining circumstances."

"Come," said one of my companions, "let's go watch a truly humorous fellow. He doesn't need a girl, he amuses himself all alone."

We repaired to the hole, having been informed that in the adjoining room, the one selected for his activities, there was a pierced chair and beneath it a chamber pot we had been busy filling for four days and in which there must have been at least a dozen large turds. Our man arrives. He was an elderly tax-farmer of about seventy years. He shuts the door, goes straight to the pot he knows to be brimming with the goodies he has ordered for his sport. He takes up the vessel and, seating himself in an armchair, passes a full hour gazing lovingly at all the treasure whereof he has been made the proprietor; he sniffs, inhales, he touches, he handles, seems to lift one turd out after another in order to contemplate them the better. Finally become ecstatic, from his fly he pulls a nasty old black rag which he shakes and beats with all his might; one hand frigs, the other burrows into the pot and scoops out handfuls of divine unction. He anoints his tool, but it remains as limp as before. There are moments, after all, when Nature is so stubborn that even the excesses we most delight in fail to awake a response. He did all in his power, and unavailingly, for nothing resulted or rose gloriously up, but by dint of abuse meted out by the same hand that had just been steeped in the ordure, the ejaculation occurred, he trembled, thrilled, fell backward, smelled, breathed deeply, rubbed his prick, and discharged upon the heap of shit which had just so inspired him.

Another gentleman dined with me one evening. We were alone together, and twelve large plates filled with the same meats were brought in and combined with the remnants of an earlier course. He sniffed these new dishes, sampled their aromas, and after he had finished eating, bade me frig him upon the one that had struck him as the most handsome.

A young crown attorney used to pay according to the number of enemas one was willing to receive at his hands; when I crossed swords with him, I agreed to accept seven, he administered them all himself; thus, seven times over had I to mount a little stepladder, while he, stationed underneath me, frigged himself until I spewed out over his prick the entire charge with which he had lubricated my bowels.

As may be readily imagined, the entire evening was devoted to unclean activities of roughly the same species that had been treated in story, and that Messieurs turned to this kind of sport will be all the more easily understood in the light of their general enthusiasm for this passion; it was of course Curval who carried matters the furthest, but his three colleagues were scarcely less infatuated with the novelties laid out before them. The little girls' eight steaming turds were arranged amidst the supper's dishes, and at the orgies the competition was doubtless even keener for those of the little boys; and thus ended the ninth day whose term they saw arrive with the greatest pleasure, for they had high expectations for the morrow, which was destined to provide them with more amply detailed anecdotes treating a subject they adored.

The Tenth Day

(Remember to be more guarded in the beginning and more gradually to disclose what is to be clarified here.)

The farther we advance, the more thoroughly we may inform the reader about certain facts we were obliged to no more than hint at in the earlier part of the story. We are able, for example, presently to advise him of the purpose of the morning visits and searches conducted in the children's quarters, the cause of their punishment when in the course of these inspections delinquents were found, and just what were the delights Messieurs tasted in the chapel: the subjects were expressly forbidden to go to the toilet or in any other place to move their bowels without individual and particular permission, this in order that there be held in reserve matters which could, as the occasion rose, be doled out to those who desired them. The visit served to determine whether anyone had neglected to comply with this order; the officer of the month carefully inspected all the chamber pots and other receptacles, and if he found any that were not empty, the subject concerned was immediately inscribed in the punishment register. However, provision had been made for those who could hold back no longer: they were, a little before the midday meal, to betake themselves to the chapel Messieurs had converted into a privy so designed that our libertines were able to enjoy the pleasure which the satisfaction of these pressing needs had the power to procure them, and the others, who had been allowed, or who had been able, to keep their loads, had the opportunity to be rid of them at some time or another during the day and in that manner which most pleased the friends, and above all in that particular manner upon which full details will subsequently be provided, for these details will compass all the manners of indulging in this voluptuous delight.

And there was yet another cause which led to the distribution of punishment, and it was the following one: what is called in France the bidet ceremony did not exactly please our friends; Curval, for example, could not bear to have the subjects with whom he came to grips wash themselves; Durcet's attitude was identical, and so it was that the one and the other would notify their duennas of the subjects with whom they planned to amuse themselves the next day, and these subjects were forbidden to wipe, rub, or wash themselves in any way and under any circumstances, and the two other friends, who did not share this abhorrence of tidiness and for whom dirt was not by any means essential, nevertheless concurred with Curval and Durcet, aided in maintaining and agreeable state of affairs, and it after having been told to be impure a subject took it into his head to be clean, he was straightway added to the fatal list.

That is what happened that morning to Colombe and Hébé; they had shitted during the previous night's orgies and, knowing that they were listed to serve coffee on the following day, Curval, who planned to amuse himself with both of them and who had even advised them that they would be expected to fart, had recommended that things be left just as they were. The children did nothing to themselves before going to bed. Inspection arrived, and Durcet, aware of the instructions Curval had given, was perfectly amazed to find them as neat as a pin;

forgetfulness was the excuse they offered, but their names went down in the register nevertheless.

No chapel permissions were granted that morning. (We should like the reader to make a particular effort to remember what we mean by such an expression; this will dispense us from having to repeat our explanations.) Calculations of what would be required during the storytelling period forbade any prodigality until that time.

Upon this day the boys' masturbation lessons were suspended, for they had entirely served their purpose, and every one of the little lads frigged as expertly as the cleverest whore in Paris. Zéphyr and Adonis led the pack in skill, speed, and deftness, and there are few pricks which would not ejaculate nigh to bleeding were they to be ministered by little hands as nimble and delicious as theirs.

Nothing worth citing occurred until coffee; it was served by Giton, Adonis, Colombe, and Hébé; these four children had, by way of preparation, been stuffed with every decoction which is best able to provoke winds, and Curval, who had proposed to be treated to farts, received a generous quantity of them. The Duc had himself sucked, or rather licked, by Giton, whose little mouth simply could not manage to engulf the enormous machine tendered him. Durcet performed some choice little horrors with Hébé, the Bishop thigh-fucked Colombe. Six o'clock sounded, they moved into the auditorium where, everyone having taken his post, Duclos began to recount what you shall read:

A new companion had very recently come to Madame Fournier's; owing to the role she is going to play in the account of the passion which follows, I believe I should give you at least a rough sketch of her. She was a young seamstress, debauched by the seducer I earlier mentioned having observed at Guérin's, and she also worked for Fournier. She was fourteen, had chestnut-brown hair, sparkling brown eyes, the most voluptuous little face in all the world, skin lily white and satin smooth, very trimly made she was, although rather inclining to fleshiness, from which slight disadvantage there resulted the sweetest, cutest, the plumpest ass, the fairest, oh 'twas possibly the finest ass in Paris. I was stationed at the hole in the partition and soon beheld the man who was to deflower her, for she was yet a maid on the other side, nothing could be plainer. Such a tidbit could only have been fed to someone very much beloved of the house: he was the venerable Abbé de Fierville, equally renowned for his wealth and his debauchery, and he had the gout to his very fingertips. He arrives swathed to the eyes in a mantle, installs himself in the chamber, examines all the equipment he is about to use, prepares everything, and then the little girl arrives; her name is Eugénie. Somewhat frightened by her first lover's grotesque face, she lowers her gaze and blushes.

"Come hither, come hither," says the libertine, "and show me your behind."

"Oh, Monsieur . . ." murmurs the shy little thing.

"Come, come," fumes the old roué, "nothing worse than these novices; she just can't imagine anyone should wish to look at an ass. Well, by the Saviour, get your damned skirts up."

And, stepping closer for fear of displeasing Fournier, whom she has promised to be very obedient, she finally pulls her skirt halfway up from behind.

"Higher, do you hear, higher," cries the pleasant old rascal. "Do you suppose I'm going to bother to do it myself?"

And in due time the beautiful ass is completely exposed. The man of God scrutinizes it, has her stand straight, has her bend forward, has her squeeze her legs tight together, has her separate them and, leaning her over the bed, spends a moment crudely, nay, uncouthly rubbing all his frontward privities, which he has brought to light and with which he now prods and pushes Eugénie's matchless bum, as if to electrify himself, as if to attract to himself some of that lovely child's essential heat. From this he passes to kisses, he falls to his knees in order to be more at his ease, and with both hands holding those superb buttocks as far apart as possible, both his tongue and lips rummage about in search of treasure.

"They're right," says he, "you do have a passably fine ass. Have you been shitting recently?"

"Just a little while ago, Father," the little one answers. "Madame had me do that before coming up."

"Why, that's nice . . . and so there's nothing left in your bowels," says the lecher. "Well, we're going to see."

And catching up the syringe, he fills it with milk, returns to behind his object, brandishes the nozzle, plunges it into the vent, and shoots out the fluid. Having been told what to expect, Eugénie submits to everything; no sooner is the remedy in her entrails than he lies down on the bed and orders Eugénie to come at once and straddle him. "Now," says he, "if you've got anything to do, have the kindness to do it in my mouth." The timid creature has taken her place as she has been told to do, she pushes, the libertine frigs himself, his mouth, sealed hermetically to her asshole, catches every drop of the precious liquid that leaps out of it. He swallows it all, giving evidence of the greatest scrupulousness in this matter, and just when he swills down the final mouthful, his fuck escapes and he is hurled into a delirium. But what is this strange mood, this cloud of loathing which, as in the case almost every other libertine, comes to darken a mind whence the entire illusion has fled? Brutally casting the little girl far from him once he has done, the saintly man readjusts his cleric's garb, says that he has been cheated, deceived, for this child, he swears, had not priorly shitted, no, they'd lied, she'd come to him full of shit, and he'd swallowed half her turd, fie upon them. It is to be noted that Monsieur l'Abbé wanted milk only, not shit. He grumbles, he curses, he storms, says he won't pay, won't ever come back, says he'll be damned if he'll stir himself for little snotfaces like this one, and goes off shouting a thousand other invectives I'll surely have occasion to report to you in connection with another passion in which they play a major role rather than, as in this instance, a very subordinate one.

"Well, by God," Curval remarked, "there you have a very fastidious man who'll get upset over swallowing a little shit when there are I don't know how many who feast upon it."

"Patience, Sire, patience," said Duclos, "allow my recitals to succeed each other in the order you yourselves dictated and you shall see the superior libertines you allude to achieve wonders on the stage."

My turn came two days later. Instructions had been given me, and I stayed away from the water closet for thirty-six hours. My hero was an elderly ecclesiastic who served as chaplain to the King; like the aforementioned athlete he too was crippled with gout: he was only to be approached if one were naked, but one's front and breast had to be very thoroughly covered; much emphasis had been placed upon this latter article, and I had been warned that were he to catch the least glimpse of those parts, it would prove a heavy misfortune, I'd never be able to get him to discharge. I approach, he studies my behind with extreme attentiveness, asks my age, asks whether it is true I have a great urge to shit, inquires as to the kind of shit I ordinarily produce, is it soft? is it hard? and a thousand other questions the asking of which, it seems to me, has the effect of animating him, for, as he chatters away his prick gradually lifts its head and leans toward me. That prick, approximately four inches in length by two or three around, had, despite its brilliant sheen, something of so humble and so pitiful an air that one all but needed spectacles to be certain of its existence. Solicited by my man thus to do, I laid firm hands on it, and noticing that my motion were rather well irritating his desires, he made ready to consummate the sacrifice.

"But is it a truly authentic desire, my child," says he, "this desire to shit you mention? For I don't care to be deceived; come, let's see whether you do indeed have shit in your ass."

And so saying, he buries his right hand's longest finger in my fundament, while with his left hand he sustains the erection I have excited in his desire. That plummeting finger had no need to search far, the chaplain was swiftly persuaded I had, quite as I said, the sincerest wish to shit, and when his gropings contacted the object of our mutual concern, he flew into a perfect ecstasy:

"Ah, by God's belly," he cries, "she tells the truth, the chicken is about to lay, and I feel the egg."

Enchanted, the bawdy old priest passes a moment kissing my bum, and observing the haste I am in and that I shall soon be unable to restrain the insurgent turd, he has me climb aboard on apparatus quite similar to the one your Lordships have here in the chapel; once seated, my behind perfectly exposed to his view, I was able to lodge my complaint in a receptable located two or three inches from his nose. This apparatus had been built expressly for the chaplain, and he employed it frequently, for scarcely a day went by without him coming to Fournier's to assist in delivering either some girl attached to the house or some other from outside it. An armchair drawn close allowed him to observe the process from a point of vantage situated just below the ring supporting my ass.

When we had taken our positions upon our respective thrones, he ordered me to commence the operation. For prelude, I release a series of farts; he inhales them. The turd hoves into sight at last; he begins to pant.

"Shit, my little one, shit away, my angel," he cries, all afire. "Show me the turd coming forth out of your lovely ass."

And he aids the delivery, pressing his fingers about my anus, he facilitates the eruption; he frigs himself, he observes, he is drunk with lust, pleasure's excess finally transports him completely, he loses his head; his cries, his sighs, his fingerings, everything convinces me he is nearing the final stage and, turning my head toward him, I find I have judged correctly, for there is his miniature engine splattering a few drops of sperm into the same pot I have just filled. The chaplain left in a good humor, and even assured me he expected he would honor me with another visit, which promise I knew very well to be false, for it was common knowledge that he never saw the same girl twice.

"Well, I appreciate his feelings in the matter," declared the Président, who was kissing Aline's ass. "One must be in our deplorable situation, one must be reduced to rack and ruin in order to be able to bear having the same ass shit twice."

"Monsieur le Président," spoke up the Bishop, "there is a certain halting tone in your voice which leads me to suspect your prick is in the air."

"Tush," Curval replied, "I'm merely kissing the buttocks of Mademoiselle your daughter, who hasn't even the courtesy to let fly one wretched little fart."

"I am then enjoying better luck than you," the Bishop announced, "for Madame your wife, lo and behold! has just presented me with the most beautiful and the bulkiest turd. . . ."

"Silence, gentlemen, silence, I say!" came from the Duc, whose voice seemed muffled as if by something covering his head. "Silence, by Jesus! we are here to listen, not to act."

"Which is therefore to say, I take it, that you are doing nothing," inquired the Bishop, "and is it in order to listen that you are wallowing under three or four assholes?"

Well, you know, he's right. Go on, Duclos, it were wiser that we hear about foolish acts than commit them. We must save our strength."

And Duclos was on the point of resuming when they all heard the usual shouts and customary blasphemies that accompanied the Duc's discharges; surrounded by his quatrain, his fuck was escaping him as with Sophie, Zéphyr, and Giton he performed countless little wantonries of a kind very analogous to those Duclos had been describing.

"Great God!" Curval exclaimed, "I can't tolerate these bad examples; there's nothing that makes me discharge like a discharge, and would you believe it? here's that little whore," he added, referring to Aline, "who only a moment ago could accomplish nothing at all and who is presently doing everything one could ask for

. . . but no matter, I'll keep my grip. Ah, you bitch, shit away, shit your head off, it will get you nowhere, I don't intend to give up my seed."

"I see very well, Messieurs," said Duclos, "that after having perverted you it is my responsibility to restore you to reason, and to do so I am going to resume my story without waiting for your command."

"No, don't you do it," cried the Bishop, "I am not as continent as Monsieur le Président, not I, my fuck's itching me, and it's got to be shed."

Wherewith, he was seen very publicly to perform things the structure of this very complex fiction prevents us from revealing at this stage, but things whose delightful influence very rapidly brought leaping forth the fuck whose mounting pressure had discomfited the Bishop's thrice-blessed balls. As for Durcet, absorbed in Thérèse's ass, nothing was heard from him, and in all likelihood Nature refused him what she lavishly granted the others, for he was not as a rule mute when accorded her favors. Seeing that now at last calm had been restored, Duclos went on with her lubricious exploits.

A month later, I came to grips with a man whom one had almost to violate in order satisfactorily to carry out an operation somewhat akin to the one I related several minutes ago. I shit upon a dish, I bring it to him and thrust it under his nose while he sits in an armchair quietly reading a book, seemingly unaware of my presence. He looks up, falls to swearing, asks how the devil can the girl have the insolence to do such a thing in his presence, but all the same it's a queer turd she's got there, he contemplates it, handles it; I ask forgiveness for the liberty I have taken, he continues to mumble incoherencies at me, and then discharges with his eyes fixed on the morsel of shit; and in so doing he says he'll find me again someday, that sooner or later he'll see to it that I get what I deserve.

A fourth gentleman employed none but women of seventy or more in practices which were quite similar; I watched him enact his rite with an old creature who could not have been less than eighty. He was reclining upon a sofa, the matron was straddling him; she deposited her strange old package on his belly while frigging a wrinkled, shriveled prick which scarcely discharged at all.

At Fournier's establishment we had another curious article of furniture: a kind of toilet chair, provided with the usual hole and set against the wall; things were so arranged that a man could lie in such a way that while his body extended into the neighboring room, his shoulders passed through an opening and his head occupied the place usually reserved for the chamber pot. I had been appointed to the task, and kneeling between his legs, I sucked his prick as best I could throughout the operation. Well, this extraordinary ceremony consisted in having a workman, who was paid to act a part whose full consequences he neither knew nor divined; in having, I say, a man of the people enter the room containing the chair, climb upon it, and do his business squarely upon the face of the patient over whom I was toiling; but the shit bearer had absolutely to be a poor drudge fetched in from the humblest milieu, he had as well to be old and ugly, he was inspected before being put to work, and were he to lack any of these qualities, our libertine would have nothing to do with him. During all this, I saw nothing but heard rather a lot: the instant of collision was also that of my man's discharge, his fuck sprang down my throat the same moment the turd splashed upon his face, and when he emerged from beneath the chair and got to his feet, I saw by the state he was in that he had been handsomely served. By chance, after the exercise was over, I happened to meet the fellow who had performed so brilliantly; he was from the Auvergne, a good honest chap who earned his livelihood working with stonemasons; he seemed delighted to earn a crown by doing naught but ridding himself of what he would have had one way or another to expel from his bowels, and this little chore struck him as infinitely less arduous than carrying his hod. He was, what for his looks, quite dreadful to behold and must have been over forty.

"Faith," muttered Durcet, "I think that should do it."

And passing into his closet with the eldest of the fuckers, with Thérèse and Desgranges, he was heard braying and whinnying some minutes later; he returned but was disinclined to inform the company of the precise nature of the excesses whereunto he had surrendered himself.

Supper was announced; it proved at least as libertine as ever, and after the meal, the four friends having been moved to spend the evening away from one another instead of frolicking together as they customarily did, the Duc went off to the boudoir at the end of the corridor, taking with him Hercule, Martaine, his daughter Julie, Zelmire, Hébé, Zélamir, Cupidon, and Marie.

Curval commandeered the auditorium, providing himself with what companionship Constance could afford him, for she fell to trembling every time she found herself with him, and he did exceedingly little to allay her fears; he also took Fanchon, Desgranges, Bum-Cleaver, Augustine, Fanny, Narcisse, and Zéphyr.

The Bishop went into the drawing room with Duclos who, that evening, revenged herself upon the fickle Duc, who had led Martaine away from him; Aline, Invictus, Thérèse, Sophie, the charming little Colombe, Céladon, and Adonis completed the prelate's entourage.

Durcet remained in the dining room. It was cleared, rugs and cushions were brought in and strewn all about. He encloseted himself, I say, with Adelaide, his beloved wife, with Antinoüs, Louison, Champville, Michette, Rosette, Hyacinthe, and Giton.

More the redoubling of lecherous appetites than any other reason had doubtless dictated this arrangement, for brains were heated to such a point that evening that it was unanimously agreed no one would go to bed; it was perfectly incredible what was achieved in each room by way of infamies and impurities.

Toward dawn, their Lordships decided to return to table, although they had taken abundant drink throughout the night; everyone trooped into the dining room, there was an indistinct, promiscuous pell-mell, the cooks were awakened and soon sent in scrambled eggs, toast, onion soup, and omelettes. Drinking was resumed, the company grew very merry, all save Constance who was plunged in inconsolable sadness. Curval's hatred was growing just as certainly as was her poor belly; she had that night during the orgies experienced the effects of his hostility, she had suffered everything but blows, for Messieurs had agreed to leave the pear to ripen; she had, I say, blows excepted, undergone every imaginable mistreatment; she though to complain to Durcet and to her husband, the Duc: they both bade her go to the devil and remarked that she must surely have been guilty of some fault which was hidden from their eyes, yes, surely, else how could she thus ever have displeased that most virtuous and most gentle of mortals; they wagged their heads and walked away. And then they all went to bed.

The Eleventh Day

They did not rise till late that day, and dispensing with all the usual ceremonies, went directly to table once they had got up from their beds. Coffee, served by Giton, Hyacinthe, Augustine, and Fanny, was largely uneventful, although Durcet could not do without some farts from Augustine, and the Duc thrust his brave instrument between Fanny's lips. Now, as from the desire to what the desire causes 'tis ever but a single step with personages such as our heroes, they went unswervingly toward satisfying themselves; happily Augustine was prepared, she blew a steady breeze into the little financier's mouth, and he came nigh to stiffening; as for Curval and the Bishop, they confined themselves to fondling the two little boys' behinds, and then our champions moved to the auditorium.

One day little Eugénie, who was becoming more familiar with the rest of us and whom six months in the whorehouse had only rendered all the prettier, Eugénie, I say, one day accosted me and lifting her skirts, bade me look at her ass. "Do you see, Duclos, how Fournier wants me to keep my behind today?"

An inch-thick patch of shit covered her sweet little asshole.

"And why does she want you to wear that?" I asked her.

"It's for the sake of an old gentleman who is coming this afternoon," she explained, "and he expects a beshitted ass."

"Well, well," said I, "he'll be very pleased with you I'm sure, for yours couldn't possibly be more thickly encrusted."

And she told me that Fournier's was the hand that had smeared her thus. Curious to witness the impending scene, I flew to the spy hole as soon as dear little Eugénie was summoned. The principal actor was a monk, but one of those monks we call gros bonnets, a Cistercian, tall, heavy, vigorous, and nearing sixty. He caresses the child, kisses her upon the mouth, and demanding to know whether she is neat and clean, he hoists her petticoats personally to verify a constant state of cleanliness whereof Eugénie gives him full assurance, although knowing nothing could be further from the truth; but she had been instructed so to speak to him.

"What's this, my little rascal?" exclaims the monk upon catching sight of that formidable mess. "What? Do you dare tell me you are neat and tidy when your ass is as filthy as this? Why, by the Virgin, I'm sure 'tis a fortnight since this bum's been wiped. 'Tis very troubling indeed, for I like things to be clean, I do, and it truly looks as if I had better look into the situation."

While speaking he had deposited Eugénie upon a bed, knelt behind her buttocks, and begun to pry them apart with both his hands. One would have thought that, at the outset, he purposed simply to observe the state of affairs, which caused him great surprise, but little by little he becomes accustomed to things as they are, sees here a virtue where he had seen only a fault before, sticks out his tongue and moves his head closer, sets to polishing the gem, the clods and spots he removes, the pristine object they conceal inflames his senses, his prick gets up, his nose, mouth, and tongue seem simultaneously to be at work, his ecstasy appears so delicious he is all but deprived of the power to speak, his fuck finally mounts - he grasps his prick, frigs it, and as he discharges, finishes cleaning that anus, which is now so fresh and pure one would scarcely suppose it had been nasty no more than a minute or two before.

But the libertine was not yet ready to bring the affair to a conclusion, this voluptuous mania of his constituted a mere preliminary; he gets to his feet, bestows further kisses upon his little partner, exposes to her view a great ass of very evil aspect and very unclean, and he orders her to give it a thorough shaking, to socratize it; this brings his prick up furiously again, he now returns to Eugénie's ass, overwhelms it with renewed caresses, lickings, and so forth, but what he did after that it is not for me to relate, nor would it properly figure in these introductory narrations; you will, Messieurs, have the great kindness to allow Madame Martaine to tell you of the behavior of a villain with whom she was only too well acquainted; and in order to avoid all questions, my Lords, which your own regulations forbid me to treat, or resolve, I continue on to another episode.

"Just one word, Duclos," said the Duc, who then queried the storyteller in an indirect language which enabled her to make lawful reply. "Was it big with the monk? Was this Eugénie's first time? . . ."

"Yes, Sire, the first, and the monk's was about the size of yours."

"Ah, fuck my eyes!" muttered Durcet; "a damned pretty demonstration, I'd like to have seen that."

You would perhaps have been equally curious, Duclos said as she picked up the thread of her narrative, about the individual who, a few days later, passed into my hands. Outfitted with a vessel containing eight or ten great turds gathered from all quarters and whose authors he would have been very distressed to have identified, I was with my own hands to rub him from head to toe with this fragrant pomade. Not an inch on his body was neglected, not even his face, and when I had massaged his prick, which I frigged at the same time, the infamous pig, who all the while stared contentedly at himself in a mirror, left evidence of his humble virility between my palms.

And at last, gentlemen, we have arrived; I can now advise you that the homage is about to be made in the veritable temple. I had been told to hold myself in

readiness, I kept my bowels closed for two long days. It was a commander of the
Order of the Knights of Malta with whom I was to break a lance; he used to see
a different girl every morning for these exercises; the following scene transpired
at his home.

"Very fair buttocks," was his opinion as he embraced my behind. "However, my
child," he continued, "there's more to it than simply having a comely ass, you
know. That comely ass must know how to shit. Tell me, have you the urge?"

"Such an urge I'm dying to satisfy it, Monsieur," I confessed.

"Well, by Jesus, that's delicious!" exclaimed the commander, "that's what is
called excellent service to society, but look here, my little duck, would you like to
shit in this chamber pot I'm offering you?"

"In faith, Monsieur," I made answer, "what with the need I have to shit, I'd do
it anywhere, I'd even shit in your mouth."

"No! In my mouth, you say? Why, bless me, that is delicious, and that's
precisely the place I myself had in mind for you," he added, setting the pot aside.

"Well, Monsieur, let's make haste, bring up your mouth," said I, "for indeed I'll
not be able to hold back much longer."

He places himself on the couch, I climb astride him, while operating I frig him,
he supports my haunches with his hands and receives, piece by piece, everything
I deposit in his avid mouth. He is thrilled by it all, nears his ecstasy, my wrist is
hardly needed to bring forth the floods of semen which salute my performance;
I frig, conclude my shitting, our man loses himself and his seed altogether, and I
leave him delighted with me, or at least so he has the kindness to say to Fournier,
at the same time requesting the services of another girl for the morrow.

The personage who came next employed more or less the same approach to the
problem, but simply kept the morsels in his mouth for a longer period. He reduced
them to a fluid, rinsed his mouth with them for a quarter of an hour, and spat out
little more than dingy water.

Yet another had, if that is possible, a still more bizarre eccentricity; he liked to
find four turds in the pot beneath a pierced chair, but those four turds could not
be mixed with so much as a single drop of urine. He would be shut up alone in the
room containing this treasure, never did he allow a girl with him, and every
precaution had to be taken to insure his solitude, he could not bear the thought
he might be observed, and when at last he felt secure he went into action; but I
am absolutely unable to tell you what he did, for no one had ever seen him; all
that is known is that when he had left the room, the pot was discovered perfectly
empty and as tidy as can be. But what he did with his four turds only the devil can
tell you, if indeed he knows. He may perhaps have thrown them away somewhere,
but, then again, he could also have done something else with them.

However, what would lead one to suspect he did not do that something else
with them is that he left the procuring of those four turds entirely up to Fournier,
and never made the least inquiry about their origin. One day, in order to observe
whether what we were about to say would alarm him - for his alarm might have

provided us with a clue about the fate of those turds - we told him that the ones he had been served that day had come from several persons suffering from syphilis. He laughed good-naturedly with us, was not in the slightest disturbed, which reaction was not to be expected from someone who had employed rather than cast away the turds. When we sought, upon one or two occasions, to push our questions a little further, he bade us be silent, and never were we to learn more of the matter.

That concludes what I have to tell you this evening, said Duclos; tomorrow I propose to relate my new mode of life, or rather the new turn my same mode of life took, when I met Monsieur d'Aucourt; and as for the charming passion you so heavily favor, I hope to have the honor to entertain you with examples of it for at least another two or three days.

Opinions were divided about the fate of the turds in the episode Duclos had just recounted, and while arguing and reasoning about them, Messieurs had a few produced for themselves; and the Duc, eager to make everyone aware of the taste he was developing for Duclos, exhibited to the entire assembly his libertine manner to amuse himself with her, and the dexterity, aptitude, and promptness, accompanied by the most stirring language, wherewith she knew so artfully how to satisfy him.

Supper and the orgies transpired without any unusual incident, nothing of importance took place before the afternoon of the next day, and so we may move directly to the recitations wherewith Duclos brightened the 12th of November.

The Twelfth Day

The new mode of life I was about to begin, said Duclos, obliges me to draw your attention, Messieurs, to my personal appearance and character at the time; one is better able to figure the pleasures being described if one is first acquainted with the object that procures them. I had just attained my twenty-first year. My hair was brown, but nevertheless my skin was of a most agreeable whiteness. The abundance of hair covering my head fell in floating and perfectly authentic curls to just above my knees. I had the eyes you behold me now to have, and they have always been judged lovely. My figure was rather full although tall, supple, and gracious. With what regards my behind, that part of the anatomy in which libertines today take such a keen interest, it was by common consent superior to the most sublime specimens one is likely ever to see, and there were few women in Paris who had an ass as deliciously molded; it was full, round, very plump, and exceedingly soft, generous, I say, but without its ampleness detracting anything from its elegance, the least gesture immediately discovered that heavenly little rosebud you so cherish, Messieurs, and which, I do indeed like yourselves believe, is a woman's most magical attraction. Although I had been for a long season active in libertinage, my ass could not have been healthier or looked more untried; its splendid condition was in part owing to the good constitution Nature had granted me and in part to the extreme prudence I exercised on the battlefield, scrupulously avoiding encounters capable of damaging my most precious asset. I had very little love for men, I had never had but one attachment; I had a libertine maid, but it was extraordinarily libertine, and after having described my charms it is only fitting that I say a word or two about my vices. I love women, Messieurs, I don't deny it. Not however to the uncommon degree my good colleague, Madame Champville, loves them; she will probably tell you that she has ruined herself for them; I have simply always preferred them to men in my pleasures, and those they have procured me have always exerted a more powerful sway over my senses than masculine delights. Apart from this fault, I have had another of adoring to steal: I have refined this mania to an unbelievable point. Entirely convinced that all possession should be equally distributed in the world and that it is only strength and violence which are opposed to this equality, foremost law of Nature, I have striven to rectify the actual scheme and to do my utmost to re-establish the proper balance. And had it not been for this accursed compulsion I might perhaps still be with the benevolent mortal of whom I shall speak next.

"You say you have done considerable stealing?" said Durcet.

"An astonishing amount, Monsieur; had I not always spent what I filched, I would be wealthy today."

"But was there not more to it than that?" the financier pursued. "Some aggravating detail, such as, for instance, forced entry, abuse of confidence, manifest deceit?"

"Everything under the sun," Duclos assured him. "I did not think it worth dwelling on these matters which would also have disturbed the smooth unfolding of my history, but since it is evident they might amuse you, in future I'll not forget to cite my thefts.

"As well as that fault, I have always been reproached for another: I am said to have a hard heart, a very bad one indeed; but is that fault really mine? or is it not rather from Nature we have our vices as well as our perfections? and is there anything I can do to soften this heart she caused to be insensible? I don't believe I have ever in all my life wept over my troubles, and I can safely assure you I have never dropped a tear for the afflictions of others; I loved my sister, and I lost her without the least twinge of grief, you were witness to the stoic indifference with which I greeted news of her undoing; I would, by God, see the universe perish without a sniffle or a sigh."

"That is how one must be," said the Duc, "compassion is a fool's virtue. Close examination reveals that it is never anything but compassion which costs us delights. But with that toughened heart of yours, you must have committed crimes, for, you know, insensibility leads straight to nothing else."

"My Lord," Duclos replied, "the regulations prescribed for our narrations prevent me from apprising you of a great many things; my companions will supply what you have ordained I omit. I do have one word to say, however: when later on they attempt to represent themselves to you as villains, you may be perfectly sure I have never been any better than they."

"That, I should say, is doing justice to oneself," Blangis observed. "Well, go on with your tales; we'll have to be content with what you tell us, for we have ourselves set bounds to your discourses; but remember that when we, you and I, have a little chat together, I'll insist upon hearing of your various peccadillos."

"And I shall conceal none of them from you, Sire. May it be that after having heard me out you shall have no cause to repent of your indulgence toward one of the King's worst subjects." Wherewith she lifted up her voice and addressed the assembly again:

Despite all these defects, and above all that of being thoroughly unappreciative of the value of the humiliating sentiment of gratitude, which I consider as naught but an injurious burden to humanity and one which completely degrades the pride and self-respect implanted in us by Nature, with all these deficiencies, I say, my companions were nevertheless very fond of me, and of them all I was the most sought after by men.

Such was my situation when a rich landowner named d'Aucourt came to have a party at Fournier's; as he was one of her steadfast clients, but one who preferred girls brought in from outside the house to those residing in it, he was held in the highest esteem, and Madame, who felt I had absolutely to make his acquaintance, gave me notice two days beforehand not to waste an ounce of the precious matter for which he had a greater passion than any of the other men I had met with until then; but from the details you will be able to judge of all this for yourselves. D'Aucourt arrived, and having eyed me up and down, he scolded Madame Fournier for having waited so long to supply him with this pretty creature. I thanked him for his gallantry, and up we went together. D'Aucourt was about fifty years of age, heavy-set, fat, but his face was pleasant to see, there was animation in his features, he was witty and, what pleased me most of all about him, he had a gentleness and honesty of character which enchanted me from the first moment.

"You must have the world's loveliest ass," said he, drawing me to him and burrowing his hand beneath my skirts. His hand went directly to my behind. "I am a connoisseur, and girls of your figure and general look almost invariably possess striking asses. Why, look here, didn't I tell you so?" he continued, after briefly palpating the object, "how fresh and round it is!"

And nimbly turning me around as with one hand he lifted my skirts to my waist and with the other fondled the article, he fell to work examining the altar to which he addressed his prayers.

"Jesus!" he cried, "by the Saviour, 'tis really one of the finest asses I have clapped eyes on in all my days and, believe me, I have studied many. . . . Spread . . . Great God, behold that strawberry! . . . allow me to suck it . . . devour it . . . 'tis really a beautiful ass indeed, this one . . . eh, tell me, dearie, have they given you the instructions?"

"Yes, Monsieur."

"They told you I have them shit?"

"Yes, Monsieur."

"But your health?" went on the capitalist, "there's nothing amiss?"

"Never fear, good sir."

"It's simply, d'ye see, that I carry things rather far," he went on, "and if you have the least illness or symptom, then I run a great risk."

"Sir," said I, "you can do absolutely anything you please, I guarantee you I am as fit and sound and safe as a newborn babe; you may act in confidence."

After this preamble, d'Aucourt had me bend around toward him and, all the while keeping my buttocks spread wide, and gluing his mouth to mine, he sucked my saliva for fifteen minutes or so; he withdrew his mouth in order to expectorate a little "fuck," and then returned to his amorous mouth pumping.

"Spit into my mouth, spit," he repeated, "from time to time, fill it with saliva."

And then I felt his tongue run over my gums, drive as far as possible into my mouth, and I had the impression it was endeavoring to draw everything out of me.

"Excellent," said he, "I'm getting stiff. Let's go to work."

Then he fell to contemplating my buttocks again, ordering me to encourage the rise of his prick. I pulled out a strange little engine three inches thick and only five long; it was as hard as a cobblestone and full of fire.

"Remove your skirts," d'Aucourt told me, "while I take off my breeches; your buttocks and mine too have to be thoroughly at their ease for the ceremony we are about to execute."

Then, once I had obeyed him:

"Lift your blouse further up, that's it, close to your corset," he continued, "and see to it your behind is absolutely disencumbered. . . . Lie on your stomach upon the bed."

He fetched up a chair and seated himself by the bed, then returned to caressing my bum, the mere sight of which appeared to intoxicate him; he spread my buttocks for a moment and I felt his tongue sound deep into my entrails, this, said he, in order beyond any shadow of equivocation to verify whether indeed the hen were inclined to lay; I report his own expressions to you. All this while, I was not touching him, not at that stage, he was himself lightly stroking the dry little member I had just brought from its lair.

"Are you ready, my child?" he asked. "For it is high time we undertake our task; your shit seems to me as it should be, I've established that, remember to shit gradually, a little at a time, and always wait until I have consumed one morsel before pushing out the next. My operation takes quite a while, so don't be in haste. A light slap on your ass will notify you that I'm ready for more, but see to it that I get no more than a bite."

Having then adopted the most comfortable position, he glued his mouth to the object of his worship, and in less time than it takes to tell I delivered a gobbet of shit the size of a pigeon's egg. He sucked it, turned it a thousand times about in his mouth, chewed it, savored it, at the end of three or four minutes I distinctly saw him swallow it; I push again, the same ceremony is repeated, and as I had a prodigious charge to be rid of, ten times over he filled his mouth and emptied it, and even after all was done he seemed famished still.

"That is all, Monsieur," I said when I had finished, "I'm pushing in vain now."

"It's all over, is it, my little dear? Why, then I believe I'll discharge, yes, discharge while paying my respects to this superb ass. Oh, Great God, what pleasure you give me! I've never eaten more delicious shit, I'd swear to that before any jury. Give it to me, bring it hither, hither, my angel, bring me your matchless ass to suck, let me devour it."

And thrusting what seemed to be twelve inches of tongue through my anus and while doing so manualizing himself, the libertine spatters his fuck over my legs, not without uttering a host of obscene words and oaths necessary, apparently, to the crowning of his ecstasy.

When at last it was all over, he sat down, invited me to sit beside him and, regarding me with great interest, asked whether I were not tired of the life of the brothel and if I should not be pleased to come across someone who would extricate me from it; seeing he had taken a fancy to me, I began to demur, and to spare you a long story which could not possibly be of any interest to you, after an hour of debating I let myself be won over, and it was decided that on the following day I would take up quarters in his home in return for twenty louis per month and board; that as he was a widower, I could conveniently occupy a large apartment in his town house; that I would have a maid to wait upon me and the society of three of his friends and their mistresses with whom he got together for libertine suppers four times each week, sometimes at his own establishment, sometimes at one of theirs; that my one obligation, and occupation, would be to eat a great deal, and always the fare he had served to me, because, doing what he did, it were essential I be fed on a diet which accorded with his taste - to eat a great deal, I say, to sleep long and soundly in order that my digestion be good and thorough, to purge myself regularly once a month, and to shit in his mouth twice every day; that this rate of shit consumption, or rather of shit production, ought not to frighten me because, by stuffing me with food, as he planned to do, I would perhaps hear the call not twice but three times a day. The capitalist presented me with a very pretty diamond in token of his eagerness to conclude the bargain; then he embraced me, told me to settle my affairs with Fournier and to be ready the following morning, at which time he would come to fetch me himself. My farewells were quickly said; my heart regretted nothing, for it knew nothing of the art of forming attachments, but my pleasures regretted the loss of Eugénie, with whom for six months I had enjoyed an exceedingly intimate liaison; I left. D'Aucourt received me with wonderful graciousness and himself took me to the very pretty suite which was to be my new habitation; I was soon fully installed. I was expected, indeed condemned, to eat four meals whence were excluded a great number of things I should have adored having: I had to go without fish, oysters, salted meat, eggs, and every kind of dairy product; but on the other hand I was so well recompensed that in truth I had no real grounds for complaint. The basis of an ordinary repast consisted of an immense quantity of breast of chicken, of boned fowl prepared and presented in every imaginable fashion, little beef or other red meat, nothing that contained grease, very little bread or fruit. I had to eat these foods even for breakfast in the morning and, in the afternoon, at tea; at these hours, they were served me without bread, and d'Aucourt gradually induced me entirely to abstain from bread; ever since then I've not eaten it at all, and I've also given up heavy soups. The result of this diet, as my lover had calculated, was two bowel movements per day, and the stools were very soft, very sweet, somewhat small but, so d'Aucourt maintained, of an exquisite taste which could not be obtained by ordinary nourishment; and d'Aucourt was a man whose opinion deserved to be accorded some weight, for he was a connoisseur. Our operations were performed when he awoke and when he retired for the night. Their details were more or less what I have already given you: he would always begin with a prolonged sucking of my mouth, which I had always to present him in its natural state, that is to say, unwashed: I was only allowed to rinse it out afterward. He would not, furthermore, discharge every time he dined, our arrangements did not in any way bind him to fidelity. D'Aucourt kept me as the pièce de résistance, I was the roast beef, as it were, but that did not prevent him from sallying forth every morning for a nibble of lunch somewhere else.

Two days after I had arrived, his comrades in debauch came for an evening at his home, and as each of the three boasted, in the taste we are presently analyzing, a superficially different although fundamentally identical passion, by your leave, Messieurs, every little example adding to our collection, I shall devote a few words to the fantasies in which they indulged themselves.

The guests arrived. The first was an elderly parliamentarian, in his sixties, and named d'Erville; his mistress was a woman of forty, exceedingly handsome, and having no visible defect other than certain excess of flesh: her name was Madame du Cange. The second was a retired military officer of between forty-five and fifty, he was called Desprès, his mistress was an attractive young person of twenty-six, blond, and having as lovely a body as you may hope to find: her name was Marianne. The third was an abbot, sixty years old, Du Coudrais by name; his mistress was a lad of sixteen, pretty as a star, whom the good ecclesiastic passed off as his nephew.

The table was laid in that part of the house near my chambers; the meal was festive, the fare delicate, and I remarked that the young lady and the youth were on a diet very similar to mine. Characters declared themselves while we dined; it was impossible to be more a libertine than d'Erville; his eyes, his speech, his gestures, everything about him proclaimed debauchery, libertinage was painted in his every line; there was more of the restrained, the deliberate in Desprès, but lust was none the less the soul of his existence; as for the abbot, he was the world's most arrant, boldest atheist: blasphemies flew from his lips with virtually every word he pronounced; with regard to the ladies, they emulated their lovers, tattled and chattered a blue streak but in a rather agreeable tone; the young boy struck me as being as great a fool as he was a pretty one, and du Cange, who seemed smitten by him, cast a series of tender glances toward him, every one of which he failed even to notice.

All propriety had vanished by the time dessert arrived, and the conversation had become as filthy as the goings on: d'Erville congratulated d'Aucourt upon his latest acquisition and begged to know whether my ass had any merit, and if I shitted pleasantly.

"Oh, by God," my capitalist replied with a smile, "you've only to establish the facts for yourself; we hold our goods in common, you know, and lend one another our mistresses quite as willingly as we do our purses."

"Why," d'Erville murmured, "I believe I will have a peek."

Taking me by the hand at once, he proposed that we repair to a closet together. As I was hesitating, du Cange raised her brows and said in a rude voice:

"Be off with you, Mademoiselle, we don't stand on ceremony here. I'll look after your lover while you're away."

And d'Aucourt, whose eyes I consulted, having made a sign of approbation, I followed the old legislator. 'Tis he, Messieurs, and the other two as well, who are going to offer you the three demonstrations of the taste we are currently studying and which should compose the better part of today's narrations.

As soon as I was closeted with d'Erville, he, very much warmed by the drink he had imbibed, kissed me upon the mouth with extreme enthusiasm, and in so doing belched a few hiccups into my mouth, which nearly made me eject from that orifice what, a few minutes later, he seemed to have the most pressing desire to see emerge from another. He lifted my skirts, examined my behind with all the lubricity of a consummate libertine, then informed me he was not at all surprised at d'Aucourt's choice, for indeed, said he, I had one of the most beautiful asses in Paris. He besought me to commence with a few farts, and after he had absorbed a half dozen of them, he returned to kissing my mouth, the while fondling me and vigorously spreading my buttocks.

"Are you beginning to feel the need?" he asked.

"I feel little else," I replied.

"Very well, my pretty child, be so good as to shit upon this dish."

He had brought with him one of white porcelain, he held it while I pushed, and scrupulously examined the turd as it emerged from my behind, a delicious spectacle which, so he maintained, intoxicated him with pleasure. When I had finished, he picked up the plate, ecstatically inhaled the voluptuous product it contained, handled, kissed, sniffed the turd, then telling me he could bear it no longer, and that it was now lust wherewith he was drunk thanks to this, the most sublime piece of shit he had ever seen, he bade me suck his prick; although there was nothing in any way agreeable about this operation, fear of angering d'Aucourt by not co-operating with his friend induced me to accede to everything. He settled himself in an armchair, or rather sprawled sideways in it, having deposited the plate on a neighboring table upon which he also rested half his body, his nose buried in the shit; he extended his legs, and I, having drawn up a low chair and having pulled from his fly a mere suspicion of a very soft prick instead of a real member, despite my repugnance I fell to sucking this miserable relic, hoping that a mouthing would give it at least a little consistency. It did not: once I had taken the wretched object into my mouth, the libertine started his operation and thrust into his the pretty little egg, all bright and new, which I had just laid for him; he did not eat it, he battened upon it: the game lasted three minutes, during which his squirmings, shudderings, contortions, declared a very ardent and a very expressive delight. But it was all in vain, not a trace of solidity appeared in that ugly little stub of a tool which, after having wept tears of chagrin into my mouth, withdrew itself more ashamed than ever and left its master in that prostration, in that abandon, in that exhaustion which is the certain consequence of a potent draught of pleasure.

"Ah," said the parliamentarian, "I forswear my faith; never have I seen anyone shit like that."

Upon returning to the dining room we found only the abbot and his nephew, and as they were operating, I can give you the essential particulars at once. Whereas the others exchanged mistresses in this little society, nothing could induce Du Coudrais to do so: always content with what he had, he never accepted a substitute for it; he would not have been able, I was informed, to amuse himself with a woman; but in every other respect, he and d'Aucourt were alike. He went about his ceremony in the same way, what was more, and when we entered the room the youngster was lying belly down upon the edge of a divan, presenting his ass to his dear uncle who, kneeling down before it, was lovingly receiving into his mouth and steadily consuming all the lad was producing, the while frigging an exceedingly small prick we observed dangling between his thighs. The abbot discharged, our presence notwithstanding, and swore that the boy was shitting better with every day that passed.

Marianne and d'Aucourt, who were amusing themselves together, soon reappeared and were followed by Després and du Cange who, they said, had only been cuddling and volleying while waiting for me.

"Because," said Després, "she and I are old acquaintances, whereas you, my lovely queen, you whom I see for the first time, inspire in me the most ardent desire for a more thorough amusement."

"But," I objected, "Monsieur d'Erville has taken it all; I have nothing more to offer you."

"Why indeed!" he said with a merry laugh, "indeed, I ask nothing from you, I'll furnish all that is needed. I merely require your fingers."

Curious to learn the meaning of this enigma, I accompany him, and as soon as we are alone together, he asks to kiss my ass for a brief minute. I raise it toward him and after two or three licks and sucks at the hole, he unbuttons his breeches and bids me do unto him what he has just done in my behalf. His posture excited my suspicions: he was seated facing the back of a chair, by clinging to which he kept his balance, and beneath him was a pot waiting to be filled; and so, observing he was ready to perform all by himself, I asked why it were necessary for me to kiss his ass.

"Nothing could be more necessary, my heart," he replied; "for my ass, in all of France the most capricious of asses, never shits save when kissed."

I obeyed, but took care to stay clear of danger; perceiving my cautious maneuvering:

"Closer, for God's sake, get closer, sweetie," he said in an imperious tone. "Are you afraid of a little shit?"

And so at last, in order to be friendly, I brought my lips to the vicinity of the hole; but he no sooner felt them there than he tripped the spring, the eruption was so violent one of my cheeks was splashed from temple to chin. He needed but one shot to submerge the plate; never in my life had I seen such a turd: all by itself it would easily have filled a very deep salad bowl. Our man snatches it up, takes it with him, and lies down on the edge of the bed, presents his entirely beshitted ass, and orders me to play with it while he feasts upon what has just darted out of his entrails. Filthy as his bum was, I had to obey. "His mistress doubtless does as much," I said to myself; "I must be as obliging as she." I plunge three fingers into the murky aperture pleading for my attentions; our man is beside himself with joy, he falls upon his own excrements, daubs his face with them, wallows in them, feeds upon them, one of his hands holds the plate, the other jostles his prick rising up majestically between his thighs; I redouble my efforts, they are not in vain, I feel his anus contract around my fingers, this reports that his erector muscles are about to launch the seed, the prospect delights me, the plate is licked clean, and my partner discharges.

Once again back in the salon, I find my inconstant d'Aucourt with the lovely Marianne; the rascal had also made use of her. The only one who remained was the page boy, with whom, I believe, he might also have come to terms had the jealous abbot only consented to relinquish him for half an hour. When everyone had returned, they all spoke of removing their clothes and of performing a few extravagances in front of each other. The idea struck me as excellent, for it would enable me to see Marianne's body, which I had the greatest desire to examine; it proved delicious, firm, fair, splendidly proportioned, and her ass, which I fondled several times in a joking manner, seemed to me a veritable masterpiece.

"What do you want with such a pretty girl?" I asked Desprès. "For the pleasure you appear to cherish places no emphasis upon looks."

"Ah," said he, "you don't know all my mysterious little ways."

I was absolutely unable to learn more about them, and although I lived for more than a year with d'Aucourt, and was present at every get-together, neither Desprès nor Marianne wished to clarify anything to me, and I remained in entire ignorance of their secret intelligences which, of whatever kind they may have been, did not prevent the taste her lover used to satisfy with me from being an authentic and distinct passion worthy in every respect of inclusion in our anthology. Whatever he did with Marianne, I supposed, must have been merely episodic and either has been or certainly will be related at some one of our sessions.

After some rather indecent libertine stunts, some farts, yet a few more little turds or turdlets, we had considerable talk and sounding impieties on the part of the abbot, who seemed to locate one of his most perfect lecheries in ungodly conduct and discourse; after all this, everyone put on his clothes again and went off to bed. The next morning, as usual, I appeared in d'Aucourt's room as he was preparing to arise, and neither of us reprimanded the other for our little infidelities of the evening before. He said that, with the exception of myself, he knew of no girl who shitted better than did Marianne; I put several questions to him, asking what she did with a lover who was so admirably self-sufficient, and d'Aucourt replied that all this was a secret between the two of them and they had never seemed willing to disclose it. And we, my own lover and I, went on with our usual little tricks.

I was not as confined at d'Aucourt's house as I had been before; I sometimes ventured abroad; he had complete faith, he told me, in my honesty, I could very well see what danger I would be exposing him to were I to impair my health, and he left me to my own devices. With what regarded the health in which, most selfishly, he took such a keen interest, I did nothing to betray his trust, but as for the rest, I considered myself free to do just about everything that would earn me any money. And so, being repeatedly solicited by Fournier who was eager to arrange parties for me at her establishment, I lent my talents to every project wherefrom I was assured an honorable profit. I was no longer one of her crew, I was a young lady kept by a farmer-general; would I have the great kindness to give Madame Fournier an hour of my valuable time and pass at her establishment on such and such a day, etc., etc. You may fancy how well that paid. It was in the course of these brief distractions that I encountered the new shit worshiper I'll discuss next.

"Just one instant," put in the Bishop. "I did not want to interrupt you until you reached the end of a chapter; you seem to be at one now. Would you therefore have the kindness to shed some additional light upon two or three essential points in this latest party? When you celebrated the orgies after your interview with Després, did the abbot, who until then had been caressing his bardash only, commit acts of infidelity? In a word, did he lay hands upon you? did the others desert their women for the boy?"

"Monseigneur," said Duclos, "the abbot never once left his little boy; he scarcely so much as glanced at us even though we were naked and all but on top of him. But he toyed with d'Aucourt's ass and Després' and also d'Erville's: he kissed them, sucked them, d'Aucourt and d'Erville shitted into his mouth and he swallowed the better part of each of those two turds. But he would not touch the women. The same was not true of the three other friends relative to his youthful bardash; they kissed him, licked his asshole, and Desprès went off alone with him for I have no idea what exercise."

"Excellent," said the Bishop. "You observe that you failed to mention everything, and that what you have just recounted forms still another passion, since it figures the taste of a man who has other men shit in his mouth, and quite mature men at that."

"That is true, Monseigneur," Duclos admitted, "I confess my error but am not sorry for it, because the soiree has drawn to a close and has indeed been overlong. The bell we are about to hear struck would have indicated that I did not have sufficient time to end the story I was preparing to begin, and with your gracious leave we will postpone it until tomorrow."

The bell did indeed ring and as no one had discharged during the sitting and as every prick was, however, mightily aloft, they only betook themselves to supper after promising to make good their loss at the orgies. But the impetuous Duc was never able to postpone important business and having ordered Sophie to present her buttocks, he had that lovely child shit, and he swallowed her turd for dessert. Durcet, the Bishop, and Curval, all similarly occupied, concluded the same operation, the first with Hyacinthe, the second with Céladon, the third with Adonis. The last named, having failed to give ample satisfaction, was inscribed in the punishment book, and Curval, swearing like a trooper, revenged himself upon Thérèse's ass, which exploded, at point-blank range, the most ponderous turd imaginable. The orgies were eminently libertine and Durcet, forsaking youthful turds, said that for the evening's games he would have none but what his three old friends could yield him. They humored him with passing fair performances, and the little libertine discharged like a stallion while devouring Curval's shit. Night came at last to restore some measure of calm to so much intemperance, and to restore as well our libertines' desires and faculties.

The Thirteenth Day

The Président, who that night lay with Adelaide, his daughter, having sported with her until he felt asleep about to claim him, had therewith relegated her to the pallet beside his bed in order that Fanchon might have her place, for he was ever eager to have the old duenna by his side when lust awoke him, which occurred almost every night; toward three in the morning, he opened his eyes with a start and fell to swearing and blaspheming like the true rascal he was. He would at such times be gripped by a lubric furor which now and again became dangerous. That is why he was so fond of having that trusty old Fanchon near him, for no one was so skillful at calming him, whether by offering herself or by immediately bringing him one of the objects lying in his bedchamber.

On that particular night, the Président, instantly recollecting some infamies he had perpetrated upon his daughter just before falling asleep, called for her at once

with the intention of repeating them; but she was not there. Imagine the
consternation and the commotion created by such an incident. Curval springs
from bed in a towering rage, asks where his daughter is; candles are lit, everyone
hunts about, the place is ransacked, nothing's to be found; the last place searched
is the girls' apartments. Every bed is examined, and at last the interesting Adelaide
is discovered seated in her nightgown near Sophie's cot. Those two charming girls,
united by their similarly tender natures, their piety, virtuous sentiments, candor,
and absolutely identical amenity, had been seized by the most beautiful affection
for each other and they were exchanging comforting words, consoling one
another for the dreadful fate that had been reserved for them. No one had
perceived their commerce until then, but what followed proved that this was not
the first time they had got together, and it was discovered as well that the elder
of the was cultivating the other's finer sentiments, and had especially pleaded with
her not to stray from her religion and her duties toward God, Who would one day
comfort and console them for all their woes.

I leave it to the reader to picture Curval's fury and stormy reaction when he
located the lovely missionary; he seized her by the hair and, overwhelming her
with invectives, all very harsh, dragged her to his chamber, where he tied her to
his bedpost and left her until the next morning to ponder over her indiscretion.
All of the friends having rushed to the scene, it will also be readily imagined with
what haste and decision Curval had the two delinquents' names written down in
the register. The Duc argued passionately in favor of instantaneous correction,
and what he proposed was not by any means mild; but the Bishop having
countered with a very reasonable objection to what his brother was urged to do,
Durcet was content simply to include them on the agenda. There was no way of
attacking the duennas; they were all four bedded in Messieurs' chambers that
night. This fact accounted for the imperfect administration of the household, and
arrangements were made whereby, in future, there would always be at least one
duenna in the girls' quarters and another in the boys'. Their lordships retired to
bed again, and Curval, whom anger had rendered more than cruelly impudicious,
did things to his daughter we cannot yet describe, but which, by precipitating his
discharge, at least put him quietly to sleep.

All the hens in the chicken coop had been so terrified that, on the morrow, no
misbehavior was discovered, and amongst the boys, only Narcisse, whom, the
evening before, Curval had forbidden to wipe his ass, wishing to have it nicely
beshitted at coffee, which this child was scheduled to serve, and who had
unfortunately forgot his instructions, only Narcisse, I say, had cleaned his anus
and he had done so with extreme care. It was in vain the little chap explained
that his mistake could be repaired, since, said he, he wanted to shit there and
then; he was told to keep what he had, and that he would be none the less
inscribed in the fatal book; which inscriptions the redoubtable Durcet instantly
performed before his eyes, thus to make him sense all the enormity of his fault, a

veritable sin and possibly by itself capable of upsetting or, who knows? of preventing Monsieur le Président's discharge.

Constance, whom they did not hinder because of her state, Desgranges, and Bum-Cleaver were the only ones who were granted chapel permission; everyone else received the order not to draw the cork until the evening toasts.

The preceding night's events provided the dinner's conversation; they made game of the Président for permitting the bird to fly from its cage, etc.; some champagne restored his gay spirits, and the company sallied forth to coffee. Narcisse, Céladon, and Zelmire distributed it, so did Sophie, who was greatly ashamed of herself; she was asked how often the thing had happened, she replied that it had occurred only twice, and that Madame de Durcet gave her such good counsel that indeed she thought it most unjust to punish them both for it. The Président assured her that what she called good counsel was, in her situation, the very worst, that the devotion wherewith Madame de Durcet had been filling her head would serve no purpose save to get her punished every day, and that, in her present circumstances, she was to have no masters and no gods save his three confreres and himself, no religion save that of blindly serving and obeying them in everything. And, all the while he was delivering this sermon, he had her kneel between his legs and bade her suck his prick, which the poor little thing did all atremble. As always partisan to thigh-fuckery, the Duc, obliged as he was to abstain from the capital practice, impaled Zelmire in this style, meanwhile having the little girl shit in his cupped hand and gobbling it up as quickly as it was received, and all that while Durcet was inducing Céladon to discharge into his mouth, and the Bishop was industriously extracting a turd from Narcisse. A few minutes, no more, were set aside for the nap that they found such an aid to digestion; then, having taken up their posts in the auditorium, Duclos faced the gathering and began the day's narrative.

The gallant octogenarian Fournier had in mind for me, Messieurs, was an official from the auditing bureau, short, pudgy, and with an extremely unpleasant face. He set a pot between us, we squatted down back to back and shitted simultaneously; he seizes up the pot, with his fingers stirs the two turds, mixes them, swallows the batter while I promote his discharge, an eruption which takes place in my mouth. He barely even glanced at my behind. Nor did he do any kissing, but his ecstasy was very sharp and compelling all the same: he pranced all about the room, swearing while he gulped and ejaculated, and then took himself off, giving me four louis for this strange ceremony.

However, my landowner became more fond of me with each passing day, and more trusting too, and this trust, which I lost no time in abusing, soon became the cause of our eternal separation. . . . One day when he had left me alone in his library, I noticed that, before going out for the day, he had filled his purse with money taken from a deep drawer entirely filled with gold. "Ah, what a capture!" I said to myself, and having from that very instant conceived the idea of making off with this sum, I set to watching for the means and opportunity whereby to appropriate it: d'Aucourt never locked the drawer, but he carried with him the key to his library, and having discovered that this door and lock were both very frail, I fancied it would take little effort to break the one and the other. Having adopted the plan, I concentrated upon nothing but taking advantage of the first time d'Aucourt was absent the entire day; that used to be the case twice a week, when he went off for private bacchanals in the company of Desprès and the abbot; Madame Desgranges will perhaps describe what occurred during these outings, they lie beyond my province. The favorable moment was soon at hand; d'Aucourt's valets, as libertine as their master, never failed to go with him to these parties, and so I found myself almost alone in the house. Full of impatience to put my project into execution, I go straightway to the door of the library, break the thin panel with a blow of my fist, rush to the drawer, find it unlocked as I knew it would be. I remove everything it contains; my prize amounts to not less than three thousand louis. I fill my pockets, rifle other drawers; a splendid jewel case catches my eye, I pick it up, but what was I not to find in the other drawers of that bountiful secretary! . . . Fortunate d'Aucourt! What great good luck for you that your imprudence was not discovered by anyone else but me; the secretary contained enought to have had him broken on the wheel, Messieurs, that is all I can tell you. Quite apart from the transparent and expressive notes addressed to him by Desprès and the abbot pertaining to their secret commerce, there was every kind of furniture needed for the performing of those infamies. . . . But I halt myself here; the boundaries you have prescribed to my depositions prevent me from saying more; Desgranges will treat the whole matter. As for myself, the theft once effected, I left at once, shuddering to think of all the dangers I had perhaps been exposing myself to by frequenting the company of such scoundrels. I crossed over to London and, as my sojourn in that city, where for six months I dwelt in the most comfortable style, offers nothing that could be of any outstanding interest to your Lordships, you will permit me to pass quickly over this part of my story. I had maintained contact with no one in Paris but Fournier; however, she advised me of the hue and cry the landowner had raised over this paltry little robbery, and I finally resolved to put an end to this blathering: I took up pen and paper and very coolly informed him that she who had happened upon his money had also discovered other things, and that if he were determined to continue to search for the culprit, I would as bravely as possible endure my fate and very certainly depose, with the same judge who would question me upon what I had done with the contents of the small drawers, a detailed statement of what I had found in the larger ones. Our man fell as silent as a tomb; and as six months later their three-partied debauchery came broadly to light and as they themselves left France for security abroad, I returned to Paris and, must I avow my misbehavior? I returned, Messieurs, as poor as I had been before dispossessing d'Aucourt, and such were my straits I was obliged to put myself back in Madame Fournier's safekeeping. As I was no more than twenty-three at the time, I did not want for adventures; I am going to ignore those exterior to my domain and recount, with your Lordships' indulgent permission, only the ones wherein I know now that you take some interest.

A week after my return, a barrel brimming with shit was placed in the chamber appointed for pleasures. My Adonis arrives; he proves to be a saintly ecclesiastic, but one so habituated to those pleasures, so blasé, that he was no longer capable of being stirred save by the excesses I shall describe. I was naked when he entered. For a moment he regards my buttocks, then, after having fingered them rather brutally, he tells me to undress him and help him get into the barrel. I remove his garments, aid him to climb in, the old pig slides down into his element; a hole has been specially bored for the purpose and, fifteen seconds after having immersed himself, his prick, almost stiff, pops through the aperture; he orders me to frig it, covered as it is with filth and horrors. I do as I am told, he ducks his head down into the shit, splashes in shit, swallows shit, shouts, discharges, and, clambering out, trots off to immerse himself in a bath, where I leave him in the hands of two house servants who spend a quarter of an hour scrubbing him clean.

Another one appeared shortly afterward. I had shitted and pissed into a pot a week before and had carefully preserved the mixture; this period was necessary before matters reached the stage our latest libertine desired. He was a man of thirty-five, and my guess was that he was connected with finance. Upon entering he asked where the pot was; I handed it to him, he sniffed it experimentally.

"You're perfectly certain that was done a week ago?" he asked.

"Monsieur," I replied, "I am prepared to answer for its age; you will notice the first signs of mildew there, some moldiness near the edge."

"Why, indeed, it looks as if it will do very nicely," he agreed, "it's the mold I adore, you know. Never too moldy to suit me. Show me, if you please," he continued, "the pretty ass that shitted what we have here."

I presented it.

"That's it," said he, "put it right there opposite me so that I can see it while eating its creation."

We arrange ourselves, he samples a little tidbit, is thrilled by the taste, plunges directly ahead, and in no time has devoured that exquisite lunch, only interrupting his chewing to scan my bum; but there was no other episode, he did not even draw his prick from his breeches.

A month passed, another unusual fellow came to our door, and this one would deal with none but Fournier herself. What an object he selected, Great God! she had been sixty-eight summers, an erysipelas was eating every inch of her hide, and the eight rotten teeth decorating her mouth communicated so fetid an odor it was all but impossible to speak with her at a distance of under five yards; but it was these shortcomings and nothing else that enchanted the lover with whom she was to take a tumble. Most eager to observe the contest, I run to the spy hole: the Adonis was an elderly doctor, but younger nevertheless than she. He takes her in his arms, kisses her mouth for a good fifteen minutes, then, having her present an ancient, wrinkled ass such as you see on a very old cow, he kisses and sucks it avidly. A syringe is brought in, three half bottles of liqueur too; Aesculapius' worshiper loads his syringe and pumps the healing drink into the entrails of his Iris; she receives the potion, holds it, the doctor does not cease kissing her, he licks every square of her body.

"Ah, my friend," the old lady cries at last, "I can contain myself no longer, not another second, prepare yourself, dear friend, I'm going to have to give it back."

Salerno's scholar kneels, from his fly pulls forth a dark, wrinkled stub of a device, which he pounds and coaxes with emphasis, Fournier settles her great ugly ass upon his mouth, pushes, the doctor imbibes, a turd or two doubtless emerge with the liquid, he gasps but it all goes down, the libertine discharges and falls backward, dead drunk. 'Twas thus this debauchee satisfied two passions at a single stroke: his wine bibbery and his lewdness.

"One moment," said Durcet. "Those excesses always give me an erection. Desgranges," he pursued, "I fancy you possess an ass closely resembling the one Duclos has just figured; come apply it to my face."

The old procuress obeyed.

"Let it go, release it," Durcet said in a muffled voice, for he was speaking from between that pair of awe-inspiring buttocks. "Give it to me, buggress, never mind if it's not liquid, I am perfectly able to chew, and I always swallow whatever comes my way."

And the operation was concluded while the Bishop was performing a similar one with Antinoüs, Curval with Fanchon, and the Duc with Louison. But our four athletes, fully acquainted with all these extravagances and totally at their ease while committing them, performed with absolute effortlessness and even nonchalance: the four deposits were consumed without a single drop of fuck being shed in any quarter.

"Well, on with your story, Duclos, finish up for the day," the Duc said; "if we are no more tranquil than before, we are at least less impatient and better able to pay attention."

"Alas, Messieurs," our heroine answered, "I fear that the anecdote I have still to relate this evening is far too simple, too mild for the state you are in. 'Tis a pity, but no matter; its turn has come, it must keep its place." And she continued as follows:

The hero of the adventure was an old brigadier in the King's army; he had to be stripped to the skin, then swaddled like an infant; when he was thus prepared, I had to shit while he looked on, bring him the plate and, with the tips of my fingers, feed him my turd as if it were pap. Everything is done according to prescription, our libertine swallows it all and discharges in his swaddling clothes, the while simulating a baby's cry.

"Let us then have recourse to children," said the Duc, "since you leave us with a children's story; Fanny, my dear," he continued, "come to your old friend and shit in his mouth, and remember to suck his prick while you are about it, for it seems to have to discharge again."

"Let thy will be done," murmured the Bishop. "Come hither, Rosette; you have heard the orders given to Fanny. Then do as she."

"May the same orders apply to you," Durcet said to Hébé, who responded to his call.

"When in Rome," said the wise Curval, "do as the Romans do, my little one. Augustine, emulate your companions, cause simultaneously to flow both my fuck into your mouth and your shit into mine."

And all these things were done; upon this occasion, all those worthies came; from everywhere the sounds of farting and falling shit were to be heard, discharges too, and, much lust sated, they betook themselves to the table, their appetite was passing strong. But at the orgies, refinements were employed, the little ones were sent off to bed. Those delicious hours were spent with none but the elite fuckers, the four ladies-in-waiting, the four storytellers. Messieurs became completely drunk and performed horrors of such absolute filthiness that I should not be able to describe them without doing an injustice to the less libertine tableaux I have yet to offer my readers. Curval and Durcet were carried away unconscious, but the Duc and the Bishop, quite as cool as if nothing had happened, were perfectly able to pass the rest of the night indulging in their ordinary riot.

The Fourteenth Day

It was discovered upon that day that the weather had lent its approval to our libertines' infamous enterprises, and had removed them to an even greater distance from the probability they would be spied upon by mortal eyes; an immense blanket of snow had fallen, it filled the surrounding vale, seeming to forbid even to wild beasts access to our scoundrels' retreat; of all human beings, there was not one that existed who could dare hope to reach where they lay fast. Ah, it is not readily to be imagined how much voluptuousness, lust, fierce joy are flattered by those sureties, or what is meant when one is able to say to oneself: "I am alone here, I am at the world's end, withheld from every gaze, here no one can reach me, there is no creature that can come nigh where I am; no limits, hence, no barriers; I am free." Whereupon, thus situate, desires spring forth with an impetuosity which knows no bounds, stops at nothing, and the impunity that electrifies them most deliciously increases all their drunkenness. There, nothing exists save God and one's conscience; well, what weight may the former exert, of what account may God be in the eyes of an atheist in heart and brain? and what sway is the conscience to enjoy, what influence upon him who is so accustomed to vanquishing remorse, routing guilt, that so to do becomes for him a game, nay, a little pleasure? Luckless flock delivered to the murderous tooth of such villains; how would you have trembled had you not still been in ignorance of what lay in store for you!

That day was a festival, the second week had ended, the second marriage was to be celebrated; Messieurs were in a glad humor and thought not but to frolic on that holiday. The marriage to take place was that of Narcisse and Hébé, but, cruel fate it was also decreed that the bride and groom were both doomed to be punished that same evening; and thus, from the warm embrace of hymeneal pleasures they were to move directly to the more bitter lessons taught in this school, how unkind! Little Narcisse, who was not a dull fellow, remarked this irony, but Messieurs none the less proceeded to the usual ceremonies. The Bishop officiated, the couple was conjoined in very holy matrimony, and they were permitted to do to each other, before the public's eyes, all they wanted to do; but, who would have believed it? the order was of a too liberal scope, or too well understood, and the little husband, who had an aptitude for learning, perfectly delighted with the prospect before him but unable to introduce himself into his pretty wife, was however about to deflower her with his fingers, and would have, had he been given his way. Firm hands intervened just in time, and the Duc, making off with Hébé, thigh-fucked her on the spot, while the Bishop did likewise with Narcisse.

Dinner came next, the newly-wedded couple were admitted to the feast, and as they had been given and commanded prodigiously to eat, both upon leaving the table shitted handsomely, one for Durcet's benefit, the other for Curval's, who, after having swallowed those little products of childhood, smacked their lips and declared 'twas delicious.

Coffee was served by Augustine, Fanny, Céladon, and Zéphyr. The Duc bade Augustine frig Zéphyr, and the latter shit in the nobleman's mouth at the same time he discharged; the operation was a stunning success, so much so that the Bishop wanted to duplicate it with Céladon; Fanny attended to the frigging, and the little fellow received orders to shit in Monseigneur's mouth the moment he felt his fuck flow. But the young operatives succeeded less brilliantly than had their companions: Céladon was never able to co-ordinate his shitting with his discharge; however, as this exercise was merely a test of skill, and as the regulations made no mention of the subjects being obliged to excel in it, no punishment was inflicted upon him.

Durcet gleaned shit from Augustine, and the Bishop, firmly erect, had Fanny suck him while she shat in his mouth; he discharged, and as his crisis was violent, he brutalized Fanny somewhat but, unhappily, failed to find adequate grounds for having her punished, great as was his apparent wish to arrange something for her. A greater tease than the Bishop never lived; no sooner would he finish discharging than he would wish for nothing better than to see his pleasure-object gone to the devil; everyone was familiar with his character, and the little girls, the wives, and the little boys dreaded nothing as much as helping him to be rid of his fuck.

The midday nap over, they passed into the auditorium, the company distributed itself, and Duclos resumed the thread of her narrative:

I sometimes used to go into town for parties, said she, and as they were usually more lucrative, Fournier did her best to procure as many of that kind as she could.

She once sent me to the home of an elderly Knight of Malta who opened a kind of wardrobe filled with cubbyholes, each of which housed a porcelain chamber pot containing a turd; the old rake had made arrangements with a sister of his, abbess of one of the most considerable convents in Paris; that obliging girl, upon his request, every morning sent him a crate of fresh shit produced by her prettiest little pensionnaires. He filed away each performance according to a classifying system, and when I arrived he bade me take down such and such a number, and it proved to be the most venerable. I presented the pot to him.

"Oh yes," said he, "that belongs to a girl of sixteen, lovely as the day. Frig me while I eat her gift."

The entire ceremony consisted in twiddling his device and in dressing my bum before his eyes while he ate, then in replenishing the pot he had just emptied. He watched me do it, wiped my asshole clean with his tongue, and discharged while sucking my anus. After that, the wardrobe is closed and locked, I receive my pay, and our man, whom I visited at an early hour in the morning, curls up and goes blissfully back to sleep.

Another, more extraordinary in my opinion, was an elderly monk. He enters, demands eight or ten turds from the first person he sees, girl or boy, it's all the same to him. He mixes them into a paste which he next kneads like dough, bites into the lump and, eating at least half of it, discharges into my mouth.

A third, and of all the men I have met in my life he aroused the greatest disgust in me, a third, I say, ordered me to open my mouth wide. I was naked, lying upon a mattress on the floor, and he was astride me; he popped his stool into my mouth and the villain then lay down beside me, ate what I spat out, and sprayed his fuck over my teats.

"Well, well, that's a pleasant one!" cried Curval; "by Jesus, I do indeed believe I want to shit, I really must try to. Whom shall I take, Monsieur le Duc?"

"Who?" said Blangis. "By my faith, I recommend Julie, my daughter; she is right there under your hand. You are fond of her mouth, put it to use."

"Thank you for the advice," said Julie sullenly. "What have I done to have you say such things?"

"Why, since the idea upsets her," said the Duc, "and since she's a good girl, take Mademoiselle Sophie: she's healthy, pretty, and she's only fourteen, you know."

"Very well, it's to be Sophie, that's decided," said Curval, whose turbulent prick was beginning to gesticulate.

Fanchon approaches the victim, the poor little wretch's tears start to fall at once. Curval laughs lightly, brings up his great, ugly, and dirty behind, pushes it down upon that charming visage, and gives us the image of a toad about to insult a rose. He is frigged, the bomb bursts, Sophie loses not so much as a crumb, and the crapulous magistrate's tongue and lips reclaim what he has launched; he swallows it all in just four mouthfuls while his prick is being rubbed upon the belly of the poor little creature who, the operation once over, vomits her very guts out, and directly upon the nose of Durcet who has come up posthaste to miss nothing, and who is frigging himself while being covered.

"Off you go, Duclos!" said Curval. "On with your tales, and rejoice at the effect of your discourses; do they not carry the day?"

And therewith Duclos resumed, warmed to the very cockles of her heart by the staggering success which had greeted her anecdote.

The man with whom I held correspondence directly after the one whose example has just seduced you, said Duclos, insisted that the woman he was presented have indigestion; in consequence, Fournier, who had given me no foreknowledge of the thing, had me, during dinner, swallow a certain laxative drug which softened what my bowels contained, indeed rendered it fluid, as if my stool had become transformed into the effect of an enema. Our man arrives and after several preliminary kisses bestowed upon the object of his whole veneration, which, by now, was becoming painfully inflated by gases, I beseech him to start without further delay; the injection is ready to escape, I grasp his prick, he pants, swallows everything, asks for still more; I furnish him with a second deluge, it is soon followed by a third, and the libertine's anchovy finally spits upon my fingers the unequivocal evidence of the sensation he has received.

The next day I treated with a personage whose baroque mania will perhaps find some worshipers amongst yourselves, Messieurs. First of all, he was installed in the room next to the one in which we ordinarily operated and in whose wall was that hole so conveniently placed for observations. He was left alone to arrange himself; a second actor awaited me in the adjoining chamber: he was a cab driver we had picked up at random and who was fully apprised of the situation; as I was too, our cast knew the various roles to perfection. It was a question of having the Phaëthon shit squarely opposite the hole, so that the libertine hidden on the other side of the partition would miss nothing involved in the spectacle. I catch the turd upon a plate, see to it that it lands intact, spread the driver's buttocks, press around his anus, I neglect nothing that can make shitting comfortable; as soon as my man has done all he has to do, I snatch up his prick and get him to discharge over the shit, and all that well within sight of our observer; finally, the package ready, I dash into the other room.

"Here you are, take it quickly, Monsieur," I exclaim, "it's nice and warm."

There is no necessity to repeat the invitation; he grasps the dish, offers me his prick, which I frig, and the rascal bolts everything I tender him while he exhales his fuck in tune with my diligent hand's elastic movements.

"And what was the driver's age?" Curval asked.

"About thirty," Duclos answered.

"Why, that's nothing at all," said Curval. "Durcet there will tell you whenever you like that we once knew an individual who did the same thing, and with positively the same attendant circumstances, but with a man of sixty or seventy who had to be found in the lowest sewer of misery and filth."

"And, you know," said Durcet, "it's only pretty that way." The financier's little engine had been gradually lifting its head ever since Sophie's aspersion. "I shall at any given time be happy to do it with the eldest of veterans."

"You're stiff, Durcet," said the Duc, "don't deny it, for I know you: whenever you start that nasty boasting it's because your fuck is coming to a boil. So hold, good friend; though not so seasoned in years as you might like, still, to appease your intemperance, I offer you all I have in my entrails, and I believe you will find it enough to make a meal upon."

"Ah, by God's belly!" cried Durcet, "you always serve your guests well, my dear Duc."

The Duc entering Durcet's alcove, the latter kneels down before the buttocks which are to fill him to overflowing with good cheer; the Duc grunts once, twice, a prodigy tumbles out, the banker swallows and, transported by this crapulous excess, discharges while swearing he has never tasted so much pleasure.

"Duclos," said the Duc, "come do for me what I have done for our good friend."

"My Lord," our storyteller replied, "you will recall that I it this morning, and that you swallowed it."

"Why, yes, 'tis true," the Duc admitted. "Very well then, hither, Martaine, I must have recourse to you, for I want none of those children's asses; I feel my fuck readying to come, but, you know, it comes reluctantly, and so we need something out of the ordinary."

But Martaine's case was that of Duclos, Curval had gobbled her shit that morning.

"What! by fuck," cried the Duc, "am I then to fail to find a turd this evening?"

Whereupon Thérèse advanced and offered the dirtiest, the broadest, and the most stinking possible of asses you, dear reader, may hope to behold.

"Well, that will do, that will do perfectly," said the Duc, assuming the posture, "and if in my present disorder this infamous ass I've got here does not produce its effect, I don't know what I'll have to resort to."

Dramatic moment; Thérèse pushes; the Duc receives! and the incense was quite as dreadful as the temple whence it emerged, but when one is as stiff as the Duc was stiff, 'tis never excess of filth one complains of. Drunk with joy, the scoundrel swallowed every ounce, and directly into Duclos' face, for she was frigging him, shot the most indubitable proof of his male vigor.

Then to table; the ensuing orgies were devoted to the distribution of justice; that week there were seven delinquents: Zelmire, Colombe, Hébé, Adonis, Adelaide, Sophie, and Narcisse; the gentle Adelaide was granted no quarter. Zelmire and Sophie also bore away a few marks of the treatment they had undergone and, without giving further particulars, since circumstances do not permit us to give them yet, everyone retired to bed, and in Morpheus' arms recovered the strength requisite to make further sacrifices to Venus.

The Fifteenth Day

Rarely would the day following correction offer fresh signs of misbehavior. There were none upon this one, but as strict as ever in the article of permission to shit in the morning, Messieurs granted this favor to no one but Hercule, Michette, Sophie, and Desgranges, and Curval came perilously near to discharging while watching the storyteller at work. Not overmuch was accomplished at coffee, the friends were content to fondle buttocks and to suck one or two assholes; the hour sounded, everyone went promptly to establish himself in the amphitheater. Duclos faced her audience once again and addressed the company in this wise:

There had lately come to Fournier's a little girl of twelve or thirteen, the age preferred by that singular gentleman I mentioned to you; but I truly doubt whether in a very long time he had debauched anything so cunning, so innocent, or so pretty. She had fair hair, was tall for her years and fit to be painted, her physiognomy was tender and voluptuous, her eyes the loveliest one could hope to see, and in all her charming person there was something sweet and intriguing which turned her into a very enchantress. But what was the degradation to which the such a host of attractions was about to be subjected! and how shameful was the debut being prepared for them! She was the daughter of a tradesman in lingerie, purveyor to the Palace and a man of comfortable means, and his daughter surely had been destined for a happier fate than this of playing the whore; but the more the man of whom it is a question was able, by means of his perfidious seductions, to beguile his victims to their ruin, and the more thorough the depravation into which he guided them, the greater his pleasure, the fiercer his ecstasy. Little Lucile, directly after her arrival, was scheduled to satisfy the disgusting and unclean caprices of a man who, not merely content to have the most crapulous tastes, wished, still better, to inflict them upon a maid.

He arrives at the house; he proves to be an old notary stuffed with gold and who, together with his wealth, has all the brutality that avarice and luxury excite when combined in a seasoned spirit. The child is exhibited to him; pretty as she may be, his first reaction is disdain; he grumbles, he grits his teeth, mutters and swears, and says that it damned well seems as if one can no longer find a pretty girl in Paris; he demands, at last, whether there is proof positive she is a virgin, he is assured that, yes, the article is mint, Fournier offers to show it to him.

"What? look at a cunt, I? Madame Fournier! I, look at a cunt! I certainly hope you propose the thing in jest; have you noticed me spending much time considering those objects since I have been coming to you? I use them, to be sure, but in a manner which, I believe, attests no great fondness for them."

"Very well, Monsieur," Fournier said, "you will have to take the house's word for it: I declare that she is as much a maid as a child born five minutes ago."

They go upstairs together and, as you may well conceive, curious about the forthcoming tête-à-tête, I go and establish myself at the hole. Poor little Lucile was overcome by a shame only to be described by superlative expressions, hence not to be described at all, for those expressions are needed to represent the impudence, the brutality, and the ill-humor of her sixty-year-old lover.

"Well, what the devil are you doing there, are you a stone?" says he in a harsh voice. "Do I have to tell you to get your skirts up? I should have been looking at your ass two hours ago. . . . Don't stand there like an idiot, move."

"But, Monsieur, what am I to do?"

"Why, Jesus Christ, are such questions still asked? What are you to do? Pick up your skirts and show me that damned ass I'm paying to see."

Lucile obeys, trembling like a leaf, and discloses a little white ass just as darling and sweet as would be that of Venus herself.

"Hum . . . looks all right," mutters the brute, "bring it nearer. . . ."

Then, getting a firm grip upon the two buttocks and separating them forcefully: "You're damned certain no one's ever done anything to you here?"

"Oh, Monsieur, no one has ever touched me. . . ."

"Very well. Now fart."

"But, Monsieur, I can't."

"Well, try, for Christ's sake, make yourself fart."

She struggles, frowns, squints, a little breath of aromatic wind does escape and produces a little echo upon entering the infected mouth of the old libertine, who seems delighted.

"Do you want to shit?" he asks.

"No, Monsieur."

"Well, I do, I've something copious to get rid of, if you're interested in the pertinent facts; so prepare yourself to satisfy this particular need of mine . . . take off your skirts."

They are removed.

"Lie down upon that sofa. Raise your thighs."

Lucile settles herself, the old notary arranges and poses her so that her wide--flung legs display her cunt to the fullest advantage, in which open and prominent position it may be readily employed as a chamber pot. So to use it was his heavenly intention; in order that the container respond more perfectly to what is to be demanded of it, he begins by widening it as much as possible, devoting both hands and all his strength to the task. He takes his place, pushes, a turd lands in the sanctuary Cupid himself would not have disdained having for a temple. He turns around, eyes his work, and with his fingers presses and thrusts the filthy excrement into the vagina and largely out of sight; he establishes himself astride Lucile once again, and ejects a second, then a third stool, and each is succeeded by the same ceremony of burial. Finally, having deposited his last turd, he inserts and tamps it down with such brutal zeal that the little one utters a cry, and by means of this disagreeable operation perhaps loses the precious flower, Nature's ornament, offered the child as a gift to Hymen. This was the moment at which our libertine's pleasure attained its crisis: to have filled the young and pretty cunt to overflowing with shit, to crowd it with shit and stuff it with yet more, that was his supreme delight: all the while in action, he opens his fly and draws out a species of prick, very flaccid it is, and he shakes it, and as he toils away in his disgusting manner, he manages to spatter upon the floor a few drops of thin, discolored sperm, whose loss may be credited solely to the infamies he has been performing. Having concluded his business, he takes himself off, Lucile washes, and that is that.

Some time later, I found myself with another individual whose mania struck me as no less unpleasant: he was an elderly magistrate at the high court. One was obliged not only to watch him shit, no, there was more to it than that: I had to help him, with my fingers, facilitate the matter's emergence by pressing, opening, agitating, compressing his anus, and when once he had been freed of his burden, I had with utmost care to clean the soiled area with my tongue.

"Well, by God! there's a bit of taxing drudgery, I own," said the Bishop. "The four ladies you see here, and they are our wives, or our daughters, or our nieces, these ladies nevertheless have to perform that same chore every day, you know. And what the devil, I ask you, what the devil is a woman's tongue good for if not to wipe assholes? I frankly cannot think of any other use to put it to. Constance," the Bishop pursued, turning to the Duc's lovely wife, who happened to be upon his couch, "give Duclos a little demonstration of your proficiency in the thing; here you are, I'll offer you a very untidy ass, it hasn't been cleaned since this morning, I've been keeping it this way for you. Off you go, display your abilities."

And the poor creature, only too well accustomed to these horrors, executed them as a dutiful, a thoughtful wife should; ah, great God! what will not dread and thralldom produce!

"Oh, by Jesus," said Curval, presenting his ugly, beslimed asshole to the charming Aline, "she'll not be the only one to give examples of excellence. Get to work, little whore," said he to that beautiful and virtuous girl, "outdo your companion."

And the thing was accomplished.

"Why, Duclos," said the Bishop, "I think we might proceed now; we only wished to point out that your man's request had nothing of the unusual about it, and that a woman's tongue is fit to nothing if to wipe an ass."

The amiable Duclos fell to laughing and continued:

You will permit me, Messieurs, said she, to interrupt the catalogue of passions for an instant that I may apprise you of an event which has no bearing upon them; it has only to do with me, but as you have ordered me to recount the interesting episodes in my life, even when they are not related to the anthology of tastes we are compiling, I think that the following ought not be passed by in silence.

I had been a great while at Madame Fournier's, had long since become the first ranked according to seniority, and in her entire entourage was the girl in whom she had the greatest confidence. It was I who most often arranged the parties and received the funds. Fournier had gradually taken the place of the mother I had lost, she had aided me in time of trouble, watched over my welfare, had written faithfully to me when I had been abroad in England, upon my return had as a friend opened her house to me when, in difficult circumstances, I desired to take asylum with her once again. Twenty times over she had lent me money, and often had never asked for it back. The opportunity arrived to show my gratitude and to respond to her limitless faith in me, and you shall judge, Messieurs, with what eagerness my soul opened itself to virtue's entrance and what an easy access it had thereinto: Fournier fell ill, and her first thought was to call me to her bedside.

"Duclos, my child, I love you," said she, "well you know it, and I am going to prove it by the absolute trust I am about to place in you. Despite your mind, which is not a good one, I believe in you incapable of wronging a friend; I am very ill, I am old, I do not know what is to become of me. But I may die soon; I have relatives who will of course be my heirs. I can at least leave them something, and want to: I have a hundred thousand francs in gold in this little coffer; take it, my child," said she, "here, I give it to you, but upon condition you dispose of this money in keeping with my instructions."

"Oh, my dear mother," said I, stretching forth my arms to her, "I beseech you, these precautions distress me; they shall surely prove needless, but if unhappily they were to prove necessary, I take oath and swear exactly to carry out your intentions."

"I believe you, my child," said she, "and that is why my eyes have settled upon you; that little coffer, then, contains one hundred thousand francs in gold; I have scruples, a few scruples, my dear friend, I feel remorseful for the life I have led, the quantity of girls I have cast into crime and snatched away from God. And so I wish to do two things by means of which it is my hope the divinity will be led to deal less severely with me: I think of charity now, and of prayer. You shall take fifteen thousand francs of this money, and you shall give it to the Capuchins on the rue Saint-Honoré, so that those good fathers will say a perpetual mass for the salvation of my soul; another sum, also of fifteen thousand francs, shall be set aside, and when I have closed my eyes, you shall surrender it to the curé of the parish and beg him to distribute it amongst the poor dwelling in this quarter of the city. Charity is a very excellent thing, my child; nothing better repairs in the eyes of God the sins we have committed in this world. The poor are His children, and beloved of Him is he who gives them succor and comfort; never is God more to be pleased than by alms distributed to the needy. There lies the true way of gaining Heaven, my child! As for the remainder, immediately I am dead you shall take sixty thousand francs to one Petignon, a shoemaker's apprentice in the rue du Bouloir: this poor lad is my son, he knows nothing of his origins: he is the bastard issue of adultery. Upon dying, I want the unhappy orphan to benefit from those marks of tenderness I have never shown him while alive. Ten thousand francs are left; I beg you to keep them, my dear Duclos, keep them as a feeble token of my fondness for you, may they be some kind of recompense for the trouble you shall have to take in seeing to the distribution of the rest of my fortune. And may this little sum aid you to resolve to abandon the dreadful trade we follow, a calling wherein there is no salvation, nor any hope. For one is not a whore forever."

Innerly delighted to be entrusted with such a handsome sum, and thoroughly determined, for fear of becoming confused by Fournier's intricate instructions upon sharing it, to keep her fortune intact and for myself alone, I produced a flood of very artificial tears and cast myself into the old matron's arms, reiterated many oaths of fidelity, and turned all my thoughts thenceforth to devising means to prevent the cruel disappointments certain to occur were a return to sound health to bring about a change in her resolutions. The means presented itself the very next day: the doctor prescribed and emetic, and as I was in charge of nursing her, it was to me he handed the medicine, drawing my attention to the fact the package contained two doses, and warning me to be sure to administer only one at a time because, were both given her, death would be the result; were the first to have no effect, or an insufficient one, the second could be employed later, if need be. I promised the doctor to take the greatest possible care, and immediately he had turned his back, banishing from my heart all those futile sentiments which would have stopped a timorous spirit, putting to rout all remorse and all frailty, and thinking exclusively of my gold, of the sweet charm of making it mine, and of the delicious titillation one experiences every time one concerts an evil deed, the certain prognostic of the pleasure it will give, dwelling, I say, upon all that and upon nothing else, I straightway dropped both doses into a glass of water and offered the brew to my dear friend's lips; she swallowed it down without a moment's delay and thereby, just as rapidly, found the death I had sought to procure her.

I cannot describe to you what feelings possessed me when I saw my scheme had succeeded; each of the retchings wherewith she exhaled her life produced a truly delicious sensation throughout my entire being; thrilled, I listened to her, I watched her, I was perfectly intoxicated with joy. She stretched her arms toward me, addressed me a last farewell, I was overwhelmed with pleasurable sensations, I was already forming a thousand plans for spending the gold. I had not long to wait; Fournier expired that same afternoon; the prize belonged to me.

"Duclos," said the Duc, "be truthful: did you frig yourself? did crime's piercingly voluptuous sensation attain your organs of pleasure?"

"Yes, my Lord, I confess it did; thanks to my prank I discharged five times before nightfall."

"It is then true," the Duc intoned in a loud and authoritative voice, "it is then true that crime has of itself such a compelling attractiveness that, unattended by any accessory activity, it may be itself suffice to inflame every passion and to hurl one into the same delirium occasioned by lubricious acts. Well, what say you?"

"Why, my Lord," Duclos answered, "I say I had my employer honorably buried, appropriated the bastard Petignon's inheritance, wasted not a penny on perpetual masses, nor did I bother to make a single charitable distribution, for, as a matter of fact, I have always beheld charity with the most authentic horror, regardless of the speeches, such as Fournier's, that I have heard pronounced in its favor. I maintain that there must be poor in this world, that Nature wishes that such there be, that she requires it, and that it is to fly in the face of her decrees to pretend to restore equilibrium, if it is disorder she wants."

"What's this!" said Durcet. "Do you then have principles, Duclos? I am very pleased to observe this in you; for, as you appear to realize, any relief given to misfortune, any gesture that lightens the load of the distressed, is a real crime against the natural order. The inequality she has created in our persons proves that this discordance pleases Nature, since 'twas she established it, and since she wishes that it exists in fortunes as well as in bodies. And as the weak may always redress matters by means of theft, the strong are equally allowed to restore inequality, or protect it, by refusing to give aid to the wretched. The universe would cease on the spot to subsist were there to be an exact similarity amongst all beings; 'tis of this disparity there is born the order which preserves, contains, directs everything. One must therefore take great care not to disturb it; moreover, in believing that it is a good thing I do for this miserable class of men, I do much ill to another, for indigence is the nursery to which the wealthy and powerful repair in quest of the objects their lust or cruelty needs; I deprive the rich man of that branch of pleasure when, by raising up the downtrodden, I inhibit this class from yielding to him. And thus my charities have done nothing but put one part of humankind very modestly in my debt and done prodigious harm to the other. Hence, I regard charity not only as something evil in itself, but, what is more, I consider it a crime against Nature who, having first made differences apparent to our eyes, has certainly never intended ideas of eliminating them to occupy our heads. And so, far from giving alms to the poor, consoling the widow, succoring the orphan, if it is according to Nature's true intentions I wish to act, not only do I leave these wretches in the state Nature put them into, but I even lend Nature a strong right arm and aid her by prolonging this state and vigorously opposing any efforts they make to change it, and to this end I believe any means may be allowed."

"What!" cried the Duc, "even stealing from and ruining them?"

"Oh my, yes," the financier replied, "even augmenting their number, since this class serves another, and since, by increasing the size of the one, though I may do it a modicum of harm, I shall perform a great service for the other."

"That, my friends, is a very harsh system indeed," said Curval. "Haven't you heard tell of the sweet pleasures of doing good unto others?"

"Abusive pleasures!" Durcet answered at once. "That delight you allude to is nothing like the one I recommend; the first is illusory, a fiction; the second is authentic, real; the first is founded upon vile prejudices, the second upon reason; the first, through the agency of pride, the most false of all our sensations, may provide the heart with a brief instant's titillation; the other is a veritable mental pleasure-taking, and it inflames every other passion by the very fact it runs counter to common opinions. In a word, one of them gets this prick of mine stiff," Durcet concluded, "and I feel practically nothing from the other."

"But must the one criterion for judging everything be our feelings?" asked the Bishop.

"The only one, my friend," said Durcet; "our senses, nothing else, must guide all our actions in life, because only their voice is truly imperious."

"But God knows how many thousand crimes may be the result of such a doctrine," the Bishop observed.

"God knows, yes, and do you suppose that matters?" Durcet demanded; "for it is enjoyable, isn't it? Crime is a natural mode, a manner whereby Nature stirs man, makes him to move. Why would you not have me let myself be moved by Nature in this direction as well as in the direction of virtue? Nature needs virtuous acts, and vicious ones too; I serve Nature as well by performing the one as when I commit the other. But we have entered into a discussion which could lead us far; suppertime is approaching, and Duclos has still ground to cover before completing her task. Go on, charming girl, pursue your way, and believe me when I say you have just acknowledged an act and a doctrine which make you deserving of our eternal esteem and of that of every philosopher."

My first idea when once my good patron had been inhumed was to assume the direction of her house and to maintain it on the same footing she had found so profitable. I announced this project to my colleagues, and they all, Eugénie above the rest, for she was my best beloved, I say, promised to regard me as their new mother. I was not too young to pretend to the title, being then nearly thirty and possessed of all the intelligence and good sense one must have to govern a convent. And so it is, Messieurs, that I shall conclude the story of my adventures not as a public whore, but as an abbess, pretty enough and still youthful enough sometimes, indeed often, to treat directly with our clients; and treat with them I did: I shall in the sequel take care to notify you each time I took personal charge of the problem at hand. All Fournier's customers remained to me, I knew the secret of acquiring additional ones: my apartments were kept very neat and clean, and an excessive submissiveness inculcated in my girls, whom I selected with discrimination, hugely flattered my libertines' caprices.

The first purchaser to arrive was an old treasurer of the Exchequer, a former friend of the departed Fournier; I gave him little Lucile, over whom he waxed very enthusiastic. His habitual mania, quite as filthy as disagreeable for his partner, consisted in shitting upon his Dulcinea's face, of smearing his excrement over all her features, and then of kissing her in this state, and of sucking her. Out of friendship for me, Lucile allowed the old satyr to have his way very completely with her, and he discharged upon her belly as he lay kissing and licking his disgusting performance.

Not long afterward, we had another; Eugénie was also assigned to cope with him. He had a barrel full of shit trundled in, plunged the naked girl into it, and licked every inch of her body, swallowing what he removed, and not finishing until he had rendered her as clean as she had been prior to her immersion. That one was a celebrated lawyer, a rich man and a very well-known one; he possessed, for the enjoyment of women, none but the most modest qualities, which lack he remedied by this species of libertinage he had lovingly cultivated all his life.

The Marquis de R_____, one of Fournier's oldest clients, came shortly after her death to express his sorrow upon learning that she was no more; he also assured me he would patronize the house just as faithfully as before and, to convince me of his devotion, wanted to see Eugénie that same evening. This old rake's passion consisted in first bestowing prodigious kisses upon the girl's mouth; he swallowed all the saliva it were possible to drain from her, then kissed her buttocks for a quarter of an hour, called for farts, and finally demanded the major thing. After it had been done, he kept the turd in his mouth and, making the girl bend down over him, he had her embrace him with one hand and frig him with the other; and while he was tasting the pleasure of this masturbation and tickling her beshitted asshole, the girl had to eat the turd she had deposited in his mouth. Although he was prepared to pay very well, he used to find exceedingly few girls who were willing to cooperate in this little abomination, and that is why the Marquis would come regularly to me: he was as eager to remain one of my clients as I was to have him make frequent visits to my establishment. . . .

At this point the Duc, very hot indeed, said that as the supper hour was hard upon them, he would like, before going to table, to execute the last-cited fantasy. And this is how he went about it: he had Sophie come to him, received her turd in his mouth, then obliged Zélamir to run up and eat Sophie's creation. This idiosyncrasy might perhaps have been a delight for anyone else but a child like Zélamir; as yet insufficiently mature, hence unable to appreciate the delicious, he manifested disgust only, and seemed about to misbehave. But the Duc threatened him with everything his anger might produce were the boy to hesitate another instant; the boy obeyed. The stunt struck the others as so engaging that each of them imitated it, more or less, for Durcet held that favors had to be parceled out fairly; was it just, he asked, for the little boys to eat the girls' shit while the girls went hungry? no, surely not, and consequently he had Zéphyr shit in his mouth and ordered up Augustine to eat the marmalade, which that lovely and interesting girl promptly did, her repast being as promptly succeeded by the racking vomitings.

Curval imitated this variation and received his dear Adonis' turd, which Michette consumed, not without a duplication of Augustine's histrionics; as for the Bishop, he was content to emulate his brother, and had the delicate Zelmire excrete a confiture Céladon was induced to gobble up. Accompanying all this were certain unmistakable signs of repugnance which, of course, were of the greatest interest to libertines in whose view the torments they inflict are unexcelled for inspiring satisfaction. The Bishop and the Duc discharged, the two others either could not, or would not, and all four went in to supper, where Duclos' action was the object of the loftiest encomiums.

"A very intelligent creature," observed the Duc, whose regard for the storyteller could not have been more profound. "Intelligent, I say, to have sensed that gratitude is nonsense, an hallucination, and that ties of fondness or of any other sort ought never either to make us pause or even to suspend the effects of crime, because the object which has served us can claim no right to our heart's generosity; that object employs itself only in our behalf, its mere presence humiliates a stout soul, and one must either hate of be rid of it."

"Very true," said Durcet, "so true that you'll never see a man of any wit seek to make others grateful to him. Fully certain that benevolence creates nothing but enemies, he practices only the arts his wisdom approves for his safety."

"One moment," interrupted the Bishop. "It is not at giving you pleasure he who serves you is laboring, but he is rather striving simply to gain an ascendancy over you by putting you in his debt. Well, I ask, what does such a scheme deserve? He does not say, as he serves you: I serve you because I wish to do good for you. No, he simply says: I put you under obligation in order to lower you and to raise myself above you."

"These reflections seem to me," said Durcet, "abundantly to prove how abusive are the services usually rendered, and how absurd is the practice of good. But, they will tell you, one does good for its own sake and for one's own; 'tis all very well for them whose weakness of spirit permits them to enjoy such little delights, but they who are revolted by them, as are we, great God! would be great fools to bother over such tepid stuff."

This doctrine having fired their imaginations, Messieurs drank a great deal, and the orgies were celebrated with vivacity and brio. Our like-thinking libertines sent the children off to bed, chose to spend a part of the night tippling with no one but the four elders and the four storytellers, and in their company to vie with one another in infamies and atrocities. As amongst these twelve individuals there was not one who was not worthy of the noose, the rack, and probably the wheel, I leave it to the reader to picture what was said and done. For from words they passed to deeds, the Duc got hot again, and I don't know just why it happened or how, but they say Thérèse bore the marks of his affection for weeks. However all that may be, let us allow our actors to move from these bacchanals to the chaste bed of the wife that had been prepared for each of the four, and let us see what transpired at the castle on the morrow.

The Sixteenth Day

Our heroes rose as bright and fresh as if they had just arrived from confession; but upon close inspection, one might have noticed that the Duc was beginning to tire a little. Blame for this could have been bestowed upon Duclos; there is no question but that the girl had entirely mastered the art of procuring him delight and that, according to his own words, his discharges were lubricious with no one else, which would corroborate the idea that these matters depend solely upon caprice, upon idiosyncrasy, and that age, looks, virtue, and all the rest have nothing whatever to do with the problem, that it all boils down to a certain tactfulness which is much more often found possessed by beauties in the autumn of life than by those others of no experience whom the springtide yet crowns with all her show.

There was as well another creature in the company who was beginning to make herself very amiable and to attract considerable attention; we are referring to Julie. She was already announcing signs of imagination, debauchery, and of libertinage. Astute enough to sense that she stood in need of protection, clever enough to caress those very persons for whom perhaps she did not at heart have a very great fondness, she contrived to become Duclos' friend, this in order to try to achieve some favor in the eyes of her father upon the others. Every time her turn came to lie with the Duc, she would adopt Duclos' techniques and emulate them so successfully, give proof of such skill, so much consideration, that the Duc was always sure of obtaining delicious discharges whenever he used those two creatures to procure them. Nevertheless, his enhusiasm for his daughter was waning prodigiously, and perhaps without Duclos' assistance, for the narrator consistently spoke well in her behalf, she would never have been able to occupy a place in his good graces. Her husband, Curval, was roughly of the same mind regarding her, and although, by means of her impure mouth and kisses, she still managed to wheedle a few discharges from him, disgust was dangerously near to becoming his predominating attitude toward her: one might even have said that the fires of his hostility were fanned by her impudicious caresses. Durcet held her in no esteem, she had not made him discharge more than twice since the adventures at Silling had started. And so it seemed that no one but the Bishop remained to her, and he indeed was fond of her libertine jargon, and judged hers to be the world's finest ass; and it is certain that Nature had furnished her with one as lovely as that which had been given to Venus. She hence made the most of that part, for she wished absolutely to please at whatever the price; as she felt an extreme need for a protector, she sought to cultivate Duclos.

At the chapel appeared that day no more than three persons: Hébé, Constance, Martaine; no one had been found at fault that morning. After the three subjects had ridded themselves of their freight, Durcet was taken by an impulse to be delivered of his. The Duc, who since early morning had been fluttering and buzzing about the financier's behind, seized the opportunity to satisfy himself and, sending away everyone but Constance, whom they kept as an aide, they encloseted themselves in the chapel. The Duc was appeased by the generous mouthful of shit he had from Durcet; these gentlemen, however, did not limit themselves to that prelude, and afterward Constance reported to the Bishop that they had performed infamies for a good thirty minutes. But what is one to expect? they had been friends, as I have said, since childhood, and since then had never ceased reminding one another of their schoolboy pleasures. As for Constance, she served no great purpose during this tête-à-tête; she wiped asses, sucked and frigged a few pricks, and that was about all.

They retired to the salon, the four friends conversed there for a while, and the midday meal was announced. It was, as usual, splendid and libertine and, after some lewd fingerings and bawdy colling, and a few scandalous remarks which spiced their lascivious byplay, they returned to the salon where Zéphyr and Hyacinthe, Michette and Colombe were waiting to serve coffee. The Duc thigh-fucked Michette, and Curval, Hyacinthe; Durcet fetched shit out of Colombe, and the Bishop dropped some in Zéphyr's mouth; Curval, recollecting one of the passions Duclos had related the day before, was moved to shit in Colombe's cunt; old Thérèse, who was supervising the day's quartet, placed Colombe in a suitable posture, and Curval performed. But as he produced colossal turds, proportioned by the immense quantity of victuals wherewith he stuffed himself every day, almost all of his creation spilled upon the floor and it was, so to speak, only superficially he beshitified that pretty little virgin cunt which had not, one would have thought, been intended by Nature to be used for such disagreeable pleasures.

Deliciously frigged by Zéphyr, the Bishop yielded his fuck philosophically, joining, to the delights he was feeling, that other offered by the wonderful spectacle being enacted about him. He was furious, he scolded Zéphyr, he scolded Curval, he fumed and grumbled at everyone. He was given a large glass of elixir whereby they hoped his faculties would be restored, Michette and Colombe settled him upon a sofa for his nap and stood by him while he slept. He woke amply refreshed and, in order to give him additional strength, Colombe sucked him for a moment or two; his engine responded by showing some positive signs of life, and they went next into the auditorium. The Bishop had Julie on his couch; as he was rather fond of her, the sight of her improved his mood. The Duc had aline; Durcet, Constance; the Président, his daughter. Everything being ready, the lovely Duclos installed herself upon her throne and began thus:

There is nothing more untrue than to say money acquired through crime brings no happiness. No greater error, I assure you; my house prospered; never had so many clients come there during Fournier's administration. It was then an idea occurred to me, a rather cruel idea, I admit, but one which, I dare flatter myself in believing, will not be altogether displeasing to your Lordships. It seemed to me that when one had not done unto another the good one ought to have done him, there existed a certain wicked voluptuousness in doing him ill, and my perfidious imagination suggested a little libertine mischief at the expense of that same Petignon, my benefactress' son, and the individual to whom I had been charged to surrender a fortune which, doubtless, would have proven very welcome to that wretch, and which I had already begun to squander upon trifles. The occasion arrived in this way: the poor shoemaker, married to a girl of his own class and sort, had, as the unique fruit of this unfortunate marriage, a daughter of about twelve; I had been to told that, together with all the lovely features of childhood, she possessed all the attributes of the most tender beauty. This child, then being brought up humbly but nevertheless as carefully as the parents' indigence could permit, for she was the joy and light of their life, this child, I say, struck me as a capture well worth making.

Petignon had never come ot the house, he knew nothing of the legal rights that were his; immediately after Fournier had mentioned him to me, my first move was to obtain information about him and those around him, and thus I learned that he possessed a treasure in his house. At about the same time the Comte de Mesanges came to me; a famous libertine of whose profession Desgranges will doubtless have at least one occasion to speak, the Comte requested me to provide him with a maid of no more than thirteen at whatever the price. I don't know what he wanted with the article, for he passed for a man with very rigorous scruples when it was a question of women, but his proposal was simple enough: after having, with the help of experts, established her virginity, he said he would buy her from me for a fixed sum and, from this moment on, she would be his, he would be her master, and, he added, the child would be removed, perhaps permanently, from France.

As the Comte was one of my habitués - you shall see him enter upon the scene very soon - I set everything in motion in an effort to satisfy him; Petignon's little daughter seemed to me exactly what he needed. But how was I to get my hands upon her? The child never left the house, it was there she received her education; so carefully was she supervised, so circumspectly that I began to despair of the prize. Nor was I able to employ that masterful debaucher of girls I mentioned some time ago; he was away from the city, and the Comte was urging me to hurry. And so I could find only one means, and this means could not have been better designed to serve the secret little wickedness which was impelling me to commit this crime, for the crime was aggravated by it. I resolved to embroil husband and wife in some kind of difficulty, to strive to get both of them imprisoned, and in this way removing some of the obstacles between the child and myself, I fancied I would encounter no trouble in luring her into the snare. Wherewith I consulted one of my friends, a skilled barrister whom I trusted and who was capable of anything; I put him on the scent, he went directly to work: he compiled information, made inquiries, located creditors, aroused them, supported their claims, in brief, it took less than a week to lodge husband and wife behind bars. From then on everything was easy; an adroit scout accosted the little girl, who had been abandoned to the care of some poor neighbors, she was led to me. Her appearance perfectly matched the reports I had received: she had a sweet, a soft, a fair skin, the roundest little ornaments, charms perfectly shaped. . . . In a word, it were difficult to find a prettier child.

As she cost me, all told, about twenty louis, and as the Comte wished to pay a flat price for her and, having once bought her outright, wished neither to hear another word about the transaction nor have further dealings with anyone, I let her go for one hundred louis; it being essential to my interests that no one get wind of my part in the thing, I was content with a net profit of sixty louis, given my attorney another twenty to create just that kind of stir which would prevent her parents from having news of their daughter for a long time. But news did reach them; the girl's disappearance was impossible to conceal. The neighbors who had been guilty of negligence excused themselves at best they were able, and as for the poor shoemaker and his wife, my man-of-law managed matters so well that they were never able to remedy the accident, for both of them died in jail some eleven years after I had made off with my prey. I reaped a twofold advantage from that little mishap, since it simultaneously assured me undisputed ownership of the child I was negotiating to sell and also assured me 60,000 francs for my trouble. As for the child, the Comte was satisfied with her; never did he encounter any difficulties, never did I, no, not a word was said, and it is more than likely Madame Desgranges will finish her story; I know no more about it. But it is high time to return to my own adventures, and to the daily events which may offer you the voluptuous details we have listed.

"Oh by God!" Curval broke in, "I adore your prudence - there is something in your method which bespeaks a meditated villainy, an orderliness which pleases me more than I can say. And as for that rascality of having given the final stroke to a victim you had until then only scratched . . .ah, that seems to me a refinement of infamy which deserves a place amongst our own masterpieces."

"I wonder, however," said Durcet, "whether I might not have done worse, for, after all, those parents could have obtained their release from jail: there are God knows how many fools in the world who think of nothing but helping such people. Those eleven years during which they lingered on meant worry for you."

"Monsieur," Duclos answered him, "when one does not enjoy the influence you have in society, when for one's little pranks one is forced to employ second-rate allies, caution often becomes very necessary, and at such times one dares not do all one would like."

"True, true," said the Duc, "she was unable to go any further."

And the amiable creature took up the thread of her narrative.

Dreadful it is, my Lords, said that accomplished girl, to have still to relate turpitudes in kind like to those I have been speaking about for several days; but you have required that I cite everything which might bear an even faint resemblance to this great genre of abomination, and insisted too that I suppress nothing. But three more examples of these filthy atrocities and we shall then continue on to other fantasies.

The first I propose to mention is that of an elderly administrator of the demesne, a man of I should say three score and six. He would have the woman remove all her clothes and, after having fondled her buttocks with less delicacy than brutality, he would promptly order her to shit on the floor before his eyes, in the middle of the room. When he had relished this prospect, he would in his turn step up and lay his own turd next to hers, then, combining them with his hands, he would oblige the girl to get down on all fours and eat the hash, and while eating she was to present her behind, which she was to have brought to the party in a most maculated state. While the ceremony was in progress he would manualize himself, and used to discharge as soon as the last bite had vanished. There were few girls, as your Lordships may readily believe, who would consent to submit themselves to such vile use, but all the same the administrator had to have them youthful and healthy. . . . Well, I used somehow to find what he needed, for everything is to be found in Paris; however, the merchandise came dear.

The second example of the three I have left to cite of this species also required what might be termed a furious docility on the girl's part; but as this libertine wished her to be extremely young, I had less trouble supplying him: children lend themselves to these games more readily than do mature women. I located a pretty little shopgirl of twelve or thirteen for the gentleman whom we are about to see in action; he arrives, has the girl take off only the clothing that covers her from the waist down; he toys with her behind for a brief moment, gets her to fart a little, then gives himself four or five copious enemas which, subsequently, he obliges his little partner to receive into her mouth and to swallow as the cascade tumbles out of his rectum. Meanwhile, as he was seated astride her chest, he employed one hand to frig a rather thick device and with the other he kneaded and pinched her mons veneris and, in order that he might do it all as he wished, he had to have a completely hairless cunt to work with. This individual wanted to continue on even after his sixth explosion, for his discharge was not yet achieved. The little girl, convulsed with vomiting, managed to articulate her disinclination to proceed, she begged to be spared, he laughed at her, introduced a seventh draught, expelled it, and his fuck finally did indeed flow.

An elderly banker provides us with the last example of these unclean horrors - or rather the last example of a man for whom they were the principal element, for I must warn you that we shall have repeated occasion to behold them as accessories to the main endeavor. He had to have a handsome woman, but one aged from forty to forty-five and with an extremely flabby pair of breasts. Immediately they were encloseted together he would have her remove all she was wearing from the waist up, and having brutally handled her teats, would cry: "These damned cow dugs! what good are such tripes, eh? What are they for if not to wipe my ass upon?" Next he would squeeze them, twist them, wring them, twine them together, tug them, pound them, spit upon them, kick and trample them, all the while saying, what a damned infamous thing is a flabby tit, he could not imagine what Nature had intended these bags of skin for, why had Nature spoiled and dishonored woman's body with these things? etc. After all these preposterous remarks he would remove every stitch of his clothing. My God, what a body! how am I to describe it to your Lordships! 'Twas no more than a disgusting ulcer, a running sore, pus seemed to cover him from head to toe, I could smell his infected odor even in the adjacent room from which I was observing the ritual; such was the relic which, however, the woman had to suck.

"Suck?" said the Duc.

Yes, Messieurs, Duclos affirmed, suck from top to bottom, every square inch of his body had to be sucked, the tongue was to neglect nothing, to explore it all; I had forewarned the girl, but apparently in vain. She'd not expected this; for upon catching sight of that ambulatory corpse she shrank away in horror.

"What's this, bitch?" says he, "do I disgust you? Why, that's a pity, for you're going to have to suck me, your tongue is going to have to lick every part of my body. Come now! Stop playing the shy little girl; others have done the job, see to it that you do it as well as they. That's enough, I tell you, no nonsense."

Ah, they speak true when they say that with money one can accomplish anything; the poor creature I had given him was in the extremest misery, and her was a chance to earn two louis: she did everything she was told, and the podagrous old scoundrel, thrilled by the sensation of a tongue straying softly over his hideous body and sweetening the bitter pungency devouring him, frigged himself voluptuously during the entire operation. When it had been completed, and completed, as you may well suppose, despite the horrible revulsion of the luckless woman, when it was done, I say, he had her lie down upon the floor on her back, he got astride her, shitted all over her bubs, and squeezing his performance between them, he used them, first one, then the other, to wipe his ass. But with what regards his discharge, I saw not so much as a hint, and some time later I learned that it required several such operations before he could be induced to part with his liquor; and as he was a man who seldom twice visited the same place, I saw no more of him and, to tell the truth, was by no means sorry.

"Upon my soul," the Duc observed, "I find the conclusion of that man's operation very reasonable indeed, and I too have never been able to believe that teats were intended for anything but bumwipes."

"One may be certain," said Curval, who at the moment was rather brutally handling those belonging to the sweet and tender Aline, "one may be certain indeed that a tit is a very infamous object. I never catch sight of one without being plunged straightway into a rage. Upon seeing these things I experience a certain disgust, a certain repugnance assails me . . . only a cunt has a worse and more decided effect upon me."

And so saying, he flung himself into his closet, dragging Aline by the breast and calling out to Sophie and Zelmire, his quatrain's two girls, and Fanchon to follow him. One cannot be sure of precisely what he did, but a loud scream, clearly a woman's, was heard by the others in the auditorium, and shortly afterward came the bellowings that usually indicated the Président had discharged. He returned. Aline was weeping and held a kerchief over her breast, and as these events rarely created any stir, or, at best, a few chuckles, Duclos went on with her story at once.

Several days later I myself took care, said she, of an old monk whose mania, more wearying to the hand, was rather less revolting to the stomach. He presented me with a great ugly behind covered with skin as tough as bull's hide and as wrinkled as a dried leaf; the task here was to knead his ass, to handle it, drub and thump it, squeeze it with all my strength, but when I reached the hole, nothing I did seemed sufficiently violent: I had to catch up the skin, rub it, pinch it, roll it between my fingers, use my nails, and it was thanks only to the vigor of my ministrations his fuck finally emerged. He attended to his own frigging while I abused his bum and vent, and I was not even obliged to show him my ankles. But that man must have made a very fierce and old habit of those manipulations, for his behind, although slack and hanging, was nevertheless upholstered by a skin as horny and as thick as leather.

The next day, doubtless having spoken highly of me and my dexterity to his friends in the monastery, he sent one of his brethren upon whose ass one had to bestow slaps, indeed blows of the hand, and stout ones at that; but this new ecclesiastic, more of a libertine and an examiner, preceded his rite by a meticulous inspection of his woman's buttocks, and my ass was kissed, nuzzled, tongued ten or twelve times over, the intervals being filled by blows aimed at his. When his hide had taken a scarlet hue, his prick got bravely up, and I can certify that it was one of the noblest engines I had palmed and fingered until that day. He put it into my hand, recommending that I frig it while continuing to slap him with the other.

"Unless I am gravely mistaken," said the Bishop, "we have finally reached the article of passive fustigation."

"Yes, Monseigneur," replied Duclos, "we have, and as my task for today has been fulfilled, you will consent to allow me to postpone until tomorrow the beginning of fustigatory tastes; we shall devote several soirees to dealing with them."

As nearly half an hour remained before supper, Durcet said that, to stimulate his appetite, he wished to give his entrails a few rinses; his announcement made something of an impression upon the women, who began to tremble; but sentence had been decreed, there was no revoking it. Thérèse, his servant that day, assured him she introduced the tube with wonderful skill; from the assertion she passed to the proof, and as soon as the little financier felt his bowels loaded, he singled out Rosette, beckoned her to him, and bade her open her mouth. There was some balking, a few complaints and a word or two of pleading, but the capital thing was obedience and, sure enough, the poor little girl swallowed two eruptions, having been granted the option or regurgitating them afterward. And regurgitate them she did, and soon. Happily, the supper bell sounded, for the financier was getting ready to begin again. But the prospect of a meal changed the disposition of their Lordships' minds, they went to taste different pleasures. A few turds were lodged on a few bubs at the orgies, and a great deal of shit was gleaned from asses; within the assembly's full view, the Duc consumed Duclos' turd, while that splendid girl sucked him, and while the bawdy fellow's hands roamed here and there, his fuck came out in a thick spray; Curval having imitated him with Champville, the friends began to speak of retiring for the night.

The Seventeenth Day

The terrible antipathy the Président had for Constance was manifest in daily outbursts: he had spent the night with her, having made a bilateral arrangement with Durcet, to whom he returned her the following morning with the most bitter complaints about her behavior.

"Since because of her condition," said he, "the society seems loath to expose her to the customary punishments for fear she be brought to bed before the time we have appointed to pluck her fruit, at least, by Jesus," said he, "we should find some means or other to punish the whore when she chooses to play the fool."

Ah, but what is that spirit of evil that inhabits libertines? Some glimmer of it may be obtained by analyzing Constance's prodigious fault. O reader, what do you suppose it was had waked Curval's wrath? Even worse than you may have dreamt: she had most unfortunately turned her front toward her master when he had called for her behind, ah yes, and such sins are not to be forgiven. But the worst part of her error was her denial of the fact; she declared, and there seemed some basis to her contention, that the Président was calumniating her, that he was seeking naught but her downfall, that she never lay with him but he would invent some such untruth; but as the law was precise and formal on this point, and as women's speeches were given no credence whatever in that society, but one question remained posed: how in future was this female to be chastised without risking the spoilage of the fruit ripening in her? It was decided that for each misdemeanor she would be obliged to eat a turd and, consequently, Curval insisted that she begin there and then. Approbation greeted his demand. They were at the time breakfasting in the girls' quarters, word was dispatched, Constance was summoned, the Président shitted in the center of the room, and she was enjoined to approach his creation on hands and knees and to devour what the cruel man had just wrought. She cast herself upon her knees, yes, but in this posture begged pardon, and her solicitations went unheeded; Nature had put bronze in those breasts where hearts are commonly to be found. Nothing more entertaining than the grimaces and affected airs to which the poor woman resorted before capitulating, and God knows how amused Messieurs were by the scene. At last, however, decisive action had to be taken, Constance's very soul seemed to burst before she was half done, but it had all to be done nevertheless, and every ounce disappeared from the tiles on the floor.

Excited by what he was witnessing, each of our friends, while watching, had himself frigged by a small girl; Curval, singularly aroused by the operation and benefiting from the wondrous skill of Augustine's enchanted fingers, feeling himself nigh to overflowing, called to Constance, who had scarcely finished eating her mournful breakfast.

"Hither, come to me, whore," said he, "after having bolted some fish one needs a little sauce, good white sauce. Come get a mouthful."

Well, there was no escaping that ordeal either, and Curval, who, while operating, was having Augustine shit, opened the sluices and let fly into the mouth of the Duc's miserable wife, and at the same time swallowed the fresh and delicate little turd the interesting Augustine had hatched for him.

The inspection tours were conducted, Durcet found shit in Sophie's chamber pot. The young lady sought to excuse her error by maintaining that she had been suffering from indigestion.

"Not at all," Durcet observed as expertly he handled the turd, "that is not true: indigestion produces diarrhea, soup, my dear, and this article looks very sound to me."

And straightway taking up his baneful notebook, he wrote down the name of that charming creature, who did her best to hide her tears and refrained, at Durcet's request, from deploring her situation. Everyone else had abided by the regulations, but in the boys' chamber, Zélamir, who had shitted the previous evening during the orgies and who had been told not to wipe his little bum, had tidied it up none the less, disobeying the orders. These were the crimes of the first magnitude: Zélamir's name was inscribed. Notwithstanding the boy's delinquency, Durcet kissed his ass and had himself sucked for a brief moment, then Messieurs passed on to the chapel, where they beheld the shitting of two subaltern fuckers, Aline, Fanny, Thérèse, and Champville. The Duc received Fanny's performance in his mouth, and he ate it, the Bishop's mouth caught the two fuckers' turds, one of which the prelate devoured, Durcet made Champville's his own, and the Président, despite his discharge, gulped down Aline's with all the avidity he had exhibited while consuming what Augustine had done for him.

Constance's scene had heated the company's imagination, for it had been a long time since Messieurs had indulged themselves in such extravagances so early in the morning. Dinner conversation dealt with moral science. The Duc declared he could not understand why in France the law smote so heavily against libertinage, since libertinage, by keeping the citizens busy, kept them clear of cabals and plots and revolutions; the Bishop observed that, no, the laws did not exactly aim at the suppression of libertinage, but at its excesses. Whereupon the latter were analyzed, and the Duc proved that there was nothing dangerous in excess, no excess which could justly arouse the government's suspicion, and that, these facts being clear, the official attitude was not only cruel but absurd; what other word was there to describe bringing artillery to bear upon mosquitoes?

From remarks they progressed to effects, the Duc, half-drunk, abandoned himself in Zephyr's arms, and for thirty long minutes sucked that lovely child's mouth while Hercule, exploiting the situation, buried his enormous engine in the

Duc's anus. Blangis was all complacency, and without stirring, without the flicker of an eyelash, went on with his kissing as, virtually without noticing it, he changed sex. His companions all gave themselves over to other infamies, and then they sallied forth to coffee. As they had just played a multitude of silly little pranks, the atmosphere was calm, and this was perhaps the one coffee hour during the entire four months' outing when no fuck was shed. Duclos was already upon the tribune, awaiting the company; when everyone had taken his place, she addressed her auditors in this wise:

I had recently suffered a loss in my house, and it had a deep effect upon me in every sense. Eugénie, whom I loved with a passion and who, thanks to her most extraordinary complaisance in whatever was connected with the possibility of earning me money, had been especially useful to me, Eugénie, I say, had just been spirited away. It happened in the strangest fashion: a domestic, having first paid the price settled upon, came to conduct her, so he said, to a supper that was to be held outside the city; her participation in the affair would be worth seven or eight louis. I was not at the house at the time the transaction took place, for I should never have allowed her to leave with someone I didn't know, but the domestic applied directly to her and she agreed to go. . . . I have never seen her since.

"Nor shall you ever again," said Desgranges. "The party proposed was her last one, and it will be my agreeable task to add the denouement to that lovely girl's history."

"Great God!" cried Duclos. "She was so beautiful, that girl . . . only twenty, her face was so sweet, she was so delicate. . . ."

"And, one might add, her body was the most superb in Paris," Desgranges said. "All those charms conspired to her undoing, but go on with what you were saying, let's not become mired down in circumstances."

Lucile was the girl who took her place, Duclos continued, both in my heart and in my bed, but not in the household's activities, for she had not by any means Eugénie's submissive temper nor her great understanding.

All the same, it was to her hands I entrusted, not long afterward, that certain Benedictine prior who used to pay me a visit now and again, and who had in past times been wont to frolic with Eugénie. After the good father had warmed her cunt with his tongue and thoroughly sucked her mouth, the major phase of the process began: Lucile took the whip and plied it lightly over his prick and balls, and he discharged from a limp machine; the gentle rubbing, the mere application of the lash produced his orgasm. His greatest pleasure used to consist in watching the girl slash with her whip at the drops of fuck as they spattered from his prick.

The next day, I myself took charge of a gentleman upon whose bare behind one had to lay one hundred carefully counted whip strokes; before his beating he prepared himself by kissing one's behind and while being lashed he frigged himself.

A third, with whom I had dealings some time later, had even heavier demands to satisfy; he also gilded each detail with additional ceremony: I received notice of his intended arrival a week in advance, and during that time I had to avoid washing any part of my body, and above all was to spare my cunt, my ass, my mouth; and furthermore, as soon as I learned he was to come, I selected three cat-o'-nine-tails and immersed them in a pot full of mixed urine and shit, and kept the whips soaking there until he presented himself. He was an elderly collector of the salt tax, a man of considerable means, a widower, without children, and he treated himself to such parties all the time. The first thing that interested him was to determine whether I had scrupulously abstained from ablutions, as he had enjoined me; I assured him I had followed his instructions to the letter; he wished proof, and began by applying a kiss to my lips. This experience must have convinced him, for he then suggested we go up to the room, and I realized that had he, upon kissing me, discovered I had cleansed my mouth in any way at all, he would not have wished to continue with the party. We go up together, as I say, he regards the whips steeping in the pot, then, bidding me undress, he sets to sniffing every part of my body, above all the orifices he had expressly forbidden me to wash; as I had honored his prescription in perfect faith and in every article, he doubtless discovered the aroma he desired to be there, for I saw him grow restless, appear anxious to be off, and heard him exclaim: "Ah, by fuck, that's what I want, that's just what I want!" I proceeded to fondle his ass: it was sheathed in what positively resembled boiled leather in color, texture, and toughness. After having spent a minute caressing, handling, poking about those gnarled, storm-beaten hindquarters, I seized a cat-o'-nine-tails and, without drying it, I gave him ten stinging cuts, putting all my strength into the blows; but this beginning produced not a tremor, he not only remained impassive, but my blows put not so much as the faintest scratch upon that unshakable citadel. Having opened with this prologue, I sank three of my fingers into his anus, took firm hold, and began to rattle him with might and main, but our man was insensible to the same degree here as elsewhere; my struggles failed to be acknowledged by so much as a sigh. These two initial ceremonies completed, his turn came to act; I lay belly down upon the bed, he knelt, spread my buttocks, and alternately shot his pilgrim tongue into this hole and into the other, and they, one may be sure, were, in keeping with his instructions, not entirely unaromatic. After he had done considerable sucking, I took up another whip, laid on a second time and socratized him again, he knelt as before and returned to his licking, and so it went, each of us doing his part at least fifteen times over. Finally, giving me further instructions and bidding me guide my movements in consonance with the state of his prick, which I was to observe carefully but which I was not to touch, when next he knelt I unleashed my turd. It shot squarely into his face, he fell back, exclaimed that I was an insolent creature, and discharged while frigging himself and while uttering cries that might have been heard in the street had I not taken the precaution of drawing the shutters. But the turd fell to the floor, he did naught but stare at and smell it, neither putting it in his mouth nor even touching it; he had received at least two hundred lashes, and I may assure you . . . his body bore not a trace of what it had sustained, his horny ass, fortified by years of rude usage, betrayed not the least mark.

"Well, by God's bum button!" chortled the Duc, "there's an ass, Président, worth as much as the curiosity you drag about."

"Oh yes, yes," said Curval, a stammer in his voice, for Aline was frigging him, "yes indeed, that fellow seems to have both my buttocks and my tastes, for, you know, I am infinitely opposed to the use of the bidet, but I prefer a longer abstinence: I usually set the period at a minimum of three months."

"Président, your prick's stiff," the Duc said.

"Do you think so?" Curval replied. "Faith, you'd best consult Aline here, she'll be able to tell you what's what, as for myself, you know, I'm so accustomed to that particular state of affairs that I rarely notice when it ends or when it begins. There is only one thing I can tell you with complete confidence, and that is that at this very moment I'd hugely like to have my hands upon a very impure whore; I'd like her to present me with a bucketful of shit, fill a bowl to above the rim, I'd like her ass to stink from shit, I'd like her cunt to smell like a beach covered with dead fish. But hold! Thérèse, O thou whose filth is as old as the hills, thou who since baptism hast not wiped thine ass, and whose infamous cunt breeds a pestilence three leagues on every side, come bring all that to my nose's delectation, I beg thee, and to that put a fine wet turd, if 'twould please thee."

Thérèse approaches, with foul and evil charms, with parts disgusting and withered and wounded she rubs the magistrate's face, upon his nose she excretes the desired turd, Aline does frig amain, the libertine discharges, and Duclos therewith resumes the story she has to tell.

An elderly rascal, who used to receive a new girl every day for the operation I am going to describe, besought one of my friends to persuade me to visit him, and at the same time I was given information about the ceremony regularly performed at the lecher's home. I arrive, he examines me with a phlegmatic glance, the kind of glance one encounters among habitual libertines, and which in an instant arrives at an infallible estimate of the object under scrutiny.

"I have been told you have a fine ass," said he in a drawling tone, "and as for the past sixty years I have had a decided weakness for fine cheeks, I should like to see whether there is any foundation to your reputation . . . lift your skirts."

That last phrase, energetically spoken, sufficed as an order; not only did I offer a view of the treasure, but I moved it as near as possible to his connoisseur's nose. At first I stand erect, then little by little I bend forward and exhibit the object of his devotion in every form and aspect most apt to please him. With each movement, I feel the old scoundrel's hands wander over the surface, scouting the terrain, probing the geography, sometimes creating a more consolidated effect, sometimes attempting to give it a more generous cast, compressing here, broadening there.

"The hole is ample, very ample," says he, "appearances attest a furious sodomistical prostitution."

"Alas, Monsieur," I concede, "we are living in an age when men are so capricious that in order to please them, one must indeed be prepared for virtually anything, and consent to it all."

Whereupon I feel his mouth glue itself hermetically to my asshole, and his tongue strive to penetrate into the chasm; I seize my opportunity, as I have been advised, and profiting from my situation, slide out, directly upon his probing tongue, the warmest, most humid, densest eructation. The maneuver displeases him not at all, but on the other hand does little to animate him; finally, after I have unleashed half a dozen winds, he gets to his feet, leads me to his bed, and points to an earthenware crock in which four cat-o'-nine-tails are marinating. Above the crock hang several whips suspended from gilded hooks.

"Arm yourself," murmurs the roué, "take a cat-o'-nine-tails and one of those other weapons, here is my ass. As you observe, it is dry, lean, and exceedingly well seasoned. Touch it."

I do so; he continues:

"You notice," says he, "that it's old, toughened by severe treatment, and it's not to be warmed save by the most incredibly excessive attacks. I am going to keep myself in this posture," and while speaking he stretched out upon the bed and rested his knees on the floor. "Employ those instruments, first one, then the other, now the cat-o'-nine-tails, now the whip. This is going to take a little time, but you will receive an unequivocal sign when the climax approaches. As soon as you see something out of the ordinary happening to this ass of mine, hold yourself in readiness to imitate what you see it doing; we will then exchange places, I shall kneel down before your splendid buttocks, you shall do what you shall have observed me do, and I'll discharge. But above all do not become impatient; I warn you once again: this business is not to be accomplished in haste."

I begin, I alternate weapons in accordance with the prescription. But, my God! what nonchalance, what stoicism! I was drenched in sweat; that my strokes be more freely applied he had suggested I roll my sleeves to above the elbow. Three-quarters of an hour went by and I was still beating him, putting every ounce of strength into my blows, sometimes tearing at his stubborn flesh with the cat-o'-nine-tails, sometimes with the steel-tipped thongs, three-quarters of an hour, I say, and it seemed as if I had got nowhere. Still, silent, our lecher was as quiet as death; one might say he was mutely savoring the interior stirrings of delight quickened by this ordeal, but there was no outward sign of pleasure, not a single indication of pleasure's influence even upon his skin. I proceeded. By and by I heard a clock strike two and realized I had been at work three whole hours; then all of a sudden I see his rump rise, his buttocks part, I slash and send my thongs whistling between certain crevices; a turd emerges, falls, I whip away, my blows send the shit flying to the floor.

"Courage," I say to him, "we're within sight of port."

And then my man gets up in a rage; his prick, hard and in fierce revolt, is glued to his belly.

"Do what I did," says he, "imitate me, I need nothing now but shit and you'll have my fuck."

I promptly adopt the position he has just abandoned, he kneels as he said he would, and into his mouth I lay an egg which I have been holding in store for him for three days. As he receives it his fuck leaps, and he flings himself backward, shouting with joy, but without swallowing, and indeed without keeping the turd in his mouth for more than a second. In conclusion let me say, Messieurs, that, your Lordships excepted, for you are without doubt superior examples of this species, I have seen few men convulse more frantically, few who have manifested a more trenchant delight; he came nigh to swooning as he gave vent to his fuck. That séance was worth two louis.

But no sooner did I return to the house than I found Lucile come to grips with another old chap who, without having laid a finger upon her, without any preliminaries, had simply ordered her to fustigate him from the small of the back to just above the knees; Lucile was using a cat-o'-nine-tails soaked in vinegar, was endowing her blows with all the force she could muster, and this individual ended his ritual by having her suck him. The girl knelt before him when he gave her the signal and, adjusting his old weary balls so that they dangled upon her teats, she took the flabby engine in her mouth whereinto the chastened sinner hastened to weep for his transgressions.

And Duclos having therewith put a period to what she had to relate that day, and the supper hour not yet having arrived, Messieurs delivered themselves of a few smutty comments while waiting.

"You must be done up, Président," gibed the Duc. "I've seen you discharge twice today, and you're hardly accustomed to such feats of liberality."

"Let's wager on a third," replied Curval, who was pawing Duclos' buttocks.

"Why, certainly, as much as you like and as often," the Duc returned.

"And I ask for only one condition," Curval said, "and that is to be allowed to do whatever I like."

"Oh, I'm afraid not," the Duc answered, "for you know very well that there are certain things we have mutually promised not to do before the appointed time indicated on our schedules: having ourselves fucked was one of them - before proceeding to that we were, according to prior agreement, to wait until some example of that passion were cited to us, but by your common request, gentlemen, we ceded on that point and suspended the restriction. There are many other pleasures and modes of taking them we ought to have forbidden ourselves until the moment they were embodied in story, and which we have instead tolerated, provided the experiments are conducted in privacy - in, that is to say, either our closets or our bedchambers. You, Président, surrendered yourself to one with Aline just a short while ago; did she utter that piercing scream for no reason at all? and has she no motive for keeping her breast covered now? Very well then, choose from amongst those mysterious modes, or from one of those we permit in public, and I'll wager one hundred louis you'll not be able to derive your third from one of those legitimate sources."

The Président then asked whether he might be allowed to repair to the boudoir at the end of the corridor and to take along the subjects he deemed necessary to success; his request was granted, although it was stipulated that Duclos would have to be witness to the goings on, and that her word would be accepted upon the existence of the discharge or upon Curval's failure to produce it.

"Agreed," said the Président, "I accept the conditions."

And by way of a preliminary, he had Duclos give him five hundred lashes within view of the assembly; that accomplished, he led away his dear and devoted friend Constance, in whose behalf his colleagues besought Curval to do nothing which might damage her pregnancy; the Président also took with him his daughter Adelaide, Augustine, Zelmire, Céladon, Zéphyr, Thérèse, Fanchon, Champville, Desgranges, Duclos, of course, and three fuckers besides.

"Why fuck my eyes!" exclaimed the Duc, "there was nothing in the bargain that said he could recruit an army."

But the Bishop and Durcet took the Président's side in the matter of manpower and firmly reminded Blangis that the terms of the wager included no limitation upon numbers. The Président led his band away, and at the end of thirty minutes, an interval the Bishop, Durcet, and the Duc, with the few subjects remaining to them, did not pass in holy orison, thirty minutes later, I say, Constance and Zelmire returned in tears, and the Président reappeared soon afterward with the rest of his force; Duclos then related the mighty things he had done, paid homage to his vigor, and certified that in all fairness and justice he merited the crown of myrtle. The reader will kindly allow us to suppress the text of Duclos' report, for the architecture of our novel bids us conceal the precise circumstances of what transpired in that remote boudoir; but Curval had won his wager, and that, we consider, is the essential point.

"These hundred louis," he remarked upon receiving them from the Duc, "will be useful in paying a fine which, I fear, shall soon be levied upon me."

And here is still another thing the explanation of which we pray the reader will permit us to postpone until the appropriate moment arrives; for the time being he need but observe how that rascal Curval would anticipate his misdeeds well in advance, and how, with unruffled calm, he would accept the fact that they would bring down upon him certain and merited punishment, a fatal necessity he faced unflinchingly and with a proud smile.

Between that time and the opening of the next day's narrations absolutely nothing out of the ordinary transpired, and therefore we propose to conduct the reader to the auditorium at once.

The Eighteenth Day

Beautiful, radiant, bejeweled, grown more brilliant with each passing day, Duclos thus started the eighteenth session's stories:

A tall and stoutly constructed creature named Justine had just been added to my entourage; she was twenty-five, five feet six inches tall, with the husky arms and solid legs of a barmaid, but her features were fine all the same, her skin was clear and smooth, and she had as splendid a body as one might wish. As my establishment used to be swarming with a crowd of those old rakehells who are incapable of experiencing the faintest pleasure save when heated by the lash or torture, I thought that a pensionnaire like Justine, furnished as she was with the forearm of a blacksmith, could be nothing but a very real asset. The day following her arrival, I decided to put her fustigatory talents to the test; I had been given to understand she wielded a whip with prodigious skill, and hence matched her against an old commissar of the quarter whom she was to flog from chest to shin and then, on the other side, from the middle of his back to his calves. The operation over with, the libertine simply hoisted the girl's skirts and planted his load upon her buttocks. Justine comported herself like a true heroine of Cythera, and our good old martyr avowed to me afterward that I had got my hands on a treasure, and that in all his days no one had ever whipped him as that rascal had.

To demonstrate how much I counted upon her contribution to our little community, a few days later I arranged a meeting between Justine and an old veteran of many a campaign on the fields of love; her required a round thousand strokes all over his body, he would have no part of himself spared, and when he was afire and nicely bloodied, the girl had to piss into her cupped hand and smear her urine over those areas of his body which looked to be most seriously molested. This lotion rubbed on, the heavy labor had to be begun again, then he would discharge, the girl would carefully collect his fuck, once again using her cupped hand, and she would give him a second massage, this time employing the balm wrung from his prick. Another triumph for my new colleague, and every succeeding day brought her further and more impassioned acclaim; but it was impossible to exercise her arm on the champion who presented himself this time.

This extraordinary man would have nothing of the feminine but womanish dress: the wearer of the costume had to be a man; in other words, the roué wanted to be spanked by a man got up as a girl. And what was the instrument she had to use on him? Don't think for a moment he was content with a birch ferule or even a cat, no, he demanded a bundle of osier switches wherewith very barbarously one had to tear his buttocks. Actually, this particular affair seeming to have somewhat of the flavor of sodomy, I felt I ought not become too deeply involved in it; but as he was one of Fournier's former and most reliable clients, a man who had been truly attached to our house in fair weather and in foul, and who, furthermore, might, thanks to his position, be able to render us some service, I raised no objections and, having prettily disguised a young lad of eighteen who sometimes availed us of his services and who had a very attractive face, I presented him, armed with a handful of switches, to his opponent.

And a very entertaining contest it was - you may well imagine how eager I was to observe it. He began with a careful study of his pretended maiden, and having found him, evidently, much to his liking, he opened with five or six kisses upon the youth's mouth: those kisses would have looked peculiar from three miles away; next, he exhibited his cheeks, and in all his behavior and words seeming to take the young man for a girl, he told him to fondle his buttocks and knead them just a little rigorously; the lad, whom I had told exactly what to expect, did everything asked of him.

"Well, let's be off," said the bawd, "ply those switches, spare not to strike hard."

The youth catches up the bundle of withes and therewith, swinging right merrily, lays fifty slashing blows upon a pair of buttocks which seem only to thirst for more; already definitely marked by those two score and ten stripes, the libertine hurls himself upon his masculine flagellatrice, draws up her petticoats, one hand verifies her sex, the other fervently clutches her buttocks, he knows not which altar to bow down before first, the ass finally captures his primary attentions, he glues his mouth to its hole, much ardor in his expression. Ah, what a difference between the worship Nature is said to prescribe and that other which is said to outrage her! O God of certain justice, were this truly an outrage, would the homage be paid with such great emotion? Never was woman's ass kissed as was that lad's; three or four times over his lover's tongue entirely disappeared into the anus; returning to his former position at last, "O dear child," cried he, "resume your operation."

Further flagellation ensued, but as it was livelier, the patient met this new assault with far more courage and intrepidity. Blood makes its appearance, another stroke brings his prick bounding up, and he engages the young object of his transports to seize it without an instant's delay. While the latter manipulates him, he wishes to render the youth the same service, lifts up the boy's skirts again, but it's a prick he's now gone in quest of; he touches it, grasps, shakes, pulls it, and soon introduces it into his mouth. After these initial caresses, he calls for a third round of blows and receives a storm of them. This latest experience puts him in a perfect tumult; he flings his Adonis upon the bed, lies down upon him, simultaneously toys with his own prick and his companion's, then presses one upon the other, glues his lips to the boy's mouth and, having succeeded in warming him by means of these caresses, he procures him the divine pleasure at the same moment he is overwhelmed himself: both discharge in harmony. Enchanted by the scene, our libertine sought to placate my risen indignation, and at last coaxed a promise from me to arrange for further delights in the same kind, both with that young fellow and with any others I could find for him. I attempted to work at his conversion, I assured him I had some charming girls who would be happy to flog him and who could do so quite as well; no, said he, none of that, he would not so much as look at what I had to offer him.

"Oh, I can readily believe it," said the Bishop. "When one has a decided taste for men, there's no changing, the difference between boy and girl is so extreme that one's not apt to be tempted to try what is patently inferior."

"Monseigneur," said the Président, "you have broached a thesis which merits a two-hour dissertation."

"And which will always conclude by giving further support to my contention," said the Bishop, "because the fact that a boy is superior to a girl is beyond doubt or dispute."

"Beyond contradiction too," Curval agreed, "but nevertheless one might still inform you that a few objections have been here and there raised to your doctrine and that, for a certain order of pleasures, such as Martaine and Desgranges shall discuss, a girl is to be preferred to a boy."

"That I deny," said the Bishop with emphasis, "and even for such pleasures as you allude to the boy is worth more than the girl. Consider the problem from the point of view of evil, evil almost always being pleasure's true and major charm; considered thus, the crime must appear greater when perpetrated upon a being of your identical sort than when inflicted upon one which is not, and this once established, the delight automatically doubles."

"Yes," said Curval, "but that despotism, that empire, that delirium born of the abuse of one's power over the weak. . . ."

"But the same is no less true in the other case," the Bishop insisted. "If the victim is yours, thoroughly in your power, that supremacy which when using women you think better established than when using men, is based upon pure prejudice, upon nothing, and results merely from the custom whereby females are more ordinarily submitted to your caprices than are males. But give up that popular superstition for a moment, view the thing equitably and, provided the man is bound absolutely by your chains and by the same authority you exert over women, you will obtain the idea of a greater crime; your lubricity ought hence to increase at least twofold."

"I am of the Bishop's mind," Durcet joined in, "and once it is certain that sovereignty is fully established, I believe the abuse of power more delicious when exercised at the expense of one's peer than at a woman's."

"Gentlemen," said the Duc, "I should greatly prefer you to postpone your discussions until mealtime. I believe these hours have been reserved for listening to the narrations, and it would seem to me proper were you to refrain from employing them upon philosophical exchanges."

"He is right," said Curval. "Go on with your story, Duclos."

And that agreeable directress of Cytherean sport plunged again into the matter she had to relate.

Another elderly man, said she, this one a clerk at parliament, paid me a call one morning, and as during Fournier's administration he had been accustomed to dealing exclusively with me, tradition bade him solicit an interview with me now. Our conference consisted in slapping his face with gradually increasing force, and in frigging him the while; that is to say, one had at first to slap him gently, then, as his prick assumed consistency, one slowly augmented the force of one's blows, and finally a series of truly bone-shattering cuffs would provoke his ejaculation. I had so well apprehended the precise nature of his eccentricity that my twentieth slap brought his fuck springing out.

"The twentieth, you say? Why, by Jesus," exclaimed the Bishop, "my prick would have gone dead limp by the third."

"There you are, my friend," the Duc declared, "to each his own peculiar mania, we ought never blame nor wonder at another's; tolerance, I say. Say on, Duclos, give us one more and have done."

My last example for the evening, said Duclos, originally was told to me by one of my friends; she had been living for two years with a man whose prick never stiffened until one had first bestowed a score of fillips upon his nose and tweaked it, pulled his ears till they bled, and bitten his buttocks, chewed his prick, nipped his balls. Aroused by these potent preliminary titillations, his prick would shoot aloft like a stallion's, and while swearing like a demon he'd almost always discharge upon the visage of the girl at whose hands he had been receiving this exhilarating treatment.

Of all that had been recounted during that afternoon's sitting, only the masculine fustigations had affected their Lordships' brains which, now passing hot, were only cooled after prolonged use of the fantasy which had fired their enthusiasm; thus it was the Duc had Hercule flog him until blood seeped from his pores, Durcet employed Invictus to the same effect, the Bishop made use of Antinoüs, and Bum-Cleaver ministered to Curval. The Bishop, who had done nothing that day, did finally discharge at the orgies, they say, while eating the turd Zélamir had been preparing for forty-eight hours. And then they went to bed.

The Nineteenth Day

That morning, after having made some observations upon the shit the subjects were producing for lubricious purposes, the friends decided that the society ought to try something Duclos had spoken of in her narrations: I am referring to the suppression of bread and soup from all the tables save Messieurs'. These two articles were withdrawn, and replaced by twice the former quantity of fowl and game. They hoped to remark some improvement, and in less than a week an essential difference in the community's excrements was indeed perceived: they were more mellow, softer, dissolved more readily, had an infinitely more subtle flavor, and the friends discovered that d'Aucourt's advice to Duclos had been that of a consummate libertine thoroughly penetrated with an appreciation of such matters. It was pointed out, however, that this new diet might have some effect upon breaths:

"Well, what does that matter?" asked Curval, to whom the Duc had addressed his objection; "'tis very faulty reasoning to maintain that, to give pleasure, a woman's mouth or a youth's must be absolutely clean and sweet smelling. Setting aside all idiosyncrasy for a moment, I most willingly grant you that he who requires stinking breath and a foul mouth is moved by depravation only, but for your part you must grant me that a mouth entirely bereft of odor gives not the slightest pleasure when kissed. There must always be some kind of spice to the thing, some flavor there, for where's the joy if it's not stung alive? the joy's asleep, I say, and it's only waked by a little filth. However clean may be the mouth, the lover who sucks it assuredly does an unclean thing, and there is no doubt at all in his mind that it is that very uncleanness that pleases him. Give a somewhat greater degree of strength to the impulse and you'll want that mouth to be impure. If it fall short of smelling of rot or the cadaver, well, be patient, the taste will develop, but that it have nothing but an odor of milk and honey or infancy, that, I tell you, is insufferable. And so the diet we're going to subject them to will, at the worst, lead not at all to corruption, but only to a certain alteration, and that is all that's necessary."

The morning searches brought nothing to light . . . the youngsters were keeping strict watch over their conduct. No one requested toilet permission, and the company sat down at table. Adelaide, one of the servants at the meal, having been enjoined by Durcet to fart in a champagne glass, and having been unable to comply, was directly entered in the fatal book by her unfeeling husband who, since the beginning of the week, had been continually endeavoring to find her at fault.

Coffee came next; it was handed round by Cupidon, Giton, Michette, and Sophie. The Duc thigh-fucked Sophie, and while so doing had her shit upon his hand; the nobleman took that pretty little packet and smeared it over his face, the Bishop did precisely the same thing with Giton and Curval with Michette, but as for Durcet, he popped his little device into Cupidon's mouth as that charming boy squeezed out his turd. There were, notwithstanding, no discharges and, having risen from their nap, Messieurs went to hear Duclos.

A man we had never seen previously, said that amiable whore, came to the house and proposed a rather unusual ceremony: he wished to be tied to one side of a stepladder; we secured his thighs and waist to the third rung and, raising his arms above his head, tied his wrists to the uppermost step. He was naked. Once firmly bound, he had to be exposed to the most ferocious beating, clubbed with the cat's handle when the knots at the tips of the cords were worn out. He was naked, I repeat, there was no need to lay a finger upon him, nor did he even touch himself, but after having received a savage pounding his monstrous instrument rose like a rocket, it was seen to sway and bounce between the ladder's rungs, hovering like a pendulum and, soon after, impetuously launch its fuck into the middle of the room. He was unbound, he paid, and that was all.

The following day he sent us one of his friends whose buttocks and thighs, member and balls had to be pricked with a golden needle. Not until he was covered with blood did he discharge. I handled that commission myself, and as he constantly shouted to me to thrust deeper, I had almost to bury the needle in his glans before seeing his fuck squirt into my palm. As he unleashed it, he thrust his face against mine, sucked my mouth prodigiously, and that was all there was to it.

A third - and he too was an acquaintance of his two predecessors - ordered me to flail every bit of his body with nettles. I soon had him streaming blood, he eyed himself in a mirror, and it was not before he saw his body reduced to a scarlet shambles that he let fly his fuck, without touching anything, fondling anything, without requiring anything else of me.

Those excesses entertained me hugely, I took a secret delight in participating in them; and all my whimsical clients were equally delighted with me. It was at about the period of those three scenes that a Danish nobleman, having been sent to me for pleasure parties of a very different character, which others have been designated to discuss, had the imprudence to arrive at my establishment with ten thousand francs in diamonds, as much in other gems, and five hundred louis in cash. The prize was too handsome to be allowed to get away; between the two of us, Lucile and I managed to rob the Dane of his last sou. He thought to lodge a complaint, but as I used to pay a heavy bribe to the police, and as in those days one did just about whatever one pleased with gold, the gentleman was ordered to put a stop to his wailing, and his belongings became mine, or rather most of them did, for, in order to assure myself of little clear title to that treasure, I had to yield a few precious stones to the minions of the law. Never have I committed a theft, and I would have you remark this interesting fact, without encountering some stroke of good fortune the next day; this latest windfall was a new client, but one of those daily clients one may truly consider a brothel's bread and butter.

This individual was an old courtier who, weary of the homages he used unendingly to receive in the palaces of kings, like to visit whores and enjoy a change of role. He wanted to start with me; very well, said I, and we began without further ado. I had to make him recite his lessons and recite his little speeches, and every time he made a mistake, he had to get down on his knees and receive, sometimes on his knuckles, sometimes on his behind, vigorous blows of a leathern ferule such as the regents use in schoolrooms. It was also my task to keep a sharp eye out for signs of emotion; once the fire had been lit, I would snatch up his prick and shake it skillfully, scolding him all the while, calling him a little libertine, a very scurvy fellow, a worry to His Majesty, and other childish names which would cause him to come very voluptuously. The identical ceremony was to be executed five times each week at my establishment, but always with a different and properly instructed girl, and for this service I received a stipend of twenty-five louis per month. I knew so many women in Paris I had no trouble promising him what he asked and keeping my word; I had that charming pupil in my house for a decade, toward the end of which period he decided to pack his bags and go off to pursue his studies in hell.

However, I too was aging with the passing years, and although I had the kind of face which retains its beauty, I was beginning to notice that my visitors were men more and more often conveyed to me by whim and accident. I still had some staunch and dependable suitors even at thirty-six, and the rest of the adventures in which I took a hand belong to the period between that time and my fortieth year.

Though thirty-six years old, as I say, the libertine, whose mania I am going to relate in closing today's session, would have nothing to do with anyone else. He was an abbot of sixty or thereabouts, for I received no one but gentlemen of a certain age, and every woman who would like to seek her fortune in our trade will doubtless see fit to impose the same rules barring irresponsible youth from her house. The holy man arrives, and as soon as we are closeted together he begs to see my bum.

"Ah, yes, there's the world's finest ass," he says admiringly. "But, unfortunately, that is not the apparatus which is to provide me with the pittance I intend to consume. Here, take hold," says he, putting his buttocks into my hands, "that's the source whence all good things do come. . . . Be so kind as to help me shit."

I bring up a porcelain pot and place it upon my knees, the abbot backs toward me, stoops, I press his anus, pry it open, and, to be brief, agitate it in every way I think likely to hasten his evacuation. It takes place, an enormous turd fills the bowl, I offer it to its author, he seizes it, precipitates himself upon it, devours it, and discharges after fifteen minutes of the most violent flogging which I administer upon the same behind that shortly before laid such a splendid egg for his breakfast. He swallowed it all; he had so nicely judged the situation that his sperm did not appear until the last mouthful vanished. All the while I plied my whip, I excited him with steady stream of comments such as: "Well, then, little rascal, what's this?" and, "Why, here's a nasty little chap, can you really eat shit that way?" and, "I'll teach you, you funny little whoreson bastard; perform such disgraceful things, will you?"

And it was by dint of these actions and speeches that the libertine attained the summit of joy.

At this point, Curval was moved to give the company a before-supper demonstration in fact of what Duclos had described in words. He summoned Fanchon, she extracted shit from him, and the libertine devoured it while the old sorceress drubbed him with all the strength of her skinny but sinewed arm. That lubric exhibition having inspired his confreres, they began hunting for shit wherever any might be found, and then Curval, who had not discharged, mixed the rest of his turd with Thérèse's, whom he had excrete without further ado.

The Bishop, accustomed to making use of his brother's delights, did the same thing with Duclos, the Duc with Marie, little Durcet with Louison. It was atrocious, why, it was unthinkable to employ such decrepit old horrors when such pretty objects stood ready at one's beck and call; but, oh how well 'tis known, satiety is born in the arms of abundance, and when in the very thick of voluptuous delights one takes an even keener pleasure in torments.

These unclean stunts over and done with, and the doing having cost only one discharge, and 'twas the Bishop who produced it, the friends went to table. Having involved themselves in a series of foul activities, they thought best not to change horses in midstream, and for the orgies would have only the four old duennas and the four storytellers; everyone else was packed off to bed. Their Lordships said so many things, did so many more, that all four came like geysers, and our libertine quartet did not retire until overcome with drink and exhaustion.

The Twentieth Day

Something very humorous indeed had occurred the night before: absolutely drunk, the Duc, instead of gaining his bedchamber, had installed himself in young Sophie's bed, and despite all the child could say, for she knew perfectly well what he was doing violated the rules, he would not be budged, and continued with great heat to maintain he was damned well where he belonged, namely, in his bed with Aline, who was listed as his wife for the night. But as he was allowed certain privileges with Aline which were still forbidden with the little girls, when he sought to put Sophie in the posture that favored the amusements of his choice, and when the poor child, to whom no one had as yet ever done such a thing, felt the massive head of the Duc's prick hammer at her young behind's narrow gate and contrive to batter a thoroughfare, the poor little creature fell to uttering dreadful screeches, and, leaping up, fled naked about the room. The Duc followed hard on her heels, swearing like a demon, still mistaking her for Aline. "Buggress!" he roared, "dost think it the first time?" And fancying he has overtaken her and has her at last, he falls upon Zelmire's bed, thinking it his own, and embraces that little girl, supposing Aline has decided to behave reasonably. The same proceedings with Zelmire as a moment ago with Sophie, because the Duc most decidedly wishes to attain his objective; but immediately Zelmire perceives what he is about, she imitates her companion and duplicates her resistance, pronounces a terrible scream, and leaps away.

However, Sophie, the first to take to flight, collects her wits and, seeing full well that there is but one way to put an end to this quid pro quo, sets off in search of light and some cool-headed individual capable of restoring order, and consequently she thinks to look for Duclos. But Duclos had behaved like a pig at the orgies and got herself blind drunk, Sophie comes upon her stretched out unconscious in the middle of the Duc's bed, and fails absolutely to bring her to her senses. Desperate, knowing not to whom under such circumstances she may apply, hearing all her comrades calling for help, she gathers up courage and enters Durcet's apartment; the financier is lying with his daughter, Constance, and Sophie blurts out what has been happening. Constance at any rate did rise from the bed, despite the efforts the drunken Durcet made to restrain her by saying he wanted to discharge; she took a candle and accompanied Sophie to the girls' chamber: she discovered the poor little dears, all in their nightgowns, clustered in the center of the room, and the Duc pursuing now one of them, now another, still persuaded he was dealing with no one but Aline, whom he swore was become a witch that night and had many shapes. Constance finally showed him his error, and entreating him to allow her to guide him back to his room, where, she assured him, he would find a very submissive Aline only too eager to do all he chose to demand of her, the Duc who, thoroughly besotted and acting as always in the very best of faith, really had no other design than to plant his staff in Aline's ass, let himself be taken to her; that lovely girl was there to greet him, and he went to bed; Constance withdrew from the room, and calm was restored generally.

They laughed very heartily all the next day over that nocturnal adventure, and the Duc declared that if, by great misfortune, he were in such a case to happen all accidentally to obliterate a maidenhead, he would not, so it seemed to him, be liable or justly subject to a fine because, intoxicated, he could not be held accountable for his actions; but, oh no, the others assured him, he was mistaken in that, he would indeed have to pay.

They breakfasted amidst their sultanas as usual, and all the little girls avowed they'd been furiously afraid. Not one, however, was found at fault despite the night's alarms; similarly, everything was in order in the boys' quarters, and coffee, like dinner, offering nothing extraordinary, they passed into the auditorium where Duclos, entirely set to rights after the previous evening's riot, amused the company with the following five episodes:

It was once again I, Messieurs, who went on the stage in the play I am about to describe to you. The other person in the drama was a medical man; the doctor's first act was to examine my buttocks, and as he came to the conclusion they were superb, he spent more than an hour doing nothing but kissing them. He at last confessed his little foibles: they were all connected with shit and shitting, as I had surmised, and knowing what was expected of me, I adopted the appropriate posture. I filled the white porcelain pot I used to employ for this sort of enterprise. Immediately he is the master of my turd, he raises it to his mouth and begins tucking it away; he has no sooner taken a bite than I pick up a bull's pizzle - that was the instrument wherewith I was to caress his bum - I shout threats and imprecations at him, then strike, scold him for the dreadful things he is wont to do, the infamous things, and without heeding me, the libertine swallows the last mouthful, discharges, and is off with the speed of light, having tossed a louis onto the table.

Shortly afterward another came to the house, and I entrusted him to Lucile, who had truly to struggle to make him discharge. He had first of all to be sure the turd that was to be served up to him originated with an old beggar woman, and to convince him, I had to have the old crone operate before his own eyes. I gave him a venerable dame of seventy, covered with ulcers and wens and other signs of erysipelas, and whose last tooth had fallen from her gums fifteen years before. "Good, that's excellent," said he, "precisely the sort I need." Then, enclosing himself with Lucile and the turd, that equally skillful, complacent, and determined girl had to excite him to the point at which he would eat that very mature lump. He sniffed it, stared at it, even touched it, but that was all, he could not seem to make himself go further. Whereupon Lucile, having to resort to something more persuasive than rhetoric, thrust the fire tongs into the fire and, drawing them out red-hot, announced she proposed to burn his buttocks if he did not obey her on the spot and eat his luncheon. Our man trembles, has another try: the same disgust, he recoils. As good as her word, Lucile lowers his breeches and, bringing to light an ass of very evil aspect and scarred all over, discolored and withered by operations in this same kind, she deftly singes his cheeks. The lecher swears, Lucile applies her iron again, now scorches and finally produces a very definite and sufficiently profound burn in the middle of his ass; pain screws him up to resolution at last, he bites off a mouthful, additional burnings excite him further, and little by little the work is completed. The downing of the last nibble of shit coincided with his discharge, and I have seen exceedingly few as violent; he emitted loud cries and screams, howled like a wolf and rolled on the floor; I thought he had been seized by a frenzy or an attack of epilepsy. Delighted with the patient understanding he had encountered in our house, the libertine promised to be my regular customer, provided I would give him the same girl but a different old woman each time.

"The more repulsive the source," said he, "the better you'll be paid for the yield. You have simply no idea," he added, "to what lengths my depravity carries me; I hardly dare acknowledge it to myself."

Upon his recommendation, one of his friends visited us the next day, and this individual's depravity carried him, in my opinion, a great deal further, for instead of a relatively mild branding, he had to be soundly beaten with red-hot tongs, and the author of the turd offered him had to be the oldest, filthiest, most disgusting thief we could find. A degenerate old valet of eighty, whom we had had in the house for ages, pleased him wonderfully well for his operation, and, rolling his eyes, smacking his lips, he gobbled up the old devil's turd while it was still warm and while the good Justine, using tongs heated to such a temperature they could hardly be held, thrashed his bum. And she was furthermore obliged to snatch up great bits of his flesh with the instrument, and all but roast them.

Another had his buttocks, belly, balls, and prick stabbed with a heavy cobbler's awl, and all this with more or less the same circumstances, that is to say, until he would eat a turd I presented to him in a chamber pot. He was not, however, curious about the turd's origins.

Messieurs, it is not easy to imagine to what lengths men are driven in the delirium of their inflamed imaginations. Have I not beheld one who, acting according to the same principles, required me to shower bone-breaking blows of a cane upon him as he ate a turd which, before his own eyes, he had us fish up out of the depths of the house's privy? and his perfidious discharge did not flow into my mouth until he had devoured the last spoonful of that foul muck.

"Well, you know, everything's imaginable and even possible," said Curval as he pensively fondled Desgranges' buttocks. "I am convinced one can go still further than that."

"Further?" said the Duc who at that moment was mauling the bare behind of Adelaide, his wife for the day. "And what the devil would you have one do?"

"Worse!" replied Curval, something of a hiss in his voice. "It seems to me one never sufficiently exploits the possible."

"I entirely agree with the Président," spoke up Durcet, then in the act of embuggering Antinoüs, "and I have the feeling my mind is capable of further improvements upon all those piggish stunts."

"I think I know what Durcet means," said the Bishop who, for the time being, was idle, or who rather had not yet begun to operate.

"Well, what the devil does he mean?" the Duc demanded to know.

Whereupon the Bishop stood up and went to Durcet's alcove; the two men whispered together, the Bishop then moved on to where Curval was, and the latter said, "That's it, exactly!" And then the Bishop spoke in the Duc's ear.

"By fuck!" His Highness exclaimed, "I'd never have thought of that one."

As these gentlemen said no more that might shed light on the thing, we have no way of knowing just what Durcet did mean or what the Duc declared he would never have thought of. And even were it that we knew, I believe we would be well advised to keep knowledge of the thing strictly to ourselves, at least in the interest of modesty, for there are an infinite number of things one ought merely to indicate, prudent circumspection requires that one keep a bridle on one's tongue; there are such things, are there not, as chaste ears? one may now and again encounter them, and I am absolutely convinced the reader has already had occasion to be grateful for the discretion we have employed in his regard; the further he reads on more secure shall be our claim to his sincerest praise upon this head, why, yes, we feel we may almost assure him of it even at this early stage. Well, whatever one may say, each one has his own soul to save, and of what punishment, both in this world and in the next, is he not deserving who all immoderately were to be pleased to divulge all the caprices, all the whims and tastes, all the clandestine horrors whereunto men are subject when their fancy is free and afire? 'twould be to reveal secrets which ought to be sunk in obscurity for humanity's sake, 'twould be to undertake the general corruption of manners and to precipitate his brethren in Jesus Christ into all the extravagances such tableaux might feature in very lively color and profusion; and God, Who seeth even unto the depths of our hearts, this puissant God Who hath made heaven and earth and Who must one day judge us, God alone knoweth whether we have any desire to hear ourselves reproached by Him for such crimes.

Messieurs put the finishing touches on several horrors they had begun; Curval, to cite one example, had Desgranges shit, the others occupied themselves with either that same distraction, or with some others not much more improving, and their Lordships then went to supper. At the orgies, Duclos having overheard the friends discussing the new diet we alluded to earlier, whose purpose was to render shit more abundant and more delicate, at the orgies, I say, Duclos noted that she was truly astonished to find connoisseurs like themselves unaware of the true secret whereby turds are made both very abundant and very tasty. Questioned about the measures which ought to be adopted, she said that there was but one: the subject should be given a mild indigestion; there was no need to make him eat what he did not like or what was unwholesome, but, by obliging him to eat hurriedly and between meals, the desired results could be obtained at once. The experiment was performed that same evening: Fanny was waked - no one had paid any attention to her, and she had gone to bed after supper - she was immediately required to eat four large plain cakes, and the next morning she furnished one of the biggest and most beautiful turds they had been able to procure from her up until that time. Duclos' suggested system was therefore approved, although they upheld their decision to do away with bread; Duclos said they were well advised to be rid of it; the fruits produced by her method, said she, would only be better. From that time on not a day passed but they'd gently upset those pretty youngsters' digestions in one way or another, and the results were simply beyond anything you could imagine. I mention this in passing so that, should any amateur be disposed to make use of the formula, he may be firmly persuaded there is none superior.

The remainder of the evening having brought nothing extraordinary, everyone retired in order to be freshly rested for the following day's wedding: the brilliant match to be made was destined to unite Colombe and Zélamir, and this ceremony was to be the basis for celebrating the third week's festival.

The Twenty-First Day

Preparations for that ceremony were started early in the morning; they were of the usual sort but, and I have no idea whether or not it was by a stroke of chance, the inspection uncovered signs of the young bride's misbehavior. Durcet declared he had found shit in her chamber pot; she denied having put it there, asserting that, to cause her to be punished, the duenna had come and done the thing during the night, and that governesses often planted such evidence when they wished to embroil the children in difficulties. Well, she defended herself very eloquently and to no purpose whatever, for she was not carefully heard, and as her little husband-to-be was already on the list, the prospect of correcting both of them was the cause of great amusement.

Nevertheless, the young bride and groom, once the mass had been said, were conducted with much pomp to the salon where the ceremony was to be completed before mealtime; they were both of the same age, and the little girl was delivered naked to her husband, who was permitted to do whatever he wanted. Is there any voice so compelling as example's? And where if not in Silling were it possible to receive very bad examples and the most contagious ones? The young man sped like an arrow to its mark, hopped upon his little wife, and as his prick was greatly stiff, although not yet capable of a discharge, he would inevitably have got his spear in her . . . but mild as would have been the damage done her, the source of all Messieurs' glory lay in preventing anything from harming the tender flower they wished alone to pluck. And so it was the Bishop checked the lad's impetuous career, and profiting from his erection, straightway thrust into his ass the very pretty and already very well-formed engine wherewith Zélamir was about to plumb his young spouse. What a disappointment for that young man, and what a discrepancy between the old Bishop's slack-sprung vent and the strait and tidy cunt of a little thirteen-year-old virgin! But Zélamir was having to deal with people who were deaf to common-sense arguments.

Curval laid hands on Colombe and thigh-fucked her from in front while licking her eyes, her mouth, her nostrils, in a word, her entire face. Meanwhile, he must surely have been rendered some kind of service, for he discharged, and Curval was not a man to lose his fuck over silly trifles.

They dined, the wedded couple appeared at the meal and again in the salon for coffee, which that day was served by the very cream of the subjects, by, I wish to say, Augustine, Zelmire, Adonis, and Zéphyr. Curval wished to stiffen afresh, had absolutely to have some shit, and Augustine shot him as fine an artifact as it were in human power to create. The Duc had himself sucked by Zelmire, Durcet by Colombe, the Bishop by Adonis. The last named shitted into Durcet's mouth after having dispatched the Bishop. But no sign of fuck; it was becoming rare, they had failed to exercise any restraint at the outset of the holiday, and as they realized the extreme need of seed they would have toward the end, Messieurs were growing more frugal. They went next to the auditorium where the majestic Duclos, invited to display her ass before starting, exposed that matchless ensemble most libertinely to the eyes of the assembly, and then began to speak:

Here is still another trait of my character, Messieurs, said that sublime woman; after having made you well enough acquainted with it, you will be so kind as to judge what I intend to omit from what I am going to tell you . . . and you will, I trust, dispense me from having to say more about myself.

Lucile's mother had just fallen into a state of the most wretched poverty, and it was only by the most extraordinary stroke of chance that this charming girl, who had received no news at all of her mother since having fled her house, now learned of her extreme distress: one of our street scouts - hard in pursuit of some young girl for a client who shared the tastes and designs of the Marquis de Mesanges, for a client, that is to say, who was eager to make an outright and final purchase - one of our scouts came in to report to me, as I was lying in bed with Lucile, that she had chanced upon a little fifteen-year-old, without question a maid, extremely pretty, and, she said, closely resembling Mademoiselle Lucile; yes, she went on, they were like two peas in a pod, but this little girl she'd found was in such bedraggled condition that she'd have to be kept and fattened for several days before she'd be fit to market. And thereupon she gave a description of the aged woman with whom the child had been discovered, and of the frightful indigence wherein that mother lay; from certain traits, details of age and appearance, from all she heard concerning the daughter, Lucile had a secret feeling the persons being discussed might well be her own mother and sister. She knew she had left home when the latter was still very young, hence it was hard to be sure of the thing, and she asked my permission to go and verify her suspicions.

At this point my infernal mind conceived a little horror; its effect was to set my body afire. Telling the street scout to leave the room, and being unable to resist the fury raging in my blood, I began by entreating Lucile to frig me. Then, halting halfway through the operation:

"Why do you want to go to see that old woman?" I asked Lucile; "what do you propose to do?"

"Why, but don't you see," said Lucile, whose heart was still undeveloped, "there are certain things that one is expected to do . . . I ought to help her if I can, and above all if she turns out to be my mother."

"Idiot," I muttered, thrusting her away from me, "go sacrifice alone to your disgusting popular prejudices, and for not daring to brave them, go lose the most incredibly fine opportunity to irritate your senses by a horror that would make you discharge for a decade."

Bewildered by my words, Lucile stared at me, and I saw I had to explain this philosophy to her, for she apparently had not the vaguest understanding of it. I therefore did lecture her, I made her comprehend the vileness, the baseness of the ties wherewith they seek to bind us to the author of our days; I demonstrated to her that for having carried us in her womb, instead of deserving some gratitude, a mother merits naught but hate, since 'twas for her pleasure alone and at the risk of exposing us to all the ills and sorrows the world holds in store for us that she brought us into the light, with the sole object of satisfying her brutal lubricity. To this I added roughly everything one might deem helpful in supporting the doctrine which same right-thinking dictates, and which the heart urges when it is not cluttered up with stupidities imbibed in the nursery.

"And what matters it to you," I added, "whether that creature be happy or wretched? Does her situation have anything to do with yours? does it affect you? Get rid of those demeaning ties whose absurdity I've just proven to you, and thereby entirely isolating this creature, sundering her utterly from yourself, you will not only recognize that her misfortune must be a matter of indifference to you, but that it might even be exceedingly voluptuous to worsen her plight. For, after all, you do owe her your hatred, that has been made clear, and thus you would be taking your revenge: you would be performing what fools term an evil deed, and you know the immense influence crime exerts upon the senses. And so here are two sources of pleasure in the outrages I'd like to have you inflict upon her: both the sweet delights of vengeance, and those one always tastes whenever one does evil."

Whether it was that I employed a greater eloquence in exhorting Lucile than I do in recounting the fact to you now, or whether it was because her already very libertine and very corrupt spirit instantly notified her heart of the voluptuous promise contained in my principles, she tasted them, and I saw her lovely cheeks flush in response to that libertine flame which never fails to appear every time one violates some prohibition, abolishes some restraint.

"All right," she murmured, "what are we to do?"

"Amuse ourselves with her," said I, "and make some money at the same time; as for pleasure, you can be sure to have some if you adopt my principles. And as for the money, the same thing applies, for I can make use of both your old gray-haired mother and your young sister; I'll arrange two different parties which will prove very lucrative."

Lucile accepts, I frig her the better to excite her to commit the crime, and we turn all our thoughts to devising plans. Let me first undertake to outline the first of them, since it deserves to be included in the category of passions I have to discuss, although I shall have to alter the exact chronology in order to fit it into the sequence of events, and when I shall have informed you of this first part of my scheme, I shall enlighten you upon the second.

There was a man, well placed in society and exceedingly wealthy, exceedingly influential and having a disorder of the mind which surpasses all that words are able to convey; as I was acquainted with him only as the Comte, you will allow me, however well advised of his full name I may be, simply to designate him by his title. The Comte was somewhat above thirty-five years of age, and all his passions had reached their maximum strength; he had neither faith nor law, no god and no religion, and was above all else endowed, like yourselves, Messieurs, with an invincible horror of what is called the charitable sentiment; he used to say that to understand this impulse was totally beyond his powers, and that he would not for an instant assent to the notion that one dare outrage Nature to the point of upsetting the order she had imposed when she created different classes of individuals; the very idea of elevating one such class through the bestowing of alms or aid, and thus of overthrowing another, the idea of devoting sums of money, not upon agreeable things which might afford one pleasure, but rather upon these absurd and revolting relief enterprises, all this he considered an insult to his intelligence or a mystery his intelligence could not possibly grasp. Thoroughly instilled, nay, penetrated though he was with these opinions, he reasoned still further; not only did he derive the keenest delight from refusing aid to the needy, but he ameliorated what was already an ecstasy by outrageously persecuting the humble and injured. One of his higher pleasures, for example, consisted in having meticulous searches made of those dark, shadowy regions where starving indigence gnaws whatever crust it has earned by terrible toil, and sprinkles tears upon its meager portion. He would stiffen at the thought of going abroad not only to enjoy the bitterness of those tears, but even . . . but even to aggravate their cause and, if 'twere possible, to snatch away the wretched substance that kept the damned yet amongst the living. And this taste of his was no whim, no light fantasy, 'twas a fury; he used to say that he knew no more piercing delight, nothing that could more successfully arouse him, inflame his soul, than these excesses I speak of. Nor was this rage of his, he one day assured me, the fruit of depravation; no, he had been possessed by this mania since his youngest years, and his heart, perpetually toughened against misery's plaintive accents, had never conceived any gentler, milder feelings for it.

As it is of the greatest importance you be familiar with the subject, you must first of all know that the same man had three different passions: the one I am going to relate to you, another, which Martaine will explain to you later when she refers to this same personage, and a third, yet more atrocious, which Desgranges will doubtless reserve for the end of her contribution as doubtless one of the most impressive upon her list. But we'll begin with the one on mine.

Straightway I had informed the Comte of the nest of misery I had discovered for him, of the inhabitants of that nest, he was transported with joy. But it so happened that business intimately connected with his fortune and having an important bearing upon his advancement, which he took much care not to neglect, in that he held them vital to his misconduct, business, I say, was going to occupy his attention for the next two weeks, and as he did not want to let the little girl slip through his fingers, he preferred sacrificing the pleasure the first scene promised him, and to be certain of enjoying the second. And so he ordered me to have the child kidnaped at whatever cost, but without delay, and to have her deposited at the address he indicated to me. And in order to keep you in suspense no longer, my Lords, that address was Madame Desgranges', for she was the agent who furnished him with material for his third class of secret parties. And now to return to the objects of all our maneuvering.

So far, we had done little but locate Lucile's mother, both to set the stage for the recognition scene between mother and daughter and to study the problems associated with the kidnaping of the little girl. Lucile, well coached in her part, only greeted her mother in order to insult her, to say that it was thanks to her she had been hurled into libertinage, and to these she added a thousand other similarly unkind remarks, which broke the poor woman's heart and ruined the pleasure of rediscovering her daughter. During this first interview, I thought I glimpsed the appropriate way to talk with the woman, and pointed out to her that, having rescued her elder child from an impure existence, I was willing to do as much for the younger one. But the stratagem did not succeed, the poor wretch fell to weeping and said that nothing in the world would induce her to part with the one treasure she had left, that the little girl was her one resource, she herself was old, infirm, that the child cared for her, and that to be deprived of her would be to lose life itself. At this juncture, Messieurs, I must confess, and I do so with shame, that I felt a faint stirring in the depths of my heart; it advised me that my voluptuous pleasure was bound only to be increased by the horrible refinements I was about to give to my meditated crime, and having informed the old lady that shortly thereafter her daughter would come to pay her a visit with a man of great influence, who could perhaps render her great services, we left, and I bent all my efforts to employing the lures and devices I usually relied upon to snare game. I had carefully examined the little girl, she was worth my going to some trouble: fifteen years of age, a pretty figure, a very lovely skin, and very pretty features. She arrived three days later, and after having examined every part of her body and found nothing but what was very charming, dimpled, and very neat despite the poor nourishment she had for so long had to put up with, I passed her along to Madame Desgranges: this transaction marked the beginning of our commercial relations.

His private affairs attended to, our Comte reappeared; Lucile conducts him to her mother's home, and 'tis at this point begins the scene I wish to describe. The old mother was found in bed, the room was without heat although we were then in the midst of a bitterly cold winter; beside her bed sat a wooden crock containing milk. The Comte pissed into the crock as soon as he had entered. To prevent any possible trouble, and in order to feel himself the undisputed master of the fort, the Comte had posted two of his minions, a pair of strapping lads, on the stairway, and they were to offer a stubborn obstacle to any undesirable coming up or going down.

"My dear old buggress," intoned the Comte, "we have come here with your daughter, you see her there, and a damned pretty whore she is, upon my soul; we have come here, I say, to relieve what ails you, wretched old leper that you are, but before we can help you, you must tell us what's amiss. Well, go on, speak," he said, seating himself and beginning to palpate Lucile's buttocks, "go on, I say, itemize your sufferings."

"Alas!" said the good woman, "you come with that vixen not to help me but to insult me."

"Vixen? How's this," said the Comte, "you dare use insults with your daughter? By God," he went on, rising to his feet and dragging the old thing from her litter, "get out of that bed, get down on your knees, and ask to be forgiven for the language you have just employed."

There was no resist.

"And you, Lucile, lift your skirts and have your mother kiss your cheeks, and I am damned certain she wants nothing more than to kiss them, eager as she must be for some kind of reconciliation."

The insolent Lucile rubs her ass upon the seamed and wrinkled visage of her dear old mother; overwhelming her with a tirade of playful epithets, the Comte permits the poor woman to crawl back into bed, and then resumes the conversation. "I tell you once again," he says, "that if you recite all your troubles to me, I'll take the best care of you."

The woe-ridden are credulous; and they love to lament. The old woman made them privy to all her sufferings, and complained especially, with great bitterness, of the theft of her daughter; she sharply accused Lucile of having had a hand in it and of knowing where the child presently was, since the lady with whom she had come a little while ago had proposed to take her under her wing; that was the basis for her supposition (and there was considerable logic in the way she argued) that this same lady had taken her away. Meanwhile, the Comte, directly facing Lucile's ass, for by this time he had got her to step out of her skirts, the Comte, I say, now and again kissing that handsome ass and frigging himself uninterruptedly, listened, put questions to her, requested details, and regulated all the titillations of his perfidious lust according to the old woman's replies. But when she said that the absence of her daughter, thanks to whose work she was procure her wherewithal, was going to lead her gradually but inexorably to the grave, since she had nothing and for four days had been kept barely alive by that small quantity of milk he had just spoiled:

"Why, then, bitch," said the Comte, aiming his prick at the old creature and continuing to explore Lucile's buttocks, "why, then go ahead and croak, you foul old whore, do you suppose the world will be any worse off without you?"

And as he concluded his question he loosed his sperm.

"Were that to happen," he observed, "I believe I'd have only one regret, and that would be not having myself hastened the event."

But there was moreto it than that, the Comte was not the sort of a man to be appeased by a mere discharge; Lucile, fully aware of the role she was to play, now that he had been relieved, busied herself preventing the old woman from noticing what he was about, and the Comte, rummaging through every corner of the room, came upon a silver goblet, the last vestige of the material well-being that had once upon a time been this poor wretch's; he put the goblet in his pocket. This fresh outrage having put new hardness into his prick, he again dragged the old woman from her bed, stripped her naked, and bade Lucile frig him upon the matron's withered old frame. Once again nothing could be done to stop him, and the villain darted his fuck over that ancient flesh, redoubled his insults, and said that the poor wretch could rest perfectly assured he was not yet done with her, and that she would soon have news of himself and of her little girl who, he wished to have her know, was in his power. He then proceeded to that last discharge, his transports of lust were ignited by the horrors wherewith his perfidious imagination was already in a ferment, by the ruin of the entire family he was contemplating, and he left. But in order not to have to return to this affair, hear, Messieurs, how I surpassed myself in villainy. Seeing that he might have confidence in me, the Comte informed me of the second scene he was preparing for the benefit of the old woman and her little daughter; he told me he wanted the child brought to him without delay and, as he wanted to reunite the whole family, he wished to have me cede Lucile to him too, for he had been deeply moved by her lovely ass; he made no effort to conceal that his purpose was to ruin Lucile as well as her ass, together with her mother and sister.

I loved Lucile. But I loved money even more. He offered me an unheard-of price for these three creatures, I agreed to everything. Four days later, Lucile, her little sister and her aged mother were brought together; Madame Desgranges will tell you about that meeting. As for your faithful Duclos, she continues and resumes the thread of her story this anecdote has interrupted; indeed, she wonders whether she ought not have recited it at some later time, for, esteeming it a very stirring episode, she considers it would have proven a fitting climax to her contribution.

"One moment," said Durcet, "I cannot hear such stories without being affected, their influence upon me would be difficult to describe. I have been restraining my fuck since the middle of the tale, kindly allow me to unburden myself now."

And he dashed into his closet with Michette, Zélamir, Cupidon, Fanny, Thérèse, and Adelaide; several minutes later his shouts began to ring out, and soon after the uproar started, Adelaide emerged in tears, saying that all this made her very unhappy, and wondering why they had to excite her husband with such dreadful stories; she who told them, Adelaide declared, not others, ought by rights to be the victim. During the interim the Duc and the Bishop had not wasted an instant, but the manner in which they operated belonging to the class of procedures circumstances compel us still to mask from the reader's view, we beg him to suffer the curtain to remain down, and to allow us to move on to the four tales Duclos had yet to relate before bringing this twenty-first meeting of the assembly to a close.

A week after Lucile's departure, I handled a rascal blessed with a rather curious mania. Warned several days in advance of his intended arrival, I had let a great number of turds accumulate in my one-holed chair, and I had induced one of my young ladies to add a few more to the collection. Our man appeared costumed as a Savoyard rustic; 'twas in the morning, he swept out my room, removed the pot from beneath the chair, and went out to empty it (this emptying, I might note in parantheses, took a considerable length of time); when he returned he showed me how carefully he'd cleaned it out and asked for his payment. But, and this of course was all stipulated in our prior agreement, instead of giving him a coin, I seize the broom and fall to belaboring him with the handle.

"Your payment, villain?" I cry, "why, here's what you deserve."

And I bestow at least a dozen blows upon him. He seeks to escape me, I pursue him, and the libertine, whose critical moment has arrived, discharges all the way down the stairs, bawling out at the top of his voice that they're cracking his skull, that they want to kill him, and that he's got himself into the house of a scoundrel, she's not by any means the honest woman he at first took her for, etc.

Another carried, in a small pocket case, a little knotty stick which he kept for an unusual purpose; he wanted me to insert the stick into his urethral canal, and, having plunged it in to a depth of three inches, to rattle it with utmost vigor, and with my other hand to pull back his foreskin and frig his poor device. At the very instant he discharged, one had to pull out the stick, raise one's skirts in front, and he would discharge upon one's mound.

Six months later I had to do with an abbot who wanted me to take a burning candle and direct the drops of molten tallow so that they fell upon his penis and balls; it required nothing more than the sensation this ceremony produced to bring about his discharge. His machine required no touching, but it remained limp throughout; before they would yield fuck, his genitals had to be given such a heavy coating of wax that toward the end there was no recognizing this strange object as a part of the human anatomy.

That ecclesiastic had a friend who loved nothing so much as to offer his bum to be perforated by a multitude of gold pins, and when thus decorated, his hindquarter far more resembling a pincushion than an ordinary ass, he would sit down, the better to savor the effect he cherished, and, presenting one's very wide-spread buttocks to him, he would twiddle his member and discharge into one's vent.

"Durcet," said the Duc, "I should very much like to see that sweet chubby ass of yours studded all over with golden pins, ah yes, I'm persuaded 'twould thus appear more interesting than ever."

"Your Grace," quoth the financier, "you know that for forty years it has been my glory and my honor to imitate you in all things; I but ask you to have the kindness to set me an example, and you have my word that I will follow it."

"God's loin-scum!" exclaimed the good Curval, who had not until now been heard from, "by His sacred seed, I do declare that story about Lucile has made me stiff! I've held my peace, but my head's been at work none the less. Look here," said he, exhibiting his prick standing high, "see whether I do not say true. I've a furious impatience to hear the denouement of the story of those three buggresses; I have the highest hope they'll meet one another in a common grave."

"Softly there, softly," said the Duc, "let's not anticipate events. Were you not stiff, Monsieur le Président, you'd not be in such a hurry to hear talk of wheels and gibbets. You resemble a great many other of Justice's servitors, whose pricks, they say, rise up every time they pronounce the sentence of death."

"Never mind the magistrature," Curval replied, "the fact remains that I am enchanted by Duclos' doings, that I find her a charming girl, and that her story of the Comte has put me in a dreadful state, and in this state, I say, I could be easily persuaded to go abroad, stop a carriage on the highway, and rob its occupants."

"Ah, Président, take care," said the Bishop; "keep a hand upon yourself, my dear fellow, else we'll cease to be in safety here. One such slip, and the least we could expect would be the noose for all of us."

"The noose? Ah, the noose, yes . . . but not for us. However, I don't for a minute deny I'd myself gladly condemn these young ladies here to be hanged, and especially Madame la Duchesse, who's lying like a cow upon my sofa and who, merely because she's got a spoonful of modified fuck in the womb, fancies no one dares touch her any more."

"Oh," said Constance, "'tis surely not with you I count upon being respected because of my state. Your loathing for pregnant women is only too notorious."

"A prodigious loathing, isn't it?" said Curval with a chuckle, "why, indeed it is prodigious."

And, transported by enthusiasm, he was, I believe, on the verge of committing some sacrilege against that superb belly, when Duclos intervened.

"Come, Sire, come with me," said she; "since 'tis I who have caused the hurt, I'd like to repair it."

And together they passed into the secluded boudoir, followed by Augustine, Hébé, Cupidon, and Thérèse. It was not long before the Président's braying resounded through the castle, and despite all Duclos' attentions, little Hébé returned weeping from the hurlyburly; there was even more to it than tears, but we dare not yet disclose just what it was had set her to trembling. A little patience, friend reader, and we shall soon hide nothing from your inquisitive gaze.

And now Curval himself returns, grumbling between his teeth and swearing that all those dratted laws prevent a man from discharging at his ease, etc.; their Lordships sit down at table. After supper they withdrew to mete out punishment for the misbehavior that had accrued during the week, but the guilty were not that evening in great number: only Sophie, Colombe, Adelaide, and Zélamir merited correction, and received it. Durcet, who since the beginning of the evening had waxed very hot, and who had been particularly inspired by Adelaide, granted her no quarter; Sophie, whom they had detected shedding tears during the story of the Comte, was punished for that misdemeanor as well as for her former one, and the Duc and Curval, we understand, treated the day's little newlyweds, Zélamir and Colombe, with a severity that almost bordered upon barbarity.

The Duc and Curval, in splendid form and singularly wrought up, said they had no wish to retire, and having had a quantity of beverages fetched in, they passed the night drinking with the four storytellers and Julie, whose libertinage, increasing every day, gave her the air of a very amiable creature who deserved to be ranked among these objects for whom Messieurs had some regard. The following morning, while making his rounds, Durcet found all seven of them dead drunk. The naked girl was discovered lodged between her father and her husband and in a posture which gave evidence of neither virtue nor decency in libertinage; it was plain enough to the financier that (to hold the reader in suspense no longer) they had both enjoyed her simultaneously. Duclos, who, from all appearances, had functioned as an instrument to this crime, lay sprawled near the compact trio, and the others were strewn in a confused heap in the corner opposite the fire, which someone had taken care to keep burning throughout the night.

The Twenty-Second Day

As a result of these all-night bacchanals, exceedingly little was accomplished on the twenty-second day of November; half the customary exercises were forgot, at dinner Messieurs appeared to be in a daze, and it was not until coffee they began to come somewhat to their senses. The coffee was served them by Rosette and Sophie, Zélamir and Giton. In an effort to return to his usual old self, Curval had Giton shit, and the Duc swallowed Rosette's turd; the Bishop had himself sucked by Sophie, Durcet by Zélamir, but no one discharged. They moved dutifully into the auditorium; the matchless Duclos, weak and quesy after the preceding day's excesses, took her place with drooping eyelids, and her tales were so brief, they contained so few episodes, were recounted so listlessly, that we have taken it upon ourselves to supply them, and in the reader's behalf to clarify the somewhat confused speech she made to our friends.

In keeping with prescription, she recounted five passions: the first was that of a man who used to have his ass frigged with a tin dildo priorly charged with warm water, the which liquid was pumped into his fundament at the same instant he ejaculated; nothing else was required to obtain that effect, he needed no one else's ministry.

The second man had the same mania, but was wont to use a far greater number of instruments; initially, he called for a very minute one, then gradually increased the caliber, ascending the scale by small fractions of an inch until he reached a weapon with the dimensions of a veritable fieldpiece, and only discharged upon receiving a torrent from its muzzle.

Far more of the mysterious was required to please the third one's palate: at the outset of the game, he had an enormous instrument introduced into his ass, then it was withdrawn, he would shit, would eat what he had just rendered, and next he had to be flogged. The flogging administered, it was time to reinsert the formidable device in his rectum, then once again it was removed, and it was the whore's turn to shit, and after that she picked up the whip again and lashed him while he munched what she had done; a third time, yes, a third time the instrument was driven home, and that, plus the girl's turd he finished eating, was sufficient to complete his happiness.

In her fourth tale, Duclos made mention of a man who would have all his joints bound with strings; in order to make his discharge even more delicious, his neck itself was compressed, and, half choking, he would shoot his fuck squarely at the whore's asshole.

And in her fifth, she referred to that individual who used to tie a slender cord tightly to his glans; the girl, naked, would pass the other end of the cord between her thighs, and walk away from him, drawing the cord taut and offering the patient a full view of her ass; he would then discharge.

Truly exhausted after having fulfilled her task, the storyteller begged to leave to retire, and she was allowed to. A few moments were devoted to uttering smutty comments upon this and that, and then the four libertines went to supper, but everyone felt the effects of our two principal actors' disorderliness. At the orgies they were also as prudent and restrained as 'twere possible for such debauchees to be, and the entire household went more or less quietly to bed.

The Twenty-Third Day

"But how is it possible to shout and roar the way you do when you discharge?" the Duc demanded of Curval upon bidding him good morning on the 23rd. "Why the devil must you scream that way? I've never seen such violent discharges."

"Why, by God," Curval replied, "is it for you, whom one can hear a league away, to address such a reproach to a modest man like myself? Those little murmurs you hear, my good friend, are caused by my extremely sensitive nervous system; the objects which excite our passions create such a lively commotion in the electrically charged fluid that flows in our nerves, the shock received by the animal spirits composing this fluid is of such a degree of violence, that the entire mechanism is rattled by these effects, and one is just as powerless to suppress one's cries when overwhelmed by the terrible blows imparted by pleasure, as one would be when assailed by the powerful emotions of pain."

"Well, you define the thing very well, Président, but what was the delicate object that could have produced such a vibration in your animal spirits?"

"I was very energetically sucking Adonis' prick, his mouth, and his asshole, for I was cast down with despair at not being able to do more to my couch companion; all the while I made the best of my hard situation, Antinoüs, seconded by your dear daughter Julie, labored, each in his own way, to evacuate the liquor whose eventual outpouring occasioned the musical sounds which, you say, struck your ears."

"And it all worked so well that now, today," said the Duc, "you're as weak as a baby."

"No, your Grace, not at all," Curval declared; "deign but to observe my career, my motions today, and but do me the honor of judging my style and vehemence in sport, and you shall see me conduct myself quite as ever, and assuredly as well as you yourself."

They were at this point in the conversation when Durcet arrived to say breakfast was being served. They passed into the qirls' quarters, where those eight charming little houris were distributing cups of coffee and hot water; the Duc therewith demanded to know of Durcet, the month's steward and presiding officer, why was it the coffee was being served with water?

"You'll have it with milk whenever you wish," said the financier. "Would you prefer it thus now?"

The Duc said that yes, he would.

"Augustine, my dear," Durcet said, "a little milk in Monsieur le Duc's cup, if you please."

Thereupon the little girl, prepared for any eventuality, placed Blangis' cup beneath her ass, and through her anus squeezed three or four spoonfuls of milk, very clear and perfectly fresh. This cunning feat produced much pleasant laughter, everyone requested milk in his coffee. All the asses were charged in the same way Augustine's was: 'twas an agreeable little surprise the month's director of games had thought to give his colleagues. Fanny poured some into the Bishop's cup, Zelmire into Curval's, and Michette into the financier's; the friends took a second round of coffee, and the four other girls performed over these new cups the same ceremony their comrades had over the first cups; and so on and on; the whole thing entertained their Lordships immoderately. It heated the Bishop's brain; he affirmed he wanted something beside milk, and the lovely Sophie stepped forth to satisfy him. Although all eight definitely wished to shit, they had been strongly urged to exercise self-restraint while dispensing the milk, and this first time to yield absolutely nothing else.

Next, they paid the little boys a good-morning visit; Curval induced Zélamir to shit from him, the Duc applauded what Giton brought to light. Two subaltern fuckers, Constance, and Rosette provided the spectacle in the chapel latrine. Rosette was one of those upon whom the old formula for promoting indigestion had beed tried out; at coffee, she had had the world's worst time keeping her milk free of foreign ingredients, and now, seated upon the throne, she released the most superb turd you could hope to lay eyes upon. Duclos was congratulated, they said her system was a resounding success, and from then on they used it every day; never once did it fail them. The conversation at the dinner was enlivened by the breakfast's pleasantry, and a number of other things of the same kind were invented and proposed; we shall perhaps have occasion to mention them in the sequel.

After-dinner coffee was served by four subjects of the same age: to wit, Zelmire, Augustine, Zéphyr, and Adonis. The Duc thigh-fucked Augustine while tickling her anus with his thumb, Curval did the same thing with Zelmire, but may or may not have used his thumb, his hand was not in clear view; the Bishop toiled between Zéphyr's tightly squeezed legs, and the financier fucked Adonis' mouth. Augustine announced that she was ready to shit, how would they like her to do a little shit? The poor dear could not wait another moment, she too had been exposed to the indigestion-producing experiments. Curval beckoned her to him, opened his mouth, and the delightful little girl dropped a monstrous turd into it; the Président gobbled it up in a trice, not without unleashing a veritable stream of fuck into Fanchon's hands.

"There you are," he said to the Duc, "you see that night-time merriment has no damaging effect upon the following day's pleasures; you're lagging behind, Monsieur le Duc."

"I'll not be behind for long," said the latter, to whom Zelmire, inspired by an urge no less imperious, was rendering the same service Augustine had a moment before rendered Curval. And, yes, as he pronounces those words, the Duc topples over, utters piercing shrieks, swallows shit, and discharges like a madman.

"Enough of this," said the stern, austere voice of the Bishop, moderation's exponent; "at least two of us must preserve our strength for the stories."

Durcet, who, unlike the Duc and Curval, had no surfeit of fuck to fling carelessly about, assented wholeheartedly, and after the shortest possible nap, they installed themselves in the auditorium, where, in the following terms, the spellbinding Duclos resumed her brilliant and lascivious history:

Why is it, Messieurs, the radiant creature inquired, that in this world there are men whose hearts have been so numbed, whose sentiments of honor and delicacy have been so deadened, that one sees them pleased and amused by what degrades and soils them? One is even led to suppose their joy can be mined nowhere save from the depths of opprobrium, that, for such men, delights cannot exist elsewhere save in what brings them into consort with dishonor and infamy. To what I am going now to recount to you, my Lords, to the various instances I shall lay before you in order to prove my assertion, do not reply, saying that 'tis physical sensation which is the foundation of these subsequent pleasures; I know, to be sure, physical sensation is involved herein, but be perfectly certain that it does not exist in some sort save thanks to the powerful support given it by moral sensation, and be sure as well that, were you to provide these individuals with the same physical sensation and to omit to join to it all that the moral may yield, you'd fail entirely to stir them.

There very often came to me a man of whose name and quality I was ignorant, but who, however, I knew most certainly to be a man of circumstance. The kind of woman with whom I married him made no difference at all: beautiful or ugly, old or young, it was all the same to him; his partner had only to play her role competently, and that role was as follows: ordinarily, he would come to the house in the morning, he would enter, as though by accident, into a room where a girl lay upon a bed, her skirts raised to above her waist and in the attitude of a woman frigging herself. Immediately his entrance was noticed, the woman, as if surprised, would spring from the bed.

"What are you doing here, villain?" she would ask very crossly; "who gave you permission to disturb me?"

He would beg forgiveness, his apologies would go unheeded, and all the while showering him with a renewed deluge of the harshest and most biting invectives, she would fall to giving him furious kicks upon the posterior, and she would become all the more certain of her aim as the patient, far from dodging or shielding his behind, would unfailingly turn himself and present the target within easy range, although looking for all the world as if he wished only to escape this punishment and flee the room. The kicking is redoubled, he cries to be spared, blows and curses are the only replies he receives, and as soon as he feels he is sufficiently excited, he promptly draws his prick from his breeches, which he has hitherto kept tightly buttoned, and lightly giving his device three or four flicks of the wrist, he discharges while rushing away under an unremitting storm of kicks and abuses.

A second personage, either tougher or more accustomed to this sort of exercise, would not enter the lists save with a street porter or some other stout rascal willing to sweat for his hire. The libertine enters furtively while his opponent is busily counting his money; the churl cries thief; whereupon the hard language and blows begin. Whereas with the former debauchee, the blows were scattered somewhat over his body, this one, keeping his breeches down about his ankles, wishes to receive everything squarely in the center of his unclothed bum, and that bum has to be buffeted by a good heavy boot, amply studded with hobnails and well coated with mud. At the moment he felt himself about to discharge, our gentleman ceased to parry the blows; planted firmly in the middle of the room, his breeches still lowered, and agitating his prick with all his strength, he braved his enemy's assaults, and, at this crucial juncture, dared him do his worst, insulting him in his own turn, and swearing he was about to die of pleasure. The more vile, the more lowly the man I found for this stalwart libertine, the more scurvy his antagonist, the heavier and the more filthy his boot, the more overpowering would be my client's ecstasy; I had to employ the same tact and discrimination in selecting his assailant that I would have had to devote to embellishing and beautifying another man's woman.

A third wished to find himself in what in a whorehouse is called the harem, at the same instant two other men, paid so to do and on hand for no other purpose, began a dispute. Both would turn upon our libertine, he would ask to be spared, would throw himself upon his knees, would not be listened to, and one of the two champions would directly snatch up a cane and fall to belaboring him all the while he crept to the entrance of another room where he would take refuge. There he would be received by a girl, she would console him, caress him as one might a child who has come to be comforted, she would raise her skirts, display her ass, and the libertine, all smiles, would spray his fuck upon it.

A fourth required the same preliminaries, but as soon as the strokes of the cane began to rain down upon his back, he would frig himself within sight of all. Then this last operation would be suspended for a moment; there would, however, be no interruption in the dual attack of blows and oaths; then he'd get hot again, frig some more, and when they saw his fuck was about to fly, they'd open a window, pick him up by the waist, and fling him out; he would land upon a specially prepared dung heap after a fall of no more than six feet. And that was the critical moment; he had been morally aroused by the foregoing preliminaries, and his physical self only became so thanks to his fall; 'twas never but upon that dung heap he loosed his fuck. When one went to look from the window, he was gone; there was an obscure little door below (he had a key to it), and he'd disappear through it at once.

A man paid for the purpose and dressed like a rowdy would abruptly enter the chamber in which the man who furnishes us with the fifth example would be lying with a girl, kissing her ass while awaiting developments. Accosting the expectant libertine, the bully, having forced the door, would insolently ask what right he had thus to meddle with his mistress and then, laying his hands upon his sword, he would tell the usurper to defend himself. All confused, the latter would fall to his knees, ask pardon, grovel on the floor, kiss his rival's feet too, and swear he was ready to relinquish the lady at once, for he had no desire to fight over a woman.

The bully, whom his adversary's pliability rendered all the more insolent, now called his enemy a coward, a contemptible fellow, a whoreson ass-fucker, and a dog, and threatened to carve up his face with the edge of his sword. And the more ugly became the one's behavior, the more humble and fawning became the other's. Finally, after a few minutes of debate, the assailant offered to make a settlement with his enemy:

"I see damned well that you've got no guts at all," said he, "and so I'll let you go, but upon condition you kiss my ass."

"Oh, Monsieur, I'll do whatever you like," said the other, enchanted by this solution, "I'd even kiss it if 'twere all beshitted, if you wish, provided you do me no harm."

Sheathing his sword, the bully directly pulled down his breeches, the libertine, only too delighted, leapt enthusiastically to work, and while the young man let fly half a dozen farts at his nose, the old rake, having attained the summit of ecstasy, loosed his fuck and swooned with pleasure.

"Every one of those excesses makes sense to me," Durcet said in a faltering tone, for the little libertine was stiff after hearing tell of these turpitudes. "Nothing more logical than to adore degradation and to reap delight from scorn. He who ardently loves the things which dishonor, finds pleasure in being dishonored and must necessarily stiffen when told that he is. Turpitude is, to certain spirits, a very sound cause of joy. One loves to hear oneself called what one wishes only to merit being, and it is truly impossible to guess how far a man may go in this direction, provided he be ashamed of nothing. 'Tis once again the story of certain sick persons whom nothing delights like the disintegration of their body."

" 'Tis all a question of cynicism," was Curval's deliberated opinion, pronounced while toying with Fanchon's buttocks. "Who is unaware that even punishment produces enthusiasms, and have we not seen certain individual's pricks stiffen into clubs at the same instant they find themselves publicly disgraced? Everyone knows the story of the brave Marquis de S____ who, when informed of the magistrates' decision to burn him in effigy, pulled his prick from his breeches and exclaimed: 'God be fucked, it has taken them years to do it, but it's achieved at last; covered with opprobrium and infamy, am I? Oh, leave me, for I've got absolutely to discharge'; and he did so in less time than it takes to tell."

"Those are undisputed facts," the Duc commented, nodding gravely. "But can you explain to me their cause?"

"It resides in our heart," Curval replied. "Once a man has degraded himself, debased himself through excesses, he has imparted something of a vicious cast to his soul, and nothing can rectify that situation. In any other case, shame would act as a deterrent and incline him away from the vices to which his mind advises him to surrender, but here that possibility has been eliminated altogether: 'tis the first token of shame he has obliterated, the initial call he has definitively silenced, and from the state in which one is when one has ceased to blush, to that other state wherein one adores everything that causes others to blush, there is no more, nor less, than a single step. All that before affected one disagreeably, now encountering an otherwise prepared soul, in metamorphosed into pleasure, and from this moment onward, whatever recalls the new state one has adopted can henceforth only be voluptuous."

"But what a distance one must first have ventured along the road of vice to arrive at that point!" said the Bishop.

"Yes, yes, 'tis so," Curval acknowledged; "but little by little one makes one's way along, and the path one treads is strewn with flowers; one excess leads to another, the imagination, never sated, soon brings us to our destination, and as the traveler's heart has only hardened as he has pursued his career, immediately he reaches his goal, that heart which of old contained some virtues, no longer recognizes a single one. Accustomed to livelier things, it promptly shrugs off those early impressions, those soft and unsweet, those tasteless ones which till then had made it drunk, and as it strongly senses that infamy and dishonor are going surely to be the consequences of its new impulsions, in order to have nothing to fear of them, it begins by making itself familiar with them. It no sooner caresses than it is seized with a fondness for them, because they are of the same nature as its new conquests; and now that heart is fixed unalterably, forever."

"And that," the Bishop observed, "is what makes mending one's way so difficult."

"Say rather that it is impossible, my friend. And how are the punishments inflicted upon him you wish to reform ever to succeed, since, with the exception of one or two privations, the state of degradation which characterizes the situation in which you place him when you punish him, pleases him, amuses him, delights him, and inwardly he relishes the self that has gone so far as to merit being treated in this way?"

"Oh, what is this glory, jest, and riddle of the world!" sighed the Duc.

"Yes, my friend, an enigma above all else," said the grave Curval. "And that perhaps is what led a very witty individual to say that better every time to fuck a man than to seek to comprehend him."

And the arrival of supper interrupting our interlocutors, they seated themselves at table without having achieved a thing during the soiree. Natheless, at dessert, Curval, his prick as hard as a demon's, declared he'd be damned if it wasn't a pucelage he wanted to pop, even if he had twenty fines to pay, and instantly laying rude hands upon Zelmire, who had been reserved for him, he was about to drag her off to the boudoir when his three colleagues, casting themselves in his path, besought him to reconsider and submit to the law he had himself prescribed; and, said they, since they too had equally powerful urges to breach the contract, but held themselves somehow in check all the same, he should imitate them, at least out of a feeling of comradeship. And as they had straightway sent word to have Julie fetched in, for Curval was fond of her, she, upon arriving, took him directly in hand, and, together with Champville and Bum-Cleaver, they all four went into the salon; the other three friends soon joined them there, for the orgies were scheduled to begin. Upon entering, they found Curval close at grips with his aides, who, adopting the most lubricious postures and providing the most libertine exhortations, finally caused him to yield up his fuck.

In the course of the orgies, Durcet had the duennas give him two or three hundred kicks in the ass; not to be outdone, his peers had the fuckers serve them identically, and before retiring for the night, no one was exempted from shedding more or less fuck, depending upon the faculties wherewith by Nature he had been endowed. Fearing some fresh return of the defloratory whim Curval had just announced, the duennas were, through precaution, assigned to sleep in the boys' and girls' chambers. But this measure was unnecessary, and Julie, who looked after the Président all night long, the following morning turned him over to the society as limp as an empty glove.

The Twenty-Fourth Day

Piety is indeed a true disease of the soul. Apply whatever remedies you please, the fever will not subside, the patient never heals; finding readier entry into the souls of the woebegone and downtrodden, because to be devout consoles them for their other ills, it is far more difficult to cure in such persons than in others. Such was the case with Adelaide: the more that vista of debauchery and of libertinage unfolded before her eyes, the more she recoiled and sought sanctuary in the arms of that comfort-giving God she hoped one day would come and deliver her from the evils which, she saw only too well, her dreadful situation was going to bring down upon her head. No one had a more profound appreciation of her circumstances than she; her mind could not more clearly have foreseen everything that was necessarily to follow the fatal beginning of which already she had been a victim, however mildly; she wonderfully well understood that, as the stories grew progressively stronger, the men's use of her and of her companions, evolving sympathetically, would also grow more ferocious. All that, despite everything she was told, made her avidly seek out, as often and for as long as she could, the society of her beloved Sophie. No longer did she dare go in quest of her at night; her overseers were sharp-eyed, wary, and drastic steps had been taken to thwart any more of those escapades, but whenever she found herself free for an instant, she would fly to her soul mate, and upon this very morning of the day we are presently chronicling, having risen early from the Bishop's bed, where she had lain that night, she went into the young girls' quarters to chat with her dearest correspondent. Durcet, who because of his duties that month used also to rise earlier than the others, found her there and declared to her there was nothing for it, he could not both carry out his functions and overlook this infraction of the rules; the society would have to decide the matter according to its pleasure. Adelaide wept, tears were her sole weapon, and she resorted to them. The only favor she dared beg from her husband was to try to prevent Sophie from being punished; for Sophie, she argued, could not be guilty, since it had been she,

Adelaide, who had come looking for her, not Sophie who had gone in search of Adelaide. Durcet said he would report the fact as he had observed it, would disguise nothing; no one is less apt to be melted than a punisher whose keenest interest lies in punishing. And such was the case here, of course; was there anything prettier to punish than Sophie? Surely not, and what cause might Durcet have for sparing her?

Their Lordships assembled, the financier made his report. Here was an habitual offender; the Président recollected that, when he had been at the Palais de Justice, his ingenious confreres used to contend that recidivism in a man proves Nature is acting more strongly in him than education or principles; hence, by repeated errors, he attests, so to speak, that he is not his own master; hence, he must be doubly punished - the Président now reasoned just as logically and with the same inspired verve that, as had won him his schoolmates' admiration, and he declared that, as he viewed the thing, one had no choice but to invoke the law and punish the incurable Adelaide and her companion with all permissible rigor. But as the law fixed the death penalty for this offense, and as Messieurs were disposed to amuse themselves yet a little longer with these ladies before taking the final step, they were content to summon them, to make them kneel, and to read them the article out of the ordinances applying to their case, drawing their attention to the grave risk they had just run in committing such a transgression. That done, their judges pronounced a sentence thrice as severe as the one which had been executed upon them the previous Saturday, they were forced to swear they would not repeat their crime, they were advised that, should the same thing occur again, they would have to endure the extreme penalty, and their names were inscribed in the register.

Durcet's inspection added three more names to the page; two from amongst the little girls, one of the boys rounded out the morning's capture. All this was the result of the experimenting with minor indigestions; it was succeeding extremely well, but those poor children, unable to restrain themselves another moment, were beginning to tumble one after another into states of culpability: such had been the experience of Fanny and of Hébé amongst the girls, and of Hyacinthe amongst the boys. The evidence found in their pots was enormous, and Durcet frolicked about with it for a long time. Never had so many permissions been requested on any given morning, and certain subordinate personages were heard to curse Duclos for having imparted her secret. Notwithstanding the multitude of requests, leave to shit was granted only to Constance, Hercule, two second-rank fuckers, Augustine, Zéphyr, and Desgranges; they provided a few minutes' entertainment, and Messieurs sat down to dine.

"Well, now you see your mistake in allowing your daughter to receive religious instruction," Durcet said to Curval; "there's nothing to be done about her now. Those imbecilities have taken root in her head. And I told you they would, ages ago."

"In faith," said Curval, "I thought that acquaintance with them would be just one more reason she'd have for despising them, and that as she grew up she would convince herself of the stupidity of those infamous dogmas."

"What you say is all very well for reasoning minds," said the Bishop, "but one simply must not expect it to succeed with a child."

"I'm afraid we're going to be forced to resort to violent measures," said the Duc, who knew very well Adelaide could overhear him.

"Oh yes, in good time," Durcet nodded. "I can assure her that if she has no one but me for her advocate, she'll be poorly defended in court."

"Oh, I know that, Monsieur!" Adelaide stammered through her tears; "everyone is aware of your feelings toward me."

"My feelings?" protested Durcet. "But, my dear wife, I ought perhaps to begin by informing you I have never had any feelings whatsoever for a woman, and assuredly fewer for you, who belong to me, than for any other. I hate religion, as well as those who practice it, and I warn you that, from the indifference I have in your regard, I shall pass damned quickly to the most violent aversion if you continue to revere infamous and execrable illusions, phantoms which have ever been the object of my contemptuous scorn. One must first have lost one's mind to be able to acknowledge a god, and to have gone completely mad to worship such a thing. In short, I declare to you before your father and these other gentlemen that there are no lengths to which I shall not go if I ever again find you guilty of such a sin. You should have been sent to a nunnery if you wanted to pray to your fuck-in-the-ass God; there you'd have been able to worship the bugger to your heart's content."

"Ah!" put in Adelaide, groaning, "a nun, Great God, a nun, would to heaven that I were such."

And Durcet, who at the time was sitting opposite her, annoyed by her response, hurled a silver plate at her face; it would have killed her had it struck her head, for the shock was so violent the missile bent double upon crashing against the wall.

"You're an insolent creature," Curval said to his daughter, who, to avoid plate, had leapt between her father and Antinoüs. "You deserve to have your belly kicked in."

And driving her away from him with a blow of his fist:

"Go crawl on your knees and beg your husband's forgiveness," said he, "or we'll expose you to the severest ordeal you've ever dreamt of."

In tears, she cast herself at Durcet's feet, but he, having got a very solid erection from hurling the plate, and declaring he'd have given a thousand louis to have hit his mark, Durcet said that he felt an immediate, a general, and an exemplary punishment was in order; another would of course be executed on Saturday, but he proposed that this one time they do without the children's services at coffee and devote that period to amusing themselves with Adelaide. Everyone consented to the proposal; Adelaide, Louison, and Fanchon, the most wicked of the four elders and the most dreaded by the women, moved into the salon; certain considerations obliged us to draw a curtain over what transpired there. But of one thing we may be perfectly certain: our four heroes discharged during that set-to, and Adelaide was allowed to take to her bed. 'Tis for the reader to invent the combinations and scene he'd like best, and kindly consent to be conveyed, if 'twould please him to accompany us, directly to the throne room where Duclos is about to resume her narrative. All of the friends have taken their places near their wives, all, that is to say, save the Duc, who was to have Adelaide that afternoon, and who has replaced her with Augustine; everyone then being ready, Duclos begins to speak.

One day, said that talented orator, while I was maintaining before one of my fellow procuresses that I had surely seen all it were possible to see of the most furious by way of passive flagellation, in that I had flogged and witnessed others flog men with thorns and the bull's pizzle:

"Oh, by God," my colleague answered, "you still have a great deal to see, my dear, and to persuade you that you've by no means observed the worst, I'll send one of my clients around tomorrow."

And having given me notice of the hour of the visit, and advised me of the ritual expected by that elderly post-office commissioner whose name, I remember, was Monsieur de Grancourt, I made full preparations and awaited for our man; I was to give him my personal attention, the thing was so arranged. He arrives at the house, and after we have retired to a room together:

"Monsieur," I say, "I deeply regret having to make the following disclosure, but I am bound to inform you that you are a prisoner and cannot leave this place. I further regret to say that Parliament has delegated me to arrest and punish you, and the Legislature has so willed it, and I have its order in my pocket. The person who sent you to me set a trap for you, for she knew full well the implications of your coming here, and she could most assuredly have enabled you to avoid this scene. As for the rest, you know the facts in the case: 'tis not with impunity one perpetrates the black and dreadful crimes you have committed, and I consider you exceedingly fortunate to get off with so little."

Our man had listened with the keenest attention to my harangue, and immediately I had done, he burst into tears and fell down on his knees before me, imploring me to deal leniently with him.

"Well I know," said he, "that I have greatly misbehaved. I know I have affronted God and justice; but since 'tis you, my sweet lady, who are appointed to chasten me, I most earnestly entreat your indulgence in my regard."

"Monsieur," I replied, "I shall do my duty. How can you be sure I am not myself being closely watched? What makes you suppose I have it in my power to respond to your pleas for merciful compassion? Remove your clothes and adopt a docile attitude, that is all I can say to you."

Grancourt obeyed; in a trice he was as naked as the palm of your hand. But, great God! what was this body he offered to my sight! I can only compare its skin to a ruffled taffeta. Upon that whole body, marked everywhere, there was not a single spot which did not bear terrible evidence of the lash.

However, into the fire I had thrust an iron scourge garnished with pointed steel tips; I had received the weapon that morning together with the final instructions. This murderous instrument had reached a bright-red color about the same moment Grancourt had removed his last stitch. I snatched the scourge from the coals and, starting to beat him with it, gently at first, then with increasing severity, then with all my strength, and that heedless of where my blows fell, rending him from the nape of his neck to his heels, I had my man streaming blood in an instant.

"You are a villain," I told him as I brought the scourge whistling down upon his body, "you're a villain and you've committed all sorts of crimes. Nothing is sacred to you, and I've lately heard that you've poisoned your own mother."

"'Tis true, Madame, oh, 'tis only too true. I'm a monster, I'm a criminal," said he as he frigged himself. "There's no infamy I've not perpetrated and am not prepared to do again. Come now, your blows are utterly in vain, I'll never mend my ways, I find too much delight in crime. You'd have to kill me to put a stop to my joy; crime is my element, 'tis my life, I've lived in crime, I'll die in it."

And you may well imagine how, these remarks of his inspiring my arm and tongue, I redoubled my blows and invectives. The word "fuck" escaped his lips, however: that was the signal: I lay on with all my might and endeavor to strike his most sensitive parts. He skips, hops, jumps, and capers, he eludes me and, discharging, he scampers into a tub of warm water specially prepared to purify him after this bloody ceremonial. Ah, upon my soul, yes! I ceded to my friend the honor of having seen more of this sort of thing than I, and I believe we two were able to say at the time that we had seen more than all the rest of Paris, for our Grancourt's needs never varied, and for above twenty years he had been going every day to that woman's establishment for the same treatment.

Shortly afterward, that same woman arranged to have me meet another libertine whose idiosyncrasy, I fancy, will seem at least unusual to you. The scene transpired in his little house at Roule. I am introduced into a rather obscurely lit room, where I find a man lying in bed, and, posed in the center of the room, a coffin.

"You see before you," our libertine said to me, "a man reclining upon his deathbed, one who would not close his eyes without rendering a last homage to the object he worships. I adore asses, and if I am to perish, I want to die while kissing one. When life shall have fled this frame, you yourself shall lift me into that coffin, draw round the shrouds, and nail down the lid. It is my design thus to die in pleasure's embrace, and at this last moment to be served by the very object of my lubricious heats. Come . . . come," he continued in a broken, weak, gasping voice, "make haste, for I am nigh to the threshold."

I draw near to him, turn around, I exhibit my buttocks.

"Ah, wondrous ass!" he cries. "'Tis well, I am easy thus to be able to take with me to the grave the idea of a behind as pretty as that one!"

And he fondled it, opened it, nuzzled and kissed it just the way the healthiest man in the world might have done.

"Oh, indeed!" said he a moment later as he left off his task and rolled toward the wall, "well I knew 'twould not be for long I'd savor this pleasure; I do now expire, remember what I have enjoined you to do."

And so saying, he uttered a profound sigh, grew rigid, and played his part with such skill that damn me if I didn't think he was dead. I kept my wits about me; eager to see the end of this droll ceremony, I wrapped him in the shroud. He had ceased to stir, and whether it was that he knew some secret for feigning death, or whether my imagination had been affected, he felt as rigid and cold as a bar of iron; only his prick gave some hints of life: it too was rigid, but not cold, and glued to his belly, and drops of fuck seemed to come oozing from it despite his moribund condition. Directly I have him swathed in the sheet, I take him up in my arms, and it wasn't easy, for the way he'd become rigid made him as heavy as a steer. I succeeded nevertheless in transporting him to the coffin. As soon as I have laid him out, I start reciting the prayer for the dead, and finally I nail the coffin shut; that was the critical instant for him: no sooner have I driven the last nail home than he sets to screeching like a madman:

"Holy name of God, I'm coming! Get out, whore, get out, for if I catch you, you're done for!"

I'm seized by fear, I dart to the stairs, upon which I meet a tactful manservant who is thoroughly acquainted with his master's manias and who gives me two louis; I proceed to the door, while the valet hastens into the patient's bedchamber to free him from the sealed coffin.

"Now there's a quaint taste," said Durcet. "Well, Curval, what do you think of that one?"

"Marvelous," the Président replied; "there you have an individual who wishes to make himself familiar with the idea of death, and hence unafraid of it, and who to that end has found no better means than to associate it with a libertine idea. There is absolutely no doubt about it: that man will die fondling an ass."

"Nor any doubt," said Champville, "that he is proudly impious; I know him, and I shall have occasion to describe the use he makes of religion's holiest mysteries."

"I don't wonder he is an unbeliever," said the Duc. "He's clearly a man who laughs at the whole business and who wishes to accustom himself to acting and thinking the same way during his last minutes."

"For my part," the Bishop said, "I find something very piquant in that passion, and I'll not hide the fact I'm stiff from hearing about it. Continue, Duclos, go on, for I have the feeling I might do something silly, and I'd prefer to leave well enough alone for the rest of the day."

Very well, said that splendid raconteur, here's one less complex; 'tis the story of a man who for five years regularly applied at my door for the single pleasure of getting me to sew up his asshole. He used to stretch out belly down upon a bed, I would seat myself between his legs and, equipped with a stout needle and half a spool of heavy cobbler's thread, I'd sew his anus completely closed, and this fellow's skin in that area was so toughened and so used to needle thrusts that my operation would not draw a single drop of blood from his hide. While I worked, he would frig himself, and he used to discharge like a mule when I'd taken the last stitch. His ecstasy dissipated, I'd promptly undo my work, and that would be that.

Another used to have brandy rubbed over every part of his body where Nature had placed hair, then I'd put a match to those areas I'd rubbed with alcohol, and all the hair would go up in flames. He would discharge upon finding himself afire, meanwhile I'd shown him my belly, my cunt, and so forth, for that fellow had the bad taste never to want to see anything but fronts.

"But, tell me, Messieurs, did any of you know Mirecourt, today président in the upper chamber, and in those days attorney to the Crown?"

"I knew him," said Curval.

"Well, my Lord, do you know what used to be, and what I dare say still is, his passion?"

"No; and he passes, or wishes to pass, for a devout and good subject, I'd be most pleased to know."

"My Lord," Duclos said, "he likes also to be taken for an ass. . . ."

"Ah! by God! said the Duc; and turning to Curval: "what do you think of that, my friend? Damned strange taste, don't you think, for a judge? I'll wager that once he's an ass he thinks he's going to pronounce judgment. Well, what next?" he asked of Duclos.

"Next, your Grace, one must lead him by the halter, walk him about the room for an hour, he brays, one mounts astride him, and when one's in the saddle, one whips his entire body with a switch, as if to quicken his gait. He breaks into a trot, and as he's started by now to frig himself, he soon discharges and, while he does so, makes loud noises, bucks, rears, and throws the rider."

"That, I'd say, is more diverting than lubricious. And pray tell me, Duclos," the Duc went on, "did that man ever tell you he had some comrade who shared his taste?"

"Why, indeed, he did tell me so," said the amiable Duclos, entering into the joke with a merry laugh and descending from her platform, for her day's stint was over; "Yes, Sire, he told me he had a quantity of comrades, but that not all of them would allow themselves to be mounted."

The séance had come to an end, Messieurs were disposed to perform a few stunts before supper; the Duc hugged Augustine in close embrace.

"You know," he said dreamily, frigging her clitoris and directing her to grasp his prick, "you know, I'm not at all surprised that Curval is sometimes tempted to violate the pact and pop a pucelage or two, for I feel at this very moment, for example, that I could willingly send Augustine's to the devil."

"Which one?" Curval inquired.

"Both of them, bless my soul," answered the Duc; "but one must behave oneself during this sojourn; in having thus to wait a little while for our pleasures, we make them far more delicious. Well, little girl," he continued, "show me your buttocks, perhaps 'twill change the character of my ideas. . . . Bleeding Christ! look at that little whore's ass! Curval, what do you advise me to do with this thing?"

"Put some vinegar sauce on it," said Curval.

"Mercy!" exclaimed the Duc, "what a notion. But patience, patience . . . everything will come in good time."

"My very dear brother," said the Bishop in a halting voice, "there's something in your words that smells of fuck."

"Really? For indeed I have the greatest desire to lose some."

"And what prevents you?" the Bishop wanted to know.

"Oh, many things, many things," the Duc replied. "First of all, I see no shit in the pipe, and I'd like shit, and then . . . I don't know - there are so many things I'd like. . . ."

"What?" asked Durcet just before Antinoüs' turd cascaded into his mouth.

"What?" echoed the Duc. "There's, to begin with, a little infamy I simply must perform."

And retiring to the distant boudoir with Augustine, Zélamir, Cupidon, Duclos, Desgranges, and Hercule, he was heard, a minute later, to utter ringing cries and oaths which proved the Duc had finally managed to calm his brain and soothe his balls. Little precise information exists upon what he did to Augustine, but, notwithstanding his love for her, she was seen to return in tears and, ominous sign! one of her fingers had been twisted. We deeply regret not yet to be able to explain all this to the reader, but it is quite certain that these gentlemen, on the sly and before the arrival of the day heralding open season, were giving themselves over to tricks which have not so far been embodied in story, hence to unsanctioned deeds, and in so doing they were acting in formal violation of the regulations they had sworn in honor to observe; but, you know, when an entire society commits the same faults, they are commonly pardoned. The Duc came back and was pleased to see that Durcet and the Bishop had not been wasting their time, and that Curval, in Bum-Cleaver's arms, was deliciously doing everything one may possibly do with all the voluptuous objects one may possibly assemble around oneself.

Supper was served, orgies followed as usual, the household retired to bed. Lame and aching as Adelaide was, the Duc, who was scheduled to have her by him that night, wanted her there, and as he had come from the orgies rather drunk, as was his wont, it is said that he did not deal tenderly with her. But by and large the night was passed just like all the preceding nights, that is to say, in the depths of delirium and debauchery, and fair-haired Aurora having come, as the poets say, to fling open the gates of the palace where dwelt Apollo, that god, somewhat a libertine himself, only mounted his azure chariot in order to bring light to shed upon new lecheries.

The Twenty-Fifth Day

However, a new intrigue was quietly taking form within the impenetrable walls of the Château of Silling; but it did not have the dangerous significance that had been attributed to Adelaide's league with Sophie. This latest association was being hatched between Aline and Zelmire; those two young girls' conformity of character contributed greatly to their attachment to each other: both were mild-natured and sensitive, no more than thirty months separated them in age, they were both very childlike, very simple, very good-hearted: they had, in brief, almost all of the same virtues, and almost all the same vices, for Zelmire, sweet and tender, was also, like Aline, careless and lazy. They suited one another so admirably that, on the morning of the 25th, they were discovered in the same bed, and this is how it happened: being destined for Curval, Zelmire slept, as we know, in his bedchamber. Aline was Curval's bedwife that same night. But Curval, having returned dead drunk from the orgies, wished to sleep with no one but Invictus, and thus it fell out that these two little doves, abandoned and brought together by fortune, from dread of the cold both camped in the same bed and, in bed, 'twas maintained, their little fingers itched more than their dear little elbows.

Upon opening his eyes in the morning and seeing these two birds sharing the same nest, Curval demanded to know what they were doing there, and ordering them both to come instantly into his bed, he sniffed about just below each one's clitoris, and clearly recognized that both of them were still full of fuck. The case was grave: Messieurs did indeed wish the young ladies to be victims of impudicity, but they insisted that, amongst themselves, they behave decently - oh, for what will libertinage, perpetually inconsistent libertinage, not insist upon! - and if they sometimes consented to permit the ladies to indulge in a little reciprocal impurity, it all had to be both upon Messieurs' express instructions and before their eyes. And thus it was the case was brought before the council, and the two delinquents, who neither could nor dared deny the thing, were ordered to demonstrate what they had been up to, and before a crowd of spectators to display just what their individual talents were. They did as they were told, with much blushing and not a little weeping, and asked to be forgiven their mistakes. But too attractive was the prospect of having that pretty couple amongst the culprits to be punished the following Saturday; consequently, they were not forgiven, but were speedily included in Durcet's book of sorrows which, incidentally, was being very agreeably filled up that week.

This chore completed, breakfast was finished, and Durcet conducted his searches. The fatal indigestions yielded still another miscreant: 'twas the little Michette, she'd been unable to hold the bridge, she said they'd made her eat too much the night before, and these were followed by a thousand other infantile excuses which did not prevent her name from being written down. Curval, his prick jumping like a young colt, seized the chamber pot and devoured its contents. And then bringing his angry eyes to bear upon her:

"Oh yes, by Jesus," said he, "yes, by the Saviour's fuck, you shall be spanked, my little rascal, my own hand will see to that. There are rules against shitting that way; you should at least have given us notice; you know damned well that we are prepared to receive shit at any hour of the day or night."

And he fondled her buttocks very vivaciously while repeating the rules to her.

The boys were found intact, no chapel permissions were distributed to them, and Messieurs repaired to table. During the meal, there was plentiful and penetrating discussion of Aline's deed; they ascribed a holier-than-thou attitude to her, said she appeared a little hypocrite, and behold! here was proof of her real temperament at last come to light.

"How now, my friend," Durcet said to the Bishop, "is one still to lay any store by appearances, above all those that girls parade?"

'Twas unanimously agreed nothing was more deceitful than a girl, and that, as they were every one of them false, they never made use of their wits save to be more skillfully false. These observations brought the table talk around to women, and the Bishop who abhorred them, gave vent to all the hatred they inspired in him. He reduced them to the state of the vilest animals, and proved their existence so perfectly useless in this world that one could extirpate them from the face of the earth without in the slightest countercarrying the designs of Nature who, having in times past very surely found the means to create without women, would find it again when only men were left.

They proceeded to coffee; it was presented them by Augustine, Michette, Hyacinthe, and Narcisse. The Bishop, one of whose greatest uncomplex pleasures was to suck little boys' pricks, had been spending a few minutes playing this game with Hyacinthe, when all of a sudden he reared back and let out, not a shout, but a bubbling noise, for his mouth was full; his exclamation was interpreted thus: "Ah, by God's balls, my friends, a pucelage! That's the first time this little rascal has discharged, I'm sure of it!" And, truth to tell, no one had so far observed Hyacinthe carry things to that point; he was indeed thought still too young to bring it off. But he was well advanced in his fourteenth year, 'tis the age when Nature customarily heaps her favors upon us, and nothing could have been more real than the victory the Bishop thought he had achieved. None the less, the others were anxious to verify the thing, and each wishing to be witness to the adventure, they drew up their chairs in a semicircle around the young man. Augustine, the most accomplished frigger in the seraglio, received permission to manualize the lad within clear sight of the assembly, and Hyacinthe was given leave to fondle and caress her in whatsoever part of her body he desired. There's no spectacle more voluptuous than that offered by a young maid of fifteen, lovely as the day, lending herself to the caresses of a boy of fourteen and provoking, by means of the most delicious pollutions, his springtide discharge.

Hyacinthe, aided perhaps by Nature, but yet more certainly by the examples he had before his nose, fondled, handled, kissed naught but his frigger's pretty little buttocks, and it required little more than an instant of this to bring color to his cheeks, to fetch two or three sighs from his lips, to induce his pretty little prick to shoot, to a distance of one yard, five or six jets of sweet fuck white as cream, which emissions happened to land on Durcet's thigh, for the banker was seated nearest the boy and was having himself frigged by Narcisse while watching the operation. The fact once indubitably established, they caressed and kissed the child rather universally, each swore he'd love to receive a small portion of that youthful sperm, and as it appeared that, at his age and for a beginning, six discharges were not too many, in that he had after all just delivered himself of two without the least difficulty, our libertines induced him to shed another in each of their mouths.

Much heated by this performance, the Duc laid hands on Augustine and frigged her clitoris with his tongue until he had elicited several solid discharges from her; full of fire and blessed with a mettlesome spirit, that little minx shot them off in short order. While the Duc was thus polluting Augustine, nothing was more engaging than to see Durcet, come up to gather symptoms of the pleasure he was not provoking, kiss that beautiful child's mouth a thousand times over, and swallow, so to speak, the voluptuousness another was causing to circulate throughout her senses. The hour was advanced, they were obliged to omit the midday nap and to pass directly into the auditorium where Duclos had been awaiting them for a long time; as soon as everyone had arranged himself, she took up the thread of her adventures and spoke as hereafter you may read:

I have already had the honor to remark in your Lordships' presence, that it is most difficult to fathom all the tortures man invents for himself in order to find, in the degradation they produce, or the agonies, those sparks of pleasure which age or satiety have made to grow faint in him. Hard it is to credit the assertion that one such gentleman of this sort, a person of sixty years and to a singular degree jaded by all the pleasures of lubricity, used only to be able to restore his senses to life by having the flames of burning candles applied to every part of his body, and principally to the ones Nature has intended for those selfsame pleasures. He would have his thighs seared, his prick, his balls roasted, and above all else his asshole: while all this was going forward, he would be kissing an ass, and after the grievous operation had been repeated for the fifteenth or twentieth time, he would discharge while sucking the anus of the girl who'd been burning him.

Soon after that one, I had dealings with another who obliged me to use a horse's currycomb on him, to rub down his entire body with that instrument, quite as one does to the animal I have just named. Directly his body was all an open wound, I'd next rub him with alcohol, and this second torture would cause him abundantly to discharge upon my breasts - that was the battlefield he chose to spray with his fuck. I would kneel before him, squeeze his prick between my bubs, and he'd quietly wash them with his balls' acrid humor.

A third would have would have every hair on his ass plucked out one by one. While that lengthy operation was advancing, he would frig himself upon a warm turd I'd just done for him. Then, at the crisis' approach, I had, to give it the necessary encouragement, to drive the point of a scissors deep enough into each of his buttocks to draw a jet of blood. His ass was a maze of wounds and scars, I was scarce able to find an open space for my two gashes; immediately the steel entered him, he'd plunge his nose into the shit, smear it upon his face, and floods of sperm would crown his ecstasy.

A fourth put his prick in my mouth and bade me bite it as hard as I could; in the meantime, as I chewed his poor device, I was expected to lacerate his buttocks with an iron comb whose teeth were ground to sharp points; and then, at the moment I sensed his prick ready to melt - a very faint, a barely perceptible erection would tell me so - and then, I say, I'd spread his buttocks prodigiously wide, ease them close to a burning candle I'd kept in readiness on the floor, and I'd braise his asshole with it. 'Twas the burning sensation of that candle under his anus decided his emission; I'd therewith redouble my bitings, and would soon find my mouth full.

"One moment, if you please," said the Bishop. "Every time I hear of someone discharging into a mouth I am reminded of the good fortune I had earlier today, and my spirits are disposed to tasting further pleasures of the same sort."

Saying which, he draws Invictus near, for that champion wsa on duty in the Bishop's alcove that afternoon, and falls to sucking the brave fellow's prick with all the energetic lustiness of a true bugger. Fuck explodes, the prelate gobbles it up, and straightway goes to repeat the operation upon Zéphyr. The Bishop was brandishing his knobkerrie, and 'twas seldom that women would feel completely at their ease when he was in this critical state and they were near him. Unfortunately, it was his niece Aline who happened to be within range.

"What are you doing there, bitch?" he rasped; "I want men for my fun."

Aline seeks to elude him, he seizes her by the hair and, dragging her into his closet along with Zelmire and Hébé, the two girls in his quartet:

"You'll see," says he to his friends, "you'll see how I'm going to teach these wenches to slip cunts under my hand when I'm doing my best to find some pricks."

Upon his order, Fanchon accompanied the three maidens, and an instant later Aline was heard to utter very shrill cries; then came tidings of Monseigneur's discharge, reverberating howls which blended with his dear niece's dolorous accents. Everyone returned . . . Aline was weeping, squeezing and clutching her behind.

"Come show me what he did to you," said the Duc; "I love nothing better than to see traces of my distinguished brother's brutality."

Aline displayed I've no idea what, for I have never been able to discover what went on in those infernal closets, but the Duc exclaimed: "By fuck, 'tis delicious, I think I'll go off and do the same." But Curval having pointed out to him that time was growing short, and having added that he had an amusing enterprise in mind for the orgies, which scheme would demand a clear head and all his fuck, Duclos was asked to go ahead with the fifth story in order that the sitting be brought to a proper conclusion; the storyteller therewith addressed the convocation once again:

Belonging to that group of extraordinary individuals, said she, whose mania consists in wallowing in degradation and in insulting their own dignity, was a certain judge of the circuit court whose name was Foucolet. There's truly no believing the point to which that fellow would carry his furor; he had to be given a sample of almost every torture. I used to hang him, but the rope would break just in time and he would fall upon a mattress; the next instant, I would strap him to a St. Andrew's cross and make as if to break his limbs with a bar, but it was only a roll of pasteboard; I used to brand him upon the shoulder, the iron I used was warm and left a faint imprint, no more; I would flog his back in precise imitation of the public servant who performs those noble feats, and whilst I was doing all this I had to overwhelm him with a stream of atrocious invectives, bitter reproaches for various crimes, for which, during each successive operation, he would demand, a candle in his hand and wearing only his shirt, God's forgiveness and the law's, pronouncing his entreaties in a very humble and contrite tone; finally, the meeting would be brought to a close on my ass, where the libertine would yield up his fuck when his head had reached the ultimate degree of distraction.

"Well now, are you going to let me discharge in peace now that Duclos has finished?" the Duc asked Curval.

"No, not a bit of it," the Président replied; "preserve your fuck, I tell you I need it for the orgies."

"Oh, so you take me for your valet, do you?" the Duc exclaimed. "You take me for a worn-out bugger? Do you suppose that the small quantity of fuck I'm going to lose in a moment will prevent me from joining in all the infamies which are going to pop into your head four hours from now? Come now, Président, you know me better than that; banish your fears, I'll be fit again for anything inside fifteen minutes, but my good and holy brother has been pleased to give me a little example of an atrocity I'd be grief-stricken not to execute with Adelaide, your dear and estimable daughter."

And pushing her forthwith into his closet, along with Thérèse, Colombe, and Fanny, the female elements of his quatrain, he probably did there, with them, what the Bishop had done to his niece, and discharged with the same episodes, for, as not long before they heard Aline's terrible scream, so now their ears were treated to another from the lips of Adelaide and the bawdy Duc's yells of lust. Curval wished to learn which of the two brothers had been the better behaved;

he summoned the two women, and having pored at length over their two behinds, he decided that the Duc had not merely imitated, but surpassed the Bishop.

They sat down at table, and having by means of some drug or other stuffed the bowels of all the subjects, men and women, with an abundance of wind, after supper they played the game of fart-in-the-face: Messieurs, all four of them, lay back upon couches, their heads raised, and one by one the members of the household stepped up to deliver their farts into the waiting mouths. Duclos was requested to do the counting and mark down the scores; there were thirty-six farters against only four swallowers: hence there were certain persons who received as many as one hundred and fifty farts. It had been for this rousing ceremony Curval had wanted the Duc to keep himself fit, but such precautions, as Blangis had made perfectly clear, were quite unnecessary; he was too great a friend of libertinage to allow some new excess to find him unprepared; to the contrary, any new excess always had the greatest effect upon him, his situation notwithstanding, and he did not fail to produce a second discharge thanks to the humid mistral Fanchon wafted into his mouth. As for Curval, they were Antinoüs' farts which cost him his fuck, whereas Durcet bent before the gale that swept out of Martaine's asshole, and the Bishop lost all control in the face of what Desgranges offered him. The youthful beauties' efforts, 'twill be remarked, came to naught; but is it not true that it is always the crapulous individual who best executes the infamous deed?

The Twenty-Sixth Day

In that nothing was more delicious than meting out punishments, in that nothing prepared the way for so many pleasures, and those very sorts of pleasures Messieurs had mutually promised not to taste until in the stories mention thereof should permit fullest indulgence in them, the libertines sought by every imaginable means to trip the subjects into states of delinquency, and so procure themselves the joy of chastising their hapless victims; to this end, the friends, having convoked an extraordinary assembly that morning, their purpose being to deliberate upon this problem, they added several articles to the household regulations, infraction of which was necessarily to occasion punishment. Firstly, the wives, the small boys, and the girls were expressly forbidden to fart anywhere save in the friends' mouths. Instantly they were seized by the desire to break wind, they were without delay to go and find one of the friends and administer unto him what required to be set at large; a severe afflictive penalty would be the reward for disobedience. Secondly, the use of bidets and ass-wipings of any kind were absolutely outlawed; it was generally proclaimed that all subjects without exception would hereafter never wash themselves, and never under any circumstances wipe the ass after having shitted; that, whenever an ass were found clean, upon the subject concerned would lie the burden of proving it had been licked clean by one of the friends, and that friend would have to be mentioned by name. In response to which citation, the friend would be questioned, and, being in a position to procure himself two pleasures, instead of only one, to wit: that of having cleaned the ass with his tongue, and that of having punished the subject who had afforded him this first pleasure. . . . Examples of this will be provided.

Thirdly, a new ceremony was introduced: at the time of the morning coffee, at the time of their entry into the girls' quarters, and also when, after that, they passed into the boys', each of the subjects would hereafter, one by one, step forth and, in a loud and clear voice, say to each of the friends: "I don't care a fuck for God; there's shit in my ass, would you like some?" and those who should fail in an intelligible voice to pronounce both the blasphemy and the invitation, would instantly be inscribed in the dread book. The reader will readily imagine what difficulties the pious Adelaide and her young pupil Sophie had to surmount before being able to utter such infamies, and their inner struggles procured Messieurs some excellent entertainment.

The foregoing once framed in law, they turned to consider delations and decided to admit them; this barbarous means of multiplying vexations, accepted by every tyrant, was warmly embraced by these. It was decided, fourthly, that every subject who should lodge complaint against some other, would thereby earn a one-half reduction of the punishment he was to suffer for the next fault he committed. Messieurs were in no way deprived by this system, because the subject who had just accused another subject could never know the extent of the punishment a half of which, he was promised, would be suppressed; and so it was a simple matter indeed to give him precisely what one wished to give him, and still to persuade him he had got off more lightly than otherwise he might. Messieurs agreed upon and published their decision, that no delation required substantiating proof in order to be believed, and that, to be inscribed, accusation brought by anyone would suffice. The duennas' authority, furthermore, was increased, and upon the basis of their slightest complaint, whether true or false, the subject would be condemned immediately. In a word, over this small population they established all the vexation, all the injustice one could imagine, certain in the belief that the more harshly their tyranny was exercised, the greater the sum of pleasures they would derive from their privileged situation.

All this legislation composed and voted, they visited the chamber pots. Colombe was found guilty; her excuses hinged upon the food they had made her eat between meals the day before; she had, said she, been unable to resist, she was dreadfully unhappy about the whole thing, and this was the fourth successive week she had been punished. The statement was true, and she had only to blame her ass, which was the freshest, the sweetest, the best-made and most endearing little ass you could hope to see. She pointed out she'd not wiped herself, and that, she supposed, should be regarded as a point in her favor. Durcet examined her, and having indeed discovered a very thick and very broad patch of shit, he assured her that, in the light of this, she'd be treated a little less rigorously. Curval, stiff at the time, laid hands on her, and having completely cleaned her anus, he had her produce her turd and ate it while having her frig him, periodically interrupting his chewing to kiss her upon the mouth and to order her to swallow, in her turn, what of her own creation he brought to her lips. They next inspected Augustine and Sophie, who had been solemnly enjoined, after the stools they had yielded up the night before, to remain in the most impure state. Sophie's appearance conformed with her instructions, even though she had slept in the Bishop's chamber, but Augustine was as neat as a pin. Sure of her reply, she advanced proudly and said that they knew very well she had, as was her custom, lain the night in Monsieur le Duc's bedchamber, and that before going to sleep he had summoned her to his bed, where he had licked her asshole while she had frigged his prick in her mouth. When interrogated, the Duc said that he had no remembrance of the thing (although the story was completely true), that he had fallen asleep with his prick in Duclos' ass, that they could substantiate the fact. They went about the matter with all possible seriousness and gravity, they sent for Duclos who, seeing clearly what was afoot, lent her support to everything the Duc advanced, and maintained that Augustine had been called to Monsieur's bed only for a brief instant, that Monsieur had shitted into Augustine's mouth and then, upon second thought, had bade her return to the bed in order that he might eat his turd. Augustine sought to defend her thesis and dispute Duclos' contentions, but silence was imposed upon her and, although perfectly innocent, her name was written down.

Amongst the boys, whose chambers they visited next, Cupidon was found guilty; he had done the world's most gorgeous turd in his chamber pot. The Duc snatched it up and gobbled it up while the young malefactor sucked his member.

All requests for chapel permissions were refused; they then went to dine. The beautiful Constance, whom they sometimes dispensed from serving at table because of her state, was however feeling fit that day, and made her appearance naked; the sight of her belly, which was beginning somewhat to swell, made Curval's head very hot; the others, seeing his treatment of the poor creature's buttocks and breasts growing rather rough - Curval's horror for her was doubling every day, that was plain - were swayed by her entreaties and their common desire to preserve her fruit, at least until a certain date, and she was allowed to absent herself from all the day's functions, save for the narrations, wherefrom she was never excused. Curval started in again with his frightful speeches about child-breeders, he declared that if he had government of the country he would borrow their law from the inhabitants of Formosa, where pregnant women under thirty are, together with their fruit, ground in a large mortar; should that law, he protested, be introduced into France, the population would still be twice what it ought to be.

Coffee came next; it was presented by Sophie, Fanny, Zélamir, and Adonis, but served in a passing strange manner: 'twas in the children's mouths, one had to sip it therefrom. Sophie served hers to the Duc, Fanny Curval's, Zélamir the Bishop's, and Durcet got his out of Adonis. They extracted a mouthful, gargled it a moment, and returned it into the mouths of those who'd served them. Curval, who had risen from the table in a great ferment, got stiff all over again thanks to this ceremony, and when it had been completed, he laid hands on Fanny and discharged into her mouth, ordering her to swallow the whey; the threats accompanying his instructions succeeded in making the poor wretch obey without the flutter of an eyelash. The Duc and his two other confreres collected shit or farts; having finished their nap, they all trooped in to listen to Duclos, who spoke to them in this wise:

I will move with dispatch, said that amiable girl, through my last two adventures concerning these unusual men who find their delight only in the pain they are made to undergo, and then with your leave we will pass on to a different variety.

The first, while he had me frig him, naked and standing up, wanted floods of hot water poured down on us through an opening in the ceiling; our bodies were to be showered during the entire operation. It was quite in vain I argued that, while not sharing in this passion of his, I was nevertheless, like himself, to be a victim of it; he replied, assuring me I would suffer no hurt from the experience, and that these showers were good for one's health. I believed him and let him have his way; as this scene transpired in his house, the temperature of the water, a critical detail, was something lying beyond my control. It was indeed nearly boiling. Messieurs, there is no conceiving the pleasure he felt upon being drenched by it. As for myself, all the while operating with all possible speed, I screeched, yes, I confess it, I screeched like a drowning tomcat; my skin came peeling off, and I made myself the firm promise never to return to that man's house.

"Ah, buggerfuck!" exclaimed the Duc, "I have the strongest inclination to give the beauteous Aline a comparable scalding."

"Your Grace," the latter replied in a humble but decided tone, "I am not a tomcat."

And the naive candor in her childlike reply having fetched a chuckle from everyone, Duclos was asked to give the second and final example of the same genre.

It was a great deal less painful for me, said Duclos; I had simply to don a stout glove, then with this protected hand to take burning grit from a frying pan I'd been heating on a stove, and, my hand filled, to rub that fiery sand over my man's body, from head to toe. His body was so inured to this exercise that he seemed to be covered not with skin, but with leather. When one reached his prick, one had to seize it and massage it in a handful of that same sand; he'd be up like a shot. Then, with the other hand, I placed a small fire shovel, heated red-hot for this purpose, under his balls. This rubbing with one hand, the consuming heat which rose to bake his testicles, perhaps a little touching of my two buttocks, which I had to keep well exposed and within reach during the operation, this combination of elements melted him altogether and he discharged, being very careful to spill his seed upon the hot shovel where, to his unutterable delight, he watched it sizzle and evaporate in steam.

"Curval," said the Duc, "there's a man who, 'twould appear to me, has no greater fondness than have you for population."

"It looks that way to me," Curval assented; "I make no bones about the fact I love the idea of watching fuck burn."

"Oh, I know all the ideas fuck inspires in you," said the Duc with a hearty laugh. "And even were the seed to ripen, the egg to hatch, you'd perform a combustion with the same pleasure, wouldn't you?"

"Upon my soul, I do fear I would," said Curval, as he did I know not what to Adelaide that brought a loud scream from her lips.

"And who the devil do you think you are dealing with, whore?" Curval demanded of his daughter. "What are these chirpings and squallings all about? Remember the company you are in. Can't you see that the Duc's trying to talk to me of burning, provoking, instilling good manners into hatched fuck, and what are you, pray tell me, but a little something hatched out of my balls' fuck? Duclos, I say, continue, if you please," Curval added, "for I have the feeling this bitch's tears might make me discharge. And I'd prefer not to."

And here we are, said our heroine, come to details which, bringing with them characters of a more singular piquancy, will perhaps please you more. You know of course that in Paris we have the custom of exposing the dead before the doors of houses. There was a particular gentleman, well placed in society, who used to pay me twelve francs for every one of these lugubrious objects to which, in a given evening, I could lead him; his whole delight consisted in going up with me as near to them as possible, to the very edge of the coffin if we were able, and once we had posted ourselves there, I had to frig him in such wise his fuck would shoot out upon the coffin. We used to run from one to another, would often pay our respects to three or four in an evening; it all depended upon the number I had located for him in advance, and we performed the same operation beside each of them; he never touched anything but my behind while I toiled over his prick. He was a man of about thirty, and I had his trade for at least ten years. I'm sure that, during the period of our collaboration, I made him discharge upon more than two thousand coffins.

"But would he not say something during the rite?" inquired the Duc. "Did he not speak either to you or to the corpse?"

"He would shower invectives upon the deceased," Duclos replied; for example: 'Here, you rascal, here, take it, you villain, you bugger, take my fuck along with you to hell.'"

"A very unusual mania, that one," Curval commented.

"My friend," said the Duc, "you can be certain that man was one of our own sort, and that he surely did not stop at that."

"You are quite right, my Lord," spoke up Martaine, "and I shall have occasion to bring that actor back upon the stage."

Taking advantage of the silence which succeeded Martaine's interjection, Duclos went on.

Another one, said she, carrying a more or less similar fantasy a good deal further, wanted me to keep spies on the watch near the cemeteries and to bring in word every time there was a burial of some young girl whose death had been caused by anything but a dangerous disease - he was very emphatic upon that point. As soon as I had got wind of something suitable, and he always paid me very handsomely for those discoveries, we would set off after sundown, enter the cemetery by one means or another, and heading at once for the grave our informant had indicated, above which the earth had only recently been broken, we would both fall to work, dig down to the cadaver, and when once we'd uncovered it, I'd frig him over it while he spent his time handling it and, above all, if 'twere possible, its buttocks. If perchance, and it frequently occurred, he stiffened a second time, he'd therewith shit, and have me shit also, upon the corpse, and discharge thereupon, all the while palpating whatever parts of the body he could lay his hands on.

"Oh, my, but that one does strike a response in me," said Curval, "and if I have to make my confession to you here and now, I'll assure you I've done the same thing from time to time. To be sure, I added a few little episodes I dare say our rules prevent me from describing at this point. Be that as it may, my prick's got monstrously fat; spread your thighs, Adelaide. . . ."

And I've not the faintest idea what happened next; all we know is that the couch groaned beneath its burden, unmistakable sounds of a discharge pealed from the Président niche, and I am led to suppose that, very simply and very virtuously, his honor the judge had just committed incest.

"Président," the Duc called over, "I'll wager you thought she was dead."

"Why, indeed, that's true," said Curval, "else how in the world could I have discharged?"

And hearing not another word from the several alcoves, Duclos brought that evening's stories to a close with the following one:

Lest I leave you, Messieurs, with dark images and sad thoughts, I am going to conclude the soiree with the story of the Duc de Bonnefort's passion. That young lord, whom I amused five or six times, and who used frequently to see one of my close friends for the same operation, required a woman, armed with a dildo, to frig herself naked in his presence - to frig herself, I say, both before and behind and to keep it up for three hours without a moment's interruption. He has a clock there to guide you, and if you drop the work before having completed the third hour, no payment for you. He sits opposite you, he observes you, makes you turn this way, that way, some other way, exhorts you to ply the dildo more energetically, he would have you go out of your mind with pleasure, and if indeed transported by the effects of the operation, you should really swoon away with delight, 'tis very certain you will hasten his. But if you keep your head, at the precise instant the clock strikes the third hour, up he gets, approaches you, and discharges in your face.

"Truly," quoth the Bishop, "I fail to understand, Duclos, why you didn't prefer to leave us with those other images and thoughts rather than with this innocuous picture. They had some spice to them, some color, and excited us powerfully, whereas here we have some sort of milksop business which, now that the session is over, leaves us with nothing at all in our heads."

"No, she did the right thing, insofar as I'm concerned," said Julie, who was lying with Durcet, "and I give her my warmest thanks. We'll all be allowed to go to bed more peacefully now that they don't have all those frightful ideas in their heads."

"Ah, lovely Julie, you may be very gravely mistaken," said Durcet, "for I never remember anything but the earlier one when the later one displeases me; you doubt my word? why, then pray have the kindness to follow me."

And, together with Sophie and Michette, Durcet fled into his closet to discharge I don't know how, but none the less in a manner which must not have suited Sophie, for she uttered a piercing scream and emerged from the sanctuary as red as a cockscomb.

"Well," drawled the Duc, "you surely could not have wanted to confuse her with a corpse for that stunt; for you've just made her give out the most furious sign of life."

"She was afraid, that's all," Durcet explained; "ask her what I did to her and make her tell you in a whisper."

He sent Sophie to speak to the Duc.

"Ah," said the latter aloud, "there's nothing in that either to warrant screams, or, for that matter, a discharge."

And because the supper call sounded, they suspended their conversation and their pleasures in order to go and enjoy those of the table. The orgies were celebrated rather quietly, and Messieurs retired to bed in good order; not one of them had even the appearance of being drunk; and that was extremely unusual.

The Twenty-Seventh Day

The denunciations, authorized on the previous day, began early that morning; the sultanas, having remarked that, save for Rosette, they were all listed for correction, decided that all eight of themselves ought to be included in the game and promptly went to level accusations against her. They reported she had spent the whole night farting, and as this was really only a teasing they were giving her, she had the entire harem against whom to pit her denials; her name was straightway inscribed. Everything else moved along splendidly and, except for Sophie and Zelmire, who stuttered just a little, the friends were thrilled by the new compliment they had from these brazen little hussies: "God's fuck, I've an assful of shit, wouldst care for some?" And, as a matter of fact, there was shit everywhere to be had indeed, for, from fear of some temptation to wash, the governesses had removed every pot, every receptacle, every towel, and all water. The diet of meat but no bread was beginning to warm all those little unwashed mouths, Messieurs noticed that there was already a very appreciable difference in the little girls' breaths.

"Damn my eyes!" exclaimed Curval as he withdrew his tongue from Augustine's gullet; "that now signifies at least something; kissing this one makes me stiff."

Everyone agreed there had been a distinct improvement.

As there was nothing new or out of the ordinary until coffee, we are going to transport the reader directly to the salon. Coffee was served by Sophie, Zelmire, Giton, and Narcisse. The Duc said he was perfectly sure Sophie was the sort of girl who could discharge; the experiment, in his view, had absolutely to be made. He asked Durcet to keep a close eye on her and, laying her upon a divan, he simultaneously polluted the edges of her vagina, her clitoris, and her asshole, at first with his fingers, next with his tongue; and Nature triumphed: after fifteen minutes of this, the lovely girl became uneasy, troubled, she flushed crimson, she sighed, she panted, Durcet drew Curval's and the Bishop's attention to all these manifestations, for 'twas they who'd doubted her discharging capacities; the Duc suggested that, since he had always been confident of them, it was for the others to convince themselves, and so they all fell to imbibing that young fuck, and the little rascal's cunt left all their lips moist. The Duc could not resist the experiment's lubricious appeal; he got up and, squatting over the child, discharged upon her half-opened fur, then used his fingers to work as much as possible of his seed into the interior of her cunt. His head inspired by what he was watching, Curval seized the little one and demanded something other than fuck of her; she tendered her cunning little ass, the Président glued his mouth to it, the intelligent reader will have no trouble guessing what he received therefrom. Zelmire was meanwhile amusing the Bishop: she first frigged, then sucked his fundament. And all that while, Curval was having himself frigged by Narcisse, whose ass he kissed ardently. However, no one but the Duc lost his fuck; Duclos had announced some pretty stories for that afternoon which, she promised, would outdo what she had served up the day before, and Messieurs were disposed to save their forces for the auditorium. The hour having come, they passed to their alcoves, and that interesting girl expressed herself in the following manner:

A man of whose circumstances and existence I had not previously known anything, she said, and about whom I was later to learn only a little, and, therefore, a man about whom I can give you no better than an imperfect portrait, sent me a note, and in it besought me to come to his house, in the rue Blanche-du-Rempart, at nine o'clock in the evening. I had no reason to be suspicious, his note said; although I had no acquaintance of him, I could be certain that neither would I have cause to complain were I to come as he bade me do. Two louis accompanied the letter, and despite my usual cautiousness, which ought certainly to have opposed my accepting the invitation of a man of whom I knew nothing, despite all that, I took the risk, trusting to I know not what intuition which, in a very low voice, told me I had nothing to fear. And so I went; and I arrived at the given address. I am greeted by a valet who informs me that I am to undress entirely, for, he explains, it is only if I am naked that he can introduce me into his master's apartment; I execute the order, and directly he sees me in the state desired, he takes me by the hand, and having led me through several intervening chambers, finally knocks upon a door. It opens, I enter, the valet withdraws, the door closes again; but, with what regards the amount of light in the room, there was precious little difference between that place and the inside of a hat, neither light nor air penetrated into that room from any opening whatever. No sooner am I in than a naked man comes up to me and seizes me without a word; I keep my wits about me, persuaded that the whole thing surely boiled down to nothing more than a little fuck to be shed by one means or another; that job once over with, I say to myself, I'll be quits with this whole nocturnal ceremony. And so I waste not a moment placing my hand upon his groin, with the intention of draining the venom from the monster as rapidly as possible. I discover a very large prick, very hard and also very rebellious, but scarcely have I touched it than my fingers are forced away: my opponent seems not to want me to find out anything about him; I am edged toward a stool and made to sit down. The unknown libertine plumps himself down near me, and grasping my tits one after the other, he squeezes and wrings them so violently that I protest that he is hurting me. Wherewith his brutalities cease, he leads me to an elevated sofa, and has me stretch out flat upon it; then seating himself between my parted legs, he falls to doing to my buttocks what he has just left off doing to my breasts: he palpates and squeezes them with unparalleled violence, he spreads them, compresses them again, kneads them, mauls, kisses, and bites them, he sucks my asshole, and as these reiterated attacks were less dangerous on that side than they might have been on the other, I held my peace and put up no resistance, and as I let him toil over my hindquarters I wondered what could be the purpose of this mysteriousness when, after all, the things he was doing were perfectly ordinary. I was trying to guess what he was driving at when all of a sudden my man began to utter bloodcurdling shrieks:

"Run for it, you damned whore, run for it, I tell you," he shouted, "get out of here, you bitch, for I'm discharging and won't be held responsible for your life!"

As you may readily imagine, my first movement was to leap to my feet; I spied a feeble glimmer of light - it was coming through the doorway I had entered - I dashed toward it - ran into the valet who had received me at the door - flung myself into his arms. . . . He gave me back my clothes, also gave me two louis, I left the place at once, very pleased to have got off so cheaply.

"And you had excellent cause to congratulate yourself," said Martaine, "for what you were exposed to was merely a diminutive version of his ordinary passion. I shall present the man to you again, Messieurs," that worldly dame continued, "but in a more dangerous aspect."

"I expect my characterization of him will be even darker," said Desgranges, "and I wish to join Madame Martaine in assuring you that you were exceedingly fortunate to have had to put up with no more than you did, for the same gentleman has far more unusual passions."

"But let us wait and hear his entire story before arguing the point," the Duc suggested, "and, Duclos, make haste to tell us another so as to remove from our minds the image of an individual who will unfailingly arouse us if we dwell any longer on him."

The libertine with whom next I came into contact, Duclos went on, wished to have a woman who had a very handsome bust, and as that is one of my beauties, after having exposed it to his scrutiny, he preferred me to any of my girls. But what use did that wretched libertine design to make of both my breasts and my face? He had me lie down, entirely naked, upon a divan, straddled my chest, desposited his prick between my dugs, ordered me to squeeze them together as tightly as I was able, and after a brief career, the wicked fellow inundated them with fuck while expectorating at least twenty mouthfuls of thick spittle, all of which landed on my face.

"Well," grumbled Adelaide, in whose face the Duc had just been spitting, "I fail to see any necessity for imitating that infamy. Are you done now?" she continued as she wiped her face. But the Duc had not discharged.

"I'll finish when it suits my convenience, sweet child," the Duc replied to her; "bear well in mind that, alive though you may be, you are only so in order to obey and to let be done to you what we please. Proceed with your story, Duclos, for I might do something worse and, adoring this beautiful creature as I do," he said, resorting to a bit of persiflage, "I'd hardly wish entirely to outrage her."

I know not, Messieurs, Duclos said as she resumed her discourse, whether you have ever heard tell of the Commander de Saint-Elme's passion. He had a gaming house where all who came to risk their money were deftly fleeced; but the most extraordinary part of it all was that cheating his visitors used to make the Commander's prick stiffen: every time he'd pick someone's pocket he'd discharge in his breeches, and a woman with whom I used to be on the very best terms, and whom he had been keeping for a long time, once told me that sometimes the thing would heat him to such a point that he would be obliged to go to her to seek some relief from the ardor devouring him. He did not confine himself to robbing customers at roulette; every other kind of theft was just as attractive in his eyes, and no article was safe when he was in the vicinity. Were he to dine at your table, he would make off with the silverware; when he entered your study, he'd pilfer your jewels; if near your pocket, he'd appropriate your snuffbox or your handkerchief. Everything was subject to seizure: he took a keen interest in anything provided he could get his hands on it, and everything gave him a stout erection, and would even cause him to discharge once he had made it his own.

But in that eccentricity of his he was certainly less outstanding than the parliamentary judge with whom I had to cope shortly after my arrival at Fournier's establishment, and whom I had as a client for many years: his being a rather ticklish case, he would deal with no one but me.

The jurisconsult had a little apartment, which he rented the year around, looking out upon the place de Grève; an old servant lived as a caretaker in the apartment, and her only duties were these two: to keep the premises in good order and to send word to her employer whenever preparations for an execution were visible upon the square. The judge would immediately get in touch with me, tell me to hold myself in readiness; he would disguise himself and come to fetch me in a cab, and we would repair to his little apartment.

In the salon the casement window was placed in such a manner it commanded a direct view of, and was situated near, the scaffold; we would post ourselves there, the judge and I, behind a latticework screen upon one of whose horizontal slats he rested an excellent pair of opera glasses, and while waiting for the patient to make his appearance, Themis' wise henchman would amuse himself upon a bed which had been drawn close to the window; while waiting, I say, he would kiss my ass, an episode which, by the by, pleased him enormously. Finally, the crowd's hubbub would announce the victim's arrival, the man of the gown would return to his place at the window and would have me take mine beside him, with the injunction to frig his prick gently, proportioning my strokes to the progress of the execution he was about to watch, in such sort that the sperm would not escape until the moment the patient rendered up his soul unto God. Everything was arranged, the criminal mounted upon the platform, the jurist contemplated him; the nearer the patient approached to death, the more furious became the villain's prick in my hands. The axe was raised, the axe was brought down, 'twas the instant he discharged: "Ah, gentle Jesus!" he'd say, "double-fucked Christ! How I'd like to be the executioner myself, and how much better than that I'd swing the blade!"

Moreover, his pleasures' impressions would be measured by the method of execution, a hanging produced in him little more than an exceedingly mild sensation, a man being broken on the wheel threw him into a delirium, but were the criminal to be either burned alive or quartered, my client would swoon away from pleasure. Man or woman, it made no difference to him.

"I dare say," he once remarked, "that only a pregnant woman would have a stronger effect upon me, and, unfortunately, the thing cannot be brought about."

"But, your honor," I said to him upon another occasion, "through your public function you have cooperated in the destruction of this luckless victim."

"Assuredly, yes," he replied, "and that precisely is what creates all the diversion for me; I have been judging for a good thirty years and have never pronounced any but the death sentence."

"And do you suppose," I said, "that you have not, if only a little, to reproach yourself for the death of these people, which so resembles murder?"

"Splendid," he murmured; "must one, however, look at the matter so closely?"

"But in society such a thing is called a horror," I protested.

"Oh," said he, "one has got to learn how to make the best of the horror; there is in horror matter to produce an erection, you see, and the reason therefor is quite simple: this thing, however frightful you wish to imagine it, ceases to be horrible for you immediately it acquires the power to make you discharge; it is, hence, no longer horrible save in the eyes of others, but who is to assure me that the opinion of others, almost always erroneous or faulty in every other connection, is not equally so in this instance? There is nothing," he pursued, "either fundamentally good, nor anything fundamentally evil; everything is relative, relative to our point of view, that is to say, to our manners, to our opinions, to our prejudices. This point once established, it is extremely possible that something, perfectly indifferent in itself, may indeed be distasteful in your eyes, but may be most delicious in mine; and immediately I find it pleasing, immediately I find it amusing, regardless of our inability to agree in assigning a character to it, should I not be a fool to deprive myself of it merely because you condemn it? Come, come, my dear Duclos, a man's life is something of such slight importance that one may sport with it as much as one likes, just as one might with a cat's life or with that of a dog; 'tis up to the feeble and weak to defend themselves, they have virtually the same weapons we possess. And since you are so scrupulous," my man added, "my stars! what would you think of the fantasy of one of my friends!"

And, with your Lordships' leave, I shall terminate the evening by giving, as my fifth story, the account of the taste the judge related me.

This philosophical jurist told me that his friend would deal only with women scheduled to be executed. The nearer the moment that they are delivered to him borders on the moment they are going to perish, the better he pays for them. But he insists that the conference be held after they have been notified of their sentence. Thanks to his position in society within easy reach of this sort of prize, he never lets one slip through his fingers and," my informant went on, "I have seen him pay up to one hundred louis for this kind of tête-à-tête. However, he does not carnally enjoy them, or rather he requires nothing of them but that they exhibit their buttocks and shit before his eyes; for taste of shit, he maintains, there is nothing to equal what one gets from a woman who has just heard the death penalty pronounced against her. He will go to any lengths to obtain these private interviews, and of course, as you may well suppose, he does not wish to be known by the victim. He sometimes passes himself off as the confessor, or at other times as a friend of the family, and his proposals are always fortified by the promise that, if they indulge his little whimsies, he may very possibly be able to be of help to them.

"And when he has finished, when he has satisfied himself, by what, my dear Duclos," said the judge, "do you fancy he concludes his operation? Just as I do, my worthy friend; he reserves his fuck for the climax, and releases it at last when before his delighted gaze the condemned person expires."

"Ah, that's true villainy," I told him.

"Villainy?" he interrupted. "My dear child, all that's mere verbiage, prattle. Nothing's villainous if it causes an erection, and the single crime that exists in this world is to refuse oneself anything that might produce a discharge."

"And so it was he refused himself nothing," said Martaine; "Madame Desgranges and I shall have, or so I hope, occasion to entertain the company with several lubricious and criminal anecdotes relating to the same personage."

"Excellent," said Curval, "for there's a man I'm already hugely fond of. That's just the way one should reason about one's pleasures, and his philosophy pleases me infinitely. It is truly incredible the way man, already restricted in all his amusements, in all his faculties, seeks further to narrow the scope of his existence through his contemptible prejudices. For example, it is not commonly suspected what limitations he who has raised up murder as a crime has imposed upon all his delights; he has deprived himself of a hundred joys, each more delicious than the other, by daring to adopt the odious illusion which founds that particular nonsense. What the devil difference can it make to Nature whether there are one, ten, twenty, five hundred more or fewer human beings on earth? Conquerors, heroes, tyrants - do they inhibit themselves by that absurd law? Do you hear them saying that we ought not do unto others that which onto ourselves we would not have done? Forsooth, my friends, I tell you frankly that I tremble, I groan when I hear fools dare to tell me that such is the law of Nature, etc. . . . Merciful Heaven! all athirst for crimes and murders, 'tis to see to it they are committed, to inspire them Nature has wrought her law, and the one commandment she graves deep in our hearts is to satisfy ourselves at no matter whose expense. But patience; I shall perhaps soon have a better occasion to expand upon these questions, I have made the profoundest study of them, and, in communicating my conclusions to you, I hope to convince you, as convinced am I, that the single way of serving Nature is blindly to respond to her desires, of whatever kind they may be, because, for the sake of maintaining the divine balance she has struck universally, vice being quite as necessary to the general scheme as virtue, she is wont to urge us to do this, now to do that, depending upon what is at the moment necessary to her design. Yes, my friends, I shall someday discuss all that before you, but for the moment I must be still, for I have fuck that needs spilling, that devilish fellow at the executions has made my poor balls swell dreadfully."

And the Président departed for the boudoir at the end of the corridor, with him went Desgranges and Fanchon, his two dear friends, for they were as great scoundrels as he; and with him also went Aline, Sophie, Hébé, Antinoüs, and Zéphyr. I have little definite information upon what the libertine took it into his head to do in the midst of those seven persons, but his absence was prolonged and he was heard to shout: "Come, damn it, turn this way, do you hear? But that's not what I told you to do" and other ill-humored remarks interspersed with oaths to which he was known to be greatly addicted while enacting scenes of debauchery; the women finally returned, their faces very red, their hair very untidy, and with the air of having been furiously mauled and pawed in every sense. Meanwhile, the Duc and his two friends had scarcely been marking time, but of their number only the Bishop had discharged, and in a manner so extraordinary that we had better say nothing about it at present.

They went to the supper table, where Curval philosophized a little more, for, with that man, passions had not the least influence upon doctrines; firm in his principles, he was just as much an atheist, an iconoclast, a criminal after having shed his fuck as when, before, he had been in a lubricious ferment, and that precisely is how all wise, level-headed people should be. Never ought fuck be allowed to dictate or affect one's principles; 'tis for one's principles to regulate one's manner of shedding it. And whether one is stiff, or whether one is not, one's philosophy, acting independently of passions, should always remain the same.

The amusement at the orgies consisted in a verification which had not until then been undertaken, but which was interesting none the less: Messieurs were moved to decide who amonst the boys, who amongst the girls had the most beautiful ass. And so, first of all, they had the eight boys form a line: they were standing erect . . . yes, but, on the other hand, they were made to bend forward just a little, for that is the only way properly to judge an ass. The examination was both very long and very severe, opinions clashed, opinions were reversed, rectified, each ass was inspected fifteen times, and the apple was generally accorded to Zéphyr; it was unanimously agreed that it was physically impossible to find anything more perfect, better molded, better cleft.

Next they turned to the girls, who adopted the same posture. Deliberation was at first very slow, very prolonged, it proved all but impossible to decide from amongst Augustine, Zelmire, and Sophie. Augustine, taller, better made than the other two, would doubtless have triumphed had the jury been composed of painters; but libertines call rather for grace than exactitude, for fullness sooner than regularity. There was in her disfavor a shade too much of the slender and of the delicate; the two other contestants offered a carnation so fresh, so healthy, so plump, buttocks so fair and so round, a back whose line descended so voluptuously, that Augustine was eliminated from further consideration. But how were they to decide between the two who remained? After ten rounds of balloting, opinion was still equally divided.

At last, Zelmire won the prize; the two charming winners were assembled, were kissed, handled, frigged for the rest of the evening, Zelmire was ordered to frig Zéphyr who, discharging like a musket, afforded, in the throes of pleasure, the most entrancing spectacle; then, in his turn, he frigged the young lady who all but fainted away in his arms, and all these scenes, of unspeakable lubricity, brought about the loss of the Duc's fuck and of his brother's, but only mildly stirred Curval and Durcet, who agreed that what they needed were scenes far less Arcadian, far less ethereal if their weary old souls were to be cheered, and that all these winsome frolickings were only good for youngsters. They went to bed, and Curval, plunged into the thick of fresh infamies, compensated himself for the tender pastorals he had been obliged to witness.

The Twenty-Eighth Day

'Twas a wedding day, and the turn of Cupidon and Rosette to be united in holy matrimony, and by still another fateful combination of accidents, both were listed for punishment that evening. As no one was found at fault that morning, that entire part of the day was devoted to the wedding ceremony, and when it was over, the newlyweds were brought into the salon to see what they would do together. The mysteries of Venus were, as we know, often celebrated in these children's presence; although none of them had so far taken an active part in them, they were well enough grounded in the theory of the thing to be able to execute about everything that there is to do. Cupidon, his prick very rigidly aloft, insinuated his little peg between Rosette's thighs, and she lent herself to his maneuvers with all the candor of the most thorough innocence; the young lad was managing so nicely that he was probably well on the way to success when the Bishop, taking him in his arms, had put in himself what, I fancy, the child would greatly have liked to put into his little wife; all the while he perforated the Bishop's ample hole, he regarded her with eyes which declared his regrets, but she was herself soon occupied: the Duc thigh-fucked her. Curval stepped up in the lewdest fashion to fondle the ass of the Bishop's little fucker, and as that pretty little ass was found, in keeping with instructions, in the desired state, he licked it and began to stiffen. Durcet was up to the same tricks with the little girl the Duc was holding with her chest pressed to his.

However, no one discharged, and Messieurs went in to dine; the young bride and groom, who had been admitted to the table, also appeared to serve coffee, together with Augustine and Zélamir. And the voluptuous Augustine, deeply distressed over not having won the prize for beauty the night before, had, as though sulking, left her hair in just that kind of disarray which rendered her a thousand times more intriguing to see. Curval was stirred by the sight, and, examining her buttocks:

"I fail to understand how it happened that this little rascal did not win the palm," said he, "for devil take me if in all the world there exists a finer ass than this one here."

So saying, he pried it open, and inquired of Augustine whether she were ready to do her old friend a great kindness. "Oh, yes," she replied, "a very great one indeed, for I really have to get rid of what I have there." Curval rests her upon a sofa and, kneeling before that radiant behind, he devours its turd in a flash.

"Sacred name of God," says he, licking his lips, turning toward his colleagues, and pointing to the prick straining against his abdomen, "I'm in a state for furiously undertaking something or other."

"And what would it be?" asked the Duc, who was very fond of making the Président utter horrors when he was in that particular state.

"What?" said Curval. "Why, whatever infamy you wish to propose, even were it to dismember Nature and unhinge the universe."

"Come along now," said Durcet, upon seeing him cast furious glances in the direction of Augustine, "come along, let's go listen to Duclos, it's story time. I'm persuaded," he went on, addressing the others, "that if he gets the bit in his teeth, that poor little duckling is going to spend a trying quarter of an hour."

"Oh, yes!" said the inflamed Président, "a very trying one, I can vouch for that."

"Curval," said the Duc, whose prick was nodding in the air like a vengeful lance, and who had just finished eliciting some shit from Rosette, "let the others entrust the harem to the two of us, and two hours from now we'll have turned in a capital performance."

Durcet and the Bishop, at the moment calmer than their coproprietors, each took one of them by the arm, and it was thus, that is to say, breeches about their ankles and pricks aloft, that those libertines made their solemn entrance into the auditorium, where the assembly was already gathered and ready to hear Duclos' latest offerings; she, having anticipated, from those two gentlemen's state, that she would soon be interrupted, began in these terms:

A nobleman at the court, aged about fifty-five, came and asked me for one of the prettiest girls I could lay my hands on. He said nothing to indicate his favorite mania, and to satisfy any need he might have, I gave him a young dressmaker who had never yet attended a party and who was incontestably one of the loveliest creatures France could boast. I introduce them to each other and, curious to observe what is about to transpire, I quickly repair to my post at the spy hole.

"Now where in the devil has Madame Duclos been," he opened by saying, "to find an ugly chit like yourself? Has she been raking over someone's dung heap? You must have been servicing a couple of soldiers when they came to fetch you here."

And the young lady, blushing to the ears with shame, for she had been forewarned of nothing, was at a loss to know what tack to take.

"Well, get your clothes off then," the courtier continued. "My God, but you're a clumsy slut! I've seen ugly whores in my life, but never one the likes of you, nor so stupid. Well, then? Are we going to be able to get this over with today? Ah, yes, there's that body they've been praising to the skies. Sacred Mother, what are those dugs! you'd think they'd been grafted from an old cow."

And he fell to handling them brutally.

"And this belly! What could have caused those wrinkles? You surely haven't whelped twenty children at your age?"

"Not one, Monsieur, I assure you."

"Oh, I see, not one, eh! That's how all these bitches talk; listen to them a while and they'll be trying to convince you they're all virgins. . . . Well, move about, will you, turn around . . . infamous ass you've got dragging there. Flabby, disgusting buttocks - I understand now why they described you as unusual. It must have taken a lot of kicks in the ass to have arranged things this way."

And you will allow me, Messieurs, to remind you that the ass he was referring to was as beautiful an ass as one could find anywhere. Be that as it may, the girl began to grow upset; I could almost make out the flutterings of her little heart, and I saw her lovely eyes become worried, then misty. And the more troubled she became, the more energetically the scoundrel sought to mortify her. I cannot possibly remember all the ungenerous things he said to her; one would not dare say anything more stinging, more biting, to the vilest, most infamous of creatures. Finally, a lump welled up in her throat and her tears began to flow; 'twas for this last development the libertine, who had been polluting himself with might and main, had reserved the bouquet of his litanies. 'Tis impossible, once again, to render for you all the horrible observations he made upon her skin, her figure, her features, the sickening odor he declared she exhaled, how he criticized her bearing, her mind; in brief, he hunted up everything, he invented everything to humiliate her pride, and discharged all over her while vomiting atrocities a street sweeper would never dare utter. This scene had a most amusing outcome: the girl seemed to have taken it as a lesson, and it prompted her to take an oath; she swore never again to expose herself to such an adventure, and a week later I learned she had entered a convent for the rest of her life. I related this to the young man, who found it all prodigiously funny, and who later asked me for someone else to convert.

Another, Duclos continued, requested me to find him extremely sensitive girls who were awaiting news of an event whose unfavorable outcome might cause them an access of profoundest grief. I had unending difficulty finding anything to answer this description, and it was virtually impossible to pawn off a makeshift upon the connoisseur. He knew what he was about, had been playing the game for ages, and one glance was sufficient to tell him whether the blow he was to strike would reach the mark. And so I made no effort to deceive him, and managed somehow always to get him girls who were in the mental state he desired. I one day produced a maid who was expecting word from Dijon of a young man she idiolized and whose name was Valcourt. I presented the girl to the libertine.

"Where do you come from, Mademoiselle?" he asked her in a decent and respectful tone.

"From Dijon, Monsieur."

"From Dijon? Why, that's a strange coincidence, for I have just this instant had a letter from Dijon containing tidings which have sore distressed me."

"And what is the trouble?" the girl asked with great interest; "I know everyone in the town, this news you have heard may be of some importance to me."

"Oh, not at all," our man replied, "it relates only to me; it has to do with the death of a young man - I was keenly fond of him, he had just married a girl whom my brother, who also lives in Dijon, had found for him, a girl to whom he was passionately attached, and the day after the wedding, he suddenly died."

"His name, Monsieur, if you please?"

"His name was Valcourt; he was originally from Paris," and the libertine named the street and the number at which Valcourt had lived. "You cannot possibly have known him, though."

But the young girl had collapsed in a faint.

Therewith our libertine, beside himself with delight, muttered a string of oaths, unbuttoned his breeches, and set to frigging himself upon her supine body. "Ah, by Christ! that's what I want. Make haste now, hurry," he said to himself, "the buttocks, I only need the buttocks to discharge."

And turning her over, and pulling up her skirts, he darts seven or eight jets of fuck upon the motionless girl's ass, and then takes himself off without a thought either for the consequences of what he has said, or for what will become of the unhappy creature.

"And did she croak as a result?" inquired Curval, who was being fucked at a great rate.

"No," Duclos admitted, "but she fell ill and lay six weeks at death's door."

"Very fine stunt, oh my, yes!" said the Duc. "But," that scoundrel went on, "I should have preferred it had your man chosen the period of her menstruation for his disclosure."

"Yes," Curval said, "quite. But, Monsieur le Duc, tell us all the truth: your prick's in the air, I can sense it from here: you would have preferred that she drop dead on the spot."

"Well, have it your own way," called back the Duc. "Since you'd wish it so, I consent, for, you know, I've not many scruples over a girl's death."

"Durcet," said the Bishop, "if you don't send those two rascals out to discharge, there'll be a merry to-do this evening."

"Ah, by the Almighty's balls," Curval shouted toward the Bishop's niche, "you're afraid for your flock. But what difference would two more or two less make? Well, Monsieur le Duc, you've heard Monseigneur the Bishop's suggestion, let's go to the boudoir, but we'll go together, for it's all too evident these other gentlemen wish to avoid a scandal tonight."

No sooner said than done; and our two libertines had themselves followed by Zelmire, Augustine, Sophie, Colombe, Cupidon, Narcisse, Zélamir, Adonis, escorted by Bum-Cleaver, Invictus, Thérèse, Fanchon, Constance, and Julie. A brief interval ensued, then two or three women's screams were heard, then the bellowings of our two lechers, who were disgorging their fuck simultaneously. Augustine reappeared dabbing at her bleeding nose, Adelaide's breast was covered by a scarf. As for Julie, always libertine enough and clever enough to get through any ordeal unscathed, she was laughing like one in hysterics and saying that had it not been for her they'd never have been able to discharge. The rest of the troupe returned; Zélamir and Adonis still had their buttocks smeared with fuck. Having assured their confreres they had conducted themselves with all possible decency and modesty, that they might have nothing to be reproached for, and that now, perfectly calm, they were in a fit state to listen, Messieurs gave Duclos the signal to proceed and she did so in the following terms:

I sincerely regret Monsieur de Curval's precipitate haste to relieve his needs, said that superb creature, for I had two pregnant-woman stories to tell him, and they would perhaps have afforded him some real pleasure. I know his taste for the fruit-laden, and I am certain that, had he a flicker of warmth left in his bowels, these two tales would divert him.

"Tell them all the same," said Curval. "You are aware, I trust, that fucking has not the least effect upon my sentiments, and that the moment when I am most infatuated with evil is always the moment after I have performed it."

Very well, said Duclos, I have seen a man whose mania was straitly connected with observing a woman give birth; he would frig himself when seeing her labor pains begin, and used to discharge squarely upon the infant's head directly it hove into view.

A second would perch a seven-month-pregnant woman upon an isolated pedestal at least fifteen feet high. She was obliged to keep her balance, and her mind on what she was about, for if by mischance she were to have grown dizzy, she and her issue would have been definitively ruined. The libertine I speak of, very little affected by the situation of the poor creature he paid for her acrobatic skill, kept her where she was until he had discharged, and frigged himself before her while exclaiming: "Ah, the lovely statue, the beautiful ornament, the empress upon her dais!"

"Well, Curval, you'd have shaken that column, wouldn't you, eh?" said the Duc.

"Ah, not at all, you're mistaken; I have too much respect for Nature and her works. Is not the most interesting of them all the propagation of our species? is it not a kind of miracle we ought to adore incessantly, and ought we not to have the warmest interest in those who perform it? For my part, I never see a pregnant woman without being melted; think for a moment what a marvelous thing is a woman who, just like an oven, can make a little snot hatch deep in her vagina. Is there anything more beautiful, anything quite as fetching as that? Constance, dear girl, come hither, I beseech you, come let me kiss the sanctuary wherein, at this very moment, such a profound mystery is in progress."

And as he found her right there in his alcove, he was not long searching after the temple he wished to minister to. But there is reason to suppose Constance took a somewhat different view of his intentions, or, at least, that she only half believed his professions, for an instant later she was heard to vent a scream which bore no relationship at all to the consequences of a reverence or an homage. Then silence closed again; observing that all lay quiet, Duclos concluded her narrations with the following little tale:

454   Marquis de Sade

I knew a man, said she, whose passion consisted in hearing children wail and cry; he had to have a mother with a child of no more than three or four. He required this mother to give her offspring a sound thrashing; it had to be done before him, and when the little creature, aroused by this treatment, began to bawl, the mother had next to catch hold of the rogue's prick and frig it industriously, directing the glans at the child, in whose face he would discharge when the little one was singing his loudest.

"Now, I wager," the Bishop said to Curval, "that fellow was no more a friend of increase than you are."

"I dare say not," Curval conceded. "He must be, according to the argument of a lady reputed to possess a great fund of wit, he must be, I say, a great scoundrel; for, in keeping with the development of her thought, any man who loves neither animals, nor children, nor swollen-bellied women, is a monster fit to be put on the rack. Well, by that agreeable old fool's judgment, my case is heard and decided and writ off the agenda," said the Président, "for I certainly have no affection for any one of those three things."

And as it was late, and as interruptions had consumed a sizable portion of the séance, they went straight to supper. At table, they debated the following questions: what need has man for sensibility? and is it or is it not useful to his happiness? Curval proved that it was nothing if not dangerous, and that it was the first sentiment, this one of human kindness, one had to extirpate from children, by early making them grow accustomed to the most ferocious spectacles. Each of them having differently approached the problem, by many and long detours they all finally ended up agreeing with Curval. Supper over, the Duc and he were of the opinion the women and youngsters should be sent to bed, and they proposed the orgies be made an entirely masculine tournament; everyone concurred, the idea was adopted, Messieurs enchambered themselves with the eight fuckers and spent almost all the night having themselves fucked and drinking liqueurs. They stumbled to bed two hours before dawn, and the morrow brought with it both events and stories the reader will perhaps find entertaining if he will give himself the trouble to read what follows.

The Twenty-Ninth Day

There is a proverb - and what splendid things proverbs are - there is one, I say, which maintains that the appetite is restored by eating. This proverb, coarse, nay, vulgar though it be, has none the less a very extensive significance: to wit, that, by dint of performing horrors, one's desire to commit additional ones is whetted, and that the more of them one commits, the more of them one desires.

Well, such exactly was the case with our insatiable libertines. Through unpardonable harshness, through a detestable refinement of debauchery, they, as we know, had condemned their wives to render them the vilest and most unclean services upon their emergence from the privy. They were not content with that, and on the 29th of November they proclaimed a new (which appeared to have been inspired by the previous night's sodomistical libertinage), a new law, I say, which ruled that, as of the 1st of December, those wives would serve as the only pots to their masters' needs, and that the said needs, both the greater and the lesser, would never be executed anywhere save in their wives' mouths; that whenever Messieurs were moved to satisfy these fundamental urges, they would be followed about by four sultanas who would, once the urge had been satisfied, render them the service which heretofore the wives had rendered them and which the said wives would hereafter be unable to render them, since they were going to have graver employment; that the four officiating sultanas would be Colombe for Curval, Hébé for the Duc, Rosette for the Bishop, and Michette for Durcet; and that the least error or failure committed in the course of either of these operations, whether in the course of that involving the wives or in that other involving the four little girls, would be punished with prodigious severity.

The poor women had no sooner learned of this new regulation than they wept and wrung their hands, unfortunately, it was all but in vain. It was however ordained that each wife would serve her husband, and Aline the Bishop, and that for this one operation Messieurs would not be allowed to exchange them. Two of the duennas were ordered to take turns presenting themselves for the same service, and the time for their rendering it was unalterably fixed at the hour Messieurs would depart the evening orgies; it was decided that Messieurs would at all times proceed to this ritual in each other's company, that while the elders were operating, the four sultanas, while waiting to give the service required of them, would make conspicuous display of their asses, and that the elders would move from one anus to the next, to press it, open it, and encourage it generally to function. This regulation promulgated, the friends proceeded that morning to administer the punishments which had not been distributed the night before because of the decision to perform the orgies with the assistance of men only.

The operation was undertaken in the sultanas' quarters; they were all eight taken care of, and after them came Adelaide, Aline, and Cupidon, who also were included upon the fatal list; the ceremony, with the details and all the protocol observed under such circumstances, dragged on for nearly four hours, at the end of which their Lordships descended to dinner, their heads swimming, especially Curval's head, for he, prodigiously cherishing these exercises, never took part in them without the most definite erection. As for the Duc, he had discharged in the thick of the fray, and so had Durcet. This latter, who was beginning to develop a very mischievous libertine testiness toward his wife Adelaide, was unable to discipline her without shudders of pleasure which ultimately loosened his seed.

Dinner was, as usual, followed by coffee; Messieurs, disposed to have some neat little asses on hand, had appointed Zéphyr and Giton to serve the cups, and to these two might have added a large number of others; but there was not one sultana whose ass was in anything like an appropriate state. In accordance with schedule, the coffee-serving team was rounded out by Colombe and Michette.

456 Marquis de Sade

Curval, examining Colombe's ass, the bedaubed condition whereof, in part the Président's own work, generated some singular desires in him, thrust his prick between her thighs from behind, while so doing fondling her buttocks vivaciously; now and again, as it moved to and fro, his engine, as if through maladdress, nudged up against the dear little hole he would have given a kingdom to perforate. For a moment he studied it attentively.

"O sacred God," he said, turning to his friends, "I'll pay the society two hundred louis on the spot for leave to fuck this ass."

Reason prevailed, however, he kept a grip upon himself and did not even discharge. But the Bishop had Zéphyr discharge into his mouth and yielded up his own sanctified fuck as he swallowed that delicious child's; Durcet had himself kicked in the ass by Giton, then had Giton shit, and remained chaste. Messieurs removed to the auditorium, where each father, by an arrangement which was encountered rather frequently, had his daughter on his couch beside him; breeches lowered, they listened to our talented storyteller's five tales.

It seemed as though, since the day I had so exactly executed Fournier's pious will, happiness smiled ever more warmly upon my house, said that distinguished whore. Never had I had so many wealthy acquaintances.

The Benedictine prior, among my most faithful clients, one day came to tell me that, having heard of a quite remarkable fantasy and having subsequently observed it performed by one of his friends who was wild about it, he had a powerful desire to enact it himself, and hence he asked me for a girl well fledged with hair. I gave him a big creature of twenty-eight years who had veritable thickets both under the arms and upon her mound. "Splendid," said the prior upon beholding the goods, "that's just what I need." And as he and I were very closely attached to each other, as we had taken many a gay tumble together, he made no objections when I requested leave to watch him at work. He had the girl undress and half recline upon a couch, her arms extended above her head, and, armed with a sharp pair of scissors he set to cropping the hear beneath her arms. Once he had clipped away every bit of it, he turned to her mound, and barbered it also, but so thoroughly that when he was done one would never have believed the least vestige of hair had ever grown on any of the areas he had worked over. The job done, he kissed the parts he'd shorn and spurted his fuck upon that hairless mound, in a perfect ecstasy over the fruit of his labor.

Another required a doubtless much more bizarre ceremony: I am thinking now of the Duc de Florville; I was advised to bring him one of the most beautiful women I could find. A manservant welcomed us at the Duc's mansion, and we entered by a side door.

"We will now prepare this attractive creature," the valet said to me; "for there are several adjustments to be made in order that she be in a state to amuse my Lord the Duc . . . come with me."

By way of detours and corridors equally somber and immense, we finally reached a lugubrious suite of rooms, lighted only by six tapers placed on the floor around a mattress covered with black satin; the entire room was hung in funereal stuffs, and the sight, as we entered, woke the worst apprehensions in us.

"Calm your fears," said our guide, "you will not suffer the least hurt; but be ready for anything," he added, speaking to the girl, "and above all see to it that you do everything I tell you."

He had her remove all her clothes, loosened her coiffure, and indicated she was to leave her hair, which was superb, to hang free. Next, he bade her lie down upon the mattress surrounded by tall candles, enjoined her to feign death and to be exceedingly careful, throughout the whole of the scene to follow, neither to stir nor breathe more deeply than she had to.

"For if unhappily my master, who is going to imagine you are really dead, perceives you are only pretending, he'll be furious, will leave you at once, and surely will not pay you a sou."

Directly he had placed the girl upon the pallet in the attitude of a corpse, he had her twist her mouth in such a way as to give the impression of pain, her eyes too were to suggest she had died in agony; he scattered her tresses over her naked breast, lay a dagger beside her, and near her heart smeared chicken's blood, painting a wound the size of one's hand.

"I repeat to you," he said to the girl, "be not afraid, you have nothing to say, nothing to do, you have simply to remain absolutely still and to draw your breath at the moments when you see he is farthest from you. And now, Madame," the valet said to me, "we may withdraw from the room. Come with me, please; that you not be worried about your girl, I am going to place you where you will be able to hear and watch the entire scene."

We quit the room, leaving the girl, who was not without her misgivings, but whom the manservant's speeches had reassured somewhat. He conducts me to a small chamber adjoining the apartment where the mystery is to be celebrated, and through a crack between two panels, over which the black material was hung, I could hear everything. To see was still easier, for the material was only crepe, I could distinguish objects on the other side quite as clearly as if I had been in the room itself.

The valet drew the cord that rang a bell, that was the signal, and a few minutes later we saw a tall, thin, wasted man of about sixty enter upon the stage. Beneath a loose-flowing dressing robe of India taffeta he was completely naked. He halted upon coming through the doorway; I had best tell you now that the Duc, supposing he was absolutely alone, had not the faintest idea his actions were being observed.

"Ah, what a beautiful corpse!" he exclaimed at once. "Death . . . 'tis beautiful to behold. . . . But, my God, what's this!" said he upon catching sight of the blood, the knife. "It must have been an assassin . . . only a moment ago . . . ah, Great God, how stiff he must be now, the person who did that."

And, frigging himself:

"How I would have loved to see him strike that blow!"

And fondling the corpse, moving his hand over its belly:

"Pregnant? . . . No, apparently not. What a pity."

And continuing to explore with his hands:

"Superb flesh! It's still warm . . . a lovely breast."

Wherewith he bent over her and kissed her mouth with incredible emotion:

"Still drooling," he said; "how I adore this saliva!"

And once again he drove his tongue almost into her gullet; no one could possibly have played the role more convincingly than did that girl, she lay stock-still, and whenever the Duc drew near she ceased entirely to breathe. Finally, he rolled her over upon her stomach:

"I must have a look at this lovely ass," he murmured.

And after having scanned it:

"Jesus Christ! What matchless buttocks!"

And then he opened them, kissed them, and we distinctly saw him place his tongue in that cunning little hole.

"Oh, upon my word!" he cried, sweating with admiration, "this is certainly one of the most superb corpses I have ever seen in my life; happy he who took this girl's life, oh, enviable person, what pleasure he must have known!"

The very idea made him discharge; he was lying beside her, squeezing her, his thighs glued against her buttocks, and he discharged upon her asshole, giving out unbelievable signs of pleasure, and, as he yielded his sperm, crying like a demon:

"Ah fuck, fuck, ah good God, if only I had killed her, if only I had been the one!"

Thus the operation ended, the libertine rose and disappeared; we entered the room to resurrect our brave little friend. She was exhausted, unable to budge: constraint, fright, everything had numbed her senses, she was about ready in all earnestness to become the character she had just personified so expertly. We departed with four louis the valet gave us; as you may well imagine, he doubtless surrendered no more than half of our pay.

"Ye living gods!" cried Curval, "now that is a passion! To say the least, the thing has flavor, aroma."

"I'm as stiff as a mule," said the Duc; "I'll stake my fortune on it, that fellow had other tricks up his sleeve."

"Right you are, my Lord," said Martaine; "he now and again employed a greater realism. I think Madame Desgranges and I have evidence to prove it to you."

"And what the devil are you going to do while waiting?" Curval asked the Duc.

"Don't disturb me, don't disturb me," the Duc shouted, "I'm fucking my daughter, I'm pretending she's dead."

"Rascal," Curval rejoined, "that makes two crimes in your head."

"Ah, by fuck," said the Duc, "would that they were more real. . . ."

And his impure seed burst into Julie's vagina.

"Well now, Duclos, what comes next? Go on with your stories," said he as soon as he had finished his affair, "go on, my dear friend, don't allow the Président to discharge, for I can hear him over there effecting an incestuous connection with his daughter; the funny little fellow is working up some evil ideas in his head; his parents have made me his tutor, they expect me to keep an eye on his behavior and I'd be distressed were it to become perverted."

"Too late," said Curval, "too late, old man, I'm discharging; ah, Christ be doublefucked, 'tis a pretty death."

And while encunting Adelaide, the scoundrel fancied to himself, as had the Duc, that he was fucking his murdered daughter; O incredible distraction of the mind of a libertine, who can naught hear, naught see, but he would imitate it that instant!

"Duclos, you must indeed continue," said the Bishop, "else I'll be seduced by those bawdy fellows' example, and in my present state I might carry things a good deal further than they."

Some time after that last adventure I went alone to the home of another libertine, said Duclos, whose mania, more humiliating perhaps, was not however so saturnine. He receives me in a drawing room whose floor was covered with a very handsome rug. He bids me remove all I am wearing and then, having me get down on my hands and knees:

"Let's see," says he, stroking and patting the heads of two great Danes lying on either side of his chair, "let's see whether you are as nimble and quick as my dogs. Ready? Go get it!"

And with that he tosses some large roasted chestnuts on the floor; speaking to me as if I were an animal, he says:

"Go fetch them!"

I run on all fours after a chestnut, thinking it best to play the game with good humor and enter into the spirit of his eccentricity; I run along, I say, I endeavor to bring back the chestnuts, but the two dogs, also springing forward, outrun me, seize the chestnuts, and take them back to their master.

"Well, you're clearly in need of some practice before you'll be in good form," said the gentleman; "it's not, by chance, that you are afraid my dogs might bite you? Don't worry yourself about them, my dear, they'll do you no harm, but inwardly, you know, they'll look down upon you if they see that you're a clumsy creature. So let's try again - try harder. Here's your chance to get even . . . bring it back!"

Another chestnut thrown, another victory carried off by the dogs, another defeat for me; well, to make a long story short, the game lasted two hours, during which I managed to get the chestnut only once and to bring it back in my mouth to him who had thrown it. But whether triumphant or bested, never did the dogs do me any harm; on the contrary, they seemed to be having a good time playing and to be amused by me, quite as though I were a dog too.

"That's enough," said the gentleman. "You've worked hard enough; it's time to eat."

He rang, a servant entered.

"Bring some food for my animals," he said.

And a moment later the servant returned, carrying an ebony feeding trough which was filled with a kind of very delicate chopped meat. He set the trough on the floor.

"Very well," my gentlemen said to me, "get down and eat with my dogs, and try to put on a better show while eating than you did while playing."

There was nothing for me to reply; I had to obey. Still on all fours, I plunged my head into the trough; the trough was very clean, the food very good, I fell to munching away beside the dogs, which very politely moved over, leaving me peacefully to my share. And that was the critical instant for our libertine; the humiliation of a woman, the degradation to which he reduced her, wonderfully stimulated his spirits.

"Oh, the buggress!" said he, frigging himself assiduously, "the tramp, look at her there, gorging herself with the dogs, that's how one should deal with all women, and if they were to be handled thus, we'd have no more sauciness from them, ah no! Domestic animals like those dogs, why should they not be treated in the same way? Ah! impudent bitch that you are, whore, slime, scum!" he cried, stepping near and spraying his fuck over my bum, "buggress, I'll have you eat with my dogs."

And that was the end of that; our man vanished, I dressed promptly, and lying by my mantelet I found two louis, the current price and doubtless the one the rogue was accustomed to paying for his pleasures.

At this point, Messieurs, Duclos continued, I am obliged to retrace my steps and, by way of conclusion to the evening's narrations, to recount two adventures I had during my youth. As they are somewhat on the strong side, they would have been out of place amidst the mild escapades with which you had me start at the beginning of the month; and so I set them aside and kept them for the end of my contribution.

I was only sixteen at the time, and was still with Madame Guérin; I had been sent to the home of a man of unchallenged distinction, and, upon arriving there, was simply told to wait in a small antechamber, told to be at my ease, told to be sure to obey the lord who would soon be coming to sport with me; but they were careful not to tell me anything else: I'd not have had such a fright if I'd been forewarned, and our libertine would certainly not have had as much pleasure. I had been in the room for about an hour when the door opened at last. It was the master of the house himself.

"What the devil are you doing here," he demanded with an air of surprise, "at this time of day? . . . What about it, whore!" he cries, seizing me by the throat and all but choking the breath out of me, "what about it! Has the slut come here to rob me?"

He calls to someone, a trustworthy servant immediately appears.

"La Fleur," says his angry master, "I've got a thief here; she was hiding when I came in. Strip her and prepare to carry out the orders I give you."

La Fleur does as he is told, I am despoiled of my clothes in a trice, they are tossed aside as they are peeled off my body.

"Very well," the libertine says to his servant, "go find a sack, then sew this creature up inside it and toss her into the river."

The valet goes to find the sack. I leave it to you to wonder whether I did not take advantage of these few moments to cast myself at the nobleman's feet and beg him to spare me, assuring him that it was Madame Guérin, his usual procuress, who had herself sent me to his house. But the lewd gentleman will have none of it, he grasps my two buttocks, and kneading them brutally between his fists:

"Why, fuck my eyes," says he, "I think I'll feed this pretty ass to the fish."

That was the single lubricious action he seemed inclined to permit himself, and until then he had exposed nothing which might have led me to suppose libertinage had something to do with the scene. The valet returns, bringing a sack with him; despite all my protests, and they were heated, I am dumped into it, the mouth of the sack is sewn up, and La Fleur lifts me upon his shoulders. It was then I heard the effects of our libertine's mounting crisis; he had probably begun to frig himself as soon as I had been put in the sack. At the same instant La Fleur raised me to his shoulders, the villain's fuck departed him.

"Into the river, into the river, do you hear me, La Fleur?" he said, stammering with pleasure. "Yes, into the river with her, and you'll slip a stone into the sack, so that the whore will drown all the more quickly."

And that was all he had to say, I was borne out, we went into the adjacent room where La Fleur, having ripped open the sack, returned me my clothes, gave me two louis, and also gave me some unequivocal proof of the manner, radically unlike his master's, in which he conducted himself in the pursuit of happiness; then I returned to Guérin's. I severely scolded Guérin for having sent me there so poorly prepared; to placate me, she arranged another party: it took place two days later, and I was even less well prepared for the battle I was to wage with this new foe.

More or less as in the adventure I have just related, I was to go and wait in an antechamber of the apartment belonging to a farmer-general, but this time I waited in the company of the valet who, sent thither by his master, had come to fetch me at Guérin's. To while away the time before my gentleman's arrival, the valet diverted me by bringing out and displaying several precious stones kept in a desk drawer in the room.

"Bless me," said the good pander, "were you to take one or two of them I don't fancy it would make much difference; the old Croesus is so damned rich I wager he doesn't even know how many of 'em or what kind he's got here in his desk. Go right ahead, if you like, don't bother yourself about me, I'm not the sort of fellow to betray a little friend."

Alas! I was only too well disposed to follow this perfidious advice; you know my predilections, I've told you about them; and so, without his having to say another word, I put my hand upon a little gold box worth seven or eight louis, not daring to make off with any more valuable object. That was all that rascal of a valet desired, and to avoid having to return to the matter later on, I afterward learned that, had I refused to take something, he would, without my being aware of it, have slipped a jewel or two into my pocket. The master arrives, greets me with kindness and courtesy, the valet leaves the room, we two remain there together. This man, unlike the other, amused himself in a very real sense; he scattered a profusion of kisses over my ass, had me flog him, fart in his mouth, he put his prick in mine, and in one word had his fill of every kind and shape of lubricity save for that sometimes sought in the cunt; but 'twas all to no purpose, he did not discharge. The propitious moment for that had not yet come, all this he had been doing was secondary, preparatory; you will soon see to what it was leading.

"Why, my stars!" he suddenly exclaimed, "it had entirely slipped my mind. There's a domestic still waiting in the other room for a gem I just a moment ago promised to give him for his master. Excuse me, my dear, but I really must keep my word to him; then we'll get back to work."

Guilty of the little larceny I'd just committed at the instigation of that accursed valet, you may well suppose that this remark made me tremble. I thought for an instant to stop him, confess to the theft, then I decided it would be better to play innocent and run the risk. He opens the desk, looks through first one drawer then the next, rummages about, and failing to find what he is after, he darts furious glances at me.

"You slut, you alone," says he, "apart from a valet in whom I have entire confidence, you have been the only person to enter this room during the past three hours; the article is missing; you must have taken it."

"Oh, Monsieur," I say, shaking in every limb, "you may be sure I am incapable . . ."

"Damn your eyes," he roars (now, you will remark that his breeches were still unbuttoned, that his prick was protruding from them, that this prick held a vertical slope; all this, you would suppose, ought to have enlightened me and dispelled my fears, but I had all but lost my head, and noticed nothing), "come along, buggress, my valuable has got to be found."

He ordered me to strip; twenty times I besought him on bended knee to spare me the humiliation of such a search, he would be moved by nothing, nothing melted him, he himself angrily tore off my clothes, and as soon as I was naked, he went through my pockets and, of course, it was not long before he came across the box.

"Ah, you bitch!" he cried, "I need no more than that to be convinced. So, buggress, you come to a man's house to steal from him?"

And immediately summoning his lieutenant:

"Go bring an officer of the police at once," he said.

"Oh, Monsieur!" I cried, "have pity upon my youthful truancy, I have been beguiled into this, 'twas not done of my own will, I was told to . . ."

"Well," the lecherous gentleman interrupted, "you will explain all that to the officer, for I'll be damned if I don't mean to put a stop to all this crime."

The valet leaves again; the libertine, still wearing a blinding erection, flings himself into an armchair and while he fumbles about his crotch, he showers a thousand invectives upon me.

"This tramp, this monster," said he, "she comes to my house to rob me, I who wanted to give her the reward her services deserve . . . ah, by God, we shall see."

As he utters these words a knock is heard at the door, and I see a gendarme enter.

"Officer," says the master of the premises, "I have a thieving wench here I wish to put in your safekeeping, and I turn her over to you naked, for I put her in that state in order to search her clothing; there is the girl, over there are her garments, and here is the stolen article; I urge you to have her hanged, officer, and good night to you."

Whereupon he reeled backward, sat down in his chair, and discharged.

"Yes, hang the bitch, by sweet Jesus, I want to see her hanged, officer, do you understand me? Hang her, that's all I ask of you!" he fairly screamed.

The pretended gendarme leads me away with my clothes and the damning box, takes me into a nearby room, removes his uniform, and reveals himself to be the same valet who received me and incited me to steal; so upset had I been, I'd not recognized him hitherto.

"Well, well!" said he, "were you frightened?"

"Alas," I murmur, hardly able to speak, "out of my very wits."

"It's all over," he said, "and here is your money."

So saying, he presents me with the same box I had stolen, 'tis a gift from his master, he restores my clothes to me, hands me a glass of brandy, and escorts me back to Madame Guérin's.

"That's an odd and pleasant mania," the Bishop observed; "the major part of it can be extracted for use in other connections. My one criticism is that it contains an excess of delicacy; you know, of course, that I don't greatly favor mixing fine feelings with libertinage. Leave that element out of it, I say, and from that story one may learn the infallible method of preventing a whore from complaining, regardless of the iniquitous ways one might be disposed to take with her. One has only to proffer the bait, draw her into the trap, and when you've caught her redhanded, why then you are at liberty to do what you wish with her, there's nothing more to fear, she won't dare emit a peep for fear either of being accused or the object of your recriminations."

"It is indeed," said Curval, "and I am sure that had I been in that gentleman's place, I would have permitted myself to go somewhat further, and you, my dear Duclos, might not have got off so lightly."

The stories having been long that evening, the supper hour arrived before Messieurs had the opportunity to indulge in any frolicking. They thus repaired to table firmly resolved to make the most of the period following the meal. It was

then that, having assembled the entire household, they decided to determine
which of the little girls and boys could be justifiably ranked as mature men and
women. To establish the critical facts, Messieurs thought best to frig everyone of
the one sex and of the other about whom they had any doubts, or rather
suspicions; amongst the women, they were sure of Augustine, Fanny, and Zelmire:
these three charming little creatures, aged between fourteen and fifteen, all
discharged in response to the lightest touch; Hébé and Michette, each being only
twelve, were hardly worth considering, and so it was simply a question of
experimenting with Sophie, Colombe, and Rosette, the first of whom was
fourteen, the latter two being thirteen years old.

Amongst the boys, it was a matter of common knowledge that Zéphyr, Adonis,
and Céladon shot their fuck like grown men; Giton and Narcisse were too young
to bother putting through their paces; the abilities of Zélamir, Cupidon, and
Hyacinthe remained to be ascertained. The friends formed a circle about a pile of
well-stuffed pillows arranged on the floor, Champville and Duclos were nominated
for the pollutions; one, owing to her qualities as a tribade, was to act as the young
girls' fricatrice, the other, absolute mistress of the art of frigging the male member,
was to pollute the three little lads. They entered the ring formed by the friends'
chairs and filled with pillows, and there Sophie, Colombe, Rosette, Zélamir,
Cupidon, and Hyacinthe were turned over to Champville and Duclos; and each
friend, the better to appreciate the spectacle, took a child between his thighs: the
Duc appropriated Augustine, Curval had Zelmire to do his bidding, Durcet
entrusted himself to Zéphyr's skill, the Bishop favored Adonis to supply his needs.

The ceremony began with the boys; Duclos, her breasts and ass uncovered, her
sleeve rolled to the elbow, mobilized all her many talents and set to polluting each
of those delicious Ganymedes one after the other. The human hand could not
possibly have wandered and tugged, squeezed and patted more voluptuously; her
wrist, her fingers flew with a deftness . . . her movements were of a delicacy and
of a willfulness . . . she offered those little boys her mouth, her breast, her ass,
made all of herself available with such art that there could be no question but that
they who were not finally to discharge had not yet the power to do so. Zélamir and
Cupidon hardened, but all Duclos' lore, all her agility, was quite in vain. With
Hyacinthe, however, the storm burst after the sixth flick of the wrist: fuck leapt
over Duclos' breast, and the child went half out of his mind while fondling her ass.
Messieurs were careful to observe that throughout the entire operation it had
never once occurred to the lad to touch her in front.

The girls' turn came next; virtually naked, her hair very elegantly arranged and
equally stylish in every other part of herself, Champville did not look thirty years
old, although she was fifty if a day. The lubricity of this operation, whence, as a
thoroughgoing tribade, she expected to mine the greatest pleasure, animated her
large dark-brown eyes which, since her youth, had always been extremely
handsome. She put at least as much verve, daring, and brilliance into her actions
as Duclos had into hers, she simultaneously polluted the clitoris, the entrance to

the vagina, and the asshole, but Nature developed nothing worthy of notice in Colombe and Rosette; there was not even the faintest appearance of pleasure in their expressions. But things were not thus with the beautiful Sophie: the tenth digital foray brought her fainting upon Champville's breast; little broken sighs, little panting sounds, the tender shade of crimson which sprang into her lovely cheeks, her parted lips which grew moist, everything manifested the delirium whereinto Nature had hurled her, and she was declared a woman. The Duc, his device as solid as a mace, ordered Champville to frig her a second time, and when she discharged afresh, the villain chose that moment to mix his impure fuck with that young virgin's. As for Curval, he had wrought his fell deed between Zelmire's thighs, and the two others theirs with the young boys they held locked between their legs.

The company retired for the night, and the following morning having furnished no event which deserves to be cited in this catalogue of exceptional feats, and dinner having furnished nothing, nor coffee, we shall remove at once to the auditorium, where the magnificently arrayed Duclos appears once again upon the platform, this time to end, with five new stories, the one hundred and fifty narrations which have been entrusted to her for the thirty days of the month of November.

The Thirtieth Day

I am not sure, Messieurs, said the beauteous storyteller, whether you have heard of the caprice, quite as unusual as dangerous, for which the Comte de Lernos is celebrated, but my several liaisons with him having afforded me a thorough acquaintance of his maneuvers, and as I found them most extraordinary indeed, I believe they ought to be included amongst the delights you have ordered me to detail. The Comte de Lernos' passion to lead into evil as many girls and married women as he is able, and apart from the books he employs to seduce them, there is truly no sort of device he will not invent to deliver them up to men; he either exploits their secret yearnings by uniting them with the object upon whom they only think longingly, or he finds them lovers if such they are lacking. He has a house devoted to nothing else, and in it all the matches he has made are tested when the individuals concerned come to grips. He unites them, guarantees them freedom from intrusion, provides them with all the facilities needed for recreation, and then goes into an adjoining chamber to enjoy the pleasure of spying upon them while they are in action. But the point to which he multiplies these disorders simply defies belief, nor would one credit an account of the immense number of obstacles he is willing to surmount in order to form these little marriages. He has associates in nearly every convent in Paris and amongst a vast quantity of married women, and this army is led by a general of such great skill that not a day passes but at least three or four little skirmishes are fought in his house. Never does he fail to watch the voluptuous jousts - without the participants suspecting his presence - but once he has gone to take up his observation post at the hole, as he stands watch all alone, no one knows how he proceeds to his discharge, nor what its character is; nothing but the fact is known, and that is all; I thought none the less that it was worthy of being mentioned to you.

The fantasy of the elderly Président Desportes will perhaps prove more amusing to you. Fully informed of the etiquette observed at the home of this habitual debauchee, I arrive at his house toward ten o'clock in the morning and, perfectly naked, I present my buttocks to be kissed; he is seated in an armchair, very grave, very solemn, and the first thing I do is fart in his face. My président is irritated, he gets to his feet, seizes a bundle of switches he has close at hand, and falls to pursuing me; my first impulse is to get out of his way.

"Impudent hussy," says he, chasing after me all the while, "I'll teach you to come to my home to behave in this outrageous fashion."

I'm to flee, he's to follow on my heels; I finally gain a narrow alley, I take cover in an impregnable retreat, but, lo! there he is, he's somehow managed to get at me. The président's threats and imprecations redouble as he sees he has me trapped; he brandishes the switches, threatens to use them upon me: I creep into a corner, cower there, put on a terrified air, I shrink to the size of a mouse; this terrified, groveling attitude of mine finally awakes his fuck, and the roué squirts it over my breasts while shouting with pleasure.

"What! Do you mean to say he didn't give you a single lick with the switches?" the Duc demanded.

"He didn't bring them within a yard of me," Duclos replied.

"A very patient individual, that one," Curval remarked; "my friends, I believe we all agree that we are somewhat less so when we have in our hands the instrument Duclos mentions."

"But you need only a small amount of patience, Messieurs," said Champville, "for I shall shortly present to you other samples of the same breed, but they'll be rather less mild tempered than Madame Duclos' président."

And Duclos, observing that silence had succeeded these comments, saw she could continue with her stories, and proceeded in the following manner:

Soon after this adventure had befallen me, I went to the town house of the Marquis de Saint-Giraud, whose fantasy consisted in seating a naked woman upon a children's swing and having her swing to a great height, back and forth. Each time you pass by his nose, he's waiting for you, and you've got either to let fly a fart at him or expect a slap upon your ass. I did my best to satisfy him; I received several slaps, but also gave him some overpowering farts. And the Marquis having finally discharged after an hour of this monotonous and fatiguing ceremony, the swing was brought to a halt, and my audience came to an end.

About three years after I had become the mistress of Fournier's establishment, a man came to make an unusual proposal to me: he wished me to find libertines who would amuse themselves with his wife and daughter, the only condition being that he be hidden in a place whence he could observe everything that transpired. Not only would whatever money I might earn from their employment be mine, but, he went on, he planned to give me an additional two louis for every encounter I could arrange for them; and there was only one final condition to the bargain: for his wife's partners he wished none but men of a certain taste, and for his daughter, men addicted to another kind of whimsy: his wife's men were all to shit upon her breasts, and the procedure to be observed with his daughter involved having the men raise her skirts, broadly expose her behind in front of the hole through which he would be doing his spying, and then discharge into her mouth. He would surrender the merchandise for the said passions, but for no others. After having made this gentleman promise to accept all responsibility in the event his wife and daughter brought complaint for having been made to come to my house, I agreed to all he wanted and in my turn promised that the two ladies would be furnished in strict accordance with his instructions. He arrived with his wares the very next day: madame was a woman of thirty-six, not very pretty, but tall and majestically formed, with a great air of sweet mildness and of modesty; her daughter was fifteen years old, blond, rather inclining toward heaviness, with the most tender, most winning countenance in all the world. . .

"Indeed, Monsieur," quoth his wife, "you have us do strange things. . . ."

"I know, my dear, I know," said the lecher, "and it mortifies me, but so it must be. Accept your lot, do as you're told, there's nothing for it, I shall not give over. And if you balk in the slightest way at the propositions and the actions we are going to submit you to - you, Madame, and you, Mademoiselle - I shall tomorrow convey you to a place I know, and it is highly unlikely you'll ever return alive from it."

Wherewith the wife she a tear or two; as the man for whom I intended her was waiting, I requested her to pass without further delay into the chamber I had set aside for their bout; mademoiselle would remain in another room with one of my girls, she would be perfectly safe there and would be notified when her turn had come. At this cruel moment there were a few more tears, and it seemed clear to me that this was the first time the brutal husband had required such a thing of his wife; unhappily, her debut was arduous, for aside from the baroque taste of the individual to whom I was surrendering her, he was an imperious and brusque old libertine who would surely not treat her with any excess of courtesy or consideration.

"That will do, no more tears," said the husband. "Bear in mind that I am watching your conduct, and that if you do not give ample satisfaction to the thoughtful gentleman who is going to take you in hand, I will come in myself and force you to do his bidding."

She enters the arena, the husband and I go into the neighboring room from which we are to watch it all. It is difficult to imagine the point to which this old scoundrel's imagination was excited by contemplating his miserable wife being made a victim of some stranger's brutality; he was thrilled by each thing she was forced to do; that poor humiliated woman's modesty and candor beneath the atrocious assaults of the libertine engaged to exercise her, composed a delicious spectacle for her husband. But when he saw her thrown brutally to the floor, and when the old ape to whom I had delivered her shit upon her chest, and her husband saw the tears, beheld the horrified shudders of his wife as she first heard proposed and then saw this infamy executed, he could restrain himself no longer, and the hand with which I was frigging him was straightway soaked with fuck. This first scene ended at last, and if it had afforded him pleasure, it was as nothing compared to the climax produced by the second. It was only with great difficulty, and above all with numerous and grave threats, that we succeeded in getting the young lady to enter the ring; she had witnessed her mother's tears but knew nothing of what had been done to her. The poor little girl raised all kinds of objections; we finally helped her make up her mind. The man to whom I turned her over was fully instructed of all that was required to be done: he was one of my regular clients whom I delighted with this windfall and who, to express his gratitude, consented to all I prescribed.

"Oh, the lovely ass!" cried the libertine father once his daughter's stud displayed her entirely naked. "Oh, sacred Jesus, what adorable buttocks!"

"Gracious!" I exclaimed, "am I to take it that this is the first time you have set eyes on them?"

"Yes, indeed it is," said he, "I required this expedient to enjoy the spectacle; but if 'tis the first time I see that superb ass, you may rest assured it shall not be the last."

I frigged him at a lively pace, he grew ecstatic; but when he saw the appalling things that young virgin was being forced to submit to, when he saw a consummate libertine's hands straying over that extraordinary body which had never before suffered such fondlings, when he saw her compelled to sink to her knees, open her mouth, when he saw a fat prick introduced into it, and saw that engine discharge inside, he tottered backward and, swearing like one possessed, shouting that he'd never in his life tasted any pleasure as keen as this, he left certain proof of his statements between my fingers. Their adventure had drawn to a conclusion, the two poor women retreated, weeping abundant tears, and the husband, but too enthusiastic over the drama they had enacted for him, doubtless found the means to persuade them to provide him with additional performances, for I received that family at my house for more than six years and, always following the orders the husband gave me, I made those two unlucky creatures acquainted with practically all the different passions I have mentioned in the course of my thirty days of storytelling; there were, to be sure, ten or twelve of the passions they had no opportunity to satisfy, because we did not practice them in my house.

"Oh, yes," said Curval, "there are many ways to prostitute a wife and a daughter. As if these bitches were made for anything else! Are they not born for our pleasures, and from that moment onward, must they not satisfy them at no matter what price? I've had a quantity of wives," said the Président, "and three or four daughters of whom, thank God, I've only one left, and if I'm not mistaken Monsieur le Duc is fucking Mademoiselle Adelaide at this very instant; but had any one of those creatures ever balked at being prostituted, in any of the numerous manners of prostitution I regularly submitted them to, may I be damned alive or condemned never to fuck anything but cunts for the rest of my life - which is worse - if I'd not have blown their bloody brains out."

"Président, your prick is in the air again," said the Duc; "your fucking remarks always betray you."

"My prick in the air? No," the Président said, "but I am on the verge of getting some shit from our dear little Sophie, and I have high hopes her delicious turd will precipitate something. Oh, upon my soul, even more than I'd suspected," said Curval, after he'd gobbled up the hash; "by the good God I'd like to fuck, I believe that my prick is taking on some consistency. Who from amongst you, Messieurs, would like to accompany me into the boudoir?"

"I'd be honored," said Durcet, dragging along Aline, whom he had been pawing steadily for an hour.

And our two libertines, having summoned Augustine, Fanny, Colombe, Hébé, Zélamir, Adonis, Hyacinthe, and Cupidon, and enlisted Julie and two duennas, Martaine and Champville, Antinoüs and Hercule, absented themselves for half an hour, at the end of which they returned triumphant, each having yielded up their vital liquor to the sweetest excesses of crapulence and debauchery.

"Move on," Curval said to Duclos, "give us your final tale, dear friend. And if it manages to make this prick of mine dance up again, you shall be able to congratulate yourself upon having wrought a miracle, for in faith, it is at least a year since I've lost so much fuck at a single sitting. On the other hand, it is true that . . ."

"Very well," the Bishop interrupted, "that will do; if we listen to you, we will hear something much worse than the passion Duclos is likely to describe to us. And so, since that would be to retreat from the stronger to the weaker, permit us to bid you be silent and listen instead to our storyteller."

That gifted whore thereupon terminated her recitations with the following passion:

The time has finally arrived, my Lords, to relate the passion of the Marquis de Mesanges to whom, you will recall, I sold the daughter of the unfortunate shoemaker, Petignon, who perished in jail with his wife while I enjoyed the inheritance his mother had left for him. As 'twas Lucile who satisfied him, you will allow me to place the story in her mouth.

"I arrive at the Marquis' mansion," that charming girl told me, "at about ten o'clock in the morning. As soon as I enter, all the doors are shut.

"'What are you doing here, little bitch?' says the Marquis, all afire. 'Who gave you permission to disturb me?'

"And since you gave me no prior warning of what was to happen, you may readily imagine how terrified I was by this reception.

"'Well, take off your clothes, be quick about it,' the Marquis continues. 'Since I've got my hands on you, whore, you'll not get out of here with your skin intact . . . indeed, you're going to perish - your last minutes have arrived.'

"I burst into tears, I fall down at the Marquis' feet, but nothing would bend him. And as I was not quick enough in undressing, he himself tore my clothes off, ripping them away by sheer force. But what truly petrified me was to see him thrown them one after another into the fire.

"'You'll have no further use for these,' he muttered, casting each article into a large grate. 'No further need for this mantelet, this dress, these stockings, this bodice, no,' said he when all had been consumed, 'all you'll need now is a coffin.'

"And there I was, naked; the Marquis, who had never before seen me, contemplated my ass for a brief space, he uttered oaths as he fondled it, but he did not bring his lips near it.

"'Very well, whore' said he, 'enough of this, you're going to follow your clothes, I'm going to bind you to those andirons; yes, by fuck, yes indeed, by sweet Jesus, I'm going to burn you alive, you bitch, I'm going to have the pleasure of inhaling the aroma of your burning flesh.'

"And so saying he falls half-unconscious into an armchair and discharges, darting his fuck upon the remnants of my burning clothes. He rings, a valet enters and then leads me out, and in another room I find a complete new outfit, clothes twice as fine as those he has incinerated."

That is the account of it I had from Lucile; it remains now to discover whether 'twas for that or for worse he employed the girl I sold him.

"For something far worse," said Desgranges; "I am glad you have introduced the Marquis to their Lordships, for I believe I too shall have something to say about him."

"May it be, Madame," Duclos said to Desgranges, "and you, my amiable companions," she added, speaking to her two other colleagues, "may it be that you speak with greater energy than have I, with livelier images, brighter diction, superior wit, and more persuasive eloquence. 'Tis now your turn, I have done, and I would but beseech Messieurs to have the kindness to forgive me if I have perchance bored them in any wise, for there is an almost unavoidable monotony in the recital of such anecdotes; all compounded, fitted into the same framework, they lose the luster that is theirs as independent happenings."

With these words, the superb Duclos respectfully saluted the company, bowed, and descended from her throne; she next went from alcove to alcove and was generally applauded and caressed by all the friends. Supper was served, Duclos was invited to sit at the table, a favor which had never before been accorded to a woman. Her conversation was quite as agreeable as her storytelling had been, and by way of recompense for the pleasure she had given them, Messieurs named her to be the governor-general of the two harems, and the four friends also made the promise, in an aside, that no matter what the extreme treatment to which they might expose the women in the course of the sojourn, she would always be dealt with gently, and very certainly taken back with them to Paris, where the society would amply reward her for the trouble she had gone to in order to help Messieurs procure themselves a little good cheer. She, Curval, and the Duc so completely besotted themselves at supper that they were practically incapacitated and barely managed, with the expense of much effort, to reach the orgies, which they soon left, allowing Durcet and the Bishop to carry on alone, and betook themselves to the remote boudoir; Champville, Antinoüs, Bum-Cleaver, Thérèse, and Louison accompanied them, and one may be perfectly confident that they uttered and had done to them at least as many horrors and infamies as, at their end, their two more sober friends were able to invent.

Everyone repaired to his bed at two in the morning, and 'twas thus the month of November ended, thus came to a close the first phase of this lubricious and interesting holiday, for whose second part we will not keep the public waiting if to our consideration it has kindly received what we have chronicled so far.

Mistakes I Have Made

I have been too explicit, not sufficiently reticent, about the chapel activities at the beginning; must not elaborate upon them until after the stories in which they are mentioned.

Said too much about active and passive sodomy; conceal that until the stories have discussed it.

I was wrong to have made Duclos react strongly to the death of her sister; that doesn't sort with the rest of her character; change it.

If I said Aline was a virgin upon arrival at the château, that was an error: she isn't, and could not be. The Bishop has depucelated her in every sector.

And not having been able to reread all this, there must be a swarm of other mistakes.

When later I put the text in final order, I must be particularly careful to have a notebook beside me at all times; I'll have to put down very exact mention of each happening and each portrait as I write it; otherwise, I'll get horribly confused because of the multitude of characters.

For the Second Part, begin with the assumption Augustine and Zéphyr are already sleeping in the Duc's bedchamber in the First Part; likewise Adonis and Zelmire in Curval's, Hyacinthe and Fanny in Durcet's, Céladon and Sophie in the Bishop's, even though none of them has been deflowered yet.

Part the Second

The 150 Complex Passions, or Those Belonging to the Second Class, Composing the Thirty-one Days of December Spent in

Hearing the Narrations of Madame Champville; Interspersed
Amongst Which Are the Scandalous Doings at the Château
During That Month; All Being Set down in the Form of a
Journal. (Draft)

THE 1ST OF DECEMBER: Champville assumes the task of storytelling and relates the one hundred and fifty following tales (the number of each precedes the tale).

1. Won't depucelate any save those aged between three and seven, but only cuntishly. 'Tis he who deflowers Champville at the age of five.

2. He ties a girl of nine in a curled-up position and depucelates her from behind.

3. He wishes to rape a girl of twelve or thirteen, and depucelates her while holding a pistol against her heart.

4. He likes to frig a man upon a maiden's cunt, he uses the fuck for pomade, and next encunts the maid while she is held by the man.

5. He wishes to depucelate three girls in succession, one in the cradle, one at the age of five, the other at seven.

THE 2ND. 6. He'll not depucelate anyone who is not between nine years old and thirteen. His prick is enormous; four women are needed to hold the virgin. The same individual Martaine speaks of, who only embuggers three-year-olds, the same hell-inspired individual.

7. He has his valet depucelate the maid, aged ten to twelve, before his eyes, and during the operation touches them nowhere save upon the ass. He now fondles the girl's, now the valet's. Discharges upon the valet's ass.

8. He wishes to depucelate a girl destined to be married the following day.

9. He wishes the marriage to be performed, and to depucelate the bride at some time between the hour of the mass and the moment the couple retires to bed.

10. He would have his valet, a very ingenious personage, go about marrying girls left and right and bring them to his master, who therewith fucks them, and next sells them to procuresses.

THE 3RD. 11. He must be provided with two sisters; he depucelates them.

12. He marries the girl, depucelates her, but 'tis all a fraud, the marriage is a fraud, once he's fucked her, he leaves her.

13. He will only fuck a maid, and then only immediately after another man has deflowered her while he has watched. He must have her cunt muddied up with sperm.

14. This one depucelates with an artificial engine, very large, and, without introducing himself, discharges upon the hole he has cleared.

15. He will have none but maids of rank and distinction and pays for them in accordance with their wealth. This individual proves to be the Duc, who will admit having depucelated more than fifteen hundred of them over a period of thirty years.

THE 4TH. 16. He forces a brother to fuck his sister in his presence, then fucks her afterward; he obliges both to shit before-hand.

17. He forces a father to fuck his daughter after he has himself had her maidenhead.

18. He brings his nine-year-old daughter to the brothel, and while she is held by a procuress, depucelates her. He has had twelve daughters; has had all twelve maidenheads.

19. Must have virgins between the ages of thirty and forty to fuck.

20. He will depucelate no one but nuns, and spends immense sums of money to get them; he fucks several.

'Tis the evening of the 4th of December, at the orgies, the Duc depucelates Fanny, who is held by the four governesses and ministered by Duclos. He fucks her twice in a row, she faints, the second time he fucks her while she is unconscious.

THE 5TH. To celebrate the fifth week's festival, Hyacinthe and Fanny are joined in matrimony, the marriage is consummated very publicly.

21. He would have the mother hold her daughter, he first fucks the mother, then depucelates the daughter while she is held by the mother. The same one Desgranges mentions on the 20th of February.

22. He likes adultery only; one must locate women for him who are generally known to be virtuous and well behaved, he makes them disgusted with their husbands.

23. He enjoys having the husband come himself to prostitute his wife and hold her while he fucks her. (Messieurs imitate that passion forthwith.)

24. He places a married woman upon a bed, encunts her while that woman's daughter, suspended above, presents him with her cunt to be licked; the next instant he effects a reversal and encunts the daughter while kissing the mother's asshole. When he has done licking the daughter's cunt, he has her piss; then he kisses the mother's asshole and has her shit.

25. He has four daughters, legitimate and wedded; he wishes to fuck all four: he makes all four of them conceive and bear children so as someday to have the pleasure of depucelating the children he has had by his daughters and whom their husbands suppose to be their own.

Apropos of which the Duc recounts - but his anecdote cannot be numbered amongst the stories because, Messieurs being unable to duplicate it, it does not compose a passion - the Duc recounts, I say, that he once knew a man who fucked three children he had by his mother, amongst whom there was a daughter whom he had marry his son, so that in fucking her he fucked his sister, his daughter and his daughter-in-law, and thus he also constrained his son to fuck his own sister and mother-in-law. Curval recounts another unusual history, that of a brother and a sister who reached an agreement whereby each would surrender his children to the other: the sister had a boy and a girl, so did the brother. They mixed the pudding in such wise that sometimes they fucked their nephews, sometimes their own children, and sometimes their first cousins, or else the brothers and sister would fuck while the father and mother, that is to say, the brother and sister, fucked one another also.

That evening, Fanny is surrendered cuntwardly to the assembly, but as the Bishop and Monsieur Durcet do not fuck cunts, she is only fucked by Curval and the Duc. Henceforth, she wears a small ribbon aslant, like a baldric, and after the loss of both her pucelages she will wear a very wide pink ribbon.

THE 6TH. 26. He has himself frigged while a woman is being frigged about the clitoris, and he wishes to discharge at the same time the girl does, but he discharges upon the buttocks of the man who frigs the girl.

27. He kisses the asshole of one girl while a second girl frigs his ass and a third his prick; they then exchange tasks, so that, when all is said and done, each of the three has her ass kissed, each frigs his prick, each frigs his ass. Farts are required of them all.

28. He licks the cunt of one girl while fucking a second in the mouth and while his asshole is being licked by a third; then exchange of positions as above. The cunts must discharge, he swallows their balm.

29. He sucks a beshitted ass, has a tongue frig his own beshitted asshole, and frigs himself upon a beshitted ass; the three girls then exchange positions.

30. He has two girls frigged before his eyes, and alternately fucks the friggeresses from the rear, but in the cunt, while they continue with their sapphotizings.

Zéphyr and Cupidon are upon that day discovered in the act of frigging each other, but they have not yet had recourse to reciprocal embuggery; they are punished. Fanny is much encunted at the orgies.

THE 7TH. 31. He would have an older girl introduce a younger girl to bad habits; the older must frig her, give her wicked advice, and end up by holding her while he fucks her, whether virgin or not.

32. He calls for four women; he fucks two of them orally, two cuntwardly, taking great care not to insert his prick in a mouth until having first had it in a cunt. While all this is going on, he is closely followed by a fifth woman, who throughout frigs his asshole with a dildo.

33. This libertine requires a dozen women, six young, six old and, if 'tis possible, six of them should be mothers and the other six their daughters. He pumps out their cunts, asses and mouths; when applying his lips to the cunt, he wants copious urine; when at the mouth, much saliva; when at the ass, abundant farts.

34. He employs eight women to frig him; each of the eight must be situated in a different posture. (This had better be illustrated by a drawing.)

35. Wishes to have three men and three women fucking each other in divers attitudes.

THE 8TH. 36. He forms twelve groups of two girls each; they are so arranged only their asses are visible to him; all the rest of their bodies must be concealed from his sight. He frigs himself while studying all those buttocks.

37. He has six couples simultaneously frig themselves in a room paneled with mirrors; each couple is composed of two girls frigging each other in various and equally lubricious postures. He is in the middle of the room, he regards both the couples and their reflections, and discharges in the middle of it all, having been frigged by an old woman. He has kissed the buttocks of every participant in this drama.

38. He has four streetwalkers besot themselves with wine and then fight with each other while he looks on; and when they are thoroughly drunk, they one after another vomit into his mouth. He favors the oldest and ugliest women possible.

39. He has a girl shit in his mouth, but does not eat her turd, and while the first girl is in action, a second sucks his prick and frigs his ass; while discharging, he shits into the hand of the girl who is socratizing him. The girls exchange places.

40. He has a man shit into his mouth and eats while a little boy frigs him, then the man frigs him and he has the boy shit.

That evening, at the orgies, Curval depucelates Michette, in front: she is held by the four duennas and ministered by Duclos; this arrangement is the conventional one and is observed upon all occasions; therefore we will not allude to it again.

THE 9TH. 41. He fucks one girl in her mouth just after having shitted into the same receptacle; a second girl is lying on top of the first, with the first girl's head between her thighs, and upon the face of the second girl a third girl drops a turd, and he, while thus fucking his own turd in the first girl's mouth, eats the shit deposited by the third girl upon the second girl's face, and then they alternate roles, in such wise that each girl enacts all three of them.

42. Thirty girls pass through his hands during a given day, and he has them all shit into his mouth, consumes the turds of the three or four prettiest. He repeats this party five times a week, which means that he sees 7800 girls a year. When Champville first encounters him, he is seventy years old and has been in business for fifty.

43. He sees twelve girls every morning and swallows their dozen turds; he sees them all at the same time.

44. He places himself in a bathtub; thirty women come up one after another and piss and shit into it till it is full; he discharges while paddling about in all that.

45. He shits in the presence of four women, requires them to watch and indeed help deliver him of his turd; next, he wishes them to divide it into equal parts and eat it; then each woman does a turd of her own. He mixes them and swallows the entire batter, but his shit-furnishers have got to be women of at least sixty.

That evening Michette's cunt is put at the disposal of the assembly; thereafter she wears the little sash.

THE 10TH. 46. He has girls A and B shit. Then he forces B to eat A's turd, and A to eat B's. Then both A and B shit a second time; he eats both their turds.

47. He requires a mother and her three daughters, and he eats the girls' shit upon the mother's ass, and the mother's shit upon one daughter's ass.

48. He obliges a daughter to shit into her mother's mouth and to wipe her ass with her mother's teats; next, he eats the turd in the mother's mouth, and afterward has the mother shit into her daughter's mouth, whence, as before, he eats the turd.

49. He wishes a father to eat his son's turd, then he eats the father's.

50. He would have the brother shit in his sister's cunt, and he eats the turd; the sister then must shit in her brother's mouth. He eats this second turd, too.

THE 11TH. 51. Champville announces she is now going to speak of impieties, and makes mention of a man who wishes the whore, while frigging him, to pronounce dreadful blasphemies; in his turn he utters terrible ones. His amusement during their dialogue consists in kissing her ass; he does no more than that.

52. He would have a girl come with him to a church, and frig him there, especially at the time the holy sacrament is exposed. He situates himself as near to the altar as possible, and fondles her ass while she performs her task.

53. He goes to confession for the sole purpose of making his confessor's prick rise aloft; he lists a quantity of infamous misdeeds, and frigs himself in the confessional all the while he speaks.

54. He wishes the girl to go and make her confession, then fucks her orally the moment she emerges from the confessional.

55. He fucks a whore throughout a mass being said in his private chapel, and discharges when the Host is raised.

That evening, the Duc depucelates Sophie cuntwardly, and while doing so blasphemes considerably.

THE 12TH. 56. He buys a confessor, who yields him his place; thus he is able to hear the young pensionnaires' confessions and to give them the worst possible advice while pardoning them their sins.

57. He would have his daughter go to confess to a monk he has previously bribed, and he is placed where he can overhear everything; but the monk demands that the penitent keep her skirts raised high while she catalogues her faults, and her ass posted within plain sight of the father: thus he is able to hear his daughter's confession and contemplate her ass at the same time.

58. Has mass celebrated for completely naked whores; while observing the spectacle, he frigs his prick upon another girl's ass.

59. He has his wife go to confess to a monk he has bought: the monk seduces the wife and fucks her in front of her husband, who is hidden. If the wife refuses, he emerges from hiding and helps the monk force her.

On that day they celebrate the sixth week's festival with the marriage of Céladon and Sophie, which union is consummated, and in the evening Sophie's cunt is put generally to use, and she dons the sash. Because of this event only four passions are recounted on the 12th.

THE 13TH. 60. Fucks whores on the altar at the same moment mass is about to be said; they have their naked asses on the sacred stone.

61. He has a naked girl sit astride and bend forward over a large crucifix; he fucks her cunt from behind while she is thus crouched down in such wise the head of Christ frigs her clitoris.

62. He farts and has the whore fart in the chalice, he pisses thereinto and has her piss thereinto, he shits thereinto and has her shit thereinto, and finally he discharges into the chalice.

63. He has a small boy shit upon the paten, and he eats this while the boy sucks him.

64. He has two girls shit upon a crucifix, he shits thereupon when they have finished, and he is frigged against the three turds covering the idol's face.

THE 14TH. 65. He breaks up a crucifix, smashes several images of the Virgin and the Eternal Father, shits upon the debris and burns the whole mess. The same man has the mania of bringing a whore to hear the sermon and having himself frigged while listening to the word of God.

66. He takes communion and, the wafer still in his mouth, has four whores shit upon it.

67. He has her go to communion and fucks her in the mouth when she returns.

68. He interrupts a priest in the midst of saying mass in his private chapel, interrupts him, I say, in order to frig himself into the chalice, obliges the whore to frig the priest thereinto, and forces the latter to quaff the mead.

(Passion Number 69 omitted by Sade.)

70. He intervenes directly the Host is consecrated and forces the priest to fuck the whore with the Host.

Upon this day Augustine and Zelmire are found frigging together; they are both rigorously punished.

THE 15TH. 71. He has the girl fart upon the Host, himself farts thereupon, and then swallows the Host while fucking the whore.

72. The same man who had himself nailed into a coffin - Duclos mentioned him - compels the whore to shit upon the Host; he also shits upon it and flings the whole affair into a privy.

73. Frigs the whore's clitoris with the Host, has her discharge upon it, then buries it in her cunt and fucks her, discharging upon it in his turn.

74. Chops it up with a knife and has the crumbs rammed into his asshole.

75. Has himself frigged and then discharges upon the Host and finally, when he is restored to perfect calm and after his fuck has flowed, feeds biscuit and all to a dog.

The same evening, the Bishop consecrates a Host and Curval destroys Hébé's maidenhead with it, he drives it into her cunt and discharges thereupon. Several others are consecrated, and the already depucelated sultanas are all fucked with Hosts.

THE 16TH. Profanation, Champville announces, lately the principal element in her stories, will from now on be no more accessory, and what, to borrow the brothel term, are known as little ceremonies are going to provide the main ingredient in the following complex passions. She asks her auditors to remember that everything connected with that will be presented merely as secondary matter, but that the difference subsisting between her stories and the examples Duclos has given, is that Duclos always pictured a man with one woman, whereas she, Champville, will always show several women administering to a single man.

76. He has himself flogged by one girl during mass, he fucks a second girl orally, and he discharges when the Host is elevated.

77. He has two women gently flog his ass with a martinet; each woman bestows ten stripes, alternating them with asshole friggery.

78. He has himself whipped by four different girls while farts are being launched into his mouth: the girls take turns, so that each will have had a chance both to whip and to fart.

79. He has himself whipped by his wife while he fucks his daughter, next by his daughter while he fucks his wife; this is the same individual Duclos spoke of, the same man who prostituted his wife and daughter in her whorehouse.

80. He has himself whipped simultaneously by two girls, one flogs the front of him, the other his rear, and when at last he has been well stimulated, he fucks one of them while the other plies the lash, then the second while the first flogs him.

That same evening Hébé's cunt is made available to the public, and she wears the little sash, not being entitled to the large one until she has lost both her pucelages.

THE 17TH. 81. He has himself flogged while kissing a boy's ass and while fucking a girl in the mouth, then he fucks the boy in the mouth while kissing the girl's asshole, the while constantly receiving the lash from another girl, then he has the boy flog him, orally fucks the whore who'd been whipping him, and then has himself flogged by the girl whose ass he had been kissing.

82. He has himself whipped by an old woman, fucks an old man in the mouth, and has the daughter of this aged couple shit into his own mouth, then changes so that, ultimately, everyone takes his turn in each role.

83. He has himself whipped while frigging himself and while discharging upon a crucifix propped up by a girl's buttocks.

84. He has himself whipped while fucking a whore from the rear, using his prick to tamp a Host into her fundament.

85. He passes an entire brothel in review; he receives the lash from all the whores while kissing the madame's asshole and receiving therefrom into his mouth both wind and rain and hailstones.

THE 18TH. 86. He has himself whipped by teams of cab drivers and chimney sweeps who pass two at a time, one plying the lash, the other farting in his mouth; he employs ten or twelve in a morning.

87. He has himself held by three girls, he gets down on hands and knees, a fourth girl mounts astride him and thrashes him; each member of the quartet takes her turn mounting and flogging him.

88. Naked, he puts himself in the midst of six girls; he is conscience-stricken, asks to be forgiven, casts himself down upon his knees. Each girl decrees a penance, and he is given one hundred strokes for each penance he refuses to do: 'tis the girl he refuses who whips him. Well, these penances are all exceedingly unpleasant: one would like to shit into his mouth; another have him lick up her spittle from the floor; a third is menstruating and would have him lick her cunt clean; the fourth hasn't washed her feet, will he kindly lick between her toes; the fifth has snot awaiting his tongue, etc.

89. Fifteen girls arrive in teams of three: one whips him, one sucks him, the other shits; the she who shitted, whips; she who sucked, shits; she who whipped, sucks. And so he proceeds till he has had done with all fifteen; he sees nothing, heeds nothing, is wild with joy: a procuress is in charge of the game. He renews this party six times each week.

(This one is truly charming and has my infinite recommendation; the thing has got to move very briskly along, each girl must bestow twenty-give strokes of the whip, and it is between whippings that the first sucks and the third shits. If you would prefer fifty strokes from each girl, that will total up to seven hundred fifty, a very agreeable figure, not by any means excessive.)

90. Twenty-five whores soften up his ass with a quantity of slaps and fondlings; he is not sent away until his ass has become completely insensible.

That evening the Duc is flogged while culling Zelmire's forward maidenhead.

THE 19TH. 91. He has himself tried by a jury of six whores; each knows the role she is to play. He is sentenced to be hanged. And hanged he is; but the cord snaps: 'tis the instant he discharges. (Relate this to similar ones Duclos described.)

92. He arranges six old women in a semicircle; while three young whores lash him, the six crones spit in his face.

93. A girl frigs his asshole with the handle of a cat-o'-nine-tails, a second girl whips his thighs and prick from the front; 'tis thus he is made eventually to discharge over the tits of the whipper posted before him.

94. Two women flay him with bulls' pizzles while a third, kneeling before him, causes him to discharge upon her breasts.

She recounts only four that day because of the marriage of Zelmire and Adonis which marks the seventh week's conclusion, and which is consummated, Zelmire having been depucelated, with what regards the cunt, the night before.

THE 20TH. 95. He struggles with six women, the cuts of whose whips he pretends to wish to avoid; he strives to snatch the whips from their hands, but they are too strong for him and fustigate him none the less. He is naked.

96. He runs the gauntlet between two ranks of twelve girls who are wielding switches; he is whipped all about the body and discharges after the ninth race.

97. He has the soles of his feet whipped, then his prick, then his thighs while, as he lies upon a couch, three women successively mount astride him and shit in his mouth.

98. Three girls alternately flog him, one with a martinet, one with a bull's pizzle, the other with a cat-o'-nine-tails. A fourth, kneeling before him and whose asshole the lecher's lackey is frigging, sucks the master's prick while frigging the lackey's, which he has discharge upon his sucker's buttocks.

99. He is amidst six girls: one pricks him with a needle, the second uses pincers on him, the third burns him, the fourth bites him, the fifth scratches him, the sixth flagellates him. All that everywhere upon his body, indiscriminately. He discharges in the thick of this activity.

That evening Zelmire, depucelated on 18th of December, is surrendered cuntwardly to the assembly - to, that is to say, Curval and the Duc, who alone of the four friends fuck cunts. Once Curval has fucked Zelmire, his hatred for Adelaide and Constance redoubles; he wishes to have Constance minister to Zelmire.

THE 21ST. 100. He has himself frigged by his lackey while the girl, naked, balances upon a narrow pedestal; all the while he is being frigged, she may neither budge nor lose her equilibrium.

101. He has the procuress frig him while he fondles her buttocks; and meanwhile, between her fingers, the girl holds a very short candle which she must not drop until the roué has spat out his fuck; he is very careful not to discharge before the girl's fingers have been seared.

102. He sups at an immense table; for light, he has six burning candles, each inserted in the ass of a naked girl lying upon the dining table.

103. While he takes his supper he has a girl kneel on sharp pebbles, and if in the course of the entire meal she stirs, she is not paid. Above her are two tilted candles whence hot tallow spills upon her bare back and breasts. She need but make the slightest movement and she is packed off without being paid a sou.

104. He obliges her to remain four days in a very narrow iron cage, wherein she can neither sit nor lie down; he feeds her through the bars. He is the one Desgranges will mention in connection with the turkey's ballet.

That same evening, Curval depucelates Colombe's cunt.

THE 22ND. 105. He wraps a girl and a cat in a large blanket, has her stand and dance about; the cat bites, scratches her as she falls to the floor; but, come what may, she must skip and leap, and continue her antics until the man discharges.

106. He massages a woman with a certain substance which causes her skin to itch so violently that she scratches herself till her blood flows; he watches her at work, frigging himself the while.

107. He gives a woman a potion to drink, it halts her menstruating, and thus he makes her run the risk of grave illness.

108. He makes her swallow a medicine intended for horses, it causes her horrible gripes and colics; he watches her suffer and shit all day long.

109. He rubs a naked girl with honey, then binds her to a column and releases upon her a swarm of large flies.

That same evening, Colombe's cunt is put at the free disposition of the company.

THE 23RD. 110. He places the girl upon a pivot which revolves with prodigious speed. She is naked and bound and turns until he discharges.

111. He keeps a girl suspended head downward until he discharges.

112. Makes her swallow a heavy dose of emetic, persuades her she has been poisoned, and frigs himself while watching her vomit.

113. Kneads and mauls her breasts until they are entirely black and blue.

114. Kneads and maltreats her ass for three hours; he repeats this rite for nine days in succession.

THE 24TH. 115. He has a girl climb a tall ladder until she is at least twenty feet above the ground, at which point a rung cracks and she falls, but upon mattresses prepared in advance; he walks up to her and discharges upon her body the very moment she lands, and sometimes he chooses this instant to fuck her.

116. He slaps a girl's face with all his strength and discharges while so doing; he is seated in a comfortable chair and the girl is upon her knees, facing him.

117. Beats her knuckles with hickory ferrules.

118. Powerful slaps upon her buttocks until her behind is scarlet.

119. Inserts the nozzle of a bellows in her asshole; he inflates her.

120. He introduces an enema of almost boiling water into her bowels, then amuses himself observing her writhe, and discharges upon her ass.

That evening, Aline's ass is soundly slapped by the four colleagues, who keep it up until her ass is crimson; a duenna holds her by the shoulders. A few slaps are bestowed upon Augustine's ass, too.

THE 25TH. 121. He has some pious women recruited for his pleasure, beats them with a crucifix and rosaries, and then has each of them pose as a statue of the Virgin upon an altar, but pose in a cramped position from which they are not to budge. They must remain thus throughout an exceedingly long mass; when at last the Elevation occurs, each woman is to shit upon the Host.

122. Has her run naked about a garden at night, the season is winter, the weather freezing; here and there are stretched cords upon which she trips and falls.

123. When she has removed all her clothes, he casts her, as if by accident, into a vat of nearly boiling water and prevents her from climbing out until he has first discharged upon her body.

124. Naked, on a wintry day she is secured to a post in the middle of a garden and there she remains until she has repeated five Pater Nosters and five Hail Marys, or until he has yielded his fuck, which another girl excites to flow as he contemplates the spectacle.

125. He spreads a powerful glue upon the rim of a privy seat and sends the girl in to shit; directly she sits down, her ass is caught fast. Meanwhile, from the other side a small charcoal brazier is introduced beneath her ass. Scorched, she leaps up, leaving an almost perfect circle of skin behind her.

That evening profane tricks are played at the expense of Adelaide and Sophie, the two believers, and the Duc depucelates Augustine, of whom he has been passionately fond for weeks; thrice he discharges into her cunt. And that same evening the idea enters his head to have her run naked through the courtyard, dreadful though the weather be. He proposes the idea with great energy and in forceful language, but his confreres regretfully reject it, saying that Augustine is very pretty and that the program calls for her further use; and, the Bishop points out, she still has not been depucelated aft. The Duc offers to pay two hundred louis into the common fund if the society will allow him to take her down into the cellars at once; he is again refused. He wishes at least that she have her ass spanked; she receives twenty-five blows from each friend. But the Duc applies his with his fist and discharges a fourth time between the eighteenth and nineteenth. He requisitions her for his bed and that night encunts her thrice again.

THE 26TH. 126. He gets the girl thoroughly drunk, she lies down to sleep. While asleep, her bed is raised. Toward the middle of the night, she reaches down for her chamber pot; not finding it within reach, she gropes further and tumbles out upon a mattress; the man awaits her there and fucks her as soon as she has fallen.

127. He has her run naked about the garden, he follows after her, brandishing a cabman's whip, but only threatens her with it. She is obliged to run until she falls from weariness; at which instant he springs upon her and fucks her.

128. He bestows one hundred strokes, ten at a time, with a martinet of black silk; between each series of blows, he kisses the girl's ass with great fervor.

129. He flogs her with a cat-o'-nine-tails whose thongs have been steeped in brandy, and does not discharge until the girl's blood is flowing. Then he discharges upon her buttocks.

Champville recounts only four passions on the 26th of December because it is the day of the eight week's festival. It is celebrated by the marriage of Zéphyr and Augustine, both of whom belong to the Duc and lie at night in his chamber; but prior to the ceremony, His Grace would have Curval flog the boy while he, Blangis, flogs the girl; and 'tis done. Each receives a hundred lashes, but the Duc, more than ever aroused by Augustine because she has made him discharge frequently, lays on very emphatically and is content with nothing short of much blood.

In connection with that evening's entertainments, we must fully explain the character of the Saturday punishments - how they are meted out and how many lashes are distributed. You might draw up a list itemizing the crimes and, to the right, the appropriate number of lashes.

THE 27TH. 130. He likes to whip none but little girls between the ages of five and seven, and always finds a pretext so as to make it appear as if he were punishing them.

131. A woman comes to confess to him, he is a priest; she recites all her sins, and by way of penance, he gives her five hundred lashes.

132. He receives four women and gives each six hundred lashes.

133. He has the same ceremony performed in his presence by two valets, one relieving the other when his arm is fatigued by the whipping; twenty women are dealt with, each merits six hundred strokes: the women are not bound. He frigs himself while the work is in progress.

134. He flogs only boys aged from fourteen to sixteen, and he has them discharge into his mouth afterward. Each is warmed by one hundred lashes; he always sees two at a sitting.

Augustine's cunt is surrendered that evening; Curval encunts her twice and, like the Duc, wishes to whip her when he has had done with her. Both gentlemen fall upon that charming girl like ravenous beasts; they propose a contribution of four hundred louis to the common fund in exchange for permission to take her in hand together that same evening; their offer is rejected.

THE 28TH. 135. He has a naked girl enter a chamber; whereupon two men fall upon her and each whips one of her buttocks until it is raw. She is bound. When 'tis over, he frigs the men's pricks upon the whore's bleeding ass, and frigs himself thereupon also.

136. She is bound hand and foot to the wall. Facing her, and also attached to the wall, is a blade of steel adjusted to the height of her belly. If she strives to avoid a blow, it is forward she must lunge; she cuts herself. If she wishes to avoid the blade, she must fling herself backward toward the lash.

137. He flogs a girl, giving her one hundred lashes the first day, two hundred the second, four hundred the third, etc., etc., and ceases on the ninth day.

138. He has the whore descend on all fours, climbs upon her back and faces her buttocks; he squeezes his legs tight about her ribs. Once in the saddle, he brings his lash down upon her ass and curls the thongs round to her cunt, and as for this operation he employs a martinet, he has no trouble directing his blows so that they carry into the vagina's interior, and that is just what he does.

139. He must have a pregnant woman, he has her bend backward over a cylinder which supports her back. Her head, on the other side of the cylinder, rests upon the seat of a chair and is secured to it; her hair is strewn about, her legs tied as far apart as possible and her swollen belly appears stretched exceedingly taut; her cunt fairly yawns in his face. 'Tis upon her belly he beats a tattoo, and when his whip has brought a profusion of blood into sight, he walks round to the other side of the cylinder and discharges upon her face.

N.B.-According to my notes, the adoptions do not occur until after defloration, hence say that the Duc adopts Augustine at this point. Verify whether or not this is true, and whether the adoption of the four sultanas does not occur at the very beginning, and whether at the beginning it is not said that they sleep in the bedrooms of the friends who have adopted them.

That evening, the Duc repudiates Constance, who therewith falls into the greatest discredit; however, they treat her with some consideration, because of her pregnancy, in connection with which Messieurs have certain plans. Augustine now passes for the Duc's wife, and hereafter performs none but a wife's functions upon the sofa and in the chapel. Constance descends in rank to below that of the governesses.

THE 29TH. 140. He works exclusively with girls of fifteen, and he flogs them with sting nettles and holly until they are bleeding; his taste in asses is highly developed, he is not easy to please.

141. Flogs only with a bull's pizzle, continuing until the buttocks are in tatters; he uses four women one after another.

142. Flogs only with steel-tipped martinets, discharges only when blood is flowing generally.

143. The same man of whom Desgranges will speak on the 20th of February requires pregnant women; he flogs with a bullwhip, by means of which he is able to remove respectable chunks of flesh from the buttocks; from time to time he aims a blow or two at her belly.

Rosette is flogged that evening, and Curval has her forward maidenhead. The intrigue between Hercule and Julie is brought to light; she has been having herself fucked. When scolded for her misbehavior, she replies libertinely; she is therewith whipped extraordinarily. Then, because Messieurs are fond of her, and also of Hercule, who has given yeoman service so far, they are pardoned and frolicked with.

THE 30TH. 144. He places a candle at a certain height. Attached to the middle finger of her right hand is a piece of bread soaked in wax and set afire; if she does not make haste, she'll be burned. Her task is, with this bit of ignited bread, to light the other candle set high upon the shelf; she is obliged to leap in order to reach it; the libertine, armed with a leathern-thonged whip, lashes her with all his strength, to encourage her to leap higher and to light the candle more quickly. If she succeeds, there's an end to the game; if not, she is flogged till she falls unconscious.

145. He flogs first his wife, then his daughter, and prostitutes them at the brothel in order to have them whipped while he looks on, but this is not the same man of whom we have already spoken.

146. Whips with a cat-o'-nine-tails, from the nape of the neck to the calves of the legs; the girl is bound, he excoriates her entire back.

147. Whips breasts only; he insists that they be exceedingly large. And pays twice the sum when the woman is pregnant.

Rosette's cunt is delivered up to the society that evening; after Curval and the Duc have thoroughly fucked it, they and their colleagues thoroughly whip it. She is down on her hands and knees; Messieurs take care to drive the martinet's steel tips well up into her.

THE 31ST. 148. He whips the face only, using a bundle of dry switches; he must have charming faces. Desgranges will refer to him on the 7th of February.

149. Using switches, he impartially lashes the entire body, sparing nothing, face, cunt, and breasts included.

150. Gives two hundred blows of the bull's pizzle, these being distributed evenly up and down the backs of lads aged from sixteen to twenty.

151. He is in a room, four girls arouse and flog him; when at last he is all afire, he leaps upon a fifth girl, who is naked and awaiting him in the next room and, wielding a bull's pizzle, he assails whatever of her he can reach, maintaining the hail of blows until he discharges; but in order that his ejaculation arrive sooner and the patient suffer less, he is not sent into the second room until his discharge is imminent.

Champville is applauded, the same honors are bestowed upon her that were given Duclos, and that evening both storytellers dine with Messieurs. Later, at the orgies, Adelaide, Aline, Augustine, and Zelmire are condemned to be whipped with switches all over the body save upon the breasts, but as the friends are to sport with them for another two months, they are treated circumspectly.

Part the Third

The 150 Criminal Passions, or Those Belonging to the Third Class, Composing the Thirty-one Days of January Passed in Hearing the Narrations of Madame Martaine; Interspersed Amongst Which Are the Scandalous Doings at the Château During That Month; All Being Set down in the Form of a Journal. (Draft)

THE 1ST OF JANUARY. 1. He loves nothing but to have himself embuggered, and he is never able to find too thick a prick. But, says Martaine, she'll not lay much emphasis upon this passion which is too simple a taste and one wherewith her auditors are far too well acquainted.

2. He wishes to depucelate none but little girls between the ages of three and seven, in the bum. This is the man who had her pucelage in this manner: she was four years old, the ordeal caused her to fall ill, her mother implored this man to give aid, money. But his heart was of flint. . . .

And this man is the same one of whom Duclos spoke on the 29th of November; the same again who appears in Champville's story of the 2nd of December. He has a prick of colossal proportions, he is enormously rich. He depucelates two little girls every day: one of them in the cunt, in the morning, as Champville related on the 2nd of December, the other in the bum, in the afternoon; and he has a quantity of other passions as well. Four women held Martaine when he embuggered her. His discharge lasts six minutes, and he bellows like a bull while it is in progress. His simple, straightforward, and adroit method of threading her needle, even though she was a young thing of four; describe all that.

3. Her mother sells the pucelage of Martaine's older brother to a man who sodomizes boys only, and who would have them exactly seven years old.

4. She is now thirteen, her brother fifteen; they go to the home of a man who constrains the brother to fuck his sister, and who alternately fucks now the boy's ass, now the girl's, while they are in each other's clutches.

Martaine proudly describes her ass; Messieurs request her to display it, she exhibits it from the platform.

The man she has just spoken of, she continues, is the same person who figured in Duclos' story of the 21st of November, the Comte, and who will appear in Desgranges' of the 24th of February.

5. He has himself fucked while embuggering the brother and sister; the same personage Desgranges will refer to on the 24th of February.

That same evening, the Duc depucelates the bum of Hébé, who is merely twelve. The operation succeeds only at the price of infinite trouble: she is held by the four duennas and administered by Duclos and Champville. And as there is to be a festival on the morrow, in order that things run smoothly then, Hébé's ass is also, on the evening of the 1st of January, surrendered to the society, and all four friends take full advantage of it. She is carried away unconscious; has been buggered seven times.

(Martaine must not say that she has a uterine deformity; that would be false.)

THE 2ND. 6. He has four girls fart in his mouth all the while he embuggers a fifth, then he changes girls. All rotate: all fart, all are embuggered; he does not discharge until he has finished with the fifth ass.

7. Amuses himself with three small boys: embuggers and has each of them shit, puts all three to each task, and frigs the boy who is inactive.

8. He fucks the sister in the mouth while having her brother shit into his mouth, then he reverses their roles, and during both exercises he is embuggered.

9. He embuggers none but girls of fifteen, but only after having, by way of preliminary, flogged them with all his strength.

10. For an hour he pinches and molests her buttocks and asshole, then embuggers her while she is flogged with exceeding violence.

The ninth week's festival is celebrated upon that day: Hercule weds Hébé and fucks her cuntwardly. Curval and the Duc take turns sodomizing first the husband, then the wife.

THE 3RD. 11. He embuggers only during mass, and discharges at the moment of the Elevation of the Host.

12. He embuggers only while kicking a crucifix about in the dust; the girl must treat it with like contempt.

13. The man who amused himself with Eugénie on Duclos' eleventh day has the girl shit, wipes the well-beshitted ass; he possesses an outsized prick, and embuggers, ploughing into the asshole behind a consecrated Host.

14. Embuggers a youth, has a second youth embugger him, both ploughing, as above, behind a protective Host; upon the nape of the neck of the boy he is

embuggering rests another Host, and a third youth shits thereupon. He discharges thus, without changing position, but while uttering fearful blasphemies.

15. He embuggers the priest while the latter is in the act of saying mass, and when the priest has performed the consecration, the fucker withdraws for a moment; profiting from this brief interval, the priest buries the Host in his ass, the fucker returns straightway to work and re-embuggers him, tamping in the wafer.

That evening, Curval, with a Host depucelates in the bum the young and charming Zélamir. And Antinoüs fucks the Président with another Host; while fucking, the Président's tongue pushes a third into Fanchon's asshole.

THE 4TH. 16. He likes to embugger none but very aged women while they are being lashed.

17. Embuggers only very aged men while being fucked.

18. Has a regular intrigue with his son.

19. Will embugger none but monsters, or blackamoors, or deformed persons.

20. In order to combine incest, adultery, sodomy and sacrilege, he embuggers his married daughter with a Host.

That evening the four friends avail themselves of Zélamir's ass.

THE 5TH. 21. He has two men alternately fuck and flagellate him while he embuggers a young boy and while an old man sheds a turd into his mouth. He eats the turd.

22. Two men take turns fucking him, one in the mouth, the other in the ass; this exercise must last no less than three hours by the clock. He swallows the fuck emanating from him who fucks him in the mouth.

23. He has himself fucked by ten men, whom he pays so much by the discharge; during a given day he withstands as many as twenty-four without himself discharging.

24. For the purposes of ass-fuckery, he prostitutes his wife, his daughter, and his sister, and watches the proceedings.

25. He employs eight men at a time: one in his mouth, one in his ass, one beneath his left testicle, one beneath his right; he frigs two others, each with one hand, he lodges a seventh between his thighs and the eighth frigs himself upon his face.

That evening, the Duc deflowers Michette's ass and causes her frightful pain.

THE 6TH. 26. He has an elderly man embuggered in his presence; several times over the prick is removed from that ancient asshole, it is placed in the mouth of the examiner, who sucks it, then sucks the old man's prick, sucks his asshole, and penetrates it while he who has been fucking the old man now embuggers the lecher, and is lashed by the lecher's governess. For the lecher is still a young man.

27. He vigorously constricts the neck of the fifteen-year-old girl he is embuggering - choking her neck has the effect of tightening her anus; meanwhile, he is flogged with a bull's pizzle.

28. He has large spheres of quicksilver inserted into his bowels. These spheres rise up in his entrails, then descend, and during the excessive titillation caused thereby, he sucks pricks, swallows fuck, has shit out of whores' asses, bolts turds. This ecstasy lasts a good two hours.

29. He would have himself embuggered by the father while he sodomizes that father's son and daughter.

Michette's ass is surrendered to the company that evening. Durcet selects Martaine for his bedroom companion, following the precedent established by the Duc, who has Duclos, and by Curval, who has Fanchon; Martaine has begun to exert upon Durcet much the same lubricious influence Duclos exerts upon Blangis.

THE 7TH. 30. He fucks a turkey whose head is gripped between the legs of a girl lying on her belly - while in action he looks quite as if he were embuggering the girl. While he is at work he is being sodomized, and the moment he discharges, the girl cuts the turkey's throat.

31. He fucks a goat from behind while being flogged; the goat conceives and gives birth to a monster. Monster though it be, he embuggers it.

32. He embuggers bucks.

33. Wishes to see a woman discharge after having been frigged by a dog; and he shoots the dog dead while its head is between the woman's thighs. But he does not harm the woman.

34. Embuggers a swan after having popped a Host up into its ass; then strangles the bird upon discharging.

This same evening, the Bishop embuggers Cupidon for the first time.

THE 8TH. 35. He has himself placed in a specially prepared wickerwork structure provided with an opening at one end; against this opening he places his asshole after having anointed it with mare's fuck. The structure he is in represents a mare's body and is covered with horsehide. A genuine horse is fetched in, mounts the artificial mare, embuggers him and meanwhile he fucks a pretty white bitch he has with him in the basket.

36. He fucks a cow, it conceives and gives birth to a monster which, shortly thereafter, he fucks.

37. In a similar basket he places a woman who receives a bull's member in her cunt. He watches this entertaining spectacle.

38. He has a tamed serpent which he introduces into his anus; while being thus sodomized, he embuggers a cat in a basket. Firmly contained therein, the animal can do him no harm.

39. He fucks a she-ass while having himself embuggered by an ass. (For this delight an elaborate machine is indispensable. We will give a description of it elsewhere.)

That evening, Cupidon's ass is presented to the society.

THE 9TH. 40. He fucks the nostrils of a goat which meanwhile is licking his balls; and during this exercise, he is alternately flogged and has his asshole licked.

41. He embuggers a sheep while a dog is licking his asshole.

42. He embuggers a dog whose head is cut off while he discharges.

43. He obliges a whore to frig a donkey, he is fucked while observing this spectacle.

44. He fucks a monkey's asshole, the animal is enclosed in a basket; while being sodomized, the monkey is tormented in order that its anus will constrict about the libertine's member.

That evening, the tenth week's festival is celebrated by the marriage of Bum-Cleaver and Michette; the union is consummated, 'tis a dolorous experience for the bride.

THE 10TH. Martaine announces that she is going to move on to another passion, and that the whip, of central importance in Champville's contributions of December, will enjoy only a secondary one in hers.

45. The procuress is obliged to find him girls guilty of some felony or other; he arrives, frightens them, says that they are going certainly to be arrested but that he will take it upon himself to protect them provided they will submit to a violent fustigation, and, afraid as they are, they let themselves be whipped till they bleed.

46. Has a woman with beautiful hair brought to him, saying he simply wishes to examine her hair; but he cuts it off very traitorously and discharges upon seeing her melt into tears and bewail her misfortune, at which he laughs immoderately.

47. With all sorts of attendant ceremonies, she enters a dark room. She sees no one there, but overhears a conversation regarding her - give details of this conversation - which is of a nature to frighten her nearly to death. Finally, she receives a deluge of slaps and blows without knowing whence they come; she hears the cries accompanying a discharge, then is taken out of the room.

48. She enters a kind of subterranean sepulcher which is lit by nothing but a few oil lamps; they reveal all the horror of the place. After a moment, during which she is able to observe everything, all the lamps are extinguished, a horrible series of screams and the rattling of chains are heard, she collapses in a swoon; if she does not faint, the noises are multiplied until finally she does fall unconscious from terror. Once unconscious, a man swoops down upon her and embuggers her, then abandons her, and valets later come to her rescue; he must have very young and very inexperienced girls. Novices, if possible.

49. She enters a similar place, but provide a few details to distinguish it from the sepulcher above. She is stripped, thrust naked into a coffin, the coffin's lid is nailed down, and the rhythm of the hammer driving the nails finally excites the man's discharge.

That afternoon, Zelmire was taken down to the cellars we have previously mentioned, which had been prepared in the manner we have just described. The four friends are there, naked and equipped with weapons; Zelmire swoons, and while she is unconscious, Curval depucelates her bum. The Président has been seized by the very same sentiments of love (mixed with lubric rage) for this girl that the Duc has for Augustine.

THE 11TH. 50. The same Duc de Florville, of whom Duclos spoke on the 29th of November, and of whom Desgranges, in her fifth story, will speak on the 26th of February, wishes to have the corpse of a beautiful and recently murdered girl placed upon a bed covered with black satin; he fondles the body, explores its every nook and cranny, and embuggers it.

51. Another individual requires two corpses, those of a boy and of a girl, and he embuggers the youth's dead body while kissing the buttocks of the girl's and driving his tongue into its anus.

52. He receives the girl in a small room filled with most convincing wax representations of dead bodies, they are all pierced in various ways. He recommends that the girl make her choice, saying he intends to kill her in whatever way she prefers, inviting her to choose the corpse whose wounds please her most.

53. He binds her to an authentic corpse, knee to knee, mouth to mouth, and flogs her until the back of her body is covered with blood.

Zelmire's ass is made the evening's treat, but before being served up, she is subjected to a trial, and she is advised that she will be killed that night; she believes what she is told but, instead of dispatching her, Messieurs are content each to give her a hundred lashes after having generously embuggered her, and Curval takes her to bed with him. She is further embuggered all night.

THE 12TH. 54. The girl must be menstruating. She arrives at his home, a valet conducts her to a room in the cellar where the libertine stands awaiting her, but he is near a kind of reservoir of icy water, more than twelve feet across and eight deep; it is concealed in such a way the girl does not notice it. She approaches the man, he topples her into it, and discharges the instant he hears the splash; she is pulled back out at once, but as she is menstruating, severe disability is the very frequent result of her adventure.

55. He lowers her into a very deep well and shouts down after her that he is about to fill it with large stones; he flings in a few clods of earth to frighten her, and discharges into the well, his seed landing on the naked whore's head.

56. He has a pregnant woman brought to him and terrifies her with threats and words, flogs her, continuing his ill-treatment of her until she either has a miscarriage there and then, or will surely have one when she returns home. If she disgorges her fruit while under his roof, she receives double payment.

57. He locks her into a black dungeon, surrounded by cats, rats, and mice; he gives her to understand she has been put there for the rest of her life, and every day he goes to her door, frigs himself, and banters with her.

58. He inserts sheafs of straw in her ass, ignites them, and watches her buttocks sizzle as the straw burns short.

That evening, Curval announces he will take Zelmire to be his wife, and does indeed publicly marry her. The Bishop officiates at the wedding, the Président repudiates Julie who therewith falls into the greatest discredit, but her libertinage speaks strongly in her favor and the Bishop is disposed to protect her somewhat until the time shall arrive for him to declare himself entirely for her - he will so declare himself later on.

More clearly than ever before, upon this particular evening his associates notice Durcet's teasing hatred for Adelaide; he torments her, vexes her, she wails and is melancholy. And her father, the Président, does not by any means give her his support.

THE 13TH. 59. He attaches a girl to a St. Andrew's cross suspended in the air, and whips her with all his might, flaying her entire back. After which, he unties her and casts her out through a window, but mattresses are there to lighten her fall, upon hearing which he discharges. Give further details of the scene in order to justify his reaction.

60. He has her swallow a drug which unhinges her imagination and causes her to see horrible things in the room. She fancies the room is being flooded, sees the water rise, climbs upon a chair, but still the water mounts, reaches her, and she is told that she has no alternative but to leap in and swim; she plunges, but falls upon the stone floor and injures herself badly. 'Tis at this point the libertine discharges; previously, he has taken much pleasure in kissing her ass.

61. He holds her suspended by a rope that runs up through a pulley affixed to the top of a tower; he stands at a window, she hangs directly outside and opposite him. He frigs himself and threatens to sever the rope as he discharges. While all this is afoot he is being flogged, and earlier he induces the whore to shit for him.

62. She is held by four slender cords, each attached to one of her limbs. She is held thus in a very cruel and painful position; a trap door is opened beneath her and a charcoal brazier, very hot, is discovered to her view: if the cords break, she falls thereupon. The roué meddles with the cords, strains them, cuts one while discharging. Sometimes he suspends the girl in the same attitude, places a weight upon her belly, then suddenly jerks all four cords, pulling her up, and in so doing rupturing her stomach and tearing her muscles. She remains where she is until he discharges.

63. He binds her to a low stool; suspended a foot above her head is a dagger whose point is filed needle sharp; the dagger hangs by a hair - if the hair snaps, the dagger drives into her skull. The libertine frigs himself while watching his victim's anxious contortions. An hour later, he frees her and bloodies her buttocks with light jabs of the same dagger which, he would like to have her remark, pricks very nicely; he discharges upon her bloodsoaked ass.

That evening, the Bishop depucelates Colombe's bum, and after his discharge lashes her with a whip, for he cannot bear to have a girl cause him to discharge.

THE 14TH. 64. He embuggers a young novice who knows nothing of the ways of the world, and as he discharges, he fires two pistol shots very close to her ear. The powder singes her hair.

65. He makes her sit down in an armchair balanced on springs; her weight releases a number of springs connected to iron rings which bind her tightly to the chair. Certain levers and gears advance twenty daggers until their points graze her

skin; the man frigs himself, the while explaining that the least movement of the chair will cause her to be stabbed. He sprays his fuck upon her, in so doing touching the chair very delicately with his foot.

66. A bascule carries her down into a small crypt hung in black and furnished with a prie-dieu, a coffin, and an assortment of death's heads. She sees six specters armed with clubs, swords, pistols, sabers, poignards, and lances, and each is about to pierce her in a different place. Overcome by fear, she sways, is about to fall; the man enters, catches her in his arms, and flogs her until he is weary, then discharges as he embuggers her. If she is unconscious at the time he enters, and this is frequently the case, his lash restores her to her senses.

67. She enters a room in a tower, in its center she sees a large charcoal brazier; upon a table, poison and a dirk; she is allowed to choose the manner whereby she is to perish. It generally happens that she selects poison. 'Tis a variety of opiate which plunges her into a profound drowsiness; while the spell lasts, the libertine embuggers her. He is the same personage Duclos cited on the 27th of November and of whom Desgranges will say more on the 6th of February.

68. The same gentleman who will figure in Desgranges' story of the 16th of February goes through the entire ceremony of preparing to decapitate the girl; just as the blow falls, a rope suddenly snatches the girl's body away, the axe-blade sinks three inches into the block. If the rope does not drag the girl away, she dies. He discharges while bringing down the axe. But prior to this, he has embuggered her as she lies with her neck upon the block.

Colombe's ass is plumbed by the society that evening, and Messieurs pretend to cut off her head. They are accomplished actors.

THE 15TH. 69. He slips a noose around the whore's throat and hangs her. Her feet rest upon a stool, a cord is tied to one leg of the stool, he sits in an armchair, watching and having the whore's daughter frig him. When he discharges, he pulls the cord, the whore hangs, he leaves, valets enter and cut the whore down. A leech lets some blood from one of her veins and she returns to life, but these attentions are given her without the libertine's knowledge. He goes off to bed with the whore's daughter and sodomizes her all night long, while doing so telling her he has hanged her mother. Have Martaine say that Desgranges will refer to him again.

70. He holds the girl by the ears and walks her around the room, discharging as he parades with her.

71. He pinches the girl's body, nipping her everywhere save upon the breast, till she turns black and blue.

72. He pinches her breasts, molests them, and kneads them until they are completely bruised.

73. He writes letters and words upon her breasts, working with a needle which has a poisoned tip; her breasts become infected, and she suffers excruciatingly.

74. Drives between one and two thousand pins into her breasts, and discharges when he has covered them.

More libertine with every passing day, Julie is discovered frigging herself with Champville. The Bishop affords her additional protection and thereafter admits her into his bedchamber, as the Duc has Duclos, Durcet Martaine, and Curval Fanchon. Julie confesses that at the time of her repudiation, having been condemned to sleep in the stables with the other animals, she appealed to Champville and was taken into her chamber; they have been bedding together ever since.

THE 16TH. 75. He buries large hatpins in the girl's flesh, dotting her entire body, her nipples included; he discharges after having driven home the last pin. Desgranges will return to the same enthusiast in her fourth story of the 27th of February.

76. He gives her a great deal to drink, then sews up her cunt and asshole; he leaves her thus sealed up till he remarks she is nigh to collapsing from the need to piss and shit, two activities which are impossible in the state she is in; or else he waits until the weight of the shit and the pressure of the piss finally breaks the stitches.

77. Four gentlemen enter the room and cuff the girl, strike and kick her until she falls. When she is down, all four mutually frig one another and discharge.

78. She is deprived of air, then given air, then 'tis taken away again. She is lodged within a pneumatic machine.

To celebrate the end of the eleventh week, the wedding of Colombe and Antinoüs takes place that day, and is consummated. The Duc, who has been indulging in some prodigious cunt-fuckery with Augustine, has been seized by a lubricious fury: he has had Duclos hold her, and has given her three hundred lashes distributed between the middle of her back and her calves, and, after that, has embuggered Duclos while kissing Augustine's flogged ass. Directly after having molested her, he does some foolish things, for his head is completely giddy: he has her sit beside him at table, will touch no food save what he has out of her mouth, dotes upon her, and does a thousand other things, all very illogical and very libertine. But he and his confreres are men of that strange turn of character.

THE 17TH. 79. He binds the girl belly down upon a dining table and eats a piping hot omelette served upon her buttocks. He uses an exceedingly sharp fork.

80. He immobilizes her head above a grill, lights a brisk fire, and roasts her until she loses consciousness, embuggering her steadily.

81. He gently toasts the skin of her breasts and buttocks, proceeding very gradually, and using sulphur-tipped matches.

82. He uses candles and extinguishes them again and again by snuffing them out in her cunt, her asshole, and upon her nipples.

83. With a match he sears her eyelids; this prevents her from sleeping soundly that night, for she cannot close her eyes.

That evening, the Duc depucelates Giton, who finds the experience discomfiting, for the Duc is enormous, fucks with great brutality, and Giton is, after all, only twelve.

THE 18TH. 84. Pointing a pistol at her heart, he obliges her to chew and swallow a live coal, and then he washes out her cunt with aqua fortis.

85. He has her dance the olivettes. Naked, she is to dance round four pillars; but the only path her naked feet can tread is studded with shards of broken glass and bits of sharp metal and pointed tacks and nails; by each pillar stands a man, a bundle of switches in his hand, and he lashes whichever side of her body she offers every time she passes by him. She is thus obliged to run a certain number of turns around, it all depending upon whether she is more or less attractive. The most beautiful are harried the most.

86. He strikes her violently in the face until the blows of his fist bring blood from her nose, and he continues yet a while longer, the blood notwithstanding; he discharges and mixes his fuck with the blood she has lost.

87. Employing very well-heated tongs, he pinches her flesh, and mainly her buttocks, her mons veneris and her breasts. Desgranges will have more to say about this personage.

88. Upon various parts of her naked, reclining body, especially the more sensitive areas, he places little mounds of gunpowder, then sets fire to them.

Giton's ass is made public property that evening, and after this ceremony, he is flogged by Curval, the Duc, and the Bishop, who have fucked him.

THE 19TH. 89. He inserts a cylinder of gunpowder in her cunt, removes the cylinder, leaves the powder there; he puts a match to the charge and ejaculates upon seeing the flames dart forth. Earlier, he has kissed her ass.

90. He soaks her everywhere from head to foot with brandy, brings a match near and entertains himself with the spectacle of this poor girl all covered with flames. Then he discharges. He repeats the same operation two or three times.

91. He gives her bowels a rinsing with boiling oil.

92. He introduces a red-hot iron into her anus, another into her cunt, after having thoroughly whipped the latter.

93. He likes to trample upon a pregnant woman until she aborts. Prior to this he whips her.

That same evening, Curval depucelates Sophie's bum, but this ordeal succeeds another: she has first been given one hundred lashes by each of the friends and is streaming blood. Directly Curval has discharged into her ass, he offers to pay the society five hundred louis for permission to take her down to the cellars that very evening and to be given a free hand with her. Curval's request is rejected, he re-embuggers her, and upon emerging from her ass after this second discharge, he gives her a kick which sends her sprawling upon a mattress fifteen feet away. He revenges himself upon Zelmire, whom he flogs till his arm aches.

THE 20TH. 94. He appears to be caressing the girl who is frigging him, she suspects nothing; but at the moment he discharges, he seizes her head and batters it against the wall. The blow is so strong and so unexpected that she usually falls unconscious.

95. They are four libertines assembled; they judge a girl, and, ultimately disagreeing upon what punishment to inflict, decide to sentence her individually. All in all, she receives one hundred strokes of the whip; each juror metes out twenty-five of them: the first flogs her from the back to the loins, the second from the loins to the calves, the third from the neck to the navel, breasts included, the fourth from the belly to the shins.

96. Using a pin, he pricks each of her eyes, each nipple, and her clitoris.

97. He drops molten sealing wax upon her buttocks, into her cunt, and upon her breasts.

98. He opens the veins in one arm and bleeds her until she faints.

Curval suggests they bleed Constance because of her pregnancy; and bled she is, until she collapses, 'tis Durcet who acts as her leech. That evening, Messieurs avail themselves of Sophie's ass, and the Duc proposes she be bled also, it could not possibly do her any harm, no, on the contrary, they might make a nice pudding of her blood for tomorrow's luncheon. His idea is acclaimed, Curval now plays the leech, Duclos frigs him while he operates, and he wishes to make the puncture at the same moment his fuck departs his balls; and he makes a generous puncture, but his blade finds the vein none the less. Despite it all, Sophie has pleased the Bishop, who adopts her for his wife, repudiating Aline, who falls into the greatest discredit.

THE 21ST. 99. He bleeds both of her arms and would have her remain standing while her blood flows; now and again he stops the bleeding and flogs her, then opens the wounds again, and this continues until she collapses. He only discharges when she faints. Earlier in the game he had her shit for him.

100. He bleeds her from all four of her limbs and from her jugular vein too, and frigs himself while watching the five fountains of blood.

101. He lightly scarifies her flesh, concentrating upon her buttocks, but neglecting her breasts.

102. He scarifies her vigorously, cutting deep, devoting particular attention to her breasts and especially to her nipples, and to the environs of her asshole when he turns his attentions to her behind. Next, he cauterizes the wounds with a red-hot iron.

103. He is bound hand and foot, as if he were a wild beast, and he is draped in a tiger's skin. When thus readied, he is excited, irritated, whipped, beaten, his ass is frigged; opposite him is a plump young girl, naked and tied by her feet to the floor, by her neck to the ceiling, in such wise she cannot stir. When the roué is all a-sweat, his captors free him, he leaps upon the girl, bites her everywhere and above all her clitoris and her nipples, which he generally manages to remove with his teeth. He roars and cries like a ferocious animal, and discharges while shrieking. The girl must shit, he eats her turd upon the floor.

That evening, the Bishop depucelates Narcisse; he is surrendered to the society the same evening, so that the festival of the 23rd will not be disturbed. Before embuggering him, the Duc has him shit into his mouth and render him, together with the turd, his predecessors' fuck. And then, after having sodomized the lad, Blangis scourges him.

THE 22ND. 104. He pulls out her teeth and scratches her gums with needles. Sometimes he heats the needles.

105. He breaks one of her fingers, several upon occasion.

106. Employing a heavy hammer, he flattens one of her feet.

107. He removes a hand, sawing through the wrist.

108. While discharging, he batters in her front teeth with a hammer. He is very fond of sucking her mouth before proceeding to the major phase of his operation.

The Duc depucelates Rosette in the rear that evening, and the same instant his prick sounds her ass, Curval extracts one of the little girl's teeth - this in order that she may experience two terrible pains at the same time. So that the morrow's festival not be disturbed, her ass is made generally available that same evening. When Curval has discharged thereinto (and he is the last of the four to do so), he sends the child spinning with a blow of his fist.

THE 23RD. Because of the holiday, only four are related.

109. He amputates one foot.

110. He breaks one of her arms as he embuggers her.

111. Using a crowbar, he breaks a bone in her leg and embuggers her after doing so.

112. He ties her to a stepladder, her limbs being attached in a peculiar manner, a cord is tied to the ladder; he pulls the cord, the ladder falls. Sometimes she breaks one limb, sometimes another.

Upon that day Invictus was married to Rosette; their wedding celebrated the twelfth week's festival. That evening, Rosette is bled after she has been fucked, and Aline is likewise bled after Hercule has fucked her; both are bled in such a way their blood spurts upon our libertines' thighs and pricks. Messieurs frig themselves while looking on, and discharge when both have fainted.

THE 24TH. 113. He cuts off one of her ears. (See to it that you specify what these persons do by way of a prelude to their major stunt.)

114. He slits her lips and nostrils.

115. After having sucked and bitten it, he pierces her tongue with a hot iron.

116. He tears several nails from her fingers, and also from her toes.

117. He cuts off one of her fingers at the last joint.

And, upon close questioning, the storyteller having said that, provided the wound is dressed at once, such a mutilation has no undesirable aftereffects, Durcet straightway cuts the end off one of Adelaide's fingers, for his lewd jesting and teasing have been increasingly directed against her. His practical joke fetches a discharge from him, his flow of fuck is accompanied by unheard-of transports.

That same evening, Curval depucelates Augustine's ass, even though she is now the Duc's wife. Her anguish, her sufferings. Curval rages against her afterward; he conspires with the Duc to take her down to the cellars without further delay, and they tell Durcet that if they are granted permission to carry out the expedition, they in their turn will allow him to dispatch Adelaide at once, but the Bishop delivers an impassioned sermon to those truants, and obtains the promise that they will restrain themselves yet a little longer for the sake of their own pleasure. Curval and the Duc hence limit themselves to giving Augustine a ferocious whipping. Both lash her at once.

THE 25TH. 118. He distills fifteen or twenty drops of molten lead into her mouth and burns her gums with aqua fortis.

119. After having had her lick his beshitted ass with her tongue, he snips off the end of that same tongue, then, when once she is mutilated, he embuggers her.

120. He employs a machine involving a hollow steel bit which bores holes in the flesh and which, when removed, takes with it a round chunk of flesh which is as long as the drill has penetrated; the machine bores on automatically if not withdrawn.

121. He transforms a boy of ten or twelve into a eunuch.

122. With a pair of pliers isolating and raising each nipple, he cuts off the same with a pair of scissors.

That same evening, Augustine's ass is made generally available. While embuggering her, Curval had wished to kiss Constance's breast, and upon discharging, he made off with a nipple in his teeth, but as her wound was treated and bandaged at once, Messieurs assured one another that the accident would have no harmful effect upon the child in her womb. Curval says to his colleagues, in answer to their pleasantries upon his mounting rage against Constance, that he has no control over the fury she inspires in him.

When in his turn the Duc embuggers Augustine, his own powerful feelings for that beautiful girl are exhaled with incomparable violence: had the others not kept an eye upon him, he would have injured her, either while mauling her breasts or squeezing her neck with all his strength as he discharged. Once again he asks the society to put her in his power, but he is requested to wait for Desgranges' narrations. His brother entreats him to be patient and abstain until he himself sets an example by dispatching Aline; haste, the Bishop points out, makes waste; and why spoil the latter part of the holiday by upsetting a schedule admirably designed to guarantee them a daily fare of moderation, wherein only happiness lies? However, the Duc will not listen to reason, he cannot any longer hold himself in check, and so, since he absolutely must torture the lovely girl, he is allowed to inflict a light wound upon her arm. He executes it upon the fleshy part of her left forearm, sucks blood from the cut he has made, and discharges; Augustine is so skillfully patched up that four days later no trace of the Duc's teeth marks is to be seen.

THE 26TH. 123. He breaks a bottle of thin glass against the face of the girl, who is bound and unable to protect herself; before doing so, he sucked her mouth with great vigor and sucked her tongue also.

124. He tears off both her legs, ties one of her hands behind her back, puts a little stick into her free hand, and invites her to defend herself. Then he attacks

her, wielding his sword with great vigor and dexterity, wounds her here and there, and finally discharges upon her wounds.

125. He stretches her upon a St. Andrew's cross, goes through the ceremony of breaking her, strains but does not dislocate three of her limbs, but does definitely break the fourth, either an arm or a leg.

126. Pistol in hand, he has her stand facing to the right and lets fly with a charge which grazes her two breasts; he aims to shoot away one of her little nipples.

127. He has her crouch down twenty feet away and present her buttocks; he shoots a bullet up her ass.

That same evening, the Bishop depucelates Fanny's bum.

THE 27TH. 128. The same man of whom Desgranges will speak on the 24th of February flogs a pregnant woman upon the belly until she miscarries; she must lay the egg in his presence, and he lashes her till she does.

129. He very tidily castrates a young lad of sixteen or seventeen after having embuggered and whipped him.

130. He must have a maiden brought to him, he slices off her clitoris with a razor, then deflowers her with a cylinder of heated iron, driving the device home with hammer blows.

131. This personage performs an abortion when the woman's pregnancy has entered its eighth month. He forces her to drink a certain brew which brings the child out dead in a trice. Upon other occasions, this libertine by his art causes the child to be born from the mother's asshole. But the child emerges dead, and the woman's life is gravely imperiled.

132. He severs an arm.

That evening, Fanny's ass is made generally available, Durcet rescues her from a torture his colleagues had been preparing for her; he takes her to be his wife, has the Bishop perform the marriage, and repudiates Adelaide, who is submitted to the torture originally readied for Fanny. It is however a paltry business after all: the Duc embuggers her while Durcet breaks her finger.

THE 28TH. 133. He cuts off both hands at the wrist and cauterizes the wounds with a hot iron.

134. He removes the tongue, cutting it at the roots, and cauterizes it with a hot iron.

135. He amputates one leg, usually having someone else cut it off while he embuggers her.

136. He extracts all her teeth, replacing each one with a red-hot nail, which he secures in place with a hammer; he does this directly after having fucked the woman in the mouth.

137. He removes one eye.

Julie is roundly whipped by everyone that evening and all her fingers are pricked with a needle. This latter operation takes place while the Bishop, who is passing fond of her, embuggers her.

THE 29TH. 138. Allowing molten sealing wax to flow thereupon, he blinds and ultimately dissolves first one eye, then the other.

139. He neatly slices off one breast, then cauterizes the wound with a hot iron. Desgranges will here interject that 'tis this same man who made off with the nipple she is missing, and that she is positively certain he ate it after having cooked it upon a griddle.

140. He amputates both buttocks after having flogged and embuggered her. It is believed that he too eats the meat.

141. He shaves off both her ears.

142. Clips off all the extremities, to wit: ten fingers, ten toes, two nipples, one clitoris and the end of the tongue.

That evening, Aline, after a vigorous whipping given her by the four friends and an embuggery the Bishop performs for the last time, is condemned to have a finger on either hand and a toe on either foot cut off by each friend. Thus she loses a total of eight parts.

THE 30TH. 143. He carves away several chunks of flesh, selecting them from divers areas upon her body; he has them roasted and obliges her to eat them with him. Desgranges will mention the same man on the 8th and 17th of February.

144. He cuts off a young boy's four limbs, embuggers the trunk, feeds him well and allows him so to live; as the arms and legs were not severed too close to the body, the boy lives for quite a while. And the surgeon embuggers him steadily for approximately a year.

145. He chains one of the girl's hands and secures the chain to the wall; he leaves her thus, without food. Near her is a large knife, and just beyond her reach sits an excellent meal: if she wishes to eat, she has but to cut through her forearm; otherwise, she dies of starvation. Prior to this he has embuggered her. He observes her through a window.

146. He manacles both mother and daughter; in order that they both survive, one has got to get to the food placed not far away: survival, that is, means that one must sacrifice a hand. He amuses himself listening to them discuss their dilemma, and argue about who is to resolve it.

She recounts only four stories, for that evening the thirteenth week's festival is to take place. During it, the Duc, acting in the capacity of a woman, is married to Hercule, who is to be the husband; acting now as a man, the Duc takes Zéphyr to be his wife. The young bardash who, as the reader is aware, possesses the prettiest ass amongst the eight boys, is dressed as a girl, and so clad appears as beautiful as the goddess of love. The ceremony is consecrated by the Bishop and transpires within the sight of the entire household. The dear little Zéphyr surrenders his virginal bum to the Duc, who finds all his pleasure therein, but much trouble making a successful entry; Zéphyr is rather badly torn, and bleeds profusely. Hercule fucks the Duc throughout this operation.

THE 31ST. 147. He plucks out both her eyes and leaves her locked in a room, saying that she has before her what she needs to eat, that she has but to get up and search for it. But in order to reach the food she must cross a broad plate of iron, which, of course, she cannot see, and which is kept heated to a very high temperature. Situated at a window, he amuses himself watching how she manages: will she burn herself, or will she prefer to perish from hunger? She has been, previously, very soundly whipped.

148. He subjects her to the rope torture; this consists in having one's four limbs tied to ropes, then one is raised high in the air and suddenly dropped from a considerable height, then raised, then dropped; each fall dislocates and sometimes breaks the limbs, because one never quite falls to the ground, the ropes halting one just a short distance above it.

149. He inflicts upon her a quantity of deep wounds into which he pours boiling pitch and molten lead.

150. The moment after she gives birth to a child, he binds her hand and foot, and ties her child not far away from her. The infant wails, she is unable to get to it. And thus she must watch it expire. Then he steps up and lashes the mother, aiming his whip-strokes at her cunt and managing the thing so that the interior of her vagina is well tickled. He himself is usually the child's father.

151. He gives her copiously to drink, then sews up her cunt, her asshole and her mouth as well, and leaves her thus until the water bursts through its conduits, or until she dies.

(Determine why there is one too many; if one is to be deleted, suppress the last, for I believe I have already used it.)

That same evening, Messieurs avail themselves of Zéphyr's ass, and Adelaide is condemned to a rude fustigation, after which a hot iron is brought very close to the interior of her vagina, to her armpits, and she is slightly scorched beneath each nipple. She endures it all like a heroine and frequently invokes God. This further arouses her persecutors.

PART THE FOURTH

the 150 Murderous Passions, or Those Belonging to the Fourth Class, Composing the Twenty-eight Days of February Spent in Hearing the Narrations of Madame Desgranges; Interspersed Amongst Which Are the Scandalous Doings at the Château During That Month; All Being Set down in the Form of a Journal. (Draft)

Begin by giving a full description of the new situation which exists in February; there has been a radical change in the appearance of things. The four original wives have been repudiated, but the Bishop has extended his protection to Julie, whom he keeps near him as a kind of servant to wait upon him; Duclos has been allowed to share her quarters with Constance, whose fruit Messieurs are eager to keep from spoiling; Aline and Adelaide have been driven out of house and home and now sleep amongst animals intended for their Lordships' table. The sultanas Augustine, Zelmire, Fanny, and Sophie have replaced the wives and now fulfill all their functions, to wit: as wipers in the chapel, as waitresses at the meals, as couch companions, as Messieurs' bed companions at night. Apart from the fucker, who changes from day to day, Messieurs have:

The Duc: Augustine, Zéphyr, and Duclos in his bed, together with his fucker; he sleeps surrounded by the four of them, and Marie occupies a sofa in his bedchamber;

Curval: the Président likewise sleeps amidst Adonis, Zelmire, a fucker, and Fanchon; his room is otherwise empty;

Durcet sleeps amidst Hyacinthe, Fanny, a fucker, and Martaine (check the foregoing), and he has Louison lie upon a neighboring divan.

The Bishop sleeps amidst Céladon, Sophie, a fucker, and Julie; Thérèse sleeps upon the divan.

Which reveals that each of the little ménages, Zéphyr and Augustine, Adonis and Zelmire, Hyacinthe and Fanny, Céladon and Sophie, all of whom are married, belong, husband and wife, to a single master. Only four little girls remain in the girls' harem, and four in the boys'. Champville sleeps in the girls' quarters, Desgranges in the boys' quarters. Aline is in the stable, as we pointed out, and Constance is in Duclos' room, but alone there since Duclos spends every night in the Duc's bed.

Dinner is always served by the four sultanas (by, that is to say, the four new wives), and supper by the remaining four sultanas; a quatrain always serves coffee; but the quatrains formerly allocated to each niche in the auditorium are now reduced in number to one boy and one girl.

The reader will recall our mention of the pillars in the auditorium; at the beginning of each séance, Aline is attached to one of them, Adelaide to the other, their buttocks facing out toward the alcoves, and near each pillar is a little table covered with assorted punitive instruments; and so it is the two women are at all times ready to receive the lash. Constance has permission to sit with the storytellers. Each duenna keeps close to her couple, and Julie, completely unclothed, wanders from couch to couch, taking orders and executing them upon the spot. As always, one fucker per couch.

Such is the situation when Desgranges begins her narrations. The friends have also ruled, in a special decree, that, during this month, Aline, Adelaide, Augustine, and Zelmire shall be surrendered to Messieurs' brutal passions, and that Messieurs are at liberty, upon the described day, either to immolate them privately or to invite whichever of their friends they please to witness the sacrifice; and that with what regards Constance, she shall be employed for the celebration of the final week, a full explanation of which shall be given in due time and place. Should the Duc and Curval, who by this arrangement are to be made widowers, be disposed to take another wife to care for their needs until the end of the holiday, they shall be able to do so by making a selection from amongst the four remaining sultanas. But the pillars will remain ungarnished when the two women who garnish them now shall have been bidden a last farewell.

Desgranges starts, and after having reminded her auditors that henceforth the tales shall be those of an exclusively murderous character, she says that she will be careful, as their Lordships have enjoined her to be, to enter into the most minute details, and above all to indicate with what ordinary caprices these libertine assassins preface their more serious exercises; thus, their Lordships will be able to perceive and judge their relationships and associations, and to see how an example of simple libertinage, rectified and elaborated by an unmannerly and unprincipled individual, may lead straight to murder, and to what kind of murder. Then she begins.

THE 1ST OF FEBRUARY. 1. He used to enjoy amusing himself with a beggarwoman who had not had a bit to eat in three days, and his second passion is to leave a woman to die of hunger in a dungeon; he keeps a close watch upon her and frigs himself while examining her, but does not discharge until the day she perishes.

2. He maintains her in her prison cell, toying with her for a long season, gradually diminishing her daily portion of food; beforehand, he has her shit, and eats her turd upon a platter.

3. He formerly liked to suck the mouth and swallow its saliva; in recent days he has developed the passion of immuring a woman in a dungeon with food to last no more than a fortnight; on the thirtieth day, he enters her prison and frigs himself upon the corpse.

4. First, he would have her kiss, then he would slowly destroy her by preventing her from drinking although feeding her all she wanted to eat.

5. He would flog, then later kill the woman by depriving her of sleep.

That same evening, Michette, after having eaten a big supper, is hung head downward until she has vomited everything upon Curval, who stands frigging himself beneath her and eating the manna that descends from on high.

THE 2ND. 6. His first passion was to have her shit into his mouth, and he would eat it as it emerged; nowadays he feeds her a diet of worthless bread and cheap wine. A month on this fare and she starves to death.

7. He was once a great cunt-fucker; now he gives the woman a venereal distemper by injection, but of such virulence she croaks in very short order.

8. As a youth, he was fond of receiving vomit in his mouth, now, by means of a certain decoction, he gives her a deathly fever which results in her speedy demise.

9. He was once wont to gather shit from assholes, presently injects an enema containing toxic ingredients dissolved in boiling water or aqua fortis.

10. Once a famous fustigator, today he binds a woman to a pivot upon which she uninterruptedly revolves until dead.

That evening, an enema of boiling water is given to Rosette the moment after the Duc has finished embuggering her.

THE 3RD. 11. He used to like to slap the whore's face; as a mature man, he twists her head around until it faces backward. When so adjusted, one may simultaneously look at her face and at her buttocks.

12. Addicted to bestiality as a youngster, he now likes to have a girl depucelated by a stallion while he looks on. She ordinarily dies.

13. Once an ass-fucker, he now buries the girl up to her waist and maintains her thus till the lower half of her body rots.

14. Previously, he was wont to frig her clitoris, and he still does so, but more vigorously, employing one of his servants to keep at the work until the girl expires.

15. Gradually perfecting his passion over the years, a fustigator now flogs every part of a woman's body until she perishes.

That evening, the Duc would have Augustine, endowed with an unusually sensitive clitoris, frigged thereupon by Duclos and Champville, who relieve each other at the post and continue the task until the little lady falls unconscious.

THE 4TH. 16. His earlier passion was to squeeze the whore's neck, in later years he would tie the girl by the neck. Before her sits a sumptuous meal, but to reach it she must strangle; otherwise she dies of hunger.

17. The same man who slew Duclos' sister and whose taste is to subject the flesh to a prolonged mauling, abuses the breasts and buttocks with such furious violence that his treatment of the whore proves fatal to her.

18. The man Martaine mentioned on the 20th of January, he who formerly adored bleeding women, now kills them by dint of repeated bloodlettings.

19. He whose passion in times past was to make a naked woman run until she dropped from exhaustion, in this age of unbridled libertinage shuts her up in a steaming bathhouse where she dies of asphyxiation.

20. He whom Duclos cited earlier, the gentleman who liked to be wrapped in swaddling clothes and fed whoreshit in a spoon rather than pap, swathes a girl so tightly in baby's blankets that he kills her.

Shortly before the company moved into the auditorium that afternoon, Curval was found embuggering one of the scullery maids. He pays the fine; the girl is ordered to reappear at the evening's orgies, where the Duc and the Bishop embugger her in their turn, and she receives two hundred lashes from the hand of each of them. She's a strapping country girl, twenty-five, in satisfactory health, and has a fine ass.

THE 5TH. 21. His first passion is for bestiality, his second is to sew the girl into an untanned donkey's skin, her head protruding; he feeds and cares for her until the animal's skin shrinks and crushes her to death.

22. He of whom Martaine spoke on the 15th of January and who liked to hang a girl for his amusement, currently amuses himself by hanging her by her feet until the blood rushing to her head kills her.

23. Duclos' libertine of the 27th of November who liked to besot his whore, today inserts a funnel into her mouth and floods her with liquids till she dies therefrom.

24. Once he was wont to mistreat nipples, but has progressed since then and now buckles a sort of small iron pot over each breast and lowers her over a stove; the iron heats, and she is allowed to perish thus in frightful pain.

25. His whole delight used to consist in watching a woman swim, but he now casts her into a pond and fishes her out half-drowned, then hangs her by the feet to encourage the water to drain out of her. Once she has returned to her senses, into the pond she goes again, and so on and so forth, till she gives up the ghost.

Upon that day and at the same hour, another kitchen servant is found being embuggered, this time by the Duc; he pays the fine, the servant is summoned to the orgies, where everyone cavorts with her, Durcet making good use of her mouth, the others of her bum, and even of her cunt, for she is a virgin, and she is condemned to receive two hundred lashes from each of her employers. She is a girl of eighteen, tall and well made, her hair is auburn in color, and she owns a very fair ass.

That same evening, Curval utters the opinion that it is a matter of extreme urgency that Constance be bled again on account of her pregnancy; the Duc embuggers her, and Curval bleeds her while Augustine frigs his prick against Zelmire's buttocks and while someone else fucks Zelmire. Upon discharging, he executes the puncture; his aim is true.

THE 6TH. 26. As a young man he used to kick a woman in the ass, tumbling her into a brazier, whence she would emerge before suffering excessively. He has lately refined this stunt, now obliges a girl to stand upright between two blazing fires: one cooks her in front, the other behind; and there she remains until the fat on her body melts.

Desgranges announces that she is going to describe murders which, bringing on a prompt death, cause very little suffering.

27. In former times he would impede respiration by constricting the neck with his hands or by blocking the nose and mouth, but these days he deposits the whore between four mattresses and she suffocates.

28. He of whom Martaine said a few words and who used to allow his victim a choice from among three manners of dying (see the 14th of January) has of late begun to blow out the whore's brains, denying her any say in the matter; he embuggers, and upon discharging, pulls the trigger.

29. The man Champville referred to on the 22nd of December as the libertine who made the girl dance with the cat, presently flings the whore from the top of a tower. She lands on sharp gravel. He discharges upon hearing her land.

30. That gentleman who liked to throttle his partner while embuggering her, and whom Martaine described on the 6th of January, has advanced to the stage at which, as he embuggers her, he slips a black silk cord about her neck and

strangles her while discharging; this delight, says Desgranges, is one of the most exquisite a libertine can procure himself.

Upon that day, Messieurs celebrate the festival of the fourteenth week, and, in the guise of a woman, Curval becomes Bum-Cleaver's wife, and, as a man, takes Adonis to be his helpmeet; 'tis not till then that child is depucelated, and the event occurs very publicly, while Bum-Cleaver is fucking the Président.

Messieurs besot themselves at supper. And they flog Zelmire and Augustine about the loins, the buttocks, the thighs, the belly, the cunt, and the groin, then Curval has Zelmire fucked by Adonis, his new wife, and embuggers both of them one after the other.

THE 7TH. 31. He once liked to fuck a drowsy woman; he does much better now: he kills her with a strong dose of opium and encunts her during her death-sleep.

32. The same roué she referred to very recently, and who subjects the whore to a series of duckings, has still another passion: tying a stone to her neck, he drowns the woman.

33. Whereas once he was content to slap her face, now he carries matters further: he pours molten lead into her ear while she is asleep.

34. He was fond of whipping her face; Champville spoke of him on the 30th of December (verify that); but now he dispatches the girl with a quick hammer blow upon the temple.

35. This libertine would previously allow a candle to burn out in a woman's anus; today, he attaches her to a lightning rod during a thunderstorm and awaits a fortuitous stroke.

36. A sometime fustigator. He has her bend over with her behind facing the muzzle of a small piece of artillery. The ball enters her ass.

That day 'tis the Bishop they discover with his prick lodged in the third kitchen servant's asshole. He pays the fine, the Duc and Curval embugger and cunt-fuck her, for she is also a virgin, then she is given a total of eight hundred stripes, two hundred by each friend. She is Swiss, nineteen, very fair of skin, very plump, and has a splendid ass. The cooks complain and say that the service will not be able to continue any longer if Messieurs go on fussing about with the help, and the society agrees to a truce extending until March.

Rosette loses a finger that evening, and the wound is cauterized with fire. She is sandwiched between Curval and the Duc during the operation: one fucks her ass, the other her cunt. Adonis' ass is made generally available that same evening; and so it is that the Duc cunt-fucks one servant and Rosette at the orgies and ass-fucks the same servant, ass-fucks Rosette too, and Adonis. He is tired.

THE 8TH. 37. His whole delight once lay in beating a woman's entire body with a bull's pizzle; 'twas to him Martaine alluded as the man who strained all four of his victim's limbs on the rack and broke but one of them. He likes now thoroughly to break the woman on the wheel, but he chokes her to death when he has finished exercising her.

38. Martaine's gentleman who would feign a decapitation and have the woman snatched from beneath the blade at the last moment, now severs her head in all good faith. He discharges as the blow falls. He frigs himself.

39. Martaine's libertine of the 30th of January who was wont to perform an extensive scarification, now consigns his victims to perish in dungeons.

40. He used to be a whipper of pregnant women's bellies, has latterly perfected that by causing an enormous weight to fall on the pregnant woman's belly, thereby crushing her and her fruit at one stroke.

41. Formerly, he was known to be fond of the sight of a girl's bare neck, which he would squeeze and molest somewhat; that mild passion has been replaced by the insertion of a pin in a certain spot upon the woman's neck. The pin kills her at once.

42. At the beginning he would gently burn various parts of the body with a candle flame, more recently he has begun to hurl women into a glowing furnace where they are consumed instantly.

Durcet, his prick very stiff and who during the storytelling has ventured forth twice to flog Adelaide awaiting him at her pillar, proposes to lay her lengthwise in the fire, and after she has had sufficient time to quake over an idea Messieurs would be nothing loath to put into execution, they burn her nipples for the sake of their convenience; Durcet, her husband, burns one, her father, Curval, burns the other. This exciting operation causes both to discharge.

THE 9TH. 43. In his young years a pin-pricker, he has got himself a more formidable weapon: discharges while thrice driving a dagger into the woman's heart.

44. He used to adore burning gunpowder in the cunt, but has since improved his passion: he attaches a slender but attractive girl to a large rocket, the fuse is ignited, the rocket ascends, then returns to earth with the girl still attached.

45. The same personage who put gunpowder in all the orifices of a woman's body, now wedges cartridges into them; they explode simultaneously, sending the members flying in every direction.

46. First passion: he enjoyed secreting an emetic in the girl's food, unbeknownst to her; his second passion: he mixes a certain powder with her snuff, or sprinkles it on some flowers, she inhales and straightway falls dead.

47. First passion: he would flog her breasts and neck; refinement thereof: he aims a blow of a crowbar at her throat, it fells her forever.

48. Duclos spoke of him on the 27th of November, Martaine on the 14th of January (verify the dates): the whore enters and shits before the rake, he scolds her; brandishing a whip, he pursues her, she thinks to take refuge in a loft. A door opens, she spies a little stairway, believes she will be safe, rushes up the steps, but one of them gives way and she plunges into a large vat of boiling water; she dies, scalded, drowned, asphyxiated. His tastes are previously to have the woman shit and to lash her while she is doing so.

Curval had solicited and obtained shit from Zelmire that morning; now, directly the aforementioned tale is concluded, the Duc demands further shit from her. She cannot produce any; she is promptly condemned to have her ass pricked with a golden needle until it is covered with blood; in that it is the Duc whose interests have suffered as a result of her refusal, he is the one who recovers damages.

Curval requests shit of Zéphyr; the latter replies, saying that the Duc had him shit that morning. This the Duc denies, Duclos is called to give evidence, she supports Blangis' contention even though it is false. Consequently, Curval has the right to punish Zéphyr, despite the fact he is the Duc's bardash, just as the Duc has punished Zelmire, who is Curval's wife. The Président flogs Zéphyr until the lad streams blood, then tweaks his nose six times; the tweaks fetch forth more blood, and that makes the Duc roar with laughter.

THE 10TH. Desgranges says that she is now going to discuss murders of imposture and duplicity in which the manner is of principal significance; that is to say, the murder itself is merely incidental. Wherewith, says she, poisonings will be presented first.

49. A man whose caprice consisted in bum-fuckery and in no other kind, now envenoms all his wives; he is presently on his twenty-second. Never does he fuck them save in the ass, nor have they ever been deflowered otherwise.

50. A bugger invites a number of friends to a banquet, and with each succeeding course a few of them are stricken with stomach cramps which prove fatal.

51. Duclos spoke of him on the 26th of November, Martaine on the 10th of January; he is a bugger, pretends that it is relief he is giving the poor, distributes food, but 'tis poisoned.

52. A treacherous bugger regularly employs a drug which, sprinkled on the ground, very wonderfully kills whosoever walks thereupon; he sprinkles it about rather frequently, and over wide areas.

53. A bugger, equally skilled in alchemy, uses another substance which causes death after inconceivable torture; the death throes last a good two weeks, and no doctor has ever been able to diagnose or treat the ailment. He takes the keenest pleasure in paying you a visit while you are in the toils.

54. A sodomizer of men and women makes use of yet another powder which deprives you of your senses and renders you as if dead. And such you are believed to be, you are buried, and full of despair, you die in your coffin, into which you have no sooner been placed than you regain consciousness. He endeavors to find the exact place you have been buried, to place an ear to the ground and listen for a few screams; if indeed he hears your cries, 'tis enough to make him swoon with pleasure. He thuswise slew part of his family.

While joking and making merry that evening, Messieurs give Julie a powder concealed in her food, which causes her frightful cramps; they advise her that she is poisoned, she believes it, she wails, is beside herself. While watching her convulsions, the Duc has Augustine frig him directly opposite Julie. Augustine has the great misfortune of allowing the repuce to slip back over the Duc's glans, and that is something which displeases the Duc extremely: he was just about to discharge, the girl's carelessness prevents it. He declares he is going to cut off one of that buggress' fingers and, as good as his word, does so, slicing a digit from the hand that failed him, and while cutting, he has his daughter Julie, still persuaded she is poisoned, crawl up to him and complete his discharge. Julie is cured that same evening.

THE 11TH. 55. A consummate bugger would frequently dine at the home of friends or acquaintances and would never fail to poison the individual his host cherished most dearly amongst all living creatures. He employed a powder which finally slew after causing two days of atrocious agony.

56. An erstwhile breast-abuser has perfected his passion: he poisons infants being suckled by their nurses.

57. He once used to love to receive back into his mouth milk enemas he had injected into his partner's rectum; his later passion: he administers toxic injections which kill while causing horrible spasms and colics.

58. A crafty bugger of whom she will have occasion to say more on the 13th and the 26th, used to love to set fire to poorhouses, and would always see to it that a quantity of persons were consumed, above all children.

59. Another bugger liked to cause women to die in childbirth; he would come to pay his respects, bringing along a powder whose odor would cause spasms and convulsions ending in death.

60. The man to whom Duclos referred during her twenty-eighth evening enjoys watching a woman bear a child; he murders it immediately it emerges from the womb and within full view of the mother, and does so while feigning to caress it.

That evening, Adelaide is first dealt a hundred lashes by each friend, and then, when she is well bloodied, shit is demanded of her; she gave some that morning to Curval, who swears 'tis not so. Consequently, they burn her two breasts, the palm of each hand, spill drops of molten sealing wax upon her thighs and belly, fill her navel therewith, burn her pubic hair after having doused it with cognac. The Duc attempts to pick a quarrel with Zelmire, and the Président severs a finger from each of her hands. Augustine is scourged about the cunt and asshole.

THE 12TH. Messieurs assemble in the morning and decide that the four governesses, who are no longer of much use to the society and whose functions the four storytellers shall henceforth be perfectly able to carry out, may just as well provide the society with a little amusement; Messieurs therefore decree that the elders shall be martyrized one after another, the first sacrifice being scheduled for the evening of that same day. The four storytellers are invited to replace the elders; they accept upon condition they shall suffer no ill-treatment. Messieurs promise to subject them to none.

61. The three friends, d'Aucourt, the abbot, and Desprès, of whom Duclos spoke on the 12th of November, are now living abroad and still enjoying each

other's company, and this is one of their common passions: they require a woman whose pregnancy is in its eighth or begun its ninth month, they open her belly, snatch out the child, burn it before the mother's eyes, and in its place substitute a package containing sulphur and quicksilver, which they set afire, then stitch the belly up again, leaving the mother thus to perish in the midst of incredible agonies, while they look on and have themselves frigged by the girl they have with them. (Verify the girl's name.)

62. He was fond of depucelating, has gradually broadened his scope of activity: he has a great number of children by several women, then, when they reach the age of five or six, he depucelates them, boys and girls alike, and directly he has fucked them, throws them into a blazing oven. Or he sometimes throws them in at the same moment he discharges.

63. The man Duclos mentioned on the 27th of November, Martaine on the 15th of January, and she herself on the 5th of February, whose taste was to play at hanging, to see hanged, etc., this same fellow, I say, hides some of his personal effects in his domestics' wardrobes and declares he has been robbed. He strives to have his servants hanged, and if he succeeds goes to watch the spectacle; if not, he locks them in a room and strangles them to death. While operating, he discharges.

64. An inveterate shit-lover, he of whom Duclos spoke on the 14th of November, has a specially prepared commode at his home; he engages his intended victim to sit down upon it, and once the victim is seated, the seat buckles, gives way, and precipitates the sitter into a very deep ditch filled with shit, in which evironment she is left to die.

65. A man to whom Martaine made reference and who would amuse himself watching a girl fall from a ladder, has perfected his passion thus (but find out which man) :

He situates the girl upon a little trestle on the edge of a deep ditch filled with water; on the farther side of it is a wall which seems to be all the more inviting, what for the ladder leaning against it. But to reach the ladder she must cross the moat, and she becomes all the more willing to spring into the water as the fire burning behind the trestle moves gradually closer to her. If she hesitates too long, the fire will reach her, consume her, and as she does not know how to swim, she will be drowned if she plunges into the water. While she is considering what to do, the fire approaches, and she finally elects to struggle with a different element and endeavor to get to the wall. It frequently happens that she drowns; if so, the game is over. But if by good fortune she reaches the other bank and then the ladder, and starts to climb it, toward the top there is a rung which breaks beneath her weight and she drops into a hole covered over with a thin layer of earth, and the hole contains a bed of live coals upon which she perishes. Hard by the scene, the libertine observes it with the keenest interest, frigging himself industriously.

66. The same man Duclos spoke of on the 29th of November, the same who bumwise depucelated Martaine when a little girl of five, and also the same with

whom Desgranges announces she will conclude her narrations (the hell episode), this individual, I say, embuggers the prettiest girl of sixteen or eighteen the procuress can find for him. Sensing his crisis about to arrive, he releases a spring, upon the bare and completely unadorned neck of the girl descends a machine furnished with steel teeth; the machine begins to move laterally and gradually saws through the pinioned neck while the libertine occupies himself with completing his discharge. Which always takes a very long time.

That very evening Messieurs discover the intrigue involving Augustine and one of the subaltern fuckers; he has not yet fucked her, but to attain his ends has suggested that they both escape from the castle, and he has outlined to her a very easy way to do so. Augustine confesses that she was about to grant him what he sought from her in order to save herself from a place where she believes her life to be in danger. 'Tis Fanchon who discovers and reports everything. The traitorous quadrumvirate leap upon the fucker without warning, bind him hand and foot, and take him down to the cellars, where the Duc embuggers him with extreme vigor and without pomade, while the Président saws through his neck and the other two apply red-hot irons to all parts of his body.

This scene transpires directly after dinner is over and hence coffee is omitted that day; the work completed, everyone repairs to the auditorium as usual, then to supper, and amongst themselves Messieurs debate whether, in return for having disclosed the conspiracy, they ought not accord Fanchon a reprieve, for their decision that morning was to maltreat her the same evening. The Bishop declares himself against sparing her, and says that it would be unworthy of them to yield to the sentiment of gratitude, and that, for his part, he will always be seen to favor any decision likely to afford the society one pleasure more, just as he will always vote against any motion apt to deprive it of a pleasure. And so, after having punished Augustine for lending herself to the subversive scheme, first by obliging her to watch her lover's execution, then by embuggering her and making her believe her head would be cut off as well, next by actually pulling out two of her teeth, an operation performed by the Duc while Curval was embuggering that beautiful girl, finally by giving her a sound whipping, after all that, I say, Fanchon is led into the arena, made to shit, given a hundred lashes by each of the friends, and then the Duc deftly shaves off her left nipple. She raises a storm, criticizing their behavior toward her and describing it as unjust. "Were it just," says the Duc, wiping his razor, "it would surely fail to give us an erection." Whereupon they dress the old whore's wounds, eager to preserve her for further ordeals.

Their Lordships perceive that indeed there had been faint but definite rebellious stirrings amongst the subaltern fuckers; the prompt sacrifice of one of them has, however, thoroughly quelled their murmurs. Like Fanchon, the three other duennas are divested of all responsibility, removed from office, and replaced by the four storytellers and Julie. They tremble, do the old dames; but by what shifts are they to escape their fate?

THE 13TH. 67. A great connoisseur of the ass, he declares his love for a girl and, having arranged a boating party, lures her upon the water in a small boat, the which has been prepared for the outing, springs a leak, founders; the girl is drowned. He sometimes pursues his objective by different means: will, for example, lead a girl out upon a high balcony, have her lean upon the railing, which gives way; and once again the girl dies.

68. A man, while making his apprenticeship in life, was content first to whip and then to embugger; now, having reached a mature age, entices the girl to enter a specially prepared room; a trap door yields beneath her step, she falls into a cellar where the rake awaits her; he plunges a knife into her breasts, her cunt, and into her asshole as she lies stunned by her fall. Next, he casts her, dead or still alive, into another cellar, over which a stone drops into place; she tumbles upon a heap of other corpses, and she expires in a great fit if life has not already departed her sore-beset frame. And he is very careful to administer delicate stabs, for he would prefer that she live a little and finally perish in the cellar mentioned latterly. Prior to all this, he of course embuggers and flogs her and discharges; 'tis coolly and with utmost method he proceeds to her undoing.

69. A bugger has the girl mount astride an untamed, unbroken horse which unseats her, drags her along a rocky terrain, and finally pitches her over a precipice.

70. Martaine's hero of the 18th of January whose juvenile passion was to distribute little mounds of gunpowder upon the girl's body, has made significant progress. He lays the girl in a special bed; when properly tucked in, the bed gives way, dropping her into a large brazier of live coals, but she is able to scramble out of it; however, he is standing by and, as she repeats her attempts to escape the fire, he drives her back, wielding a pitchfork and with it aiming stout blows at her belly.

71. The gentleman she mentioned on the 11th, who likes to burn down poorhouses, endeavors to lure a beggar, whether a man or a woman, from out of one and into his own home, upon the pretense of bestowing charity; he embuggers his victim, then breaks his back and leaves him thus discomfited to die in a dungeon.

72. He who was wont to defenestrate a woman, hurling her upon a dung heap, the same man of whom Martaine spoke, by way of second passion executes the following one: he allows the girl to sleep in a room she is acquainted with and whose window she knows to be not far above the ground; she is given opium, when in a deep slumber she is conveyed to another chamber, identical with the first but having a window high above the ground which, on this side of the house, is strewn with sharp rocks. Next, the libertine enters where she lies sleeping, makes a dreadful noise, terrifies her; she is informed that she is about to die. Knowing the drop from the window to the ground to be short, she leaps through it, but falls thirty feet and lands upon the murderous rocks, killing herself. No one has so much as laid a finger upon her.

In the character of a woman, that great histrionic, the Bishop, marries Antinoüs, whose role is that of a husband, and also weds Céladon, whom he takes to be his wife, and 'tis that evening the child is embuggered for the first time.

This ceremony celebrates the festival of the fifteenth week; to complete the holiday, the prelate wishes to expose Aline to some severe vexations, for his libertine rage against her has been quietly but steadily mounting: she is hanged, then quickly cut down, but while seeing her however briefly aloft, everyone discharges. Durcet opens her veins, this treatment restores her to life; the next day she appears none the worse for wear, but suspension has added an inch to her height; she relates what she experienced during the ordeal. The Bishop, for whom everything is an occasion of jollity and everyone the object of game that day, cuts one of old Louison's nipples clean off her breast; whereupon the other two duennas see very clearly what their fate is to be.

THE 14TH. 73. A man whose simple taste was to flog a girl, perfects it by every day removing morsels of flesh the size of a pea from the girl's body, but her wounds are not dressed, and thus she perishes over a low fire, as it were.

Desgranges announces that she will now deal with exceedingly painful murders wherein 'tis the extreme cruelty which comprises the main element; Messieurs more strongly than ever urge her to furnish abundant details.

74. He who was fond of letting blood daily relieves his victim of a half ounce of it, continuing till she is dead. Messieurs greet this example with hearty applause.

75. He who was wont to prick the ass with many pins every day administers a more or less superficial gash with a poignard. The blood is stanched, but the wound is not treated, neither does it mend, and thus 'tis a slow death she dies. A fustigator (75) quietly and slowly saws off all four limbs, one after the other.

76. The Marquis de Mesanges, of whom Duclos spoke in connection with the shoemaker Petignon's daughter, bought by the Marquis from Duclos, and whose first passion was to undergo four hours of flogging without discharging, for a second passion places a little girl in the hands of a giant fellow who holds the child by the head over a large charcoal brazier which burns her very slowly; the victims must be virgins.

77. His first passion: little by little to burn the breasts and buttocks with the flame of a match; his second: over every part of the girl's body to plant a forest of sulphur-coated slivers, which he lights one by one. He watches her die in this way.

"Nor is there anymore painful way to die," observes the Duc, who then confesses to having surrendered himself to this infamous pastime, and to having discharged vigorously thanks to it. They say that the patient lives six hours, sometimes eight.

Céladon's ass is made generally available that evening; the Duc and Curval indulge themselves heavily. Constance's pregnancy is still on the Président's mind; he suggests that she be bled, and bleeds her himself while discharging in Céladon's ass, then he lops off one of Thérèse's nipples while embuggering Zelmire, and the Duc sodomizes the duenna during the amputation.

THE 15TH. 78. Once beguiled by the charms of a mouth to suck and saliva to swallow, he is now of sterner stuff: every day he inserts a funnel into the girl's mouth and pours a small dose of molten lead down her throat; she gives up the ghost on the ninth day.

79. First a finger-twister, he currently breaks all her limbs, tears out her tongue, gouges out her eyes, and leaves her thus to live, diminishing her sustenance day by day.

80. A perpetrator of sacrilege, the second one Martaine mentioned on the 3rd of January, he secures a beautiful youth to a tall cross, binding him with cords and leaving him there as food for ravens.

81. An armpit-sniffer and -fucker, to whom Duclos alluded, binds a woman hand and foot and hangs her by a rope looped under her arms; he goes every day to prick some part of her body so that the blood will attract flies; her death is by slow degrees.

82. A passionate admirer of asses rectifies his worship: he now seals a girl in an underground cave where she has food to last three days; before leaving her, he inflicts several wounds upon her body, thuswise to render her death more painful. He wishes to have them virgins and spends a week embracing their asses before organizing their destruction.

83. Formerly he loved to fuck very youthful mouths and asses; his later improvement consists in snatching out the heart of a living girl, widening the space that organ occupied, fucking the warm hole, replacing the heart in that pool of blood and fuck, sewing up the wound, and leaving the girl to her fate, without help of any kind. In which case the wait is not long.

Still wroth with the lovely Constance, Curval maintains that there is no reason under the sun why one cannot successfully bear a child even though one has a broken limb, and therefore they fracture that unlucky creature's arm the same evening. Durcet slices off one of Marie's nipples after she has been well warmed by the lash and made copiously to shit.

THE 16TH. 84. A fustigator refines his passion: he learns and then practices the art of gently removing flesh from bones; he then extracts the marrow, usually by sucking it out, and pours molten lead into the cavity.

At this point the Duc loudly exclaims that he'll not fuck another ass while he lives if that isn't the very ordeal he has had in mind for his beloved Augustine; that poor girl, whom Blangis has been embuggering for some time, utters cries and sheds a torrent of tears. And as thanks to her misbehavior she interferes with his discharge and frustrates it effectively, he withdraws, takes hold of his engine in one hand, and while with the other he gives her a dozen slaps which resound through that wing of the castle, he manages his discharge very satisfactorily by himself.

85. A bugger uses an ingenious machine to chop the girl into small pieces: this is a Chinese torture.

86. Weary of his early fondness for girls' pucelages, his latest passion is to impale a girl upon the point of a sharp pickaxe introduced into her cunt; there she sits, as if upon a horse, he ties a cannon ball to each of her legs, the pick works deeper, and she is left to her own devices and a slow death.

87. A fustigator flays the girl thrice over; he soaks her fourth layer of skin with a devouring escharotic which brings about death accompanied by hideous agonies.

88. His first passion was to sever a finger; his second is to pluck up some flesh with a pair of red-hot tongs, to cut off the flesh with a pair of scissors, then to burn the wound. He is quite apt to spend as long as four or five days whittling away a girl's body piecemeal, and she ordinarily dies while the cruel operation is still advancing.

Sophie and Céladon have been found amusing themselves together and are punished that evening; both are whipped over their entire bodies by the Bishop, whose chattels they are. Sophie loses two fingers to the shears, Céladon as many; but he recovers very quickly. The Bishop is no less eager to use them in his pleasures, however they be maimed.

Fanchon returns to the center of the stage. After having been beaten with a bull's pizzle, the soles of her feet are burned, each thigh, before and behind, is burned also, her forehead too, and each hand as well, and Messieurs extract all her remaining teeth. The Duc's prick is almost continually wedged into her ass throughout this lengthy operation.

Mention that it has been prescribed by law that a subject's buttocks shall be left intact until the day the said subject reaches the end of his career.

THE 17TH. 89. Martaine's gentleman of the 30th of January and the same one she herself described on the 5th of February, pares away a girl's breasts and buttocks, eats them, and upon her wounds puts plasters which so violently burn the flesh that they are her undoing. He also forces her to eat her own flesh, which he has had grilled.

90. A bugger cooks up a little girl in a double boiler.

91. A bugger: he has her roasted alive on a spit directly after embuggering her.

92. A man whose initial passion was to have little girls and boys embuggered in his presence by massive and ponderous pricks, impales the girl, a spear in her ass, and leaves her thus to die while he studies her contortions.

93. Another bugger: attaches a woman to a wheel, it is then set in motion and, without having done her any previous harm, he allows her to die a very pretty death.

That evening, the Bishop, his spirits in a great ferment, wishes to have Aline tormented, his rage against her has reached its fever pitch. She makes her appearance naked, he has her shit and embuggers her, then, without discharging, he withdraws in a towering fury from that enchanting ass and injects a rinse of boiling water into it, obliging her to squirt it out at once, while it is still boiling hot, upon Thérèse's face. After that, Messieurs hack off all the fingers and toes Aline has left, break both her arms and burn them with red-hot pokers. She is next flogged, beaten, and slapped, then the Bishop, still further aroused, cuts off one of her nipples, and discharges.

Wherewith they transfer their attentions to Thérèse, the interior of her vagina is seared, her nostrils, tongue, feet, and hands are all burned too; then she is given six hundred lashes with a bull's pizzle. Out come the rest of her teeth, fire is introduced into her throat. A witness to these harsh proceedings, Augustine falls to weeping; the Duc lashes her belly and cunt until he has drawn a suitable amount of blood therefrom.

THE 18TH. 94. A flesh-sacrifier in his early days, his adult entertainment consists in quartering girls by bending four saplings, attaching an arm or leg to each, and releasing the trees, which spring back erect.

95. A fustigator suspends her from a machine which lowers a girl into and immediately lifts her out of a fire, then repeats the operation until there is very little left of the patient.

96. He once loved to extinguish candles by snuffing them out upon flesh; today, he envelopes her in sulphur and uses her for a torch, being careful to prevent the fumes for choking her.

97. A sodomist: rips the intestines from a young boy and a young girl, puts the boy's into the girl, inserts the girl's into the boy's body, stitches up the incisions, ties them back to back to a pillar which supports them both, and he watches them perish.

98. A man who was fond of inflicting light burns, improves his passion: he now roasts his victim upon a grill, turning him over and over again.

Michette is, that evening, exposed to the libertines' fury; all four begin by whipping her, then each tears out one of her teeth, they cut off four fingers (each friend amputates one), her thighs are burned in four places, two in front and two behind, the Duc manhandles one of her breasts until it is truly unrecognizable, sodomizing Giton in the meantime.

Louison is next on the bill of fare; she is made to shit, she is given eight hundred strokes with the bull's pizzle, she is divested of all her teeth, her tongue is burned, as is her asshole, her vagina, and her remaining nipple, and so are six places upon her thighs.

When everyone has retired to bed for the night, the Bishop goes in search of his brother, they wake Desgranges and Duclos, and the four of them take Aline down into the cellars; the Bishop embuggers her, the Duc embuggers her, they pronounce the death sentence, and by means of excessive torments which last until daybreak, they execute it. Upon returning, they exchange words of unqualified praise for these two storytellers and advise their colleagues to undertake no serious projects without their help.

THE 19TH. 99. He places the woman so that the base of her spine bears upon the sharpened head of a tall post, her four limbs are held in the air only by light cords; the effects of her suffering make the lecher laugh incontinently, the torture is frightful.

100. A man who used to enjoy cutting small steaks from the girl's rump has become absolutely a butcher: he has the girl sandwiched between two heavy planks, then slowly and carefully sawed in two.

101. An embuggerer of both sexes has brother and sister fetched in; he declares to the brother that he is about to die a horrible death, and shows the young man all the deployed tackle he proposes to use; however, the libertine continues, he will save the brother's life if he will fuck his sister and strangle her at once. The young man agrees, and while he fucks his sister, the libertine embuggers now one of them, now the other. Then the brother, fearing for his life, deprives her sister of hers, and the moment he completes that operation, both he and his dead sister tumble through a trap door into a capacious charcoal brazier, wherein the libertine wathces them be consumed.

102. A bugger compels a father to fuck his daughter in his presence. Next, the father holds the daughter, the bugger sodomizes her; after which he informs the father that the girl absolutely has to perish, but that he has the alternatives of killing her himself by strangling her, which will cause her little suffering, or, in that other case, if her prefers not to kill his daughter, then he, the libertine, will do the work, but the father shall have to witness it all, and his child's agonies will be atrocious.

Rather than see her undergo frightful tortures, the father decides to kill his daughter with a noose of black silk, but while he is preparing to dispatch her, he is seized, bound, and before his eyes his child is flayed alive, then rolled upon burning iron nails, then cast into a brazier, and the father is strangled; this, says the libertine, is to teach him a lesson not to be so eager to choke the life out of his own children, for 'tis barbaric. Afterward, he is dumped into the same brazier wherein his daughter perished.

103. A great devotee of asses and of the lash brings together mother and daughter. He tells the girl that he is going to kill her mother if she, the girl, does not consent to the sacrifice of both her hands; the little one agrees, they are severed at the wrist. Whereupon these two creatures are separated; a rope suspended from the ceiling is slipped around the girl's neck, she stands upon a stool; another cord runs from the stool into the next room and the mother is requested to hold the end. She is then invited to tug on the cord: she pulls it without knowing what she is doing, she is led directly into the first room to contemplate her work, and during that moment of her keenest distress, she is smitten down by a saber blow aimed at her head from behind.

Jealous of the pleasure the two brothers had the night before, Durcet, that evening, is moved to suggest that they vex Adelaide, whose turn, he assures the society, is soon to come. And so Curval, her father, and Durcet, her husband, worry her thighs with white-hot thongs while the Duc's unlubricated member sounds her ass. The tip of her tongue is pierced, the ends of both her ears are shorn away, with the aid of instruments Messieurs dispossess her of four teeth, and then she is given a savage whipping. That same evening, the Bishop bleeds Sophie while her dearly beloved friend, Adelaide, watches the blood issue from the child's veins; the fountains are kept turned on until Sophie loses consciousness; as he bleeds her, the Bishop embuggers her, remaining in her ass throughout the operation.

While Curval is sodomizing him, Narcisse loses a pair of fingers, then Marie is hailed into court, red-hot irons are thrust into her cunt and asshole, more irons are applied to six places upon her thighs, upon her clitoris, her tongue, upon her one remaining breast, and out come the remainder of her teeth.

THE 20TH. 104. Champville's of the 5th of December, the man who was wont to have the mother prostitute her son and hold him while he embuggered the lad, improves his taste by bringing the mother and son together. He tells the mother that he is about to kill her, but will spare her if she will murder her son. In case she refuses to do so, he slits the boy's throat before the woman's eyes. Or if she consents: then she is bound to her son's dead body and left quietly to meditate and finally to die.

105. A very incestuous personage assembles two sisters after having embuggered both of them; he binds them to a machine, each has a knife in her hand: the machine is set in motion, the girls are brought suddenly together and mutually kill each other.

106. Another devotee of incest requires a mother and her four children. They are locked into a room; he observes them through a small barred window. He gives them nothing to eat in order to study the effects of famine upon this woman, and to discover which of her children she will eat first.

107. Champville's of the 29th of December, who liked to flog pregnant women, calls for a mother and daughter, both of whom must be gravid: they are tied to a pair of steel plates one set above the other; the women face one another; the machine starts, the jaws of the vise close with great speed and power, the two women are ground to dust, together with their fruit.

108. A very buggerish gentleman entertains himself in the following manner: he assembles lover and mistress:

"There is in all the world but one person who stands in the way of your happiness," says he, taking the lover aside; "I am going to put that individual in your power."

And he leads him into an obscurely lit chamber containing a bed; upon it someone lies asleep. Greatly aroused, the young man takes dagger in hand and stabs his enemy. When he has had done, he is permitted to recognize his mistress' dead body: 'twas she he slew; he kills himself in despair, or if he does not, the libertine kills him with a shot from a rifle, fired at a distance, not daring to enter the room with the furious young man who still has a weapon in his hand. Previously, he fucked the youth and his beloved too, they singly yielded to him in the hope he would help them and bring them together, it is after having enjoyed them he rids the world of them.

In celebration of the sixteenth week, Durcet, as a woman, marries Invictus, who enacts a masculine role; and as a man he takes Hyacinthe to be his wife; the ceremonies are performed that evening and, by way of festivity, Durcet wishes to torment Fanny, his feminine wife. Consequently, her arms are burned, so are her thighs in six separate places, two teeth are extracted from her mouth, she is flogged; Hyacinthe, who loves her and who is her husband thanks to the voluptuous arrangements hitherto described. Hyacinthe, I say, is obliged to shit into Fanny's mouth, and she to eat the turd.

The Duc pulls out one of Augustine's teeth and immediately afterward fucks her in the mouth. Fanchon reappears, she is bled, and while blood flows from her arm, her arm is broken; next, they remove her toenails and sever the fingers from both her hands.

THE 21ST. She announces that the following examples are of buggers who wish to commit exclusively masculine murders.

109. He buries the muzzle of a shotgun in the boy's ass, the weapon is loaded with buckshot and he has just finished fucking the lad. He pulls the trigger; the gun and his prick discharge simultaneously.

110. He obliges the lad to watch his mistress being mutilated, and to eat her flesh, principally her buttocks, breasts, and heart. He has the option of eating these meats, or of dying of hunger. As soon as he has devoured them, if 'tis that he elects to do, the libertine inflicts several deep wounds upon him and leaves him thus to bleed to death; if he abstains from eating, he then starves to death.

111. He tears off the youth's testicles and, a short while later, serves them up to him in a ragout, then, in place of the stolen treasure, substitutes spheres of quicksilver and fills his voided scrotum with sulphur a-plenty, which cause such violent suffering that the patient succumbs. During his agony, the libertine embuggers him and increases the boy's trouble by burning him here, there and everywhere with sulphur-impregnated slivers, and by scratching, picking, and further burning these wounds.

112. He drives a long spike through the victim's asshole and thus nails him to a slender pole, and leaves him to sigh away his last hours, or days.

113. He embuggers, and whilst sodomizing, opens the cranium, removes the brain, and fills the cavity with molten lead.

Vigorously fustigated beforehand, Hyacinthe's ass is made generally available that evening. Narcisse is presented to the assembly: off come his balls with a snip of the scissors. Adelaide is summoned forth, a red-hot fire shovel is brushed over the rear of her thighs, they burn her clitoris, pierce her tongue, lash her breasts with cruel instruments, cut off the two little buttons on her breasts, break both her arms, carve away her remaining fingers, tear the hair from her cunt, tear a handful of hair from her head, pull out six of her teeth. Thus discomfited, she causes Messieurs to discharge every one save the Duc who, his livid prick straining upward, demands leave to exercise Thérèse all alone. Leave so to do is accorded him; using a pocketknife, he pries out all her nails and, as he proceeds, burns her fingers with a candle, then he fractures one of her arms, and still he does not discharge; very wroth, he leaps upon Augustine, encunts her and tears out one of her teeth as he spills his seed into her womb.

THE 22ND. 114. He breaks a young boy on the rack, then affixes him to a wheel upon which he is left to expire: upon the wheel he is turned in such a way as to expose his buttocks, and the scoundrel, his tormentor, has his table set beneath the wheel, and dines there every day until the patient is no more.

115. He flays a young boy, rubs his body with honey, and invites the flies to the feast.

116. He slices off his prick and breasts, nails one of his feet to a post, one of his hands to another post, and thus he is left to expire with however little dignity.

117. The same man who had made Duclos take supper with his dogs, owns a lion too, and, arming a boy with a light stick, introduces the youngster into the lion's cage. They boy's defense only further arouses the animal; the libertine watches the contest and discharges when the loser is completely devoured.

118. Clothed in a mare's skin, his asshole smeared with mare's fuck, a small boy is surrendered to an excited horse. The libertine observes their struggle and the boy's death.

Giton is subjected to tortures that evening: the Duc, Curval, Hercule, and Bum-Cleaver penetrate his ass ungreased. He is whipped very lustily, Messieurs extract four of his teeth, cut off four of his fingers (as always, each friend has a share in the despoiling of the victim), and Durcet crushes one of his balls between thumb and forefinger. All four gentlemen soundly flog Augustine. Her glorious ass is soon washed in blood, the Duc embuggers her while Curval severs one of her fingers, then Curval marches into the breach while the Duc six times sears her thighs with a hot iron; Blangis snips away yet another finger the same instant his colleague discharges, and despite all this rough treatment, she spends the night, a stormy one, in the Duc's bed. Marie sustains a broken arm, her fingernails are drawn out, her fingers burned.

That same night, Durcet and Curval, seconded by Desgranges and Duclos, accompany Adelaide to the cellars. Curval gives her a farewell embuggering, then they cause her to die in the throes of terrible sufferings, which you will give in full detail.

THE 23RD. 119. He places a young boy in a machine which stretches him, dislocating his bones; he is meticulously and thoroughly broken, then removed from the machine, given a chance to recover his breath, exposed to the process again; and so it continues for several days, until the patient's death.

120. He has a pretty girl pollute and fatigue a young boy; he is drained very dry indeed, but still the girl toils over him, he is given no nourishment, and eventually dies in horrible convulsions.

121. In the space of a single day, he performs four operations upon the young man: a gallstone removal, a trepanning, the excision of a fistula in the eye, of one in the anus. He knows just enough about surgery to botch all four operations; then he abandons the patient, giving him no further help and watching him expire.

122. After having sheared off the boy's prick and balls, using a red-hot iron he hollows out a cunt in the place formerly occupied by his genitals; the iron makes the hole and cauterizes simultaneously: he fucks the patient's new orifice and strangles him with his hands upon discharging.

123. He massages him with a currycomb; when he has generally abraded his flesh in this fashion, he rubs him with alcohol, ignites it, resumes his combing, rubs again with alcohol, relights the torch, proceeding in this wise till death makes further care unnecessary.

That same evening, Narcisse's turn arrives to be vexed; fire is applied to his thighs and little prick, then Messieurs crush his two balls.

They turn again to Augustine upon the recommendation of the Duc, whose spiteful attitude toward her seems only to have worsened; they burn her thighs and armpits, a very hot bar of iron is rammed into her cunt. She faints, the Duc waxes all the more furious, he shears off one of her nipples, drinks her blood, breaks both her arms, and tears out her cunt hair, all her teeth, and cuts off every finger left on her hands, cauterizing the wounds with fire. And once again 'tis in his bed she sleeps, or rather lies, that night, for if one is to believe Duclos, he fucks her fore and aft the whole night long, repeatedly telling her that the day about to dawn will be her last.

Louison appears, they break one of her arms, burn her tongue, her clitoris, tear out all her nails, and burn the tips of her bleeding fingers. Curval sodomizes her in this state and, in his rage, twists and manhandles one of Zelmire's breasts while discharging. Not content with those abuses, he catches hold of her again and whips her until he cannot lift his arm.

THE 24TH. 124. The same man Martaine referred to on the 1st of January wishes to embugger the father while his two children observe, and as he discharges, he stabs one child to death with one hand, and with his other strangles the other.

125. His first passion was to flog the bellies of pregnant women; his second is to assemble six of them whose pregnancy has reached the end of the eighth month: he ties them back to back, their bellies prominently thrust forward: he splits open the belly of the first, perforates the belly of the second with dagger thrusts, gives a hundred kicks to the third's, a hundred blows of a club deflates the belly of the fourth, he burns the fifth's, applies a rasp to the sixth's, and then, using a truncheon upon her belly, he finishes off whichever amongst them has survived his treatment.

Curval interrupts the narrations with some furious scene or other, this passion having had a great effect upon his mind.

126. The seducer mentioned by Duclos assembles two women. Says he to the first: "Deny God and religion if you wish to live," but his valet has whispered to her, telling her to say nothing, for if she does, she shall surely be killed, but by keeping silent she shall have nothing to fear. Hence, she is mute; he blows out her brains, murmuring, "There's one for God." He calls the second; struck by the example of the first and remembering what she has been told before entering the room, that she has no choice but to renounce belief in God and religion if she is to save herself, she assents to all he proposes: he blows out her brains: "And there's another for the Devil." The villain plays that little game every week.

127. He is a great bugger and he is fond of giving dances, but the ceiling in the salon is of a special order, it collapses as soon as the room is filled, and nearly everyone perishes. Were he to remain living in the same city for any length of time, he would be detected, but he moves frequently; he is eventually found out, but only after having given his fiftieth dance.

128. Martaine's of the 27th of January, whose taste is to promote abortions, establishes three pregnant women in three cruel postures, composing an artistic group. Thus situated, they give birth while he looks on, then he ties each infant to its mother's neck until the little creature either dies or is eaten, for the libertine keeps the women just where they are and gives them no food. The same personage has yet another passion: he has two women whelp in his presence, blindfolds them, and after having himself indentified the infants by some mark, he puts them side by side and bids each woman go and recover each her own offspring; if the ladies are not mistaken, he permits their young to live, but if they are in error, he carves up the children with a saber.

Narcisse is presented at the evening orgies. While the Bishop sodomizes the little fellow, Durcet relieves him of his remaining digits and inserts a red-hot needle into his urethral canal. They bid Giton step forth, he is kicked about, 'tis a lively game of ball they play with him, three of the friends fracture one of his legs while the Duc embuggers him.

Zelmire's turn: they roast her clitoris, sear her tongue, bake her gums, extract four of her teeth, burn her thighs in six places before and behind, snip away her nipples, unfinger both her hands, and when she is thus prepared to afford pleasure, Curval embuggers her. But he does not discharge.

Up steps Fanchon. Their attentions cost her an eye.

Escorted by Desgranges and Duclos, the Duc and Curval make a journey to the cellars with Augustine in the course of that night; her ass has been preserved in excellent condition, 'tis now lashed to tatters, then the two brothers alternately embugger her, but guard their seed, and then the Duc gives her fifty-eight wounds in the buttocks, pours boiling oil into each gash. He drives a hot iron into her cunt, another into her ass, and fucks her wounded charms, his prick sheathed in a sealskin condom which worsens the already lamentable state of her privities. That accomplished, the flesh is peeled away from the bones of her arms and legs, which bones are sawed in several different places, then her nerves are laid bare in four adjacent places, the nerve ends are tied to a short stick which, like a tourniquet, is twisted, thus drawing forth the aforesaid nerves, which are very delicate parts of the human anatomy and, which, when mistreated, cause the patient to suffer much. Augustine's agonies are unheard-of.

She is given some respite and allowed to recruit her strength, then Messieurs resume work, but this time, as the nerves are pulled into sight, they are scraped with the blade of a knife. The friends complete that operation and now move elsewhere; a hole is bored in her throat, her tongue is drawn back, down, and passed through it, 'tis a comical effect, they broil her remaining breast, then, clutching a scalpel, the Duc thrusts his hand into her cunt and cuts through the partition dividing the anus from the vagina; he throws aside the scalpel, reintroduces his hand, and rummaging about in her entrails, forces her to shit through her cunt, another amusing stunt; then, availing himself of the same entrance, he reaches up and tears open her stomach. Next, they concentrate upon her visage: cut away her ears, burn her nasal passages, blind her eyes with molten sealing wax, girdle her cranium, hang her by the hair, attach heavy stones to her feet, and allow her to drop: the top of the skull remains dangling.

She was still breathing when she fell, and the Duc encunted her in this sorry state; he discharged and came away only the more enraged. They split her belly, opened her, and applied fire to her entrails; scalpel in hand, the Président burrows in her chest and harasses her heart, puncturing it in several places. 'Twas only then her soul fled her body; at the age of fifteen years and eight months thus perished one of the most heavenly creatures ever formed by Nature's skillful hand. Etc. Her eulogy.

THE 25TH. That morning, the Duc takes Colombe to be his wife and hereafter she performs all a wife's functions.

129. A great connoisseur of the ass and a man mightily fond thereof, he embuggers the mistress while the lover looks on, then the lover while his mistress watches, then he nails the lover over the mistress' body and leaves them to expire, mouth to mouth.

Such will be the end of Céladon and Sophie, who are in love, and Messieurs interrupt the storyteller to oblige Céladon himself to spread a little hot sealing wax on his dear Sophie's thighs; while obeying the instructions, he collapses: while lying unconscious, he is embuggered by the Bishop.

130. He who was wont to amuse himself by throwing a girl into water and pulling her out, has as his second passion that of casting seven or eight whores into a pond and watching them thrash about, for they are poor swimmers. He tenders them an iron pike, but it is heated red hot; still they cling to it, but he thrusts them away, and that they the more certainly perish, he has amputated one limb from each of them before throwing them in.

131. His earlier caprice was to cause vomiting; his improvement thereof is, by using a secret means, to spread the plague throughout an entire provence: he has

brought about the death of a truly incredible number of people. He also poisons wells and streams.

132. Fond of employing the whip, he has three pregnant women locked in an iron cage, and with them he imprisons their three children; a fire is lit beneath the cage, its occupants caper and dance more and more in earnest as the floor heats; the women take the children in their arms, and finally fall and die in this manner.

(That one belongs somewhere further above; move it to its proper place.)

133. 'Twas he who pricked with an awl; more of a man today, he seals a pregnant woman in a chest whose interior is studded with sharp nails; he then has the chest rolled and dragged through the garden.

These tales of pregnant women being chastised have proven as woeful to Constance's ears as they have delighted Curval's; she sees only too well what the future holds in store for her. As her fatal hour is drawing nigh, Messieurs are of the opinion her vexations may be inaugurated: her thighs are burned in six places, molten wax is allowed to trickle upon her navel, and her breasts are teased with pins.

Giton appears, a burning needle is run through his little member, his little balls are stabbed, four of his teeth are extracted.

Then comes Zelmire, whose death is not far off; deep into her cunt runs a red-hot poker, six wounds are inflicted upon her breasts, a dozen upon her thighs, needles are driven into her navel, each friend bestows twenty strong blows upon her face. They forcibly remove four of her teeth, her eye is pricked, she is whipped, she is embuggered. While in the act of sodomizing her, Curval, her husband, gives her intelligence of her death, scheduled for the morrow; she declares she is not sorry to learn the tidings, for 'twill put a period to her sorrows.

Rosette steps forward; four teeth are jerked from her mouth, each of her shoulders is branded, her thighs and calves are gashed and hacked; she is then embuggered while several hands worry her breasts.

And now Thérèse advances; out comes an eye, a hundred blows of the bull's pizzle rain down upon her scrawny back.

THE 26TH. 134. A bugger takes his stand at the foot of a tower; the earth about him is studded with sharpened steel rods pointing upward; his associates pitch several children of both sexes from the top of the tower. He has previously embuggered them, and now enjoys seeing them impaled a second time. 'Tis, he considers, very thrilling to be splashed by their blood.

135. The same personage she cited on the 11th of February, whose tastes ran to instigating combustions, also delights in binding six pregnant women to bundles of inflammable materials; these he sets afire, and if his victims undertake to save themselves, he awaits them, pitchfork in hand, skewers them and hurls them back into the blaze. However, when half-roasted, the floor gives way and they spill into a large vat of boiling oil, wherein they finally perish.

136. He is the nobleman Duclos spoke of, who has no fondness for the poor and who bought Lucile, her mother, and her sister, and whom Desgranges has

also cited (verify this); another of his passions is to assemble a family of beggars over a mine and to watch those luckless creatures blown to bits.

137. A notorious sodomist, in order to combine that crime with those of incest, murder, rape, sacrilege, and adultery, first inserts a Host in his ass, then has himself embuggered by his own son, rapes his married daughter, and kills his niece.

138. Greatly partisan to asses, he strangles a mother while embuggering her; when she is dead, he turns her over and cunt-fucks her corpse. While discharging, he kills her daughter with a knife, slashing her breasts, then he embuggers the girl even though she is dead; then apparently convinced there is still some life in his victims, and fancying they are jet capable of suffering, he hurls the cadavers into a fire and discharges as he watches them burn. Duclos spoke of this wealthy individual on the 29th of November: 'twas he who liked to see the girl lying on the pallet covered with black satin; he is also the same man who figured in Martaine's first tale of the 11th of January.

The evening's program begins with Narcisse. One of his hands is lopped off. Giton loses a hand too.

The interior of Michette's cunt is burned, the same treatment is given Rosette's, and then both girls are burned upon the body and breasts. But Curval, who has lost control of himself, violates the society's charter and cleaves an entire breast from Rosette's chest, all the while embuggering Michette.

Thérèse makes a further appearance; she receives two hundred blows of the bull's pizzle and loses her other eye.

Curval goes in search of the Duc that night when all is still and, accompanied by Desgranges and Duclos, those two champions take Zelmrire down to the cellars where the most refined tortures are put to use upon her: they are all much more painful, more severe than the others employed upon Augustine, and the two men are still hard at work by the time breakfast arrives the following morning. That enchanting girl dies at the age of fifteen years and two months. 'Twas she who could boast the most beautiful ass in the harem of little girls. And thus deprived of a wife, the Président weds Hébé the next day.

THE 27TH. The seventeeth and last week's festival is postponed until the morrow, in order that the holiday may coincide with the end of the narrations; Desgranges recounts the following passions:

139. A man Martaine described on the 12th of January, the one who set off fireworks in the woman's ass, has, for his second, this other passion: he ties two pregnant women together so that they form a ball and fires them from a large mortar.

140. He was a scratcher and scab picker; he now places two pregnant women in a room and obliges them to fight with knives (he observes them from a safe position); they are naked, he threatens them with a gun he keeps trained upon them, and promises to shoot them dead if they begin to dally and falter. If they kill each other, why, that is precisely what he wishes, if not, sword in hand, he rushes

into the arena and, after killing one, he disembowels the other and burns her entrails with aqua fortis, or with pieces of red-hot metal.

141. A man who once liked to flog pregnant women's bellies has reformed: he presently binds a pregnant girl to a wheel and beneath it, fixed in a chair and unable to move, sits the girl's mother, her head flung back, her mouth open and ready to receive all the ordures and rubbish which flow out of the corpse, and the infant, too, if the girl gives birth to it.

142. Martaine's of the 16th of January, whose joy was to prick asses, attaches a girl to a machine studded with sharp iron points; he fucks her as she lies upon that bed, with every blow of his loins he drives her upon the nails, then he turns her over and fucks her asswise, that she may also be punctured on the other side. When he has finished that phase of the operation, he lays a second plank above her, and it is likewise provided with nails; the planks are brought together by means of bolts, thus dies the patient, crushed and stabbed in a multitude of places. The pressing is carried out gradually, she is given ample opportunity to savor her pain.

143. A fustigator stretches a pregnant woman out upon a table; he nails her thereto, first driving a fiery nail into each eye, one into her mouth, another into either breast, then he burns her clitoris and nipples with a taper, and slowly saws her knees halfway through, breaks her legs, and ends by hammering a red-hot spike, of enormous size, into her navel: it undoes both mother and child. He likes to have her ready to give birth.

Messieurs whip Julie and Duclos that evening, but from amusement, since they are both amongst the inhabitants of Silling who shall transfer their residence to Paris: nevertheless, Julie's thighs are burned in two places, and she is depilated.

Sentenced to die the next day but unaware of her impending fate, Constance appears; her nipples are scorched, molten wax is allowed to trickle down over her belly, she yields four teeth, Messieurs prick the white of her eyes with needles.

Narcisse, also due to be immolated on the 28th of February, enters upon the stage; he loses an eye and four teeth.

Giton, Michette, and Rosette, destined to accompany Constance to the grave, each surrenders an eye and four teeth, Rosette her two nipples to the knife and six chunks of flesh, some of them carved from her arms, some from her thighs; all her fingers are neatly severed, and hot irons are introduced into her cunt and bum. Both Curval and the Duc discharge twice.

Up steps Louison; she weathers a storm of one hundred blows of the bull's pizzle; Messieurs pluck out one of her eyes and, most cynically, bid her swallow it. Down it goes.

THE 28TH. 144. A bugger: has two girls brought to him, they are fast friends, he ties them mouth to mouth, and by their side sits an excellent meal; but they cannot get to it, and he watches them bite and eat each other when hunger begins to exert its influence upon them.

Marquis de Sade

145. A man who as a boy was wont to flog pregnant women, now shuts six of this sort into a round cage formed by large iron hoops: they are all facing one another. Little by little, the hoops contract, little by little they are brought together, slowly they are flattened, gradually all six are crushed, their fruit crushed too. But prior to this he has cut a buttock and a breast from each and fashioned six collars therefrom; each woman wears one as you might a fur tippet.

146. Another pregnant-woman beater binds two of these objects each to the end of a long tilting pole; a clever machine, into which the other ends of the poles are inserted, bumps and bangs the women against each other. These repeated collisions are their mutual undoing, and he discharges. He makes every effort to procure himself a mother and daughter, or two sisters.

147. That Comte of whom Duclos spoke at length, and to whom Desgranges alluded once before on the 26th, he who purchased Lucile, Lucile's mother, and Lucile's little sister, of whom Martaine also spoke in her fourth tale on the 1st of January, this Comte, I say, has another passion still: 'tis to suspend three women over three holes. The first woman hangs by her tongue, beneath her is a very deep well; the second hangs from her breasts, underneath her lies a charcoal brazier; the scalp of the third has been loosened, she hangs by her hair over a pit studded with pointed iron rods. When the weight of their bodies causes these women to fall free - when the scalp is torn from the head of the third, when the breasts of the second tear loose from her torso, when the tongue of the first is torn from her mouth - they only escape one difficulty in order to encounter a new one. Whenever possible, he suspends three pregnant women, or three women from the same family; such was his unkind use of Lucile, her sister, and her mother.

148. The last passion.

(But why the last? Where are the other two? They were all there in the original outline.)

Desgranges recounts the last passion:

The nobleman who indulges in this final passion we shall designate as the infernal caprice or, more simply, as the hell passion, has been cited four times: by Duclos in the last story she told on the 29th of November; by Champville, when referring to a personage who depucelates nine-year-olds only; by Martaine, as he who depucelates three-year-olds in the bum; by Desgranges who mentioned him in an early connection (establish that connection more precisely). He is a man of some forty years, enormous in stature and furnished with the member of a stallion: his prick is very near to nine inches in circumference and a foot in overall length; he is exceedingly wealthy, a very powerful lord, very harsh, very cruel, his heart is of stone. He has a house on the outskirts of Paris which he uses for no purposes other than the gratification of this passion.

The surroundings wherein he savors his delight is a spacious room, simply decked, but padded everywhere, the floor covered with mattresses; upon entering the room one sees a single long casement window, the room has no other opening save for the door; that window looks down upon an underground cellar, twenty feet below the salon where he busies himself, and looking out, one sees the mattresses which break the fall of the girls as he flings down into the cellar, a description whereof we shall give shortly. He requires fifteen girls for this party; their ages must be between fifteen and seventeen, neither more, nor less; he employs six procuresses in Paris, as well as twelve in the provinces, and they are to spare no efforts, no expense to find him everything of the most charming that may possibly be found of that age, and as it is collected, the material is sent to a country convent over which he has absolute control, and there, in that nursery, the girls ripen, and from it he selects the fifteen objects for his debauch, which is regularly executed every fortnight.

That evening before the ceremony begins, he personally examines the said material, the least defect in which warrants its rejection; he insists that his creatures be perfect models of beauty. Escorted by a procuress, they arrive at the house and are lodged in a room adjacent to the pleasure-salon. They are first exhibited to him in this adjoining chamber, all fifteen are naked. He touches, feels, fondles, experiments with them, he scrutinizes them, sucks their mouths, and one after the other has them all shit into his mouth. But he does not swallow.

This initial operation performed with dreadful seriousness, he brands each upon the shoulder, imprinting a number in her flesh; it is to indicate the order in which he will receive them. That done, he goes alone into the salon, where he remains for a brief space: no one knows what he does in this moment of solitude. Then he knocks. Girl Number 1 is cast into his lair. And she is properly cast into it: the procuress flings her toward him, he catches her in his arms, she is naked. He shuts the door, takes up switches and begins to flail her ass; after that he sodomizes her with his gigantic prick. Never does he need any help. He does not discharge. His prick retires, still rock-hard; he seizes the switches again and returns to lashing the girl's back, the front and back of her thighs, then he lays her down again and deflowers her cunt; next, he goes back to beating her, now upon the breasts, both of which he seizes and grinds and kneads with all his strength, and he is a strong man. And now he picks up an awl and six times stabs her body, driving his point once into each bruised breast.

After all that has been done, he opens the casement window, places the girl in the middle of the room, standing erect, at attention, facing the window; he stands behind her and, when all is ready, gives her a kick in the ass of such startling violence that she flies across the room, crashes against the windowsill, topples over it, and vanishes into the cellar. But before launching her, he slips a ribbon around her neck, thereby to signify which torture, according to his best belief, will be most suitable for that particular patient, which torture will prove most voluptuous to inflict upon her, and his acuity and judgment in these matters, his tact and discrimination are truly wonderful.

And thus the girls pass one by one through his hands, the identical ceremony awaits them all, and thus he makes away with thirty maidenheads in a given day, and performs those heroic feats unscathed: not a drop of fuck does he lose. The subterranean apartment into which the girl tumble is furnished with fifteen different assortments of frightful torture machines, and an executioner, wearing the mask and emblems of a demon, wearing also the colors of his specialty, presides over each apparatus. The ribbon placed about the girl's neck corresponds in color with the torture to which she has been condemned, and directly she falls into the pit, the appropriate executioner steps forward, having recognized his victim, and drags her to the machine of which he has charge, but the tortures do not begin until the fifteenth has entered the gallery and been claimed by her demon. As soon as the entire complement has descended, our man, by now in a furious state after having depucelated thirty orifices without discharging, I say, makes his entrance into the infernal repair; he is practically naked, his prick glued against his belly. Everything is ready, all the tortures are in motion, and they proceed simultaneously, amidst much noise.

The first torture engine is a wheel upon which the girl is strapped and which, rotating uninterruptedly, bears against an outer circle studded with razors which everywhere scratch and tear and slice the unfortunate victim, but as the blades do not bite deep, only superficially, she turns for at least two hours before dying.

The second: the girl lies two inches above a red-hot iron plate which slowly melts her.

Third: she is attached by the waist to a piece of burning iron, and all her limbs are twisted and frightfully dislocated.

Fourth: the four limbs attached each to a spring which slowly moves away, gradually stretching her arms and legs until they are detached and the trunk falls into a brazier.

Fifth: a red-hot cast-iron bell is place over her head, but the bonnet is several sizes too large, the iron does not touch her, but her brain slowly melts, her head is slowly grilled.

Sixth: she is chained inside an iron tub of boiling oil.

Seventh: she is held standing before a machine which, six times a minute, shoots a small dart into her body, and each time into a different place; the machine does not stop until she is entirely feathered.

Eighth: her feet anchored in a furnace, a mass of lead very gradually descends upon her head, thrusting her further into the oven.

Ninth: her executioner continually pricks her with a red-hot iron goad; she is bound before him, he thus meticulously works over every inch of her body.

Tenth: she is chained to a pillar underneath a large glass dome, twenty famished reptiles devour her alive.

Eleventh: a cannon ball attached to each foot, she is suspended by one hand, and if she falls, 'tis into a furnace.

Twelfth: a hook is driven through her mouth; thus she hangs, a deluge of burning pitch incessantly pouring over her body.

Thirteenth: the nerves are pulled from her flesh and tied to cords which draw them further, and meanwhile burning nails are driven into her body.

Fourteenth: alternately torn with tongs and whipped upon her cunt and ass with martinets whose steel tips are heated red hot, and from time to time scratched with burning iron rakes.

Fifteenth: she is poisoned by a drug which burns and rends her entrails, which hurls her into frightful convulsions, causes her to utter hideous screams, and insures her death; but it is slow, and she is the last to succumb. This is one of the most terrible of the ordeals.

The villain walks about the torture chamber as soon as he arrives there, spends fifteen minutes contemplating each operation while swearing like of the damned and overwhelming the patient with unmentionable invectives. When toward the end he can bear no more of it and his fuck, captive for so long, is ready to escape him, he falls into a comfortable armchair whence he can observe the entire spectacle, two of the demons approach him, display their asses and frig him, and he squirts his seed while pronouncing shouts so stentorian that they rise above and totally blot out the din his fifteen patients are producing. And now he gets to his feet and leaves the gallery, the coup de grâce is given the girls who are not yet dead, their bodies are buried, and there's an end to it until the next fortnight comes round.

Wherewith Desgranges terminates her contribution; she is congratulated, toasted, acclaimed, etc. . . . .

Upon the morning of that day there had been the most ominous preparations for the great holiday Messieurs were meditating. Curval, detesting Constance as he does, had been cunt-fucking her at a very early hour and while fucking her had imparted grave news to her. Coffee was served by the five victims, to wit: Constance, Narcisse, Giton, Michette, and Rosette. Horrid things were perpetrated in the salon; during the recitations the reader has just perused, the quatrains Messieurs had been able to arrange had been composed of naked children. And as soon as Desgranges had brought her narrations to a term, Fanny had been marched to the fore: her remaining fingers and toes had been hacked off, and Curval had embuggered her without pomade, so had the Duc, so had the four first-rank fuckers.

Sophie was led into the center of the stage; Céladon, her lover, had been obliged to burn the interior of her cunt, all her fingers had been severed, her four limbs bled, her right ear had been torn away, her left eye gouged out. Céladon had been constrained to lend his assistance in all these operations, and his least frown or lowest murmur was rewarded by a flogging with an iron-tipped martinet. Supper had come next, the meal had been voluptuous, Messieurs drank naught but sparkling champagne and liqueurs.

The torturing was arranged for the orgy hour; as the friends sat at dessert, word was brought to them that everything was in readiness, they descended and found the cellars agreeably festooned and very properly furnished. Constance lay upon a kind of mausoleum, the four children decorated its corners. As their asses were still in excellent condition, Messieurs were able to take considerable pleasure in molesting them; then at last the heavier work was begun: while embuggering Giton, Curval himself opened Constance's belly and tore out the fruit, already well-ripened and clearly of the masculine sex; then the society continued, inflicting tortures upon those five victims. Their sufferings were long, cruel, and various.

Upon THE 1ST DAY OF MARCH, remarking that the snows have not yet melted, Messieurs decide to dispatch the rest of the subjects one by one. Messieurs devise new arrangements whereby to keep their bedchambers staffed, and agree to give a green ribbon to everyone whom they propose to take back with them to France; the green favor is bestowed, however, upon condition the recipient is willing to lend a hand with the destruction of the other victims. Nothing is said to the six women in the kitchen; Messieurs decide to do away with the three scullery maids, who are well worth toying over, but to spare the cooks, because of their considerable talents. And so a list is drawn up; 'tis found that, to date, the following creatures had already been sacrificed:

Wives: Aline, Adelaide, and Constance: 3

Sultanas: Augustine, Michette, Rosette, and Zelmire: 4

Bardashes: Giton and Narcisse: 2

Fuckers: one subaltern: 1

Total: 10

The new ménages are arranged:

The Duc takes unto himself, or under his protection: Hercule, Duclos, one cook: 4

Curval takes: Bum-Cleaver, Champville, one cook: 4

Durcet takes: Invictus, Martaine, one cook: 4

And the Bishop: Antinoüs, Desgranges, Julie: 4

Total: 16

Messieurs decide that, upon a given signal, and with the aid of the four fuckers and the four storytellers, but not the cooks whom they do not wish to employ for these purposes, they will seize all the others, making use of the most treacherous possible means and when their victims least expect it; they will lay hands upon all the others, I say, save for the three scullions, who will not be seized until later on; it is further decided that the upstairs chambers will be converted into four prisons, that the three subaltern fuckers, manacled, will be lodged in the strongest of these prisons; Fanny, Colombe, Sophie, and Hébé in the second; Céladon, Zélamir, Cupidon, Zéphyr, Adonis, and Hyacinthe in the third; and the four elders in the fourth; that one subject will be dispatched every day; and that when the hour arrives to arrest the three scullions, they will be locked into whichever of the prison happens to be empty.

These agreements once reached, Messieurs appoint each storyteller the warden of one prison. And whenever they please, Messieurs will amuse themselves with these victims, either in their prison or in one of the larger rooms, or in their Lordships' bedchambers, depending upon Messieurs' individual preference. And so, as we have just indicated, one subject is dispatched daily, in the following order:

On the 1st of March: Fanchon.

On the 2nd: Louison.

On the 3rd: Thérèse.

On the 4th: Marie.

On the 5th: Fanny.

On the 6th and the 7th: Sophie and Céladon together, for they are lovers, and they perish nailed one to the other, as we have hitherto explained.

On the 8th: one subaltern fucker.

On the 9th: Hébé.

On the 10th: another subaltern fucker.

On the 11th: Colombe.

On the 12th: the last of the subaltern fuckers.

On the 13th: Zélamir.

On the 14th: Cupidon.

On the 15th: Zéphyr.

On the 16th: Adonis.

On the 17th: Hyacinthe.

On the morning of the 18th, Messieurs and their cohorts seize the three scullions, lock them in the prison formerly occupied by the elders, and dispatch one upon that day.

A second upon the 19th.

And the last upon the 20th.

Total: 20.

The following recapitulation lists the inhabitants of the Château of Silling during that memorable winter:

Masters: 4

Elders: 4

Kitchen staff: 6

Storytellers: 4

Fuckers: 8

Little boys: 8

Wives: 4

Little girls: 8

Total: 46

Whereof thirty were immolated and sixteen returned to Paris.

FINAL ASSESSMENT

Massacred prior to the 1st of March,

in the course of the orgies: 10

Massacred after the 1st of March: 20

Survived and came back: 16

Total: 46

With what regards the tortures and deaths of the last twenty subjects, and life such as it was in the household until the day of departure, you will give details at your leisure and where you see fit, you will say, first of all, that thirteen of the sixteen survivors (three of whom were cooks) took all their meals together; sprinkle in whatever tortures you like.

Notes

Under no circumstances deviate from this plan, everything has been worked out, the entirety several times re-examined with the greatest care and thoroughness.

Detail the departure. And throughout the whole, introduce a quantity of moral dissertation and diatribe, above all at the suppers.

When you produce the final version, keep a notebook; in it you will place the names of all the principal characters and the names of all those who play important roles, such as they who have several passions and who will appear several times in the romance, as, for example, the hell libertine; leave a wide margin beside their names and, as you recopy, fill it with everything you come across that has any bearing upon them; this note is very essential, it is the sole way to keep your work clear of obscurities and to avoid repetitions.

Edulcorate Part The First, it is much too strong; things develop too rapidly and too far in it, it cannot possibly be too soft, mild, feeble, subdued. Above all, never have the four friends do anything until it has first been recounted. You have not been sufficiently scrupulous in that connection.

In Part The First, say that the man who mouth-fucks the little girl prostituted by her father is the same man, of whom she has already spoken, who fucks with a dirty prick.

Do not forget to place somewhere in December the scene of the little girls serving supper, squirting liqueurs from their asses into Messieurs' glasses; you announced such a scene but failed to include it in the plan.

Supplementary Tortures

-By means of a hollow tube, a mouse is introduced into her cunt, the tube is withdrawn, the cunt sewn up, and the animal, unable to get out, devours her entrails.

-She is made to swallow a snake which in similar wise feeds upon her entrails.

Addenda

In general, describe Curval and the Duc as two hot-blooded and imperious scoundrels, 'tis thus you conceived them in the plan and in Part The First, and figure the Bishop as a cool, reasoning and tough-minded villain. As for Durcet, he must be mischievous, a teaser, false, traitorous, perfidious. In accordance with which, have them do everything that conforms with such characters.

Carefully recapitulate all the names and the qualities of all the personages your storytellers mention; this to avoid repetition.

Upon one page in your notebook of characters draw the plan of the château, room by room, and in the blank space next to this page, itemize all the things done in each room.

This entire great roll was begun the 22nd of October, 1785, and finished in thirty-seven days.

Florville and Courval
(or Fatalism)

Monsieur de Courval had just turned fifty-five. Vigorous and healthy, he could reasonably expect to live another twenty years. Having had nothing but unpleasantness from his first wife, who had long ago abandoned him in order to throw herself into a life of debauchery, and being obliged, on the basis of unequivocal testimony, to assume that this creature was in her grave, he began contemplating the idea of again entering into the bonds of matrimony, this time with a sensible woman who, by the kindness of her character and the excellence of her morals, would make him forget his earlier mishaps.

Unfortunate in his children as well as in his wife, he had had only two: a girl whom he had lost at a very early age, and a boy who, at the age of fifteen, had abandoned him as his wife had done, unfortunately in order to pursue the same licentious ways. Believing that nothing would ever bind him to this monster, Monsieur de Courval planned to disinherit him and bequeath all his possessions to the children he hoped to have with the new wife he wanted to take. He had an income of fifteen thousand francs a year; he had formerly been in business, and this was the fruit of his work. He was living on it in a respectable manner, with a few friends who all cherished and esteemed him, and saw him either in Paris, where he had an attractive apartment on the Rue Saint-Marc, or, more often, on a charming little estate near Nemours, where he spent two-thirds of the year.

This upright man confided his plan to his friends. When they expressed approval of it, he urged them to ask among their acquaintances to learn whether any of them knew a woman between the ages of thirty and thirty-five, either unmarried or a widow, who might fulfill his wishes.

Two days later one of his former colleagues came to tell him that he thought he had found exactly what he needed.

"The girl I'm proposing to you," this friend said to him, "has two things against her; I'll begin by telling them to you, so that I can console you afterward by describing her good qualities. It's certain that her parents are not alive, but no one knows who they were or where she lost them. All that's known is that she's a cousin of Monsieur de Saint-Prât, a reputable man who acknowledges her, holds her in great esteem, and will gladly express to you his enthusiastic and well-deserved praise of her. She has no inheritance from her parents, but Monsieur de Saint-Prât gives her four thousand francs a year. She was brought up in his house and spent her whole youth there. So much for her first fault, let's go on to her second: an affair at the age of sixteen, and a child who's no longer alive. She never seen the father again. Those are the things against her; now for a few words about those in her favor.

"Mademoiselle de Florville is thirty-six, but she looks no more than twenty-eight, it would be difficult to imagine a more pleasing and interesting face. Her features are soft and delicate, her skin has the whiteness of a lily, and her brown hair hangs down almost to her feet. Her fresh, appealing mouth is like a springtime rose. She's very tall, but she has such an excellent figure, and so much grace in her movements, that no one is unfavorably impressed by her height, which might otherwise give her a rather hard appearance. Her arms, her neck and her legs are all shapely, and she has a kind of beauty that will not grow old for a long time.

"As for her conduct, it's extreme regularity may not please you. She doesn't like social activities, and she leads a secluded life. She's very pious and very conscientious in the duties of the convent in which she lives. While she edifies everyone around her by her religious qualities, she also enchants everyone who sees her by the charms of her mind and the sweetness of her character . . . In short, she's an angel on earth, sent by heaven for the happiness of your old age."

Monsieur de Courval, delighted by this description, eagerly asked his friend to let him see the girl in question.

"I don't care about her birth," he said. "As long as her blood is pure, what does it matter who transmitted it to her? And her adventure at the age of sixteen doesn't alarm me, either: she's made up for that failing by many years of virtuous conduct. I'll simply consider that I'm marrying a widow; having decided to take a woman between thirty and thirty-five, it would have been hard for me to maintain a foolish insistence on virginity. So nothing displeases me in your proposal, and I can only urge you to let me see the object of it."

Monsieur de Courval's friend soon granted his wish: three days later he invited him to dinner with the young woman of whom he had spoken. It would have been difficult not to be enchanted at first sight by that charming girl. She had the features of Minerva herself, disguised beneath those of love. Since she knew what was at issue, she was even more reserved than usual. Her discretion, her modesty and the nobility of her bearing, combined with her many physical charms, her gentle character and her keen, well-developed mind, left poor Courval so enraptured that he begged his friend to hasten the conclusion.

He saw her several more times, in his friend's house, in his own, and in Monsieur de Saint-Prât's. Finally, in response to his earnest entreaties, she told him that nothing could be more pleasing to her than the honor he wanted to bestow on her, but that her conscience would not allow her to accept it until she herself had related the vicissitudes of her life to him.

"You haven't been told everything, monsieur," she said, "and I can't consent to be yours unless you know more about me. Your esteem is so important to me that I don't want to risk losing it, and I would certainly not deserve it if, taking advantage of your illusions about me, I were to agree to be your wife without giving you a chance to judge whether or not I'm worthy of it."

Monsieur de Courval assured her that he knew everything, that it was he, rather than she, who ought to have misgivings about his worthiness, and that if he was fortunate enough to please her, she had no reason to trouble herself about anything. But she held firm: she told him emphatically that she would not consent to anything until he had been thoroughly informed by her. He had to give in to her; all he was able to obtain from her was that she would come to his estate near Nemours, that all preparations would be made for the wedding he desired, and that she would become his wife the day after he had heard her story.

"But, monsieur," said that gracious girl, "since all those preparations may be in vain, why make them? What if I should persuade you that I'm not meant for you?"

"You'll never prove that to me, mademoiselle," replied the honest Courval. "I defy you to prove it to me. Let us go, I beg you, and don't oppose my plans."

It was impossible to make him change his mind. Everything was arranged and they went to his estate. They were alone, however, as Mademoiselle de Florville had demanded: the things she had to say were not to be revealed to anyone except the man who wanted to marry her, so no one else was admitted. The day after their arrival that beautiful and interesting girl asked monsieur de Courval to listen to her, and told him the events of her life in these words:

Mademoiselle de Florville's Story

Your intentions with regard to me, monsieur, make it imperative that you be deceived no longer. You've seen Monsieur de Saint-Prât; you've been told that I'm related to him, and he himself was kind enough to say so, and yet you were greatly deceived on that point. My family is unknown to me; I've never had the satisfaction of knowing to whom I owe my birth. A few days after I was born, I was found in a green taffeta bassinet on Monsieur de Saint-Prât's doorstep. Attached to the canopy over my bassinet was an anonymous letter which said simply:

Since you have been married for ten years without having a child and still want one every day, adopt this one. Her blood is pure: she is the fruit of a virtuous marriage, and not of debauchery; she comes from an honorable family. If she does not please you, you can have her taken to a foundling home. Do not make any inquiries, because none of them would be successful. It is impossible to tell you anything more.

I was immediately taken in by the good people at whose house I'd been left. They brought me up, took the best possible care of me, and I can say that I owe them everything. Since there was no indication of my name, it pleased Madame de Saint-Prât to name me Florville.

I had just reached the age of fifteen when I had the misfortune of seeing my foster mother die. Nothing could express the grief I felt at losing her. I had become so dear to her that just before her death she begged her husband to allot me an income of four thousand francs a year and never to abandon me. Monsieur de Saint-Prât granted these two requests. He was also kind enough to acknowledge me as a cousin of his wife and to draw up a marriage contract for me under that title, as you have seen.

He made it clear to me, however, that I could no longer stay in his house. "I'm a widower, and still young," that virtuous man said to me. "If you and I were to live under the same roof now, it would give rise to doubts which we don't deserve. Your happiness and your reputation are dear to me: I don't want to endanger either of them. We must part, Florville, but I will never abandon you as long as I live, and I don't even want you to go outside of my family. I have a widowed sister in Nancy. I'm going to send you to her. You can count on her friendship the same as mine. With her, you'll still be before my eyes, so to speak, and I can continue to take care of everything that will be required to complete your education and establish you in life."

I wept when I heard this news. It gave me an additional sorrow which bitterly renewed my grief over the death of my foster mother. But I was convinced of the soundness of Monsieur de Saint-Prât's reasoning, so I decided to follow his advice. I left for Lorraine in the company of a lady from that region to whom I had been entrusted. She brought me to Madame de Verquin, Monsieur de Saint-Prât's sister, with whom I was to live.

Madame de Verquin's house was quite different from Monsieur de Saint-Prât's. In his, I had seen decency, religion and morality reign supreme; in hers, frivolity, independence and the pursuit of pleasure were enthroned.

When I'd been there only a few days, Madame de Verquin warned me that my prudish air displeased her, that it was outrageous to come from Paris with such awkward manners and such a ridiculous strain of virtue in one's character, and that if I wanted to get along with her I'd have to adopt another tone. This beginning alarmed me. I won't try to make myself appear better than I am, monsieur, but everything contrary to morality and religion has always displeased me so intensely, I've always been so strongly opposed to anything that offends virtue, and the sins to which I've been driven in spite of myself have caused me so much remorse, that I must confess to you that you won't be rendering me a service if you bring me back into the world. I wasn't made to live in it, it makes me feel shy and morose. The deepest seclusion is what best suits the state of my soul and the inclinations of my mind.

These reflections, still badly formulated and not sufficiently ripened at such an early age, save me neither from Madame de Verquin's bad advice nor from the calamities into which her enticement was to plunge me. The constant company and hectic pleasures with which I was surrounded, the examples and words of others -- everything combined to lead me astray. I was told that I was pretty, and, unfortunately for me, I dared to believe it.

The Normandy regiment was garrisoned in Nancy at that time. Madame de Verquin's house was a meeting place for the officers. All the young women came too, and it was there that all the amorous intrigues of the town were begun, broken off and recomposed.

It was unlikely that Monsieur de Saint-Prât knew all about his sister's conduct. With his austere morality, how could he have consented to send me to her if he

had known her well? This consideration held me back and prevented me from
complaining to him. And, if I must confess everything, it's even possible that I had
little desire to complain to him. The impure air I was breathing had begun to
pollute my soul, and, like Telemachus on Calypso's island, I might not have
listened to Mentor's advice.

One day the shameless Madame de Verquin, who had been trying to corrupt
me for a long time, asked me whether I was sure I'd brought a pure heart with me
to Lorraine, and whether I hadn't left a lover behind me in Paris.

"I've never even thought of the failings you suspect me of," I replied "and your
brother will answer for my conduct . . ."

"Failings?" interrupted Madame de Verquin. "If you have one, it's being too
innocent for your age. I hope you'll correct it."

"Oh, madame !   Is that the kind of language I ought to hear from such a
respectable lady?"

"Respectable? Ah, not another word ! I assure you, my dear, that respect is
the feeling I care least about. Love is what I want to inspire. I'm not yet old
enough for respect. Follow my example, my dear, and you'll be happy. . . .By the
way, have you noticed Senneval?" added that siren, referring to a
seventeen-year-old officer who often came to her house.

"Not particularly," I replied. "I can assure you that I see them all with the same
indifference."

"That's just what you mustn't do, my young friend. From now on, I want us to
share our conquests. You must have Senneval. He's my handiwork, I've taken the
trouble to develop him. He's in love with you. You must have him. . . ."

"Oh, madame, please don't insist on it ! Really, I'm not interested in anyone
! "

"You must do it: I've already made arrangements with his colonel, who's my
current lover, as you've seen."

"Please leave me free to make my own choice. I'm not at all inclined toward the
pleasures you cherish."

"Oh, that will change ! Some day you'll like them as much as I do. It's easy not
to cherish something you don't know yet, but it's inadmissible to refuse to know
something that was made to be adored. In short, the whole thing has already been
planned: Senneval will declare his passion to you this evening, and I don't want
you to make him wait too long before you satisfy it, otherwise I'll be angry with
you--seriously angry."

At five o'clock the company gathered. Since the weather was hot, card games
were organized outside in the groves. Things had been so well arranged that
Monsieur de Senneval and I found that we were the only ones who were not
playing cards, so we were obliged to talk with each other.

It would be pointless to conceal the fact that as soon as that charming and
witty young man had told me of his love for me, I felt irresistibly drawn toward
him. When I later tried to understand that attraction, I found that everything

about it was obscure to me. It seemed to me that it wasn't the effect of an ordinary feeling: its characteristics were hidden from me by a veil before my eyes. On the other hand, at the very moment when my heart flew toward him, an invincible force seemed to hold it back, and in that tumult, that ebb and flow of incomprehensible ideas, I was unable to decide whether I was right to love Senneval or whether I ought to flee from him forever.

He was given ample time to confess his love to me . . . Alas, he was given too much ! I had time enough to appear responsive to him. Taking advantage of my agitation, he demanded an admission of my feelings. I was weak enough to tell him that he was far from displeasing me, and three days later I was sinful enough to let him enjoy his victory.

The malicious joy of vice in its triumphs over virtue is a truly extraordinary thing. Madame de Verquin was ecstatic when she learned that I'd fallen into the trap she'd set for me. She made fun of me, laughed at me, and finally assured me that what I'd done was the simplest, most reasonable thing in the world, and that I could receive my lover in her house every night without fear; because she would see nothing. She said she was too busy to concern herself with such trifles, but that she would admire my virtue nevertheless, because I would probably limit myself to the one lover I had just chosen, while she, lacking my modesty and reserve, had to contend with three of them at once.

When I took the liberty of telling her that such promiscuity was odious, that it presupposed neither sensitivity nor sentiment, and that it reduced our sex to the level of the vilest species of animals, she burst out laughing and said, "'Gallic heroine,' I admire you and don't blame you. I know very well that at your age sensitivity and sentiment are gods to whom one sacrifices pleasure. At my age, it's different: completely disillusioned about those phantoms, one gives them a little less power; sensual pleasures that are more real are preferred to the silly delusions that fill you with enthusiasm. Why should we be faithful to men who aren't faithful to us? Isn't it enough to be weaker without also being more gullible? A woman who has qualms about such actions is foolish . . . Take my advice, my dear: vary your pleasures while your age and your charms allow you to do it, and abandon your absurd faithfulness. It's a gloomy, repugnant virtue that's unsatisfying in itself and never impresses others."

These words made me shudder, but I saw clearly that I no longer had the right to oppose them; the criminal co-operation of that immoral woman had become necessary to me, and I had to treat her with consideration. This is one of the fatal disadvantages of vice: as soon as we abandon ourselves to it, it places us in bondage to people whom we would otherwise scorn. And so I accepted all of Madame de Verquin's obligingness. Every night Senneval gave me new proof of his love, and I spend the next six months in such a passionate turmoil that I scarcely had time to think.

My eyes were opened by a disastrous consequence: I became pregnant. I nearly died of despair when I discovered my condition. Madame de Verquin was amused by it. "However," she said, "we must save appearances. Since it wouldn't be very decent for you to have your baby in my house, Senneval's colonel and I have made some arrangements. He's going to give Senneval a leave. You'll go to Metz, he'll join you there a few days later, and then, with his aid, you'll give birth to the illicit fruit of your love. Afterward, you'll both come back here, one after the other, the same as you'll have left."

I had to obey. As I've already said, monsieur, we place ourselves at the mercy of all men and all situations when we've been unfortunate enough to sink into sin; we give rights over ourselves to everyone in the world, we become the slaves of every living being as soon as we forget ourselves to the point of becoming the slaves of our passions.

Everything took place as Madame de Verquin had said. On the third day, Senneval and I were in Metz together, in the house of a midwife whose address I'd been given before I left Nancy, and there I gave birth to a boy. Senneval, who had never stopped showing the most tender and delicate feelings for me, seemed to love me even more as soon as I had doubled his existence, as he put it. He was full of consideration for me; he begged me to leave his son to him, swore that he would take all possible care of him for the rest of his life, and wouldn't think of returning to Nancy until he had fulfilled his obligations to me.

It was not until he was about to leave that I dared to point out to him how unhappy I was going to be because of the sin he had made me commit, and to suggest that we atone for it by consecrating our union before the altar. Senneval, who hadn't expected this, became upset.

"Alas," he said, "it's not within my power. I'm still a minor, so I'd have to have my father's consent. What would our marriage be without it? Besides, I'm by no means a good match for you. As Madame de Verquin's niece" (this was what everyone in Nancy believed) "you can expect something better. Believe me, Florville, the best thing we can do is to forget our mistakes. You can count on my discretion."

These words came as a shock to me, and they made me painfully aware of the enormity of my sin. My pride prevented me from replying, but my grief was all the more bitter. If anything had hidden the horror of my conduct from me, it was, I confess, the hope of making amends for it some day by marrying my lover. What a credulous girl I was ! Although I should no doubt have been enlightened by Madame de Verquin's perversity, I hadn't believed that a man could amuse himself by seducing an unfortunate girl and then abandoning her, that the sentiment of honor, so highly respected among men, could be totally inoperative with regard to us, and that our weakness could justify an insult which one man could not inflict on another without risking his life. I saw that I was both the victim and the dupe of the man for whom I would gladly have given my life. This terrible realization nearly put me into my grave. Senneval didn't leave me; he took care of me the same as before, but he never spoke of my suggestion again, and I had too much pride to mention the cause of my despair to him a second time. He went away as soon as he saw that I'd recovered.

Determined never to go back to Nancy, and realizing that I was seeing my lover for the last time in my life, I felt all my wounds reopening when I said good-by to him. But I had the strength to withstand that final blow . . . How cruel he was !

He left, he tore himself away from my bosom wet with my tears, without shedding a single tear of his own !

Such is the result of the vows of love we're foolish enough to believe ! The more sensitive we are, the more completely our seducers forsake us . . . The traitors ! The degree to which they abandon us is in proportion to our efforts to keep them with us.

Senneval had taken his child and placed him in a country home where it was impossible for me to find him. He wanted to deprive me of the sweet consolation of cherishing and bringing up that tender fruit of our union. It was as though he wanted me to forget everything that might still bind us to each other, and I did, or rather I thought I did.

I decided to leave Metz immediately and not go back to Nancy. I didn't want to quarrel with Madame de Verquin, however. Despite her faults, the fact that she was so closely related to my benefactor was enough to make me treat her with consideration all my life. I wrote to her in the most courteous possible terms, giving my shame over what I'd done in Nancy as my reason for not wanting to return there, and asking her to give me her permission to go back to her brother in Paris. She replied promptly that I was free to do as I pleased, and that I could always count on her friendship. She added that Senneval had not yet returned, that no one knew where he was, and that I was a fool to be so distressed by such trifles.

As soon as I received this letter I went back to Paris and hurried to throw myself at Monsieur de Saint-Prât's feet. My silence and my tears soon informed him of my unhappiness. But I was careful to accuse only myself; I never told him of his sister's deliberate efforts to lead me astray. With his kind, trusting nature, he had never suspected her disorderly life, and believed her to be the most respectable of women. I did nothing to destroy his illusion, and this conduct on my part, which Madame de Verquin knew about, preserved her friendship for me.

Monsieur de Saint-Prât pitied me, made me even more keenly aware of the wrong I'd done, and finally forgave me for it.

"Ah, my child," he said with the gentle gravity of an honorable soul, so different from the odious delirium of crime, "my dear daughter, now you know what it costs to forsake virtue . . . Its practice is so necessary and so intimately bound up with our existence that there's nothing but unhappiness for us as soon as we abandon it. Compare the tranquillity of the state of innocence in which you left this house to the terrible turmoil in which you've returned to it. Do the weak pleasures you savored during your downfall compensate for the torments that now rend your heart? Happiness lies only in virtue, my child, and all the sophisms of its detractors will never bring us a single one of its enjoyments. Ah, Florville, you may be sure that those who deny or oppose those sweet enjoyments do so only out of jealousy, for the barbarous pleasure of making others as guilty and unhappy as themselves. They've blinded themselves and want to blind everyone else; they're mistaken and they want everyone else to be mistaken. But if one could see into the depths of their souls, one would find only sorrow and remorse: all those apostles of crime are full of wretchedness and despair. There's not one of them who, if he were sincere, if he could tell the truth, wouldn't admit that his foul words or his dangerous writings had been guided only by his passions. And who can seriously maintain that the foundations of morality can be shaken without risk? Who would dare to say that doing and desiring well must not necessarily be man's purpose? And how can someone who does only evil expect to be happy in a society whose most powerful interest is that good should be constantly multiplied? But will not even that apologist of crime shudder when he has uprooted from every heart the only thing from which he can expect his preservation? Who will restrain his servants from ruining him if they have ceased to be virtuous? Who will prevent his wife from dishonoring him if he has convinced her that virtue is useless? Who will hold back the hands of his children if he has dared to wither the seeds of good in their hearts? How will his freedom and his possessions be respected if he has said to the powerful, 'Impunity goes with you, and virtue is only an illusion? No matter what that unhappy man's condition, whether he be a husband or a father, rich or poor, a master or a slave, dangers will spring up on all sides of him, and daggers will be raised above his heart from all directions. If he has dared to destroy in man the only duties which balance his perversity, you may be sure that the poor wretch will perish sooner or later, the victim of his own horrible systems.

"Let us leave religion for the moment and, if you like, let us consider man alone. Who would be stupid enough to think that if he breaks all the laws of society, that society which he has outraged can leave him in peace? Is it not in the interest of man, and the laws, he has made for his safety, always to try to destroy whatever is obstructive or harmful? A certain amount of influence or wealth may give the wicked man a fleeting glow of well-being, but how short its duration will be ! He will soon be recognized, unmasked and made an object of public hatred and contempt. Will he then find the apologists of his conduct? Will his partisans come forward to console him? None of them will acknowledge him. Now that he no longer has everything to offer them, they will all cast him off like a burden. Misfortune will surround him, he will languish in disgrace and sorrow, and, no longer having even his own heart as a refuge, he will soon die in despair."

"What, then, is this absurd reasoning of our adversaries? What is this impotent effort to diminish virtue, to dare to say that anything which is not universal is illusory, and that since virtues are only local, none of them can have any reality? What ! Is there no virtue because each person has had to make its own? If different climates and different kinds of temperament have made different kinds of restraints necessary, if, in a word, virtue has multiplied in a thousand forms, does this mean that there is no virtue on earth? One might as well doubt the reality of a river because it splits off into a thousand different streams. What better proof of the existence and necessity of virtue is there than man's need to adapt it to all his different moral codes and to make it the basis of all of them?

"If anyone can find me a single people which lives without virtue, a single one for which benevolence and kindness are not fundamental bonds . . . I will go further: If anyone can show me even an association of criminals which is not held together by a few principles of virtue, then I will abandon its cause. But if, on the contrary, it can be demonstrated to be useful everywhere, if there is no nation, class, group or individual that can do without it, if no man, in short, can live either happily or safely without it, then, my child, am I wrong to urge you never to depart from it?

"You see where your first lapse has led you, Florville ! " continued my benefactor, clasping me in his arms. "If error should solicit you again, if seduction on your weakness should set new traps for you, remember the misery of this first lapse, think of the man who loves you as though you were his own daughter and whose heart is torn by your failings, and you will find in these reflections all the strength required by devotion to virtue, which I want to instill in you forever."

In accordance with these same principles, Monsieur de Saint-Prât didn't offer to let me stay in his house, but he suggested that I go and live with one of his relatives, a woman as famous for the lofty piety of her life as Madame de Verquin was for her immorality. This arrangement pleased me greatly, Madame de Lérince accepted me gladly, and I was installed in her house less than a week after my return to Paris.

Ah, monsieur, what a difference between that respectable woman and the woman I had just left ! If vice and depravity had established their dominion in Madame de Verquin, it was as though Madame de Lérince's heart had become the sanctuary of all the virtues. I had been frightened by Madame de Verquin's depravity; I was consoled by Madame de Lérince's edifying principles. I had found only bitterness and remorse in listening to Madame de Verquin; I found only sweetness and consolations in abandoning myself to Madame de Lérince . . . Ah, monsieur, let me describe that adorable woman whom I shall always love ! It's a tribute that my heart owes to her virtues, and it's impossible for me to resist it.

Madame de Lérince was about forty years old; she still had the bloom of youth, and her air of candor and modesty did much more to make her face beautiful than the divine proportions that nature had given to her features. Some of those who knew her thought that a little too much nobility and majesty made her rather awesome at first sight, but what might have been taken for pride became softened as soon as she spoke. She had such a pure and beautiful soul, such perfect graciousness and such complete frankness that, in spite of oneself, one always became aware of tender feelings gradually arising beside the veneration she inspired at first.

There was nothing exaggerated or superstitious in Madame de Lérince's religion. The principles of her faith resided in an extreme sensibility. The idea of the existence of God, the worship owed to that Supreme Being: such were the keenest enjoyments of that loving soul. She avowed openly that she would be the most wretched of creatures if some sort of perfidious enlightenment should ever force her mind to destroy in her the respect and love she had for her religion.

Still more strongly attached, if possible, to the sublime morality of her religion that to its practices and ceremonies, she made that excellent morality the rule of all her actions. Slander never soiled her lips; she would not tolerate even a jest which might hurt someone's feelings. Full of affection and compassion for others, finding them interesting even in their faults, she was solely concerned with either carefully hiding those faults or gently admonishing them. If others were unhappy, nothing was as gratifying to her as relieving their unhappiness. She didn't wait for the poor to come and implore her aid; she sought them out, she sensed their distress before they expressed it, and joy could be seen shining from her face when she had consoled a widow or provided for an orphan, when she had brought prosperity to a poor family, or when her hands had broken the chains of adversity. And there was nothing harsh or austere with all this: if the pleasures proposed to her were pure, she indulged in them with delight. She even invented pleasures herself, for fear others might be bored in her company.

Wise and enlightened with the moralist, profound with the theologian, she inspired the novelist and smiled on the poet, she astonished the legislator and the statesman, and directed the games of a child. She had every kind of intelligence, but the kind that shone most brightly in her was recognized chiefly by her special care and charming attention in bringing out the intelligence of others or expressing appreciation of it. Living in retirement by inclination, cultivating her friends for their own sake, Madame de Lérince, who could have served as a model for either sex, made all those around her enjoy the peaceful happiness and heavenly delight which is promised to the honest man by the holy god whose image she was.

I won't bore you, monsieur, with the monotonous details of my life during the seventeen years I was fortunate enough to live with that adorable woman. Discussion of morality and piety, as many benevolent acts as it was possible for us to perform: such were the duties that filled our days.

"People are frightened away from religion, my dear Florville," Madame de Lérince once said to me, "only because awkward guides point out nothing but its restraints to them, without offering them its sweetness. Can there be a man absurd enough to open his eyes to the universe and still dare not to agree that such wonders could only be the work of an all-powerful God? Once this first truth has been realized --- and does one require anything more than one's heart in order to become convinced of it? -- how can anyone be so cruel and barbarous as to refuse his homage to the benevolent God who created him?

"But the diversity of religions is cited as an objection: their falsity is thought to be proved by their multitude. What sophistry !   Is not the existence of a supreme God proved more irrefutably by this unanimity of all peoples in recognizing and serving a God, and by this tacit avowal imprinted in the hearts of all men, than by the sublimities of nature? What !   Man cannot live without adopting a God, he cannot question himself without finding evidence of Him within himself, he cannot open his eyes without seeing traces of Him everywhere, and yet he dares to doubt His existence !

"No, Florville, there are no atheists in good faith. Pride, stubbornest, the passions: those are the destructive weapons of that god who constantly revivifies Himself in man's heart or reason. And when each beat of that heart and each bright ray of that reason offer me that incontestable Being, shall I refuse my homage to Him? Shall I rob Him of the tribute which His goodness allows my weakness? Shall I not humiliate myself before His greatness, and ask Him to help me endure the miseries of life and participate in His glory some day? Shall I not aspire to the favor of spending eternity in His bosom, or shall I risk spending that eternity in a frightful abyss of torments because I've refused to accept the indubitable proofs of that great Being's existence which He has been kind enough to give me? My child, does that appalling choice permit even a moment's reflection? Ah, you who stubbornly refuse to let yourselves recognize the letters of fire that God has traced in the depths of your hearts, be just for at least a moment, and, if only out of pity for yourselves, yield to this invincible argument of Pascal's: 'If there is no God, what does it matter to you if you believe in Him, what harm does it do you? And if there is a god, what risks will you be taking if you refuse Him your faith?'

"But you say, skeptics, that you don't know what tribute to pay to this God; you're repelled by the multitude of religions. Very well, examine them all, I have no objections; then afterward come and tell me sincerely in which one of them you find the most grandeur and majesty. Deny if you can, Christians, that the religion in which you were fortunate enough to be born is the one where characteristics appear to you the holiest and most sublime; seek elsewhere such great mysteries, such pure dogmas, such consoling morality; find in another religion the ineffable sacrifice of a God in favor of His creature, see in it more beautiful promises, a more appealing future, a greater and more sublime God ! No, you cannot, philosopher of the day; you cannot, slave of your pleasures whose faith changes with the physical state of your nerves, so that you are impious in the fire of the passions and a believer as soon as they are calmed; you cannot, I tell you. Sentiment constantly acknowledges the God your mind combats. He always exists beside you, even in the midst of your errors. Break the chains which bind you to crime and that holy and majestic God will never leave the temple He has built in your heart.

"It is in the depths of the heart, my dear Florville, even more than in the mind, that we must seek the necessity of that god whom everything indicates and proves to us. It is also from the heart that we must receive the necessity of the worship we devote to Him. And it is the heart alone, my dear friend, that will soon convince you that the noblest and purest of all religions is the one in which we were born. Let us therefore practice that sweet and consoling religion with exactitude and joy. May it fill our most beautiful moments in this world, may we cherish it until we are gradually led to the end of our life, and may it be by a path of love and delights that we go to place in the bosom of God that soul which emanated from Him, which was formed solely to know Him, and which we should have enjoyed only to believe in Him, and which we should have enjoyed only to believe in Him and worship Him."

That's how Madame de Lérince spoke to me, that's how my mind was strengthened by her advice, and how my soul was refined beneath her holy wing. But, as I've told you, I'm going to pass in silence over the little details of my life in that house and dwell only on what's essential. It's my sins that I must reveal to you, generous and sensitive man, and when heaven has allowed me to live peacefully in the path of virtue, I have only to be thankful and remain silent.

I continue to write to Madame de Verquin. I heard from her regularly twice a month. I should no doubt have stopped writing to her, and I was more or less obliged to do so by my better principles and the reformation of my life, but what I owed to Monsieur de Saint-Prât, the hope of perhaps receiving news of my son some day, and, most of all, I must confess, a secret feeling which still drew me toward the place to which cherished people had bound me in the past -- all these things made me inclined to continue our correspondence, which she was courteous enough to maintain regularly. I tried to convert her, I praised the sweetness of the life I was leading, but she called it an illusion. She never stopped making fun of my resolutions or combating them, and, still firm in her own, she assured me that nothing in the world could weaken them. She told me of the new girls she had converted to her principles for her own amusement, and she claimed that their docility was much greater than mine. Their multiple lapses from virtue, said that perverse woman, were little triumphs which she was always delighted to win, and the pleasure of leading those young hearts into evil consoled her for not being able to do as much of it as her imagination dictated to her.

I often asked Madame de Lérince to lend me her eloquent pen in order to overthrow my adversary, and she was glad to do so. Madame de Verquin replied to us; her sophisms, sometimes very powerful, forced us to resort to the more victorious arguments of a sensitive soul, in which was inevitably found, Madame de Lérince rightly claimed, everything that could destroy vice and confound unbelief.

I occasionally asked Madame de Verquin for news of the man I still loved, but she was always either unwilling or unable to give me any.

The time has come, monsieur; I must tell you of the second catastrophe of my life, the cruel event that breaks my heart each time it presents itself to my imagination. When you have heard it and learned from it the horrible crime of which I am guilty, you will no doubt give up the flattering plans you made with regard to me.

Although Madame de Lérince's house was as orderly as I've described it to you, she nevertheless opened it to a few friends. One day Madame de Dulfort, a middle-aged lady who had once belonged to the household of the Princess of Piedmont, and who came to see us very often asked Madame de Lérince for permission to introduce to her a young man who had been expressly recommended to her, and whom she would be glad to bring into a house where the examples of virtue he would constantly receive could not fail to contribute to forming his heart. My protectress apologized at first, saying that she never received young men; then, vanquished by her friend's earnest entreaties, she consented to see the Chevalier de Saint-Ange.

He appeared. Whether from a presentiment or any other reason you may care to name, monsieur, as soon as I saw that young man I began to quiver all over without being able to determine the cause. I was on the verge of fainting. . . . Not seeking the reason for that strange reaction, I attributed it to some inner indisposition, and Saint-Ange stopped troubling me.

But while he had agitated me at first sight, a similar reaction had also taken place in him, as he later told me himself. He was filled with great veneration for the house into which he had been admitted that he didn't dare to forget himself to the point of revealing the flame that was consuming him. And so three months went by before he ventured to say anything about it to me; but his eyes expressed his feelings so vividly that it was impossible for me to mistake their meaning. Determined not to relapse into a sin which had caused the greatest unhappiness of my life, and strengthened now by better principles, I was ready a score of times to inform Madame de Lérince of the feelings I thought I discerned in Saint-Ange; but at the last moment I was always held back by the alarm I was afraid of causing her, and so I said nothing. This was undoubtedly the wrong decision, for it was the cause of the frightful disaster I will soon relate to you.

We were in the habit of spending six months of every year in Madame de Lérince's attractive country house five miles outside of Paris. Monsieur de Saint-Prât often came to see us there. Unfortunately for me, he had an attack of gout that year and was unable to come. I say "unfortunately for me," monsieur, because, having naturally more confidence in him that in Madame de Lérince, I would have told him things I was never able to bring myself to tell anyone else, and telling them to him would no doubt have prevented the deadly accident that happened.

Saint-Ange asked Madame de Lérince for permission to come with us, and since Madame de Dulfort also requested this favor for him, it was granted.

Everyone in our group was rather uneasy about our lack of knowledge of this young man; nothing very clear or definite was known about his life. Madame de Dulfort had told us he was the son of a provincial gentleman to whom she was related. As for Saint-Ange himself, he sometimes forgot what Madame de Dulfort had said and referred to himself as Piedmontese, a claim which seemed rather well supported by the way he spoke Italian. Although he was old enough to something in life, he hadn't yet embarked on any career and showed no inclination to do so. He had a very handsome face, worthy of an artist's brush. His manners were excellent, he always spoke courteously, and he gave every indication of being well bred; but through all this there was a prodigious intensity, a kind of impetuosity in his character which sometimes frightened us.

The curb he had tried to impose on his feelings had only made them grow. As soon as he was in Madame de Lérince's country house it became impossible for him to conceal from me. I trembled . . . but I summoned up enough self-control to show him only pity.

"Really, monsieur," I said to him, "you must have a false idea of your own worth, or else you have time to waste, since you spend it with a woman twice your age. But even assuming that I should be foolish enough to listen to you, what ridiculous aims would you dare to form concerning me?"

"My only aim would be to bind myself to you by the holiest of ties, mademoiselle. How little respect you would have for me if you thought I had any other ! "

"Let me assure you, monsieur, that I would never offer the public the strange spectacle of a woman of thirty-four marrying a boy of seventeen."

"Ah, cruel woman, would you be aware of that slight difference if your heart contained even a thousandth of the fire that's consuming mine?"

"It's certain, monsieur, that for my part I'm quite calm. I've been calm for many years; and I hope I shall continue for as long as it pleases God to let me languish on this earth."

"You deprive me of even the hope of moving you to pity some day."

"I go further: I dare to forbid you to speak to me of your madness any longer."

"Ah, fair Florville, do you want my life to be miserable?"

"I want it to be peaceful and happy."

"It can be neither without you."

"No, not until you've destroyed the ridiculous feelings you never should have conceived. Try to overcome them, try to control yourself, and your tranquility will return."

"I can't."

"You don't want to. We must part before you can succeed. If you spend two years without seeing me, your agitation will pass, you'll forget me, and you'll be happy."

"Ah, never ! Never shall I find happiness anywhere but at your feet. . . ."

Just then the others rejoined us, so our first conversation stopped at that point.

Three days later, Saint-Ange succeeded in being alone with me again and tried to resume our discussion in the same tone as before. This time I imposed silence on him so sternly that his tears flowed abundantly. He left me abruptly, after telling me that I was driving him to despair and that he would soon take his own life if I continued to treat him as I was doing. Then he turned around, hurried back to me like a madman and said, "Mademoiselle, you don't know the soul you're insulting ! No, you don't know it. . . . Let me tell you that I'm capable of going to violent extremes . . . extremes that you may be far from thinking of . . . Yes, I'll resort to them a thousand times rather than renounce the happiness of belonging to you." And he left in terrible grief.

I was never more strongly tempted to speak to Madame de Lérince than I was then, but, as I've already said, I was restrained by the fear of harming Saint-Ange. I said nothing. For a week he fled from me, scarcely speaking to me, avoiding me at table, in the drawing room, and during our walks. All this was no doubt done in order to see whether his change of conduct would make an impression on me. It would have been an effective means if I had shared his feelings, but I was so far from doing so that I hardly seemed to be aware of his maneuvers.

Finally he came up to me in the garden and said, in the most violent state imaginable, "Mademoiselle, I've at last succeed in calming myself. Your advice has had the effect on me that you expected: you can see how tranquil I've become. I've tried to find you alone only because I want to tell you good-by . . . Yes, I'm going away from you forever, mademoiselle, I'm going away . . . You'll never again see the man you hate . . . Oh, no, you'll never see him again ! "

"I'm glad to hear of your plan, monsieur. I like to think that you've become reasonable at last. But," I added smiling, "your conversion doesn't seem very real to me."

"Well, then, how should I be, mademoiselle, in order to convince you of my indifference?"

"Quite different from the way I see you now."

"But at least when I'm gone, when you no longer have the pain of seeing me, perhaps you'll believe that all your efforts have finally succeeded in making me reasonable."

"It's true that only your departure would convince me of it, and I'll continue to advise you to leave."

"Then I must be terribly repulsive to you ! "

"You're a charming man, monsieur, who ought to pursue conquests of a different value and leave me in peace, because it's impossible for me to listen to you."

"But you will listen to me ! " he said furiously. "Yes, cruel woman, you'll listen, no matter what you say, to the feelings of my fiery soul, and to the assurance that there's nothing in the world I won't do either to deserve you or to obtain you . . . And don't believe in my pretended departure," he went on impetuously. "I told you about it only to test you . . . Do you really think I'd leave you? Do you think I could tear myself away from the place where you are? I'd rather die a thousand deaths ! Hate me, traitress, hate me, since that's my unhappy fate, but never hope to overcome the love for you with which I'm burning . . . "

When he spoke these last words he was in such a state that, by a mischance which I've never been able to understand, I was deeply moved and turned away from him to hide my tears. I left him in the thicket where he had joined me. He didn't follow me. I heard him throw himself on the ground and abandon himself to the excess of a horrible delirium . . . and I must admit to you, monsieur, that although I was quite certain of having no feeling of love for him, whether from commiseration or memory it was impossible for me not to give vent to my own emotion.

"Alas," I said to myself, yielding to my sorrow, "Senneval spoke to me in the same way ! It was in the same terms that he expressed his passion to me . . . And also in a garden, a garden like this one . . . He told me he would always love me, and yet he cruelly deceived me ! Good heavens, he was the same age ! . . . Ah, Senneval, Senneval, are you trying to take away my peace of mind again? Have you reappeared in this seductive guise to drag me into the abyss a second time? Away, coward, away ! I now abhor even your memory ! "

I wiped my eyes and stayed in my room till supper time. I then went downstairs. But Saint-Ange didn't appear, having announced that he was ill. And the next day he was adroit enough to let me see only serenity on his face. I was deceived by him: I really believed he had exercised enough self-control to overcome his passion. I was mistaken, the treacherous deceiver ! . . . Alas, what am I saying, monsieur? I no longer owe him invectives . . . I owe him only my tears and my remorse.

He appeared so calm only because he had already made his plans. Two days went by like this, and toward the evening of the third he publicly announced his departure. He made arrangements with Madame de Dulfort, his protectress, concerning their common affairs in Paris.

We all went to bed . . . Forgive me, monsieur, for the agitation which the story of that terrible catastrophe arouses in me in advance; it never presents itself to my memory without making me shudder with horror.

Since it was a very hot night, I lay down on my bed almost naked. As soon as my maid left, I put out my candle. A sewing bag had unfortunately remained open on my bed, because I'd just cut some gauze I was going to need the next day. My eyes had scarcely begun to close when I heard a sound . . . I quickly sat up. I felt a hand seize me . . .

"This time you won't get away from me, Florville," said Saint-Ange, for it was he. "Forgive the excessiveness of my passion, but don't try to escape from it. I must make you mine ! "

"Infamous seducer ! " I cried. "Get out immediately, or fear the effects of my anger ! "

"I fear nothing except not being able to possess you cruel girl ! " said that ardent young man, throwing himself on me so skillfully and in such a state of frenzy that I became his victim before I was able to do anything to prevent it . . .

Enraged by his audacity and determined to do anything rather than submit to it any further, I broke away from his and snatched up the scissors that were lying at my feet. But even in my fury I retained a certain amount of self-control: I sought his arm, intending to stab him in it, much more to frighten him by my resolution than to punish him as he deserved. When he felt my movements he redoubled the violence of his own.

"Traitor ! " I cried, stabbing what I thought was his arm, "Get out this instant ! And blush with shame for your crime ! "

Oh monsieur, a fatal hand had guided mine! The poor young man uttered a cry and fell to the floor. I quickly lit a candle and bent over him . . . Good heavens! I had stabbed him in the heart! He died . . . I threw myself onto his bleeding body and feverishly clasped it to my agitated bosom . . . I pressed my mouth to his, trying to bring back his departed soul. I washed his wound with my tears . . .

"Ah, you whose only crime was to love me too much," I said in the frenzy of despair, "did you deserve such a death? Should you have died by the hand of the woman for whom you would have sacrificed your life? Unhappy young man, image of him whom I once adored, if all I must do is to love you in order to bring you back to life, let me tell you at this cruel moment when you can unfortunately no longer hear me, let me tell you, if your soul is still palpitating, that I wish I could revive you at the cost of my own life . . . I want you to know that I was never indifferent to you, that I never saw you without emotion, and that my feelings for you were perhaps far superior to the weak love that burned in your heart."

With these words I fell unconscious onto the body of that unfortunate young man. My maid came in, having heard the sound of my fall. She brought me back to my senses, then she joined me in trying to revive Saint-Ange. Alas, all our efforts were in vain. We left that fateful room, carefully locked its door, took the key with us and immediately hurried to Monsieur de Saint-Prât's house in Paris. I had him awakened, gave him the key to that sinister chamber and told him my horrible story. He pitied me and consoled me, and then, even though he was ill, he went straight to Madame de Lérince's house. Since it was quite close to Paris, he arrived as everyone was getting up, before the events of the night had become known. Never have friends or relatives conducted themselves better. Far from imitating those stupid or ferocious people whose only concern in such crises is to make known everything that can bring dishonor or unhappiness to themselves and those around them, they acted in such a way that even the servants scarcely had any suspicion of what had occurred.

At this point, Mademoiselle de Florville broke off her narrative because of the tears that were choking her; then she said to Monsieur de Courval, "Well, monsieur now will you marry a woman capable of such a murder? Will you hold in your arms a creature who deserves the full severity of the law, a wretched creature who is constantly tormented by her crime, and who has never had a peaceful night since that cruel moment? No monsieur, there has never been a single night when my unfortunate victim hasn't presented himself to me covered with the blood I tore from his heart ! "

"Be calm, mademoiselle, be calm, I beg you," said Monsieur de Courval, mingling his tears with hers. "With the sensitive soul you've been given by nature, I understand your remorse. But there's not even the shadow of a crime in that fatal event. It was a terrible misfortune, of course, but that's all. There was nothing premeditated in it, nothing heinous; your only desire was to ward off an odious attack . . . In short, it was a murder committed by chance, in self-defense. Put your mind at rest, mademoiselle, I insist on it . . . The sternest tribunal would do nothing except wipe your tears. Ah, how mistaken you were if you were afraid that such an event would make you lose the rights to my heart which your personal qualities have given you. No, no, fair Florville, far from dishonoring you, it enhances your virtues in my eyes, and only makes you worthier of a consoling hand that will make you forget your sorrows."

"Monsieur de Saint-Prât also said what you've been kind enough to tell me," said Mademoiselle de Florville, "but the reproaches of my conscience can't be stifled by the great kindness you've both shown me, and nothing will ever soothe its remorse. But it doesn't matter; let me go on, monsieur, because you must be apprehensive about the outcome of all this."

And Mademoiselle de Florville continued her story:

Madame de Dulfort was grief-stricken; aside from Saint-Ange's intrinsic attractiveness he had been so specially recommended to her that she couldn't fail to lament his loss. But she saw the reasons for silence, she realized that a public scandal would only ruin me without bringing her protégé back to life, and she said nothing. Madame de Lérince, despite the severity of her principles and the extreme propriety of her morals, behaved still better, if that's possible, because prudence and humanity are the distinctive characteristics of true piety. She began by telling her household that I had capriciously decided to go back to Paris during the night in order to enjoy the cool weather, that she had been informed of this whim on my part, and that she had no objection to it because she herself was planning to go to Paris that evening for supper. On this pretext, she sent all her servants there. As soon as she was alone with Monsieur de Saint-Prât and Madame de Dulfort, she sent for the parish priest. Madame de Lérince's pastor was as wise and enlightened as herself; he gave Madame de Dulfort an official attestation without raising any objections, and then, with two of his servants, he secretly buried the unfortunate victim of my fury.

When these precautions had been taken, everyone reappeared and took an oath of secrecy. Monsieur de Saint-Prât came to calm me by telling me about everything that had been done to make sure that my act would remain shrouded in oblivion. He seemed to want me to resume my life in Madame de Lérince's house as before. She was ready to receive me. I told him I couldn't bring myself to do it. He then advised me to seek diversion. Madame de Verquin, with whom I'd never ceased to be in correspondence, as I've already told you, monsieur, was still urging me to come and spend a few months with her. I discussed this idea with her brother, he approved of it, and a week later I went to Lorraine. But the memory of my crime pursued me everywhere and nothing was able to calm me.

I often awoke in the middle of the night, thinking I could still hear poor Saint-Ange's moans and cries; I saw him bleeding at my feet, reproaching me for my barbarity, assuring me that the memory of my horrible act would hound me to the end of my days, and that I didn't know the heart I'd pierced.

One night I dreamed that Senneval - that wretched lover whom I hadn't forgotten, since he alone still drew me toward Nancy - showed me two corpses: that of Saint-Ange and that of a woman who was unknown to me. He shed tears on both of them, and pointed to a nearby coffin bristling with thorns, which seemed to have been opened for me. I awoke in a state of terrible agitation; a multitude of confused feelings arose in my soul, and a secret voice seemed to say to me, "Yes, as long as you live, your poor victim will draw tears of blood from you which will become more agonizing every day and the goad of your remorse will constantly grow sharper, rather than duller."

Such was the state in which I reached Nancy, monsieur. A thousand new sorrows were awaiting me there; once the hand of fate descends upon us, its blows increase until they crush us.

I went to visit Madame de Verquin; she had asked me to come in her last letter, and she had said that she was looking forward to seeing me, but little did I realize the conditions under which we were going to share the joy of seeing each other again. She was on her deathbed when I arrived. Merciful heaven, who would have thought it! She had written to me only two weeks before, telling me of her present pleasures and announcing others to come. Such are the plans of mortals: it's while they're forming them, in the midst of their amusements, that merciless death comes to cut the thread of their days; living without ever concerning themselves with that fateful moment, as though they were going to be on earth forever, they vanish into the dark cloud of immortality, uncertain of the fate that lies in store for them.

Allow me, monsieur, to interrupt the story of my adventures a few moments to tell you about Madame de Verquin's death, and to describe to you the frightening stoicism which accompanied her to the grave.

After an escapade that was foolish for her age (she was then fifty-two), Madame de Verquin had jumped into the water to cool herself. She fainted and was brought home in an alarming state. Pneumonia set in the following day, and on the sixth day she was told that she had no more than twenty-four hours to live. This news didn't frighten her; she knew I was going to come, and she ordered that I be received.

I arrived on the very evening when, according to her doctor, she was going to die. She'd had herself placed in a room furnished with the greatest possible taste and elegance. She was lying, casually dressed, on a voluptuous bed whose lilac-colored silk curtains were pleasantly set off by garlands of natural flowers.

Every corner was adorned by bouquets of carnations, jasmine, tuberoses and roses; she was pulling off the petals of some of them, and she'd already covered her bed and the whole room with them. She held out her hand to me as soon as she saw me.

"Come, Florville," she said, "embrace me on my bed of flowers . . . How tall and beautiful you've become ! Ah, yes, my child, virtue has done you good . . . You've been told about my condition . . . You've been told about it, Florville . . . I know about it too . . . In a few hours I'll be gone; I'd never have thought I'd have so little time to spend with you when I saw you again . . . "

She saw my eyes fill with tears. "Come, come, foolish girl," she said, "don't be childish . . . Do you really think there's any reason to feel sorry for me? Haven't I had as much pleasure as any other woman in the world? I'm losing all the years when I'd have had to give up my pleasures, and what would I have done without them? The truth is that I don't pity myself at all for not living to be older than I am now. Before long, no man would have wanted me, and I've never had any desire to live to an age when I'd arouse repugnance. Only believers have any reason to fear death, my child; always between heaven and hell, not knowing which will open to receive them, they're torn by anxiety. As for me, I hope for nothing, and I'm sure of being no more unhappy after my death than I was before my life. I'm going to sleep peacefully in the bosom of nature, without regret or grief, without remorse or apprehension. I've asked to be buried in my bower of jasmine; my place is already being prepared in it. I'll be there, Florville, and the atoms that come from my disintegrating body will nourish the flowers I've loved most of all. And next year," she went on, stroking my cheek with a bouquet of those flowers, "when you smell them you'll be inhaling your dead friend's soul; the fragrance will force its way into the fibers of your brain, give you pleasant ideas and make you think of me."

My tears began to flow again. I clasped the hands of that unfortunate woman and tried to make her exchange her frightful materialistic ideas for a less impious viewpoint, but as soon as she became aware of my intention she pushed me away in alarm.

"Oh, Florville," she cried, "please don't poison my last moments with your errors ! Let me die in peace. I hated those errors all my life, and I'm not going to adopt them now that I'm about to die."

I said nothing. What could my feeble eloquence have done against such firmness? I would only have distressed her without converting her; simple human kindness opposed it. She pulled her bell cord and I immediately heard sweet, melodious music which seemed to be coming from an adjoining room.

"This is how I intend to die, Florville," said that Epicurean. "Isn't it better than being surrounded by priests who would fill my last moments with turmoil, alarm and despair? No, I want to teach your pious believers that it's possible to die in peace without being like them. I want to convince them that it doesn't require religion, but only courage and reason."

Three by Marquis de Sade

Time was passing. A notary came in; she had sent for him. The music stopped. She dictated a few last wishes. She had no children and she had been a widow for a number of years, so she was able to dispose of many things as she saw fit; she left legacies to her friends and her servants. Then she took a little coffer from a writing desk near her bed.

"Here's all I have left now," she said, "a little cash and a few jewels. Let's amuse ourselves the rest of the evening. There are six of you in my room now; I'm going to divide all this into six parts and we'll have a lottery. Each one of you will keep whatever he wins."

I was amazed by her composure. It seemed incredible to me that she could have so many things with which to reproach herself, and yet approach her last moment with such calm - a pernicious effect of unbelief. If the horrible deaths of some wicked people make us shudder, how much more frightened we ought to be by such steadfast impenitence !

What she wanted was done. She had a magnificent meal served. She ate from several dishes and drank liqueurs and Spanish wines, for the doctor had told her that in her condition it didn't matter.

The lots were drawn and each of us received nearly two thousand francs in gold or jewels. This little game was scarcely over when she was seized with a violent attack.

"Well, is this it?" She asked the doctor, still with complete serenity.

"I'm afraid so, madame."

"Then come, Florville," she said, holding out her arms to me, "come and receive my last farewells. I want to die on the bosom of virtue . . . "

She clasped me tightly in her arms and her beautiful eyes closed forever.

Being a stranger in that house and no longer having any reason to stay there, I left immediately. I leave you to imagine the state I was in, and how much that spectacle still darkened my mind.

The gap between Madame de Verquin's way of thinking and mine was too great to allow me to love her with complete sincerity. Furthermore, she was the first cause of my dishonor and all the calamities that had followed it. And yet that woman, sister of the only man who had really taken care of me, had never treated me with anything but kindness and had continued to do so even on her deathbed. My tears were therefore quite sincere, and their bitterness redoubled when I reflected that, with her excellent qualities, that miserable creature had involuntarily brought on her own perdition, and that, already cast out from God's bosom, she was no doubt painfully undergoing the punishment she had earned by her depraved life. However, the thought of god's supreme goodness came to soothe the distress that these ideas had caused in me. I fell to my knees and dared to pray the almighty to forgive that unfortunate soul; even though I myself had great need of heaven's mercy, I dared to implore it for someone else. To sway heaven as much as was in my power, I added two hundred francs of my own money to what I had won in Madame de Verquin's lottery and had it all distributed among the poor of her parish.

Her last wishes were scrupulously respected; she had made her arrangements so well that they could not fail to be carried out. She was buried in her bower of jasmine. At her head was a black marble obelisk on which this single word was carved: Vixit

Thus died the sister of my dearest friend. Full of intelligence and knowledge, richly endowed with charms and talents, Madame de Verquin could have deserved, if she had behaved differently, the love and esteem of all those who knew her; instead, she obtained only their contempt. Her licentiousness had increased as she grew older. Someone who has no principles is never more dangerous than at the age when he has ceased to blush: depravity corrupts his heart, he refines his first failings, and gradually he begins to commit crimes, thinking he is still only indulging in follies. But I was constantly surprised by the incredible blindness of Madame de Verquin's brother. Such is the distinctive mark of candor and goodness; virtuous people, never suspecting the evil of which they themselves are incapable, are readily taken in by the first scoundrel who seizes upon them, and that's why there's so much ease and so little glory in deceiving them. The insolent rogue who does it is only working to demean himself, and without even proving his talent for vice, he only lends greater brilliance to virtue.

In losing Madame de Verquin, I'd also lost all hope of learning anything about my lover and my son; as you can well imagine, I hadn't dared to question her about them when I saw the terrible state she was in.

Crushed by this catastrophe and exhausted from a journey made in a painful state of mind, I decided to rest for a time in Nancy, at the inn where I already had a room, without seeing anyone at all, since Monsieur de Saint-Prât had seemed to want me to conceal my name. It was there that I wrote to my dear protector, having resolved not to leave until I'd received his answer:

A wretched girl who is nothing to you, monsieur, and who can lay claim only to your pity, endlessly troubles your life; instead of speaking to you only of the grief you must be feeling over the loss you have just suffered, she dares to speak to you of herself, to ask you for your orders and to await them . . .

But it was ordained that misfortune was to follow me everywhere, and that I was to be constantly either a witness or a victim of its sinister effects.

One evening I came back to the inn rather late after having gone out for a breath of fresh air with my maid and a footman whom I had hired temporarily on arriving in Nancy. Everyone else had already gone to bed. As I was about to go into my room, a woman in her early fifties, tall and still beautiful, whom I'd known by sight since my arrival at the inn, suddenly came out of her room, next to mine, and, armed with a dagger, rushed into a room across the hall. My natural inclination was to see . . . I hurried forward followed by my servants, and in the twinkling of an eye, before we had time to stop her or even call out to her, we saw that wretched woman throw herself on another woman, stab her in the heart a dozen times, then go back to her room in a frenzied state, without having seen us. We thought at first that she'd gone mad; we couldn't understand her crime, for which no motive was apparent to us. When I saw that my maid and my footman were about to cry out, an overpowering impulse, whose cause was unknown to me, made me order them to remain silent, seize them by the arm, pull them into my room and close the door behind us.

We soon heard a frightful commotion: the woman who had just been stabbed had managed to stagger to the head of the stairs, screaming horribly. Before she died she was able to name her murderer. Since it was known that we were the last to enter the inn, we were arrested at the same time as the murder. However, since the victim's accusation had cast no suspicions on us, we were merely ordered not to leave the inn until the end of the trial.

The murderer was imprisoned, but she admitted nothing and firmly maintained that she was innocent. My servants and I were the only witnesses. We were summoned to testify. I had to speak, and I also had to conceal the agitation that was secretly devouring me. I deserved death as much as the woman my forced testimony was going to send to the scaffold, for although the circumstances had been different, I was guilty of the same crime. I would have given anything to avoid that cruel testimony. It seemed to me as I spoke that with each word a drop of blood was torn from my heart. But our statements had to be complete; we reported everything we had seen.

We later learned that no matter how firmly convinced the authorities may have been that the crime was committed by that woman, whose motive had been to do away with a rival, it would have been impossible to convict her if it hadn't been for us, because a man involved in the situation had fled and might have been suspected; but the poor woman's doom was sealed by our testimony - especially that of my footman, who happened to be attached to the inn where the crime had been committed - which we could not have refused to give without placing ourselves in danger.

The last time I confronted her, she examined me with great astonishment and asked me how old I was.

"I'm thirty-four," I replied.

"Thirty-four? . . . And you're from this province?"

"No, madame."

"Your name is Florville?"

"Yes, that's what I'm called."

"I don't know you," she said, "but you're an honest woman, and you're said to be respected in this town; unfortunately that's enough for me . . . Mademoiselle," she went on with agitation, "I had a dream in which you appeared to me in the midst of the horrors that now surround me. You were there with my son . . . Yes, I'm a mother, and an unhappy one, as you can see. You had the same face, the same figure, the same dress . . . And the scaffold was before my eyes . . . "

"A dream," I exclaimed, "a dream, madame ! " I immediately recalled my own dream, and I was struck by her features: I recognized her as the woman who had appeared to me with Senneval, near the coffin bristling with thorns. Tears welled up in my eyes. The more I examined that woman, the more I was tempted to retract my testimony. I wanted to ask to be executed in her stead, I wanted to flee and yet I couldn't tear myself away . . .

Having no reason to doubt my innocence, the officials merely separated us when they saw the terrible state in which she'd placed me. I went back to my inn in despair, overwhelmed by a multitude of feelings whose cause I couldn't discern. The next day, that miserable woman was put to death.

On that same day I received Monsieur de Saint-Prât's answer. He urged me to come back. Nancy was, of course, no longer very pleasant to me, after the grim scenes it had just offered me, so I left it immediately and set out for Paris, pursued by the new ghost of that woman, who seemed to cry out to me at every moment, "It's you who've sent me to my death, wretched girl, and you don't know who it is that your own hand has pushed into the grave ! "

Crushed by all these afflictions and persecuted by an equal number of sorrows, I asked Monsieur de Saint-Prât to find me a retreat in which I could end my days in the deepest solitude, and in the most rigorous duties of my religion. He suggested the one in which you found me, monsieur. I took up residence in it that same week, and from then on I left it only twice a month, to visit my dear protector and to spend a little time with Madame de Lérince. But heaven, which seems determined to deal me a painful blow every day, didn't let me enjoy my friendship with Madame de Lérince for long: I had the misfortune of losing her last year. Her affection for me required that I stay with her during those cruel moments, and she, too, breathed her last in my arms.

But who would have believed it, monsieur? Her death was less peaceful than Madame de Verquin's. Since Madame de Verquin had never hoped for anything, she wasn't afraid of losing everything. Madame de Lérince seemed to dread seeing the object of her hope disappear. I had noticed no remorse in Madame de Verquin, who should have been overwhelmed by it; Madame de Lérince, who had never given herself any reason for remorse, felt it keenly. At her death, Madame de Verquin regretted only that she hadn't done enough evil; Madame de Lérince died regretting the good she hadn't done. One covered herself with flowers and lamented only the loss of her pleasures, the other wanted to die on a cross of ashes, and was grieved by the memory of the hours she hadn't devoted to virtue.

I was struck by these contrasts. A little laxity stole over my soul. "Why," I said to myself, "isn't virtue rewarded with calm at that time, when it seems to be granted to misconduct?" But then strengthened by a heavenly voice that seemed to thunder from the depths of my heart, I immediately cried out, "Is it for me to fathom God's will? What I see only assures me of one more merit. Madame de Lérince's fear was the solicitude of virtue; Madame de Verquin's cruel indifference was only the last aberration of crime. Ah, if I have a choice in my last moments, may God grant me the favor of frightening me like Madame de Lérince, rather than numbing me like Madame de Verquin ! "

Such is the last of my adventures, monsieur. For the past two years I've been living at the Convent of the Assumption, where my benefactor placed me. Yes, monsieur, I've been living there for two years, and not once have I had a moment of rest, not once have I spent a night without seeing the image of poor Saint-Ange and the unfortunate woman whose execution. I caused in Nancy. Now you know the state in which you found me, and the secret things I had to reveal to you. Wasn't it my duty to inform you of them before yielding to the feelings that had deceived you? Now you can see whether it's possible for me to be worthy of you, and whether a woman whose soul is torn by sorrow could bring any joy to your life. Take my advice, monsieur: stop deluding yourself, let me return to the stern seclusion which is the only kind of existence that befits me. If you were to tear me away from it, you would constantly have before your eyes the frightful spectacle of remorse, grief and misfortune.

By the time she had thus ended her story, Mademoiselle de Florville was in a state of violent agitation. Naturally animated, sensitive and delicate, she could not fail to be deeply affected by such a recital of her tribulation.

Monsieur de Courval did not feel that the later events of her story presented any more valid reasons for changing his plans that the earlier ones had done. He did everything he could to calm the woman he loved.

"Let me say again, mademoiselle," he said to her, "that there are fateful and singular things in what you've just told me, but that I don't see a single one that ought to alarm your conscience or damage your reputation. An affair at the age of sixteen, so be it, but there were many excuses on your side: your age, Madame de Verquin's effort to lead you astray, a young man who was no doubt very charming . . . and whom you've never seen since then, have you, mademoiselle? He added with a touch of anxiety. "And you'll probably never see him again . . ."

"Oh, certainly not ! " said Florville, sensing the reasons for his anxiety.

"Well, then, mademoiselle," he said, "let's conclude our arrangements, I beg you, and let me convince you as soon as possible that there's nothing in your story that could diminish, in the heart of an honest man, either the consideration owed to all your virtues or the homage demanded by all your charms."

She asked for permission to return to Paris again to consult her protector for the last time, and promised that she would raise no further objections. He could not refuse to let her fulfill that virtuous duty. She left, and came back a week later with Saint-Prât. Monsieur de Courval showered courteous attentions on him; he made it abundantly clear to him how greatly flattered he was to be able to marry the girl he was kind enough to protect, and he begged him to go on acknowledging her as his relative. Saint-Prât responded graciously to Courval's attentions and continued to give him extremely advantageous notions concerning Mademoiselle de Florville's character.

At last came the day that Courval had desired so much. The ceremony took place, and when the contract was read he was surprised to learn that, without telling any, Monsieur de Saint-Prât had, in consideration of Florville's marriage, doubled the income of four thousand francs a year which he was already giving her, and bequeathed her a hundred thousand francs to be paid to her after his death.

She shed abundant tears when she saw her protector's new kindnesses to her, and at the bottom of her heart she was glad to be able to offer the man who was good enough to marry her a fortune at least equal to his own.

Cordiality, pure joy and reciprocal assurance of esteem and attachments presided over the celebration of that wedding . . . of that fateful wedding whose torches were secretly extinguished by the Furies.

Monsieur de Saint-Prât spend a week in Courval's country house, along with our bridegroom's friends, but the newlyweds did not return to Paris with them: they decided to stay in the country until the beginning of winter, to give themselves time to put their affairs in order so that they would be able to establish a good household in Paris. Monsieur de Saint-Prât was instructed to find them a pleasing residence near his own, to enable them to see each other more often.

Monsieur and Madame de Courval had already spent nearly three months together in the sweet anticipation of all those agreeable arrangements, and they were already certain of her pregnancy, which they had hastened to announce to the good Monsieur de Saint-Prât, when an unexpected event blighted the well-being of the happy couple and changed the tender roses of wedlock into the mournful cypresses of sorrow.

At this point my pen stops . . . I ought to ask my readers for mercy, beg them to go no further . . . Yes, let them stop immediately if they do not wish to shudder with horror . . . Sad condition of mankind on earth, cruel effect of the capriciousness of fate . . . Why should the unhappy Florville, the most virtuous, charming and sensitive girl in the world, have found herself, through an almost inconceivable series of fateful events the most abominable monster that nature could have created?

One evening that tender, loving wife was sitting beside her husband, reading an incredibly gloomy English novel which was causing a great stir at the time.

"There's someone who's almost as unfortunate as I am," she said, throwing down the book.

"As unfortunate as you?" said Monsieur de Courval, clasping his beloved wife in his arms. "Oh, Florville, I thought I'd made you forget your misfortunes ! I see I was mistaken . . . Did you have to say it to me so harshly?"

But Madame de Courval had become as though insensitive: she did not even utter a word in response to his caresses. With an involuntary movement, she pushed his away in alarm, hurried over to a sofa, lay down on it and burst into tears. It was in vain that the worthy Courval threw himself at the feet of the woman he worshiped and begged her either to calm herself or at least tell him the cause of her sudden despair. She continued to repulse him and turn away from him when he tried to dry her tears, until finally, no longer doubting that a pernicious memory of her former passion had come to inflame her anew, he could not help reproaching her a little on the subject.

For a time she listened to him without answering, then she stood up and said, "No, monsieur, you're mistaken in giving that interpretation to the sorrow that overwhelmed me just now. I'm frightened not by memories, but by forebodings . . . I see myself happy with you, monsieur -- yes, very happy -- and I wasn't born for happiness. It's impossible for me to go like this much longer; my destiny is such that the dawn of happiness is always the lightning which precedes a thunderbolt . . . That's what make me shudder: I'm afraid we weren't destined to live together. Perhaps tomorrow I shall no longer be your wife . . . A secret voice cries out from the depths of my heart that all this happiness is only a shadow which is about to vanish like a flower that springs up and is cut down in a single day. So don't accuse me of being capricious or becoming cold toward you, monsieur: I'm guilty only of excessive sensibility and an unhappy tendency to see everything in its most sinister aspect -- a painful result of my afflictions . . . "

Monsieur de Courval was still at her feet, unsuccessfully trying to calm her by his caresses and his words when suddenly (it was about seven o'clock on an evening in October) a servant was insistently asking to speak to Monsieur de Courval. Florville shuddered. Involuntary tears streamed down her cheeks, her legs became unsteady and she sat down; she tried to speak, but her voice died on her lips.

More concerned with his wife's condition than with what his servant had just told him, Monsieur de Courval curtly ordered him to tell the visitor to wait, then he hurried to Florville's aid. But, afraid of succumbing to the secret emotion that was gripping her, and wishing to hide her feelings from the stranger whose arrival had been announced, she stood up forcefully and said, "It's nothing, monsieur, it's nothing . . . Let the gentleman come in."

The servant left and returned a moment later, followed by a man thirty-seven or thirty-eight years old whose face, though quite attractive, bore the marks of a deeply rooted sorrow.

"Father ! " cried the stranger, throwing himself at Monsieur de Courval's feet. "Will you recognize a wretched man who's been separated from you for twenty-two years, and who's been all too severely punished for his cruel misconduct by the calamities that have constantly overwhelmed him ever since he left you?"

"What ! You're my son? Good heavens ! . . . By what event . . . Ingrate ! What made you remember my existence?"

"My heart . . . that heart which has never stopped loving you, despite its guilt . . . Listen to me, father, I have greater misfortunes than my own to reveal to you; please sit down and hear me. And you, madame," continued young Courval, turning to his father's wife, "please forgive me if, immediately after paying my respects to you for the first time in my life, I'm forced to relate some terrible family catastrophes which it's no longer possible to conceal from my father."

"Speak, monsieur, speak," stammered Madame de Courval, looking at him with haggard eyes, "the language of unhappiness isn't new to me: I've known it ever since my childhood."

Staring at her with a kind of involuntary agitation, the young man said to her, "You've been unhappy, madame? Ah, merciful heaven, can you have been as unhappy as we?"

They sat down. Madame de Courval's state would be difficult to describe. She glanced at the visitor, looked down at the floor, sighed from inner turmoil. Monsieur de Courval was weeping while his son tried to calm him and begged him to lend him his attention. Finally the conversation took a more orderly turn.

"I have so many things to tell you, monsieur," said young Courval, "that you'll have to allow me to omit the details and tell you only the main facts. And I want you and madame to give me your word not to interrupt me until I've finished.

"I left you when I fifteen, monsieur. My first impulse was to go to my mother, whom I was blind enough to prefer to you. She'd been separated from you for many years. I rejoined her in Lyons. Her scandalous life alarmed me so much that I had to flee from her to preserve what remained of the sentiments I owed to her. I went to Strasbourg, where the Normandy regiment was garrisoned . . . "

Madame de Courval started, but controlled herself.

"My colonel took a certain interest in me," young Courval went on. "I attracted his attention and he made me a second lieutenant. The following year, I went with the regiment to Nancy, where I fell in love with Madame de Verquin's young niece. I seduced her, had a son by her, then cruelly abandoned her."

At these words, Madame de Courval quivered and a low moan escaped from her chest, but she continued to be firm.

"That wretched adventure was the cause of all my misfortunes. I placed the poor girl's child in the home of a woman who lived near Metz, and who promised to take care of him. A short time later I returned to my regiment. My conduct was strongly condemned. Since the young lady hadn't been able to reappear in Nancy, I was accused of having ruined her. Too charming not to have interested the whole town, she found avengers there. I fought a duel, killed my adversary and went to Turin with my son, after going back to Metz to get him.

"I spent twelve years in the service of the King of Sardinia. I won't describe the mishaps I encountered there; they were countless. It's only by leaving France that one learns to miss it. Meanwhile my son was growing and showing great promise. I became acquainted in Turin with a French lady who had accompanied one of our princesses who married into that court. When this respectable lady took an interest in my misfortunes, I ventured to ask her to take my son to France so that he could finish his education there. I promised her that I would order my affairs well enough to be able to come and take him from her care in six years.

She consented, took my poor child to Paris, spared no effort to give him a good upbringing, and regularly sent me news of him.

"I came a year earlier than I'd promised. I went to the lady's house, filed with the sweet expectation of embracing my son, of holding in my arms that token of a sentiment which I had betrayed, but which still burned in my heart . . . "Your son is no longer living," my worthy friend said to me with tears in her eyes. "He was a victim of the same passion that brought such unhappiness to his father. We'd taken him to the county. He fell in love there with a charming girl whose name I've sworn not to reveal. Carried away by the violence of his love, he tried to take by force what she'd refused him out of virtue . . . She stabbed him, intending only to frighten him, but she pierced his heart and he fell dead . . . "

At this point Madame de Courval fell into a kind of stupor which for a moment made the two men fear that she had suddenly lost her life. Her eyes were glazed, her pulse had stopped. Monsieur de Courval, who was all too clearly aware of the appalling way in which those deplorable events were related, told his son to be silent and hurried to his wife. She regained consciousness and said with heroic courage, "Let your son go on, monsieur. Perhaps I haven't yet reached the end of my afflictions."

Not understanding her sorrow over events that seemed to concern her only indirectly, but discerning something incomprehensible in her face, young Courval looked at her with emotion. Monsieur de Courval took his son's hand and, after distracting his attention from Florville, told him to go on with his story without dwelling on any unnecessary details, for it contained mysterious circumstances that were of the greatest interest.

"In despair over the death of my son," continued young Courval, "and no longer having anything to hold me in France--except you, father, but I didn't date to approach you and I dreaded your anger---I decided to travel to Germany . . . Ill-fated father, I still haven't told you the most painful part of my story," he said, wetting his father's hands with his tears. "I beg you to summon up your courage.

"When I arrived in Nancy I learned that a Madame Desbarres--this was the name my mother had adopted in her disorderly life, as soon as she had made you believe she was dead--had just been imprisoned for having stabbed her rival to death, and that she was perhaps going to be executed the next day."

"Oh, monsieur ! " exclaimed poor Florville, throwing herself in her husband's arms with tears and heart-rending cries. "Oh, monsieur, do you see the full extent of my afflictions?"

"Yes, madame, I see everything," said Monsieur de Courval, "but please let my son finish."

Florville restrained herself, but she had almost stopped breathing, all her feelings were impaired, and all her muscles were frightfully taut.

"Go on, my son, go on," said the unhappy father. "In a few minutes I'll explain everything to you."

"Well, monsieur," said young Courval, "I made inquiries to see if there was any confusion of names. I found that it was unfortunately all too true that the criminal was my mother. I asked to see her and my request was granted. I threw myself into her arms. 'I'm going to die guilty,' the poor woman said to me, 'but there's a terrible stroke of fate in the events that have led me to my death. A certain man was going to be suspected of my crime, and he would have been, because all the evidence was against him, but a woman and her two servants who happened to be in the inn saw me commit the murder, and I was so preoccupied that I didn't notice them. Their testimony was the sole cause of my death sentence. But no matter; I have only a little time left to talk to you, and I don't want to waste it on futile complaints. I have some important secrets to tell you; listen to them, my son.

"'As soon as my eyes are closed, go to my husband and tell him that among all my crimes there's one which he never knew, and which I finally confessed . . . You have a sister, Courval. She was born a year after you. I adored you and I was afraid she would be a drawback to you some day because your father might make a dowry for her by taking some of the money you would inherit. To keep it intact for you, I decided to get rid of my daughter and do everything in my power to make sure my husband would have no more children from our marriage. My disorders led me into other failings and forestalled the effect of those new crimes by making me commit other and more terrible ones; but as for my daughter, I mercilessly resolved to kill her. I was about to carry out that infamous plan, acting in concert with the wet nurse, whom I had amply compensated, when she told me that she knew a man who had been married for many years and constantly wanted children without being able to have them, and that she could rid me of my daughter without committing a crime, and in a way that might give her a happy life. I quickly accepted. That same night my daughter was left on the doorstep of that man with a note in her bassinet. As soon as I'm dead, hurry to Paris and beg your father to forgive me, not to curse my memory, and to claim his daughter for his own.'

"With these words, my mother kissed me and tried to calm the frightful agitation into which I'd been plunged by what she'd just told me . . . Father, she was executed the next day. Then a terrible illness nearly put me in my grave; for two years I hovered between life and death, with neither the strength nor the courage to write to you. The first use I've made of my recovered health has been to come and throw myself at your feet, to beg you to forgive my unfortunate mother, and to give you the name of the man who can tell you what has become of my sister: he's Monsieur de Saint-Prât."

Monsieur de Courval was deeply perturbed; all his senses were frozen, he nearly lost consciousness, his condition became alarming.

As for Florville, who had been torn to pieces for the past quarter of an hour, she stood up with the serenity of someone who had just come to a decision and said to Courval, "Well, monsieur, now do you believe that a more horrible criminal than the wretched Florville can exist anywhere in the world? Recognize me, Senneval, recognize me as your sister, the girl you seduced in Nancy, your son's murderer, your father's wife, and the infamous creature who led your mother to the scaffold . . . Yes, gentlemen, those are my crimes. When I look at either of you I see an object of horror; I either see my lover in my brother, or my husband in my father. And if I look at myself, I see only the abominable monster who stabbed her son and caused her mother's death. Do you think the Almighty can have enough torments for me? And do you think I can go on living any longer with the afflictions that are torturing my heart? No, I still have one more crime to commit, and it will avenge all the others."

The poor girl immediately leapt forward, snatched one of Senneval's pistols and shot herself in the head before either of the two men had time to realize her intention. She died without saying another word.

Monsieur de Courval fainted. His son, dazed by those horrible scenes, called for help as best he could. Florville no longer had any need for assistance: the shadows of death had already spread over her brow, and her features had been doubly contorted by the throes of despair and the upheaval of a violent death. She lay in a pool of her own blood.

Monsieur de Courval was carried to his bed. He was at death's door for two months. His son, in an equally painful state, was nevertheless fortunate enough to see his affection and care bring back his father's health. But after all the blows which fate had so cruelly rained down upon their heads, they decided to withdraw from the world. Austere solitude has taken them from their friends forever, and now, in the bosom of piety and virtue, each of them is peacefully finishing a sad and oppressive life which was given to him only to convince him, as well as those who will read this tragic story, that it is only in the darkness of the tomb that man can find the calm which the wickedness of his fellow man, the disorder of his passions, and, above all, the decrees of his fate, will always refuse to him on this earth.

Made in the USA
Columbia, SC
13 January 2021